CHUNG KUO
THE BROKEN WHEEL

D0188146

Chung Kuo. The words mean "Middle Kingdom," and since 221 B.C., when the first emperor, Ch'in Shih Huang Ti, unified the seven Warring States, it is what the "black-haired people," the Han, or Chinese, have called their great country. The Middle Kingdom—for them it was the whole world; a world bounded by great mountain chains to the north and west, by the sea to east and south. Beyond was only desert and barbarism. So it was for two thousand years and through sixteen great dynasties. Chung Kuo *was* the Middle Kingdom, the very center of the human world, and its emperor the "Son of Heaven," the "One Man." But in the eighteenth century that world was invaded by the young and aggressive Western powers with their superior weaponry and their unshakable belief in progress. It was, to the surprise of the Han, an unequal contest and China's myth of supreme strength and self-sufficiency was shattered. By the early twentieth century, China—Chung Kuo—was the sick old man of the East: "a carefully preserved mummy in a hermetically sealed coffin," as Karl Marx called it. But from the disastrous ravages of that century grew a giant of a nation, capable of competing with the West and with its own Eastern rivals, Japan and Korea, from a position of incomparable strength. The twenty-first century, "the Pacific Century," as it was known even before it began, saw China become once more a world unto itself, but this time its only boundary was space.

Also by David Wingrove

CHUNG | KUO

BY | DAVID WINGROVE

BOOK 2:
THE BROKEN WHEEL

A DELL BOOK

Published by
Dell Publishing
a division of
Bantam Doubleday Dell Publishing Group, Inc.
1540 Broadway
New York, New York 10036

ISBN: 0-440-20928-5

Reprinted by arrangement with Delacorte Press, New York, New York

Printed in the United States of America

Published simultaneously in Canada

November 1991

10 9 8 7 6 5 4

RAD

FOR ROSE AND IAN,

"A new sound from the old keys."

Keep away from sharp swords
Don't go near a lovely woman.
A sharp sword too close will wound your hand,
Woman's beauty too close will wound your life.
The danger of the road is not in the distance,
Ten yards is far enough to break a wheel.
The peril of love is not in loving too often,
A single evening can leave its wound in the soul.

—MENG CHIAO , *Impromptu, eighth century* A.D.

CONTENTS

BOOK 2
The Broken Wheel

Ascher, Emily—Trained as an economist, she joined the *Ping Tiao* revolutionary party at the turn of the century, becoming one of its policy-formulating Council of Five. A passionate fighter for social justice, she was also once the lover of the *Ping Tiao's* unofficial leader, Bent Gesell.

De Vore, Howard—A onetime Major in the T'ang's Security forces, he has become the leading figure in the struggle against the Seven. A highly intelligent and coldly logical man, he is the puppet master behind the scenes as the great "War of the Two Directions" takes a new turn.

Ebert, Hans—Son of Klaus Ebert and heir to the vast GenSyn Corporation, he has been promoted to Major in the Security forces, and is admired and trusted by his superiors. Ebert is a complex young man, a brave and intelligent officer; he also has a selfish, dissolute, and rather cruel streak.

Fei Yen—Daughter of Yin Tsu, one of the heads of "The Twenty-Nine," the minor aristocratic families of Chung Kuo. Her marriage to the murdered Prince Li Han Ch'in has been nullified, and she is set to marry Han's brother, the young Prince Li Yuan. The classically beautiful "Flying Swallow" is fragile in appearance, but surprisingly strong-willed and fiery.

Haavikko, Axel—Smeared by the false accusations of his fellow officers, Lieutenant Haavikko has spent the best part of a decade in debauchery and self-negation. At core, however, he is a good, honest man, and circumstances will raise him from the pit into which he has fallen.

Kao Chen—Once an assassin from the Net, the lowest levels of the great City, Chen has raised himself from his humble beginnings and is now a Captain in the T'ang's Security forces. As friend and helper to Karr, he is one of the foot-soldiers in the War against DeVore.

Karr, Gregor—Major, later Colonel, in the Security forces, he was recruited by General Tolonen from the Net. In his youth he was a "blood"—a to-the-death combat fighter. A huge, giant of a man, he is the "hawk" Li Shai Tung plans to fly against his adversary De-Vore.

Lehmann, Stefan—Albino son of the former Dispersionist leader Pietr Lehmann, he has become a lieutenant to DeVore. A cold, unnaturally dispassionate man, he seems to be the very archetype of nihilism, his only aim to bring down the Seven and their great City.

Li Shai Tung—T'ang of Europe and one of the Seven, the ruling Council of Chung Kuo, Li Shai Tung is now in his seventies. For many years he was the fulcrum of the Council and unofficial spokes-man for the Seven, but the murder of his heir, Han Ch'in, weak-ened him, undermining his once-strong determination to prevent Change at all costs.

Li Yuan—Second son of Li Shai Tung, he has become heir to City Europe after the murder of his brother. Thought old before his time, his cold, thoughtful manner conceals a passionate nature, expressed in his wooing of and marriage to his dead brother's wife, Fei Yen.

Shepherd, Ben—Son of Hal Shepherd, the T'ang's chief advisor, and great-great-grandson of City Earth's architect. Shepherd was born and brought up in the Domain, an idyllic valley in the southwest of England where, deciding not to follow in his father's footsteps and become advisor to Li Yuan, he pursues instead his calling as an artist, developing a whole new art form, the Shell, which will eventually have a cataclysmic effect on Chung Kuo society.

Tolonen, Jelka—Daughter of Marshal Tolonen, Jelka has been brought up in a very masculine environment, lacking a mother's influence. However, her genuine interest in martial arts and in weaponry and strategy mask a very different side to her nature; a side brought out by violent circumstances.

Tolonen, Knut—Marshal of the Council of Generals and onetime General to Li Shai Tung, Tolonen is a big, granite-jawed man and the staunchest supporter of the values and ideals of the Seven. Possessed of a fiery, fearless nature, he will stop at nothing to protect his masters, yet after long years of War even his belief in the necessity of stasis has been shaken.

Tsu Ma—T'ang of West Asia and one of the Seven, the ruling Council of Chung Kuo, Tsu Ma has thrown off his former dissolute ways as a result of his father's death and become one of Li Shai Tung's greatest supporters in Council. A strong, handsome man, he has still, however, a weakness in his nature; one which is almost his undoing.

Wang Sau-leyan—Fourth and youngest son of Wang Hsien, T'ang of Africa, he has been placed closer to the center of political events by the murder of his two eldest brothers. Thought of as a wastrel, he is, in fact, a shrewd and highly capable political being who is destined—through circumstances of his own devising—to become the harbinger of change inside the Council of the Seven.

Ward, Kim—Born in the Clay, that dark wasteland beneath the great City's foundations, Kim has a quick and unusual bent of mind. His vision of a giant web, formulated in the darkness, had driven him up into the light of the Above. However, after a traumatic fight and a long period of personality reconstruction, he has returned to things not quite the person he was. Or so it seems, for Kim has lost none of the sharpness that has made him the most promising young scientist in the whole of Chung Kuo.

LIST OF CHARACTERS

THE SEVEN AND THE FAMILIES

Chi Hsing—T'ang of the Australias.

Hou Tung-po—T'ang of South America.

Li Feng Chiang—brother and advisor to Li Shai Tung.

Li Shai Tung—T'ang of Europe.

Li Yuan—second son of Li Shai Tung and heir to City Europe.

Pei Ro-hen—head of the Pei Family (one of the "Twenty-Nine" Minor Families).

Tsu Ma—T'ang of West Asia.

Wang Hsien—T'ang of Africa.

Wang Sau-leyan—fourth son of Wang Hsien.

Wang Ta-hung—third son of Wang Hsien and heir to City Africa.

Wei Chan Yin—eldest son of Wei Feng and heir to City East Asia.

Wei Feng—T'ang of East Asia.

Wu Shih—T'ang of North America.

Yin Chan—Minor-Family Prince; son of Yin Tsu.

Yin Fei Yen—"Flying Swallow," Minor-Family Princess; daughter of Yin Tsu.

Yin Sung—Minor-Family Prince; son of Yin Tsu.

Yin Tsu—head of Yin Family (one of the "Twenty-Nine" Minor Families).

Yin Wu Tsai—Minor-Family Princess and cousin of Fei Yen.

FRIENDS AND RETAINERS OF THE SEVEN

Auden, William—Captain in Security.

Chang Li—Chief Surgeon to Li Shai Tung.

Chang Shih-sen—personal secretary to Li Yuan.

Ch'in Tao Fan—Chancellor of East Asia.

Chu Ta Yun—Minister of Education for City Europe.

Chuang Ming—Minister to Li Shai Tung.

Chung Hu-yan—Chancellor to Li Shai Tung.

Ebert, Berta—wife of Klaus Ebert.

Ebert, Hans—Major in Security and heir to GenSyn.

Ebert, Klaus Stefan—Head of GenSyn (Genetic Synthetics) and advisor to Li Shai Tung.

Erkki—guard to Jelka Tolonen.

Fan Liang-wei—painter to the court of Li Shai Tung.

Fest, Edgar—Captain in Security.

Fischer, Otto—Head of Personal Security at Wang Hsien's palace in Alexandria.

Haavikko, Axel—lieutenant in Security.

Haavikko, Vesa—sister of Axel Haavikko.

Heng Yu—Minister of Transportation for City Europe.

Hoffmann—Major in Security.

Hua—personal surgeon to Li Shai Tung.

Hung Feng-chan—Chief Groom at Tongjiang.

Hung Mien-lo—advisor to Wang Ta-hung and Chancellor of City Africa.

Kao Chen—Captain in Security.

Karr, Gregor—Major in Security.

Lautner, Wolfgang—Captain in Security Personnel at Bremen.

Lung Mei Ho—secretary to Tsu Ma.

Nan Ho—Li Yuan's Master of the Inner Chamber.

Nocenzi, Vittorio—General of Security, City Europe.

Panshin, Anton—Colonel in Security.

Pearl Heart—maid to Li Yuan.

Russ—Captain in Security.

Sanders—Captain of Security at Helmstadt Armory.

Scott—Captain of Security.

Shepherd, Ben—son of Hal Shepherd.

Shepherd, Beth—wife of Hal Shepherd.

Shepherd, Hal—advisor to Li Shai Tung and Head of Shepherd family.

Shepherd, Meg—daughter of Hal Shepherd.

Sun Li Hua—Wang Hsien's Master of the Inner Chamber.

Sweet Rain—maid to Wang Hsien.

Sweet Rose—maid to Li Yuan.

Tender Willow—maid to Wang Hsien.

Tolonen, Helga—aunt of Jelka Tolonen.

Tolonen, Jelka—daughter of Knut Tolonen.

Tolonen, Jon—brother of Knut Tolonen.

Tolonen, Knut—Marshal of the Council of Generals and father of
Jelka Tolonen.
Wang Ta Chuan—Li Shai Tung's Master of the Inner Palace.
Wu Ming—servant to Wang Ta-hung.
Ying Chai—assistant to Sun Li Hua.
Ying Fu—assistant to Sun Li Hua.
Yu—surgeon to Li Yuan.

DISPERSIONISTS

Berdichev, Soren—head of SimFic (Simulated Fictions) and leader of the
Dispersionists.
DeVore, Howard—former Major in Li Shai Tung's Security forces.
Douglas, John—Company Head.
Kubinyi—lieutenant to DeVore.
Lehmann, Stefan—albino son of former Dispersionist leader Pietr
Lehmann and Lieutenant to DeVore.
Wiegand, Max—lieutenant to DeVore.

PING TIAO

Ascher, Emily—economist and member of the Council of Five.
Gesell, Bent—unofficial leader of the *Ping Tiao* and member of the
Council of Five.
Mach, Jan—maintenance official for the Ministry of Waste Recy-
cling and member of the Council of Five.
Mao Liang—Minor-Family Princess and member of the Council of
Five.
Shen Lu Chua—computer expert and member of the Council of Five.
Yun Ch'o—lieutenant to Shen Lu Chua.

OTHER CHARACTERS

Barycz, Jiri—scientist on the Wiring Project.
Beattie, Douglas—alias of DeVore.
Chan Wen-fu—friend of Heng Chian-ye.
Chuang Lian—wife of Minister Chuang.
Ebert, Lutz—half brother of Klaus Ebert.

Ellis, Michael—assistant to Director Spatz.

Ganz, Joseph—alias of DeVore.

Golden Heart—young prostitute bought by Hans Ebert for his household.

Hammond, Joel—Senior Technician on the Wiring Project.

Heng Chian-ye—son of Heng Chi-po and nephew of Heng Yu.

Herrick—an illegal-implant specialist.

Kao Ch'iang Hsin—infant daughter of Kao Chen.

Kao Wu—infant son of Kao Chen.

Kung Wen-fa—Senior Advocate from Mars.

Ling Hen—henchman for Herrick.

Liu Chang—brothel keeper/pimp.

Loehr—alias of DeVore.

Lotte—student at Oxford; sister of Wolf.

Lo Wen—personal servant to Hans Ebert.

Lu Cao—*amah* (maidservant) to Jelka Tolonen.

Lu Ming-shao—"Whiskers Lu," Triad boss.

Lu Nan Jen—the "Oven Man."

Lu Wang-pei—murder suspect.

Mi Feng—"Little Bee," maid to Wang Hsien.

Mu Chua—Madam of the House of the Ninth Ecstasy, a singsong house, or brothel.

Novacek, Lubos—merchant; father of Sergey Novacek.

Novacek, Sergey—sculptor and student at Oxford.

Reynolds—alias of DeVore.

Schenck, Hung-li—Governor of the Mars Colony.

Siang Che—martial arts instructor to Jelka Tolonen.

Spatz, Gustav—Director of the Wiring Project.

Sweet Flute—*mui tsai* to Madam Chuang Lian.

T'ai Cho—tutor and "guardian" to Kim Ward.

Tarrant—company head.

Tissan, Catherine—student at Oxford.

Tong Chou—alias of Kao Chen.

Tsang Yi—friend of Heng Chian-ye.

Tung T'an—Senior Consultant at the Melfi Clinic.

Turner—alias of DeVore.

Wang Ti—wife of Kao Chen.

Ward, Kim—Clayborn orphan and scientist.

Wolf—student at Oxford and brother of Lotte.

The Sound of Jade

At rise of day we sacrificed to the Wind God,
When darkly, darkly, dawn glimmered in the sky.
Officers followed, horsemen led the way;
They brought us out to the wastes beyond the town,
Where river mists fall heavier than rain,
And the fires on the hill leap higher than the stars.
Suddenly I remembered the early levees at Court
When you and I galloped to the Purple Yard.
As we walked our horses up Dragon Tail Way
We turned and gazed at the green of the Southern Hills.
Since we parted, both of us have been growing old;
And our minds have been vexed by many anxious cares;
Yet even now I fancy my ears are full
Of the sound of jade tinkling on your bridle-straps.

—PO CHU-I, *To Li Chien* (A.D. 819)

IT WAS NIGHT and the moon lay like a blinded eye upon the satin darkness of the Nile. From where he stood, on the balcony high above the river, Wang Hsien could feel the slow, warm movement of the air like the breath of a sleeping woman against his cheek. He sighed and laid his hands upon the cool stone of the balustrade, looking out to his right, to the north, where in the distance the great lighthouse threw its long sweeping arm of light across the delta. For a while he watched it, feeling as empty as the air through which it moved; then he turned back, looking up at the moon itself. So clear the nights were here. And the stars. He shivered, the bitterness flooding back. The stars . . .

A voice broke into his reverie. "*Chieh Hsia?* Are you ready for us?"

It was Sun Li Hua, Master of the Inner Chamber. He stood just inside the doorway, his head bowed, his two assistants a respectful distance behind him, their heads lowered. Wang Hsien turned 'and made a brief gesture, signifying that they should begin; then he turned back, staring up at the stars.

He remembered being with his two eldest sons, Chang Ye and Lieh Tsu, on the coast of Mozambique in summer. A late summer night with the bright stars filling the heavens overhead. They had sat there around an open fire, the three of them, naming the stars and their constellations, watching the Dipper move across the black velvet of the sky until the fire was ash and

the day was come again. It was the last time he had been with
them alone. Their last holiday together.

And now they were dead. Both of them lying in their coffins,
still and cold beneath the earth. And where were their spirits
now? Up there? Among the eternal stars? Or was there only one
soul, the *hun*, trapped and rotting in the ground? He gritted his
teeth, fighting against his sense of bitterness and loss, hardening
himself against it. But the bitterness remained. Was it so? he
asked himself. Did the spirit soul—the *p'o*—rise up to Heaven
as they said, or was there only this? This earth, this sky, and
Man between them? He shuddered. Best not ask. Best keep such
thoughts at bay, lest the darkness answer you.

He shivered, his hands gripping the stone balustrade fiercely.
Gods, but he missed them! Missed them beyond the power of
words to say. He filled his hours, keeping his mind busy with the
myriad affairs of state. Even so, he could not keep himself from
thinking of them. Where are you? he would ask himself on
waking. Where are you, Chang Ye, who smiled so sweetly? And
you, Lieh Tsu, my *ying tao*, my baby peach, always my favorite?
Where are you now?

Murdered, a brutal voice in him insisted. And only ash and
bitterness remain.

He turned savagely, angry with himself. Now he would not
sleep. Bone-tired as he was, he would lie there, sleepless, impotent against the thousand bittersweet images that would come.

"Sun Li Hua!" he called impatiently, moving the diaphanous
curtain aside with one hand. "Bring me something to make me
sleep! *Ho yeh*, perhaps, or *tou chi*."

"At once, *Chieh Hsia*."

The Master of the Inner Chamber bowed low; then went to do
as he was bid. Wang Hsien watched him go; then turned to look
across at the huge low bed at the far end of the chamber. The
servants were almost finished. The silken sheets were turned
back, the flowers at the bedside changed, his sleeping robes laid
out, ready for the maids.

The headboard seemed to fill the end wall, the circle of the
Ywe Lung—the Moon Dragon, symbol of the Seven—carved
deep into the wood. The seven dragons formed a great wheel,

their regal snouts meeting at the hub, their lithe, powerful bodies forming the spokes, their tails the rim. Wang Hsien stared at it for a while; then nodded to himself as if satisfied. But deeper, at some dark, unarticulated level, he felt a sense of unease. The War, the murder of his sons—these things had made him far less certain than he'd been. He could no longer look at the *Ywe Lung* without questioning what had been done in the name of the Seven these last five years.

He looked down sharply. Five years. Was that all? Only five short years? So it was. Yet it felt as though a whole cycle of sixty years had passed since the *New Hope* had been blasted from the heavens and war declared. He sighed and put his hand up to his brow, remembering. It had been a nasty, vicious war; a war of little trust—where friend and enemy had worn the same smiling face. They had won, but their victory had failed to set things right. The struggle had changed the nature—the very essence— of Chung Kuo. Nothing would ever be the same again.

He waited until the servants left, backing away, bowed low, their eyes averted from their lord's face. Then he went across and stood before the wall-length mirror.

"You are an old man, Wang Hsien," he told himself softly, noting the deep lines about his eyes and mouth, the ivory yellow of his eyes, the loose roughness of his skin. "Moon-faced, they call you. Maybe so. But this moon has waxed and waned a thousand times and still I see no clearer by its light. Who are you, Wang Hsien? What kind of man are you?"

He heard a noise in the passageway outside and turned, tensing instinctively; then he relaxed, smiling.

The three girls bowed deeply, then came into the room, Little Bee making her way across to him, while Tender Willow and Sweet Rain busied themselves elsewhere in the room.

Little Bee knelt before him then looked up, her sweet, unaffected smile lifting his spirits, bringing a breath of youth and gaiety to his old heart.

"How are you this evening, good father?"

"I am fine." He lied, warmed by the sight of her. "And you, Mi Feng?"

"The better for seeing you, my Lord."

He laughed softly, then leaned forward, and touched her head gently, affectionately. Little Bee had been with him six years now, since her tenth birthday. She was like a daughter to him.

He turned, enjoying the familiar sight of his girls moving about the room, readying things for him. For a while it dispelled his previous mood, made him forget the darkness he had glimpsed inside and out. He let Little Bee remove his *pau* and sit him, naked, in a chair; then he closed his eyes and let his head fall back while she began to rub his chest and arms with oils. As ever, the gentle pressure of her hands against his skin roused him. Tender Willow came and held the bowl with the lavender glaze while Sweet Rain gave him ease, her soft, thin-boned fingers caressing him with practiced strokes until he spilled his seed. Then Little Bee washed him there, and, making him stand, bound him up in a single yellow-silk cloth before bringing a fresh sleeping garment.

He looked down at her tiny, delicate form as she stood before him, fastening his cloak, and felt a small shiver pass through him. Little Bee looked up, concerned.

"Are you sure you are all right, Father? Should I ask one of your wives to come to you?"

"It's nothing, Mi Feng. And no, I'll sleep alone tonight."

She fastened the last of the tiny, difficult buttons, looking up into his face a moment, then looked down again, frowning. "I worry for you, *Chieh Hsia,*" she said, turning away to take a brush from the table at her side. "Some days you seem to carry the whole world's troubles on your shoulders."

He smiled and let her push him down gently into the chair again. "I am Seven, Mi Feng. Who else should carry the burden of Chung Kuo?"

She was silent a moment, her fingers working to unbind his tightly braided queue. Then, leaning close, she whispered in his ear. "Your son," she said. "Why not make Ta-hung your regent?"

He laughed shortly, unamused. "And make Hung Mien-lo, that rascal friend of his, a T'ang in all but name?" He looked at her sharply. "Has he been talking to you?"

"Has who been talking to me, Father? I was thinking only of your health. You need more time to yourself."

He laughed, seeing how free from subterfuge she was. "Forget what I said, Mi Feng. Besides, I enjoy my duties."

She was brushing out his hair now, from scalp to tip, her tiny, perfectly formed body swaying gently, enticingly, beside him with each passage of the brush. He could see her in the mirror across the room, her silks barely veiling her nakedness.

He sighed and closed his eyes again, overcome by a strange mixture of emotions. Most men would envy me, he thought. And yet some days I think myself accursed. These girls . . . they would do whatever I wished, without a moment's hesitation; yet there is no joy in the thought. My sons are dead. How could joy survive such heartbreak?

He shuddered and stood up abruptly, surprising Little Bee, making the others turn and look across. They watched him walk briskly to the mirror and stand there as if in pain, grimacing into the glass. Then he turned back, his face bitter.

"Ta-hung!" he said scathingly, throwing himself down into the chair again. "I was a fool to let that one be born!"

There was a shocked intake of breath from the three girls. It was unlike Wang Hsien to say such things. Little Bee looked to the others and nodded, then waited until they were gone before speaking to him again.

She knelt, looking up into his face, concerned. "What is it, Wang Hsien? What eats at you like poison?"

"My sons!" he said in sudden agony. "My sons are dead!"

"Not all your sons," she answered gently, taking his hands in her own. "Wang Ta-hung yet lives. And Wang Sau-leyan."

"A weakling and a libertine!" he said bitterly, not looking at her, staring past her into space. "I had two fine, strong sons. Good, upstanding men with all their mother's finest qualities. And now—" He shivered violently and looked at her, his features racked with pain, his hands gripping hers tightly. "This war has taken everything, Mi Feng. Everything. Some days I think it has left me hollow, emptied of all I was."

"No . . ." she said, sharing his pain. "No, my Lord. Not everything."

He let her hands fall from his and stood again, turning away from her and staring at the door that led out onto the balcony.

"It is the most bitter lesson," he said fiercely, "that a man might own the world and yet have nothing."

Little Bee swallowed and looked down. She had seen her master in many moods, but never like this.

She turned, realizing there was someone in the chamber with them. It was Sun Li Hua. He stood in the doorway, his head bowed. In his hands was the bowl with the lavender glaze Tender Willow had taken out to him only moments earlier.

"*Chieh Hsia?*"

Wang Hsien turned abruptly, facing the newcomer, clearly angered by the interruption. Then he seemed to collect himself and dropped his head slightly. He looked across at Little Bee and with a forced smile dismissed her.

"Good night, *Chieh Hsia*," she said softly, backing away. "May Kuan Yin bring you peace."

———

SUN LI HUA stood there after the maid had gone, perfectly still, awaiting his master's orders.

"Come in, Master Sun," Wang Hsien said after a moment. He turned away and walked slowly across the room, sitting down heavily on his bed.

"Are you all right, *Chieh Hsia?*" Sun Li Hua asked. He set the bowl down on the small table at the bedside then looked at his master. "Has one of the maids done something to upset you?"

Wang Hsien glanced at his Master of the Inner Chamber almost without recognition, then shook his head irritably. "What is this?" he said, pointing at the bowl.

"It is your sleeping potion, *Chieh Hsia*. Lotus seeds mixed with your own life elixir. It should help you sleep."

Wang Hsien took a deep, shuddering breath, then reached out and took the bowl in one hand, sipping from it. The *ho yeh* was slightly bitter to the taste—a bitterness augmented by the salt tang of his own *yang* essence, his semen—but not unpleasant. He drained the bowl, then looked back at Sun Li Hua, holding out the empty bowl for him to take. "You will wake me at five, yes?"

Sun Li Hua took the bowl and backed away, bowing again. "Of course, *Chieh Hsia*."

Sun Li Hua watched the old T'ang turn and slide his legs between the sheets, lower his head onto the pillow, and pull the covers up about his shoulders. Two minutes, he thought; that's all the good Doctor Yueh said it would take.

Sun Li Hua moved back, beneath the camera, waiting in the doorway until he heard the old T'ang's breathing change. Then, setting the bowl down, he took a key from inside his silks and reached up, opening a panel high up in the door's frame. It popped back, revealing a tiny keyboard and a timer unit. Quickly he punched the combination. The timer froze, two amber lights appearing at the top of the panel.

He counted to ten, then touched the EJECT panel. At once a thin, transparent card dropped into the tray beneath the keyboard. He slipped it into his pocket, put its replacement into the slot at the side, and punched SET.

"Good," he said softly, closing the panel and slipping the key back inside his silks. Then taking a pair of gloves from his pocket, he stepped back inside the bedchamber.

━━━◆◆◆◆◆━━━

SIX FLOORS BELOW, at the far end of the palace, two soldiers were sitting in a cramped guardroom, talking.

The younger of them, a lieutenant, turned momentarily from the bank of screens that filled the wall in front of him and looked across at his Captain. "What do you think will happen, Otto? Will they close all the companies down?"

Captain Fischer, Head of the T'ang's personal security, looked up from behind his desk and smiled. "Your guess is as good as anyone's, Wolf. But I'll tell you this, whatever they do there'll be trouble."

"You think so?"

"Well, think about it. The volume of seized assets is so vast that if the Seven freeze them it's certain to damage the market badly. However, if they redistribute all that wealth in the form of rewards there's the problem of who gets what. A lot of people are going to be jealous or dissatisfied. On the other hand, they can't just give it back. There has to be some kind of punishment."

The lieutenant turned back to his screens, scanning them conscientiously. "I agree. But where do they draw the line? How do they distinguish between those who were actively against them and those who were simply unhelpful?"

Fischer shrugged. "I don't know, Wolf. I really don't."

They were discussing the most recent spate of Confiscations and Demotions, a subject never far from most people's lips these days. In the past eighteen months more than one hundred and eighty thousand First Level families had been "sent down" and all their material goods confiscated by the Seven as punishment for what had been termed "subversive activities." A further five thousand families had simply vanished from the face of Chung Kuo—to the third generation as the law demanded—for active treason against the Seven. But now, with the War in its final stages and the clamor for peace growing daily, the Confiscations had become a delicate subject and a major bone of contention between those who wanted retribution and those who simply wanted to damp down the fires of resentment and bitterness that such retribution brought in its wake.

The lieutenant turned, eyeing his Captain speculatively. "I hear there's even talk of reopening the House."

Fischer looked back at his junior officer sternly, his voice suddenly hard. "You would do best to forget such talk, Lieutenant."

"Sir." The lieutenant gave a curt bow of his head, then turned back to his screens.

Fischer studied Rahn's back a moment, then leaned back, yawning. It was just after two, the hour of the Ox. The palace was silent, the screens empty of activity. In an hour his shift would be over and he could sleep. He smiled. That is, if Lotte would let him sleep.

He rubbed at his neck, then leaned forward again and began to catch up with his paperwork. He had hardly begun when the door to his right crashed open. He was up out of his seat at once, his gun drawn, aimed at the doorway.

"Sun Li Hua! What in Hell's name?"

The Master of the Inner Chamber looked terrible. His silks were torn, his hair disheveled. He leaned against the doorpost for support, his eyes wide with shock, his cheeks wet with tears. He reached out, his hand trembling violently, then shook his head, his mouth working mutely. His voice, when he found it, was cracked, unnaturally high.

"The T'ang . . ."

Fischer glanced across at the screen that showed Wang Hsien's bedchamber, then back at Sun Li Hua. "What is it, Master Sun? What's happened?"

For a moment Sun Li Hua seemed unable to speak, then he fell to his knees. A great, racking sob shook his whole body, then he looked up, his eyes wild, distraught. "Our Master, the T'ang. He's . . . dead."

Fischer had known as soon as he had seen Sun Li Hua, had felt his stomach fall away from him with fear; but he had not wanted to know—not for certain.

"How?" he heard himself say. Then, seeing what it meant, he looked across at his lieutenant, pre-empting him, stopping him from pressing the general alarm that would wake the whole palace.

"Touch nothing, Wolf. Not until I order you to. Get Kurt and Alan here at once."

He turned back to Sun. "Who else knows, Master Sun? Who else have you told?"

"No one," Sun answered, his voice barely audible. "I came straight here. I didn't know what to do. They've killed him, killed him while he slept."

"Who? Who's killed him? What do you mean?"

"Fu and Chai. I'm certain it was they. Fu's stiletto . . ."

Fischer swallowed, appalled. "They knifed him? Your two assistants knifed him?" He turned to his lieutenant. "Wolf, take two copies of the surveillance tape. Send one to Marshal Tolonen at Bremen. Another to General Helm in Rio."

"Sir!"

He thought quickly. No one knew anything. Not yet. Only he and Wolf and Sun Li Hua. And the murderers, of course; but they would be telling no one. He turned back to his lieutenant. "Keep Master Sun here. And when Kurt and Alan come have them wait here until I get back. And Wolf . . ."

"Sir?"

"Tell no one anything. Not yet. Understand me?"

▬▬▬▬

W A N G   H S I E N lay there on his back, his face relaxed, as if in sleep, yet pale—almost *Hung Mao* in its paleness. Fischer leaned across and felt for a pulse at the neck. Nothing. The flesh was cold. The T'ang had been dead an hour at least.

Fischer shuddered and stepped back, studying the body once again. The silk sheets were dark, sticky with the old man's blood. The silver-handled stiletto jutted from the T'ang's bared chest, the blade thrust in all the way up to the handle. He narrowed his eyes, considering. It would have taken some strength to do that, even to a sleeping man. And not just strength. It was not easy for one man to kill another. One needed the will for the job.

Could Fu have done it? Or Chai? Fischer shook his head. He could not imagine either of them doing this. And yet if not them, who?

He looked about him, noting how things lay. Then, his mind made up, he turned and left the room, knowing he had only minutes in which to act.

▬▬▬▬

T H E   B O A R D lay on the desk in front of DeVore, its nineteen-by-nineteen grid part overlaid with a patterning of black and white stones. Most of the board was empty; only in the top right-hand corner—in *Chu*, the West—were the stones concentrated heavily. There the first stage of the battle had been fought, with black pressing white hard into the corner, slowly choking off its breath, blinding its eyes until, at last, the group was dead, the ten stones taken from the board.

It was an ancient game—one of the ten games of the West Lake, played by those two great masters from Hai-nin, Fan Si-pin and Su Ting-an, back in 1763. DeVore played it often, from memory, stopping, as now, at the fifty-ninth move to query what Fan, playing white, had chosen. It was an elegant, enthralling game, the two masters so perfectly balanced in ability, their moves so exquisitely thought out, that he felt a shiver of delight contemplating what was to come. Even so, he could not help but search for those small ways in which each player's game might have been improved.

DeVore looked up from the board and glanced across at the young man who stood, his back to him, on the far side of the room. Then, taking a wafer-thin ice-paper pamphlet from his jacket pocket, he unfolded it and held it out.

"Have you heard of this new group, Stefan—the *Ping Tiao?*"

Lehmann turned, his face expressionless, then came across and took the pamphlet, examining it. After a moment he looked back at DeVore, his cold, pink eyes revealing nothing. "Yes, I've heard of them. They're low-level types, aren't they? Why are you interested?"

"A man must be interested in many things," DeVore answered cryptically, leaning forward to take a white stone from the bowl, hefting it in his hand. "The *Ping Tiao* want what we want—to destroy the Seven."

"Yes, but they would destroy us just as readily. They're terrorists. They want *only* to destroy."

"I know. Even so, they could be useful. We might walk the same path awhile, don't you think?"

"And then?"

DeVore smiled tightly. Lehmann knew as well as he. Then there would be war between them. A war he would win. He looked down at the board again. The fifty-ninth move. What would *he* have played in Fan's place? His smile broadened, became more natural. How many times had he thought it through? A hundred? A thousand? And always, inevitably, he would make Fan's move, taking the black at 4/1 to give himself a temporary breathing space. So delicately were things balanced at that point that to do otherwise—to make any of a dozen other tempting plays—would be to lose it all.

A wise man, Fan Si-pin. He knew the value of sacrifice: the importance of making one's opponents work hard for their small victories, knowing that while the battle was lost in *Chu*, the war went on in *Shang* and *Ping* and *Tsu*.

So it was now, in Chung Kuo. Things were balanced very delicately. And one wrong move . . . He looked up at Lehmann again, studying the tall young albino.

"You ask what would happen should we succeed, but there are other, more immediate questions. Are the *Ping Tiao* important enough? You know how the media exaggerate these things. And would an alliance with them harm or strengthen us?"

Lehmann met his gaze. "As I said, the *Ping Tiao* are a low-level organization. Worse, they're idealists. It would be hard to work with such men. They would have fewer weaknesses than those we're used to dealing with."

"And yet they *are* men. They have needs, desires."

"Maybe so, but they would mistrust us from the start. In their eyes we are First Level, their natural enemies. Why should they work with us?"

DeVore smiled and stood up, coming round the desk. "It's not a question of choice, Stefan, but necessity. They need someone like us. Think of the losses they've sustained."

He was about to say more—to outline his plan—when there was an urgent knocking at the door.

DeVore looked across, meeting Lehmann's eyes. He had ordered his lieutenant, Wiegand, not to disturb him unless it was vitally important.

"Come in!"

Wiegand took two steps into the room, then came sharply to attention, his head bowed. "I've a call on the coded channel, sir. Triple-A rated."

DeVore narrowed his eyes, conscious of how closely Lehmann was watching him. "Who is it?"

"It's Stifel, sir. He says he has little time."

"Stifel" was the code name for Otto Fischer in Alexandria. DeVore hesitated a moment, his mind running through possibilities; then nodded.

"Okay. Switch it through."

It was a nonvisual, Fischer's voice artificially distorted to avoid even the remote possibility of recognition.

"Well, Stifel? What is it?"

"The moon is down, sir. An hour past at most."

DeVore caught his breath. "How?"

"Eclipsed."

DeVore stared across at Lehmann, astonished. He hesitated a moment, considering, then spoke again.

"How many know about this?"

"Three, maybe four."

"Good. Keep it that way." He thought quickly. "Who's guarding our fallen moon?"

"No one. A camera . . ."

"Excellent. Now listen . . ."

He spelled out quickly what he wanted, then broke contact, knowing that Fischer would do exactly as he had asked.

"Who's dead?"

DeVore turned and looked at Lehmann again. His face, like the tone of his words, seemed utterly devoid of curiosity, as if the question were a mere politeness, the answer a matter of indifference to him.

"Wang Hsien," he answered. "It seems he's been murdered in his bed."

If he had expected the albino to show any sign of surprise he would have been disappointed, but he knew the young man better than that.

"I see," Lehmann said. "And you know who did it?"

"The agent, yes, but not who he was acting for." DeVore sat behind his desk again, then looked up at Lehmann. "It was Sun Li Hua."

"You know that for certain?"

"Not for certain, no. But I'd wager a million *yuan* on it."

Lehmann came across and stood at the edge of the desk. "So what now?"

DeVore met his eyes briefly, then looked down at the board again. "We wait. Until we hear from Stifel again. Then the fun begins."

"Fun?"

"Yes, fun. You'll see. But go now, Stefan. Get some rest. I'll call you when I need you."

He realized he was still holding the white stone. It lay in his palm like a tiny moon, cold, moist with his sweat. He opened out his fingers and stared at it, then lifted it and wiped it. The fifty-ninth stone.

The game had changed dramatically, the balance altered in his favor. *The moon was down. Eclipsed.*

DeVore smiled, then nodded to himself, suddenly knowing where to play the stone.

◆◆◆◆◆

THE DEAD T'ANG lay where he had left him, undisturbed, his long gray hair fanned out across the pillow, his arms at his sides, the palms upturned. Fischer stood there a moment, looking down at the corpse, breathing deeply, preparing himself. Then, knowing he could delay no longer, he bent down and put his hand behind the cold stiff neck, lifting the head, drawing the hair back from the ear.

It was not, physically, difficult to do—the flesh parted easily before the knife; the blood stopped flowing almost as soon as it had begun—yet he was conscious of a deep, almost overpowering reluctance in himself. This was a T'ang! A Son of Heaven! He shivered, letting the severed flesh fall, then turned the head and did the same to the other side.

He lowered the head onto the pillow and stepped back, appalled. Outwardly he seemed calm, almost icy in his control, but inwardly he quaked with an inexplicable, almost religious fear of what he was doing. His pulse raced, his stomach churned, and all the while a part of him kept saying to himself, What are you doing, Otto? What are you doing?

He stared, horrified, at the two thick question-marks of flesh that lay now on the pillow, separated from their owner's head; then he steeled himself and reached out to take them. He drew the tiny bag from inside his jacket and dropped them into it, then sealed the bag and returned it to the pocket.

Wang Hsien lay there, regal even in death, indifferent to all that had been done to him. Fischer stared at him awhile, mesmerized, awed by the power of the silent figure. Then, realizing he was wasting time, he bent over the corpse again, smoothing the hair back into place, hiding the disfigurement.

Nervousness made him laugh—a laugh he stifled quickly. He shuddered and looked about him again, then went to the doorway. There he paused, reaching up to reset the camera, checking the elapsed time against his wrist timer, then moved the camera's clock forward until the two were synchronized. That done, he pressed out the combination quickly. The lights at the top changed from amber to green, signifying that the camera was functioning again.

He looked back, checking the room one final time. Then, satisfied that nothing was disturbed, he backed out of the room, pulling the door to silently behind him, his heart pounding, his mouth dry with fear, the sealed bag seeming to burn where it pressed against his chest.

━━━━━━

WANG TA-HUNG woke to whispering in his room and sat up, clutching the blankets to his chest, his mind dark with fear.

"Who is it?" he called out, his voice quavering. "Kuan Yin preserve me, who is it?"

A figure approached the huge bed, bowed. "It is only I, Excellency. Your servant, Wu Ming."

Wang Ta-hung, the T'ang's eldest surviving son, pulled the blankets tighter about his neck and stared, wide-eyed, past his Master of the Bedchamber, into the darkness beyond.

"Who is there, Wu Ming? Who were you whispering to?"

A second figure stepped from the darkness and stood beside the first, his head bowed. He was a tall, strongly built Han dressed in dark silks, his beard braided into three tiny pigtails, his face, when it lifted once again, solid, unreadable. A handsome, yet inexpressive face.

"Excellency."

"Hung Mien-lo!"

Wang Ta-hung turned and glanced at the ornate timepiece beside the bed, then twisted back, facing the two men, his face twitching with alarm.

"It is almost half two! What are you doing here? What's happened?"

Hung Mien-lo sat on the bed beside the frightened twenty-year-old, taking his upper arms gently but firmly in his hands.

"It's all right, Ta-hung. Please, calm yourself. I have some news, that's all."

The young Prince nodded, but it was as if he were still in the grip of some awful dream: his eyes continued to stare, a muscle in his left cheek twitched violently. He had been this way for eighteen months now, since the day he had found his two brothers dead in one of the guest bedrooms of the summer palace, their naked bodies gray-blue from the poison, the two maids they had been entertaining sprawled nearby, their pale limbs laced with blood, their eyes gouged out.

Some said that the pale wasted-looking youth was mad; others that it was only natural for one of his sickly disposition to suffer after such a discovery. He had never been a strong boy, but now . . .

Hung Mien-lo stroked the young man's shoulder, comforting him, knowing the delicacy of what lay ahead—that what must be said might well send him deeper into madness. He spoke softly, reassuringly. "It is your father, Ta-hung. I am afraid he is dead."

For a moment it didn't register. There was a flicker of disbelief, of uncertainty. Then, abruptly, the Prince pulled himself away, scrambling back until he was pressed up against the headboard, his eyes wide, his mouth open.

"How?" he said, the words the tiniest, frightened squeak. "*How* did he die?"

Hung Mien-lo ignored the question. He spoke calmly, using the same reassuring tone as before. "You must get dressed, Ta-hung. You must come and bear witness to what has happened."

Wang Ta-hung laughed shrilly, then buried his head in his arms, shaking it wildly. "No-o-o!" he cried, his voice muffled. "No-oh! God no, not again!"

Hung Mien-lo turned and clicked his fingers. At once Wu Ming bustled off to get things ready. Yes, Hung thought, he at least understands. For now that the old T'ang is dead, Ta-hung is T'ang in his place, mad or no. Indeed, the madder the better as far as I'm concerned, for the more Ta-hung relies on me, the more power lies within my hands.

He smiled and stood, seeing how the young man cowered away from him, yet how his eyes beseeched his help. Yes, indeed, Hung Mien-lo thought; my hour has truly come, the hour I waited for so long as companion to this young fool. And now I am effectively first man in City Africa. The shaper. The orderer. The granter of favors.

Inwardly he felt exultation, a soaring, brilliant joy that had lit in him the moment he had been told; yet this, more than any other moment, was a time for masks. He put one on now, shaping his face toward sternness, to the expression of a profound grief. Satisfied, he went over to the young Prince and lifted him from the bed, standing him on his feet.

"It was so cold," the youth murmured, looking up into his face. "When I touched Chang Ye's shoulder, it was like he had been laid in ice. The cold of it seemed to burn my hand. I . . ." He hesitated, then looked down, turning his hand, lifting the palm to stare at it.

"That's done with, Ta-hung. You must get dressed now and see your father. You are the eldest now, the Head of your family. You must take charge of things."

Ta-hung stared back at him uncomprehendingly. "Take charge?"

"Don't worry," Hung said, unfastening the cord, then pulling the Prince's sleeping silks down off his shoulders, stripping him naked. "I'll be there beside you, Ta-hung. I'll tell you what to do."

Wu Ming returned and began at once to dress and groom the Prince. He was only partway through when Ta-hung broke away from him and threw himself down at Hung Mien-lo's feet, sobbing.

"I'm frightened, Mien-lo. So frightened!"

Hung glanced at Wu Ming, then reached down and hauled the Prince roughly to his feet. "Stop it! You've got to stop this at once!"

There was a moment's shocked silence, then the young Prince bowed his head. "I'm sorry, I . . ."

"No!" Hung barked. "No apologies. Don't you understand, Ta-hung? You're *T'ang* now. *Seven*. It is I who should apologize, not you, *Chieh Hsia*."

Chieh Hsia. It was the first time the words of imperial address had been used to the young man and Hung Mien-lo could see at once the effect they had on him. Though Ta-hung still shivered, though tears still coursed freely down his cheeks, he stood straighter, slightly taller, realizing for the first time what he had become.

"You understand then? Good. Then remember this. Let none but a T'ang touch you without your permission. And let no man, not even a T'ang, speak to you as I spoke then. You are T'ang now. Supreme. Understand me, *Chieh Hsia?*"

Ta-hung's voice when he answered was different, almost calm. "I understand you, Mien-lo. My father is dead and I am T'ang now."

"Good. Then, with your permission, we will go to see your father and pay our respects, neh?"

The slightest shudder passed through the young man's wasted frame, the smallest cloud of revulsion momentarily crossed the sky of his face, then he nodded. "As you say, Mien-lo. As you say."

———

WANG SAU-LEYAN heard their voices coming nearer— the rustle of silks and the sound of their soft footsteps on the tiled floor—and slid the door open, slipping out into the dimly lit corridor. He pulled the door to quietly, then turned, facing them. They came on quickly, talking all the while, not seeing him until they were almost on top of him. He saw the look of surprise on Hung Mien-lo's face, heard his brother's gasp of fear.

He smiled and gave the slightest bow. "I heard noises, Ta-hung. Voices calling softly but urgently in the darkness. What is happening, brother? Why do you wander the corridors at this early hour?"

He saw how Ta-hung looked to his friend—at a loss, his face a web of conflicting emotions—and smiled inwardly, enjoying his brother's impotence.

"I'm afraid there is bad news, Wang Sau-leyan," Hung Mien-lo answered him, bowing low, his face grave. "Your father is dead."

"Dead? But how?"

He saw how Hung Mien-lo glanced at his brother and knew at once that Ta-hung had not been told everything.

"It would be best if you came yourself, Excellency. I will explain everything then. But excuse us, please. We must pay our respects to the late T'ang."

He noted how pointedly Hung Mien-lo had emphasized the

last two words; how his voice, while still superficially polite, was a register of how he thought things had changed. Wang Sau-leyan smiled tightly at Hung, then bowed to his elder brother.

"I will get dressed at once."

He watched them go; then, satisfied, he slid the door open again and went back into his rooms.

A voice from the bed, young, distinctly feminine, called softly to him. "What was it, my love?"

He went across to her and slipping off his robe, joined her, naked beneath the sheets.

"It was nothing," he said, smiling down at his father's third wife. "Nothing at all."

━━━━━

WANG TA-HUNG stood in the doorway of his father's room staring in, fear constricting his throat. He turned and looked at Hung Mien-lo beseechingly. "I can't . . ."

"You are T'ang," Hung answered him firmly. "You can."

The young man swallowed, then turned back, his fists clenched at his sides. "I am T'ang," he repeated. "T'ang of City Africa."

Hung Mien-lo stood there a moment, watching him take the first few hesitant steps into the room, knowing how important the next few minutes were. Ta-hung had accustomed himself to the fact of his father's death. Now he must discover how the old man died. Must learn, firsthand, the fate of kings.

And if it drove him mad?

Hung Mien-lo smiled to himself, then stepped inside the room. Kings had been mad before. What was a king, after all, but a symbol—the visible sign of a system of government? As long as the City was ruled, what did it matter who gave the orders?

He stopped beside the old man's chair, watching the youth approach the bed. Surely he's seen? he thought. Yet Ta-hung was too still, too composed. Then the young T'ang turned, looking back at him.

"I knew," he said softly. "As soon as you told me, I knew he had been murdered."

Hung Mien-lo let his breath out. "You knew?" He looked

down. There, beneath him on the cushion, lay the T'ang's hairbrush. He leaned forward and picked it up, studying it a moment, appreciating the slender elegance of its ivory handle, the delicacy of its design. He was about to set it down when he noticed several strands of the old T'ang's hair trapped among the darkness of the bristles—long white strands, almost translucent in their whiteness, like the finest threads of ice. He frowned then looked back at Wang Ta-hung. "How do you feel, *Chieh Hsia*? Are you well enough to see others, or shall I delay?"

Wang Ta-hung looked about him, then turned and stared down at his father. He was still, unnaturally calm.

Perhaps this is it, thought Hung. Perhaps something has broken in him and this calmness is the first sign of it. But for once there seemed no trace of madness in Ta-hung, only a strange sense of dignity and distance, surprising because it was so unexpected.

"Let the others come," he said, his voice clear of any shade of fear, his eyes drinking in the sight of his murdered father. "There's no sense in delay."

Hung Mien-lo hesitated, suddenly uncertain, then turned and went to the door, telling the guard to bring Fischer and Sun Li Hua. Then he went back inside.

Wang Ta-hung was standing at the bedside. He had picked something up and was sniffing at it. Hung Mien-lo went across to him.

"What is this?" Ta-hung asked, handing him a bowl.

It was a perfect piece of porcelain. Its roundness and its perfect lavender glaze made it a delight to look at. Hung turned it in his hands, a faint smile on his lips. It was an old piece, too. *K'ang Hsi* perhaps . . . or perhaps not, for the coloring was wrong. But that was not what Ta-hung had meant. He had meant the residue.

Hung sniffed at it, finding the heavy, musky scent of it strangely familiar; then he turned, hearing voices at the door. It was Sun Li Hua and the Captain.

"Master Sun," he called out. "What was in this bowl?"

Sun bowed low and came into the room. "It was a sleeping potion, *Chieh Hsia*," he said, keeping his head bowed, addressing the new T'ang. "Doctor Yueh prepared it."

"And what was in it?" Hung asked, irritated by Sun's refusal to answer him directly.

Sun Li Hua hesitated a moment. "It was *ho yeh*, for insomnia, *Chieh Hsia*."

"*Ho yeh* and what?" Hung insisted, knowing the distinct smell of lotus seeds.

Sun glanced briefly at the young T'ang, as if for intercession, then bent his head. "It was mixed with the T'ang's own *yang* essence, *Chieh Hsia*."

"Ah . . ." He nodded, understanding.

He set the bowl down and turned away, looking about the room, noting the fresh flowers at the bedside, the T'ang's clothes laid out on the dresser ready for the morning.

He looked across at Fischer. "Has anything been disturbed?"

"No . . . Excellency."

He noted the hesitation and realized that although they knew how important he had suddenly become, they did not know quite how to address him. I must have a title, he thought. Chancellor, perhaps. Some peg to hang their respect upon.

He turned, looking across at the open door that led out onto the balcony. "Was this where the murderer entered?"

Fischer answered immediately. "No, Excellency."

"You're certain?"

"Quite certain, Excellency."

Hung Mien-lo turned, surprised. "How so?"

Fischer glanced up at the camera, then stepped forward. "It is all on tape, Excellency. Sun Li Hua's assistants, the brothers Ying Fu and Ying Chai, are the murderers. They entered the room shortly after Master Sun had given the T'ang his potion."

"Gods! And you have them?"

"Not yet, Excellency. But as no one has left the palace since the murder they must be here somewhere. My men are searching the palace even now to find them."

Ta-hung was watching everything with astonishment, his lips parted, his eyes wide and staring. Hung Mien-lo looked across at him a moment, then turned back to Fischer, giving a curt nod. "Good. But we want them alive. It's possible they were acting for another."

"Of course, Excellency."

Hung Mien-lo turned and went to the open door, pulling back the thin see-through curtain of silk and stepping out onto the balcony. It was cool outside, the moon low to his left. To his right the beam of the distant lighthouse cut the darkness, flashing across the dark waters of the Nile delta and sweeping on across the surrounding desert. He stood there a moment, his hands on the balustrade, staring down into the darkness of the river far below.

So, it was Fu and Chai. They were the hands. But who was behind them? Who besides himself had wanted the old man dead? Sun Li Hua? Perhaps. After all, Wang Hsien had humiliated him before his sons when Sun had asked that his brothers be promoted and the T'ang had refused. But that had been long ago. Almost three years now. If Sun, why now? And in any case, Fischer had said that Sun had been like a madman when he'd come to him, feverish with dismay.

Who, then? *Who*? He racked his brains, but no answer sprang to mind. Wang Sau-leyan? He shook his head. Why should that no-good wastrel want power? And what would he do with it but piss it away if he had it? No, Ta-hung's little brother was good only for bedding whores, not for intrigue. Yet if not he, then who?

There was an anguished cry from within the room. He recognized it at once. It was Ta-hung! He turned and rushed inside.

Ta-hung looked up at him as he entered, his face a window, opening upon his inner terror. He was leaning over his father, cradling the old man's head in the crook of his arm.

"Look!" he called out brokenly. "Look what they've done to him, the carrion! His ears! They've taken his ears!"

Hung Mien-lo stared back at him, horrified, then turned and looked at Sun Li Hua.

Any doubts he had harbored about the Master of the Inner Chamber were dispelled instantly. Sun stood there, his mouth gaping, his eyes wide with horror.

Hung turned, his mind in turmoil now. His ears! Why would they take his ears? Then, before he could reach out and catch him, he saw Ta-hung slide from the bed and fall senseless to the floor.

"Prince Yuan! Wake up, your father's here!"

Li Yuan rolled over and sat up. Nan Ho stood in the doorway, a lantern in one hand, his head bowed.

"My father?"

A second figure appeared behind Nan Ho in the doorway. "Yes, Yuan. It's late, I know, but I must talk with you at once."

Nan Ho moved aside, bowing low, to let the T'ang pass; then backed out, closing the door silently behind him.

Li Shai Tung sat on the bed beside his son, then reached across to switch on the bedside lamp. In the lamp's harsh light his face was ashen, his eyes red-rimmed.

Li Yuan frowned. "What is it, Father?"

"Ill news. Wang Hsien is dead. Murdered in his bed. Worse, word of it has got out, somehow. There are riots in the lower levels. The *Ping Tiao* are inciting the masses to rebellion."

"Ah . . ." Li Yuan felt his stomach tighten. It was what they had all secretly feared. The War had left them weak. The Dispersionists had been scattered and defeated; but there were other enemies these days, others who wanted to pull them down and set themselves atop the wheel of state.

He met his father's eyes. "What's to be done?"

Li Shai Tung sighed, then looked aside. "I have spoken to Tsu Ma and Wu Shih already. They think we should do nothing, that we should let the fires burn themselves out." He paused, then shrugged. "Tensions have been high lately. Perhaps it would be good to let things run their course for once."

"Perhaps."

Li Yuan studied his father, knowing from his uncertainty that this was a course he had been talked into, not one he was happy with.

The T'ang stared away broodingly into the far corner of the room, then turned, facing his son again.

"Wang Hsien was a good man, Yuan. A strong man. I depended on him. In Council he was a staunch ally, a wise counselor. Like a brother to me, he was. The death of his sons . . . it brought us very close."

He shook his head, then turned away, suddenly angry, a tear spilling down his cheek. "And now Wang Ta-hung is T'ang! Ta-hung, of all the gods' creations! Such a weak and foolish young man!" He turned back, facing Li Yuan, anger and bitterness blazing in his eyes. "Kuan Yin preserve us all! This is an ill day for the Seven."

"And for Chung Kuo."

When his father had gone Li Yuan got up and pulled on his robe, then crossed the room and stood by the window, staring out into the moonlit garden. It was as his father said, the Seven were made much weaker by this death. Yet Wang Hsien had been an old man. A very old man. They would have had to face the consequences of his death some day or other, so why not now? Wang Ta-hung was weak and foolish, that was true; but there were six other T'ang to lead and guide him. That was the strength of the Seven, surely? Where one might fall, the Seven would stand. So it was. So it would always be.

He turned and looked down. There, on the low table by the window, was his bow, the elegant curve of it silvered by the moonlight. He bent down and lifted it, holding the cool smooth surface of the wood against his cheek a moment. Then, abruptly, he spun about, as he'd been taught, the bow suddenly at his waist, the string tensed as if to let fly.

He shivered, then felt himself grow still, looking back.

He had not thought of it in a long time, but now it came clear to him, the memory released like an arrow across the years. He saw himself, eight years old, sat beside Fei Yen in the meadow by the lake. He could smell the faint sweet scent of jasmine, see the pale cream of her sleeve, feel once more the shudder that had run through him as it brushed deliciously against his knees. Across from them sat his brother, Han Ch'in, his booted feet like two young saplings rooted in the earth, his hands placed firmly on his knees.

Wang Sau-leyan . . . Yes, he remembered it now. Fei Yen had been talking about Wang Sau-leyan and how he had been caught in his father's bed. Ten years old, he had been. Only ten, and to be caught with a girl in his father's bed!

Li Yuan frowned, then swallowed, his mouth suddenly dry, remembering how Fei Yen had laughed, not shocked but amused by the tale. He recalled how she had fanned herself slowly, how her eyes had looked briefly inward before she raised her eyebrows suggestively, making Han guffaw with laughter. Fei Yen. His brother's wife. And now his own betrothed. The woman he would be marrying only weeks from now.

And Wang Sau-leyan? Yes, it all made sense. He remembered how Wang Hsien had exiled his youngest son, had sent him in disgrace to his floating palace, a hundred thousand *li* above Chung Kuo. And there the boy had stayed a whole year, with only the T'ang's own guards for company. A year. It was a long, long time for such a spirited child. An eternity, it must have seemed. Long enough, perhaps, to break the last thin ties of love and filial respect. What bitterness that must have engendered in the boy—what hatred of his captors.

Li Yuan looked down at the bow in his hands and shivered violently. That day with Fei Yen, it had been the day of the archery contest—the day she had let his brother best her. And yet, only two days later, Han Ch'in was dead and she a widow.

He shuddered, then saw her smile and tilt her head, showing her tiny perfect teeth. And wondered.

━━━━━━

SUN LI HUA, Master of the Inner Chamber, stood by the door, watching as the doctors examined the body. He had made his statement already, sat beneath the glaring lights of the Security cameras while monitors tested his vital body signs for abnormalities. He had passed that test and now only one thing stood between him and success.

He saw them mutter among themselves, then Fischer turned and came across to him.

"It tests out, Master Sun," he said, making a small bow. "The *ho yeh* was pure."

"I did not doubt it," Sun answered, allowing a slight trace of indignation to enter his voice. "Doctor Yueh is a trusted servant. He had served the T'ang for more than forty years."

"So I understand. And yet men can be bought, can they not?"

Fischer smiled tightly, then bowed again and walked on, leaving the room momentarily. Sun watched him go. *What does it matter what he suspects?* he thought. *He can prove nothing.*

He turned, then went across to where the doctors were busy at their work. One cradled the T'ang's head, while a second delicately examined the area where the ear had been cut away. They would make new ears from the T'ang's own genetic material, for a T'ang must be buried whole. But as to where the originals had gone, there was no sign as yet, just as there was no sign of Fu or Chai.

A mystery . . .

Sun Li Hua stared down into the old man's vacant face and took a deep breath, filled suddenly with a sense of grim satisfaction. *Yes, old man,* he thought, *you humiliated me once, before your sons. Refused to promote my brothers. Held down my family. But now you're dead and we will rise in spite of you. For another has promised to raise the Sun family high, to make it second family in all of City Africa.*

He turned away, smiling beneath the mask of grief. It had been so easy. Fu and Chai—what simpletons they'd been! He thought back, remembering how he had drugged them and taped them murdering the copy of the T'ang. But they knew nothing of that, only that they were being sought for a crime they had no memory of committing.

Trust—it was a fragile thing. Break it and the world broke with it. And Wang Hsien had broken Sun Li Hua's trust in him some years ago.

He glanced across and saw himself in the wall-length mirror opposite. *Do I look any different?* he wondered. *Does my face betray the change that's taken place in me? No. For I was different that very day, after he'd spurned me. It was then I first stuck the knife in him. Then. For the rest was only the fulfillment of that first imagining.*

He turned and saw Fischer standing there, watching him from the doorway.

"Well, Captain, have you found the murderers?"

"Not yet, Master Sun, but we shall, I promise you."

Fischer let his eyes rest on Sun a moment longer, then looked away. It was as DeVore said: Sun Li Hua was the murderer. While Sun had been in his office Fischer had had his lieutenant take a sample of his blood under the pretext of giving him a sedative. That sample had shown what DeVore had said it would show, traces of CT-7, a drug that created the symptoms of acute distress.

His shock, his overwhelming grief—both had been chemically faked. And why fake such things unless there was a reason? And then there was the camera. There was no way of proving it had been tampered with, but it made sense. Apart from himself, only Sun Li Hua knew the combination; only Sun had the opportunity. It was possible, of course, that they had simply not seen Fu and Chai go into the room, but his lieutenant was a good man—alert, attentive. He would not have missed something so obvious. Which meant that the tape of the murder had been superimposed.

But whose hand lay behind all this? Hung Mien-lo? It was possible. After all, he had most to gain from Wang Hsien's death. Yet he had seen with his own eyes how fair, how scrupulous, Hung had been in dealing with the matter. He had let nothing be rushed or overlooked, as if he, too, were anxious to know who had ordered the T'ang's death.

As he would need to. For he would know that whoever killed a T'ang might kill again.

No. *Would* kill again.

"Captain Fischer . . ."

He turned. It was Wang Ta-hung. Fischer bowed low, wondering at the same time where Hung Mien-lo had got to.

"Yes, *Chieh Hsia?*"

"Have you found them yet?"

He hesitated. It had been almost thirty minutes since they had begun searching for Sun's two assistants and still there was no trace of them.

"No, *Chieh Hsia.* I'm afraid—"

He stopped, astonished. A man had appeared in the doorway at Wang Ta-hung's back, his hair untidy, his clothing torn. In his hand he held a bloodied knife.

"Wang Sau-leyan!"

Ta-hung spun around and cried out, then took two faltering steps backward, as if he feared an attack. But Wang Sau-leyan merely laughed and threw the knife down.

"The bastards were hiding in my rooms. One cut me here." He pulled down his *pau* at the neck, revealing a thin line of red. "I stuck him for that. The other tried to take my knife from me, but he knew better after a while."

"Gods!" said Fischer, starting forward. "Where are they?"

Wang Sau-leyan straightened up, touching the wound gingerly. "Where I left them. I don't think they'll be going far."

Fischer turned and looked across at the doctors. "Quick, now! Come with me, *ch'un tzu*! I must save those men."

Wang Sau-leyan laughed and shook his head. He was staring at his brother strangely. "Do what you must, Captain. You'll find them where I left them."

Fischer turned, facing the new T'ang. "*Chieh Hsia*, will you come?"

Wang Ta-hung swallowed, then nodded. "Of course."

They met Hung Mien-lo in the corridor outside.

"You've found them, then?"

Fischer bowed, then glanced at Wang Sau-leyan. "The Prince found them, in his quarters. He has incapacitated them, it seems."

Hung Mien-lo glared at Wang Sau-leyan, then turned angrily away. "Come, then. Let's see what the Prince has left us, neh?"

━━━━━

WANG SAU-LEYAN sat on a footstool in his bedroom, letting the doctor dress the wound at his neck. Across from him Fischer was moving about the bathroom suite, examining the two corpses.

"Why?" Hung Mien-lo asked him again, standing over him almost threateningly. "Why did you kill them?"

He looked up, ignoring Hung Mien-lo, his eyes piercing his elder brother. "They were dangerous men. They killed our father. What was to stop them killing me?"

He smiled tightly, then looked back at the bathroom. He saw Fischer straighten up, turn, and come to the doorway. He had been searching the dead men's clothing, as if looking for something they had stolen.

"Where are they?" Fischer asked, looking directly at him.

Wang Sau-leyan stared back at him, irritated by his insolence. "Where are what?" he asked angrily, wincing as the doctor tightened the bandage about his shoulder.

"The ears," said Fischer, coming out into the room.

"Ears?" Wang Sau-leyan gave a short laugh.

"Yes," Fischer said, meeting the Prince's eyes. "The ears, my Lord. Where are the great T'ang's ears?"

The Prince rose sharply from his stool, pushing Hung Mien-lo aside, his broad moonlike face filled with disbelief. He strode across and stood glowering at Fischer, his face only inches from his.

"What are you suggesting, Captain?"

Fischer knelt, his head bowed. "Forgive me, my Lord. I was suggesting nothing. But the murderers took your father's ears, and now there is no sign of them."

Wang Sau-leyan stood there a moment longer, clearly puzzled, then whirled about, looking directly at his brother.

"Is this true, Ta-hung?"

"*Chieh Hsia* . . ." Hung Mien-lo reminded him, but Wang Sau-leyan ignored him.

"Well, brother? Is it true?"

Wang Ta-hung let his head fall before the fierceness of his younger brother's gaze. He nodded. "It is so."

Wang Sau-leyan took a shuddering breath then looked about him again, his whole manner suddenly defiant, his eyes challenging any in that room to gainsay him.

"Then I'm glad I killed them."

Hung Mien-lo stared at the Prince a moment, astonished by his outburst, then turned and looked across at Wang Ta-hung. The contrast was marked. Tiger and lamb, they were. And then he understood. Wang Sau-leyan had dared to have his father killed. Yes! Looking at him he knew it for a certainty. Sun had had access to the T'ang and motive enough, but only Wang Sau-leyan had had the will—the sheer audacity—to carry through the act.

It took his breath. He looked at the Prince with new eyes. Then, almost without thinking, he stepped forward and, his head bowed in respect, addressed him.

"Please, my Prince, sit down and rest. No blame attaches to you. You did as you had to. The murderers are dead. We need look no further."

Wang Sau-leyan turned, facing him, a smile coming to his lips. Then he turned toward Fischer, his face hardening again.

"Good. Then get the bodies of those vermin out of here and leave me be. I must get some sleep."

The Art of War

Though the enemy be stronger in numbers, we may prevent him from fighting. Scheme so as to discover his plans and the likelihood of their success. Rouse him, and learn the principle of his activity or inactivity. Force him to reveal himself, so as to find out his vulnerable spots. Carefully compare the opposing army with your own, so that you may know where strength is superabundant and where it is deficient.

—SUN TZU, *The Art of War*, *fifth century* B.C.

CHAPTER ONE

The Fifty-Ninth Stone

I T W A S D A W N on Mars. In the lowland desert of
the Golden Plains it was minus 114 degrees and rising.
Deep shadow lay like the surface of a fathomless sea to
the east, tracing the lips of huge escarpments; while to
the north and west the sun's first rays picked out the frozen slopes
and wind-scoured mouths of ancient craters. Through the center
of this landscape ran a massive pipeline, dissecting the plain
from north to south, a smooth vein of polished white against the
brown-red terrain.

For a time the plain was still and silent. Then, from the south,
came the sound of an approaching craft; the dull roar of its
engines carried faintly on the thin atmosphere. A moment later
it drew nearer, following the pipeline. Feng Shou Pumping
Station was up ahead, in the distance—a small oasis in the
billion-year sterility of the Martian desert—discernible even at
this range from the faint spiral curve of cloud that placed a blue-
white smudge amid the perfect pinkness of the sky.

The report had come in less than an hour earlier, an uncon-
firmed message that an unauthorized craft had been challenged
and brought down in the Sea of Divine Kings, eighty *li* northwest of Feng Shou Station. There was no more than that; but

Karr, trusting to instinct, had commissioned a Security craft at once, speeding north from Tian Men K'ou City to investigate.

Karr stared down through the dark filter of the cockpit's screen at the rugged terrain below, conscious that after eight months of scouring this tiny planet for some sign of the man, he might at last be nearing the end of his search.

At first he had thought this a dreadful place. The bitter cold, the thin unnatural atmosphere, the closeness of the horizon, the all-pervading redness of the place. He had felt quite ill those first few weeks, despite the enjoyable sensation of shedding more than 60 percent of his body weight to Mars' much smaller surface gravity. The Han Security officer who had been his host had told him it was quite natural to feel that way: it took some time to acclimatize to Mars. But he had wondered briefly whether this cold, inhospitable planet might not be his final resting place. Now, however, he felt sad that his stay was coming to an end. He had grown to love the austere magnificence of Mars. Eight months. It was little more than a season here.

As the craft drew nearer he ordered the pilot to circle the station from two *li* out.

The five huge chimneys of the atmosphere generator dominated the tiny settlement, belching huge clouds of oxygen-rich air into the thin and frigid atmosphere. Beneath them the sprawl of settlement buildings was swathed in green—hardy mosses that could survive the extreme temperatures of the Martian night. Farther out, the red sands were rimed with ice that formed a wide, uneven ring of whiteness about the Station. The generator itself was deep beneath the surface, its taproots reaching down toward the core of the planet to draw their energy. Like thirty other such generators scattered about the planet's surface, it had been pumping oxygen into the skies of Mars for more than one hundred and fifty years. Even so, it would be centuries yet before Mars had a proper atmosphere again.

Karr made a full circle of the settlement, studying the scene. There were four transports parked to the east of the pipeline, in an open space between some low buildings. At first, in the half light, they had seemed to form one single, indistinct shape—a complexity of shadows—but through the resolution of field glasses he could make out individual markings. One was a craft belonging to the settlement; another two were Security craft from out of Kang Kua in the north. The fourth was unmarked. A small, four-man flier, the design unlike anything he had seen before on Mars.

He leaned forward and tapped out that day's security code, then sat back, waiting. In a moment it came back, suitably amended, followed by an update.

Karr gave himself a moment to digest the information, then nodded to himself. "Okay. Set her down half a *li* to the south of those craft. Then suit up. I want to be ready for any trouble."

The young pilot nodded tersely, setting them down softly on the southern edge of the settlement. While the pilot suited up, Karr sat there, staring out at the settlement, watching for any sign that this might yet be a trap.

"Ready?"

The young man nodded.

"Good. Wait here. I'll not be long."

Karr took a breath, then released the hatch. As he climbed out, systems within his suit reacted immediately to the sudden changes in temperature and pressure. It was cold out here. Cold enough to kill a man in minutes if his suit failed.

There were five buildings surrounding the craft: three domes and two long, flat-topped constructions, the domes to the left, the flat-tops to the right. The pumping station itself was the largest of the domes, straddling the pipeline like a giant swelling. It was one of eight similar stations—situated at two hundred *li* intervals along the pipeline—that pumped water from the sprawling Tzu Li Keng Seng generating complex in the south to the three great northern cities of Hong Hai, Kang Kua, and Chi Shan.

Karr walked toward the huge hemisphere of the station, the tiny heat generator in his suit clicking on as he moved into the shadow of the giant pipeline. As he came nearer a door hissed open and unfolded toward the ground, forming steps. Without hesitation he mounted them and went inside, hearing the door close behind him.

He went through the air lock briskly and out into the pressurized and heated core of the station. Two Security men were waiting for him, at attention, clearly surprised that he was still suited up. They looked at him expectantly, but he went past them without a word, leaving them to follow him or not, as they wished.

He took a left turn at the first junction into a corridor that bridged the pipeline. As he did so an officer, a fresh-faced young Han, hurried down the corridor toward him.

"Major Karr. Welcome to Feng Shou. Captain Wen would like . . ."

Ignoring him, Karr brushed past and turned off to the left, taking the narrow stairwell down to the basement. Guards looked up, surprised, as he came down the corridor toward them, then stood to a hurried attention as they noticed the leopard badge of a third-ranking officer that adorned the chest of his suit.

"Forgive me, Major Karr, but the Captain says you must . . ."

Karr turned and glared at the junior officer who had followed him, silencing him with a look.

"Please tell your Captain that, as his superior officer, I've taken charge of this matter. And before you ask, no; I don't want to see him. Understand me?"

The young soldier bowed deeply and backed off a step. "Of course, Major. As you say."

Karr turned away, forgetting the man at once. These stations were all the same. There was only one place to keep prisoners securely. He marched down the narrow dimly lit passageway and stopped, facing a heavy paneled door. He waited as one of the guards caught up with him and took a bunch of old-fashioned metal keys from inside a thick pouch; then, as the door swung inward, he pushed past the man impatiently.

Hasty improvisation had made a cell of the small storeroom. The floor was bare rock, the walls undecorated ice, opaque and milky white, like a blind eye. The four men were bound at wrist and ankle.

Berdichev was sitting slumped against the wall. His gray uniform was dusty and disheveled, buttons missing from the neck; his face was thinner, gaunter than the Security profile of him. He hadn't shaved for a week or more, and he stared back at Karr through eyes red-rimmed with tiredness. Karr studied him thoughtfully. The horn-rimmed glasses that were his trademark hung from a fine silver chain about his neck, the lenses covered in a fine red grit.

He had not been certain. Not until this moment. But now he knew. Berdichev was his. After almost five years of pursuit, he had finally caught up with the leader of the Dispersionists.

Karr looked about the cell again, conscious of the other three watching him closely, then nodded, satisfied. He knew how he looked to them. Knew how the suit exaggerated his size, making him seem monstrous, unnatural. Perhaps they were even wondering what he was—machine or man. If so, he would let them know. He lit up his face plate, seeing how the eyes of the others widened with surprise. But not Berdichev. He was watching Karr closely.

Karr turned, slamming the door shut behind him; then turned back, facing them again.

He knew what they expected. They knew the laws that were supposed to govern an arrest. But this was different. They had been tried in their absence and found guilty. He was not here to arrest them.

"Well, Major Karr, so we meet up at last, eh?" Berdichev lifted his chin a little as he spoke, but his eyes seemed to look down on the giant. "Do you really think you'll get me to stand trial? In fact, do you even think you'll leave Mars alive?"

If there had been any doubt before, there was none now. It was a trap. Berdichev had made a deal with the Captain, Wen. Or maybe Wen was in another's pay—a friend of Berdichev's. Whatever, it didn't matter now. He walked over to where Berdichev was sprawled and kicked at his feet.

"Get up," he said tonelessly, his voice emerging disembodied and inhuman through the suit's microphone.

Berdichev stood slowly, awkwardly. He was clearly ill. Even so, there was a dignity of bearing to him, a superiority of manner, that was impressive. Even in defeat he thought himself the better man. It was how he had been bred.

Karr stood closer, looking down into Berdichev's face, studying the hawklike features one last time. For a moment Berdichev looked away; then, as if he realized this was one last challenge, he met the big man's stare unflinchingly, his features set, defiant.

Did he know whose gaze he met across the vastness of space? Did he guess in that final moment?

Karr picked him up and broke his neck, his back, then

dropped him. It was done in an instant, before the others had a chance to move, even to cry out.

He stepped away then stood there by the door, watching.

They gathered about the body, kneeling, glaring across at him, impotent to help the dying man. One of them half rose, his fists clenched, then drew back, realizing he could do nothing.

Karr tensed, hearing noises in the corridor outside—Captain Wen and his squad.

He took a small device from his belt, cracked its outer shell like an egg, and threw the sticky innards at the far wall, where it adhered, high up, out of reach. He pulled the door open and stepped outside, then pulled it closed and locked it. His face plate still lit up, he smiled at the soldiers who were hurrying down the corridor toward him as if greeting them; then he shot Wen twice before he could say a word.

The remaining four soldiers hesitated, looking to the junior officer for their lead. Karr stared from face to face, defying them to draw a weapon, his own held firmly out before him. Then, on the count of fifteen, he dropped to the floor.

The wall next to him lit up brightly and a fraction of a second later, the door blew out.

Karr got up and went through the shattered doorway quickly, ignoring the fallen men behind him. The cell was devastated, the outer wall gone. Bits of flesh and bone lay everywhere, unrecognizable as parts of living men.

He stood there a moment, looking down at the thermometer on the sleeve of his suit. The temperature in the room was dropping rapidly. They would have to address that problem quickly or the generators that powered the pumps would shut down. Not only that, but they would have to do something about the loss of air pressure within the station.

Karr crossed to the far side of the room and stepped outside, onto the sands. Debris from the blast lay everywhere. He turned and looked back at the devastation within. *Was that okay?* he asked silently. Did that satisfy your desire for vengeance, Li Shai Tung? For the T'ang was watching everything. All that Karr saw, he saw—the signal sent back more than four hundred million *li* through space.

He shrugged, then tapped the buttons at his wrist, making contact with the pilot.

"I'm on the sands to the west of the pipeline, near where the explosion just happened. Pick me up at once."

"At once, Major."

He turned back and fired two warning shots into the empty doorway, then strode out across the sands, positioning himself in a kneeling stance, facing the station.

Part of him saw the craft lift up over the massive pipeline and drop toward him, while another part of him was watching the doorway for any sign of activity. Then he was aboard, the craft climbing again, and he had other things to think of. There was a gun turret built into the side of the station. Nothing fancy, but its gun could easily bring down a light two-man craft like their own. As they lifted he saw it begin to turn and leaned across the pilot to prime the ship's missiles, then sent two silkworms hurtling down into the side of the dome.

A huge fireball rose into the sky, rolling over and over upon itself. A moment later the blast rocked the tiny craft.

"*Kuan Yin!!*" screamed the pilot. "What in hell's name are you doing?"

Karr glared at the young Han. "Just fly!"

"But the station . . ."

The big dome had collapsed. The two nearest domes were on fire. People were spilling from the nearby buildings, shocked, horrified by what they saw. As Karr lifted up and away from the settlement, he saw the end of the fractured pipeline buckle and then lift slowly into the air, like a giant worm, water gushing from a dozen broken conduits, cooling rapidly in the frigid air.

"*Ai ya!*" said the young pilot, his voice pained and anxious. "It's a disaster! What have you done, Major Karr? What have you done?"

"I've finished it," Karr answered him, angry that the boy should make so much of a little water. "I've ended the War."

━━━━━

FOUR HUNDRED MILLION *li* away, back on Chung Kuo, DeVore strode into a room and looked about him. The room was sparsely furnished, undecorated save for a flag that was pinned to the wall behind the table, its design the white stylized outline of a fish against a blue background. At the table sat five people: three men and two women. They wore simple, light-blue uniforms on which no sign of rank or merit was displayed. Two of them—one male, one female—were Han. This last surprised DeVore. He had heard rumors that the *Ping Tiao* hated the Han. No matter. They hated authority, and that was good enough. He could use them, Han in their ranks or no.

"What do you want?"

The speaker was the man at the center of the five; a short stocky man with dark intense eyes, fleshy lips, and a long nose. His brow was long, his thin gray hair receding. DeVore knew him from the report. Gesell was his name. Bent Gesell. He was their leader or at least the man to whom this strange organization of so-called equal individuals looked for their direction.

DeVore smiled, then nodded toward the table, indicating the transparent grid that was laid out before Gesell. "You have the map, I see."

Gesell narrowed his eyes, studying him a moment. "Half of it, anyway. But that's your point, isn't it, *Shih* Turner? Or am I wrong?"

DeVore nodded, looking from face to face, seeing at once how suspicious they were of him. They were of a mind to reject his proposal, whatever it might be. But that was as he had expected. He had never thought this would be easy.

"I want to make a deal with you—the other half of that map, and more like it, for your cooperation in a few schemes of mine."

Gesell's nostrils dilated, his eyes hardened. "We are not criminals, *Shih* Turner, whatever the media says about us. We are *Ko Ming*. Revolutionaries."

DeVore stared back at Gesell challengingly. "Did I say otherwise?"

"Then I repeat. What do you want?"

DeVore smiled. "I want what you want. To destroy the Seven. To bring it all down and start again."

Gesell's smile was ugly. "Fine rhetoric. But can you support your words?"

DeVore's smile widened. "That packet your men took from me. Ask one of them to bring it in."

Gesell hesitated, then indicated to the guard who stood behind DeVore that he should do so. He returned a moment later with the small sealed package, handing it to Gesell.

"If this is a device of some kind . . ." Gesell began. But DeVore shook his head.

"You asked what proof I have of my intentions. Well, inside that package you'll find a human ear. The ear of the late T'ang of Africa, Wang Hsien."

There was a gasp from the others at the table, but Gesell was cool about it. He left the package untouched. "Half a map and an ear. Are these your only credentials, *Shih* Turner? The map could be of anything, the ear anyone's."

He's merely playing now, thought DeVore; impressing on the others how wise he is, how cautious. Because he, at least, will have had the map checked out and will know it is of the Security arsenal at Helmstadt Canton. Likewise with the ear. He knows how easy it is to check the authenticity of the genetic material.

He decided to push. "They might. But you believe otherwise. It must interest you to know how I could get hold of such things."

Gesell laughed. "Perhaps you're a thief, *Shih* Turner."

DeVore ignored the insult but stored it in memory. He would have his revenge for that.

"The ear is easy to explain. I had Wang Hsien assassinated."

Gesell's laughter was harder; it registered his disbelief. "Then why come to us? If you can have a T'ang murdered so easily, what need have you for such"—he looked about him humorously "—small fish as we *Ping Tiao?*"

DeVore smiled. "I came here because the War has entered a new phase. And because I believe I can trust you."

"*Trust* us?" Gesell studied him closely, looking for any trace of irony in the words. "Yes. Perhaps you could. But can we trust you, *Shih* Turner? And should we even consider trusting you? I mean, what are your real motives for coming here today? Is it really as you say—to ally with us to bring down the Seven? Or do you simply want to use us?"

"I want to share what I know with you. I want to fight alongside you. If that's using you, then yes, I want to use you, *Shih* Gesell."

Gesell's surprise was marked. "How do you know my name?"

DeVore met his stare openly. "I do my homework."

"Then you'll know we work with no one."

"You used not to. But those days are past. You've suffered substantial losses. You need me. As much as I need you."

Gesell shrugged. "And why *do* you need us? Have your Above backers pulled out, then, *Shih* Turner?"

He feigned surprise, but he had known Gesell would raise this point. Had known because he himself had passed the information on to his contact inside the *Ping Tiao*.

Gesell laughed. "Come clean, *Shih* Turner. Tell us the real reason why you're here."

DeVore stepped forward, appealing suddenly to them all, not just Gesell, knowing that this was the point where he could win them over.

"It's true. The War has taken many whose funds supported my activities. But there's more to it than that. Things have changed. It's no longer a struggle in the Above between those in power and those who want to be. The conflict has widened. As you know. It's no longer a question of who should rule, but whether or not there should be rulers at all."

Gesell sat back. "That's so. But what's your role in this? You claim you've killed a T'ang."

"And Ministers, and a T'ang's son . . ."

Gesell laughed shortly. "Well, whatever. But still I ask you: why should we trust you?"

DeVore leaned forward and placed his hands on the edge of the table. "Because you have to. Alone, both of us will fail. The *Ping Tiao* will go down into obscurity, or at best earn a footnote in some historical document as just another small fanatical sect. And the Seven . . ." He heaved a huge sigh and straightened up. "The Seven will rule Chung Kuo forever."

He had given them nothing. Nothing real or substantial, anyway. As Gesell had so rightly said, all they had was half a map, an ear. That and his own bare-faced audacity in daring to knock on their door, knowing they were ruthless killers. Yet he could see from their faces that they were more than half convinced already.

"Unwrap the package, *Shih* Gesell. You'll find there's something else besides an ear inside."

Gesell hesitated, then did as DeVore had asked. Setting the ear aside, he unfolded the transparent sheet and placed it beside its matching half.

"I have three hundred and fifty trained men," DeVore said quietly. "If you can match my force we'll take the Helmstadt Armory two days from now."

Gesell stared at him. "You seem very sure of yourself, *Shih* Turner. Helmstadt is heavily guarded. It has complex electronic defenses. How do you think we can take it?"

"Because there will be no defenses. Not when we attack."

Quickly, confidently, he spelled out his plan, holding back only the way he had arranged it all. When he'd finished, Gesell looked to his colleagues. He had noted what DeVore had said, in particular the part about the high-profile media publicity the *Ping Tiao* would gain from the attack, publicity that was sure to swell their ranks with new recruits. That, and the prospect of capturing a significant stockpile of sophisticated weaponry, seemed to have swung the decision.

Gesell turned to him. "You'll let us confer a moment, *Shih* Turner. We are a democratic movement. We must vote on this."

DeVore smiled inwardly. *Democracy, my ass. It's what you want, Gesell. And I think you're clever enough to know you've no option but to go along with me.*

Giving the slightest bow, he walked out of the room. He had only to wait a few minutes before the door opened again and Gesell came out. He stood facing the *Ping Tiao* leader.

"Well?"

Gesell stared at him a moment, coldly assessing him. Then, with the smallest bow, he stepped back, holding out his arm. "Come in, *Shih* Turner. We have plans to discuss."

━━━━━━━

THE GIRL WAS DEAD. Haavikko sat there, distraught, staring at her, at the blood that covered his hands and chest and thighs, and knew he had killed her.

He turned his head slightly and saw the knife, there on the floor where he remembered dropping it; he shuddered, a wave of sickness, of sheer self-disgust washing over him. What depths, what further degradations, lay ahead of him? Nothing. He had done it all. And now this.

There was no more. This was the end of that path he had set out upon ten years ago.

He turned back, looking at her. The girl's face was white, drained of blood. Such a pretty face it had been in life, full of laughter and smiles, her eyes undulled by experience. He gritted his teeth against the sudden pain he felt and bowed his head, overcome. She could not have been more than fourteen.

He looked about the room. There, draped carelessly over the back of the chair, was his uniform. And there, on the floor beside it, the tray with the empty bottles and the glasses they had been drinking from before it happened.

He closed his eyes, then shivered violently, seeing it all again—the images forming with an almost hallucinatory clarity that took his breath. He uttered a small moan of pain, seeing himself holding her down with one hand, striking at her in a frenzy with the knife, once, twice, a third time, slashing at her breasts, her stomach, while she cried out piteously and struggled to get up.

He jumped to his feet and turned away, putting his hands up to his face. "Kuan Yin preserve you, Axel Haavikko, for what you've done!"

Yes, he saw it all now. It all led to this. The drinking and debauchery, the insubordination and gambling. This was its natural end. This grossness. He had observed his own fall, from that moment in General Tolonen's office to this . . . this finality. There was no more. Nothing for him but to take the knife and end himself.

He stared at the knife. Stared long and hard at it. Saw how the blood was crusted on its shaft and handle, remembering the feel of it in his hand. His knife.

Slowly he went across, then knelt down next to it, his hands placed on either side of it. End it now, he told himself. Cleanly, quickly, and with more dignity than you've shown in all these last ten years.

He picked up the knife, taking its handle in both hands, then turned the blade toward his stomach. His hands shook, and for the briefest moment, he wondered if he had the courage left to carry the thing through. Then, determined, he closed his eyes.

"Lieutenant Haavikko, I've come to see—"

Haavikko turned abruptly, dropping the knife. The pimp, Liu Chang, had come three paces into the room and stopped, taking in the scene.

"Gods!" the Han said, his face a mask of horror. He glanced at Haavikko fearfully, backing away; then turned and rushed from the room.

Haavikko shuddered, then turned back, facing the knife. He could not stand up. All the strength had gone from his legs. Nor could he reach out and take the knife again. His courage was spent. Nothing remained now but his shame. He let his head fall forward, tears coming to his eyes.

"Forgive me, Vesa, I didn't mean . . ."

Vesa. It was his beloved sister's name. But the dead girl had no name. Not one he knew, anyway.

He heard the door swing open again; there were footsteps in the room, but he did not lift his head. Let them kill me now, he thought. Let them take their revenge on me. It would be no less than I deserve.

He waited, resigned, but nothing happened. He heard them lift the girl and carry her away, then sensed someone standing over him.

Haavikko raised his head slowly and looked up. It was Liu Chang.

"You disgust me." He spat the words out venomously, his eyes boring into Haavikko. "She was a good girl. A lovely girl. Like a daughter to me."

"I'm sorry . . ." Haavikko began, his throat constricting. He dropped his head, beginning to sob. "Do what you will to me. I'm finished now. I haven't even the money to pay you for last night."

The pimp laughed, his disgust marked. "I realize that, soldier boy. But then, you've not paid your weight since you started coming here."

Haavikko looked up, surprised.

"No. It's a good job you've got friends, neh? Good friends who'll bail you out when trouble comes. That's what disgusts me most about your sort. You never pay. It's all settled for you, isn't it?"

"I don't know what you mean. I—"

But Liu Chang's angry bark of laughter silenced him. "This. It's all paid for. Don't you understand that? Your friends have settled everything for you."

Haavikko's voice was a bemused whisper. "Everything . . . ?"

"*Everything.*" Liu Chang studied him a moment, his look of disgust unwavering, then he leaned forward and spat in Haavikko's face.

Haavikko knelt there long after Liu Chang had gone, the spittle on his cheek a badge of shame that seemed to burn right through to the bone. It was less than he deserved, but he was thinking about what Liu Chang had said. Friends . . . What friends? He had no friends, only partners in his debauchery, and they would have settled nothing for him.

He dressed and went outside, looking for Liu Chang.

"Liu Chang. Where is he?"

The girl at the reception desk stared at him a moment, as if he were something foul and unclean that had crawled up out of the Net, then handed him an envelope.

Haavikko turned his back on the girl, then opened the envelope and took out the single sheet of paper. It was from Liu Chang.

Lieutenant Haavikko,

Words cannot express the disgust I feel. If I had my way you would be made to pay fully for what you have done. As it is, I must ask you never to frequent my House again. If you so much as come near, I shall pass on my record of events to the authorities, "friends" or no. Be warned.

Liu Chang.

He stuffed the paper into his tunic pocket then staggered out, more mystified than ever. Outside, in the corridor, he looked about him, then lurched over to the public drinking fountain inset into the wall at the intersection. He splashed his face then straightened up.

Friends. What friends? Or were they friends at all?

Liu Chang knew, but he could not go near Liu Chang. Who then?

Haavikko shivered, then looked about him. Someone knew. Someone had made it their business to know. But who?

He thought of the girl again and groaned. "I don't deserve this chance," he told himself softly. And yet he was here, free, all debts settled. Why? He gritted his teeth and reached up to touch the spittle that had dried on his cheek. Friends. It gave him a reason to go on. To find out who. And why.

———

DEVORE TOOK OFF his gloves and threw them down on the desk; then he turned and faced his lieutenant, Wiegand, lowering his head to dislodge the lenses from his eyes.

"Here." He handed the lenses to Wiegand, who placed them carefully in a tiny plastic case he had ready. "Get these processed. I want to know who those other four are."

Wiegand bowed and left. DeVore turned, meeting the eyes of the other man in the room.

"It went perfectly. We attack Helmstadt in two days."

The albino nodded, but was quiet.

"What is it, Stefan?"

"Bad news. Soren Berdichev is dead."

DeVore looked at the young man a moment, then went and sat behind his desk, busying himself with the reports that had amassed while he was away. He spoke without looking up.

"I know. I heard before I went in. A bad business, by all accounts, but useful. It may well have alienated the Mars settlers. They'll have little love for the Seven now, after the destruction of the pipeline."

"Maybe . . ." Lehmann was silent a moment, then came and stood at the edge of the desk looking down at DeVore. "I liked him, you know. Admired him."

DeVore looked up, masking his surprise. He found it hard to believe that Stefan Lehmann was capable of liking anyone. "Well," he said, "he's dead now. And life goes on. We've got to plan for the future. For the next stage of the War."

"Is that why you went to see those scum?"

DeVore stared past Lehmann a moment, studying the map on the wall behind him. Then he met his eyes again.

"I have news for you, Stefan."

The pink eyes hardened, the mouth tightened. "I know already."

"I see." DeVore considered a moment. "Who told you?"

"Wiegand."

DeVore narrowed his eyes. Wiegand. He was privy to all incoming messages, of course, but he had strict instructions not to pass on what he knew until DeVore authorized it. It was a serious breach.

"I'm sorry, Stefan. It makes it harder for us all."

The Notice of Confiscation had come in only an hour before he had gone off to meet the *Ping Tiao*, hot on the heels of the news of Berdichev's death. In theory it stripped Lehmann of all he had inherited from his father, making him a pauper, but DeVore had preempted the Notice some years back by getting Berdichev to switch vast sums from the Estate in the form of loans to fictitious beneficiaries. Those "loans" had long been spent—and more besides—on constructing further fortresses, but Lehmann knew nothing of that. As far as he was concerned, the whole sum was lost.

Lehmann was studying him intently. "How will it change things?"

DeVore set down the paper and sat back. "As far as I'm concerned it changes nothing, Stefan. All our lives are forfeit anyway. What difference does a piece of paper bearing the seals of the Seven make to that?"

There was the slightest movement in the young man's ice-pale face. "I can be useful. You know that."

"I know." Good, thought DeVore. He understands. He's learned his lessons well. There's no room for sentimentality in what we're doing here. What's past is past. I owe him nothing for the use of his money.

"Don't worry," he said, leaning forward and picking up the paper again. "You're on the payroll now, Stefan. I'm appointing you lieutenant, as from this moment. Ranking equal with Wiegand."

Yes, he thought. That should take the smile from Wiegand's face.

When Lehmann had gone he stood and went across to the

map again. In the bottom left-hand corner the carp-shaped area that denoted the Swiss Wilds was crisscrossed with lines, some broken, some solid. Where they met or ended were tiny squares, representing fortresses. There were twenty-two in all, but only fourteen of them—boxed in between Zagreb in the southeast and Zurich in the northwest—were filled in. These alone were finished. The eight fortresses of the western arm remained incomplete. In four cases they had yet to be begun.

Money. That was his greatest problem. Money for wages, food, and weaponry. Money for repairs and bribes and all manner of small expenses. Most of all, money to complete the building program: to finish the network of tunnels and fortresses that alone could guarantee a successful campaign against the Seven. The Confiscations had robbed him of many of his big investors. In less than three hours the remainder were due to meet him, supposedly to renew their commitments, though in reality, he knew, to tell him they had had enough. That was why Helmstadt was so important now.

Helmstadt. He had wooed the *Ping Tiao* with promises of weapons and publicity, but the truth was otherwise. There would be weapons, and publicity enough to satisfy the most egotistical of terrorist leaders, but the real fruit of the raid on the Helmstadt Armory would be the two billion yuan DeVore would lift from the strong room. Money that had been allocated to pay the expenses of more than one hundred and forty thousand troops in the eight garrisons surrounding the Wilds.

But the *Ping Tiao* would know nothing of that.

He turned away from the map and looked over at his desk again. The Notice of Confiscation lay where he had left it. He went across and picked it up, studying it again. It seemed simple on the face of it: an open acknowledgment of a situation that had long existed in reality, for Lehmann's funds had been frozen from the moment Berdichev had fled to Mars, three years earlier. But there were hidden depths in the document. It meant that the Seven had discovered evidence to link Stefan's father to the death of the Minister Lwo Kang; and that, in its turn, would legitimize Tolonen's killing of Lehmann Senior in the House.

It was an insight into how the Seven were thinking. For them the War was over. They had won.

But DeVore knew otherwise. The War had not even begun. Not properly. The confiscations and the death of T'angs notwithstanding, it had been a game until now, a diversion for the rich and bored, an entertainment to fill their idle hours. But now it would change. He would harness the forces stirring in the lowest levels. Would take them and mold them. And then?

He laughed and crumpled the copy of the Notice in his hand. Then Change would come. Like a hurricane, blowing through the levels, razing the City to the ground.

———

MAJOR HANS EBERT set the drinks carefully on the tray, then turned and, making his way through the edge of the crowd that packed the great hall, went through the curtained doorway into the room beyond.

Behind him the reception was in full swing; but here, in the T'ang's private quarters, it was peaceful. Li Shai Tung sat in the big chair to the left, his feet resting on a stool carved like a giant turtle shell. He seemed older and more careworn these days; his hair, once gray, was pure white now, like fine threads of ice, tied tightly in a queue behind his head. The yellow cloak of state seemed loose now on his thin, old man's frame and the delicate perfection of the gold chain about his neck served merely to emphasize the frail imperfection of his flesh. Even so, there was still strength in his eyes, power enough in his words and gestures to dispel any thought that he was spent as a man. If the flesh had grown weaker, the spirit seemed unchanged.

Across from him, seated to the right of the ceremonial *kang*, was Tsu Ma, T'ang of West Asia. He sat back in his chair, a long, pencil-thin cheroot held absently in one hand. He was known to his acquaintances as "the Horse," and the name suited him. He was a stallion, a thoroughbred in his late thirties, broad-chested and heavily muscled, his dark hair curled in elegant long pigtails, braided with silver and pearls. His enemies still considered him a dandy, but they were wrong. He was a capable, intelligent man for all his outward style; and since his father's death he had shown himself to be a fine administrator, a credit to the Council of the Seven.

The third and last man in the anteroom was Hal Shepherd.

He sat to Tsu Ma's right, a stack of pillows holding him upright in his chair, his face drawn and pale from illness. He had been sick for two weeks now, the cause as yet undiagnosed. His eyes, normally so bright and full of life, now seemed to protrude from their sockets as if staring out from some deep inner darkness. Beside him, her head bowed, her whole manner demure, stood a young Han nurse from the T'ang's household, there to do the sick man's least bidding.

Ebert bowed, crossed to the T'ang, and stood there, the tray held out before him. Li Shai Tung took his drink without pausing from what he was saying, seeming not to notice the young Major as he moved across to offer Tsu Ma his glass.

"But the question is still what we should do with the Companies. Should we close them down completely? Wind them up and distribute their assets among our friends? Should we allow bids for them? Offer them on the Index as if we were floating them? Or should we run them ourselves, appointing stewards to do our bidding until we feel things have improved?"

Tsu Ma took his peach brandy, giving Ebert a brief smile, then turned back to face his fellow T'ang.

"You know my feelings on the matter, Shai Tung. Things are still uncertain. We have given our friends considerable rewards already. To break up the 118 companies and offer them as spoils to them might cause resentment among those not party to the share-out. It would simply create a new generation of malcontents. No. My vote will be to appoint stewards. To run the companies for ten, maybe fifteen years, and then offer them on the market to the highest bidder. That way we prevent resentment and at the same time, through keeping a tight rein on what is, after all, nearly a fifth of the market, help consolidate the Edict of Technological Control."

Ebert, holding the tray out before Hal Shepherd, tried to feign indifference to the matter being discussed; but as heir to Gen-Syn, the second largest company on the Hang Seng Index, he felt crucially involved in the question of the confiscated companies.

"What is this?"

Ebert raised his head and looked at Shepherd. "It is Yang Sen's Spring Wine Tonic, *Shih* Shepherd. Li Shai Tung asked me to bring you a glass of it. It has good restorative powers."

Shepherd sniffed at the glass, then looked past Ebert at the old T'ang. "This smells rich, Shai Tung. What's in it?"

"Brandy, *kao liang*, vodka, honey, gingseng, japonica seeds, oh, and many more things that are good for you, Hal."

"Such as?"

Tsu Ma laughed and turned in his seat to look at Shepherd. "Such as red-spotted lizard and sea-horse and dried human placenta. All terribly good for you, my friend."

Shepherd looked at Tsu Ma a moment, then looked back at Li Shai Tung. "Is that true, Shai Tung?"

The old T'ang nodded. "It's true. Why, does it put you off, Hal?"

Shepherd laughed, the laugh lines etched deep now in his pallid face. "Not at all." He tipped the glass back and drank heavily, then shuddered and handed the half-empty glass to the nurse.

Tsu Ma gave a laugh of surprise. "One should sip Yang Sen's, friend Hal. It's strong stuff. Matured for eighteen months before it's even fit to drink. And this is Shai Tung's best. A twelve-year brew."

"Yes . . ." said Shepherd hoarsely, laughing, his rounded eyes watering. "I see that now."

Tsu Ma watched the ill man a moment longer, then turned and faced Ebert. "Well, Major, and how is your father?"

Ebert bowed deeply. "He is fine, *Chieh Hsia*."

Li Shai Tung leaned forward. "I must thank him for all he has done these last few months. And for the generous wedding gift he has given my son today."

Ebert turned and bowed again. "He would be honored, *Chieh Hsia*."

"Good. Now tell me, before you leave us. Candidly now. What do *you* think we should do about the confiscated companies?"

Ebert kept his head lowered, not presuming to meet the T'ang's eyes, even when asked so direct a question. Nor was he fooled by the request for candor. He answered as he knew the T'ang would want him to answer.

"I believe his Excellency Tsu Ma is right, *Chieh Hsia*. It is necessary to placate the Above. To let wounds heal and bitterness evaporate. In appointing stewards the markets will remain stable. Things will continue much as normal, and there will be none of the hectic movements on the Index that a selling-off of such vast holdings would undoubtedly bring. As for rewards, the health and safety of the Seven is reward enough, surely? It would be a little man who would ask for more."

The old T'ang's eyes smiled. "Thank you, Hans. I am grateful for your words."

Ebert bowed and backed away, knowing he had been dismissed.

"A fine young man," said Li Shai Tung, when Ebert had gone. "He reminds me more of his father every day. The same bluff honesty. Tolonen's right. He should be a general when he's of age. He'd make my son a splendid general, don't you think?"

"An excellent general," Tsu Ma answered him, concealing any small qualms he had about Major Hans Ebert. His own Security reports on Ebert revealed a slightly different picture.

"Now that we're alone," Li Shai Tung continued, "I've other news."

Both Tsu Ma and Shepherd were suddenly attentive. "What's that?" Tsu Ma asked, stubbing out his cheroot in the porcelain tray on the *kang* beside him.

"I've heard from Karr. Berdichev is dead."

Tsu Ma laughed, his eyes wide. "You're certain?"

"I've seen it with these eyes. Karr was wired to transmit all he saw and heard."

"Then it's over."

Li Shai Tung was silent a moment, looking down. When he looked up again his eyes seemed troubled. "I don't think so." He looked across at Shepherd. "Ben was right after all, Hal. We've killed the men, and yet the symptoms remain."

Shepherd smiled bleakly. "Not all the men. There's still De-Vore."

The old T'ang lowered his head slightly. "Yes. But Karr will get him. As he got Berdichev."

Tsu Ma leaned forward. "A useful man, Karr. Maybe we ought to mass-produce the fellow. Give Old Man Ebert a patent for the job."

Li Shai Tung laughed and lifted his feet one at a time from the

turtle stool. "Maybe . . ." He pulled himself up and stretched.
"First, however, I have another idea I want you to consider—
something Li Yuan has been working on these last few months.
I'm going to introduce it in Council tomorrow, but I wanted to
sound you out first."

Tsu Ma nodded and settled back with his drink, watching the
old T'ang as he walked slowly up and down the room.

"It was an idea Li Yuan had years ago, when he was eight. He
was out hawking with Han Ch'in when one of the hawks flew
high up in a tree and refused to come down to the lure. Han
Ch'in, impatient with the hawk, took the control box from the
servant and destroyed the bird."

"Using the homing-wire in the bird's head?"

"Exactly."

Tsu Ma took a sip, then tilted his head slightly. "I've never had
to do that, myself."

"Nor I," agreed Li Shai Tung. "And it was the first I had heard
of the matter when Li Yuan told me of it six months ago.
However, until then Li Yuan had not realized that the birds were
wired in that way. It made him wonder why we didn't have such
a thing for men."

Tsu Ma laughed. "Men are not hawks. They would not let
themselves be bound so easily."

"No. And that is exactly what Li Yuan told himself. Yet the
idea was still a good one. He argued it thus: if the man was a
good man he would have no fear of having such a wire put into
his head. It would make no difference. And if the man was a bad
man, then he *ought* to have the wire."

"I like that. Even so, the fact remains, men are not hawks.
They like the illusion of freedom."

Li Shai Tung stopped before Hal Shepherd and leaned forward a moment, placing his hand on the shoulder of his old
friend, a sad smile on his face; then he turned back, facing
Tsu Ma.

"And if we gave them that illusion? If we could make them
think they *wanted* the wires in their heads?"

"Easier said than done."

"But not impossible. And Li Yuan has come up with a scheme
by which the majority of men might do just that."

Tsu Ma sat back, considering. "And the technicalities of this?"

Li Shai Tung smiled. "As ever, Tsu Ma, you anticipate me. There are, indeed, problems with creating such a control system. Men's brains are far more complex than a hawk's, and the logistics of tracking forty billion separate individuals through the three hundred levels of the City are far greater than the problems involved in tracing a few hawks on an estate. It is fair to say that Li Yuan has made little progress in this regard. Which is why there is a need to invest time and money in research."

"I see. And that's what you want from the Council tomorrow? Permission to pursue this line of inquiry?"

Li Shai Tung inclined his head slightly. "It would not do for a T'ang to break the Edict."

Tsu Ma smiled. "Quite so. But rest assured, Shai Tung, in this as in other things, you have my full support in Council." He drained his glass and set it down. "And the rest of your scheme?"

Li Shai Tung smiled. "For now, enough. But if you would honor me by being my guest at Tongjiang this Autumn, we might talk some more. Things will be more advanced by then, and Li Yuan, I know, would be delighted to tell you about his scheme."

Tsu Ma smiled. "It would be my great honor and delight. But come, talking of Li Yuan, we have neglected your son and his new wife far too much already. I have yet to congratulate him on his choice."

Both men pretended not to see the flicker of doubt that crossed the old T'ang's face.

"And you, Hal?" Li Shai Tung turned to face his old friend. "Will you come through?"

Shepherd smiled. "Later, perhaps. Just now I feel a little tired. Too much Yang Sen, I guess."

"Ah. Maybe so." And, turning sadly away, Li Shai Tung took Tsu Ma's arm and led him out into the gathering in the great hall.

━━━━━

KARR LEANED across the desk and with one hand pulled the man up out of his seat, the front of his powder-blue silk tunic bunched tightly in his fist.

"What do you mean, *can't*? I'm leaving today. By the first craft available. And I'm taking those files with me."

For a moment the man's left hand struggled to reach the summons pad on his desk, then desisted. He had heard what a maniac Karr was, but he'd never believed the man would storm into his office and physically attack him.

"Don't you know who I *am*?" he screeched, his voice half-strangled. "I'm Governor of Mars. You can't do this to me!"

Karr dragged the man across the desk until he was eye to eye with him. "You're a fine one to lecture me on what can and can't be done, Governor Schenck. You were ordered to give me full assistance, but you've been nothing but obstructive since I came back to Tian Men K'ou City."

The Governor swallowed painfully. "But . . . the investigation . . . Feng Shou Station destroyed, the pipeline badly damaged."

"That's your concern. Mine is to report back to my T'ang at the earliest opportunity, and to take back with me all relevant information. You knew that. You had your orders."

"But . . ."

Karr leaned back across the desk, and threw Schenck down into his chair, then slammed his fist down on the summons pad.

"Do you want war with the Seven?"

"*What?*" Schenck's face blanched.

"Because that's what you'll get if you take any further measures to keep me here. By a special Edict of the Seven I was authorized to do as I saw fit to bring the traitor Berdichev to justice and to reclaim any files or documents relating to that same person. That I have done. Now, tell me, *Shih* Schenck, what has your investigation to do with me?"

"I . . ." he began, then saw the door open behind Karr.

Karr turned at once. "Bring the Berdichev files. At once."

The underling looked past Karr at Governor Schenck. "Excellency?"

Karr turned back to Schenck. "Well? Will you defy the Seven and sign your own death warrant, or will you do as I request?"

Schenck swallowed again, then bowed his head. "Do as he says. And while you're at it, prepare Major Karr's clearance for the *Tientsin*. He leaves us this afternoon."

"At once, Excellency."

"Good," said Karr, settling his huge frame into the tiny chair facing Schenck. "Now tell me, Governor, who ordered you to keep me here?"

———————

BACK ON CHUNG KUO, DeVore looked up from the files and stared hard at his lieutenant. "Is this all?"

Wiegand bowed his head. "For now, Excellency. But our contacts have promised us more. You'll know all you need to know about these scum before you meet with them again."

"Good. Because I want to know who's good at what, and who's responsible for what. I want to know where they came from and what they ultimately want. And I want no guesses. I want facts."

"Of course, Excellency. I'll see to it at once."

Wiegand bowed low, then turned and left. A good man, thought DeVore, watching him go. Intelligent and reliable, despite that business with Lehmann and the Notice.

He got up and walked around his desk, then stood there, studying the huge blown-up photograph of the five *Ping Tiao* leaders that Wiegand had pinned to the wall.

The simple black and white image was clear and sharp, the life-size faces of the five terrorists standing out perfectly, Gesell in their center. It had been taken ten or fifteen seconds into the meeting, the tiny lens cameras activated when he'd nodded to indicate the half-map on the table in front of Gesell. His intention had been merely to get images of the other four *Ping Tiao* leaders so they could be traced through his contacts in Security, yet what the picture captured most clearly was the intense, almost insane suspicion. DeVore smiled. He had sensed something of it at the time, but had been too engrossed in his own scheme to make anything of it. Now, seeing it so vividly—so physically—expressed, he realized he had missed something of real importance.

They were scared, yes; but it was more than that. They were on the run. Their cockiness was merely a front. Gesell's bluster masked a general fear that someone would come along and simply wipe them out. Them and everything they stood for. They had suffered too many setbacks, too many betrayals by their own kind. They were paranoid, afraid of their own shadows.

But that was good. He could use that. It would give him the whip hand when they met in two days' time.

He went through what he knew. The Han male to the far left of the picture was Shen Lu Chua, a computer systems expert, trained as a mathematician. He was in his mid-thirties, his clean-shaven face long and drawn. Beside him was a rather pretty-looking woman with finely chiseled features—a *Hung Mao*, though her dark, fine hair was cut like a Han's. Her name was Emily Ascher and she was an economist, though of more interest to DeVore was the fact that she was Gesell's lover. On the other side of Gesell—second from the right in the photo— was the Han female, Mao Liang. She was an interesting one. The fourth daughter of a quite prominent Minor Family, she had been raised and educated at First Level but had rebelled against her upbringing in her late teens; after a year of arguments at home, she had vanished into the lower levels, surfacing only now, five years later, among the *Ping Tiao*.

Last of the five—on the far right of the photo—was Jan Mach. He was a tall broad-shouldered man of thirty-three with dark shoulder-length braided hair and a thick growth of beard. He worked for the Ministry of Waste Recycling as a maintenance official. It was a good job for a *Ping Tiao* member, allowing him quick and legitimate passage between the levels; but Mach had the further advantage of being a volunteer in the Security Reserve Corps, licensed to carry a firearm. In the circles in which he operated it provided the perfect cover for his *Ko Ming* activities.

Mach alone of the five was looking away from DeVore in the picture, his eyes lowered to a writing pad on the desk before him. On the pad—in neatly formed pictograms that could be read quite clearly—was written *Jen to chiu luan lung to chiu han:* "Too many people bring chaos; too many dragons bring drought."

The detail was interesting. If Gesell was the leader, Mach was the power behind the throne. He was the one to watch, to influence, the ideologue of the group.

There was a sharp knock on the door.

"Come in!"

Lehmann stood there in the doorway. "Our guests are here, sir."

DeVore hesitated, noting how well the albino looked in uniform, then nodded. "Good. I'll be down in a short while. Take them to the dining room, and make sure they're well looked after."

Lehmann bowed and left.

DeVore turned and had one last brief look at the life-size picture of the five terrorists. "As one door closes, so another opens."

He laughed softly, then went across to his desk and pressed out the code to link him to the landing dome. His man there, Kubinyi, answered at once.

"Is everything in hand?"

"As you ordered, Excellency."

"Good. I want no foul-ups. Understand me?"

He cut contact before Kubinyi could answer, then reached across and took the file from the drawer. He paused, looking about his office, conscious of the significance of the moment. Then, with a sharp laugh of enjoyment, he slammed the drawer shut and went out.

New directions, he told himself as he marched briskly down the corridor toward the elevator. *The wise man always follows new directions.*

They turned as he entered the room. Seven of them. First Level businessmen, dressed in light-colored silk *pau*.

"Gentlemen," he said, deliberately—ironically—avoiding the normal Han term, *ch'un tzu*. "How good to see you all again."

He saw at once how tense they were, how they looked to each other for support. They were afraid of him. Afraid how he might react to the news they brought. News they thought he was unaware of. But he saw also how resigned they were. A spent force. The Seven had routed them thoroughly. The confiscations, the arrests and executions—these had shaken them badly. They saw now the true cost of their involvement.

So it is, he thought. *And now your time has passed.*

He went among them, shaking hands, making small talk, his style and manner putting them at ease. He left Douglas until last, taking the old man's hand firmly, warmly, holding his shoulder a moment, as if greeting the best of friends. Douglas was leader of the Dispersionists now that Berdichev was dead. Leader of a broken party, unwilling even to whisper its own name in public.

The news of Berdichev's death had been broken publicly only two hours before. While they were meeting, no doubt, finalizing what they would say to him this afternoon. The shock of that lay on them too. He could see it in Douglas's eyes.

"It's a sad business," he said, pre-empting Douglas. "I had nothing but respect for Soren Berdichev. He was a great man."

Douglas lowered his head slightly. The news had affected him badly. His voice was bitter and angry, but also broken. "They killed him," he said. "Like a common criminal. One of their animal-men—some GenSyn brute—did it, I'm told. Snapped his back like a twig. No trial. Nothing." He raised his eyes again and met DeVore's. "I never imagined . . ."

"Nor I," said DeVore sympathetically, placing an arm about his shoulders. "Anyway . . . Come. Let's have something to eat. I'm sure you're all hungry after your flight here. Then we'll sit and talk."

Douglas bowed his head slightly, a wistful smile on his lips softening the hurt and anger in his eyes. "You're a good man, Howard."

Little was said during the meal, but afterward, with the plates cleared and fresh drinks poured all round, Douglas came to the point.

"The war is over, Howard. The Seven have won. We must plan for the long peace."

The outer-blast shutters had been drawn back, and through the thick clear glass of the wall-length window could be seen the sunlit valley and the cloud-wreathed mountains beyond. The late afternoon light gave the room a strangely melancholy atmosphere. DeVore sat at the head of the table, his back to the window, facing them, his face in partial shadow.

"*Ai mo ta yu hsin ssu.*"

Douglas gave a slow nod of agreement. "So it is. Nothing *is* more sorrowful than the death of the heart. And that is how we feel, Howard. Weary. Heartbroken. More so now that Soren is not with us."

"And?" DeVore looked from one to another, noting how hard they found it to look at him at this moment of surrender. They were ashamed. Deeply, bitterly ashamed. But of what? Of their failure to dislodge the Seven? Or was it because of their betrayal of him? Only Douglas was looking at him.

When no one spoke DeVore stood and turned his back to them, staring out at the mountains. "I'm disappointed," he said. "I can't help it, but I am. I thought better of you than this. I thought you had more . . ." He turned, looking at them. "More *guts.*"

"We've lost," Douglas said, sitting back, suddenly defensive. "It's an unpleasant fact to face, but it's true. Things have changed drastically, even in the last few months. It would be suicide to carry on."

"I see." DeVore seemed surprised. He turned slightly aside, as if considering something unexpected.

"Surely you must have thought about it, Howard? You must have seen how things are. The arrests. The confiscations. The Seven are riding high. Anyone who shows even the slightest sign of opposing them is crushed. And no half-measures." He paused, looking about him for support. "That's how it is. I can't change that, Howard. None of us can change it. We failed. Now it's time to call it a day."

"And that's how you all feel?"

There was a murmur of agreement from around the table. DeVore sighed heavily. "I thought as we'd come so far . . ."

They were watching him now. Wondering what he would do.

DeVore tapped the file, suddenly more animated, his voice holding the slightest trace of anger. "I had plans. Schemes for new campaigns. Ways to finish what we had so successfully begun."

"Successfully?" Douglas laughed sharply. "I'm sorry, Howard, but in that you're wrong. We lost. And we lost heavily. Berdichev, Lehmann, and Wyatt. Duchek, Weis, and Barrow. They're all dead. Along with more than two thousand other, lesser members of our 'revolution.' One hundred and eighteen companies have ceased trading, their assets and holdings confiscated by the Seven. And the Seven are still there, stronger than ever, more dominant than ever."

"No. You're wrong. The Seven are weak now. Weaker than they've been in their entire history. The Council has lost four of its most experienced members in the last six years. The new T'ang are young and inexperienced. Not only that, but the older T'ang have lost the confidence, the certainty, they once possessed. Once it was considered inconceivable to challenge the Seven. But now . . ."

"Now we understand why."

DeVore shook his head, then, resignedly, sat again.

Douglas watched him a moment, then looked down. "I'm sorry, Howard. I know how you must feel. You were closer to it all than we were. The fortresses. The campaigns. These were your projects—your children, if you like. It must be hard to give them up. But it's over. We would just be throwing good money after bad if we continued to support it all."

DeVore lifted his head, then smiled and shrugged. His voice was softer, more reconciled. "Well, as you say, old friend. But you're still wrong. We shook the tree. Can't you see that? It almost fell."

Douglas looked away, his disagreement implicit in that gesture. "What will you do?"

DeVore stared down at the two files, as if undecided. "I don't know. Wind it all down here, I guess."

"And after that?"

DeVore was still staring at the folders, his hunched shoulders and lowered head indicative of his disappointment. "Go to Mars, maybe."

"Mars?"

He looked up. "They say it's where the future lies. The Seven have a weaker hold out there."

"Ah . . ." Douglas hesitated a moment, then looked about him once more. "Well, Howard. I think we've said all we came to say. We'd best be getting back."

DeVore stood up. "Of course. It was good seeing you all a last time. I wish you luck in all your ventures. And thank you, gentlemen. For all you did. It was good of you."

He embraced each one as they left, then went to the window, staring out at the jagged landscape of rock and ice and snow. He was still there, watching, ten minutes later, as their craft lifted from the hangar and slowly banked away to the right. For a moment its shadow flitted across the escarpment opposite, then, with a sudden, shocking brightness, it exploded. The shock of the explosion struck a moment later, rattling the empty glasses on the table.

He saw the fireball climb the sky, rolling over and over upon itself; heard the roar of the explosion roll like a giant clap of thunder down the valley and return a moment later. A million tiny incandescent fragments showered the mountainside, melting the snow where they fell, hissing and bubbling against the glass only a hand's width from his face. Then there was silence.

DeVore turned. Lehmann was standing in the doorway.

"What is it, Stefan?"

Lehmann looked past him a moment, as if recollecting what he had just seen. Then he came forward, handing DeVore a note. It was from Douglas. Handwritten. DeVore unfolded it and read.

> Dear Howard,
>
> I'm sorry it didn't work out. We tried. We really did try, didn't we? But life goes on. This is just to say that if ever you need anything—anything at all—just say.
>
> With deep regard,
>
> John Douglas.

DeVore stared at it a moment longer, then screwed it into a ball and threw it down. *Anything . . .* The words were meaningless. The man had given up. He and all the rest like him. Well, it was time now to go deeper, lower, to cultivate a different class of rebel. To shake the tree of state again. And shake and shake and shake. Until it fell.

THE OFFICERS CLUB at Bremen was a spacious, opulently decorated place. Dark-suited Han servants, their shaven heads constantly bowed, moved silently between the huge round-topped tables that lay like islands in an ocean of green-blue carpet. Tall pillars edged the great central hexagon, forming a walkway about the tables, like the cloisters of an ancient monastery, while fifty *chi* overhead the hexagonal paneling of the ceiling was a mosaic of famous battles, the Han victorious in all.

It was late afternoon and most of the tables were empty, but off to the right, halfway between the great double doorway and the bar, a group of eight officers was gathered about a table, talking loudly. Their speech, and the clutter of empty bottles on the table, betrayed that they were somewhat the worse for drink. However, as none of them was less than captain in rank, the duty officers smiled and turned away, allowing behavior they would not have tolerated from lesser-ranking officers.

The focus of this group was the young Major, Hans Ebert, the "Hero of Hammerfest," who had been regaling them with stories about the reception he had attended that afternoon. Now, however, the conversation had moved on into other channels, and the low, appreciative laughter held a suggestion of dark enjoyments.

Auden, seeing how things were drifting, directed the conversation back to his superior. That was his role—to keep his master central at all times. Unlike the others, he had barely touched his drink all afternoon. It was not evident, for he seemed to lift his drink as often to his lips and refill his glass as often from the bottle, but his speech, unlike the others, was clear, precise.

"And you, Hans? How is that lady you were seeing?"

Ebert looked aside, smiling rakishly. "Which of my ladies would that be, Will?"

Auden leaned forward to tap the end of his cigar against the tray, then sat back again in his chair. "You know the one. The Minister's wife."

There was a gasp of surprise and admiration. A Minister's wife! That smelled of danger. And danger was an aphrodisiac they all understood.

"Yes, tell us, Hans," said Scott, his eyes bright with interest.

Ebert sipped at his glass relaxedly, then looked about the circle of eager, watching faces.

"She's my slave," he said calmly. "I can make her do anything I want. Anything at all. Take the other day, for instance. I had her two maids strip her and hold her down while I beat her with my cane. Then, while she watched, I had her maids. Afterward, she was begging for it. But I shook my head. 'You have to earn it,' I said. 'I want you to show me how much you love your maids.' "

"*No!*" said Panshin, a rather portly Colonel. "And did she?"

Ebert sipped again. "Didn't I say she was my slave?" He smiled. "Right in front of me she got down on the floor with her maids and rolled about for more than twenty minutes, until all three of them were delirious, begging me to join them."

Fest's eyes were bulging. "And then you gave her one?"

Ebert set his glass down and slowly shook his head. "Nothing so simple. You see, I have this ritual."

"Ritual?" Scott swigged down his brandy with a quick tilt of his head, then set his glass down hard on the table. "What kind of ritual?"

"I had all three of them kneel before me, naked, their heads bowed. Then I called them forward, one at a time, to kneel before the god and kiss the god's head. As each did so they had to repeat a few words. You know the sort of thing. 'I promise to be faithful and obedient to the god and do whatever the god wishes.' That sort of thing."

"Kuan Yin!" said another of the captains, a man named Russ. "Don't tell me, and then you had all three at once."

Ebert laughed and finished his drink. "I'm afraid not. The old girl was just about to take her turn when I noticed what time it was. 'Sorry,' I told her, 'I didn't realize the time. I have to go. The T'ang awaits me.'"

"Gods!" Scott spluttered, then shook his head. "You're not kidding us, Hans. That really happened?"

"Less than six hours back."

"And what did she say?"

Ebert laughed. "What could she say? You don't keep a T'ang waiting."

"And your promise?" said Russ. "You promised you'd fuck her if she showed she loved her maids."

Ebert reached out and tipped more wine into his glass. "I'm a man of my word, Captain Russ. As you all know. When we've finished here I'll be returning to fulfill my promise."

"And her husband?" Scott asked. "Where was he while all of this was going on?"

"In his study. Reading the *Analects*."

There was a great guffaw of laughter at that, which made heads turn at nearby tables.

"Power. That's what it's really all about," said Ebert, his eyes half-closed, a faintly sybaritic smile on his lips. "That's the key to sex. Power. It's something young Li Yuan will learn this very night. Master your sexuality and the world is yours. Succumb to it and . . ." He shrugged. "Well . . . look at Fest here!"

The laughter rolled out again, dark, suggestive.

At that moment, on the threshold of the great doorway to the club, a rather dour-looking, almost ugly man, a Han, paused, looking in, his eyes drawn momentarily toward the laughter at the table to his right. He was different from the other Han inside the club in that he wore the powder-blue uniform of a Security officer, his chest patch showing him to be a Captain. But he was a Han all the same, and when he took a step across that threshold, a duty officer stepped forward, intercepting him.

"Excuse me, sir, but might I see your pass?"

Kao Chen stopped, then turned and faced the man, keeping his feelings in tight check. The man was within his rights, after all. He gave a terse bow and took his permit card from the top pocket of his tunic, then handed it to the officer. As the man studied the card intently, Kao Chen was aware that other, non-Han officers went through unhindered, even guests from other Security forces. But he had half-expected this. The color of his skin, the fold of his eyes—both were wrong here. The officer class of Security was almost totally made up of *Hung Mao*, descendants of the mercenary armies who had fought for the Seven against the tyrant Tsao Ch'un. Here Han were secondary; servants, not rulers. But he was an officer and he was thirsty. He had a right to sit and have a beer. And so he would.

The officer handed him back his pass, then gave a brief, almost slovenly salute. In terms of rank, Chen was his superior, but he was not *Hung Mao*, and so the rank meant little.

"Thank you, Lieutenant," he said tightly, then made his way through, down the plushly carpeted steps and out into the main body of the club.

He was halfway across the floor before he realized who he was walking toward. He saw Ebert's eyes widen in recognition and decided to walk past quickly, but he was not to be so fortunate. Three paces past the table he was called back.

"Hey, you! Han! Come here!"

Chen turned slowly, then came back and stood in front of Ebert, his head bowed. "Major Ebert."

Ebert leaned back arrogantly in his chair, a sneering smile on his face. "What in fuck's name do you think you're doing, Han?"

Chen felt himself go cold with anger, then remembered he was *kwai*. These were but words. And words could not hurt him. Only a knife could hurt a *kwai*. He answered Ebert calmly, civilly.

"I've just come off duty. I was hot and thirsty. I thought I would have a beer or two at the bar."

"Then you can think again. There are rules in this place. No women and no Han."

"No Han?"

He realized as soon as he said it that he had made a mistake. He should have bowed, turned around, and left. Now it was a question of face. His words, correct enough, innocuous enough in themselves, had challenged what Ebert had asserted. It did not matter that he, Kao Chen, had the right to use the club. That was no longer the issue.

Ebert leaned forward slightly, his voice hardening. "Did you hear me, *Han*?"

Chen hesitated, then lowered his head slightly, afraid to let the anger in his eyes show. "Excuse me, Major, but I am an officer in the service of the T'ang. Surely . . ."

Ebert leaned forward and threw his drink into Chen's face. "Are you stupid? Don't you understand me?"

Chen was silent a moment, then bowed again. "I apologize, Major. It was my fault. Might I buy you another drink before I leave?"

Ebert gave him a look of profound disgust. "Just go, little Han. Now. Before I beat you senseless."

Chen bowed low and backed away, mastering the pain, the fierce stinging in his eyes, his face perfectly controlled. Inside, however, he seethed; and at the doorway he looked back, hearing their laughter drift outward from the table, following him.

Laugh now, he thought; laugh good and long, Hans Ebert, for I'll not rest until my pride's restored and you lie humbled at my feet.

At the table all eyes were once again on Ebert.

"The nerve of some of them," he said, filling his glass again. "Anyway. Where were we? Ah yes . . ." He stood up, then raised his glass. "To Li Yuan and his bride! May this evening bring them clouds and rain!"

The answering roar was deafening. "To Li Yuan!" they yelled. "Clouds and rain!"

———

THE CEREMONY was over; the last of the guests had departed; the doors of the inner palace were locked and guarded. Only the two of them remained.

Li Yuan turned from the doorway and looked across. Fei Yen sat in the tall-backed chair at the far side of the room, on the dais, as if enthroned. A *chi pao* of brilliant red was draped about her small and slender figure, while her dark hair was braided with fine strands of jewels. A thin cloth of red and gold veiled her features, an ancient *kai t'ou*, as worn by the brides of the Ching Emperors for almost three centuries. Now that they were alone, she lifted the veil, letting him see her face.

She was beautiful. More beautiful than ever. His breath caught as he looked at her, knowing she was his. He knew now how his brother, Han Ch'in, must have felt in his final moments, and grieved less for him. It would be fine to die now, knowing no more than this.

He walked across to her, hesitant, aware of her eyes upon him, watching him come.

He stopped at the foot of the steps, looking at her. The huge throne dwarfed her. She seemed like a child sitting in her father's chair. Three steps led up to the dais, but standing there, his face was on the level of Fei Yen's. He studied her, conscious that in the years since he had first seen her she had grown to the fullness of womanhood.

His eyes narrowed with pain, looking at her, seeing how dark her eyes were. How deep and beautiful they were. How delicate the lashes. How finely drawn the curves of skin about the liquid centers. Eyes so dark, so vast, he felt he could lose himself in their depths.

"Well?" Fei Yen leaned forward. She was smiling at him, her hand extended. "What does my husband command?"

He felt a fresh thrill of delight course through his blood, at the same time hot and cold, both exquisite and painful. Her eyes held him, making him reach out and take her hand.

He looked down at her hand. So small and fine it was. Its warmth seemed to contradict its porcelain appearance, its strength oppose its apparent fragility. Her hand closed on his, drawing him up the steps to where she sat. He knelt, his head in her lap, her hands caressing his neck. For a moment it was enough. Then she lifted his head between her hands and made him move back, away from her.

They stood, facing each other.

Her hand went to the ruby-studded clasp at her right shoulder and released it. Slowly, with a faint silken rustle, the cloth unraveled, slipping from her body.

She stood there, naked but for the jewels in her hair, the bands of gold at her ankles and at her throat. Her skin was the white of swan's feathers, her breasts small, perfectly formed, their dark nipples protruding. Mesmerized, he looked at the curves of her flesh, the small, dark tangle of her sex, and felt desire wash over him so fiercely, so overpoweringly, he wanted to cry out.

Timidly he put out his hand, caressing her flank and then her breast, touching the dark brown nipple tenderly, as if it were the most fragile thing he had ever touched. She was watching him, her smile tender, almost painful now. Then, softly, she placed her hands upon his hips and pushed her face forward.

He moved closer, his eyes closed, his body melting. His hands caressed her shoulders, finding them so smooth, so warm, they seemed unreal; while her lips against his were soft and wet and hot, like desire itself, their sweetness blinding him.

She reached down, releasing him, then drew him down on top of her. At once he was spilling his seed, even as he entered her. He cried out, feeling her shudder beneath him. And when he looked at her again he saw how changed her eyes were, how different her mouth—a simple gash of wanting now that he was inside her.

That look inflamed him, made him spasm again, then lie still on top of her.

They lay there a long while; then, as one, they stirred, noticing how awkwardly they lay, their bodies sprawled across the steps.

He stood and tucked himself in, aware of how incongruous the action seemed, then reached down to help her up, unable to take his eyes from her nakedness.

Saying nothing, she led him through into the bridal room. There she undressed him and led him to the bath and washed him, ignoring his arousal, putting him off until she was ready for him. Then, finally, they lay there on the low wide bed, naked, facing each other, their lips meeting for tiny sips of kisses, their hands tenderly caressing each other's bodies.

"When did you know?" she asked, her eyes never leaving his.

"When I was eight," he said and laughed softly, as if he knew it was madness. For more than half his young life he had loved her. And here she was, his wife, his lover. Eight, almost nine years his senior. Half a lifetime older than he.

For a time she was silent, her eyes narrowed, watching him. Then, at last she spoke. "How strange. Perhaps I should have known." She smiled and moved closer, kissing him.

Yes, he thought, releasing her, then watching her again, seeing the small movements of her lashes, of the skin about her eyes, the line of her mouth. Cloud motion in the eyes, it seemed, the bones of her face molded and remolded constantly. He was fascinated by her. Mesmerized. He felt he could lie there forever and never leave this room, this intimacy.

They made love again, slowly this time, Fei Yen leading him, guiding him, it seemed, bringing him to a climax more exquisite than the last, more painful in its intensity.

He lay there afterward, watching the darkness in her face, the sudden color in her cheeks and at her neck and knew he would always want her. "I love you," he said finally, shaking his head slowly, as if he could not believe it. He had said the words so often in his head. Had imagined himself saying them to her. And now . . .

"I know," she said, kissing him again. Then, relaxing, she settled down beside him, her head nestling into the fold of his arm, her cheek pressed soft and warm against his chest.

CHAPTER TWO

Conflicting Voices

L I Y U A N W O K E early and, loath to disturb her, went to his desk on the far side of the room and sat there in the tight circle of the lamp's light, looking across at her. For a time he did nothing, entranced by the vision of her sleeping form; then, stirring himself, he took paper from the drawer and, after mixing water and ink from the ink block, began, writing the words in a neat, unhesitant hand down the page, right to left.

> Hot wings, perfumed like cinnamon,
> Beat about me, black as the moonless night.
> I heard your splendid cry in the silence,
> And knew the phoenix fed upon my heart.

He dipped the brush again, then looked across, realizing she was watching him.

"What are you doing, my love?"

He felt a tiny thrill, a shiver of pure delight, pass through him at her words. *My love* . . . How often he'd dreamed of her saying them. He smiled, then set the brush down.

"Nothing, my darling one. Sleep now. I'll wake you when it's time."

He picked up a tiny dragon-headed pot and shook sand over the paper to dry the ink, then lifted the sheet to blow it clean.

"Is it business?"

He looked up again, smiling. She had raised herself on one elbow and was looking across at him, her dark hair fallen loose across the silk of her shoulder.

Li Yuan folded the sheet in half and in half again, then put it in the pocket of his gown. He looked away a moment, toward the garden. It was dark outside; black, like a sea of ink pressed against the glass.

He looked back, smiling. "No."

"Then come to bed, my love. It's warm here."

He laughed softly. "Yes, but I must get ready."

There was a meeting of the Council that afternoon and there was much to do beforehand. He ought to begin. Even so, he hesitated, seeing her thus. It was his first morning with her, after all. Surely his father would understand this once?

She was watching him silently, letting the darkness of her eyes, the silken perfection of her naked shoulder, bring him to her. He stood, then went across, sitting beside her on the bed.

She leaned forward to greet him, her left hand moving between the folds of his gown to touch and caress his chest. As she did so, the covers slipped back, revealing her neck, the smooth perfection of her upper chest, the magnificence of her breasts. He looked down at them, then up into her face again.

"Fei Yen . . ."

Her lips parted slightly, her eyes widened, smiling. "Husband?"

He laughed again, a brief sound of delight. "Husband . . . It sounds so different from your lips."

"Different?"

He shivered, then leaned forward to kiss her lips, gently, softly, holding her to him momentarily. Then he released her and sat back, looking at her again. "Yes . . . like something undeserved."

There was a small movement in her mouth, then she laughed. "I have a present for you."

"A present?"

"Yes. Wait there . . ."

Li Yuan reached out and took her arm gently, stopping her.

"Hold, my love. Look at you!" His eyes traced the form of her. "What need have I for presents?"

"But this is different, Yuan. It's something I chose for you myself."

"Ah . . ." he said, releasing her, then watched, his heart pounding in his chest, as she turned from him, throwing the sheets aside to reveal the slender curve of her back. She scrambled across the huge bed, then came back, a slim package in her hand.

"Here . . ."

He took it, but his eyes were elsewhere, drinking in the beauty of her.

"Well?" she said, laughing gently at him, enjoying the way he looked at her. "Open it."

He hesitated, then looked down, tugging at the bow to free the ribbon then pulled the wrapping aside. It was a book. He opened the pages, then blushed and looked up.

"What is it?" he said quietly.

"It is a *chun hua,*" she said, coming alongside him, draping her warmth across his side and shoulder. "A pillow book. Something to excite us when we're here, alone."

He turned the pages slowly, reluctantly, pretending he had never seen its like, strangely appalled by the graphic nature of its sexual images. "Fei Yen . . . we have no need for this. Why, I have only to look at you . . ."

"I know," she said, turning his head gently with her fingers and kissing him softly on the cheek. "But this will keep our love fresh and powerful; will raise us to new heights."

He shuddered, closing his eyes, overwhelmed by the feeling of her warmth pressed up against him, the softness of her kisses against his flesh. He could smell the scent of their lovemaking on her skin. Could taste it on his tongue.

"I must get ready," he said almost inaudibly. "The Council . . ."

In answer she drew him down again, her kisses robbing him of his senses, inflaming him once more.

━━━━━

PRINCE WANG SAU-LEYAN stood on the balcony of his dead father's room, his hands resting lightly on the balustrade, his back to his brother's Chancellor. The broad sweep of the Nile lay below him, bisecting the empty landscape, its surface glittering in the morning light. He was dressed in a long silk sleeping robe of lavender decorated with butterflies, tied loosely at the waist. His feet were bare and his hair hung long, unbraided. He had been silent for some time, watching the slow hovering flight of the birds high overhead, but now he lowered his head, finally acknowledging the waiting man.

"Greetings, Hung Mien-lo. And how is my brother this fine morning?"

Hung Mien-lo inclined his head. He was dressed formally, the three tiny pigtails of his beard braided tightly with silver thread, the dark silks he wore contrasting with the vermilion sash of office.

"The T'ang is poorly, Excellency. His nerves were bad and he did not sleep. He asks that you act as regent for him at today's Council. I have the authority here, signed and sealed."

The Prince dipped his hand into a bowl on the balustrade, at his side, scattering a handful of meat onto the desert floor, then watched the vultures swoop toward the subtly poisoned bait.

"Good. And our spies? What have they reported?"

Hung Mien-lo lifted his head, studying the Prince's back. "That Li Shai Tung has a scheme. Something his son, Yuan, has proposed. I've sounded some of our friends."

"And?"

The friends were a mixture of First Level businessmen and representatives, government officials, and selected members of the Minor Families—all of them men of some influence outside the narrow circle of the Seven.

"They feel it would be best to oppose such a scheme."

"I see." He turned, looking at the Chancellor for the first time. "This scheme . . . what does it involve?"

"They want to place a device in every citizen's head, a kind of tracking beam. They believe it would allow for a more effective policing of Chung Kuo."

Wang Sau-leyan turned away. It was not a bad idea, but that was not the point. His purpose was to blunt Li Shai Tung's authority in Council, and what better way than to oppose his son? If, at the same time, he could win the support of certain influential members of the Above, then all the better. When his own plans came to fruition they would be reminded of his opposition to the scheme.

He turned, looking back fiercely at Hung Mien-lo. "It is abominable. To put things in men's heads. Why, it would make them little more than machines!"

"Indeed, Excellency. And men should not be machines to be manipulated, should they?"

Both men laughed.

"You understand me well, Chancellor Hung. Too well, perhaps. But I can use you."

Hung Mien-lo bowed low. "As your Excellency desires."

"Good." Wang Sau-leyan smiled and turned, staring out across the delta toward the distant pinnacle of the lighthouse. "Then you understand the last step we must take, you and I?"

Hung remained bowed; but his words came clear, unbowed, almost arrogant in their tone. "I understand . . . *Chieh Hsia.*"

———

AFTER THE CHANCELLOR had gone, Wang Sau-leyan stood there, watching the birds. At first they seemed unaffected by the poison, but then, first one and then another began to stagger unsteadily. One flapped its wings awkwardly, attempting to fly, lifting ten, maybe fifteen *ch'i* into the air before it fell back heavily to earth. He smiled. Six birds had taken the poison. He watched them stumble about for a time before they fell and lay still. More birds were gathering overhead, making slow circles in the cloudless sky. In a while they too would swoop. And then . . .

He turned away, tired of the game already—knowing the outcome—and went back inside.

"Sun!" he shouted impatiently. "Sun! Where are you?"

Sun Li Hua, Master of the Inner Chamber, appeared in the doorway at once, his head bent low.

"Yes, Excellency?"

"Send the maids. At once! I wish to dress."

Sun bowed and made to back away, but Wang Sau-leyan called him back.

"No . . . Send just the one. You know . . . Mi Feng."

"As you wish, Excellency."

He sniffed deeply, then crossed to the full-length dragon mirror and stood there, looking at himself. So his brother was unwell. Good. He would feel much worse before the day was out.

Wang Sau-leyan smiled and combed his fingers through his hair, drawing it back from his forehead. Then, almost whimsically, he turned his head, exposing one ear to view. That mystery—the mystery of who had taken his father's ears—remained unsolved. He had had Hung Mien-lo make a thorough investigation of the matter, but it had been without result. They had vanished, as if they had never been.

The thought brought a smile to his lips. He turned, still smiling, and saw the girl.

Mi Feng was kneeling just inside the door, her head lowered almost to her lap, awaiting his pleasure.

"Come here," he said brusquely, turning from her, moving across toward the great wardrobes that lined one side of the room. "I want you to dress me, girl."

She was his brother's maid, inherited from their father. In the wardrobe mirrors he saw her hesitate and glance up at his back.

"Well, girl? What are you waiting for? You heard me, didn't you?"

He noted her confusion, saw the way her face clouded momentarily before she bowed her head and began to move toward him.

He turned abruptly, making her start nervously.

"How is your sting, Little Bee? Did you serve my father well?"

Again he noted the movements in her face, the uncertainty, maybe even the suggestion of distaste. Well, who did she think she was? She was a servant, there to do his bidding, not the daughter of a T'ang.

She moistened her lips and spoke, her head kept low, her eyes averted. "What do you wish to wear, my Lord?"

White, he almost answered her. *White for mourning*.

"What do you suggest?" he asked, studying her more carefully, noting how delightfully she was formed, how petite her figure. "What would my father have worn to Council?"

She looked up at him, then quickly away, clearly bewildered by what was happening. "Forgive me, Prince Sau-leyan, but I am the T'ang's maid. Surely . . ."

He shouted at her, making her jump. "Be quiet, girl! You'll do as you're told or you'll do nothing, understand me?"

She swallowed, then nodded her head.

"Good. Then answer me. What would my father have worn to Council?"

She bowed, then moved past him, keeping her head lowered. A moment later she turned back, a long robe held over one arm.

"Lay it out on the bed so that I can see it."

He watched her move across to do as she was told, then smiled. Yes, the old man had chosen well with this one. He could imagine how the girl had wormed her way into the old boy's affections. She had kept his bed warm many a night, he was sure.

She had turned away from him, laying out the heavy, formal robe. He moved closer, coming up behind her, then bent down and lifted her gown up from the hem, exposing her buttocks and her lower back. She froze.

"You didn't answer me earlier," he said. "I asked you—"

"I heard you, Excellency."

Her tone was sharper than it should have been. Impertinent. He felt a sudden flush of anger wash over him.

"Put your hands out," he said, his voice suddenly cold. "Lean forward and stretch them out in front of you."

Slowly she did as she was told.

"Good," he said. "Now stay there."

He went outside onto the balcony a moment, then returned, holding a cane he had broken from the bamboo plant. It was as long as his arm and as thick as his middle finger. He swished it through the air, once, then a second time, satisfied with the sound it made; then he turned and looked across at her.

"I am not my father, Mi Feng. Nor my brother, come to that. They were weak men. They held weak ideas. But I'm not like that. I'm stronger than them. Much stronger. And I'll have no impertinence from those beneath me."

He moved closer, measuring the distance between himself and the girl, then brought the cane down hard across her buttocks.

She cried out involuntarily, her whole body tensing from the blow.

"Well?" he said, as if there were something she should say, some apology or word of mitigation. But she was silent, her body tensed against him, defiantly expectant. He shivered, angered by her silence, and lashed out, again and again, bringing the cane down wildly, impatiently, until, with a shudder, he threw it aside.

"Get up," he said, tonelessly. "Get up. I wish to be dressed."

━━━━━

FEI YEN lay there, Yuan's head cradled between her breasts, her hands resting lightly on his back, her fingertips barely touching his flesh. He was sleeping, exhausted from their last bout of lovemaking, the soft exhalation of his breath warm against her skin. It was almost noon and the bedchamber was flooded with light from the garden. If she turned her head she could see the maple, by the pathway where they had walked, so long ago.

She sighed and turned back, studying the neat shape of his head. It had been a sweet night, far sweeter than she had ever imagined. She thought of what they had done and her blood thrilled. She had fancied herself the famous concubine, Yang Kuei Fei, lying in the arms of the great T'ang emperor, Ming Huang, and at the moment of clouds and rain, had found herself transported. A *son*, she had prayed to Heaven; *let his seed grow in me and make a son!* And the joy of the possibility had filled her, making her cry out beneath him with the pleasure of it.

A son! A future T'ang! From these loins she would bring him forth. And he would be an Emperor. A Son of Heaven.

She shivered, thrilled by the thought of it, then felt him stir against her.

"What is it?" he said sleepily.

Her hands smoothed his back, caressed his neck. "I was thinking how hard it was before last night. How difficult to be alone."

He lifted his head slightly, then lay back again.

"Yes," he said, less drowsily than before. "I can see that."

He was silent for a time, his body at ease against her own, then he lifted himself up on his arms, looking down at her, his face serious. "How was it? All those years before last night. How hard was that?"

She looked away. "It was like death. As if not Han but I had died that day." She looked up at him, fiercely, almost defiantly.

"I am a woman, Yuan, with a woman's appetites." She swallowed. "Oh, you just don't know . . ." For a moment longer her face was hard with past bitterness, then it softened and a smile settled on her lips and in her eyes. "But now I am alive again. And it was you who brought me back to the living. My Prince. My love . . ."

She made to draw him down again, but he moved back, kneeling there between her legs, his head bowed. "Forgive me, my love, but I am spent. Truly I am." He laughed apologetically, then met her eyes again. "Tonight, I promise you, I will be a tiger again. But now I must dress. The Council . . ."

He turned to look at the timer beside the bed, then sat bolt upright. "Gods! And you let me sleep!" He backed away from her, then stood there on the bare floor, naked, looking about him anxiously. "I shall be late! Where is Nan Ho? Why did he not wake me?"

She laughed and stretched, then reached down and pulled the sheets up to her neck.

"I sent him away. They will excuse you this once if you are late. Besides, you needed to sleep."

"But Fei Yen . . ." Then he laughed, unable to be angry with her. She was beautiful, and, yes, he had needed to sleep. What's more, they would forgive him this once. Even so . . .

He turned from her. "All right. But now I must dress."

He was halfway to the door when she called him back. "Li Yuan! Please! You don't understand. I'll dress you."

He turned. She had climbed from the bed and was coming toward him.

"You?" He shook his head. "No, my love. Such a task is beneath you. Let me call the maids."

She laughed, then put her arms about his neck. "You will do no such thing, my Prince. I *want* to dress you. I *want* to serve you as a wife *should* serve her master."

He felt a small thrill go through him at the words. "But I . . ." Her kiss quieted him. He bowed his head slightly. "As you wish."

She smiled. "Good. But first I must bathe you. After all, you cannot go to Council smelling like a singsong house."

He laughed uneasily, then seeing how she smiled at him, felt the unease fall from him. It was impossible to be angry with her, even when her words were ill-chosen, for that too was part of the charm—the sheer delight—of her. Like porcelain she looked, yet in the darkness she had been fire; black wings of fire, beating about him wildly.

WHEN HE WAS GONE she looked around the room.

It was a strangely feminine room, unlike the rooms of her brothers. There were no saddles, no weapons of war on display. In their place were beautiful ceramic pots filled with the most exquisite miniature trees and shrubs. And in place of heavy masculine colors were softer shades, delicately chosen to complement the colors of the garden outside. She looked about her, pleased by what she saw, then went across to the desk and sat there.

She placed her left hand on the desk's broad surface, then lifted it, surprised. She licked at the tiny grains that had adhered to her palm, then understood. Of course. He had been writing.

She stood, then went back to the bed and picked up his sleeping robe. From whim, she tried it on, putting her arms into its sleeves and tying the slender sash about her waist. It was far too big for her, yet it felt somehow right to be wearing it. She laughed, then sat down on the bed, reaching into the pocket to take out the folded piece of paper.

She read it. Twice, and then a third time.

A poem. For her? It must have been. She shivered, then touched the tip of her tongue against her top teeth thoughtfully.

Yes. She could see it now: she would be everything to him. Indispensable. His wife. In all things his wife.

It was true what she had said. Or almost true. He *had* brought her back from death. From the death of all her hopes and dreams. Had given her back what she had always wanted.

And in return?

She smiled and drew his gown tighter about her. In return she would be his woman. That before all else. His helpmate and advisor. His champion and chief advocate. His lover and when he needed it, a mother to him.

Yes, and that was the clue to Li Yuan. She had known it earlier, when he had rested his head between her breasts, had known then that it was a mother he wanted. Or at least, someone to be the mother he had never had. Well, she would be that to him, among other things. And in time . . .

She shivered and slipped the poem back into the pocket of the gown.

In time she would have sons of her own. Seven sons. Each one of them a T'ang. She laughed and stood, letting the gown fall from her until she stood there, naked, lifting her arms defiantly. There! That was her dream. A dream she had shared with no one.

It seemed an impossibility, and yet she saw it clearly. It *would* be so. Yes, but first she must be practical. First she must become all things to him. She would ask him this evening, after they had made love. She would bathe him and wash his hair, and then, when he was at his sweetest, she would go down on her knees before him, pleading to be allowed always to serve him so.

He would agree. Of course he would. And then she would ask again. The maids, she would say, you must send them away. And he would do so. And then he would be hers. Completely, irrevocably hers.

━━━━━

TENDER WILLOW and Sweet Rain were talking, laughing between them as they came into the room, but seeing Little Bee stretched out facedown on her bed, they fell silent.

"What is it?" Sweet Rain asked, moving closer. "What happened?"

Mi Feng looked up, her eyes red, her cheeks wet with tears, and shook her head.

"What did he do?" Tender Willow asked, coming alongside her sister.

Mi Feng swallowed, then let her head fall again, a great sob racking her body.

The two girls sat on the bed, on either side of her, their arms about her, comforting her. But when Tender Willow leaned back, accidentally brushing against her buttocks, Mi Feng winced and gave a small moan.

The two girls exchanged looks, then nodded. Carefully, they lifted Mi Feng's robe, conscious of how she tensed.

"Kuan Yin . . ." Sweet Rain said softly, her voice pained. "What did he do this with?"

"A cane," came the whisper. "A bamboo cane."

Tender Willow stared at the cuts a moment longer, horrified, then she shuddered. "How *dare* he?" she said, outraged. "Who does he think he is? You are the T'ang's maid, not his. He cannot be allowed to act like this."

Mi Feng shook her head. A great shuddering sigh passed through her; then she spoke again, more calmly and clearly than before. "You are wrong, sister. He may do as he wishes. He is a Prince, after all. And what am I? Only a maid. A thing to be used or discarded. I learned that today, Tender Willow. I had it beaten into me. And the T'ang . . ." She laughed coldly, then swallowed, another shiver passing through her, ". . . the T'ang will do nothing."

Tender Willow met her eyes momentarily, then looked away, feeling sick. Maybe it was true. The T'ang *would* do nothing. But this was too much. The Prince had gone too far this time. Maid or not, *thing* or not, she would not allow this to happen to her sister.

"I have creams," she said gently, looking back, reaching out to touch and stroke her sister's brow, "ointments to soothe the cuts and help them heal. Lay still, Little Bee, and I'll bring them. And don't worry. Everything will be all right."

━━━━━

THE SERVANT BOWED low and backed away, his message delivered. Tsu Ma allowed himself the slightest smile, then turned, greeting the newcomer.

"You're late, Li Yuan!" he said sternly, loud enough for the others to hear, then let the hard lines of his face melt into a broad grin. He put a hand on the young man's shoulder. "Was it hard to get up this morning?"

"No . . ." Li Yuan began innocently, then blushed deeply as he saw the verbal trap and heard the great gust of laughter from the rest of the men on the great broad balcony. He looked about and saw how each face—even his father's—was filled with a tolerant, good-natured humor. All but one. A young, moon-faced man stood alone by the ornamental rail, beyond the two small groups of men. He was staring back coldly at Li Yuan, as if irritated by his arrival. At first Li Yuan did not recognize him. Then he realized who it was and looked down, frowning. Wang Sau-leyan . . .

Tsu Ma squeezed his shoulder gently, then lowered his voice. "Anyway, Yuan, come. The second session is not due to start for another half hour. There's time for talk and refreshments before then."

He turned and drew Li Yuan out of the shadows into the warm, midafternoon sunlight, then began the formality of introducing him to the T'ang and those of their sons who were attending.

Li Yuan knew them all personally. All but the last.

"I'm surprised to find you here, Wang Sau-leyan," he said, as he lifted his head.

"Surprised?" Wang Sau-leyan's eyes looked out past Li Yuan's shoulder, an expression of disdain on his pale round face. "Five years ago, perhaps. But as things are . . ." He laughed, no warmth in the laughter. "Well, my brother is unwell. His nerves . . ."

He glanced briefly at Li Yuan, then seemed to dismiss him, turning to concentrate his attention on Tsu Ma.

"Have you sounded the other T'ang about my proposal, Tsu Ma?"

Tsu Ma smiled pleasantly, concealing whatever he had been thinking. "I have broached the matter."

"And?"

Tsu Ma laughed kindly. "Well, it's difficult, cousin. If you had given them more warning, if they had had just a little more time to consider all the possible ramifications of your suggestion . . ."

Wang Sau-leyan interrupted him curtly. "What you mean is, no, they won't debate it."

Tsu Ma gave the slightest suggestion of a shrug, the smile remaining on his lips. "It was felt that it might be—how should I say?—*premature* to press the matter without consideration. But if the T'ang's regent would like to prepare something for the next meeting."

Wang Sau-leyan leaned toward Tsu Ma angrily, the words

hissing from him coldly. "Four months from now! That's far too long! Why not today? Why are they so afraid to listen to new ideas?"

Heads had turned, but Tsu Ma seemed perfectly unflustered. He smiled, his whole manner calm and polite. "I understand your impatience, Wang Sau—"

"*Impatience?* You insult me, Tsu Ma! For three hours I have listened patiently to the words of others. Have attended to their schemes. Yet now, when I beg my turn to speak, they deny me. Is that impatience?"

Li Yuan had seen the movements of the muscles in Tsu Ma's cheeks. Had known that, were he not a T'ang, Tsu Ma would have called the young Prince out and challenged him to a duel. Yet his control now in the face of such provocation was magnificent.

Tsu Ma smiled. "Forgive me, Wang Sau-leyan. My words were ill-chosen. Even so, it is neither the validity of your views nor the . . . *novelty* of your words that are at issue here. It is merely our way. All that we say here, all we decide upon, has a profound effect upon the lives of those we rule. It would not do to give less than the most serious consideration to such matters. Ill-considered change benefits no man."

"You would lecture me, Tsu Ma?"

"Not at all. I wish merely to explain the position of my fellow T'ang. These things are matters of long standing. It is how we transact our business."

"Then perhaps it ought to change."

Tsu Ma laughed. "Maybe so. Perhaps the Prince Regent would put the idea forward for the next Council to consider?"

Wang Sau-leyan lifted his chin slightly. "Perhaps . . ." He let his eyes rest momentarily on Li Yuan, then looked back at Tsu Ma, giving the slightest inclination of his head. "I thank you for your efforts, Tsu Ma. If my manner was terse, forgive me. That is my way. But do not mistake me. I too have the best interests of Chung Kuo at heart."

Li Yuan watched as Wang Sau-leyan crossed the room to greet the young T'ang of South America, Hou Tung-po, then turned back to Tsu Ma. "Well! What *was* his proposal?"

Tsu Ma smiled. "Not here," he said quietly. Then he drew Li Yuan aside, his smile suddenly broader, more natural.

"So . . . tell me, cousin. How *is* that beautiful bride of yours?"

<hr />

HELMSTADT ARMORY was a massive hexagonal block of 300 levels, isolated from the stacks surrounding it by a space fifty *ch'i* in width. That two-*li*-deep chasm was spanned, at four separate levels, by three broad connecting bridges, each bridge ending at a huge double gate, closed against intruders. To each side a whole battery of weapons—state-of-the-art equipment controlled from the guard room within—covered these entry points to the complex.

Helmstadt was considered by its makers to be invulnerable: a fortress second only to the great nerve center of Bremen. But in less than thirty seconds, if everything went according to plan, three of its gates would be open, the approaches unguarded.

DeVore crouched among his men in a side corridor on the City side of the bridge, looking down at his handset, watching through the complex's own Security cameras as his man approached the gate. The man was a lieutenant in the Armory's backup forces, called in on emergency standby after half the Armory's regular garrison had been sent to help quell the riots in Braunschweig, thirty *li* away.

The lieutenant marched up to the gate, then came to attention, holding his pass up for inspection. Two of the overhead guns had swiveled about, covering him; but now, on the computer's recognition signal, they swung back, focusing once more on the mouth of the corridor beyond.

He moved forward, placing one eye to an indented pad set into the gate, then stepped back. Three seconds passed, then a panel irised back, chest high to him, revealing a keyboard. The lieutenant inserted his card, then tapped out the coded signal.

At once the gates began to open.

Elsewhere, at a gate on the far side of the stack and at another one fifty levels down, the same thing was happening. Much now depended on timing. If just one of the gates remained unsecured, the odds would swing against them.

DeVore waited, tensed, counting. At thirty the screen of the handset went blank and he gave the signal. Immediately his men spilled out of the corridor and began to cross the bridge. If his inside man had failed they would be cut down instantly. But the guns remained silent. Beyond them, on the far side of the bridge, the great doors stayed open.

DeVore switched channels on the handset quickly, making sure. All three were blank, the transmission signals dead. He smiled, then, tucking the set inside his one-piece, followed his men out onto the bridge.

Inside, he found things well advanced. The level had been sealed off and all four of the big transit elevators secured. On the floor to one side a line of captives lay facedown, bound hand and foot. Most of the prisoners were only partly dressed, while two were completely naked. Only the five-man duty squad was fully dressed, but even they had been too surprised to put up any fight. Down below his men would be moving through the levels, securing all major entry points to the arsenal itself, isolating any remaining defenders scattered about these uppermost levels.

Much depended now on how the *Ping Tiao* fared, fifty levels down. If they could seal off the barracks and hold their gate, all would be well. But even if they didn't, it would be more their loss than his. He needed the weapons, it was true, but there was something far more important here. Something he hadn't bothered to mention in the briefing.

He turned and called the lieutenant across to him.

"Which of these is the Duty Captain?"

The lieutenant went down the line, then stopped and bent down to touch the back of one of the half-dressed men.

"Good. Take him into the guard room."

While two of his men lifted the Captain under the shoulders and dragged him away, DeVore turned to Lehmann. Of all of them he looked most at ease in the simple *Ping Tiao* clothes they were wearing.

"Stefan . . . Come here."

Lehmann came across, then followed him into the guard room.

The Captain had been placed in a chair, his back to them. One of the men was busy binding him about the chest and legs.

"Who are you?" he was demanding as DeVore entered. "You're not *Ping Tiao*. I can see that, despite your clothes and those fish symbols about your necks. You're too sharp, too well organized. Those scum wouldn't know how to break into a food store."

"You're quite right, Captain," DeVore said, coming around and sitting on the table edge, facing him.

The man's eyes widened. "DeVore!"

DeVore laughed softly, then signaled for the two men to leave. When they were gone he looked past the man at Lehmann, who nodded and turned to lock the door.

"Good," DeVore smiled. "Now to business."

The Captain glared at him defiantly. "What business? I have no business with you, DeVore."

"No?" DeVore reached into the breast pocket of his one-piece and took out something small and flat and round, its white casing like a lady's compact. Looking across at the Captain he smiled. "You have a nice family, Captain Sanders. A beautiful wife, two fine sons, and a baby girl. Well, she's divine; a pretty little thing."

Sanders watched, horrified, as DeVore opened the casing and activated the hologram within.

"You have them?" Sanders looked up at DeVore, swallowing dryly; then looked back down at the tiny holo of his family, noting the look of anguish on his wife's face, the way the boys huddled against her.

DeVore smiled. "As I said. To business."

"What do you want?"

"Six numbers and five letters."

Sanders understood at once. "The elevator . . ."

"Yes."

It was a secret one-man shaft that went down from this level to the floor of the stack. He had seen it once, when he had inspected Helmstadt eleven years earlier, had traveled down and seen first-hand how it was defended. Now he would use what he knew.

Sanders hesitated, staring at the hologram. "And if I do . . . they'll go free?"

"Of course." DeVore snapped the case shut and slipped it back into the pocket of his one-piece. "You might consider me a traitor, Captain Sanders, but I'm still a man of my word."

Sanders studied DeVore a moment longer, doubt warring with fear in his eyes; then he nodded. "All right. But it won't help you."

"No?" DeVore leaned back slightly. "Well, we'll see, eh? Just give me the code. I'll do the rest."

━━━━━

FIVE THOUSAND *li* to the east, in the great palace at Astrakhan on the shore of the great inland sea, the Seven were in Council. As was their way, they sat not at a great table but in low comfortable chairs drawn into a circle at one end of the room. Their manner seemed casual, as though they had met as friends to drink and talk of old times; yet here, on such occasions, all major policy decisions were made. Behind the T'ang, on simple stools, sat those sons who were attending—four in all, including Li Shai Tung's son, Li Yuan—while at a desk behind Tsu Ma sat two scribes. In this, the second session of the day, they had come at last to the central issue: the matter of the Confiscations. Tsu Ma was just coming to the end of his speech, leaning forward in his chair, his words a strong echo of Li Shai Tung's.

". . . but that would be folly. There's no better way to put an end to all this bitterness and rivalry. At one stroke we can stabilize the market and placate those who, however mistakenly, might otherwise feel ill-served by our generosity to those who sided with us."

Tsu Ma paused and looked about the circle of his fellow T'ang, self-assured, his mouth and eyes forming a smile. "Which is why I have no hesitation in seconding Li Shai Tung's proposal. The stewardship system will achieve the end we seek."

There was a murmur of agreement from the older T'ang, but even as Tsu Ma sat back, Wang Sau-leyan leaned forward, his round face tensed with anger, his eyes hard. He spoke bitterly, staring about him angrily, challengingly.

"Can I believe what I hear? Have we not just fought a war? A war that by the power of Heaven we won. If that is so, why should we fear the bitterness of our enemies? Why should we seek to placate them? Would they have done the same? No! They would have destroyed us. And what then? What would they have offered us? Nothing! Not even the dignity of a decent burial. And yet you sit here worrying about your enemies and their feelings. Well, I say forget them! We must reward our friends! Publicly, so all can see. What better way to encourage support for the Seven?"

Wei Feng sat forward in his chair, his face grim, his hands spread in a gesture that suggested his despair at Wang's words. "That's foolish talk, Wang Sau-leyan! Loyalty cannot be bought. It is like a tree. Long years go into its making. Your scheme would have us *buy* our friends." He laughed scornfully. "That would reduce our friendships to mere transactions, our dealings to the level of the marketplace."

Wang Sau-Leyan stared back at Wei Feng, his eyes narrowed.

"And what is wrong with the marketplace? Is it not that self-same market that gives us our power? Be honest now—what's the truth of it? Does the love of our subjects sustain us, or is it the power we wield? Is there anyone here who does not fear the assassin's knife? Is there a single one of us who would walk the lowest levels unprotected?" Wang laughed scornfully and looked about him. "Well, then, I ask again—what is so wrong with the marketplace? Wei Feng says I speak foolishly. With respect, cousin Wei, my thoughts are not idle ones. You are right when you talk of loyalty as a tree. So it was. But the War has felled the forests. And are we to wait a dozen, fifteen, years for the new seed to grow?" He shook his head. "We here are realists. We know how things stand. There is no time to grow such loyalty again. Times have changed. It is regrettable, but . . ."

He paused, spreading his hands.

"So. Let me ask again. What is wrong with rewarding our friends? If it achieves our end—if it breeds a kind of loyalty— why question what it is that keeps a man loyal? Love, fear, money—in the end it is only by force that we rule."

There was a moment's silence after he had finished. Li Shai Tung had been looking down at his hands while Wang was speaking. Now he looked up and with a glance at Tsu Ma and Wu Shih, addressed the Council.

"I hear what my cousin Wang says. Nevertheless, we must decide on this matter. We must formulate our policy here and now. I propose that this matter is put to the vote."

Wang Sau-leyan stared at him a moment, then looked down.

There was to be no delay, then? No further debate? They would have his vote now? Well, then, he would give them his vote.

Tsu Ma was leaning forward, taking a small cigar from the silver-and-ivory box on the arm of his chair. He glanced up casually. "We are agreed, then, cousins?"

Wang Sau-leyan looked about him, watching his fellow T'ang raise their hands, then let them fall again.

"Good," said Tsu Ma. "Then let us move on quickly . . ."

Wang Sau-leyan spoke up, interrupting Tsu Ma. "Excuse me, cousin, but have you not forgotten something?"

Tsu Ma met his eyes, clearly puzzled. "I'm sorry?"

"The vote. You did not ask who was against."

Tsu Ma laughed awkwardly. "I beg your pardon . . . ?"

"Six hands were raised. Yet there are seven here, are there not?"

Wang Sau-leyan looked about him, seeing the effect his words were having on his fellow T'ang. Like so much else, they had not expected this. In Council all decisions were unanimous. Or had been. For one hundred and twenty-six years it had been so. Until today.

It was Li Shai Tung who broke the silence. "You mean you wish to vote against? After all we've said?"

Wei Feng, sat beside him, shook his head. "It isn't done," he said quietly. "It just isn't our way . . ."

"Why not?" Wang asked, staring at him defiantly. "We are Seven, not one, surely? Why must our voice be single?"

"You misunderstand—" Tsu Ma began, but again Wang cut in.

"I misunderstand nothing. It is my right to vote against, is it not? To put on record my opposition to this item of policy?"

Tsu Ma hesitated, then gave a small nod of assent.

"Good. Then that is all I wish to do. To register my unease at our chosen course."

At the desk behind Tsu Ma the secretary Lung Mei Ho had been taking down everything that was said for the official record, his ink brush moving quickly down the page. Beside him his assistant had been doing the same, the duplication ensuring that the report was accurate. Now both had stopped and were looking up, astonished.

"But that has been done already, cousin Wang. Every word

spoken here is a matter of record. Your unease . . ." Tsu Ma frowned, trying to understand. "You mean you really *do* wish to vote against?"

"Is it so hard to understand, Tsu Ma?" Wang looked past the T'ang at the scribe, his voice suddenly hard. "Why aren't you writing, *Shih* Lung? Did anyone call these proceedings to a halt?"

Lung glanced at his master's back, then lowered his head, hurriedly setting down Wang's words. Beside him his assistant did the same.

Satisfied, Wang Sau-leyan sat back, noting how his fellow T'ang were glaring at him now or looking among themselves, uncertain how to act. His gesture, ineffective in itself, had nonetheless shocked them to the bone. As Wei Feng had said, it wasn't done. Not in the past. But the past was dead. This was a new world, with new rules. They had not learned that yet. Despite all, the War had taught them nothing. Well, he would change that. He would press their noses into the foul reality of it.

"One further thing," he said quietly.

Tsu Ma looked up, meeting his eyes. "What is it, cousin Wang?"

The sharpness in Tsu Ma's voice made him smile inside. He had rattled them, even the normally implacable Tsu Ma. Well, now he would shake them well and good.

"It's just a small thing. A point of procedure."

"Go on . . ."

"Just this. The Princes must leave. Now. Before we discuss any further business."

He saw the look of consternation on Tsu Ma's face, saw it mirrored on every face in that loose circle. Then the room exploded in a riot of angry, conflicting voices.

━━━━━

DEVORE BRACED HIMSELF as the elevator fell rapidly, one hand gripping the brass-and-leather handle overhead, the other cradling the severed head against his hip. They had quick-frozen the neck to stop blood from seeping against his uniform and peeled away the eyelids. In time the retinal pattern would decay, but for now it was good enough to fool the cameras.

As the elevator slowed he prepared himself, lifting the head up in front of his face. When it stopped, he put the right eye against the indentation in the wall before him, then moved it away, tapping in the code. Three seconds, then the door would hiss open. He tucked the head beneath his arm and drew his gun.

"What's happening up top?"

The guard at the desk was turning toward him, smiling, expecting Sanders; but he had barely uttered the words when DeVore opened fire, blowing him from his seat. The second guard was coming out of a side room, balancing a tray with three bowls of *ch'a* between his hands. He thrust the tray away and reached for his sidearm, but DeVore was too quick for him. He staggered back, then fell and lay still.

DeVore walked across to the desk and put the head down, then looked about him. Nothing had changed. It was all how he remembered it. In eleven years they had not even thought of changing their procedures. Creatures of habit, they were—men of tradition. DeVore laughed scornfully. It was their greatest weakness and the reason why he would win.

He went to the safe. It was a high-security design with a specially strengthened form of ice for its walls and a blank front that could be opened only by the correct sequence of light pulses on the appropriate light-sensitive panels. That too was unchanged. *It won't help you*—that's what Sanders had said. Well, Sanders and his like didn't think the way he thought. They approached things head-on. But he . . .

DeVore laughed, then took the four tiny packets from the tunic and, removing their contents, attached them to the ice on each side of the safe's rectangular front. They looked like tiny hoops, like snakes eating their own tails. Four similar hoops— much larger, their destructive capacity a thousand times that of these tiny, ringlike versions—had begun it all, ten years earlier, when they had ripped the Imperial Solarium apart, killing the T'ang's Minister Lwo Kang and his advisors. Now their smaller brothers would provide him with the means to continue that War.

He smiled, then went across to one of the side rooms and lay down on the floor. A moment later the explosion juddered the room about him. He waited a few seconds, then got up and went back inside. The guard room was a mess. Dust filled the air; machinery and bits of human flesh and bone littered the walls and floor. Where the safe had been the wall was ripped apart; the safe itself, unharmed by the explosion, had tumbled forward and now lay there in the center of the room, covered by debris.

He took off his tunic and wrapped it around the safe, then slowly dragged it across the floor and into the elevator. He looked back into the room, then reached across and pushed the button. He had no need for the head this time—there were no checks on who left the room, nor on who used the elevator to ascend. Again that was a flaw in their thinking. He would have designed it otherwise: would have made it easier to break in, harder to get out. That way one trapped one's opponent, surrounded him. As in *wei chi*.

At the top Lehmann was waiting for him, a fresh one-piece over his arm.

"How are things?" DeVore asked, stripping off quickly and slipping into the dark-green maintenance overalls.

Lehmann stared at the safe. "The *Ping Tiao* have held their end. We've begun shipping the armaments out through the top east gate. Wiegand reports that the Security channels are buzzing with news of the attack. We should expect a counterattack any time now."

DeVore looked up sharply. "Then we'd best get this out quick, eh?"

"I've four men waiting outside, and another two holding the west transit elevator. I've told the *Ping Tiao* it's out of order."

"Excellent. Anything else?"

"Good news. The rioting in Braunschweig has spilled over into neighboring *hsien*. It seems our friends were right. It's a powder keg down there."

"Maybe . . ." DeVore looked thoughtful for a moment, then nodded. "Right. Get those men in here. I want this out of here before the *Ping Tiao* find out what we've done. Then we'll blow the bridges."

LI YUAN LEFT at once, not waiting for the T'ang to resolve their dispute. He went out onto the broad balcony and stood there at the balustrade, looking out across the blue expanse of the Caspian toward the distant shoreline. Wei Feng's son Wei Chan Yin joined him there a moment later, tense with anger.

For a time neither of them spoke, then Wei Chan Yin lifted his chin. His voice was cold and clear—the voice of reason itself.

"The trouble is, Wang Sau-leyan is right. We have not adapted to the times."

Li Yuan turned his head, looking at the older man's profile. "Maybe so. But there are ways of saying such things."

Wei Chan Yin relaxed slightly, then gave a small laugh. "His manners *are* appalling, aren't they? Perhaps it has something to do with his exile as a child."

Their eyes met and they laughed.

Li Yuan turned, facing Wei Chan Yin. Wei Feng's eldest son was thirty-six, a tall, well-built man with a high forehead and handsome features. His eyes were smiling, yet at times they could be penetrating, almost frightening in their intensity. Li Yuan had known him since birth and had always looked up to him, but now they were equals in power. Differences in age meant nothing beside their roles as future T'ang.

"What does he want, do you think?"

Wei Chan Yin shrugged. He stared out past Li Yuan a moment, considering things, then looked back at him.

"My father thinks he's a troublemaker."

"But you think otherwise."

"I think he's a clever young man. Colder, far more controlled than he appears. That display back there—I think he was playacting."

Li Yuan smiled. It was what he himself had been thinking. Yet it was a superb act. He had seen the outrage on the faces of his father and the older T'ang. If Wang Sau-leyan's purpose had been merely to upset them, he had succeeded marvelously. But why? What could he gain by such tactics?

"I agree. But my question remains. What does he want?"

"Change."

Li Yuan hesitated, waiting for Wei Chan Yin to say more. But Chan Yin had finished.

"Change?" Li Yuan's laughter was an expression of disbelief. Then, with a tiny shudder of revulsion, he saw what his cousin's words implied. "You mean . . ."

It was left unstated, yet Wei Chan Yin nodded. They were talking of the murder of Wang Hsien. Chan Yin's voice sank to a whisper. "It is common knowledge that he hated his father. It would make a kind of sense if his hatred extended to all that his father held dear."

"The Seven?"

"And Chung Kuo itself."

Li Yuan shook his head slowly. Was it possible? If so . . . He swallowed, then looked away, appalled. "Then he must never become a T'ang."

Wei Chan Yin laughed sourly. "Would that it were so easy, cousin. But be careful what you say. The young Wang has ears in unexpected places. Between ourselves there are no secrets; but there are some, even among our own, who do not understand when to speak and when to remain silent."

Again there was no need to say more. Li Yuan understood at once who Wei Chan Yin was talking of. Hou Tung-po, the young T'ang of South America, had spent much time recently with Wang Sau-leyan on his estates.

He shivered again, as if the sunlight suddenly had no strength to warm him, then reached out and laid his hand on Wei Chan Yin's arm.

"My father was right. These are evil times. Yet we *are* Seven. Even if some prove weak, if the greater part remain strong . . ."

Wei covered Li Yuan's hand with his own. "As you say, good cousin. But I must go. There is much to be done."

Li Yuan smiled. "Your father's business?"

"Of course. We are our fathers' hands, neh?"

Li Yuan watched him go, then turned back and leaned across the balustrade, staring outward. But this time his thoughts went back to the day when his father had summoned him and introduced him to the sharp-faced official Ssu Lu Shan. That afternoon had changed his life, for it was then that he had learned of the Great Deception, and of the Ministry that had been set up to administer it.

History had it that Pan Chao's great fleet had landed here on the shores of Astrakhan in A.D. 98. He had trapped the *Ta Ts'in* garrison between his sea forces and a second great land-based army and after a battle lasting three days, had set up the yellow dragon banner of the Emperor above the old town's walls. But history lied. Pan Chao had, indeed, crossed the Caspian to meet representatives of the *Ta Ts'in*—consuls of Trajan's mighty Roman Empire. But no vast Han army had ever landed on this desolate shore, no Han had crossed the great range of the Urals and entered Europe as conquerors. Not until the great dictator Tsao Ch'un had come, little more than a century past.

Li Yuan shivered, then turned away, angry with himself. Lies or not, it was the world they had inherited; it did no good to dwell upon alternatives. He had done so for a time and it had almost destroyed him. Now he had come to terms with it, had made his peace with the world of appearances. And yet sometimes—as now—the veil would slip and he would find himself wishing it would fly apart and that he could say, just once, *This is the truth of things*. But that was impossible. Heaven itself would fall before the words could leave his lips. He stared back at the doorway, his anger finding its focus once more in the upstart Wang Sau-leyan.

Change . . . Was Prince Wei right? Was it change Wang Sau-leyan wanted? Did he hunger to set the Great Wheel turning once again, whatever the cost? If so, they must act to stop him. Because change was impossible. Inconceivable.

Or was it?

Li Yuan hesitated. No, he thought, not inconceivable. Not now. Even so, it could not be. They could not let it be. His father was right: Change was the great destroyer; the turning Wheel crushed all beneath it, indiscriminately. It had always been so. If there was a single reason for the existence of the Seven it was this—to keep the Wheel from turning.

With a shudder he turned back, making his way through, his role in things suddenly clear to him. Yes, he would be the brake, the block that kept the Wheel from turning.

AT THE TURN DeVore stopped and flattened himself against the wall of the corridor, listening. Behind him the four men rested, taking their breath, the safe nestled in the net between them. Ahead there were noises—footsteps, the muffled sound of voices. But whose? These levels were supposed to be empty, the path to the bridge clear.

DeVore turned and pointed to a doorway to their right. Without needing to be told, they crossed the space and went inside. Satisfied, DeVore went to the left, moving down the corridor quickly, silently, conscious of the voices growing louder as he approached the junction. Before the turn he stopped and slipped into a side room, then waited, his ear pressed to the door. When they had gone by, he slipped out again, taking the right-hand turn, following them.

Ping Tiao. He was certain of it. But why were they here? And what were they doing?

Ten of them. Maybe more. Unless . . .

There was no reason for his hunch; yet he knew, even as he had it, that he was right. They were *Ping Tiao*. But not all of them. They had taken prisoners. High-ranking Security officers, perhaps. But why? For their ransom value? Or was there some other reason?

He frowned and ran on silently, knowing that he had to get closer to them, to make sure he was right, because if they *had* taken prisoners it was something he should know; something he could use. He had agreed with Gesell beforehand that there would be no prisoners, but Gesell wasn't to be trusted.

The bridge was up ahead, the corridor on the far side of it cleared by his men earlier. But how had they found out about it? He had told Gesell nothing. Which meant they had a man inside his organization. Or had paid someone close to him for the information. Even so, they didn't know about the safe. Only he knew about that.

They were much closer now. He could hear them clearly now. Three—no, four—voices. They had slowed down as they came near the bridge, cautious now, suspicious of some kind of trap. The next turn was only twenty *ch'i* ahead. From there he would be able to see them clearly. But it was risky. If they saw him . . .

DeVore slowed, then stopped just before the junction,

hunched down, listening again. They had paused, perhaps to send one of their number ahead of them across the bridge. He waited; then, when he heard the call come back, he put his head around the corner, keeping low, where they'd not expect to see anyone.

He took it all in at a glance, then moved back sharply. Five *Ping Tiao* and eight bound prisoners. As he'd thought. They weren't in uniform, but he could tell by their mustaches and the way they tied their hair that they were officers. Such things were a sign of rank as unmistakable as the patches on the chests of their dress uniforms.

So. Gesell was taking prisoners. He would find out why, then confront the man with the fact. It would be fun to hear what excuse he would give. Meanwhile his man on the far side of the bridge could follow them, find out where they took their captives.

He smiled and was about to turn away when he heard footsteps coming back toward him.

"Go on across!" a voice called out, closer than before. "Quick now! I'll meet up with you later."

DeVore took a deep breath and drew his gun. He looked at it a moment, then slipped it back into its holster. No. He would need to be quiet. Anyway, a knife was just as effective when it came to killing a man.

He looked about him quickly, wondering whether he should hide and let the man pass, then decided against it. He was almost certain he hadn't been seen, so he would have the element of surprise.

As the footsteps came on, he flattened himself against the wall. Then, as the man turned the corner, he reached out and pulled him close, whirling him about and pinning him against his chest, his right hand going to the man's throat, the knife's blade pressed tight against the skin.

"Cry out and you're dead," he said softly in his ear.

"Turner . . ." It was a whisper of surprise.

"Shen Lu Chua," he answered quietly, tightening his grip on the Han. "What a surprise to meet *you* here."

The *Ping Tiao* leader swallowed painfully, but he held his head proudly, showing no sign of fear. "What are you doing here?"

DeVore laughed softly. "You forget who holds the knife, Shen Lu Chua. Why is Gesell taking prisoners?"

"You saw? . . . Of course."

"Well?"

"You think I'd tell you?" Shen sniffed.

"It doesn't matter. I know what Gesell intends."

Shen's mocking laughter confirmed it. This was *his* idea. And Gesell knew nothing of it. Which in itself was interesting. It meant there were splits in their ranks, divisions he could capitalize upon. But why be surprised? They were human, after all.

"You know nothing . . ."

But DeVore had stopped listening. Hugging Shen closer, he thrust the tip of the knife up through the Han's neck, into the cavern of his mouth, then let him fall. For a moment he watched Shen lie there, struggling to remove the blade, small croaking noises coming from his ruined larynx; then he stepped forward and kneeling over the man, tugged the head back sharply, breaking his neck.

━━━━━

HUNG MIEN-LO sat at the desk in his office, the small, desk-mounted screen at his side lit with figures. Standing before him, his head bowed, was the Master of the Inner Chamber, Sun Li Hua.

"You summoned me, Chancellor Hung?"

Hung Mien-lo glanced at Sun, then continued to tap in figures on the keyboard.

"You took your time, Master Sun."

Sun kept his head lowered. "I am a busy man. There was much to organize for my master."

Hung sniffed. "And which master is that, Sun?"

Sun smiled faintly. "The same master we both serve."

Hung Mien-lo raised his head and stared at Sun, then laughed and turned the screen about so that it faced the man.

"Do you recognize these figures, Master Sun?"

Sun raised his head for the first time, studying the screen. Then he looked back at Hung, his expression unchanged. "Those look like the household accounts, Chancellor."

"And so they are. But they're wrong. They've been tampered with. And not just once but consistently, from what I can make out." He touched the pad to clear the screen, then sat back, smiling. "Someone has been milking them of quite considerable sums these last four years."

Sun met his gaze openly. "And?"

Hung nodded, admiring the man's coolness. "And there are only three men who could have done it. I've questioned the other two, and it's clear that they are innocent. Which leaves you, Master Sun. Your family has prospered greatly these past four years."

"Are you accusing me of embezzlement, Chancellor Hung?"

Hung Mien-lo smiled. "I am."

Sun stared back at him awhile, then laughed. "Is that all? Why, if every official who had massaged his accounts were to be arrested, the Seven would quickly find themselves short of servants."

"Maybe so. But *you* have been caught, Master Sun. I've evidence enough to have you demoted to the Net."

Sun looked back at him, untroubled, his smile intact. He recognized the big squeeze when he saw it. "What do you want, Chancellor? What's the real reason for this meeting?"

"You think I have an ulterior motive, is that it, Master Sun?"

There was movement in Sun's squat face; then, uninvited, he sat down, his features set in a more serious expression. "We are realists, you and I. We know how the wind blows."

"What do you mean?"

Sun sat back, relaxing, his face filled with sudden calculation. "We have been fortunate, you and I. Events have moved strongly in our favor this last year. We have risen while others have fallen away. Our families are strong, our kin powerful."

"So?"

Sun's lips were smiling now, but his eyes were still cold and sharp. "What I mean is this. We should be allies, Hung Mien-lo. Allies, not enemies."

Hung Mien-lo leaned toward him, his expression suddenly hard, uncompromising. "And if I say no?"

For the first time a flicker of uncertainty crossed Sun Li Hua's face. Then, reassuring himself, he laughed. "You would not be talking to me if you had already decided. You would have had me arrested. But that's not your purpose, is it? You want something from me."

But Hung was glaring at him, angry now. "Have you no ears, man? No understanding of the situation you are in?" He shook his head, astonished. "You have dared the ultimate, Sun Li Hua. You have killed a T'ang. And even the merest whisper in some ears of your involvement would bring about your certain death."

"You have no proof . . ." Sun began, then saw that what Hung had said was true. Such a thing needed no proving; it was enough that suspicion existed. And then he understood what Hung Mien-lo had been getting at, why he had raised the matter of the embezzled funds. Demotion to the Net would make him vulnerable. Would place him beyond the protection of law and kin. He stared at his hands a moment, sobered. There was nothing he could do. Hung Mien-lo held *all* the cards.

He bowed his head. "What do you want?"

Hung Mien-lo studied Sun Li Hua a moment, savoring his victory. For some time now he had wanted to humble the man, to pull him down from his high horse. Today, forced by the Prince to act, he had taken a gamble, had wagered that what he'd guessed about Sun and the old T'ang was true. And had won. But that was only the start. The next step raised the stakes considerably. This time he gambled with his life.

Thus far his hands had been clean. Thus far others had accomplished all he had wished for, as if on his behalf. But now . . .

He took a deep breath, studying the man, making certain in his own mind that this was what he wanted. Then, calmly, his voice controlled, he answered Sun.

"I'll tell you what I want. I want you to kill again. I want you to kill the new T'ang, Wang Ta-hung."

━━━━━

EMILY ASCHER'S FACE was dark with anger, her nostrils flared, her eyes wide, glaring at Gesell. She stood face on to him, her hands on her hips, her chin tilted back challengingly.

"Go on! Confront him with it! I bet the bastard denies it!"

Gesell's chest rose and fell violently. The news of Shen's death had shaken him badly. Things had been going so well . . .

"You're sure?"

She made a sharp, bitter sound of disgust. "It was his knife. The blade with the pearled handle. The one we confiscated from him when he came to see us that time."

"I see . . ."

She leaned closer, her voice lowered to a whisper. "Then you'll kill him, neh? As you said you would if he double-crossed us?"

Gesell shuddered involuntarily, then nodded. "If it's true," he said softly. "But he'll deny it."

"Then you'll *know* it's true."

"Yes . . ." He turned and looked across to where the albino was standing, watching their exchange. "Where is he?" he demanded, his voice raised for the first time since they had come up in the elevator.

"He'll be here," Lehmann answered coldly.

"And if he's not?" Ascher said softly at his side.

"Then we die here," Gesell said, not looking at her, returning the albino's cold stare.

In the distance there was the stutter of small-arms fire, then a muffled explosion that made the floor shudder beneath their feet. The armaments had been shipped out more than fifteen minutes before. It was time to get out. But they couldn't. Not until Turner was here.

Gesell spat, then turned away, pacing up and down slowly, looking about him at the men and women gathered in the corridors nearby. "What's keeping him?" he muttered angrily. He could see how tense his people were, how quickly they had caught his mood. Under his breath he cursed Turner. Emily was right. They should never have gotten into this.

Then, as he turned back, he saw him.

"Well," he said quietly, glancing at Ascher. "Here he is now."

DeVore spoke briefly to the albino, then came across. "You're ready?"

Gesell shook his head. "Not yet. I want some answers."

"About Shen Lu Chua?"

Gesell laughed briefly, surprised by his audacity. "You're a cool one, Turner. What happened?"

DeVore was staring back at him, his whole manner candid, open. "I killed him. I had to. He attacked me."

"Why?"

"I don't know. I tried to explain to him why I was there, but he gave me no chance."

"No . . ." Gesell looked to Ascher, then back at DeVore. "I knew Shen. He wouldn't do such a thing."

"You knew him?" DeVore laughed. "Then I guess you knew he was smuggling out eight prisoners? Senior Security officers."

Gesell felt Ascher touch his elbow. "He's lying . . ."

DeVore shook his head. "No. Ask your man Mach to check on it. Shen's side-kick, Yun Ch'o, has taken them to an apartment in Ottersleben. Level Thirty-four. I think you know the place."

Gesell tensed. Maybe Turner *was* bluffing, stalling for time. But that made no sense. As he said, it was easy for Mach to check. In any case, something else was bothering him. Something Turner hadn't yet explained.

"They tell me they found the body down at One-twenty. Even if it's as you say and Shen was double-crossing us, why were *you* down there?"

He stepped back sharply as DeVore reached into his uniform jacket. But it wasn't a weapon DeVore drew from his inner pocket. It was a map. Another map. DeVore handed it across to him.

"It was too good an opportunity to miss. I knew it was down there. I'd seen it, you see. Years ago."

Gesell looked up at him again, his mouth open with surprise. "Bremen . . . Gods! It's a Security diagram of Bremen."

"A part of it. The rest I've sent on."

"Sent on?" He was about to ask what Turner meant when one of his messengers pushed through the crowded corridor behind him and came up to him, almost breathless. He made the man repeat the message, then whirled about, facing DeVore.

"There's a problem."

"A problem?" DeVore raised his eyebrows.

"It seems we're trapped. The last of the bridges has been blown."

"I know. I ordered it."

"You *what?*"

"You heard. We're not going out that way. That's what they're waiting for, don't you see? They'll have worked out what we've done and they'll be sitting there, waiting to pick us off in the side corridors on the other side of the bridge. But I'm not going to give them the opportunity. I've craft waiting for us on the roof." DeVore glanced at the timer inset into his wrist. "We've less than five minutes, however, so we'd best get moving."

Gesell glanced at the map, then looked back at Turner, astonished, the business with Shen forgotten. "You've transporters?"

"That's what I said. But let's go. Before they work out what we're up to."

"But where? Where are we going?"

DeVore smiled. "South. To the mountains."

CHAPTER THREE

Connections

W ANG SAU-LEYAN stood before the full-length dragon mirror in his dead father's room watching his own reflection while his brother's maids dressed him.

"You should have seen them! You wouldn't believe how offended they were!" He laughed and bared his teeth. "It was marvelous! They're such hypocrites! Such liars and schemers! And yet they fancy themselves so clean and pure." He turned and glanced across at the Chancellor, his mouth formed into a sneer. "Gods, but they make me sick!"

Hung Mien-lo stood there, his head lowered. He was unusually quiet, his manner subdued, but Wang Sau-leyan barely noticed him; he was too full of his triumph in Council that afternoon. Dismissing the maids, he crossed to the table and lifted his glass, toasting himself.

"I know how they think. They're like ghosts, they travel only in straight lines. But I'm not like them. They'll have prepared themselves next time, expecting me to be rude again, to trample on their precious etiquette. They'll meet beforehand to work out a strategy to deal with my 'directness.' You see if they don't. But I'll wrong-foot them again. I'll be so meek, so sweet-assed and polite they'll wonder if I've sent a double."

He laughed. "Yes, and all the time I'll be playing their game.

Undermining them. Suggesting small changes that will require further debate. Delaying and diverting. Querying and qualifying. Until they lose patience. And then . . ."

He stopped, for the first time noticing how Hung Mien-lo stood there.

"What is it, Chancellor Hung?"

Hung Mien-lo kept his head lowered. "It is your brother, Excellency. He is dead."

"Dead? How?"

"He . . . killed himself. This afternoon. An hour before you returned."

Wang Sau-leyan set the glass down on the table and sat, his head resting almost indolently against the back of the tall chair.

"How very convenient of him."

Hung Mien-lo glanced up, then quickly looked down again. "Not only that, but Li Shai Tung's armory at Helmstadt was attacked this afternoon. By the *Ping Tiao*. They took a large amount of weaponry."

Wang Sau-leyan studied the Chancellor's folded body, his eyes narrowed. "Good. Then I want a meeting with them."

The Chancellor looked up sharply. "With the *Ping Tiao*? But that's impossible, *Chieh Hsia* . . ."

Wang Sau-leyan stared at him coldly. "Impossible?"

Hung's voice when it came again was smaller, more subdued than before. "It will be . . . difficult. But I shall try, *Chieh Hsia.*"

Wang Sau-leyan leaned forward, lifting his glass again. "Make sure you do, Hung Mien-lo, for there are others just as hungry for power as you. Not as talented, perhaps, but then, what's talent when a man is dead?"

Hung Mien-lo looked up, his eyes meeting the new T'ang's momentarily, seeing the hard, cold gleam of satisfaction there. Then he bowed low and backed away.

━━━━━━

KAO CHEN STOOD in the corridor outside the temporary mortuary, his forehead pressed to the wall, his left hand supporting him. He had not thought he could be affected any longer, had thought himself inured to the worst Man could do to his fellow creatures; yet he had found the sight of the mutilated corpses deeply upsetting. The younger ones especially.

"The bastards . . ." he said softly. There had been no need. They could have tied them up and left them. Surely they'd got what they wanted? But to kill all their prisoners. He shuddered. It was like that other business with the hostages—Captain Sanders' young family. There had been no need to kill them, either.

He felt a second wave of nausea sweep up from the darkness inside him and clenched his teeth against the pain and anger he felt.

"Are you all right, sir?"

His sergeant, a *Hung Mao* ten years Chen's senior, stood a few paces distant, his head lowered slightly, concerned but also embarrassed by his officer's behavior. He had been assigned to Kao Chen only ten days before and this was the first time they had been out on operations together.

"Have you seen them?"

The sergeant frowned. "Sir?"

"The dead. Cadets, most of them. Barely out of their teens. I kept thinking of my son."

The man nodded. "The *Ping Tiao* are shit, sir. Scum."

"Yes . . ." Chen took a breath, then straightened up. "Well . . . let's move on. I want to look at their dead before I report back."

"Sir."

Chen let his sergeant lead on, but he had seen the doubt in the man's eyes. All of this looking at the dead was quite alien to him—no doubt his previous officers hadn't bothered with such things—but Chen knew the value of looking for oneself. It was why Tolonen had recruited Karr and himself, because they took such pains. They noticed what others overlooked. Karr particularly. And he had learned from Karr. Had been taught to see the small betraying detail, the one tiny clue that changed the whole picture of events.

"Here it is, sir."

The sergeant came to attention outside the door, his head bowed. Chen went inside. Here things were different, more orderly, the bodies laid out in four neat rows on trestle tables.

And unlike the other place, here the bodies were whole. These men had died in action; they had not been tied up and butchered.

He went down the first of the rows, pausing here and there to pull back the covering sheets and look at a face, a hand, frowning to himself now, his sense of "wrongness" growing with every moment. Finally, at the head of the row, he stopped beside one of the corpses, staring down at it. There was something odd— something he couldn't quite place—about the dead man.

He shook his head. No, he was imagining it. But then, as he made to move on, he realized what it was. The hair. He went closer and lifted the head between his hands, studying it. Yes, there was no doubt about it, the dead man's hair was cut like a soldier's. Quickly he went down the row, checking the other corpses. Most of them had normal short hair, styles typical of the lower levels; but there were five with the same military-style cut, the hair trimmed back almost brutally behind the ear and at the line of the nape.

"Sergeant!"

The man appeared at the doorway at once.

"Bring me a comset. A unit with a visual connection."

"Sir!"

While he waited he went down the line again, studying the men he had picked out. Now that he looked he saw other differences. Their nails were manicured, their hands smooth, uncallused. They were all *Hung Mao*, of course, but of a certain kind. They all had those gray-blue eyes and chiseled features that were so typical of the men recruited by Security. Yes, the more he looked at them, the more he could imagine them in uniform. But was he right? And, if so, what did it mean? Had the *Ping Tiao* begun recruiting such types, or was it something more ominous than that?

The sergeant returned, handing him the comset, then stood there, watching, as Chen drew back the eyelid of the corpse with his thumb and held the machine's lens over the eye, relaying an ID query through to Central Records.

He had his answer almost immediately. There were six "likelies" that approximated to the retinal print, but only one of the full-body descriptions fitted the dead man. It was as Chen had thought: he was ex-Security.

Chen went down the line, making queries on the others he had picked out. The story was the same: all five had served in the Security forces at some point. And not one of them had been seen for several years. Which meant that either they had been down in the Net or they had been outside. But what did it signify? Chen pressed to store the individual file numbers, then put the comset down and leaned against one of the trestles, thinking.

"What is it, sir?"

Chen looked up. "Oh, it's nothing, after all. I thought I recognized the man, but I was mistaken. Anyway, we're done here. Have the men finish up then report to me by four. The General will want a full report before the day's out."

"Sir!"

Alone again, Chen walked slowly down the rows, taking one last look at each of the five men. Like the other dead, they wore the *Ping Tiao* symbol—a stylized fish—about their necks and were dressed in simple *Ping Tiao* clothes. But these were no common terrorists.

Which was why he had lied to the sergeant. Because if this was what he thought it was, he could trust no one.

No. He would keep it strictly to himself for the time being, and in the meantime he would find out all he could about the dead men: discover where they were stationed and under whom they had served.

As if he didn't know already. As if he couldn't guess which name would surface when he looked at their files.

◆◆◆◆◆

NAN HO, Li Yuan's Master of the Inner Chamber, climbed down from the sedan and returning the bow of the Grand Master of the Palace, mounted the ancient stone steps that led up to the entrance of the summer palace.

At the top he paused and turned, looking back across the ruins of the old town of Ch'ing Tao. Beyond it the bay of Chiao Chou was a deep cobalt blue, the gray-green misted shape of Lao

Shan rising spectacularly from the sea, climbing three *li* into the heavens. A thousand *li* to the east was Korea and beyond it the uninhabitable islands of Japan.

It was a year since he last visited this place—a year and two days, to be precise—but from where he stood, nothing had changed. For his girls, however, that year had been long and difficult, a year of exile from Tongjiang and the Prince they loved.

He sighed and turned back, following the Grand Master through. This was the smallest of the T'ang's summer palaces and had laid unused since his great-grandfather's days. It was kept on now only out of long habit, the staff of fifty-six servants undisturbed by the needs of their masters.

Such a shame, he thought, as he made his way through the pleasantly shaded corridors into the interior. Yet he understood why. There was danger here. It was too open, too hard to defend from attack. Whereas Tongjiang . . .

He laughed. The very idea of attacking Tongjiang!

The Grand Master slowed and turned, bowing low. "Is anything the matter, Master Nan?"

"Nothing," Nan Ho answered, returning the bow. "I was merely thinking of the last time I was here. Of the crickets in the garden."

"Ah . . ." The Grand Master's eyes glazed over, the lids closed momentarily; then he turned back, shuffling slowly on.

The two girls were waiting in the Great Conservatory, kneeling on the tiles beside the pool, their heads bowed.

He dismissed the Grand Master, waiting until he had left before he hurried across and pulled the two girls up, holding one in each arm, hugging them tightly to him, forgetting the gulf in rank that lay between them.

"My darlings!" he said breathlessly, his heart full. "My pretty ones! How have you been?"

Pearl Heart answered for them both.

"Oh, Master Nan . . . it's so good to see you! We've been so lonely here!"

He sighed deeply. "Hush, my kittens. Hush now, stop your crying. I've news for you. Good news. You're leaving this place. Two weeks from now."

They looked up at him, joy in their faces, then quickly averted their eyes again. Yes, they had changed, he could see that at once. What had the Grand Master done to them to make them thus? Had he been cruel? Had there been worse things than that? Well, he would find out. And if the old man had misbehaved he would have his skin for it.

Sweet Rose looked up at him hopefully. "Li Yuan has asked for our return?"

He felt his heart wrenched from him that he had to disappoint her.

"No, my little one," he said, stroking her arm. "But he wishes to see you." *One last time*, he thought, completing the sentence in his head. "And he has a gift for you both. A special gift . . ." He shivered. "But he must tell you that. I come only as a messenger, to help prepare you."

Pearl Heart was looking down again. "Then she will not have us," she said quietly.

He squeezed her to him. "It would not be right. You know that. It was what we spoke of last time we were here together."

He remembered the occasion only too well. How he had brought them here in the dark of night, and how they had wept when he had explained to them why they must not see their beloved Prince again. He swallowed, thinking of that time. It had been hard for Li Yuan, too. And admirable in a strange way. For there had been no need, no custom to fulfill. He recalled arguing with Li Yuan, querying his word to the point where the Prince had grown angry with him. Then he had shrugged and gone off to do as he was bid. But it was not normal. He still felt that deeply. A man—a Prince, especially—needed the company of women. And to deny oneself for a whole year, merely because of an impending wedding! He shook his head. Well, it was like marrying one's dead brother's wife; it was unheard of.

And yet Li Yuan had insisted. He would be "pure" for Fei Yen. As if a year's abstinence could make a man pure! Didn't the blood still flow, the sap still rise? He loved his master dearly, but he could not lie to himself and say Li Yuan was right.

He looked down into the girls' faces, seeing the disappointment there. A year had not cured *them* of their love. No, and nor would a lifetime, if it were truly known. Only a fool thought otherwise. Yet Li Yuan was Prince and his word was final. And though he was foolish in this regard, at least he was not cruel. The gift he planned to give them—the gift Nan Ho had said he could not speak of—was to be their freedom. More than that, the two sisters were to be given a dowry, a handsome sum, enough to see them well married, assured the luxuries of First Level.

No, it wasn't cruel. But neither was it kind.

Nan Ho shook his head and smiled. "Still . . . let us go through. We'll have some wine and make ourselves more comfortable," he said, holding them tighter against him momentarily. "And then you can tell me all about the wicked Grand Master and how he tried to have his way with you."

━━━━━

CHUANG LIAN, wife of Minister Chuang, lay among the silken pillows of her bed, fanning herself indolently, watching the young officer out of half-lidded eyes as he walked about her room, stopping to lift and study a tiny statue or to gaze out at the garden. The pale-cream sleeping robe she wore had fallen open, revealing her tiny breasts; yet she acted as if she were unaware, enjoying the way his eyes kept returning to her.

She was forty-five—forty-six in little over a month—and was proud of her breasts. She had heard how other women's breasts sagged, either from neglect or from the odious task of childbearing, but she had been lucky. Her husband was a rich man—a powerful man—and had hired wet nurses to raise his offspring. And she had kept her health and her figure. Each morning, after exercising, she would study herself in the mirror and thank Kuan Yin for blessing her with the one thing that, in this world of Men, gave a woman power over them.

She had been beautiful. In her own eyes she was beautiful still. But her husband was an old man now and she was still a woman, with a woman's needs. Who could blame her if she took a lover to fill the idle days with a little joy? So it was for a woman in her position, married to a man thirty years her senior. Yet there was still the need to be discreet, to find the right man for her bed. A young and virile man, certainly, but also a man of breeding, of quality. And what better than this young officer?

He turned, looking directly at her, and smiled. "Where is the Minister today?"

Chuang Lian averted her eyes, her fan pausing in its slow rhythm, then starting up again, its measure suddenly erratic, as if indicative of some inner disturbance. It was an old game, and she enjoyed the pretense; yet there was no mistaking the way her pulse quickened when he looked at her like that. Such a predatory look it was. And his eyes, so blue they were. When he looked at her it was as if the sky itself gazed down at her through those eyes. She shivered. He was so different from her husband. So alive. So strong. Not the smallest sign of weakness in him.

She glanced up at him again. "Chuang Ming is at his office. Where else would he be at this hour?"

"I thought perhaps he would be here. If I were he . . ."

His eyes finished the sentence for him. She saw how he looked at her breasts, the pale flesh of her thighs showing between the folds of silk, and felt a tiny shiver down her spine. He wanted her. She knew that now. But it would not do to let him have her straightaway. The game must be played out—that was half its delight.

She eased up onto her elbows, putting her fan aside, then reached up to touch the single orchid in her hair. "Chuang Ming is a proper *Lao Kuan*, a Great Official. But in bed . . ." She laughed softly, and turned her eyes on him again. "Well, let us say he is *hsiao jen*, neh? A little man."

When he laughed he showed his teeth. Such strong, white, perfect teeth. But her eyes had been drawn lower than his face, wondering.

He came closer, then sat on the foot of the bed, his hand resting gently on her ankle. "And you are tired of little men?"

For a moment she stared at his hand where it rested against her flesh, transfixed by his touch; then she looked up at him again, her breath catching unexpectedly in her throat. This was not how she had planned it.

"I . . ." But his warm laughter, the small movements of his fingers against her foot, distracted her. After a moment she let herself laugh, then leaned forward, covering his hand with her own. So small and delicate it seemed against his, the dark olive of her flesh a stark contrast to his whiteness.

She laced her fingers among his and met his eyes. "I have a present for you."

"A present?"

"A first-meeting gift."

He laughed. "But we have met often, *Fu Jen* Chuang."

"Lian . . ." She said softly, hating the formality of his "Madam," even if his eyes revealed he was teasing her. "You must call me Lian here."

Unexpectedly he drew her closer, his right hand curled gently but firmly about her neck, then leaned forward, kissing her brow, her nose. "As you wish, my little lotus . . ."

Her eyes looked up at him, wide, for one brief moment afraid of him, of the power in him; then she looked away, laughing, covering her momentary slip, hoping he had not seen through, *into* her.

"Sweet Flute!" she called lightly, looking past him, then looking back at him, smiling again. "Bring the *ch'un tzu's* present!"

She placed her hand lightly against his chest, then stood up, moving past him but letting her hand brush against his hair, then rest upon his shoulder, maintaining the contact between them, feeling a tiny inner thrill when he placed his hand against the small of her back.

Sweet Flute was her *mui tsai*, a pretty young thing of fifteen her husband had bought Chuang Lian for her last birthday. She approached them now demurely, her head lowered, the gift held out before her.

She felt the young officer shift on the bed behind her, clearly interested in what she had bought him; then, dismissing the girl, she turned and faced him, kneeling to offer him the gift, her head bowed.

His smile revealed his pleasure at her subservient attitude. Then, with the smallest bow of his head, he began to unwrap the present. He let the bright red wrapping fall, then looked up at her. "What is it?"

"Well, it's not one of the Five Classics . . ."

She sat beside him on the bed and opened the first page, then looked up into his face, seeing at once how pleased he was.

"Gods . . ." he said quietly, then laughed. A soft, yet wicked laugh. "What *is* this?"

She leaned into him, kissing his neck softly, then whispered in his ear. "It's the *Chin P'ing Mei*, the Golden Lotus. I thought you might like it."

She saw how his finger traced the outlines of the ancient illustration, pausing where the two bodies met in that most intimate of embraces. Then he turned his head slowly and looked at her.

"And I brought you nothing . . ."

"No," she said, closing the book and drawing him down beside her, her gown falling open. "You're wrong, Hans Ebert. You brought me yourself."

━━━━━

THE EIGHTH BELL was sounding as they gathered in Nocenzi's office at the top of Bremen fortress. Besides Nocenzi, there were thirteen members of the General Staff, every man ranking captain or above. Ebert had been among the first to arrive, tipped off by his captain, Auden, that something was afoot.

Nocenzi was grim-faced. He convened the meeting and came swiftly to the point.

"*Ch'un tzu*, I have brought you here at short notice because this evening, at or around six, a number of senior Company Heads—twenty-six in all—were assassinated, for no apparent reason that we can yet make out."

There was a low murmur of surprise. Nocenzi nodded somberly, then continued.

"I've placed a strict media embargo on the news for forty-eight hours, to try to give us a little time, but we all know how impossible it is to check the passage of rumor, and the violent death of so many prominent and respected members of the trading community *will* be noticed. Moreover, coming so closely upon the attack on Helmstadt Armory, we are concerned that the news should not further destabilize an already potentially explosive situation. I don't have to tell you, therefore, how urgent it is that we discover both the reason for these murders and the identity of those who perpetrated them."

One of the men seated at the front of the room, nearest Nocenzi, raised his hand.

"Yes, Captain Scott?"

"Forgive me, sir, but how do we know these murders are connected?"

"We don't. In fact, one of the mysteries is that they're all so very different—their victims seemingly unconnected in any way whatsoever. But the very fact that twenty-six separate assassinations took place within the space of ten minutes on or around the hour points very clearly to a very tight orchestration of events, wouldn't you say?"

Another hand went up. Nocenzi turned, facing the questioner. "Yes, Major Hoffmann?"

"Could this be a Triad operation? There have been rumors for some time that some of the big bosses have been wanting to expand their operations into the higher levels."

"That's so. But no. At least, I don't think so. Immediate word has it that the big gang bosses are as surprised as we are by this. Two of the incidents involved small Triad-like gangs—splinter elements, possibly trying to make a name for themselves—but we've yet to discover whether they were working on their own or in the pay of others."

Ebert raised his hand, interested despite himself in this new development. He would much rather have still been between the legs of the Minister's wife, but if duty called, what was better than this?

"Yes, Major Ebert?"

"Is there any discernible pattern in these killings? I mean, were they all *Hung Mao*, for instance, or were the killings perhaps limited to a particular part of the City?"

Nocenzi smiled tightly. "That's the most disturbing thing about this affair. You see, the victims are mixed. Han and *Hung Mao*. Young and old. And the locations, as you see"—he indicated the map that had come up on the screen behind him—"are scattered almost randomly. It makes one think that the choice of victims may have been random. Designed, perhaps, to create the maximum impact on the Above. Simply to create an atmosphere of fear."

"*Ping Tiao*?" Ebert asked, expressing what they had all been thinking. Before the attack on Helmstadt it would have been unthinkable, a laughable conclusion, but now . . .

"No." Nocenzi's certainty surprised them all.

"At least, if it is *Ping Tiao*, they're slow at claiming it. And in all previous *Ping Tiao* attacks, they've always left their calling cards."

That was true. The *Ping Tiao* were fairly scrupulous about leaving their mark—the sign of the fish—on all their victims.

"There are a number of possibilities here," Nocenzi continued, "and I want to assign each of you to investigate some aspect of this matter. Is this Triad infiltration? Is it the beginning of some kind of violent trade war? Is it, in any respect, a continuation of Dispersionist activity? Is it pure terrorist activity? Or is it—however unlikely—pure coincidence?"

Captain Russ laughed, but Nocenzi shook his head. "No, it's not entirely impossible. Unlikely, yes, even improbable, but not impossible. A large number of the murders had possible motives. Gambling debts, company feuds, adultery. And however unlikely it seems, we've got to investigate the possibility."

Ebert raised his hand again. "Who'll be coordinating this, sir?"

"You want the job, Hans?"

There was a ripple of good-humored laughter, Ebert's own among it.

Nocenzi smiled. "Then it's yours."

Ebert bowed his head, pleased to be given the chance to take on something as big as this at last. "Thank you, sir."

Nocenzi was about to speak again when the doors at the far end of the room swung open and Marshal Tolonen strode into the room. As one, the officers stood and came to sharp attention, their heads bowed.

"*Ch'un tzu!*" Tolonen said, throwing his uniform cap down onto the desk and turning to face them, peeling off his gloves as he did so. "Please, be seated."

Nocenzi moved to one side as the Marshal stepped forward.

"I've just come from the T'ang. He has been apprised of the situation and has given orders that we are to make this matter our first priority over the coming days." He tapped his wrist, indicating the tiny screen set into his flesh. "I have been listening to your meeting and am pleased to see that you understand the seriousness of the situation. However, if we're to crack this one we've got to act quickly. That's why I've decided to overrule General Nocenzi and assign each of you two of the murdered victims."

Hoffmann raised his hand. "Why the change, sir?"

"Because if there's any pattern behind things, it ought to be discernible by looking at the facts of two very different murders. And with thirteen of you looking at the matter, we ought to come up with *something* pretty quickly, don't you think?"

Hoffmann bowed his head.

"Good. And Hans . . . I appreciate your keenness. It's no less than I'd expect from you. But I'm afraid I'll have to tie your hands somewhat on this one. That's not to say you won't be coordinator, but I want you to work closely with me on this. The T'ang wants answers and I've promised him that he'll have them before the week's out. So don't let me down."

Ebert met the Marshal's eyes and bowed his head, accepting the old man's decision, but inside he was deeply disappointed. So he was to be tied to the old man's apron strings yet again! He took a deep breath, calming himself, then smiled, remembering suddenly how Chuang Lian had taken his penis between her tiny delicate toes and caressed it, as if she were holding it in her hands. Such a neat little trick. And then there was her *mui tsai*—what was her name?—Sweet Flute. Ah yes, how he'd like to play that one!

He raised his eyes and looked across at Tolonen as General Nocenzi began to allocate the case files. Yes, well, maybe the Marshal would be in command nominally, but that was not to say he would be running things. Russ, Scott, Fest, Auden— these were *his* men. He had only to say to them . . .

The thought made him smile. And Tolonen, glancing across at him at that moment, saw his smile and returned it strongly.

◆◆◆◆

IT WAS WELL after ten when Chen arrived back at the apartment. Wang Ti and the children were in bed, asleep. He looked in on them, smiling broadly as he saw how all four of them were crowded into the same bed, the two-year-old, Ch'iang Hsin, cuddled against Wang Ti's chest, her hair covering her plump little face, the two boys to her right, young Wu pressed close against his older brother's back.

He stood there a moment, moved, as he always was, by the sight of them; then he went back through to the kitchen and made himself a small *chung* of *ch'a*.

It had been a long day, but there was still much to do before he could rest. He carried the porcelain *chung* through to the living room and put it down on the table, then moved the lamp close, adjusting its glow so that it illuminated only a tight circle about the steaming bowl. He looked about him a moment, frowning, then went across to the shelves, searching until he found the old lacquered box he kept his brushes and ink block in.

He put the box down beside the *chung*, then went out into the hall and retrieved the files from the narrow table by the door, beneath his tunic. He paused, then went back and hung his tunic on the peg, smiling, knowing Wang Ti would only scold him in the morning if he forgot.

Switching off the main light, he went back to the table and pulled up a chair. Setting the files down to his right, he sat back a moment, yawning, stretching his arms out to the sides, feeling weary. He gave a soft laugh, then leaned forward again, reaching for the *chung*. Lifting the lid, he took a long sip of the hot *ch'a*.

"Hmm . . . that's good," he said quietly, nodding to himself. It was one of Karr's. A gift he had brought with him last time he had come to dinner. *Well, my friend*, he thought; *now I've a gift for you.*

He reached across and drew the box closer, unfastening the two tiny catches, flipping the lid back.

"Damn it . . ." he said, starting to get up, realizing he had forgotten water to mix the ink. Instead, he reached for the *chung* again and dipped his finger; using the hot *ch'a* as a substitute. He had heard that the great poet Li Po had used wine to mix his ink, so why not *ch'a*? Particularly one as fine as this.

He smiled, then wiping his finger on his sleeve, reached across and drew the first of the files closer.

Today he had called in all the favors owed him; had pestered friend and acquaintance alike until he'd got what he wanted. And here they were. Personnel files. Income statements. Training records. Complete files on each of the five men who had died at Helmstadt. The so-called *Ping Tiao* he had checked up on. Their files and two others.

He had gone down to Central Records, the nerve-center of Security Personnel at Bremen. There, in Personnel Queries, he had called upon an old friend, Wolfgang Lautner. Lautner, one of the four senior officers in charge of the department, was an old friend. They had been in officer training together and had been promoted to captain within a month of each other. Several times in the past Chen had helped Lautner out, mainly in the matter of gambling debts.

Lautner had been only too happy to help Chen, giving him full access to whatever files he wanted, even to several that were, strictly speaking, off limits. All had gone smoothly until Chen, checking up on a personnel number that had appeared on several of the files, came up against a computer block.

He could see it even now, the words pulsing red against the black of the screen. INFORMATION DENIED. LEVEL-A CODE REQUIRED.

Not knowing what else to do, he had taken his query direct to Lautner, had sat there beside him in his office as he keyed in the Level-A code. He remembered how Lautner had looked at him, smiling, his eyebrows raised inquisitively, before he had turned to face the screen.

"Shit . . ." Lautner had jerked forward, clearing the screen; then he had turned abruptly, looking at Chen angrily, his whole manner changed completely. "What in fuck's name are you doing, Kao Chen?"

"I didn't know—" Chen had begun, as surprised as his friend by the face that had come up on the screen; but Lautner had cut him off sharply.

"Didn't know? You expect me to believe that? Kuan Yin, preserve us! He's the last bastard I want to find out I've been tapping into his file. He'd have our balls!"

Chen swallowed, remembering. Yes, he could still feel Ebert's spittle on his cheek, burning there like a badge of shame. And there, suddenly, he was, a face on a screen, a personnel coding on the files of three dead ex-Security men. It was too much of a coincidence.

Chen drew the *chung* closer, comforted by its warmth against his hands. He could still recall what Ebert had said to him, that time they had raided the Overseer's House, the time young Pavel had died; could remember vividly how Ebert had stood there, looking to the west where Lodz Garrison was burning in the darkness, and said how much he admired DeVore.

Yes, it all made sense now. But the knowledge had cost him Lautner's friendship.

He lifted the lid from the *chung* and drank deeply, as if to wash away the bitter taste that had risen to his mouth.

If he was right, then Ebert was DeVore's inside man. It would certainly explain how the *Ping Tiao* had got into Helmstadt Armory and stripped it of a billion *yuans'* worth of equipment. But he had to prove that, and prove it conclusively. As yet, it was mere coincidence.

He began, working through the files again, checking the details exhaustively, page by page, looking for something—anything—that might point him in the right direction.

He had almost finished when he heard a movement on the far side of the room. He looked up and saw young Wu in the darkness of the doorway. Smiling, he got up and went across, picking up the five-year-old and hugging him to his chest.

"Can't you sleep, Kao Wu?"

Wu snuggled into his father's shoulder. "I want a drink," he said sleepily, his eyes already closed.

"Come . . . I'll make you one."

He carried him into the kitchen, dimming the light. Then, one-handed, he took a mug from the rack and squeezed a bulb of juice into it.

"Here . . ." he said, holding it to the child's lips.

Wu took two sips, then snuggled down again. In a moment he was asleep again, his breathing regular, relaxed.

Chen set the mug down, smiling. The warm weight of his son against his shoulder was a pleasant, deeply reassuring sensation. He went back out, into the hallway, and looked across to where he had been working. The files lay at the edge of the circle of light, facedown beside the empty *chung*.

It was no good; he would have to go back. He had hoped to avoid it, but it was the only way. He would have to risk making direct inquiries on Ebert's file.

He looked down, beginning to understand the danger he was in. And not just himself. If Ebert *were* DeVore's man, then none of them was safe. Not here, nor anywhere. Not if Ebert discovered what he was doing. And yet, what choice was there? To do nothing? To forget his humiliation and his silent vow of vengeance? No. Even so, it made him heavy of heart to think, even for a moment, of losing all of this. He shivered, holding Kao Wu closer, his hand gently stroking the sleeping boy's neck.

And what if Lautner had taken steps to cover himself? What if he had already gone to Ebert?

No. Knowing Lautner, he would do nothing. And he would assume that Chen would do nothing, too. Would gamble on him not taking any further risks.

Achh, thought Chen bitterly; *you really didn't know me, did you?*

He took Wu to his bed and tucked him in, then went through to the other bedroom. Wang Ti was awake, looking back at him, Ch'iang Hsin's tiny figure cuddled in against her side.

"It's late, Chen," she said softly. "You should get some sleep."

He smiled at her and nodded. "I should, but there's something I have to do."

"At this hour?"

Again he nodded. "Trust me. I'll be all right."

Something about the way he said it made her get up onto one elbow. "What is it, Chen? What are you up to?"

He hesitated, then shook his head. "It's nothing. Really, Wang Ti. Now go to sleep. I'll be back before morning."

She narrowed her eyes, then, yawning, settled down again. "All right, my husband. But take care, neh?"

He smiled, watching her a moment longer, filled with the warmth of his love for her, then turned away, suddenly determined.

It was time to make connections. To find out whether Ebert really was in DeVore's pay.

━━━━━

OUTSIDE IT WAS DARK, the evening chill, but in the stables at Tongjiang it was warm in the glow of the lanterns. The scents of hay and animal sweat were strong in the long high-ceilinged barn, the soft snorting of the animals in their stalls the only sound to disturb the evening's silence. Li Yuan stood in the end stall, feeding the Arab from his hand.

"Excellency . . ."

Li Yuan turned, smiling, at ease here with his beloved horses. "Ah . . . Master Nan. How did it go? Are my girls well?"

Nan Ho had pulled a cloak about his shoulders before venturing outdoors. Even so, he was hunched into himself, shivering from the cold.

"They are well, my Lord. I have arranged everything as you requested."

Li Yuan studied him a moment, conscious of the hesitation. "Good." He looked back at the horse, smiling, reaching up to smooth its broad black face, his fingers combing the fine dark hair. "It would be best, perhaps, if we kept this discreet, Master Nan. I would not like the Lady Fei to be troubled. You understand?"

He looked back at Nan Ho. "Perhaps when she's out riding, neh?"

"Of course, my Lord."

"And Nan Ho . . ."

"Yes, my Lord?"

"I know what you think. You find me unfeeling in this matter. Unnatural, even. But it isn't so. I love Fei Yen. You understand that?" Li Yuan bent and took another handful of barley from the sack beside him, then offered it to the Arab, who nibbled contentedly at it. "And if that's unnatural, then this too is unnatural . . ."

He looked down at his hand, the horse's muzzle pressed close to his palm, warm and moist, then laughed. "You know, my father has always argued that good horsemanship is like good government. And good government like a good marriage. What do you think, Nan Ho?"

Master Nan laughed. "What would I know of that, my Lord? I am but a tiny part of the great harness of state. A mere stirrup."

"So much?" Li Yuan wiped his hand on his trouser leg, then laughed heartily. "No, I jest with you, Master Nan. You are a whole saddle in yourself. And do not forget I said it." He grew quieter. "I am not ungrateful. Never think that, Master Nan. The day will come . . ."

Nan Ho bowed low. "My Lord . . ."

When Nan Ho had gone, Li Yuan went outside, into the chill evening air, and stood there, staring up into the blackness overhead. The moon was low and bright and cold. A pale crescent, like an eyelid on the darkness.

And then?

The two words came to him, strong and clear, like two flares in the darkness. Nonsense words. And yet, somehow, significant. But what did they mean? Unaccountably, he found himself filled with sudden doubts. He thought of what he had said to Nan Ho of horsemanship and wondered if it were really so. Could one master one's emotions as one controlled a horse? Was it that easy? He loved Fei Yen—he was certain of it—but he also loved Pearl Heart and her sister, Sweet Rose. Could he simply shut out what he felt for them as if it had never been?

And then?

He walked to the bridge and stood there, holding the rail tightly, suddenly, absurdly obsessed with the words that had come unbidden to him. *And then? And then?*

He shivered. *And then what?* He gritted his teeth against the pain he suddenly felt. "No!" he said sharply, his breath pluming out from him. No. He would not succumb. He would ride out the pain he felt. Would deny that part of him. For Fei Yen. Because he loved her. Because . . .

The moon was an eyelid on the darkness. And if he closed his eyes he could see it, dark against the brightness inside his head.

But the pain remained. And then he knew. He missed them. Missed them terribly. He had never admitted it before, but now he knew. It was as if he had killed part of himself to have Fei Yen.

He shuddered, then pushed back, away from the rail, angry with himself.

"You are a prince. A *prince!*"

But it made no difference. The pain remained. Sharp, bitter, like the image of the moon against his inner lid, dark against the brightness there.

CHEN SAT THERE, hunched over the screen, his pulse racing as he waited to see whether the access code would take.

So far it had been easy. He had simply logged that he was investigating illicit Triad connections. A junior officer had shown him to the screen then left him there, unsupervised. After all, it was late, and hardly anyone used the facilities of Personnel Inquiries at that hour. Chen was almost the only figure in the great wheel of desks that stretched out from the central podium.

The screen filled. Ebert's face stared out at him a moment, life-size, then shrank to a quarter-size, relocating at the top right of the screen. Chen gave a small sigh of relief. It worked!

The file began, page after page of detailed service records.

Chen scrolled through, surprised to find how highly Ebert was rated by his superiors. Did he know what they thought of him? Had he had access to this file? Knowing Ebert, it was likely. Even so, there was nothing sinister here. Nothing to link him to DeVore. No; if anything, it was exemplary. Maybe it was simple coincidence, then, that Ebert had served with three of the dead men. But Chen's instinct ruled that out. He scrolled to the end of the file, then keyed for access to Ebert's accounts.

A few minutes later he sat back, shaking his head. Nothing. Sighing, he keyed to look at the last of the subfiles—Ebert's expenses. He flicked through quickly, noting nothing unusual, then stopped.

Of course! It was an *expenses* account. Which meant that all the payments on it ought to be irregular. So what was this monthly payment doing on it? The amount differed, but the date was the same each month. The fifteenth. It wasn't a bar invoice, for those were met from Ebert's other account. And there was a number noted against each payment. A Security Forces service number, unless he was mistaken.

Chen scrolled back, checking he'd not been mistaken, then jotted the number down. Yes, here it was, the link. He closed the file and sat back, looking across at the central desk. It was quiet over there. Good. Then he would make this one last query.

He keyed the service number, then tapped in the access code. For a moment the screen was blank and Chen wondered if it would come up as before—INFORMATION DENIED. LEVEL-A CODE REQUIRED. But then a face appeared.

Chen stared at it a moment, then frowned. For some reason he had expected to recognize it, but it was just a face like any other young officer's face, smooth-shaven and handsome in its strange *Hung Mao* fashion.

For a time he looked through the file, but there was nothing there. Only that Ebert had worked with the man some years before, in Tolonen's office, when they were both cadets. Then why the payments? Again he almost missed it, was slow to recognize what was staring him in the face, there on the very first page of the file. It was a number. The reference coding of the senior officer the young cadet had reported to while he had been stationed in Bremen ten years earlier. Chen drew in his breath sharply.

DeVore!

He shut the screen down and stood, feeling almost light-headed now that he had made the connection. I've got you now, Hans Ebert, he thought. Yes, and I'll make you pay for your insult.

Chen picked up his papers and returned them to his pocket, then looked across at the central desk again, remembering how his friend Lautner had reacted, the sourness of that moment tainting his triumph momentarily. Then, swallowing his bitterness, he shook his head. So it was in this world. It was no use expecting otherwise.

He smiled grimly, unconsciously wiping at his cheek, then turned and began to make his way back through the web of gangways to the exit.

Yes, he thought. I've got you now, you bastard. I'll pin your balls to the fucking floor for what you've done. But first you, Axel Haavikko. First you.

CHAPTER FOUR

Thick Face, Black Heart

D E V O R E   S T O O D there on the mountainside, the lifeless bodies of the two alpine foxes dangling from leather thongs at his back, their fur smeared with blood. In his left hand he held the crossbow he had killed them with, in his right the two blood-caked bolts he had pulled from their flesh.

It was an hour after dawn and the mountains below him were wreathed in mist. He was high up where he stood, well above the snow line. To his left, below him, the mountainside was densely wooded, the tall pines covering most of the lower slopes, stretching down into the mist. He laughed, enjoying the freshness of the morning, his breath pluming away from him. Surely there was no better sight in the world than the Alps in high summer? He looked about him; then, slipping the bolts into the deep pocket of his furs, he began to make his way down, heading for the ruins of the castle.

He was halfway down when he stopped, suddenly alert. There had been movement down below, among the ruins. He moved quickly to his right, his hand reaching for one of the bolts, hurriedly placing it into the stock and winding the handle.

He scrambled behind some low rocks and knelt, the crossbow aimed at the slopes below. His heart was beating fast. No one was supposed to be out here at this hour . . . not even his own patrols.

He tensed. A figure had come out and now stood there, one hand up to its eyes, searching the mountainside. A tall, thin figure, its angular frame strangely familiar. Then it turned, looking up the slope, its predatory gaze coming to rest on the rocks behind which DeVore was crouching.

Lehmann . . . DeVore lowered the crossbow and stood, then went down the slope, stopping some ten or fifteen *ch'i* from the albino, the crossbow held loosely in his left hand.

"Stefan! What in the gods' names are you doing here?"

Lehmann looked past him a moment, then looked back, meeting his eyes. "Our friends are getting restless. They wondered where you were."

DeVore laughed. "They're up already, eh?" He moved closer, handing the foxes over to the albino. "Here . . . hold these for me."

Lehmann took them, barely glancing at the dead animals. "I wondered where you went to in the mornings. It's beautiful, neh?"

DeVore turned, surprised, but if he hoped to find some expression of wonder in the albino's face, he was disappointed. Those pale pink eyes stared out coldly at the slopes, the distant peaks, as if beauty were merely a form of words, as meaningless as the rest.

"Yes," he answered. "It is. And never more so than at this hour. Sometimes it makes me feel like I'm the last man. The very last. It's a good feeling, that. A pure, clean feeling."

Lehmann nodded. "We'd best get back."

DeVore laughed coldly. "Let them wait a little longer. It'll do that bastard Gesell good."

Lehmann was silent a moment, his cold eyes watching the slow, sweeping movements of a circling eagle, high up above one of the nearer peaks. For a while he seemed lost in the sight, then he turned his head and stared at DeVore penetratingly. "I thought he was going to kill you over that Shen Lu Chua business."

DeVore looked back at him, surprised. "Did you?" He seemed to consider it a moment, then shook his head. "No. Gesell's far too cautious. You know the Han saying *p'eng che luan tzu kuo ch'iao?*"

Lehmann shook his head.

DeVore laughed. "Well, let's just say he's the kind of man who holds on to his testicles when crossing a bridge."

"Ah . . ."

DeVore studied the albino a moment, wondering what it would take to penetrate that cold exterior and force a smile, a grimace of anger, a tear. He looked down. Perhaps nothing. Perhaps he *was* as empty of emotions as he seemed. But that could not be. He was human, after all. There had to be something he wanted. Something that kept him from simply throwing himself from the cliff onto the rocks below.

But what?

DeVore smiled faintly, detaching himself from the problem, and looked up to find Lehmann still staring at him. He let his smile broaden as if to make connection with something behind—far back from—the unsmiling surface of that unnaturally pallid face.

Then, shaking his head, he turned, making his way across to the tower and the tunnels beneath.

━━━━━

THE PING TIAO LEADERS were waiting in the conference room, the great window wall giving a clear view of the slopes. Outside the light was crisp and clear, but a layer of mist covered the upper slopes. Even so, the view was impressive. One had a sense of great walls of rock climbing the sky.

DeVore stood in the doorway a moment, looking in. Six of them were gathered in the far left corner of the room, seated about the end of the great table, as far from the window as they could get. He smiled, then turned, looking across. Only one of them was standing by the window, looking out. It was the woman—Gesell's lover—Emily Ascher.

He went in.

Noticing him, two of the men made to stand up, but Gesell reached out to either side, touching their arms. They sat back, looking warily between Gesell and DeVore.

"Turner . . ." Gesell greeted DeVore bluntly, his whole manner suddenly alert, businesslike.

"Gesell . . ." He gave the slightest nod of acknowledgment, then went to the window, staring outward, as if unconscious of the woman standing at his side. Then he turned back, smiling. "So?"

While he'd been gone, his lieutenant, Wiegand, had shown them around the base, letting them see the mask—the surface installation—while giving no hint of the labyrinth of tunnels that lay beneath.

Gesell glanced at Mach, then looked back, a faint sneer on his lips.

"You want me to say I'm impressed—is that it, *Shih* Turner?"

"Did I say that?"

Gesell leaned forward, lacing his fingers together. "No. But you're very much a product of your level. And your level likes to impress all those beneath it with the grandeur of their works."

"That's true enough. And are you impressed? Are my works grand enough for you?"   .

DeVore kept his words light yet challenging, concealing his distaste for the man. Arrogant little bastard. He thought he knew everything. He was useful just now, admittedly—a key to things. But once he'd unlocked a few doors he could be discarded.

He waited for Gesell to respond, but it was Mach who answered him.

"It's very pretty, *Shih* Turner, but what's it all for? The enemy is in there, in the City, not out here in the Wilds. I don't see the point of building something like this."

DeVore stared back at Mach, then nodded. How astute of you, he thought. How clever to penetrate so far with just one look. But you haven't seen it all. You haven't seen the great hangars, the missile silos, the training halls. And because you haven't, you've no idea what this really is. To you this seems a mere shadow of Bremen, a great fortress designed with only one thought in mind: to protect itself against attack. But this is different. My aim is not to defend my position here but to attack my opponents. To cut their lines and penetrate their territory.

"So you think all this a waste of time?"

He saw how Mach looked to Gesell, then lowered his head slightly, letting Gesell take charge again. That concession was further confirmation of what he already suspected. The ideas, the very words the *Ping Tiao* used—these belonged to Mach. But it was Gesell who held the power. Gesell to whom Mach demurred when his words had to be turned into actions.

Gesell leaned forward. "Wasteful, yes. But not a total waste. You seem beyond the reach of the Seven here, and that's good. And I've seen how your men fight. They're well-trained, well-disciplined. In that respect we could learn from you."

DeVore hid his surprise at Gesell's candidness. "But?"

Gesell laughed and looked about him. "Well, look at this place! It's so cut off from the realities of what's going on. So *isolated*. I mean, how can you know what's happening—what's *really* happening in the levels—when you're so far from it all."

DeVore was smiling. "Is that what you think?"

He clicked his fingers. At once a panel slid back overhead and a bank of screens lowered itself into the room: screens that showed scenes from a dozen different levels of the City. Turning back, DeVore saw how impressed they were despite themselves.

"What do you want to see?" he asked. "Where would you like to go in the City? My cameras are everywhere. My eyes and ears. Watching and listening and reporting back. Taking the pulse of things."

As he spoke the images changed, moving from location to location, until, when he clicked his fingers a second time, they froze, all twelve screens showing the same image.

"But that's Shen Lu Chua's man, Yun Ch'o . . ." Gesell began, recognizing the figure below the camera.

"It's Ottersleben," said Mach quietly. "Level 34. He must have taken this earlier."

DeVore studied them, saw how Mach looked down, as if considering what this meant, then looked back up again, watching as a dozen images of himself led a dozen *Ping Tiao* assault squads in the raid on their comrade Yun Ch'o's apartment. Beside him, Gesell was leaning forward, fascinated by the unfolding action. He saw the brief fight, saw Yun Ch'o fall, mortally wounded; then watched as the eight hostages—the eight Security officers Turner had told them would be there—were led out into the corridor. When it was over Gesell looked back at Turner, smiling tightly.

"That was clever of you, Turner. A nice trick. But it doesn't mean much *really*, does it?"

"Like the T'ang's ear, you mean, or the map of Helmstadt?" DeVore laughed, then moved closer. "You're a hard man to convince, *Shih* Gesell. What must I do to satisfy you?"

Gesell's features hardened. "Show me the other maps. The maps of Bremen."

"And in return?"

But before Gesell could answer, the woman, Ascher, interrupted him.

"You're talking deals here, but it's still a mystery to me, *Shih* Turner. If you're so powerful, if you can do so much, then why do you need us? This base you've had built, the raid on Helmstadt, the killing of Wang Hsien—any one of these things is far beyond anything we could do. So why us?"

Gesell was glaring at her angrily. DeVore studied the *Ping Tiao* leader a moment, then half turned, looking back at the woman.

"Because what I can do is limited."

She laughed coldly, staring back at him, her dislike unconcealed. "Limited by what?"

"By funding. By opportunity."

"And we have those?"

"No. But you have something much more valuable. Your organization has potential. Vast potential. All this—everything I've patiently built over the last eight years—is, as *Shih* Mach so rightly described it, inflexible. Your organization is different. It's a kind of organism, capable of vast growth. But to achieve that you need to create the best climate for that growth. What we did yesterday was a beginning. It raised your public profile while giving you considerable firepower. Both things strengthened you considerably. Without me, however, you would have had neither."

Gesell interrupted. "You're wrong. You needed us."

DeVore turned back. "Not at all. I could have taken Helmstadt on my own. You've seen my men, *Shih* Gesell. You've even remarked on how good their training and discipline is. Well, I've a thousand more where they came from. And a thousand beyond them. No, I asked you to join me yesterday because such a relationship as we must forge has to be reciprocal. There has to be give and take. I gave you Helmstadt. As, in time, I'll give you Bremen. But you must give me something back. Not a great thing. I'd not ask that of you yet. But some small thing to cement our partnership. Some favor I might find it difficult to undertake myself."

"A small thing?" Gesell was staring at him suspiciously.

"Yes. I want you to kill someone for me. A child."

"A child?"

DeVore clicked his fingers. The images on the screens changed; showed a dozen separate portraits of an adolescent girl, her ash-blond shoulder-length hair loose in some shots, tied in plaits in others. Her straight-boned slender figure was caught in a dozen different poses, dressed casually as if at home, or elegantly in the latest First Level fashions.

"But that's . . ."

"Yes," DeVore said, looking up at the screens. "It's Jelka Tolonen. Marshal Tolonen's daughter."

━━━━━

JELKA HAD JUST FINISHED her exercises when her father entered the exercise hall. Her instructor, Siang Che, seeing him, bowed then backed away, busying himself at the far end of the gym.

She turned, hearing a different tread, then laughed, her young face breaking into a great beam of a smile. "Daddy! You're back early!" She ran across, reaching up to hug him to her. "What's up? I didn't expect you until the weekend."

"No," he said, smiling down at her, lowering his head to kiss her brow. "I'd almost forgotten . . ."

"Forgotten what?"

Tolonen put one hand on her shoulder. "Not here. Let's go through to your rooms. I'll talk to you once you've changed, neh?"

He stood there, looking about her room while she showered. It was not a typical young girl's room. Not by any means. In a box in one corner were flails and batons, practice swords, chucks and staffs, while high up on the wall was a brightly colored painting of Mu-Lan, the famous warrior heroine, dressed in full military armor, her expression fierce as she took up a defensive pose. Old maps and charts covered the front of the built-in wardrobes to the left, while to the right most of the wall space was filled with Jelka's own hand-drawn designs—machines and weaponry, their ugly purpose disguised somehow by the sleek elegance of her pen.

An old armchair to one side displayed a touch of luxury, heaped as it was with colorful silk cushions, but her bed was spartan, a simple dark-blue sheet covering it. Beside it, beneath a half-length mirror, was her study desk, a *wei chi* board set up to the right, books and papers stacked neatly on the left at the back. He went across and looked, interested to see what she was reading.

At the very front of the table, facedown beside her comset, was a copy of Sun Tzu's *The Art of War*, the *Ping Fa*. He picked it up and read the passage she had underlined:

> If not in the interests of the state, do not act. If you cannot succeed, do not use troops. If you are not in danger, do not fight.

He smiled. Ten thousand books had been written on the subject since Sun Tzu first wrote his treatise twenty-five hundred years before and not one had come as close to capturing the essence of armed struggle as the *Ping Fa*. He set the book down again, then studied the *wei chi* board a moment, noting how a great spur of black stones cut between two areas of white territory, separating them. There were other books piled up on the desk—the *San Kuo Yan Yi*, the *Romance of the Three Kingdoms*, Tseng Kung-liang's *Wu Ching Tsung Yao*, his *Essentials of the Martial Classics*, and the *Meng Ke* among them—but what took the Marshal's interest was a small floppy, orange-covered volume tucked away at the back of the desk. He reached across and pulled it from the pile.

It was an ancient thing, the cover curling at the edges, the paper within yellowed badly. But that was not what had caught his eye. It was the words on the cover. Or, rather, one word in particular. *China.*

He stared at the cover for a time, frowning. He had not heard that term—not seen it in print—in more than forty years. China. The name that Chung Kuo, the Middle Kingdom, had had before Tsao Ch'un. Or at least, the name it had been called in the West. He leafed through the book, reading at random, then closed it, his pulse racing. Islam and Communism. America and Russia. Soviets and Imperialists. These were lost terms. Terms from another age. A forgotten, forbidden age. He stared at the cover a moment longer, then nodded to himself, knowing what he must do.

He turned, hearing her in the next room, singing softly to herself as she dressed, then forced himself to relax, letting the anger, the tension drain from him. It was a mistake, almost certainly. Even so, he would find out who had given this to her and make them pay.

"Well?" she asked, standing in the doorway, smiling across at him. "Tell me, then. What is it?"

She saw how he looked down at the book in his hands.

"In a moment. First, where did you get this?"

"That? It was on your shelves. Why, shouldn't I have borrowed it?"

"My shelves?"

"Yes. It was in that box of things you had delivered here three weeks ago. My *amah*, Lu Cao, unpacked it and put it all away. Didn't you notice?"

"She shouldn't have," he began irritably. "They were things General Nocenzi had sent on to me. Things we'd unearthed during the Confiscations. Special things . . ."

"I'm sorry, Father. I'll tell her. But she wasn't to know."

"No . . ." He softened, then laughed, relieved that it was only that. "Did you read any of it?"

"Some." She smiled, looking inside herself a moment. "But it was odd. It presented itself as a factual account, but it read more like fiction. The facts were all wrong. Almost all of it. And that map at the front . . ."

"Yes . . ." He weighed the book in his hand a moment, then looked up at her again. "Well, I guess no harm's done. But listen. This is a forbidden book. If anyone were to find you had read even the smallest part of it . . ." He shook his head. "Well, you understand?"

She bowed her head. "As you wish, Father."

"Good. Then this other matter . . ." He hesitated, then gave a short laugh. "Well, you know how long Klaus Ebert and I have been friends. How close our families have always been."

She laughed. "*Shih* Ebert has been like an uncle to me."

Her father's smile broadened momentarily. "Yes. But I've long wished for something more than that. Some stronger, more intimate bond between our families."

"More intimate . . ." She stared at him, not understanding.

"Yes," he said, looking back at her fondly. "It has long been my dream that you would one day wed my old friend's son."

"Hans? Hans Ebert?" Her eyes were narrowed now, watching him.

"Yes." He looked away, smiling. "But it's more than a dream. You see, Klaus Ebert and I came to an arrangement."

She felt herself go cold. "An arrangement?"

"Yes. Klaus was very generous. Your dowry is considerable."

She laughed nervously. "I don't understand. Dowry? What dowry?"

He smiled. "I'm sorry. I should have spoken to you about all this before, but I've not had time. Things were so busy, and then, suddenly, the day was upon me."

The coldness melted away as a wave of anger washed over her. She shook her head defiantly. "But you can't . . ."

"I can," he said. "In fact, there's no question about it, Jelka. It was all arranged, ten years ago."

"Ten years?" She shook her head, astonished. "But I was four . . ."

"I know. But these things must be done. It is our way. And they must be done early. Hans is heir to a vast financial empire, after all. It would not do to have uncertainty over such matters. The markets . . ."

She looked down, his words washing over her unheard, her breath catching in her throat. Her father had sold her—sold her to his best friend's son. Oh, she'd heard of it. Indeed, several of her school friends had been engaged in this manner. But this was herself.

She looked up at him again, searching his eyes for some sign that he understood how she felt; but there was nothing, only his determination to fulfill his dream of linking the two families.

Her voice was soft, reproachful. "Daddy . . . how could you?"

He laughed, but his laughter now was hard, and his words, when they came, held a slight trace of annoyance.

"How could I what?"

Sell me, she thought, but could not bring herself to say the words. She swallowed and bowed her head. "You should have told me."

"I know. But I thought . . . well, I thought you would be pleased. After all, Hans is a handsome young man. More than half the girls in the Above are in love with him. And you . . . well, you alone will be his wife. The wife of a General. The wife of a Company Head. And not just any company, but GenSyn."

It was true. She ought to be pleased. Her friends at school would be jealous of her. Green with envy. But somehow the thought of that palled in comparison with the enormity of what her father had done. He had not asked her. In this, the most important thing she would ever do, he had not taken her feelings into consideration. Would he have done that if her mother had been alive?

She shivered, then looked up at him again.

"So I *must* marry him?"

He nodded tersely, his face stern. "It is arranged."

She stared back at him a moment, surprised by the hard edge to his voice, then bowed her head. "Very well. Then I shall do as you ask."

"Good." He smiled tightly, then glanced down at the timer at his wrist. "You'd best call your *amah,* then, and have her dress you. It's after eleven now and I said we'd be there by one."

She stared at him, astonished. "This afternoon?"

He looked back at her, frowning, as if surprised by her question. "Of course. Now hurry, my love. Hurry, or we'll be late."

Jelka hesitated, watching him a moment longer, seeing how he looked down at the book in his hand as if it were a mystery he needed to resolve; then she turned and went through into the other room, looking for Lu Cao.

"Well, what is it?"

Auden took Ebert to one side, out of earshot of the two guards. "I think we may have stumbled onto something."

Ebert smiled. "What kind of thing?"

"A link. A possible explanation for what happened the other night."

Ebert's smile broadened. "How good a link? Good enough to make me late for an appointment with the Minister's wife?"

Auden returned the smile. "I think so."

They went inside. The prisoner was a Han. A young man in his late twenties. He was well-dressed and neatly groomed but sweating profusely.

"Who is this?" Ebert asked, as if the man had no existence, no identity other than that which he or Auden gave him.

"He's a close relative of one of the murdered men. The victim was a merchant, Lu Tung. This is his third cousin, Lu Wang-pei. It seems he depended on Lu Tung for funds. To repay gambling debts and the like."

Lu Wang-pei had bowed his head at the mention of his name, but neither of the officers paid him the slightest attention. His eyes followed them as they moved about the room, but otherwise he was perfectly still. In this he had no choice for he was bound tightly to the chair.

Ebert looked about him at the sparsely furnished room. "So what have you found?"

"Forensic evidence shows that the bomb was hidden inside a package—a present delivered to Lu Tung's apartments only minutes before the explosion. It seems that our man here delivered that package."

"I see. So in this case we have our murderer?"

"Yes and no. Wang-pei had no idea what he was delivering. That's not to say he wasn't culpable in some small degree, because he did agree to deliver it."

"For someone else?"

Auden smiled. "That's right. For three men. Business rivals of Lu Tung's, so they claimed. It seems they bought up our friend's gambling debts, then offered to wipe the slate clean if he'd do a little favor for them."

"The package."

"Exactly. They told him they wanted to frighten his uncle. To shake him up a little."

Ebert laughed. "Well . . . And so they did!"

"Yes," Auden looked down momentarily. "And there it would end, were it not for the fact that Wang-pei here didn't trust his new friends. He secreted a camera on himself when he went to make his collection. Here."

He handed the flat 3-D image to Ebert, then watched as his initial puzzlement changed into a smile of enlightenment. "De-Vore . . ."

Auden nodded. "Yes. But it was the two at the front Wang-Pei dealt with. They did all the talking."

"And who are they?"

"One's an ex-Security man. Max Wiegand. A good man, it seems. He had an excellent service record."

"And the other?"

"We couldn't get a trace on him. But look at the pallor of his skin. He looks albinic. If so he might be wearing contact lenses to disguise the color of his eyes."

"Hmmm . . ." Ebert handed back the flat. "And what does our man here know?"

"Nothing much. I think he's telling the truth. I've checked on the gambling debts. I'd guess it happened exactly as he told us."

Ebert nodded, then turned, looking directly at the Han for the first time since he'd entered the room. "All right. Leave him with me a moment. I'll see whether we can find out anything more."

When Auden had gone, Ebert walked over and stood directly in front of the Han, looking down at him contemptuously.

"As far as I'm concerned, *Shih* Lu, I couldn't care a shit if you Han butchered one another until the corridors ran red. If that was all that was at stake here I'd let you go. But it's not. You made a mistake. A fortunate mistake for me. But for you . . ."

He lashed out viciously, catching the Han across the nose. Wang-pei drew his head back, groaning, his eyes wide with shock. Blood ran freely from his nose.

"Tell me the truth. What's your connection to these men? When did you first start working for them?"

Wang-pei began to shake his head, but Ebert hit him again; a stinging blow across the ear that made him cry out, his face distorted with pain.

"I never saw them before . . ." he began. "It's as I said—"

The third blow knocked him backward, the chair tilting out from under him. Ebert followed through at once, kicking him once, twice, in the stomach. Hard, vicious kicks that made the Han double up, gasping.

"You know nothing, eh? Nothing! You fuck-head! You pissing fuck-head chink! Of course you know nothing!"

He kicked again, lower this time. The Han began to vomit. Ebert turned away, disgusted. Of course he knew nothing. De-Vore was not that stupid. But he *had* slipped up this time. He should have kept out of it. Should have let his two henchmen do all the front work.

The door beside him opened.

"Are you all right . . . ?"

He looked across at Auden, smiling. "I'm fine. But this one's dead."

Auden stared back at him a moment, then nodded. "And the guards?"

Ebert looked back at the Han, his smile broadening. "They saw nothing. Okay? You deal with them, Will. I'll recompense you."

The Han lay there, wheezing for breath, his frightened eyes staring up at them imploringly.

Auden nodded. "All right. But why? After all, we have the link."

"Yes. And we're going to keep it, understand me? I *want* DeVore. I want to nail him. But I want it to be me. *Me.* Understand? Not some other bastard."

Auden looked down, his expression thoughtful. "I see."

"Good. Then I'll leave you to tidy things up. I've kept the Minister's wife waiting far too long already."

———◆◆◆———

CHEN WAS WAITING for Haavikko when he came out of the Officers Mess. He hung back, careful not to let the young *Hung Mao* spot him even though he could see that Haavikko was the worse for drink. He smiled bitterly. Yes, that was in the file, too, along with all the brawling, the whoring, the gambling, and all the other derelictions of duty.

But that was as nothing beside the fact of his treason. Chen felt a shiver of anger ripple through him and let his hand rest momentarily on the handle of his knife. Well, he would cut a confession from him if he had to, piece by tiny piece. Because if Haavikko was behind the butchery at Helmstadt . . .

He stopped, moving in to the side. Up ahead of him Haavikko had paused, leaning against the wall unsteadily, as if about to be sick. But when a fellow officer approached him, he turned quickly, his movements exaggerated by drunkenness, letting out a string of obscenities. The officer put his hands out before him in apology, backing away, then turned and walked off, shaking his head.

Chen felt the bile rise again. Haavikko was a disgrace. To think what he might have become. And to waste it so . . . He shook his head, then began to move again, keeping the man in sight.

Twenty levels down he watched as Haavikko fumbled with the combination to his door, then slumped against the wall, making three attempts at it before he matched his eye to the indented pad. Then Chen was moving quickly, running the last few *ch'i* as the door began to iris shut.

Haavikko swung round, his bleary eyes half-lidded, his jacket already discarded, as Chen came through into the room.

"What the fuck . . . ?"

Chen had drawn his knife, a big knife with a wickedly curved blade that glinted razor-sharp in the overhead lights. "Haavikko? Axel Haavikko?"

He saw the flicker of fear in the young man's eyes as he staggered back and almost fell against the bed.

"What . . . what you want?" The words were slurred, almost incoherent.

"I think you know . . ." Chen began, moving closer. But suddenly Haavikko was no longer awkward, his movements no longer slow and clumsy. Chen found himself thrown backward by the man's charge, the knife knocked from his hand by a stinging blow. But before Haavikko could follow up, Chen had rolled aside and jumped to his feet again, his body crouched in a defensive posture.

Haavikko was facing him, crouched, his eyes wide, watching Chen's every movement, all pretense at drunkenness peeled from him. He swayed gently, as if about to attack, but it was clear to Chen that that was not Haavikko's intention. He was waiting for Chen to go for his knife, which lay just behind him by the door. It was what he himself would have done. Chen gave the slightest nod, suddenly respectful of the man's abilities. No one, not even Karr, had ever been fast enough to knock his knife from his hand.

"Well?" Haavikko said, clearly this time, the word formed like a drop of acid. "What do you want?"

Chen lifted his chin in challenge. "I'll tell you what I want. I want answers."

Haavikko laughed bitterly. "Answers? What do you mean?" But there was a slight hesitation in his eyes, the smallest trace of fear.

"I think you know more than you're letting on. I think you've done one or two things you're ashamed of. Things that aren't even in your file."

Chen saw how he blanched at that, how the skin about his eyes tightened.

"Who sent you? Was it Liu Chang?"

"Liu Chang? Who's that?"

Haavikko snorted in disgust. "You know damned well who I mean. Liu Chang, the brothel keeper. From the Western Isle. Did he send you? Or was it someone else?"

Chen shook his head. "You've got me wrong, Lieutenant. I'm a soldier, not a pimp's runner. You forget where we are. This is Bremen. How would a pimp's runner get in here?"

Haavikko shook his head. "I'd credit him with anything. He's devious enough, don't you think?"

Who? he wondered, but said, "It's Chen . . . Captain Kao Chen."

Haavikko laughed sourly, then shook his head. "Since when did they make a Han captain?"

Slowly Chen's hand went to his jacket.

"Try anything and I'll break your neck."

Chen looked back at him, meeting his eyes coldly, his fingers continuing to search his pocket, emerging a moment later with his pass. He threw it across to Haavikko, who caught it deftly, his eyes never leaving Chen's face.

"Back off . . . Two paces."

Chen moved back, glancing about him at the room. It was bare, undecorated. A bed, a wardrobe, a single chair. A picture of a girl in a frame on the tiny bedside table. Haavikko's uniform tunic hung loosely on the door of the wardrobe where he had thrown it.

Haavikko looked at the pass, turned it in his hand, then threw it back at Chen, a new look—puzzlement, maybe curiosity—in his eyes.

Chen pocketed the pass. "You're in trouble, aren't you, Haavikko? Out of your depth."

"I don't know what you mean."

"Oh, I think you do. Your friends have dumped you in it this time. Left you to carry the can."

Haavikko laughed scathingly. "Friends? I've no friends, Captain Kao. If you've read my file, you'll know that much about me."

"Maybe. And maybe that's just another pose—like the pretense of drunkenness you put on for me earlier."

Haavikko breathed deeply, unevenly. "I saw you earlier, when I went into the Mess. When you were still there when I came out, I knew you were following me."

"Who were you meeting?"

"I wasn't meeting anyone. I went in there to find something out."

Chen narrowed his eyes. "You weren't meeting Fest, then? I noticed that he entered the Mess just before you. You used to serve with him, didn't you?"

Haavikko was silent a moment, then he shook his head. "I wasn't meeting Fest. But yes, I served with him. Under General Tolonen."

"And under Major DeVore, too."

"I was ensign to DeVore for a month, yes."

"At the time of Minister Lwo's assassination."

"That's so."

Chen shook his head. "Am I to believe this crap?"

Haavikko's lips formed a sneer. "Believe what you like, but I wasn't meeting Fest. If you must know I went in there to try to overhear what he was saying."

"Are you blackmailing him?"

Haavikko bristled. "Look, what *do* you want? Who are you working for, Captain Kao?"

Chen met the challenge in his eyes momentarily, then looked about the room again. Something had been nagging at him. Something he didn't realize until he noticed the lieutenant's patch on the tunic hanging from the cupboard door. Of course! Haavikko had been the same rank these last eight years. But why? After all, if he *was* working for Ebert . . .

Chen looked back at Haavikko, shaking his head, then laughed quietly.

Haavikko had tensed, his eyes narrowed, suspicious. "What is it?"

But Chen was laughing strongly now, his whole manner suddenly different. He sat down on the bed, looking up at Haavikko. "It's just that I got you wrong. Completely wrong." He shook his head. "I thought you were working for Ebert."

"Ebert! That bastard!" Then realization dawned on Haavikko. "Then . . ." He gave a short laugh. "Gods! And I thought . . ."

The two men stared at each other a moment, their relief—their sudden understanding—clouded by the shadow of Ebert.

"What did he do?" Chen asked, getting up, his face serious, his eyes filled with sympathy. "What did he do to you, Axel Haavikko, to make you destroy yourself so completely?"

Haavikko looked down, shivering, then met Chen's eyes again. "It's not in the file, then?"

Chen shook his head.

"No. I guess it wouldn't be. He'd see to that, wouldn't he?" He was quiet a moment, staring at Chen sympathetically. "And you, Kao Chen? What did he do to make you hate him so?"

Chen smiled tightly. "Oh, it was a small thing. A matter of face." But he was thinking of his friend Pavel and of his death in the attack on the Overseer's House. That, too, he set down against Hans Ebert.

"Well . . . What now, Kao Chen? Do we go our own ways, or is our hatred of him strong enough to bind us?"

Chen hesitated, then smiled and nodded. "Let it be so."

━━━◆◆◆◆━━━

THE REST of the *Ping Tiao* leaders had gone straight to the cruiser, clearly unnerved at being out in the open; but the woman, Ascher, held back, stopping at the rail to look out across the open mountainside. DeVore studied her a moment, then joined her at the rail, for a time simply doing as she did—drinking in the sheer grandeur of the view.

"The mountains. They're so different . . ."

He turned his head, looking at her. She had such finely chiseled features, all excess pared from them. He smiled, liking what he saw. There was nothing gross, nothing soft about her: the austere, almost sculpted beauty of her was accentuated by the neat cut of her fine jet-black hair, the trimness of her small well-muscled body. Such a strong lithe creature she was, and so sharp of mind. It was a pity. She was wasted on Gesell.

"In what way different?"

She continued staring outward, as if unaware of his gaze. "I don't know. Harder, I suppose. Cruder. Much more powerful and untamed than they seem on the screen. They're like living things . . ."

"They're real, that's why."

"Yes . . ." She turned her head slightly, her breath curling up in the cold air.

He inclined his head toward the cruiser. "And you . . . you're different, too. You're real. Not like them. This, for instance. Something in you responds to it. You're like me in that. It touches you."

Her eyes hardened marginally, then she looked away again. "You're wrong. We've nothing in common, Turner. Not even this. We see it through different eyes. We want different things. Even from this." She shivered, then looked back at him. "You're a different kind of creature from me. You served *them*, remember? I could never do that. Could never compromise myself like that, whatever the end."

"You think so?"

"I know."

He smiled. "Have it your way. But remember this when you go away from here, Emily Ascher. I know you. I can see through you, like ice."

She held his gaze a moment longer, proudly, defiantly, then looked back at the mountains, a faint smile on her lips. "You see only mirrors. Reflections of yourself in everything. But that's how your kind thinks. You can't help it. You think the world's shaped as you see it. But there's a whole dimension you're blind to."

"Love, you mean? Human understanding? Goodness?" He laughed shortly, then shook his head. "Those things don't exist. Not really. They're illusions. Masks over the reality. And the reality is like these peaks—it's beautiful, but it's also hard, uncompromising, and cold, like the airless spaces between the stars."

She was silent a moment, as if thinking about what he had said. Then she turned back to him. "I must go. But thank you for letting me see this."

DeVore smiled. "Come again. Anytime you want. I'll send my cruiser for you."

She studied him a moment, then turned away, the smallest sign of amusement in her face. He watched her climb the steps and go inside. Moments later he heard the big engines of the cruiser start up.

He turned and looked across toward the snow-buried blister of the dome. Lehmann was standing by the entrance, bare-headed, a tall, gaunt figure even in his bulky furs. DeVore made his way across, while behind him the big craft lifted from the hangar and turned slowly, facing the north.

"What is it?" he asked.

"Success," Lehmann answered tonelessly. "We've found the combination."

He let his hand rest on Lehmann's arm momentarily, turning to watch the cruiser rise slowly into the blue, then turned back, smiling, nodding to himself. "Good. Then let's go and see what we've got."

Minutes later he stood before the open safe, staring down at the contents spread out on the floor at his feet. There had been three compartments to the safe. The top one had held more than two hundred bearer credits—small "chips" of ice worth between fifty and two hundred thousand *yuan* apiece. A second, smaller compartment in the center had contained several items of jewelry. The last, which made up the bulk of the safe's volume, had held a small collection of art treasures—scrolls and seals and ancient pottery.

DeVore bent down and picked up one of the pieces, studying it a moment. Then he turned and handed it to Lehmann. It was a tiny, exquisitely sculpted figure of a horse. A white horse with a cobalt-blue saddle and trappings and a light-brown mane and tail.

"Why this?" Lehmann asked, looking back at him.

DeVore took the piece back, examining it again, then looked up at Lehmann. "How old would you say this is?"

Lehmann stared back at him. "I know *what* it is. It's T'ang dynasty—fifteen-hundred years old. But that isn't what I meant. Why was it there, in the safe? What were they doing with it? I thought only the Families had things like this these days."

DeVore smiled. "Security has to deal with all sorts. What's currency in the Above isn't always so below. Certain Triad bosses prefer something more . . . *substantial*, shall we say, than money."

Lehmann shook his head. "Again, that's not what I meant. The bearer credits —they were payroll, right? Unofficial expenses for the eight garrisons surrounding the Wilds."

DeVore's smile slowly faded. Then he gave a short laugh. "How did you know?"

"It makes sense. Security has to undertake any number of things that they'd rather weren't public knowledge. Such things are costly precisely because they're so secretive. What better way of financing them than by allocating funds for nonexistent weaponry, then switching those funds into bearer credits?"

DeVore nodded. That was exactly how it worked.

"The jewelry likewise. It was probably taken during the Confiscations. I should imagine it was set aside by the order of someone fairly high up—Nocenzi, say—so it wouldn't appear on the official listings. Officially it never existed; so no one has to account for it. Even so, it's real and can be sold. Again, that would finance a great deal of secret activity. But the horse . . ."

DeVore smiled, for once surprised by the young man's sharpness. The bearer credits and jewelry—those were worth, at best, two billion yuan on the black market. That was sufficient to keep things going for a year at present levels. In the long term, however, it was woefully inadequate. He needed four, maybe five times as much simply to complete the network of fortresses. In this respect the horse and the two other figures—the tiny moon-faced Buddha and the white-jade carving of Kuan Yin—were like gifts from the gods. Each one was worth as much—and potentially a great deal more—as the rest of the contents of the safe combined.

But Lehmann was right. What *were* they doing there? What had made Li Shai Tung give up three such priceless treasures? What deals was he planning to make that required so lavish a payment?

He met the albino's eyes and smiled. "I don't know, Stefan. Not yet."

He set the horse down and picked up the delicate jade-skinned goddess, turning it in his hands. It was perfect. The gentle flow of her robes, the serene expression of her face, the gentle way she held the child to her breast—each tiny element was masterful in itself.

"What will you do with them?"

"I'll sell them. Two of them, anyway."

Yes, he thought, Old Man Lever will find me a buyer. Someone who cares more for this than for the wealth it represents.

"And the other?"

DeVore looked down at the tiny, sculpted goddess. "This one I'll keep. For now, anyway. Until I find a better use for her."

He set it down again, beside the horse, then smiled. Both figures were so realistic, so perfect in every detail, that it seemed momentarily as if it needed only a word of his to bring them both to life. He breathed deeply, then nodded to himself. It was no accident that he had come upon these things; nor was it instinct alone that made him hold on to the goddess now. No, there was a force behind it all, giving shape to events, pushing like a dark wind at the back of everything.

He looked up at Lehmann and saw how he was watching him.

And what would you make of that, my ultra-rational friend? Or you, Emily Ascher, with your one-dimensional view of me? Would you think I'd grown soft? Would you think it a weakness in me? If so, you would be wrong. For that's my strength: that sense of being driven by the darkness.

At its purest—in those few, rare moments when the veil was lifted and he saw things clearly—he felt all human things fall from him, all feeling, all sense of self erased momentarily by that dark and silent pressure at the back of him. At such moments he was like a stone—a pure white stone—set down upon the board; a mere counter, played by some being greater than himself in a game the scale of which his tiny human mind could scarcely comprehend.

A game of dark and light. Of suns and moons. Of space and time itself. A game so vast, so complicated . . .

He looked down, moved deeply by the thought, by the cold, crystalline-pure abstraction of such a vast and universal game.

"Are you all right?" Lehmann's voice lacked all sympathy; it was the voice of mechanical response.

DeVore smiled, conscious of how far his thoughts had drifted from this room, this one specific place and time. "Forgive me, Stefan. I was thinking . . ."

"Yes?"

He looked up. "I want you to track the woman for me. To find out what you can about her. Find out if it's true what they say about her and Gesell."

"And?"

He looked down at the jade-skinned goddess once again. "And nothing. Just do it for me."

———

SHE KEPT HER SILENCE until they were back in Gesell's apartment. There, alone with him at last, she turned on him angrily, all of her pent-up frustration spilling out.

"What in the gods' names are we doing working with that bastard?"

He laughed uncomfortably, taken aback by her outburst. "It makes good sense," he began, trying to be reasonable, but she cut him off angrily.

"*Sense?* It's insane, that's what it is! The surest way possible of cutting our own throats! All that shit he was feeding us about his inflexibility and our potential for growth. That's nonsense! He's *using* us! Can't you see that?"

He glared back at her, stiff faced. "You think I don't know what he is? Sure he's trying to use us, but we can benefit from that. And what he said is far from nonsense. It's the truth, Em. You saw his setup. He *needs* us."

She shook her head slowly, as if disappointed in him. "For a time, maybe. But as soon as he's wrung every advantage he can get from us, he'll discard us. He'll crunch us up in one hand and throw us aside. As for his 'weakness'—his 'inflexibility'—we saw only what he wanted us to see. I'd stake my life that there's more to that base than meets the eye. Much more. All that 'openness' he fed us was just so much crap. A mask, like everything else about our friend."

Gesell took a long breath. "I'm not so sure. But even if it is, we can still benefit from an alliance with him. All the better, perhaps, for knowing what he is. We'll be on our guard."

She laughed sourly. "You're naive, Bent Gesell, that's what you are. You think you can ride the tiger."

He bridled and started to snap back at her, then checked himself, shaking his head. "No, Em. I'm a *realist*. Realist enough to know that we can't keep on the way we've been going these last few years. You talk of cutting our own throats . . . well, there's no more certain way of doing that than by ignoring the opportunity to work with someone like Turner. Take the raid on Helmstadt, for instance. Dammit, Emily, but he was *right*! When would we *ever* have got the opportunity to attack a place like Helmstadt?"

"We'd have done it. Given time."

He laughed dismissively. "Given time . . ."

"No, Bent, you're wrong. Worse than that, you're impatient, and your impatience clouds your judgment. There's more at issue here than whether we grow as a movement or not. There's the question of what *kind* of movement we are. You can lie to yourself all you want, but working with someone like Turner makes us no better than he. No better than the Seven."

He snorted. "That's nonsense and you know it! What compromises have we had to make? None! Nor will we. You forget—if there's something we don't want to do, we simply won't do it."

"Like killing Jelka Tolonen, for instance?"

He shook his head irritably. "That makes good sense and you know it."

"*Why*? I thought it was our stated policy to target only those who are guilty of corruption or gross injustice?"

"And so it is. But what is Tolonen if not the very symbol of the system we're fighting against."

"But his *daughter* . . . ?"

He waved her objection aside. "It's a war, Emily. Us or them. And if working with Turner gives us a bit more muscle, then I'm all for it. That's not to say we have to go along with everything he wants. Far from it. But as long as it serves our cause, what harm is there in that?"

"What *harm* . . . ?"

"Besides, if you felt so strongly about this, why didn't you raise the matter in Council when you had the chance. Why have it out with me? The decision was unanimous, after all."

She laughed sourly. "*Was* it? As I recall we didn't even have a vote on it. But that aside, I could see what the rest of you were thinking—even Mach. I could see the way all of your eyes lit up at the thought of attacking Helmstadt. At the thought of getting your hands on all those armaments."

"And now we have them. Surely that speaks for itself? And Turner was right about the publicity, too. Recruitment will be no problem after this. They'll flock in in droves."

She shook her head. "You miss my point. I . . ."

She would have said more, would have pursued the matter, but at that moment there was an urgent knocking on the door. A moment later Mach came into the room. He stopped, looking from one to the other, sensing the tension in the air between them, then turned to face Gesell, his voice low and urgent.

"I have to speak to you, Bent. Something's come up. Something strange. It's . . ." He glanced at Emily. "Well, come. I'll show you."

She saw the way they excluded her and felt her stomach tighten with anger. The *Ping Tiao* was supposedly a brotherhood—a *brotherhood*! she laughed inwardly at the word—of equals. Yet for all their fine words about sexual equality, when it came to the crunch their breeding took over; and they had been bred into this fuck-awful system where men were like gods and women nothing

She watched them go, then turned away, her anger turned to bitterness. Maybe it was already too late. Maybe Turner had done his work already as far as Bent Gesell was concerned; the germ of his thought already in Gesell's bloodstream, corrupting his thinking, silting up the once-strong current of his idealism, the disease spreading through the fabric of his moral being, transforming him, until he became little more than a pale shadow of Turner. She hoped not. She hoped against hope that it would turn out otherwise, but in her heart of hearts she knew it had begun. And nothing—nothing she nor any of them could do—could prevent it. Nothing but to say no right now, to refuse to take another step down this suicidal path. But even then it was probably too late. The damage was already done. To say no to Turner now would merely set the man against them.

She shivered, then went into the washroom and filled the bowl with cold water. While she washed her face, she ran things through her mind, trying to see how she had arrived at this point.

For her it had begun with her father. Mikhail Ascher had been a System man, a Junior Credit Agent, Second Grade, in the T'ang's Finance Ministry, the *Hu Pu*. Born in the Lows, he had worked hard, passing the exams, slowly making his way up the levels until, in his mid-thirties, he had settled in the Upper Mids, taking a Mid-Level bride. It was there that Emily had been born, into a world of order and stability. Whenever she thought of her father, she could see him as he was before it all happened, dressed in his powder-blue silks, the big square badge of office prominent on his chest, his face clean-shaven, his dark hair braided in the Han fashion. A distant, cautious, conservative man, he had seemed to her the paradigm of what their world was about, the very archetype of order. A strict New Confucian, he had instilled into her values that she still, to this day, held to be true. Values that—had he but known it—the world he believed in had abandoned long before he came into it.

She leaned back from the bowl, remembering. She had been nine years old.

Back then, before the War, trade had been regular and credit rates relatively stable, but there were always minor fluctuations, tenths, even hundredths of a percentage point. It was one of those tiny fluctuations—a fluctuation of less than 0.05 of a percent—that her father was supposed to have "overlooked." It had seemed such a small thing when he had tried to explain it to her. Only much later, when she had found out the capital sum involved and worked out just how much it had cost the *Hu Pu*, did she understand the fuss that had been made. The Senior Credit Agent responsible for her father's section had neglected to pass on the rate change and to save his own position, had pointed the finger at her father, producing a spurious handwritten note to back up his claim. Her father had demanded a tribunal hearing, but the Senior Agent—a Han with important family connections—had pulled strings and the hearing had found in his favor. Her father had come home in a state of shock. He had been dismissed from the *Hu Pu*.

She could remember that day well, could recall how distraught her mother was, how bemused her father. That day his world fell apart about him. Friends abandoned him, refusing to take his calls. At the bank their credit was canceled. The next day the lease to their apartment was called in for "Potential Default." They fell.

Her father never recovered from the blow. Six months later he was dead, a mere shell of his former self. And between times they had found themselves demoted down the levels. Down and down, their fall seemingly unstoppable, until one day she woke and found herself in a shared apartment in Level 58, a child bawling on the other side of the thin curtain, the stench of the previous night's overcooked soypork making her want to retch.

Not their fault. Yes, but that wasn't what she had thought back then. She could still recall the sense of repugnance with which she had faced her new surroundings, her marked distaste for the people she found herself among. So coarse they were. So dirty in their habits.

No, she had never really recovered from that fall. It had shaped her in every single way. And even when her aversion had turned to pity and her pity into a fiery indignation, still she felt, burning within her chest, the dark brand of that fall.

Her mother had been a genteel woman, in many ways a weak woman, wholly unsuited to the bustle of the Lows; but she had done her best and in the years that followed had tried in every way to keep the standards that her husband had once set. Unused to work, she had broken with a lifetime's habits and gone looking for work. Eventually she had found it, running a trader's stall in the busy Main where they lived. The job had bruised her tender Mid-Level sensibilities sorely, but she had coped.

Emily shuddered, remembering. *Why do you do it?* she had asked her mother whenever she returned, tearful and exhausted, from a day working the stall. The answer was always the same: *For you. To get you out of this living hell.* It was her hard work that had put Emily through college; her determination, in the face of seemingly overwhelming odds, that had given Emily her chance. But for what? To climb the levels again? To take part in the same charade that had destroyed her father? No. She was set against that path. Secretly—for she knew that even to mention it would hurt her mother badly—she had harbored other dreams.

She had joined the *Ping Tiao* eight years ago, in its earliest days, just before the War. Back then there had been a lot of talk about ultimate goals and keeping the vision pure. But eight years was a long time to keep the flame of idealism burning brightly; especially when they had had to face more than their fill of disappointments. And all that time she had been Bent's woman, his alone, fired by his enthusiasm, his vision of how things might be. But now things had changed. Now it was hard to say whether those ideals still fired them or whether, in some small way, they had become the very thing they once professed to hate.

She stared at her reflection in the mirror, trying, as she so often did, to get beyond the surface of each eye and see herself whole and clear. So hard to do, it was. So hard. She looked down again, shaking her head. There was no doubting it—her fall had opened her eyes to the evil of the world, a world in which good men and women could be left to fester in the shit-heap of the lower levels while the corrupt and the unscrupulous wallowed in undeserved luxury high above them. A world unfit for decent beings. No; and she would never feel at ease in the world while such moral discrepancies existed.

She sighed and turned from the bowl, drying her face and upper arms. So maybe Bent was right. Maybe she was just being silly about the Tolonen girl. Maybe it *would* help bring this rotten pile crashing down. And yet it didn't feel right. No. Because it wasn't Jelka Tolonen's fault, either, that she had been born into this world of levels. And so long as she had no proof that the girl was anything other than a pawn of circumstance, she would not feel happy undertaking such a task.

Not for herself, let alone for a bastard like Turner.

Besides, what *was* his motive? Why did he want the General's daughter dead? Was it as he said, to weaken the General and thus undermine the T'ang's Security forces? Or was it something personal? Some slight he'd suffered at the General's hands?

She shivered again, remembering the moment on the moun-tainside beside Turner. To think that he thought they had something—*anything*—in common! She laughed and felt the laugh turn sour, recalling his words.

Love, you mean? Human understanding? Goodness? Those things don't exist. Not really. They're illusions. Masks over the reality. And the reality is like these peaks—it's beautiful, but it's also hard, uncompromising, and cold, like the airless spaces between the stars.

Well, maybe that was how he saw it, but the truth was otherwise. It was as she had said: he was lacking a dimension, lacking, essentially, any trace of basic human feeling. The Han had a saying for the behavior of such men, *Hou lian, hei hsin*— "Thick face, black heart"—and it was never more true than of Turner. Only in his case Thick Face, Black Heart had reached its ultimate, where the face is so thick it is formless, the heart so black it is colorless. His nihilism was pure, untempered by any trace of pity. And that was why they should not be working with him; for while their paths might coincide for a time, their aims were diametrically opposed.

In time they would have to fight the man. That was, if he had not, in the meantime, robbed them of the will to fight

━━━◆━━━

THE MUI TSAI BOWED deeply, then backed away two paces, holding the door open for him.

"Major Ebert. Please, come in. My mistress offers her apologies. She is afraid she will be late."

The girl kept her head lowered, as if from politeness, but a faint flush at her neck and cheeks betrayed her embarrassment at being left alone with the young Major.

"Oh? Not ill news, I hope."

"I believe not, Excellency, but she was summoned urgently. She knew you would understand."

Ebert moved past her slowly, turning to keep his eyes on her. Yes, she was a pretty young thing. Sixteen, seventeen at most. He could see the shape of her breasts beneath the thin silk of the dress she wore, the fullness of her hips. She was a peach. An absolute peach, ripe for the picking.

He moved closer. "How long will your mistress be?"

She turned to face him, her eyes averted. "She said she would not be long, Excellency. Fifteen minutes, perhaps. Twenty at the most. Her husband . . ."

She fell silent, looking up at him, surprised. Ebert had moved closer, taking her left hand in his own, while with his other hand he held her breast.

"Good," he said, smiling. "Then come. There's time for other things, neh?"

The linen cupboard was in the next room—a tiny chamber in itself, wide drawers and rows of silk *chi pao*, full-length elegant formal dresses arrayed in a rainbow of stunning colors to either side. He had noticed it on his previous visit, had seen the cushioned floor and thought how nice it might be . . .

He pushed the girl down, onto the cushions, laughing softly, enjoying the way she looked back at him, a strange wantonness in her dark eyes.

Afterward they lay there, the soft hiss of their breathing the only sound in the silence. The scent of their lovemaking was mixed deliciously with the faded perfumes of the dresses ranged on either side above them, a sweet, musky smell that, with the warm presence of her naked body beneath him, made him stir again.

She laughed softly, then turned her head to look at him. "That was nice . . ."

"Yes . . ." He let out a small, shuddering breath. Maybe he'd offer to buy her from Chuang Lian . . .

He felt her stiffen, then draw back from him, and opened his eyes. Then he heard the sound. It came from the other room. The sound of rustling silks.

"Gods . . ." the girl whispered anxiously, searching for her dress. But Ebert was smiling. Had they been at it that long, then? Or had the Minister's wife come back earlier than expected? He pulled his trousers up over his knees, then climbed to his feet, beginning to button himself up.

The girl had pulled the dress over her head and was fumbling at the fastenings. Ebert turned to her and put his finger against his lips; then reaching past her for his belt, he pushed her back into the linen cupboard and closed the door.

Fastening the last button, his belt in his hand, he went out into the other room.

"Lian, my love . . ."

She turned, clearly not expecting him, momentarily embarrassed by her state of half-undress. Then, with a laugh, she let the garment fall from her and, her breasts exposed, put out her arms to welcome him.

"Quickly," she said, drawing him down onto the bed, her hands fumbling with the buttons of his trousers. "Gods, I've missed you . . ." She looked up at him, her eyes filled with an unnatural agitation.

"Slowly . . ." he said, pushing her down, amused by the strange urgency of her actions. "What's up, my darling? Why so tense?"

She paused, then looked away, shuddering with disgust. "Of all the times . . ." She looked back up at him, uncertain whether to say; then she looked down again, sniffing, her hands reaching out to take his. "It was my husband. He doesn't ask for me often, but when he does . . ."

Ebert laughed. "So the old man still fucks you, eh?"

He saw the brief flare of anger in her eyes. Then she relented and laughed. "He tries. But it's like trying to fuck a goldfish . . ."

"Hmmm . . ." He thought of the girl, crouched still in the linen cupboard, and felt a little shudder of desire wash through him. "And you wanted a pike . . . ?"

Her eyes met his, all pretense gone from them suddenly. But all he could see was how lined she was, how *old;* how her breasts sagged, her flesh folded upon itself at neck and stomach. He shivered, thinking of the *mui tsai,* of the taut silken surfaces of her young flesh, then leaned closer, kissing the woman's cheek and neck, closing his eyes, trying to imagine that it was Sweet Flute he was kissing. But the scent of her was different—old and faded like her flesh, her powder sickly sweet like the scent of a corpse.

He moved back, shuddering, all desire suddenly dead in him. She had just come from her husband; was unwashed from the old man's feeble groping. The thought of it made his stomach churn. He could see her under him, the old man's wrinkled, emaciated buttocks tightening as he came.

And was he to take his place now? To be the man her husband clearly couldn't be?

"What is it?" she said, her eyes narrowed, her whole body suddenly tensed.

"I . . ." He shook his head. "I'm tired, that's all. I . . ." He fished for an excuse, then remembered the Han he'd beaten earlier. "I've been on duty thirty hours. Something urgent came up and I had to see to it. A number of Senior Company men were murdered . . ."

She swallowed and looked down. "I heard . . ."

He looked at her, suddenly disgusted, not only by her but by his involvement with her. And when she reached out to touch and hold him, he drew back sharply from her.

He saw her draw her hand back, then, her face wrinkling, lift it to her nose. Her mouth fell open; she jerked her head up and glared at him, her eyes black with anger. "What's this? Is this what you mean by *duty*?" She nodded her head exaggeratedly. "Oh, I understand it now. You've been screwing my *mui tsai*, haven't you? You've been having fun here while I've been on my knees before my husband . . ."

He laughed, delighted by the image that came to mind. "On your knees, Madam Chuang?"

There was a dark flash of fury behind her eyes; she swung her hand at him, trying to slap his face, but he caught it easily and threw her back down onto the bed. Oh, he could fuck her now. Could do it to her in anger. To humiliate her. But from desire?

"What if I have?" he taunted her. "What if I tell you that your *mui tsai* fucks like a dream? That she's ten times the woman you are, eh?"

She had bared her teeth. "You're a liar. She's only a girl . . ."

He sneered at her. "You think you were hot, eh? Is that it? You think you could make me come just thinking about what you did to me, eh? Well, let me tell you, Madam Chuang . . . you weren't so good. I've had much better below the Net. Clapped out old singsong girls who'd do it for a single yuan!" He saw how she started to answer him and put his hand brutally over her mouth. "No . . . it was simply the thought of fucking a Minister's wife. Of shitting in his nest. It *amused* me. But now I'm bored. I've had enough of you, old woman. Your haggard old frame bores me."

He stood, fastening himself, pulling his belt about him, watching her all the while, contempt burning in his eyes. He could see now how weak she was, how frail under that brittle carapace of hers. She thought herself so hard, so sophisticated, but she was just a spoiled little girl grown old. Tediously old.

"I'll bury you . . ." she said quietly, almost hissing the words through her teeth. "You can smile now, but I'll destroy you, Hans Ebert. Your name will be shit by the time I'm finished with you."

He laughed dismissively. "And yours? What will your name be worth, Madam Chuang, if the truth came out? How would you hold your head up in company if it were known what appetites you harbored inside that ancient, wizened skull of yours?"

"You bastard . . ." She shivered and drew the blanket up about her breasts. "I'll have you, Ebert. See if I don't."

He went to the door, then turned, looking back in at her crouched there on the bed. "You'll have me?" He looked down, laughing; then looked back at her, his face suddenly hard, uncompromising. "*You'll* have *me?*" He shook his head, then laughed: a cruel, dismissive laugh. "Go suck on your husband's prick!"

TWO HOURS LATER, Klaus Stefan Ebert, Head of Gen-Syn, stood on the front steps of his family's mansion, his broad hand extended to his old friend, Tolonen. The Marshal had become a gray-haired stiff-mannered old man in the fifty-odd years Ebert had known him, the uniform a second skin; but he remembered a simpler, less-daunting fellow, the gay companion of his adolescence.

The two men embraced, the warmth of their greeting overriding the formality of the occasion. This was more than politics. They grinned at one another and slapped each other's back.

"I'm glad," said Tolonen, tears brimming in his eyes.

"And I," responded Ebert, holding him at arm's length and smiling fiercely into his face. "This is a day to remember, Knut. Truly a day to remember!"

Jelka stood there at the bottom of the steps, a tall, willowy girl of fourteen with long straight ash-blond hair and beautiful blue eyes. She was no longer the child Ebert remembered so vividly. Now she was not far from womanhood.

Ebert smiled and nodded. She would make his son a perfect bride.

His son, Hans, stood behind him at the top of the steps, a tall twenty-eight-year-old, broad-shouldered yet lithe of build. He was considered extremely handsome by those who dictated taste in the Above; and as heir to the mighty GenSyn Empire, he was rated the most attractive unattached male in City Europe.

Hans barely looked at his bride-to-be. There was time enough for that. He stood there, at ease, his dress uniform immaculate, his short blond hair styled fashionably with a double pigtail. He watched the two men embrace and recognized the significance of all this, his role in it. The Marshal was like a second father to him, his Commanding Officer.

It was a perfect match. Strategically, logically, it was the obvious thing to do; and when his father had suggested it, ten years ago, he had agreed at once.

As he stood there he imagined the power he would one day wield, not merely as his father's son, but as Commander of the forces of the T'ang. He had dreams. Dreams he could not share. And they began here.

He looked at his intended—the child. She was studying him: looking at him with a critical eye, as if to sum and dismiss him. He glared at her, then relented, remembering, letting his face form into a smile, as if the first were only mischief.

He looked her up and down. She possessed the unformed figure of a girl. Pretty enough, but not a woman. Not a patch on the women he knew, anyway.

He smiled and looked away. Still, he would arrange things. Make life pleasant for himself. A wife was not a jailer, after all.

They went inside, Jelka bowing her head, her cheeks flushed, as the contracts were presented and endorsed by all parties.

He signed, then straightened, looking across the table at her. In three years he would be her husband. Three years. But who knew how things would be in three years time? And the girl? In three years she would be seventeen. Again he smiled, remembering the *mui tsai*. And you, my little one? he wondered, looking across at the Marshal's daughter. What will you be like on our wedding night? Are you the frigid, nervous type, or is there fire in your loins? His smile broadened, seeing how she looked away, the color deepening at her neck. Yes, well, we'll see. And even if you prove a disappointment, there will be others—plenty of others—to sweeten my nights.

And in the meantime maybe he would buy the *mui tsai*. After all, it wasn't every woman who could make love like that. Gifted, she'd been. He turned, taking the Marshal's offered hand, smiling back fiercely at the two old men. Yes, he would buy the *mui tsai*. And later, when her temper had cooled, he would go and see Madam Chuang again, and make it up with her.

JELKA SAT at her father's side, sipping at her bowl of *ch'a*, conscious of the stifling opulence of the room. She looked about her, feeling an unease that had nothing to do with her personal situation.

She shuddered and looked down. The Eberts flaunted their wealth, displaying it with an ostentation she found quite taste-less. Ornate Ming vases rested on hideous plinths, heavy, brutal things in garish colors. In recesses of the curiously shaped room, huge canvases hung in heavy gilt frames, the pictures dark, suggestive of blood.

Across from her, Hans's two sisters were staring at her with an unconcealed hostility, the youngest a year or so older than Jelka, the oldest in her early twenties. She tried not to look at them, knowing they saw her only as a rival. More disconcerting was the creature serving them; a goatlike being, grown in GenSyn's vats. She shivered when its pink-eyed stare met her own and in a deep but toneless voice, it asked if she would like more *ch'a*. She looked at its pinched, three-toed hand and shook her head, noting the fine silk of its cuffs, the stylish cut of its trousers.

She had the oddest feeling of being in a dream, unreality piled upon unreality. Yet this was real. Was the reality of power. She looked at her future husband and saw him with a clarity that almost overwhelmed her. He was a tall young man, taller than her father, and handsome. Yet there was a cruelty, an arrogance in his handsomeness that made her shudder. She could see his pride, his intense sense of self-importance, in the way he held his head, in the cold indifference of his eyes.

Even so, it didn't reach her yet; didn't touch or move her. Three years was a long time. She could not imagine how she would feel three years from now. This much—this ritual of contracts, of pledges and vague promises—seemed a small thing to do to satisfy her father.

She smiled, looking at her father, sensing his pride in her. It pleased her, as always, and she reached out to hold and touch his arm. She saw how old man Ebert smiled at that, a tender, understanding smile. He was cut from a different cloth than the rest of his family. Beside him his wife, Berta, looked away, distanced from everything about her, her face a mask of total indifference to the whole proceeding. A tall, elegant woman, hers was a cold, austere beauty: the beauty of pine forests under snow. A rarefied, inhuman beauty.

With that same clarity with which she had seen the son, Jelka saw how Berta Ebert had shaped her children in their father's absence. Saw how their cold self-interest was a reflection of their mother's.

She held her father's arm, feeling its warmth, its strong solidity, and drew comfort from that contact. He loved her. Surely he would allow nothing that would harm her?

On the way over he had talked to her of the reasons behind this marriage. Of the need to build strong links between the Seven and the most powerful of the new, commercial Families. It was the way forward, and her union with Hans would cement the peace they had struggled hard to win. GenSyn had remained staunchly loyal to the Seven in the recent War and Li Shai Tung had rewarded them for that loyalty. Klaus Ebert had taken over mining contracts on Mars and the Uranus moons as well as large holdings in three of the smaller communications companies. Her marriage would make this abstract, commercial treaty a personal thing. Would make it a thing of flesh and blood.

She understood this. Even so, it seemed a long way off. Before then she had to finish her schooling, the rest of her childhood. She looked at Hans Ebert dispassionately, as if studying a stranger.

She turned in her seat, her cup empty, to summon the servant. It came to her without a word, as if it had anticipated her wish, bowing to her as it filled her cup. Yet before it moved back into the shadows of the room it looked up at her, meeting her eyes a second time, holding them a moment with its dark, intimate knowledge of things she did not know.

Jelka turned her head away, looking past her father, meeting the eyes of her future husband. Blue eyes, not pink. Startlingly blue. Colder, harder eyes. Different . . .

She shuddered and looked down. And yet the same. Somehow, curiously, the same.

WANG SAU-LEYAN raised the silk handkerchief to his face and wiped his eyes. For a moment he stood there, his well-fleshed body shaking gently, the laughter still spilling from his lips; then he straightened up and sniffed loudly, looking about him.

Behind him the tomb was being sealed again, the rosewood litter carried away. Servants busied themselves, sweeping the dirt path with brushes of twigs, while, to one side, the six New Confucian officials stood in a tight circle, talking quietly among themselves.

"That was rich, Heng, don't you think?" Wang said, turning to face his Chancellor, ignoring the looks of displeasure of his fellow T'ang. "I had visions of my brother getting up out of the casket to chastise the poor buggers!"

"My Lord . . ." Heng's face was a picture of dismay. He glanced about him at the gathered T'ang, then lowered his head. "It was unfortunate . . ."

"Unfortunate!" Wang's laughter rang out again. "Why, it could only have happened to Ta-hung! Who else but my brother would find himself *thrown* into his own tomb!" With the last few words Wang Sau-leyan made a mime of the casket sliding into the tomb.

It had been an accident. At the top of the steps, one of the bearers had tripped and with the balance of the casket momentarily upset, the remaining bearers had lost their grip. The whole thing had tumbled down the steps, almost throwing out its occupant. Wang Sau-leyan, following close behind, had stood there at the tomb's mouth, doubled up with laughter. He had not stopped laughing since. Throughout the ceremony, he had giggled, oblivious of the astonished looks of the officials.

Now, however, his fellow T'ang were exchanging looks, appalled by his behavior. After a moment the oldest of them, Wei Feng, stepped forward.

"What is this, Wang Sau-leyan? Have you no feelings for your dead brother? We came to honor him today, to pay our respects to his souls as they journey on. This laughter is not fitting. Have you forgotten the rites, Wang Sau-leyan? It is your duty—"

"Hell's teeth, Wei Feng, I know my duty. But it was funny. Genuinely funny. If he had not been dead already, that last fall would have killed him!" Wang Sau-leyan stared back at his fellow T'ang momentarily, then looked away. "However . . . forgive me, cousins. It seems that I alone saw the humor in the moment."

Wei Feng looked down, his anger barely contained. Never in all his years had he seen anything like it.

"There are times for humor . . ."

Wang's huff of disgust was clearly disrespectful. He moved past Wei Feng as if the older man weren't there, confronting the other T'ang.

"If my brother had been a man to respect I would have shown him some respect, but my brother was a fool and a weakling. He would never have been T'ang but for the death of my elder brothers." Wang looked about him, nodding his head. "Yes, and I know that goes for me, too, but understand me, cousins. I'll not play hollow tongue to any man. I'll speak as I feel. As I am, not as you'd have me seem. So you'll understand me if I say that I disliked my brother. I'm not glad he's dead. No, I'd not go that far, for even a fool deserves breath. But I'll not be a hypocrite. I'll shed no false tears for him. I'll save them for men who deserve them. For men I truly love. Likewise I'll keep my respect for those who deserve respect."

Tsu Ma had been staring past Wang while he spoke. Now he looked back at him, his face inexpressive, his eyes looking up and down the length of Wang Sau-leyan, as if to measure him.

"And yet your brother was T'ang, Wang Sau-leyan. Surely a T'ang deserves respect?"

"Had the man filled the clothes . . ."

"And he did not?"

Wang Sau-leyan paused, realizing suddenly what dangerous seas he had embarked upon. Then he laughed, relaxing, and looked back at Tsu Ma.

"Don't mistake me, Tsu Ma. I speak only of my brother. I knew him well. In all the long history of the Seven there was never one like him. He was not worthy to wear the imperial yellow. Look in your hearts, all of you, and tell me that I'm wrong. In all honesty, was there one of you who, knowing my father was dead, rejoiced that Ta-hung was T'ang?"

He looked about them, seeing the grudging confirmation in every face.

"Well, let us keep our respect for those that deserve it, neh? For myself I'd gladly bow to any of my cousins here. You are men who have proved your worth. You, indeed, are T'ang."

He saw how that mollified them and laughed inwardly. They were all so vain, so title-proud. And hypocrites, too; for if the truth were known they cared as little for Ta-hung as he. No, they had taken offense not at his denigration of his brother but at the implied mockery of his brother's title, for by inference it mocked them also. As for himself . . .

He moved through, between their ranks, bowing to each of them as he passed, then led them on along the pathway and up the broad marble steps into the ancient palace.

As for himself, he cared not a jot for the trappings of his title. He had seen enough of men and their ways to know how hollow a mere title could be. No, what he valued was not the title "T'ang" but the reality of the power it gave him; the ability to say and do what he had always dreamed of saying and doing. The power to offend, if offense was what he wished. To be a T'ang and not have that was to be as nothing—was to be an actor in a tiresome play, mouthing another's words, constrained by bonds of ritual and tradition.

And he would not be that.

As the servants made their way among his guests, offering wine and sweetmeats, he looked about him again, a faint smile coming to his lips as he remembered that moment at the entrance to the tomb.

Yes, he thought, it was not your fate to be T'ang, Ta-hung. You were designed for other things than kingship. And yet T'ang you became.

Wang smiled and took a cup of wine from a servant, then turned away, looking out through the window at the walled garden and the great marbled tablet of the tomb at its center.

It was unfortunate. He had not disliked his brother. Despised him, maybe—though even that was too strong a word for the mild feeling of irritation he had felt—but not hated him as he had his father and his two oldest brothers. However, Ta-hung had had the misfortune of being born before him. As a younger brother he would have been no threat, but as T'ang he had been an obstacle, a thing to be removed.

He sipped at his wine and turned his head, looking across at his Chancellor. Hung Mien-lo was talking to Tsu Ma, his head lowered in deference. Smoothing things over, no doubt. Wang looked down, smiling, pleased by his morning's work.

It was true, he *had* found the accident genuinely amusing, but he had grasped at once that it was the perfect pretext for annoying his fellow T'ang—the perfect irritant; and he had exaggerated his response. He had seen how they bridled at his irreverence. And afterward it had given him the opportunity to play the bluff, honest man. To put his heart upon his sleeve and flaunt it before them. He took a deep breath, then looked up again, noting how their eyes went to him constantly. Yes, he thought. They hate me now, but they also admire me in a grudging way. They think me crass but honest. Well, let them be mistaken on both counts. Let them take the surface-show for the substance, for it will make things easier in the days to come.

He turned again, looking back at the tomb. They were dead—every one of them who had been in the room that day he had been exiled. Father and mother, brothers and uncles. All dead. And he had had them killed, every last one.

And now I'm T'ang and sleep in my father's bed with my father's wives and my father's maids.

He drained his glass, a small ripple of pleasure passing through him. Yes. He had stopped their mouths and closed their eyes. And no one would ever again tell him what he could or couldn't do.

No one.

━━━━━

TWO HOURS LATER, Wang Sau-leyan sat in his father's room, in the big, tall-backed chair, side-on to the mirror, his back to the door.

He heard the door open, soft footsteps pad across the tiles. "Is that you, Sweet Rain?"

He heard the footsteps pause and imagined the girl bending

low as she bowed. A pretty young thing, perhaps the prettiest of
his father's maids.

"Chieh Hsia?"

He half-turned, languid from the wine he'd drunk, and put his
hand out.

"Have you brought the lavender bowl?"

There was the slightest hesitation, then, "I have, Chieh Hsia."

"Good. Well, come then. I want you to see to me as you used
to see to my father."

Again there was the slightest hesitation before she acted.
Then she came round, bowing low, and knelt before him, the
bowl held delicately in the long slender fingers of her left hand.

He had seen the film of his father's final evening, had seen
how Sweet Rain had ministered to him, milking the old man
into the lavender bowl. Well, now she would do the same for
him. But no one would be watching this time. He had turned off
the cameras. No one but he would know what he did within the
privacy of *his* bedroom walls.

He drew the gown back from his lap, exposing his nakedness.
His penis was still quite flaccid.

"Well, girl? What are you waiting for?"

He let his head fall back and closed his eyes, waiting. There
was the faint rustle of silks as she moved closer, then he felt her
fingers brush against his flesh. He shivered, then nodded to
himself, feeling his penis stir between her fingers. Such a delicate touch she had—like silk itself—her fingers caressing the
length of him slowly, tantalizingly, making his breath catch in
his throat.

He opened his eyes, looking down at her. Her head was
lowered, intent on what she was doing, the darkness of her hair
held up with a single white-jade pin.

"Is this how you touched my father?"

She glanced up. "No, Chieh Hsia. But I thought . . ."

And still her fingers worked on him, gathering the whole of
him up into that tiny nexus of pleasure, there between his legs.

"Thought what?" he said after a moment, the words barely
audible.

She hesitated, then looked up at him again, candidly this

time. "Every man is different, *Chieh Hsia*. Likewise their needs . . ."

He nodded slowly. Gods, but it was delightful. He would never have dreamed that a woman's hands could be so potent an instrument of pleasure.

Her eyes met his again. "If the T'ang would prefer, I could . . . *kiss* him there."

He shuddered. The word "kiss" promised delights beyond imagining. He gave a tiny nod. "Yes. I'd like that."

He heard her set the bowl down and let his head fall back, his eyes close, then felt her lift him to her lips. Again he shivered, drawn up out of himself by the sheer delight of what she was doing. For a while, then, he seemed to lapse out of himself, becoming but a single thread of perfect pleasure, linked to the warm wetness of her mouth, a pleasure that grew and grew . . .

He didn't hear the door open. Nor did he hear the second set of footsteps pad almost silently across the tiles toward him. But a movement in the girl in front of him—the slightest tensing of her left hand where it rested on his knee—made him open his eyes suddenly and look up, his gaze going to the mirror.

Tender Willow was almost upon him, the knife already raised in her right hand. At once he kicked out with his right leg, pushing Sweet Rain away from him, and lurched forward, out of the seat.

It was not a moment too soon. Tender Willow's knife missed his shoulder by a fraction, tearing into the silken cushioning of the chair, gashing the wooden beading. Wang turned quickly, facing her, twice her weight and a full *ch'i* taller; but still the girl came on, her face filled with hatred and disgust.

As she thrust the knife at him a second time, he moved forward, knocking her arm away, then, grabbing her neck brutally, he smashed her head down into the arm of the chair, once, then a second time. She fell and lay still.

He stood there a moment, his breath hissing sharply from him, then turned and kicked out at Sweet Rain again, catching her in the stomach so that she wheezed, her breath taken from her. His face was dark now, twisted with rage.

"You foxes . . ." he said quietly, his voice trembling. "You foul little bitches . . ."

He kicked again, catching the fallen girl fully on the side of the head, then turned back and spat on the other girl.

"You're dead. Both of you."

He looked about him, noting the broken bowl and, beside it, a single white jade pin, then bent down and recovered the knife from the floor. He straightened up, then, with a slight shudder, walked to the door and threw it open, calling the guards.

Shells

Between the retina and the higher centers of the cortex the innocence of vision is irretrievably lost—it has succumbed to the suggestion of a whole series of hidden persuaders.

—ARTHUR KOESTLER, *The Act of Creation*

That which we experience in dreams, if we experience it often, is in the end just as much a part of the total economy of our soul as is anything we "really" experience: we are by virtue of it richer or poorer.

—FRIEDRICH NIETZSCHE, *Beyond Good and Evil*

CHAPTER FIVE

The Innocence of Vision

▬▬▬▬▬▬

BEN CAME UPON the cottage from the bay path, climbing the steep slope. At the lower gate he turned, looking back across the bay. New growth crowded the distant foreshore, masking where the fire had raged five years earlier. Only at the hill's crest, where the old house had stood, did the new vegetation end. There the land was fused a glassy black.

The tall seventeen-year-old shook his head, then turned to face the cottage. Landscott was a long low shape against the hill, its old stone walls freshly whitewashed, its roof thatched. A flower garden stretched up to it, its blooms a brilliant splash of color beside the smooth greenness of the lawn. Behind and beside it other cottages dotted the hillside, untenanted yet perfectly maintained. Shells, they were. Part of the great illusion. His eyes passed over them quickly, used to the sight.

He looked down at his left hand where it rested on the gatepost, conscious of a deep, unsatisfied itch at the join between the wrist and the new hand. The kind of itch you couldn't scratch, because it was inside, beneath the flesh. The join was no longer sore, the hand no longer an unaccustomed weight at the end of his arm, as it had been for the first year. Even so, something of his initial sense of awkwardness remained.

The scar had healed, leaving what looked like a machined ridge between what was his and what had been given. The hand itself looked natural enough, but that was only illusion. He had seen what lay beneath the fibrous dermal layer. It was much stronger than his right hand and in subtle ways, much better— far quicker in its responses. He turned it, moving it like the machine it was rather than the hand it pretended to be, then smiled to himself. If he wished, he could have it strengthened and augmented, could transform it into any kind of tool he needed.

He let it fall, then began to climb again, crossing the gradual slope of the upper garden. Halfway across the lawn he slowed, then stopped, surprised, hearing music from inside the cottage. Piano music. He tilted his head, listening, wondering who it was. The phrase was faltering at first, the chords uncertain. Then, a moment later, the same chords were repeated, confidently this time, all sense of hesitation gone.

Curious, he crossed the lawn and went inside. The music was coming from the living room. He went to the doorway and looked in. At the far side of the room his mother was sitting at a piano, her back to him, her hands resting lightly on the keys.

"Mother?" Ben frowned, not understanding. The repetition of the phrase had been assured, almost professional, and his mother did not play.

She turned, surprised to see him there, a slight color at her cheeks. "I . . ." then she laughed and shook her head. "Yes, it was me. Come. I'll show you."

He went across and sat beside her on the long benchlike piano seat. "This is new," he said, looking down at the piano. Then, matter-of-factly, he added, "Besides, you don't play."

"No," she said, but began anyway—a long introductory passage, more complex than the phrase she had been playing; a fast passionate piece played with a confidence and skill the earlier attempt had lacked. He watched her hands moving over the keys, surprised and delighted.

"That's beautiful," he said when she had finished. "What was it?"

"Chopin. From the Preludes." She laughed, then turned and glanced at him, her eyes bright with enjoyment.

"I still don't understand. That was excellent."

"Oh, I wouldn't say that." She leaned back, staring down at the keyboard. "I'm rather rusty. It's a long while since I played."

"Why didn't you play before now?"

"Because it's an obsession."

She had said it without looking at him, as if it explained everything. He looked down at her hands again, saw how they formed shapes above the keys.

"I had to think of you and Meg. I couldn't do both, you understand. Couldn't play and look after you. And I wanted to bring you up. I didn't trust anyone else to do the job."

"So you gave up *this*?"

If anything, he understood it less. To have such a gift and not use it. It was not possible.

"Oh, there were plenty of times when I felt like playing. I ached to do it. It was like coming off a drug. A strong, addictive drug. And in denying that part of me I genuinely felt less human. But there was no choice. I wanted to be a mother to you, not simply a presence flitting through your lives."

He frowned, not following her. It made him realize how little he knew about her. She had always been too close, too familiar. He had never thought to ask her about herself, about her life before she had met his father.

"My own mother and father were never there, you see." Her hands formed a major chord, then two quick minors. It sounded familiar; yet, like the Chopin, he couldn't place it.

"I was determined not to do to you what they did to me. I remember how isolated I felt. How unloved." She smiled, reaching across to take his right hand—his human hand—and squeeze it.

"I see."

It awed him to think she had done that for them. He ran the piece she had played through his memory, seeing where she placed emphasis, where she slowed. He could almost feel the music. Almost.

"How does it *feel* to be able to do that?"

She drew in a long breath, looking through him, suddenly distant, her eyes and mouth lit with the vaguest of smiles; then she shook her head. "No. I can't say. There aren't the words for it. Raised up, I guess. Changed. *Different* somehow. But I can't say what, exactly."

For the first time in his life Ben felt something like envy, watching her face. Not a jealous, denying envy, but a strong desire to emulate.

"But why now?"

"Haven't you guessed?" She laughed and placed his right hand on the keyboard. "You're usually so quick."

"You're going to teach me."

"Both of you," she answered, getting up and coming behind him so that she could move his arms and manipulate his hands. "Meg asked me to. And she wouldn't learn unless you could, too."

He thought about it a moment, then nodded.

"What was that piece you were playing when I came in? It sounded as if you were learning it for the first time, yet at the same time knew it perfectly."

She leaned closer, her warmth pressed against his shoulder, her long dark hair brushing against his cheek. "It wasn't originally a piece for piano, that's why. It was scored for the string and woodwind sections of an orchestra. It's by Grieg. 'Wedding Day at Troldhaugen.' " She placed her hands on either side of his own and repeated the phrase he had heard, then played a second, similar one.

"That's nice," he said. Its simplicity appealed to him.

"You came back early," she said. "What's up? Didn't you want to go into town?"

He turned, meeting her eyes. "Father called. The T'ang has asked him to stay on a few days."

There was a brief movement of disappointment in her face. It had been three months since she had seen Hal.

"A few more days," she said quietly. "Ah well, it'll soon pass." Then, smiling, she put her hand on his arm. "Perhaps we'll have a picnic. You, me, and Meg. Like old times. What do you think?"

Ben looked back at her, seeing her anew, the faintest smile playing on his lips and in his eyes. "It would be nice," he said. But already his thoughts were moving on, his mind toying with the possibilities of the keyboard. Pushing things further. "Yes," he added, getting up and going over to her. "Like old times."

THE NEXT MORNING found Ben in the shadowed living room, crouched on his haunches, staring intently at the screen that filled half the facing wall. He was watching one of the special Security reports that had been prepared for his father some months before, after the T'ang of Africa's assassination. It was an interesting document, not least because it showed things that were thought too controversial, too inflammatory, for general screening.

The Seven had acted swiftly after Wang Hsien's death, arresting the last few remnants of opposition at First Level—thus preventing a further outbreak of the war between the factions in the Above—but even they had been surprised by the extent of the rioting lower down the City. There had been riots before, of course, but never on such a widespread scale or with such appalling consequences. Officials of the Seven, Deck Magistrates among them, had been beaten and killed. Security posts had been destroyed and Security troops forced to pull out of some stacks in fear of their lives. Slowly, very slowly, things had died down, the fires burning themselves out; and in some parts of the City—in East Asia and North America, particularly— Security had moved back within days to quell the last few pockets of resistance. Order had been restored. But for how long?

He knew it was a warning. A sign of things to come. But would the Seven heed it? Or would they continue to ignore the problems that beset those who lived in the lowest levels of the City, blaming the unrest on groups like the *Ping Tiao*?

Ben rubbed at his chin thoughtfully. To the respectable Mid-Level citizenry, the *Ping Tiao* were bogeymen, the very type and symbol of those destructive forces the War had unleashed; and MidText, the Mid-Level media channel, played heavily upon their fears. But the truth was otherwise.

The *Ping Tiao* had first come into the news eighteen months earlier, when three members of their faction had kidnapped and murdered a Mid-Level administrator. They had issued pamphlets claiming that the Administrator was a corrupt and brutal man who had abused his position and deserved his fate. It was the truth, but the authorities had countered at once, depicting the dead official as a well-respected family man who had been the victim of a group of madmen; madmen who wanted only one thing—to level the City and destroy Chung Kuo itself.

As the weeks passed and further *Ping Tiao* "outrages" occurred, the media had launched a no-holds-barred campaign against the group, linking their name with any outbreak of violence or civil unrest. There was a degree of truth behind official claims, for the tactics of the *Ping Tiao* were certainly of the crudest kind, the seemingly random nature of their targets aiming at maximum disruption. However, the extent of *Ping Tiao* activities was greatly exaggerated, creating the impression that if only the *Ping Tiao* could be destroyed, the problems they represented would vanish with them.

The campaign had worked. Or at least, in the Mid-Levels it had worked. Farther down, however, in the cramped and crowded levels at the bottom of the City, the *Ping Tiao* were thought of differently. There they were seen as heroes, their cause as a powerful and genuine expression of long-standing grievances. Support for the terrorists grew and grew; and would have continued growing but for a tragic accident in a Mid-Level crèche.

Confidential high-level sources later made it quite clear that the *Ping Tiao* had had nothing to do with what was termed "the Lyons Canton Massacre," but the media had a field day, attacking the *Ping Tiao* for what they called its "cowardly barbarism and inhumanity."

The effect was immediate. The tide of opinion turned against the *Ping Tiao* overnight, and a subsequent Security operation against the terrorists resulted in the capture and execution of over eight hundred members of the faction, most of them identified by previously sympathetic friends and neighbors.

For the *Ping Tiao* those few weeks had been disastrous. They had sunk into obscurity. Yet in the past few days they seemed to have put that behind them. Fish emblems—the symbol of the *Ping Tiao*—had been seen everywhere throughout the levels, painted on walls or drawn in blood on the faces of their victims.

But the authorities had hit back hard. MidText, for instance, had played heavily on old fears. The present troubles, they asserted, were mainly the result of a conspiracy between the *Ping*

Tiao and a small faction in the Above who financed their atrocities.

Ben froze the tape momentarily, thinking back to what Li Shai Tung had said—on that evening five years earlier—about knowing his enemy. It was on this level, accepting at face value the self-deluding half-truths of the MidText images, that Li Shai Tung had been speaking. But these men—terrorists and Company men alike—were merely cyphers, the scum on the surface of the well. And the well was deep. Far deeper than the Seven dared imagine.

He let the tape run. At once the babble began again, the screen filling once more with images of riot and despoliation.

Vast crowds surged through the lower levels, destroying guard posts and barriers, wrecking storefronts and carrying off whatever they could lay their hands on. Unfortunate officials were beaten to death in front of the camera, or bound and doused in petrochemicals before being set on fire. Ben saw how the crowd pressed in tightly about one such victim, roaring their approval as a frail, gray-bearded magistrate was hacked to death. He noted the ugly brutality in every face, and nodded to himself. Then the image changed, switching to another crowd, this one more orderly. Hastily made banners were raised on every side, demanding increased food rations, a resumption of state aid to the jobless, and an end to travel restrictions. "*Pien hua!*" they chanted in their hundred thousands, "*Pien hua!*"

Change!

There was a burning indignation in many of the faces; in others a fierce, unbridled need that had no outlet. Some waved long knives or clubs in the air and bared their teeth in ferocious animal smiles, a gleam of sheer delight in their eyes at having thrown off all restraints. For many this was their first taste of such freedom and they danced frenetically in time with the great chant, intoxicated by the madness that raged on every side.

"*PIEN HUA! PIEN HUA! PIEN HUA! PIEN HUA!*"

Ben watched the images flash up one after another, conscious of the tremendous power, the dark potency that emanated from them. It was primordial. Like some vast movement of the earth itself. And yet it was all so loosely reined, so undirected. Change, they demanded. But to what?

No one knew. No one seemed capable of imagining what change might bring. In time, perhaps, someone would find an answer to that question, would draw the masses to him and channel that dark tide of discontent. But until then, the Seven had been right to let the storm rage, the floodwaters rise unchecked; for they knew the waters would recede, the storm blow itself out. To have attempted to control that vast upsurge of feeling or repress it could only have made things worse.

Ben blanked the screen, then stood, considering what he had seen. Wang Hsien's death may have been the catalyst, but the real causes of the mass violence were rooted much deeper. Were, in fact, as old as Man himself. For this was how Man really was beneath his fragile shell of culture. And not just those he had seen on the screen, the madness dancing in their eyes, but all of Mankind. For a long time they had tried to fool themselves, pretending they were something else, something more refined and spiritual, more godlike and less animalistic than they really were. But now the lid was off the well, the darkness bubbling to the surface once again.

"Ben?"

He turned. Meg was watching him from the doorway, the morning sunlight behind her throwing her face and figure into shadow, making her look so like his mother that, momentarily, he mistook her. Then, realizing his error, he laughed.

"What is it?" she asked, her voice rich and low.

"Nothing," he answered. "Is it ready?"

She nodded, then came into the room. "What were you watching?"

He glanced at the empty screen, then back at her. "I was looking at Father's tapes. About the riots."

She looked past him. "I thought you weren't interested."

He met her eyes. "I'm not. At least, not in the events themselves. But the underlying meaning of it all—that fascinates me. Their faces—they're like windows to their souls. All their fears and aspirations show nakedly. But it takes something like this to do it, something big and frightening. And then the mask slips and the animal stares out through the eyes."

And the *Ping Tiao*, he thought. I'm interested in them, too.

Because they're something new. Something the City has been missing until now. A carp to fill an empty pool.

"Well . . . shall we go out?"

She smiled. "Okay. You first."

On the lawn beside the flower beds, their mother had spread out a picnic on a big red-and-white-checked tablecloth. As Ben came out into the open she looked across at him and smiled. In the sunlight she seemed much younger than she really was, more Meg's older sister than her mother. He sat beside her, conscious of the drowsy hum of bees, the rich scent of the blooms masking the sharp salt tang of the bay. It was a perfect day, the blue above them broken here and there by big slow-drifting cumuli.

Ben looked down at the picnic spread before them. It all looked newly created. A wide basket filled with apples lay at the center of the feast, their perfect, rounded greenness suggesting the crispness of the inner fruit. To the left his eye was drawn to the bright yellow of the butter in its circular white-china dish and, beside it, the richer, almost-honeyed yellow of the big wedge of cheddar. There was a big plate of thick-cut ham, the meat a soft pink, the rind a perfect snowy white, and next to that a fresh-baked loaf, three slices cut from it and folded forward, exposing the fluffy whiteness of the bread. Bright-red tomatoes beaded with moisture shared a bowl with the softer green of a freshly washed lettuce, while other, smaller bowls held tiny radishes and onions, peeled carrots, grapes and celery, red currants and watercress.

"It's nice," he said, looking up at his mother.

Pleased, she handed him a plate. A moment later Meg reappeared, carrying a tray on which were three tall glasses and a jug of freshly made, iced lemonade. He laughed.

"What is it?" Meg asked, setting the tray down.

"This," he said, indicating the spread laid out before them. Meg's smile faded slowly. "What's wrong? Don't you like it?"

"No," he said softly, reassuringly. "It's marvelous." He smiled, then leaned forward, beginning to transfer things to his plate.

Meg hesitated, then poured from the jug, handing him the cold, beaded glass. "Here."

He set his plate down, then took the glass and sipped.

"Hmm . . ." he said appreciatively, his eyes smiling back at her. "Perfect."

Beside him his mother was busy filling a plate for Meg. She spoke without looking at him.

"Meg tells me you've been reading Nietzsche."

He glanced across at Meg. She was looking down, a faint color in her cheeks.

"That's right." He sipped again, then stared at the side of his glass intently.

His mother turned her head, looking at him. "I thought you'd read Nietzsche."

"I did. When I was eight."

"Then I don't understand. I thought you said you could never read a thing twice."

He met her eyes. "So I thought. But it seems I was wrong."

She was silent awhile, considering, then looked back at him again. "Then you *can* forget things, after all?"

He shook his head. "It's not a question of forgetting. It's just that things get embedded."

"Embedded?"

He paused, then set his glass down, realizing he would have to explain. "I realized it months ago, when Father quoted something from Nietzsche to me. Two lines from *Ecce Homo*. The memory should have come back clearly, but it didn't. Oh, it was clear enough in one sense—I could remember the words plain enough. I could even see them on the page and recall where I was when I read them. But that was it, you see. That's what I mean by things getting embedded. When Father triggered that specific memory, it came back to me *in context*, surrounded by all the other ragbag preoccupations of my eight-year-old self."

Ben reached out and took a tomato from the bowl and polished it on his sleeve; then he looked up at his mother again, his face earnest, almost frowning.

"You see, those lines of Nietzsche's were interlaced with all kinds of other things. With snatches of music—Mahler and Schoenberg and Shostakovich—with the abstract paintings of Kandinsky and Klee, the poetry of Rilke and Donne and Basho, and God knows what else. A thousand intricate strands. Too many to grasp at a single go. But it wasn't just a case of association by juxtaposition. I found that my reading, my very under-standing of Nietzsche, was colored by those things. And try as I might, I couldn't shake those impressions loose and see his words fresh. I had to separate it physically."

"What do you mean?" Beth asked, leaning forward to take a grape from the bunch.

"I mean that I had to return to the text. To read the words fresh from the page again. Free from all those old associations."

"And?" It was Meg who asked the question. She was leaning forward slightly, watching him, fascinated.

He looked down, then bit into the tomato. He chewed for a moment, then swallowed and looked up again. "And it worked. I liberated the words from their old context."

He popped the rest of the tomato into his mouth and for a while was silent, thoughtful. The two women watched him, indulging him as always, placing him at the very center of things. The tomato finished, he took a long sip of his lemonade. Only then did he begin again.

"It's as if my mind is made up of different strata. It's all there—fossilized, if you like, and available if I want to chip away at it—but my memory, while perfect, is nonetheless selective."

Ben laughed and looked at his sister again. "Do you remember that Borges story, Meg? 'Funes the Memorious'—about the boy with perfect recall; confined to his bed, entrapped by the perfec-tion, the overwhelming detail, of past moments. Well, it isn't like that. It could never be like that, amusing as the concept is. You see, the mind accords certain things far greater significance than others. And there's a good reason for that. The undermind recog-nizes what the conscious intelligence too often overlooks—that there is a hierarchy of experience. Some things matter more to our deeper self than others. And the mind returns them to us strongly. It thrusts them at us, you might say—in dreams, and at quiet moments when we least suspect their presence."

"Why should it do that?"

Ben gave a tiny shrug. "I'm not sure." He took an apple from the basket and lifted it to his mouth. "But maybe it has to do with something programmed into us at the genetic level. A code. A key to why we're here, like the cyphers in Augustus's journal."

As Ben bit deeply into the apple, Meg looked across at her mother and saw how she had looked away at the mention of Augustus and the journal.

"But why Nietzsche?" Meg asked, after a moment. She could not understand his fascination with the nineteenth-century German philosopher. To her, the man was simply an extremist, a fanatic. He understood nothing of those purely human things that held a society together—nothing of love, desire, or sacrifice. To her mind, his thinking was fatally flawed. It was the thinking of a hermit, a misanthrope. But Man was a social species; he did not exist in separation from his fellows, nor *could* he for longer than one human lifetime. And any human culture was the product of countless generations. In secret she had struggled with the man's difficult, spiky prose, trying to understand what it was Ben saw in him; but it had served only to confirm her own distaste for his thought.

Ben chewed the piece of apple, then smiled and swallowed. "There's an almost hallucinatory clarity about his thinking that I like. And there's a fearlessness, too. He's not afraid to offend. There's nothing he's afraid to look at and investigate at depth, and that's rare in our culture. Very rare."

"So?" Meg prompted, noting how her mother was watching Ben again, a fierce curiosity in her eyes.

He looked at the apple, then shrugged and bit again.

Beth broke her long silence. "Are you working on something new?"

Ben looked away. Then it was true. He had begun something new. Yes, she should have known. He was always like this when he began something new—fervent, secretive, subject to great swings of mood.

The two women sat there, watching him as he finished the apple, core and all, leaving nothing.

He wiped his fingers on the edge of the cloth, then looked up again, meeting Meg's eyes. "I was thinking we might go along to the cove later on and look for shells."

She looked away, concealing her surprise. It was some time since they had been down to the cove, so why had he suggested it just now? Perhaps it was simply to indulge her love of shells, but she thought not. There was always more to it than that with

Ben. It would be fun, and Ben would make the occasion into a kind of game, but he would have a reason for the game. He always had a reason.

Ben laughed and reached out to take one of the tiny radishes from the bowl. "And then, tomorrow, I'll show you what I've been up to."

WARFLEET COVE was a small bay near the mouth of the river. A road led toward it from the old town, ending abruptly in a jumble of rocks, the shadow of the Wall throwing a sharp but jagged line over the rocks and the hill beyond. To the left the land fell away to the river, bathed in brilliant sunlight. A path led down through the thick overgrowth—blackberry and bramble, wildflowers and tall grasses—and came out at the head of the cove.

Ben stepped out onto the flattened ledge of rock, easing the strap of his shoulder bag. Below him the land fell away steeply to either side, forming a tiny, ragged flint-head of a bay. A shallow spill of shingle edged the sandy cove. At present the tide was out, though a number of small rockpools reflected back the sun's brilliance. Low rocks lay to either side of the cove's mouth, narrowing the channel. It was an ancient, primitive place, unchanged throughout the centuries; and it was easy to imagine Henry Plantagenet's tiny fleet anchored here in 1147, waiting to sail to Jerusalem to fight the Infidel in the Second Crusade. Further around the headland stood the castle built by Henry Tudor, Henry VII, whose son had broken with the papacy. Ben breathed deeply and smiled to himself. This was a place of history. From the town itself the Pilgrim Fathers had sailed in August 1620 to the new lands of America, and in June 1944 part of the great invasion fleet had sailed from here—five hundred ships, bound for Normandy and the liberation of Europe from Hitler and the Nazis.

All gone, he thought wryly, turning to look at his sister. All of that rich past gone, forgotten, buried beneath the ice of the Han City.

"Come on," he said. "The tide's low. We'll go by the rocks on the north lip. We should find something there."

Meg nodded and followed him, taking his hand where the path was steepest, letting him help her down.

At the far edge of the shingle they stopped and took off their shoes, setting them down on the stones. Halfway across the sand, Ben stopped and turned, pointing down and back, tracing a line. "Look!"

She looked. The sun had warmed the sand, but where they had stepped their feet had left wet imprints, dark against the almost white, compacted sand. They faded even as she watched, the most distant first, the nearest last.

"Like history," he said, turning away from her and walking on toward the water's edge.

Or memory, Meg thought, looking down at her feet. She took a step then stopped, watching how the sharp clarity of the imprint slowly decayed, like an image sent over some vast distance, first at the edges, then—in a sudden rush—at the very center, breaking into two tiny, separate circles before it vanished. It was as if the whole had sunk down into the depths beneath the sand and was now stored in the rock itself.

"Here!" he called triumphantly. She hurried over to where he was crouched near the water's edge and bent down at his side.

The shell was two-thirds embedded in the sand. Even so, its shape and coloring were unmistakable. It was a pink-mouthed murex. She clapped her hands, delighted, and looked at him.

"Careful when you dig it out, Ben. You mustn't damage the spines."

He knew, of course, but said nothing, merely nodded and pulled his bag round to the front, opening up the flap.

She watched him remove the sand in a circle about the shell, then set the tiny trowel down and begin to remove the wet hardpacked sand with his fingers. When he had freed it, he lifted it carefully between his fingers and took it to one of the rockpools to clean.

She waited. When he came back, he knelt in front of her and, opening out the fingers of her right hand, put the pale, whitepink shell down on her palm. Cleaned, it looked even more beautiful. A perfect specimen, curved and elegant, like some strange fossil fish.

"The hedgehog of the seas," he said, staring at the shell. "How many points can you count?"

It was an old game. She lifted the shell and staring at its tip— its "nose"—began to count the tiny little nodes that marked each new stage on the spiral of growth.

"Sixteen," she said, handing the shell back.

He studied it. "More like thirty-four," he said, looking up at her. He touched the tip of the shell gently. "There are at least eighteen in that first quarter of an inch."

"But they don't count!" she protested. "They're too small!"

"Small they may be, but they do count. Each marks a stage in the mollusk's growth, from the infinitesimally tiny up. If you X-rayed this, you'd see it. The same form repeated and repeated, larger and larger each time, each section sealed off behind the shellfish—outgrown, if you like. Still growing even at the creature's death. Never finished. The spiral uncompleted."

"As spirals are."

He laughed and handed her back the shell. "Yes. I suppose by its nature it's incomplete. Unless twinned."

Meg stared at him a moment. "Ben? What *are* we doing here?"

His dark-green eyes twinkled mischievously. "Collecting shells. That's all."

He stood and walked past her, scanning the sand for new specimens. Meg turned, watching him intently, knowing it was far more complex than he claimed; then she got up and joined him in the search.

Two hours later they took a break. The sun had moved behind them and the far end of the cove was now in shadow. The tide had turned an hour back and the sea had already encroached upon the sands between the rocks at the cove's mouth. Ben had brought sandwiches in his bag and they shared them now, stretched out on the low rocks, enjoying the late afternoon sunlight, the shells spread out on a cloth to one side.

There were more than a dozen different specimens on the bright green cloth—batswing and turitella, orchid spider and flamingo tongue, goldmouth helmet and striped bonnet, pelican's foot, mother-of-pearl, snakeshead cowrie, and several others—all washed and gleaming in the sun. A whole variety of shapes and sizes and colors, and not one of them native to the cold gray waters of the English south coast.

But Meg knew nothing of that.

It had begun when Meg was only four. There had been a glass display case on the wall in the hallway, and noting what pleasure Meg derived from the form and color of the shells, Hal Shepherd had bought new specimens in the City and brought them back to the Domain. He had scattered them by hand in the cove at low tide and taken Meg back the next day to "find" them. Ben, seven at the time, had understood at once; but had gone along with the deception, not wishing to spoil Meg's obvious enjoyment of the game. And when his father had suggested he rewrite his great-grandfather's book on shells to serve the deception, Ben had leaped at the opportunity. That volume now rested on the shelves in place of the original, a clever, subtle parody of it. Now he, in his turn, carried on his father's game. Only two days ago he had scattered these shells that lay now on the cloth.

Seagulls called lazily, high overhead. He looked up, shielding his eyes, then looked back at Meg. Her eyes were closed, her body sprawled out on the rock like a young lioness. Her limbs and arms and face were heavily tanned, almost brown against the pure white of her shorts and vest. Her dark hair lay in thick long curls against the sun-bleached rock. His eyes, however, were drawn continually to the fullness of her breasts beneath the cloth, to the suggestive curve of leg and hip and groin, the rounded perfection of her shoulders, the silken smoothness of her neck, the strange nakedness of her toes. He shivered and looked away, disturbed by the sudden turn of his thoughts.

So familiar she was, and yet, suddenly, so strange.

"What are you thinking?" she asked softly, almost somnolently.

The wind blew gently, mild, warm against his cheek and arm, then subsided. For a while he listened to the gentle slosh of the waves as they broke on the far side of the great mound of rock.

Meg pulled herself up onto one elbow and looked across at him. As ever, she was smiling. "Well? Cat got your tongue?"

He returned her smile. "You forget. There are no cats."

She shook her head. "You're wrong. Daddy promised me he'd bring one back this time."

"Ah." He nodded, but said nothing of what he was thinking. Another game. Extending the illusion. If their father brought a cat back with him, it too would be a copy—GenSyn, most likely—because the Han had killed all the real cats long ago.

"What are you going to call him?"

She met his eyes teasingly. "Zarathustra, I thought."

He did not rise to her bait. Zarathustra was Nietzsche's poet-philosopher, the scathingly bitter loner who had come down from his mountain hermitage to tell the world that God was dead.

"A good name. Especially for a cat. They're said to be highly independent."

She was watching him expectantly. Seeing it, he laughed. "You'll have to wait, Meg. Tomorrow, I promise you. I'll reveal everything then."

Even the tiny pout she made—so much a part of the young girl he had known all his life—was somehow different today. Transformed—strangely, surprisingly erotic.

"Shells . . ." he said, trying to take his mind from her. "Have you ever thought how like memory they are?"

"Never," she said, laughing, making him think for a moment she had noticed something in his face.

He met her eyes challengingly. "No. Think about it, Meg. Don't most people seal off their pasts behind them stage by stage, just as a mollusk outgrows its shell, sealing the old compartment off behind it?"

She smiled at him, then lay down again, closing her eyes. "Not you. You've said it yourself. It's all still there. Accessible. All you have to do is chip away the rock and there it is, preserved."

"Yes, but there's a likeness even so. That sense of things being embedded that I was talking of. You see, parts of my past *are* compartmentalized. I can remember what's in them, but I can't somehow return to them. I can't feel what it was like to be myself back then."

She opened one eye lazily. "And you want to?"

He stared back at her fiercely. "Yes. More than anything. I want to capture what it felt like. To save it, somehow."

"Hmmm . . ." Her eye was closed again.

"That's it, you see. I want to get inside the shell. To feel what it was like to be there before it was all sealed off to me. Do you understand that?"

"It sounds like pure nostalgia."

He laughed, but his laughter was just a little too sharp. "Maybe . . . but I don't think so."

She seemed wholly relaxed now, as if asleep, her breasts rising and falling slowly. He watched her for a while, disturbed once more by the strength of what he felt. Then he lay down and, following her example, closed his eyes, dozing in the warm sun.

When he woke the sun had moved further down the sky. The shadow of the Wall had stretched to the foot of the rocks beneath them and the tide had almost filled the tiny cove, cutting them off. They would have to wade back. The heavy crash of a wave against the rocks behind him made him twist about sharply. As he turned a seagull cried out harshly close by, startling him. Then he realized Meg was gone.

He got to his feet anxiously. "Meg! Where are you?"

She answered him at once, her voice coming from beyond the huge tumble of rock, contesting with the crash of another wave. "I'm here!"

He climbed the rocks until he was at their summit. Meg was below him, to his left, crouched on a rock only a foot or so above the water, leaning forward, doing something.

"Meg! Come away! It's dangerous!"

He began to climb down. As he did so she turned and stood up straight. "It's okay. I was just—"

He saw her foot slip beneath her on the wet rock. Saw her reach out and steady herself, recovering her footing. And then the wave struck.

It was bigger than all the waves that had preceded it and broke much higher up the rocks, foaming and boiling, sending up a fine spray like glass splintering before some mighty hammer. It hit the big tooth-shaped rock to his right first, then surged along the line, roaring, buffeting the rocks in a frenzy of white water.

One moment Meg was there, the next she was gone. Ben saw the huge wave thrust her against the rocks, then she disappeared beneath the surface. When the water surged back there was no sign of her.

"Meg!!!"

Ben pressed the emergency stud at his neck, then scrambled down the rocks and stood at the edge, ignoring the lesser wave that broke about his feet, peering down into the water, his face a mask of anguish, looking for some sign of her.

At first nothing. Nothing at all. Then . . . *there*! He threw himself forward into the water, thrusting his body down through the chill darkness toward her. Then he was kicking for the surface, one arm gripping her tightly.

Gasping, Ben broke surface some twenty feet out from the rocks and turned onto his back, cradling Meg against him, face up, her head against his neck.

At first the waves helped him, carrying him in toward the rocks, but then he realized what danger he was in. He turned his head and looked. As the wave ebbed, it revealed a sharp, uneven shelf of rock. If he let the waves carry them in, they might be dashed against that shelf. But what other option was there? If he tried to swim around the rocks and into the cove he would be swimming against the current and it would take too long. And he had little time if he was to save Meg. He would have to risk it.

He slowed himself in the water, trying to judge the rise and fall of the waves, then kicked out. The first wave took him halfway to the rocks. The second lifted them violently and carried them almost there.

Almost. The wave was beginning to ebb as he reached out with his left hand and gripped the ledge. As the water surged back a spear of pain jolted through his arm, making him cry out. Then he was falling, his body twisting round, his side banging painfully against the rock.

For a moment it felt as if his hand were being torn from his arm, but he held on, waiting for the water to return, his artificial fingers biting into the rock, Meg gripped tightly against him. And when it came he kicked out fiercely, forcing himself up onto the land, then scrambled backward, pushing desperately with his feet against the rock, away from the water, Meg a dead weight against him.

Ignoring the pain in his hand, he carried Meg up onto a ledge above the water and put her down, fear making his movements urgent. Her lips and the lobes of her ears were tinged with blue.

He tilted her head back, forcing her chin up, then pinched her nose shut with the finger and thumb of his left hand. Leaning over her, he sealed his lips about her open mouth and gave four quick, full breaths.

Ben moved his head back and checked the pulse at her neck. Her heart was still beating. He watched her chest fall, then, leaning forward again, breathed into her mouth, then, three seconds later, once more.

Meg shuddered, then began to gag. Quickly he turned her head, allowing her to bring up seawater and the part-digested sandwich she had eaten only an hour before. Clearing her mouth with his fingers, he tilted her head back again and blew another breath into her, then turned her head again as she gagged a second time. But she was breathing now. Her chest rose and fell, then rose again. Her eyelids fluttered.

Carefully, he turned her over, onto her front, bending her arm and leg to support the lower body, then tilted her chin back to keep the airway open. Her breathing was more normal now, the color returning to her lips.

Ben sat back on his heels, taking a deep breath. She had almost died. His darling Meg had almost died. He shuddered, then felt a faint tremor pass through him like an aftershock. Gods! For a moment he closed his eyes, feeling a strange giddiness, then opened them again and put his hand down to steady himself.

Below him another wave broke heavily against the rocks, throwing up a fine spray. The tide was still rising. Soon they would be cut off completely. Ben looked about him, noting from the length of the shadows how late it was. They had slept too long. He would have to carry her across, and he would have to do it now.

He took a deep breath, preparing himself, then put his arms beneath her and picked her up, turning her over and cradling her, tilting her head back against his upper arm. Then he began to climb, picking his way carefully across the mound of rocks and down, into shadow.

The water was almost waist deep and for the first twenty or thirty feet he lifted Meg up above it, afraid to let the chill get at her again. Then he was carrying her through horseheads of spume little more than knee deep and up onto the shingle.

He set her down on the shingle close to where they had left their sandals. She was still unconscious, but there was color in her cheeks now and a reassuring regularity to her breathing. He looked about him but there was nothing warm to lay over her, nothing to give her to help her body counter the shock it would be feeling.

He hesitated a moment; then, knowing there was nothing else to be done before help arrived, he lay down beside her on the shingle and held her close to him, letting the warmth of his body comfort her.

———

M E G W O K E before the dawn, her whole body tensed, shivering, remembering what had happened. She lay there, breathing deeply, calming herself, staring through the darkness at the far wall where her collection of shells lay in its glass case. She could see nothing, but she knew it was there—conch and cowrie, murex and auger, chambered nautilus and spotted babylon, red mitre and giant chiragra—each treasured and familiar, yet different now; no longer so important to her. She recalled what Ben had said about shells and memory, sealed chambers and growth, and knew she had missed something. He had been trying to say something to her; to seed an idea in her mind. But what?

She reached up, touching the lump on the side of her head gingerly, examining it with her fingers. It was still tender, but it no longer ached. The cut had been superficial and the wound had already dried. She had been lucky. Very lucky.

She sat up, yawning, then became still. There was a vague rustling, then the noise of a window being raised in Ben's room. For a moment she sat there, listening. Then she got up, pulled on her robe and went softly down the passage to his room. Ben was standing at the window, naked, leaning across the sill, staring out into the darkness.

Meg went to him and stood at his side, her hand on the small of his back, looking with him, trying to see what he was seeing. But to her it was only darkness. Her vision was undirected, uninformed.

She felt him shiver and turned her head to look into his face. He was smiling, his eyes bright with some knowledge she had been denied.

"It has something to do with this," he said softly, looking back at her. "With dark and light and their simple interaction. With the sunlight and its absence. So simple that we've nearly always overlooked it. It's there in the Tao, of course, but it's more than a philosophy—more than simply a way of looking at things—it's the very fabric of reality."

He shivered, then smiled at her. "Anyway . . . how are you?"

"I'm fine," she answered in a whisper.

She had a sudden sense of him. Not of his words, of the all-too-simple thing he'd said, but of his presence there beside her. Her hand still lay there on the firm, warm flesh of his back, pressing softly, almost unnoticed against his skin. She could feel his living pulse.

He was still looking at her, his eyes puzzling at something in her face. She looked down at the place where her hand rested against his back, feeling a strange connective flow, stronger than touch, aware of him standing there, watching her; of the tautness, the lean muscularity of his body.

She had never felt this before. Never felt so strange, so conscious of her own physical being, there, in proximity to his own. His nakedness disturbed her and fascinated her, making her take a long slow breath, as if breathing were suddenly hard.

As he turned toward her, her hand slipped across the flesh of his back until it rested against his hip. She shivered, watching his face, his eyes, surprised by the need she found in them.

She closed her eyes, feeling his fingers on her neck, moving down to gently stroke her shoulders. For a moment she felt consciousness slipping, then caught herself, steadying herself against him. Her fingers rested against the smooth channels of his groin, the coarse hair of his sex tickling the knuckles of her thumbs.

She looked down at him and saw how fierce and proud he stood for her. Without thinking she let her right hand move down and brush against his sex.

"Meg . . ." It was a low, desirous sound. His hands moved down her body, lifting her nightgown at the waist until his hands

held her naked hips, his fingers gently caressing the soft smoothness of her flesh. She closed her eyes again, wanting him to go
further, to push down and touch her, there where she ached for
him.

"Meg . . . ?"

She opened her eyes, seeing at once the strange mixture of
fear and hurt, confusion and desire in his eyes.

"It's all right . . ." she whispered, drawing him to her, reassuring him. She led him to the bed and lay there, letting him take
the gown from her.

It hurt. For all his gentleness, his care; it hurt to take him
inside her. And then the pain eased and she found she was
crying, saying his name over and over, softly, breathlessly, as he
moved against her. She responded eagerly, pressing up against
him again and again until his movements told her he was coming. Trembling, she held him tighter, pulling him down into
her, her hands gripping his buttocks, wanting him to spill his
seed inside her. Then, as his whole body convulsed, she gasped,
a wave of pure, almost painful pleasure washing over her. For a
time she lapsed from consciousness; then, with a tiny shudder,
she opened her eyes again.

They lay there, brother and sister, naked on the bloodied bed,
their arms about each other. Ben slept, his chest rising and
falling slowly while she watched its movement closely. She
looked at his face, at his long dark lashes, his fine, straight nose
and firm, full lips. A face the mirror of her own. Narcissistically,
she traced the shape of his lips with her fingers, then let her
hand rest on his neck, feeling the pulse there.

The look of him reminded her of something in Nietzsche,
from the section in the *Zarathustra* called "The Dance Song."
She said the words softly, tenderly, her voice almost a whisper.

> To be sure, I am a forest and a night of dark trees: but he who is
> not afraid of my darkness will find rosebowers too under my
> cypresses.
> And he will surely find too the little god whom girls love best:
> he lies beside the fountain, still, with his eyes closed.

She shivered and looked down the length of their bodies,
studying the differences that gender made between them. The

fullness of her breasts and hips, the slenderness of his. The strangeness of his penis, so very different in rest, so sweet and harmless now; all the brutality, the lovely strength of it dissipated.

She felt a warmth, an achingly sweet tenderness rise up in her, looking at him, seeing how vulnerable he was in sleep. Unguarded and open. A different creature from his waking self. She wanted to kiss him there and wake that tiny bud, making it flower splendidly once more.

Meg closed her eyes and shivered. She knew what they had done. But there was no shame in her, no regret.

She loved him. It was quite simple. Sisters should love their brothers. But her love for him was different in kind. She loved him with more than a simple, sisterly devotion. For a long time she had loved him like this, wholly, without barriers.

And now he knew.

She got up, careful not to disturb him, and put on her gown. For a moment longer she stood there, looking down at his sleeping, perfect form; then she left him, returning to her room.

And as she lay there, her eyes closed, drifting into sleep, her left hand pressed softly against her sex, as if it were his.

━━━◆◆◆━━━

"How's my invalid?"

Beth Shepherd set the tray down on the floor, then went to the window and pulled back the curtains, letting the summer sunlight spill into the room.

Meg opened her eyes slowly, smiling. "I'm fine. Really I am."

Beth sat on the bed beside her daughter and parted her hair, examining the wound. "Hmm. It looks all right. A nice clean cut, anyway." For a moment she held her hand to Meg's brow, then, satisfied that she wasn't feverish, she smiled and began to stroke her daughter's hair.

"I'm sorry . . ." Meg began, but her mother shook her head.

"Ben's told me what happened. It was an accident, that's all. You'll know better in future, won't you?"

Meg nodded. "If it weren't for Ben . . ."

Beth's fingers hesitated, then continued to comb Meg's thick, dark hair. "I'd say that made you even, wouldn't you? A life for a life."

Meg looked up at her, then away. "No. It was different. Totally different. He risked himself. He could have died."

"Maybe. But would you have done less?"

Meg hesitated, then answered quietly. "I guess not." She shivered and looked across at the glass case that held her shells. "You know, I can't imagine what it would be like here without Ben."

Beth smiled. "Nor I. But anyway, have your breakfast. That's if you feel like eating."

Meg laughed. "I'm ravenous, and it smells delicious."

Beth helped Meg sit up, plumping pillows behind her, then took the tray from the floor and set it down on her lap. There were grapefruit and pancakes, fresh orange and coffee, two thick slices of buttered toast and a small pot of honey.

Meg ate heartily, watched by her mother. When she was finished, Beth clapped her hands and laughed. "Goodness, Meg! You should fall in the water more often if it gives you an appetite like that!"

Meg sighed and lay back against the pillows, letting her mother take the tray from her and set it aside. Beth turned back to her, smiling. "Well? Are you staying in bed, or do you want to get up?"

Meg looked down, embarrassed. "I want to talk."

"Okay. What about?"

"About you, and Father. About how you met and fell in love."

Beth laughed, surprised. "Goodness! What brings this on?"

Meg colored slightly. "Nothing. It's just that I realized I didn't know."

"Well . . . all right. I'll tell you." She took a deep breath, then began. "It was like this. When I was eighteen I was a pianist. I played all the great halls of the world, performing before the very highest of First Level society—the *Supernal*, as they call themselves. And then, one day, I was asked to play before the T'ang and his court."

"That must have been exciting."

"Very." She took her daughter's hand and squeezed it gently.

"Anyway, that night, after the performance, everyone was telling me how well I'd played, but I was angry with myself. I had played badly. Not poorly, but by my own standards I had let myself down. And before the T'ang of all people. It seemed that only your father sensed something was wrong. It was he, I later found out, who had arranged the whole affair. He had seen me perform before and knew what I was capable of.

"Well. After the reception he took me aside and asked me if I'd been nervous. I had, of course. It's not every day that an eighteen-year-old is called to perform before one of the Seven. But that wasn't an excuse. I told him how ashamed I was at having let the T'ang down; and to my surprise and chagrin, he agreed with me. Right there and then he took me into the T'ang's own quarters and asking Li Shai Tung's forgiveness for intruding, made me sit at the piano again and play. 'Your best, this time, Elizabeth,' he said. 'Show the T'ang why I boasted of you.' And I did. And this time, with just your father and the T'ang listening, I played better than I'd ever played in my life."

"What did you play? Can you remember?"

Her mother smiled, looking off into the distance. "Yes. It was Beethoven's Sonata in F Minor, the *Appassionata*. It was only when I had finished that I realized I had just committed a capital offense."

Meg's mouth fell open. "Gods! Of course! It's a prohibited piece, isn't it? Like all of Beethoven's work! But what did the T'ang do?"

Beth looked down at her daughter and ruffled her hair. "He clapped. He stood up and applauded me. Then he turned to your father and said, 'I don't know what that was, Hal, and I don't want to know, but you were right to bring the girl back. She's in a class of her own.' "

"And?"

"And for a year, nothing. I thought your father had forgotten me, though I often thought of him and of what he had done for me that evening. But then, out of the blue, I received an invitation from him, asking me to come and visit the Domain."

Meg sat forward eagerly. "And that's when it all happened?"

Beth shook her head. "No. Not at all. I was flattered, naturally, but such a request was impossible to comply with. I was only nineteen. It was six years before I would come of age, and my mother and father would have forbidden me to go even if I had asked them."

"So what did you do?"

Beth laughed. "I did the only thing I could. I sent him an invitation to my next concert."

"And he came?"

"No. What happened next was strange. My father called on me. I hadn't seen him in over six months; and then, the day after I'd sent the note to Hal, there was my father, larger than life, telling me that he'd arranged a husband for me."

Meg's mouth fell open a second time. "A husband?"

"Yes. The son of an old friend of his. A rich young buck with no talent and as little intelligence."

Meg clutched her mother's hands tightly. "And you said no. You told your father you were in love with Hal Shepherd and wanted to marry him. Is that right?"

Beth laughed. "Gods, no. I had no say in it. Anyway, I wasn't in love with your father then. I quite liked him. He was handsome and intelligent, and I felt a kind of . . . affinity with him. But beyond that nothing. Not then, anyway. What I didn't realize, however, was that your father had fallen in love with me. It seems he had spent that whole year trying to forget me, but when he heard about my engagement, he went mad and challenged my intended to a duel."

Meg blinked. "He did *what*?"

"Yes." Beth laughed delightedly. "An old-fashioned duel, with swords."

"*And?*" Meg's eyes were big and round.

"Well . . . My father was horrified, naturally. My fiancé wanted to fight, but Hal had something of a reputation as a swordsman and my father was certain he would kill my future husband. He asked Hal to call on him to try to sort things out."

"And they came to an arrangement?"

Beth leaned forward. "Not straightaway. Though that's not the story my father told. You see, I listened secretly from the next room when they met. My father was angry at first. 'You can't have her,' he said. 'If you kill this man, I'll arrange a marriage with another.' 'Then I'll kill him, too!' Hal said. My father was taken aback. 'And I'll find another suitor. You can't kill them all.' But Hal was determined. His voice rang out defiantly. 'If I have to, I'll kill every last man in Chung Kuo! Don't you see? I *want* your daughter.' "

Beth laughed, then sat back, her face suddenly more thoughtful, her eyes gazing back in time. Then, more quietly, "Gods, Meg. You don't know how thrilling it is to be wanted like that."

Meg watched her mother a moment longer, then looked down, giving a small shudder. "Yes . . . And your father gave in to Hal?"

"Gods, no. He was a stubborn man. And a mercenary one. You see, he'd found out how much Hal was worth by then. All this was a kind of playacting, you understand, to put up the price."

Meg frowned, not understanding.

"He wanted a dowry. Payment for me."

Meg made a small noise of astonishment.

"Yes. And he got it, too. He threatened to stop Hal from marrying me until I was twenty-five unless he paid what he asked."

"And did he?"

"Yes. Twice what my father asked, in fact."

"Why?"

Beth's smile widened. "Because, Hal said, my father didn't know the half of what he had given life to."

Meg was silent for a while, considering. Then she looked up at her mother again. "Did you hate your father?"

Beth hesitated, a sadness in her face. "I didn't know him well enough to hate him, Meg. But what I knew of him I didn't like. He was a little man, for all his talent. Not like Hal." She shook her head gently, a faint smile returning to the corners of her mouth. "No, not like your father at all."

"Where's Ben?" Meg asked, interrupting her mother's reverie.

"Downstairs. He's been up hours, working. He brought a lot of equipment up from the basement and set it up in the living room."

Meg frowned. "What's he up to?"

Beth shook her head. "I don't know. Fulfilling a promise, he said. He said you'd understand."

"Ah . . ." *Shells*, she thought. *It has to do with shells.*
And memory.

———

BEN SAT in a harness at the piano, the dummy cage behind
him, its morph mimicking his stance. A single thin cord of
conduit linked him to the morph. Across the room, a trivee
spider crouched, its program searching for discrepancies of
movement between Ben and the morph. Meg sat down beside
the spider, silent, watching.

A transparent casing covered the back of Ben's head, attached
to the narrow horseshoe collar about his neck. Within the
casing a web of fine cilia made it seem that Ben's blond hair was
streaked with silver. These were direct implants, more than sixty
in all, monitoring brain activity.

Two further cords, finer than the link, led down from the ends
of the collar to Ben's hands, taped to his arms every few inches.
Further hair-fine wires covered Ben's semi-naked body, but the
eye was drawn to the hands.

Fine, flexible links of ice formed crystalline gloves that fitted
like a second skin about his hands. Sensors on their inner
surfaces registered muscular movement and temperature
changes.

Tiny pads were placed all over Ben's body, measuring his
responses and feeding the information back into the collar.

As he turned to face Meg, the morph turned, faceless and yet
familiar in its gestures, its left hand, like Ben's, upon its thigh,
the fingers splayed slightly.

Meg found the duplication frightening—deeply threatening—but said nothing. The piano keyboard, she noted, was
normal except in one respect. Every key was black.

"Call Mother in, Meg. She'd like to hear this."

The morph was faceless, dumb; but in a transparent box at its
feet was a separate facial unit—no more than the unfleshed
suggestion of a face, the musculature replaced by fine wiring. As
Ben spoke, so the half-formed face made the ghost-movements
of speech, its lips and eyes a perfect copy of Ben's own.

Meg did as she was told, bringing her mother from the sunlight of the kitchen into the shadows of the living room. Beth

Shepherd sat beside her daughter, wiping her hands on her apron, attentive to her son.

He began.

His hands flashed over the keys, his fingers living jewels, coaxing a strange, wistful, complex music from the ancient instrument. A new sound from the old keys.

When he had finished, there was a moment's intense silence, then his mother stood and walked across to him. "What *was* that, Ben? I've never heard its like. It was . . ." She laughed, incredulous, delighted. "And I presumed to think that I could teach *you* something!"

"I wrote it," he said simply. "Last night, while you were all asleep."

Ben closed his eyes, letting the dissonances form again in his memory. Long chordal structures of complex dissonances, overlapping and repeating, twisting about each other like the intricate threads of life, the long chains of deoxyribonucleic acid. It was how he saw it. Not A and C and G Minor, but Adenine and Cytosine and Guanine. A complex, living structure.

A perfect mimicry of life.

The morph sat back, relaxing after its efforts, its chest rising and falling, its hands resting on its knees. In the box next to its feet the eyes in the face were closed, the lips barely parted, only a slight flaring of the nostrils indicating life.

Meg shuddered. She had never heard anything so beautiful, nor seen anything so horrible. It was as if Ben were being played. The morph, at its dummy keyboard, seemed far from being the passive recipient of instructions. A strange power emanated from the lifeless thing, making Ben's control of things seem suddenly illusory: the game of some greater, more powerful being, standing unseen behind the painted props.

So this was what Ben had been working on. A shiver of revulsion passed through her. And yet the beauty—the strange, overwhelming beauty of it. She shook her head, not understanding, then stood and went out into the kitchen, afraid for him.

━━━━━

BEN FOUND HER in the rose garden, her back to him, staring out across the bay. He went across and stood there, close by her, conscious more than ever of the naked form of her beneath the soft gauze dress she wore. Her legs were bare, her hair unbraided. The faintest scent of lavender hung about her.

"What's up?" he asked softly. "Didn't you like it?"

She turned her head and gave a tight smile, then looked back. It was answer enough. It had offended her somehow.

He walked past her slowly, then stopped, his back to her, his left hand on his hip, his head tilted slightly to the left, his right hand at his neck, his whole body mimicking her stance. "What didn't you like?"

Normally she would have laughed, knowing he was ragging her, but this time it was different. He heard her sigh and turn away, and wondered, for a moment, if it was to do with what had happened in the night.

She took a step away, then turned back. He had turned to follow her. Now they stood there, face-to-face, a body's length separating them.

"It was . . ." She dropped her eyes, as if embarrassed.

He caught his breath, moved by the sight of her. She might have died. And then he would never have known. He spoke softly, coaxingly, the way she so often spoke to him, drawing him out. "It was what?"

She met his eyes. "It was frightening." He saw her shiver. "I felt . . ." She hesitated, as if brought up against the edge of what she could freely say to him. This reticence was something new in her and unexpected, a result of the change in their relationship. Like something physical in the air between them.

"Shall we walk? Along the shore?"

She hesitated, then smiled faintly. "Okay."

He looked up. The sky was clouding over. "Come. Let's get our boots and coats. It looks like it might rain."

An hour later they were down at the high-water level, their heavy boots sinking into the mud, the sky overcast above them, the creek and the distant water meadows to their left. It was low tide and the mud stretched out to a central channel which meandered like an open vein cut into a dark cheek, glistening like oil whenever the sun broke through the clouds.

For a time they walked in silence, hand in hand, conscious of their new relationship. It felt strange, almost like waking to self-consciousness. Before there had been an intimacy, almost a singularity about them—a seamless continuity of shared experience. They had been a single cell, unbreached. But now? Now it was different. It was as if this new, purely physical intimacy had split that cell, beginning some ancient, inexorable process of division.

Perhaps it was unavoidable. Perhaps, being who they were, they had been fated to come to this. And yet . . .

It remained unstated, yet both felt an acute sense of loss. It was there, implicit in the silence, in the sighs each gave as they walked the shoreline.

Where the beach narrowed, they stopped and sat on a low, gently sloping table of gray rock, side by side, facing back toward the cottage. The flat expanse of mud lay to their right now; while to their left, no more than ten paces away, the steep, packed earth bank was almost twice their height, the thickly interwoven branches of the overhanging trees throwing the foot of the bank into an intense shade. It could not be seen from where they sat, but this stretch of the bank was partly bricked, the rotting timbers of an old construction poking here and there from the weathered surface. Here, four centuries before, French prisoners from the Napoleonic Wars had ended their days, some in moored hulks, some in the makeshift jails that had lined this side of the creek.

Ben thought of those men now. Tried to imagine their suffering, the feeling of homesickness they must have felt, abandoned in a foreign land. But there was something missing in him— some lack of pure experience—that made it hard for him to put himself in their place. He did not know how it felt to be away from home. Here was home and he had always been here. And there, in that lack of knowledge, lay the weakness in his art.

It had begun long before last night. Long before Meg had come to him. And yet last night had been a catalyst—a clarification of all he had been feeling.

He thought of the words his father had quoted back at him and knew they were right. *Ultimately, no one can extract from things, books included, more than he already knows. What one has no access to through experience one has no ear for.*

It was so. For him, at least, what Nietzsche had said was true. And he had no access. Not here.

He was restless. He had been restless for the past twelve months. He realized that now. It had needed something like this to bring it into focus for him. But now he knew. He had to get out.

Even before last night he had been thinking of going to College in the City. To Oxford, maybe, or the Technical School at Strasbourg Canton. But he had been thinking of it only as the natural path for such as he; as a mere furthering of his education. Now, however, he knew there was more to it than that. He needed to see life. To experience life fully, at all its levels. Here he had come so far, but the valley had grown too small for him, too confined. He needed something more—something *other*— than what was here in the Domain.

"If I were to . . ." he began, turning to face Meg, then fell silent, for at the same time she had turned her head and begun to speak to him.

They laughed, embarrassed. It had never happened before. They had always known instinctively when the other was about to speak. But this . . . it was like being strangers.

Meg shivered, then bowed her head slightly, signaling he should speak, afraid to repeat that moment of awkwardness.

Ben watched her a moment. Abruptly, he stood and took three paces, then turned and looked back at her. She was looking up at him from beneath the dark fall of her hair.

"I've got to leave here, Meg."

He saw at once how surprised she was; how much it meant to her. There was a momentary widening of her eyes, the slightest parting of her lips, then she lowered her head. "Ah . . ."

He was silent, watching her. But as he made to speak again, she looked up suddenly, the hurt and anger in her eyes unexpected.

"Why? Is it because of last night?"

He sighed and shook his head. "It has nothing to do with us, Meg. It's me. I feel constrained here. Boxed in. It feels like I've outgrown this place. Used it up."

As he spoke he stared away from her at the creek, the surrounding hills, the small, white-painted cottages scattered among the trees. Overhead, the sky was a lid of ashen gray.

"And I *have to* grow. It's how I am." He looked at her fiercely, defiantly. "I'll die if I stay here much longer, Meg. Can't you see that?"

She shook her head, her voice passionate with disagreement. "It's not so, Ben. You've said it yourself. It's a smaller world in there. You talk of feeling boxed in, here, in the Domain. But you're wrong. *That's* where it's really boxed in. Not here. We're outside of all that. Free of it."

He laughed strangely, then turned aside. "Maybe. But I have to find that out. For myself." He looked back at her. "It's like that business with memory. I thought I knew it all, but I didn't. I was wrong, Meg. I'd assumed too much. So now I've got to find out. Now. While I still can."

Her eyes had followed every movement in his face, noting the intense restlessness there. Now they looked down, away from his. "Then I don't understand you, Ben. There's no hurry. Surely there's no hurry?"

"Ah, but there is."

She looked up in time to see him shrug and turn away, looking out across the mud toward the City.

The City. It was a constant in their lives. Wherever they looked, unless it was to sea, that flat, unfeatured whiteness defined the limits of their world, like a frame about a picture or the edge of some huge encroaching glacier. They had schooled themselves not to see it. But today, with the sky pressed low and featureless above them, it was difficult not to see it as Ben saw it—as a box, containing them.

"Maybe . . ." she said, under her breath. But the very thought of him leaving chilled her to the bone.

He turned, looking back at her. "What were you looking for?"

She frowned. "I don't follow you."

"Before the wave struck. You were about to tell me something. You'd seen something, hadn't you?"

She felt a sudden coldness on the back of her hand and looked. It was a spot of rain. She brushed at it, then looked back at her brother.

"It was a shell. One I'd never seen before. It was attached to the rock but I couldn't free it with my fingers. It was like it was glued there. A strange, ugly-looking shell, hard and ridged, shaped like a nomad's tent."

More spots of rain fell, distinct and heavy. Ben looked up at the sky, then back at her. "We'd best get back. It's going to fall down."

She went to him and took his hand.

"Go," she said. "But not yet. Not just yet."

He leaned forward, kissing her brow, then moved back, looking at her, his dark green eyes seeing nothing but her for that brief moment. "I love you, Megs. Understand that. But I can't help what I am. I have to go. If I don't . . ."

She gave the smallest nod. "I know. Really. I understand."

"Good." This time his lips touched hers gently, then drew away.

She shivered and leaned forward, wanting to kiss him once again, but just then the clouds burst overhead and the rain began to come down heavily, pocking the mud about their feet, soaking their hair and faces in seconds.

"Christ!" he said, raising his voice against the hard, drumming sound of the rain. For a moment neither of them moved; then Meg turned and, pointing to the bank, yelled back at him.

"There! Under the trees!"

Ben shook his head. "No. Come on! There's half a day of rain up there. Let's get back!" He took her hands, tugging at her, then turned and, letting her hands fall from his, began to run back along the shore toward the cottage. She caught up with him and ran beside him, laughing now, sharing his enjoyment of the downpour, knowing—suddenly knowing without doubt—that just as he had to go, so he would be compelled to return. In time. When he had found what he was looking for.

Suddenly he stopped and, laughing, throwing his hands up toward the sky, turned his eyes on her again. "It's beautiful!" he shouted. "It's bloody beautiful!"

"I know!" she answered, looking past him at the bay, the tree-covered hillsides misted by the downpour, the dour-looking cottages on the slope before them.

Yes, she thought. *You'll miss this in the City. There it never rains. Never in ten thousand years.*

CHAPTER SIX

Compulsions

━━━━━━━━━━

THAT NIGHT he dreamed.

He was floating above a desert, high up, the jet-black lavatic sands stretching off to the horizon on every side. Tall spirals of dust moved slowly across the giant plain, like fluted pillars linking heaven and earth. A cold wind blew. Over all, a black sun sat like a sunken eye in a sky of bloodied red.

He had come here from dead lands, deserted lands, where temples to forgotten gods lay in ruins, open to the sky; had drifted over vast mountain ranges, their peaks a uniform black, the purest black he'd ever seen, untouched by snow or ice; had glided over plains of dark, fused glass, where the image of his small, compacted self flew like a Doppelganger under him, soaring to meet him when he fell, falling as he rose. And now he was here, in this empty land, where color ended and silence was a wall within the skull.

Time passed. Then, with a huge, almost animal shudder that shook the air about him, the sands beneath him parted, the great dunes rolling back, revealing the perfect smoothness of a lake, its red-tinged waters like a mirror.

He fell. Turning in the air, he made an arrow of himself, splitting the dark, oily surface cleanly. Down he went, the coal-black liquid smooth, unresistant, flowing about his body like cold fire.

Deep he went, so deep that his ears popped and bled. His

lungs, like flowers, blossomed in the white cage of his chest, bursting, flooding his insides with a fiery hotness. For a moment the blackness was within, seeping into him through every pore; a barrier through which he must pass. Then he was through; freed from his normal, human self. And still he sank, like a spear of iron, down through the blackness; until there, ten miles beneath the surface, the depths were seared with brightness.

The lake's bed was white, like bone; clean and polished and flat, like something made by men. It glowed softly from beneath, as if another land—miraculous and filled, as bright as this was dark—lay on the far side of its hard, unyielding barrier.

He turned his eyes, drawn to something to his left. He swam toward it.

It was a stone. A dark, perfect circle of stone, larger than his palm. It had a soft, almost dusted surface. He touched it, finding it cool and hard. Then, as he watched, it seemed to melt and flow, the upper surface flattening, the thin edge crinkling. Now it was a shell, an oyster, its circumference split by a thin, uneven line of darkness.

His hand went to his waist; he took the scalpel from its tiny sheath, then slipped its edge between the plates. Slowly, reluctantly, they parted, like a moth's wings opening to the sun.

Inside was a pearl of darkness—a tiny egg so dark, so intensely black, that it seemed to draw all light into itself. He reached out to take it; but even as he closed his left hand about the pearl, he felt its coldness burn into his flesh then fall, like a drop of heaven's fire, onto the bed below.

Astonished, he held the hand up before his face and saw the perfect hole the pearl had made. He turned the hand. Right through. The pearl had passed right through.

He shivered. And then the pain came back, like nothing he had ever experienced.

Ben woke and sat upright, beaded in sweat, his left hand held tightly in his right, the pain from it quite real. He stared at it, expecting to see a tiny hole burned through from front to back, but there was no outward sign of what was wrong. It spasmed again, making him cry out, the pain unbelievable—worse than the worst cramp he had ever had.

"Shit!" he said under his breath, annoyed at himself for his weakness. Control the pain, he thought. Learn from it. He gritted his teeth and looked at the timer on the wall beside his bed. It was just after five.

He must have damaged the hand, getting Meg out of the water.

When the pain subsided he got up, cradling the hand against his chest, and began to dress. It was more difficult than he had imagined, for the slightest awkward movement of the hand would put it into spasm again, taking his breath. But eventually it was done and quietly he made his way out and down the passageway.

The door to Meg's room was open. Careful not to wake her, he looked inside. Her bed was to the left against the far wall, the window just above her head. She lay on her stomach, her hair covering her face, her shoulders naked in the shadow, her right arm bent above the covers. The curtains were drawn, the room in partial darkness; but a small gap high up let in a fragment of the early morning sun, a narrow bar of golden light. It traced a contoured line across the covers and up the wall, revealing part of her upper arm. He stared at it a moment, oblivious of the dull pain in his hand, seeing how soft her flesh seemed in this light.

For a moment he hesitated, wondering if he should wake her. *And if he did?*

He shivered, remembering how she had come to him in the night, and felt that same strong stirring of desire. Though it disturbed him, he could not lie to himself. He wanted her. More now than before. Wanted to kiss the softness of her neck and see her turn, warm and smiling, and take him in her arms.

The shiver that ran up his spine was like the feeling he had when listening to an exquisite piece of music or on first viewing a perfect work of art. But how so? he wondered. Or was all art grounded in desire?

The fingers of his damaged hand clenched again. He took a sharp intake of breath against the pain and leaned his shoulder against the doorpost. It was the worst yet and left him feeling cold and weak, his brow beaded with sweat. He would have to have it seen to today. This morning, if possible. But first there was something he must do.

He went down and unlatched the door that led into the garden. Outside the air was sharp, fresh, the sky clear after the rain. Long shadows lay across the glittering, dew-soaked grass, exaggerating every hump and hollow, making the ground seem rutted and uneven. The roses were beaded with dew, the trestle table dark and wet.

He was still a moment, listening to the call of birds in the eaves above him and in the trees down by the water. It was strange how that sound seemed always not to breach but to emphasize the underlying silence.

The pain came again, more bearable this time. He braced himself against it, then, when it was fading, lifted the injured hand to his face. There was the faintest scent of burning. A sweet, quite pleasant scent. He pressed it against his cheek. It was warm. Unnaturally warm.

Cradling the hand against his chest, he stared out across the lawn toward the shadowed bay. The tide was high. Sunlight lay in the trees on the far side of the water, creeping slowly toward the waterline.

He smiled. This much never changed: each day created new, light flying out from everything, three hundred meters in a millionth of a second, off on its journey to infinity.

He went down, across the lawn, and onto the narrow gravel path that led, by way of an old, rickety gate, into the meadows. The grass here was knee high, uncut since his father had left three months earlier, the tall stems richly green and tufted. He waded out into that sea of grass, ignoring the path that cut down to the meandering creek, making for the Wall.

There, at the foot of the Wall, he stopped, balanced at the end of a long rib of rock that protruded above the surrounding marshland. The Wall was an overpowering presence here, the featureless whiteness of its two *li* height making a perfect geometric turn of 120 degrees toward the southeast. It was like being in the corner of a giant's playbox, the shadow of the Wall so deep it seemed almost night. Even so, he could make out the great circle of the Seal quite clearly, there, at the bottom of the Wall, no more than thirty paces distant.

Ben squatted and looked about him. Here memory was dense. Images clustered about him like restless ghosts. He had only to close his eyes to summon them back. There, off to his left, he could see the dead rabbit, sunk into the grass. And there, just beyond it, his father, less than a year ago, looking back toward him but pointing at the Seal, explaining the new policy the Seven had drawn up for dealing with incursions from the Clay. He turned his head. To his right he could see Meg, a hundred, no, a thousand times, smiling or thoughtful, standing and sitting, facing toward him or away, running through the grass or simply standing by the creek, looking outward at the distant hills. Meg as a child, a girl, a woman. Countless images of her. All stored, hoarded in his mind. And for what? Why such endless duplication of events?

He shuddered, then turned, looking back at the cottage, thinking how ageless it seemed in this early morning light. He looked down, then rubbed the back of his left hand with his right, massaging it. It felt better now, more relaxed, which made him think it was some form of cramp. But did machines get cramp?

He breathed deeply, then laughed. And what if we're all machines? What if we're merely programmed to think otherwise?

Then the answer would be yes, machines get cramp.

It was strange, that feeling of compulsion he had had to come here. Overpowering, like his desire for Meg. It frightened him. And even when it was purged, it left him feeling less in control of himself than he had ever been. Part of that, of course, was the drugs—or the absence of them. It was over a week now since he had last taken them. But it was more than that. He was changing. He could feel it in himself. But into what? And for what purpose?

He stared at the Seal a moment longer, then looked away, disturbed. It was like in his dream. The bottom of the lake: that had been the Wall. He had sunk through the darkness to confront the Wall.

And?

He shivered. No, he didn't understand it yet. Perhaps, being what he was—schizophrenic—he *couldn't* understand it. Not from where he was, anyway. Not from the inside. But if he passed through?

He stared at the Wall intently, then looked down. And if his father said no? If his father said he couldn't go to College?

Ben got to his feet, turning his back upon the Wall. If Hal said no he would defy him. He would do it anyway.

━━━━━

"Again, Meg. And this time try to relax a bit. Your fingers are too tense. Stretch them gently. Let them *feel* for the notes. Accuracy is less important than feeling at this stage. Accuracy will come, but the feeling has to be there from the start."

Meg was sitting beside her mother at the piano. It was just after nine and they had been practicing for more than an hour already, but she was determined to master the phrase—to have something to show Ben when he returned.

She began again. This time it seemed to flow better. She missed two notes and one of the chords was badly shaped; yet for all its flaws, it sounded much more like the phrase her mother had played than before. She turned and saw Beth was smiling.

"Good, Meg. Much better. Try it again. This time a little slower."

She did as she was bid, leaning forward over the keys. This time it was note-perfect and she sat back, pleased with herself, feeling a genuine sense of achievement. It was only a small thing, of course—nothing like Ben's achievement—yet it was a start: the first step in her attempt to keep up with him.

She looked around again. Her mother was watching her strangely.

"What is it?"

Beth took her hand. "You're a good child, Meg. You know that? Nothing comes easy to you. Not like Ben. But you work at it. You work hard. And you never get disheartened. I've watched you labor at something for weeks, then seen Ben come along and master it in a few moments. And always—without fail—you've been delighted for him. Not envious, as some might be. Nor bitter. And that's . . ." She laughed. "Well, it's remarkable. And I love you for it."

Meg looked down. "He needs someone."

"Yes. He does, doesn't he?"

"I mean . . ." Meg placed her free hand gently on the keys, making no sound. "It must be difficult being as he is. Being so alone."

"Alone? I don't follow you, Meg."

"Like Zarathustra, up in his cave on the mountainside. Up where the air is rarefied, and few venture. Only with Ben, the mountain, the cave, are in his head."

Beth nodded thoughtfully. "He's certainly different."

"That's what I mean. It's his difference that makes him alone. Even if there were a hundred thousand people here, in the Domain, he would be separate from them all. Cut off by what he is. That's why I have to make the effort. To try to reach him where he is. To try to understand what he is and what he needs."

Beth looked at her daughter, surprised. "Why?"

"Because he's Ben. And because I love him."

She reached out and gently brushed Meg's cheek with her knuckles. "That's nice. But you don't have to worry. Give him time. He'll find someone."

Meg looked away. Her mother didn't understand. There *was* no one else for Ben. No one who would ever understand him a tenth as well. Not one in the whole of Chung Kuo.

"Do you want to play some more?"

Meg shook her head. "Not now. This afternoon, perhaps?"

"All right. Some breakfast, then?"

Meg smiled. "Yes. Why not?"

━━━━━

THEY WERE IN the kitchen, at the big scrubbed-pine table, their meal finished, when there were footsteps on the flagstones outside. The latch creaked, then the door swung outward. Ben stood in the doorway, looking in, his left arm held strangely at his side.

"That smells good."

His mother got up. "Sit down. I'll cook you something."

"Thanks. But not now." He looked at Meg. "Are you free, Megs? I need to talk."

Meg looked across at her mother. She had been about to help her with the washing. "Can I?"

Beth smiled and nodded. "Go on. I'll be all right."

Meg got up, taking her plate to the sink; then she turned back, facing him. "Where have you been . . . ?" She stopped, noticing how he was holding his left arm. "Ben? What have you done?"

He stared at her a moment, then looked toward his mother. "I've damaged the hand. I must have done it on the rocks." He held it out to her. "I can barely use it. If I try to it goes into spasm."

Beth wiped her hands, then went to him. She took the hand carefully and studied it, Meg at her side, her face filled with concern.

"Well, there's no outward sign of damage. And it was working perfectly well yesterday."

Ben nodded. "Yes. But that stint at the piano probably didn't help it any."

"Does it hurt?" Meg asked, her eyes wide.

"It did when I woke up. But I've learned how not to set it off. I pretend the problem's higher up. Here." He tapped his left shoulder with his right hand. "I pretend the whole arm's dead. That way I'm not tempted to try to use the hand."

Beth placed his arm back against his side, then turned away, looking for something in the cupboards. "Have you notified anyone?"

He nodded. "Two hours ago, when I came in from the meadows. They're sending a man this afternoon."

She turned back, a triangle of white cloth between her hands. "Good. Well, for now I'll make a sling for you. That'll ease the strain of carrying it about."

He sat, letting his mother attend to him. Meg, meanwhile, stood beside him, her hand resting gently on his shoulder.

"Why was the keyboard black? I mean, totally black?"

He turned, looking up at her. "Why?"

Meg shrugged. "It's been playing on my mind, that's all. It just seemed . . . strange. Unnecessary."

Beth, kneeling before him, fastening the sling at his shoulder, looked up, interested in what he would say.

He looked away. "It's just that I find the old-style keyboard distracting. It preconditions thought; sets the mind into old patterns. But that all-black keyboard is only a transitional stage. A way of shaking free old associations. Ultimately I want to develop a brand-new keyboard—one better suited to what I'm doing."

"There!" Beth tightened the knot, then stood up. "And what *are* you doing?"

Ben met her eyes candidly. "I don't know yet. Not the all of it, anyway." He stood, moving his shoulder slightly. "Thanks. That's much easier." Then he looked across at Meg. "Are you ready?"

She hesitated, wondering for a moment if she might persuade him to listen to the piano phrase she had learned that morning, then smiled and answered him softly. "Okay. Let's go."

IT WAS LATE morning, the sun high overhead, the air clear and fresh. They sat beneath the trees on the slope overlooking the bay, sunlight through the branches dappling the grass about them, sparkling on the water below. Above them, near the top of the hillside, obscured by a small copse of trees, was the ruined barn, preserved as it had been when their great-great-great-grandfather, Amos, had been a boy.

For two hours they had rehashed the reasons why Ben should leave or stay. Until now it had been a reasonably amicable discussion, a clearing of the air, but things had changed. Now Meg sat there, her head turned away from her brother, angry with him.

"You're just pig stubborn! Did you know that, Ben? Stubborn as in stupid. It's not the time. *Not now.*"

He answered her quietly, knowing he had hurt her. "Then when is the time? I have to do this. I *feel* I have to. And all the rest . . . that's just me rationalizing that feeling. It's the feeling—the instinct—that I trust."

She turned on him, her eyes flashing. "Instinct! Wasn't it you who said that instinct was just a straitjacket—the Great Creator's way of showing us whose fingers are really on the control buttons?"

He laughed, but she turned away from him. For once this was about something other than what *he* wanted. This was to do with Meg, with *her* needs.

"Don't make it hard, Megs. Please don't."

She shivered and stared outward, across the water, her eyes burning, her chin jutting defiantly. "Why ask me? You'll do what you want to anyway. Why torment me like this, when you know you've decided already what you're going to do?"

He watched her, admiring her, wanting to lean forward and kiss her neck, her shoulder. She was wearing a long nut-brown cotton dress that was drawn in below the breasts and buttoned above. The hem of it was gathered about her knees, exposing the tanned flesh of her naked calves. He looked down, studying her feet, noting the delicacy of the toes, the finely rounded nails. She was beautiful. Even her feet were beautiful. But she could not keep him here. Nothing could keep him. He must find himself. Maybe then he could return. But for now . . .

"Don't chain me, Meg. Help me become myself. That's all I'm asking."

She turned angrily, as if to say something, then looked down sharply, her hurt confusion written starkly on her face.

"I want to help you, Ben. I really do. It's just . . ."

He hardened himself against her, against the pity he instinctively felt. She was his sister. His lover. There was no one in the world he was closer to and it was hard to hurt her like this, but hurt her he must, or lose sight of what he must become. In time she would understand this, but for now the ties of love blinded her to what was best. And not just for him, but for the two of them.

"Keep me here, Meg, and it'll die in me. It'll turn inward and fester. You know it will. And I'll blame you for that. Deep down I'll come to hate you for keeping me here. And I never want to hate you. Never."

She met his eyes, her own moist with unshed tears. Then she turned and came to him, holding him, careful not to hurt his damaged arm, her head laid warmly, softly, on his right shoulder.

"Well?" he said after a while. "Will you support me against Father?"

He noticed the slight change in her breathing. Then she moved back away from him, looking at him intently, as if reading something in his face.

"You think he'll try to stop you?"

Ben nodded. "He'll make excuses. The uncertainty of the times. My age."

"But what if he's right, Ben. What if it is too dangerous? What if you *are* too young?"

"Too young? I'm seventeen, Meg. Seventeen! And apart from that one visit to Tongjiang, I've never seen anything other than this; never been anywhere but here."

"And is that so bad?"

"Yes. Because there's more to life than this. Much more. There's a whole new world in there. One I've no real knowledge of. And I need to experience it. Not at second hand, through a screen, but close up."

She looked down. "What you were saying, Ben, about me chaining you. I'd never do that. You know I wouldn't. And I *can* free you. But not in there. Not in the City." She raised her eyes. "This is our place. Right here, in the Domain. It's what we've been made for. Like the missing pieces of a puzzle." She paused, then, more earnestly: "We're not like them, Ben. We're different. Different *in kind*. Like aliens. You'll find that out."

"All part of Amos's great experiment, eh?"

"Maybe . . ." But it wasn't what she had meant. She was thinking less of genetic charts than of something deeper in their natures, some sense of connection with the earth that they had, and that others—cut off by the walls and levels of the City— lacked. It was as if they were at the same time both more and less advanced as human beings: more primitive and yet more exalted spiritually. They were the bridge between heaven and earth, the link between the distant past and the far future. For them, therefore, the City was an irrelevancy—a wrong direction Man had taken—and for Ben to embrace it was simply foolish, a waste of his precious time and talents.

Besides which, she needed him. Needed him as much— though he did not see it yet—as he needed her. It would break her heart to see him go.

"Is that all?" he asked, sensing she had more to say.

She answered him quietly, looking away past him as she spoke. "No. It's more than that. I worry about you. All this business with morphs and mimicry. I fear where it will take you."

"Ah . . ." He smiled and looked down, plucking a tall stem of grass and putting it to his mouth. "You know, Meg, in the past there was a school of thought that associated the artist with Satan. They argued that all art was blasphemy, an abrogation of the role of the Creator. They claimed that all artists set them-

selves up in place of God, making their tiny satanic palaces—
their Pandemoniums—in mimicry of God's eternal City. They
were wrong, of course, but in a sense it's true. All art is a kind of
mimicry, an attempt to get closer to the meaning of things.

"Some so-called artists are less interested in understanding
why things are as they are than in providing a showcase for their
own egotism, but in general true art—art of the kind that *sears*
you—is created from a desire to understand, not to replace.
Mimicry, at that level, is a form of worship."

She laughed softly. "I thought you didn't believe in God."

"I don't. But I believe in the reality of all this that surrounds
us. I believe in natural processes. In the death of stars and the
cycle of the seasons. In the firing of the synapses and the
inexorable decay of the flesh. In the dark and the light."

"And in the City, too?"

He smiled. "That, too, is a process; part of the natural flow of
things, however 'unnatural' it might seem. The City is an expression of human intelligence, which, after all, is a natural
thing. It's too easy to dismiss its artificiality as an antithesis to
nature, when it really is an attempt to simplify and thus begin to
understand the complexity of natural processes."

"And to control those processes."

"Yes, but there are levels of control. For instance, what controls *us* that makes us want to control other things? Is it all just
genetics? And even if it is, what reason is there for that? We've
been asking ourselves that question since DNA was first isolated, and we're still no closer to an answer."

She looked away sharply, as if suddenly tired of the conversation. "I don't know, Ben. It all seems suddenly so bleak. So dark."

Again he misread her comment, mistook its surface content for
its deeper meaning. "Yes," he said, staring out across the water.
"But what is darkness? Is it only a space waiting to be filled? Or
has it a purpose? Something other than simple contrast?"

"Ben . . ."

He looked back at her, surprised by the brittle tone she had
used. She was looking at him strangely. "Yes?"

"What about us? How do we fit in with all these processes?"

"We're a focus, a filter . . ."

But she was shaking her head. "No. I didn't mean that. I

meant *us.* You and me. Is that just process? Just a function of the universe? Is what I feel for you just another fact to be slotted into the great picture? Or is there more to it than that? Are there parts of it that just don't fit?"

Again the bitterness in her voice surprised him. He had thought it was resolved between them, but now he understood: it would never be resolved until he was gone from here.

"Three years," he said. "That's all I'll need. You'll be, what, seventeen—my age now—when I come back. It's not long, Meg. Really it isn't."

She stood, moving away, then stood at the edge of the trees, above him, her back turned.

"You talk of dying if you stay. But I'll die if you go. Don't you understand that, Ben? Without you here it'll be like I'm dead." She turned to him, her eyes wide with hurt and anger. "You're my eyes, my ears, the animating force behind each moment of my day. Without you, I don't exist!"

He gave a short laugh, surprised by her intensity. "But that's silly, Meg. Of course you exist. Besides, there's Mother . . ."

"Gods! You really *don't* understand, do you?"

There was that same strange, unreadable movement in her face; then, abruptly, she turned away, beginning to climb the slope.

Ben got up awkwardly and began to follow her, making his way between the trees, careful not to knock his useless arm; but she was running now, her whole body leaning into the slope as she struggled to get away from him.

At the edge of the trees he stopped, wincing from the sudden pain in his hand, then called out to her. "Meg! Stop! Please stop!"

She slowed and stood there, just below the barn, her back to him, her head lowered, waiting.

Coming to her, he moved around her, then lifted her face with his good hand. She was crying.

"Meg . . ." he said softly, torn by what he saw. "Please don't cry. There's no reason to cry. Really there isn't."

She swallowed, then looked aside, for a moment like a hurt four-year-old. Then, more defiantly, she met his eyes again, bringing up a hand to wipe the tears away.

"I love you," he said gently. "You know that."

"Then make love to me again."

He laughed, but his eyes were serious. "What, here?"

She stared back at him challengingly. "Why not?"

He turned her slightly. From where they stood they could see the cottage clearly down below.

She turned back, her eyes watching him closely, studying his face. "All right. Up there, then. In the barn."

He turned and looked, then nodded, a shiver passing down his spine.

She reached down, taking his good hand, then led him up the slope. At the barn door she turned, drawing him close, her arms about his neck. It was a long passionate kiss, and when she pulled away from him her eyes were different. Older than he remembered them, more knowing. A stranger's eyes.

She turned and led him through. Inside, the barn was filled with shadows. Bars of sunlight, some broad, some narrow, slanted down from gaps between the planks that formed the sides of the barn, creating broken veils of light from left to right.

"Quick," she said, leading him further in, "before Mother calls us in for lunch."

He smiled and let himself be led, thrilled by the simple pressure of her hand against his own.

"Here," she said, looking about her. A barrier of wooden slats formed a stall in the far left-hand corner, a space the size of a small storeroom, filled waist-high with old hay. The warm, musty smell of the hay was strong but pleasant. Light, intruding from two knotholes higher up, laced the shadows with twin threads of gold. Meg turned and smiled at him. "Lie down. I'll lie on top of you."

He sat, easing himself down onto the hay, feeling it yield beneath him, then let his head fall back, taking care not to jolt his hand. Lying there, looking up at her, his left arm still cradled in its sling, he felt like laughing.

"Are you sure this is such a good idea?"

Her smile, strange, enigmatic at first, widened as she slowly undid the buttons at the front of her dress, then pulled it up over her shoulders. Beneath the dress she was naked.

Ben felt his breath catch in his throat. "Meg . . ."

She bent over him and eased the sling from his arm, then straddled him, the soft, warm weight of her pressed down against him as she began to unbutton his shirt.

Meg's face lay but a short space from his face, her lips slightly parted, the tip of her tongue peeping through, her eyes concentrating on her busy fingers. But Ben's eyes were drawn to her breasts, to the hard, provocative shapes of her nipples.

He reached up and cupped her left breast in his hand, feeling its smooth warmness, then eased forward until his lips brushed against the budlike nipple.

Meg shuddered, her fingers faltering a moment. Ben drew back slightly, looking up into her face once more. Her eyes were closed, her lips parted more fully, reminding him fleetingly of one of those ancient paintings of religious ecstasy. He shivered, then leaned forward again, drawing the breast back to his mouth, his tongue wetly tracing the stiff brown berry of the nipple, teasing it with his teeth and lips and tongue, conscious of Meg pressing herself down into him with each small motion.

He lay back again, ignoring the dull pain of the reawakened pulse in his hand, watching as her eyes slowly opened, smiling back at him.

For a while he lay there, letting her undress him. Then she climbed above him again, the smooth warmth of her flesh against his own making him shiver with anticipation.

"Close your eyes . . ."

He lay there, letting her make love to him, slowly at first, then, as the ancient rhythm took her, wildly, urgently; her hands gripping his shoulders tightly, her face changed, unrecognizable, her teeth clenched fiercely, her eyes staring wildly down at him. In it he saw a reflection of the agony he was suffering from his damaged hand. That lay beside him, quivering, the fingers clenched tight, trapped in a prolonged spasm that was as painful as her lovemaking was delightful. Faster and more furious she moved, until, with a shudder that brought on his own orgasm, she arched her back and cried out, forcing herself against him as if to breach him: as if to press through the flesh that separated them and *become* him.

Afterward he lay still, the pain in his hand ebbing slowly.

Meg lay across him, sleeping, her dark hair fanned across his chest. Two small bands of light lay across their shadowed bodies like golden ribbons joining their flesh, striping them at chest and hip, tracing the contours of their expired lust.

Ben looked down the length of their bodies, studying the play of shadow within shadow, noting where flesh seemed to merge with flesh. The scent of their lovemaking filled the tiny space, mingling with the smell of old hay. It seemed part of the shadows, the dust-specked bands of light.

He closed his eyes, thinking. What had she meant by this? To show her love for him? Her need? Perhaps. But needs were of different kinds. She had been wrong earlier. Though she thought so now, she would not die for missing him. She would wait, as she always waited, knowing he would be back. But he— he *had* to go. He would go mad—literally, mad—if he did not leave this place. Each day now it grew worse. Each day the feeling grew in him, feeding his restlessness, stoking the fire of dissatisfaction that raged in his belly.

Out. He had to get out. Or "in" as she preferred to call it. Whichever, he had to get away. Far away from here. Even from those he loved.

"Ben . . . ! Meg . . . !"

The calls were muted, distant, from the slope below the barn. Meg stirred and lifted her head slowly, turning to face him.

"What's that?"

He smiled and leaned forward, kissing her nose. "It's all right. It's only Mother calling us in. It must be lunchtime."

"Ah . . ." She started to relax again, then pushed herself up abruptly, suddenly awake. "Only Mother!"

"Mind—" he said, wincing at the pain that shot up his arm where she had bumped into his hand.

Her face was all concern. "Oh, Ben, I'm sorry . . ."

Then they were laughing, clutching each other, Ben's hand held out to one side as he embraced her. And outside, more distantly, moving away from them now, the call came again.

"Ben . . . ! Meg . . . !"

BETH STOOD in the gateway at the bottom of the lower garden, relaxed, her apron tied loosely about her dress, waiting for them. She had let her hair down and she was smiling.

"Where were you?" she said as they came up to her. "I was looking everywhere. Didn't you hear me calling?"

Meg looked away, but Ben went straight to his mother. "We were in the barn," he said casually. "It was warm in there and musty. We were talking, then we fell asleep. We must have missed you calling."

"I see," she said, smiling, ruffling his hair.

"I'm sorry," he said, falling in beside her while Meg walked on ahead. "Lunch isn't spoiled, I hope."

Beth smiled and shook her head. "I wasn't calling you for lunch. It's your father. He's home."

Meg turned. "Daddy . . ." Then, without a further word, she raced up the slope and disappeared inside the house.

Ben walked beside his mother, taking her arm. "Is he okay?"

"What do you mean?"

Ben stopped, looking at her. Her voice had seemed strange, her answer too defensive. His query had been politeness, but she had taken it for something more meaningful.

"What's wrong with him?" he asked.

Beth looked away. "I don't know. He seems much older, somehow. Tired." She shrugged.

"Perhaps it's overwork. Things have been bad in there."

"Yes . . ." She smiled wistfully. "Maybe that's it."

They walked on. Up ahead, from inside the cottage, they could hear Meg's squeals of delight. Then she appeared, cradling what looked like a tiny, animated fur hat. She thrust the bundle at Ben.

"Isn't he just adorable?"

Ben held the kitten up to his face, meeting its strange, alien eyes. "Hello there, Mog. I'm Ben."

Meg took the kitten back at once. "Don't hurt him. And it's not Mog. It's Zarathustra."

"Of course." Ben reached out and rubbed the kitten between the ears, then moved past Meg into the doorway.

His father was sitting just inside, in the deep shadow of the hallway. Seeing Ben, his face creased into a smile.

"Ben! How are you, lad?"

"I'm fine," he answered, moving inside, feeling his mother's hand on his shoulder. "And you, Father?"

"I've been busy. Run ragged, you might say. I feel like I've put the whole world to rights these last few days."

Hal Shepherd sat back in the tall-backed, armless chair, his arms stretched wide in a gesture of expansiveness. The old fire still burned in his eyes, but Ben could see at once that he was ill. He saw the lines of tiredness and strain, the redness at the corner of his eyes, the way his muscles stood out at his neck when he spoke, and knew it was more than simple fatigue.

"The kitten's beautiful. What is it? GenSyn?"

Hal shook his head. "No, Ben. It's a real kitten. We confiscated its parents from Madam Moore the day the warrant was signed for her husband's arrest. It seems there are a few cats left in the Wilds. Moore must have smuggled it in through quarantine for her."

"Or bribed his way."

"More likely . . ." Hal took a deep breath—awkwardly, Ben thought—then smiled again. "I brought something back for you, too, Ben."

"A dog?"

Hal laughed, for a moment almost his old, vital self. "Now that *would* be something, wouldn't it? But no, I'm afraid not. Although I've a feeling that, as far as you're concerned, you might find it a lot more interesting than a dog."

"What is it?"

Hal's smile remained while he studied his son; as if this was a sight he had not expected to see again. Then with a brief glance past him, at Beth, he said, "It's downstairs. In the cellar workrooms. I've rigged one of them up ready for you to try."

Ben frowned, trying to work out what his father meant, then he understood. "It's a *pai pi*! You've brought back a *pai pi*!"

"Not one, Ben. Eight of them."

"Eight!" Ben laughed, astonished. "Christ! Where did you get them? I thought they'd all been destroyed years ago. They've been banned for more than sixty years, haven't they?"

"That's right. But there are collectors among the Above. Men who secretly hold on to banned technology. These were found in the collection of a First-Level Executive."

Ben understood at once. "The Confiscations . . ."

"Exactly. The man was a Dispersionist. We were going to destroy them; but when I told Li Shai Tung of your interest, he signed a special order permitting me to take them out of the City. Here in the Domain, you see, the Edict has no power. We Shepherds can do as we wish."

"Can I try one now?"

Beth, her hand still on Ben's shoulder, answered for her husband. "Of course. Meg and I will get dinner ready while you're downstairs."

Meg, coming in from outside, protested. "That's unfair! Why can't I join them?"

Hal laughed. "Well . . . Ben might be a bit embarrassed."

"What do you mean?" Meg asked, cuddling the struggling kitten under her chin.

"Just that it's a full-body experience. Ben has to be naked in the harness."

Meg laughed. "Is that all?" She turned away slightly, a faint color in her cheeks. "He was practically naked when he was working with the morph."

Hal looked at his son, narrowing his eyes. "You've been using the morph, Ben? What for?"

"I'll tell you," Ben said, watching Meg a moment, surprised by her sudden rebelliousness. "But later. After I've tried the *pai pi.*"

━━━━

THE CELLARS beneath the cottage had been added in his great-great-grandfather's time, but it was only in the last decade that his father had set up a studio in one of the large, low-ceilinged rooms. Beneath stark artificial lighting, electronic equipment filled two-thirds of the floor space, a narrow corridor between the freestanding racks leading to a cluttered desk by the far wall. To the left of the desk a curtain had been drawn across, concealing the open space beyond.

Ben went through. The eight *pai pi* lay on the desk, the small, dark, rectangular cases small enough to fit into the palm of his hand. He picked them up, one at a time, surprised by the weight of them. They looked like lozenges or like the "chops" executives used to seal official documents, each one imprinted with the logo of the manufacturing company. *Pai pi*—the name meant, literally, "a hundred pens"—provided full-body experiences, a medium that had blossomed briefly in the earliest days of the City as an entertainment for the very rich. The cassettes themselves were only the software, the operational instructions; the hardware stood off to one side.

Hal pulled back a curtain. "There! What do you think?"

The couch was a work of art in itself, its curved, boatlike sides inlaid in pearl and ivory, the dark, see-through hood shaped like the lid of an ancient sarcophagus. At present the hood was pulled back, like a giant insect's wing, exposing the padded interior. Dark blue silks—the same blue-black the sky takes on before the dark—masked the internal workings of the machine, while depressed into the padded silk was a crude human shape. Like the instruments of some delicious mechanism of torture, fine filaments extended from all parts of the depression, the threadlike wires clustered particularly thickly about the head. These were the "hundred pens" from which the art form derived its name, though there were only eighty-one in actuality. When the machine was operational, these input points fed information to all the major loci of nerves in the recipient's body.

"It's beautiful," said Ben, going close and examining the couch with his fingers. He bent and sniffed at the slightly musty innards. "I wonder if he used it much?"

It was a deceptively simple device. A tiny, one-man dream palace. You laid down and were connected up; then, when the hood was lowered, you began to dream. Dreams that were supposed to be as real as waking.

He turned, facing his father again. "Have you tried it out?"

"One of the technicians did. With permission, of course."

"And?"

Hal smiled. "Why don't you get in? Try it for yourself."

He hesitated, then began to strip off, barely conscious of his father watching, the fascination of the machine casting a spell over him. Naked, he turned, facing his father. "What now?"

Hal came up beside him, his movements slower, heavier, than Ben remembered, then bent down beside the machine and unfolded a set of steps.

"Climb inside, Ben. I'll wire you up."

Fifteen minutes later he was ready, the filaments attached, the hood lowered. With an unexpected abruptness it began.

He was walking in a park, the solid shapes of trees and buildings surrounding him on every side. Overhead the sky seemed odd. Then he realized he was inside the City and the sky was a ceiling fifty *ch'i* above him. He was aware of the ghostly sense of movement in his arms and legs, of the nebulous presence of other people about him, but nothing clear. Everything seemed schematic, imprecise. Even so, the overall illusion of walking in a park was very strong.

A figure approached him, growing clearer as it came closer, as if forming ghostlike from a mist of nothingness. A surly-looking youth, holding a knife.

The youth's mouth moved. Words came to Ben, echoing across the space between them.

"Hand over your money or I'll cut you!"

He felt his body tense, his mouth move and form words. They drifted out from him, unconnected to anything he was thinking.

"Try and get it, scumbag!"

Time seemed to slow. He felt himself move backward as the youth lunged with the knife. Turning, he grabbed the youth's arm and twisted, making the knife fall from his hand. He felt a tingle of excitement pass through him. The moment had seemed so real, the arm so solid and actual. Then the youth was falling away from him, stumbling on the ground, and he was following up, his leg kicking out, straight and hard, catching the youth in the side.

He felt the two ribs break under the impact of his kick, the sound—exaggerated for effect—seeming to fill the park. He moved away—back to normal time now—hearing the youth moan, then hawk up blood, the gobbet richly, garishly red.

He felt the urge to kick again, but his body was moving back, turning away, a wash of artificial satisfaction passing through him.

Then, as abruptly as it began, it ended.

Through the darkened glass of the hood he saw the dark shape of his father lean across and take the cassette from the slot. A moment later the catches that held down the hood were released with a hiss of air and the canopy began to lift.

"Well? What do you think?"

"I don't know," Ben answered thoughtfully. "In some ways it's quite powerful. For a moment or two the illusion really had me in its grasp. But it was only for a moment."

"What's wrong with it, then?"

Ben tried to sit up but found himself restrained.

"Here, let me do that."

He lay back, relaxing as his father freed the tiny suction pads from the flesh at the back of his scalp and neck.

"Well . . ." Ben began, then laughed. "For a start it's much too crude."

Hal laughed with him. "What did you expect, Ben? Perfection? It was a complex medium. Think of the disciplines involved."

"I have been. And that's what I mean. It lacks all subtlety. What's more, it ends at the flesh."

"How do you mean?"

"These . . ." He pulled one of the tiny suckers from his arm. "They provide only the vaguest sensation of movement. Only the shadow of the actuality. If they were somehow connected directly to the nerves, the muscles, then the illusion would be more complete. Likewise the connections at the head. Why not input them direct into the brain?"

"It was tried, Ben. They found that it caused all kind of problems."

"What kind of problems?"

"Muscular atrophy. Seizures. Catalepsy."

Ben frowned. "I don't see why. You're hardly in there longer than three minutes."

"In that case, yes. But there were longer tapes. Some as long as half an hour. Continual use of them brought on the symptoms."

"I still don't see why. It's only the sensation of movement, after all."

"One of the reasons they were banned was because they were

so addictive. Especially the more garish productions, the sex and violence stims, for instance. After a while, you see, the body begins to respond to the illusion: the lips form the words, the muscles make the movements. It's that unconscious mimicry that did the damage. It led to loss of control over motor activity and, in a few cases, to death."

Ben peeled the remaining filaments from his body and climbed out.

"Why were the tapes so short?"

"Again, that's due to the complexity of the medium. Think of it, Ben. It's not just a question of creating the visual backdrop—the environment—but of synchronizing muscular movement to fit into that backdrop."

"Nothing a good computer couldn't do, surely?"

"Maybe. But only if someone were skilled enough to program it to do the job in the first place."

Ben began to pull his shirt on, then paused, shaking his head. "There were other things wrong with it, too. The hood, for instance. That's wrong. I had a sense all the while of the world beyond the machine. Not only that, but there was a faint humming noise—a vibration—underlying everything. Both things served to distance me from the illusion. They reminded me, if only at some deep, subconscious level, that I *was* inside a machine. That it *was* a fiction."

Hal went over to the desk and sat, the strain of standing for so long showing in his face. "Is that so bad, Ben? Surely you have the same in any art form? You know that the book in your hands is just paper and ink, the film you're watching an effect of light on celluloid, a painting the result of spreading oils on a two-dimensional canvas. The medium is always there, surely?"

"Yes. But it doesn't have to be. Not in this case. That's what's so exciting about it. For the first time ever you can dispense with the sense of 'medium' and have the experience direct, unfiltered."

"I don't follow you, Ben. Surely you'll always be aware that you're lying inside a machine, no matter how good the fiction?"

"Why?" Ben buttoned the shirt, pulled on his pants and trousers, and went over to his father, standing over him, his eyes burning. "What if you could get rid of *all* the distractions? Wouldn't that change the very nature of the fiction you were creating? Imagine it! It would seem as real as this now—as me talking to you here, now, you sitting there, me standing, the warm smell of oil and machinery surrounding us, the light just so, the temperature just so. Everything as it is. Real. As real as real, anyway."

"Impossible," Hal said softly, looking away. "You could never make something that good."

"Why not?" Ben turned away a moment, his whole body fired by a sudden enthusiasm. "What's preventing me from doing it? Nothing. Nothing but my own will."

Hal shrugged, then looked back at his son, a faint smile of admiration lighting his tired features momentarily. "Perhaps. But it's not as easy as that, Ben. That little clip you experienced. How long do you think it was?"

Ben considered. "Two minutes. Maybe slightly longer."

Hal laughed, then grew more serious. "It was two minutes and fourteen seconds, and yet it took a team of eight men more than three weeks to make. It's a complex form, Ben. I keep telling you that. To do what you're talking about, well, it would take a huge team of men years to achieve."

Ben turned, facing his father, his face suddenly very still. "Or a single man a lifetime?"

Hal narrowed his eyes. "What do you mean?"

"I mean myself. My calling. For months now I've been experimenting with the morph. Trying to capture certain things. To mimic them, then reproduce them on a tape. But this . . . these *pai pi* . . . they're the same kind of thing. Stores of experience. Shells, filled with the very yolk of being. Or at least they could be."

"Shells . . . I like that. It's a good name for them."

Strangely, Ben smiled. "Yes. It is, isn't it. Shells."

Hal studied his son a moment longer then looked down. "I had another reason for showing these to you. Something more selfish."

"Selfish?"

"Yes. Something I want you to help me with."

"Ah . . ."

The hesitation in Ben's face surprised him. "There's something I have to ask you first," Ben said quickly. "Something I need from you."

Hal sat back slightly. So Beth was right. Ben *was* restless here. Yes, he could see it now. "You want to leave here. Is that it?"

Ben nodded.

"And so you can. But not now. Not just yet."

"Then when?"

Again, the hardness in Ben's voice was unexpected. He had changed a great deal in the last few months. Had grown, become his own man.

"Three months. Is that so long to wait?"

Ben was still a moment, considering, then shook his head. "No. I guess not. You'll get me into Oxford?"

"Wherever you want. I've already spoken to the T'ang."

Ben's eyes widened with surprise.

Hal leaned forward, concealing his amusement, and met his son's eyes defiantly. "You think I don't know how it feels?" He laughed. "You forget I was born here, too. And I, too, was seventeen once, believe it or not. I know what it's like, that feeling of missing out on life. I know it all too well. But I want something from you in return. I want you to help me."

Ben took a breath, then nodded. "All right. But how?"

Hal hesitated, then looked away. "I want to make a *pai pi* . . . a shell. For your mother. Something she can keep."

Ben frowned. "I don't understand. Why? And what kind of shell?"

Hal looked up slowly. He seemed suddenly embarrassed, awkward. "Of myself. But it's to be a surprise. A present. For her birthday."

Ben watched his father a moment, then turned and looked back at the ornate casing of the machine. "Then we should make a few changes to that, don't you think? It looks like a coffin."

Hal shuddered. "I know . . ."

"We should get workmen in . . ." Ben began, turning back, then stopped as he saw how his father was staring down at his hands. Hands that were trembling like the hands of a very old man.

Ben's voice was almost a whisper. "What's wrong?"

He saw how his father folded his hands together, then looked up, a forced smile shutting out the fear that had momentarily taken hold of his features.

"It's nothing. I . . ."

He stopped and turned. Meg was standing just behind him. She had entered silently.

"The man's come," she said hesitantly.

"The man?"

Meg looked from one to the other, disturbed by the strange tension in the room; aware that she had interrupted something. "The man from ProsTek. He's come to see to Ben's hand."

"Ben's hand?" Hal turned, looking across at Ben, then he laughed. A brief, colorless laugh. "Of course. Your mother said."

Ben's eyes didn't leave his father for a moment. "Thanks. Tell Mother I'll be up."

She hesitated, wanting to ask him what was wrong, but she could see from the look of him that she was excluded from this.

"Ben?"

Still he didn't look at her. "Go on. I told you. I'll be up."

She stood there a moment longer, surprised and hurt by the sudden curtness in his voice. Then, angered, she turned and ran back down the space between the racks and up the steps.

At the top of the steps she stopped, calming herself. Hal had said no. That was it! And now Ben was angry with her, because she didn't want him to go either. Meg shivered, her anger suddenly washed from her; then, giving a soft laugh of delight, she pushed the door open and went through.

▬▬▬▬▬

THE HAND LAY on the table, filaments trailing from the precisely severed wrist like fine strands of hair. It was not like the other hand. This one shone silver in the light, its surfaces soft and fluid like mercury. Yet its form suggested heaviness and strength. Meg, staring at it from across the room, could imagine the being from which it had been cut: a tall, faceless creature with limbs on which the sunlight danced like liquid fire. She could see him striding through the grass below the cottage. See the wood of the door splinter like matchwood before his fist.

She shuddered and turned, looking back at the man kneeling at Ben's side. As she looked he glanced up at her and smiled: a polite, pleasant smile. He was a Han. Lin Hou Ying, his name was. A tiny, delicate man in his sixties, with hands that were so small they seemed like a child's. Hands so doll-like and delicate, in fact, that she had asked him if they were real.

"These?" He held them up to her, as if for her appraisal. Then he had laughed. "These hands are mine. I was born with them. But as to what is real . . ."

He had almost finished removing the damaged hand by now. As she watched, he leaned close, easing the pressure on the vise that held the hand, then bent down and selected one of the tiny instruments from the case on the floor beside his knee. For a moment longer he was busy, leaning over the hand, making the final few adjustments that would disconnect it.

"There," he said, finally, leaning back and looking up into Ben's face. "How does that feel?"

Ben lifted his left arm up toward his face, then turned it, studying the clean line of the stump. "It's strange," he said, after a moment. "The pain's gone. And yet it feels as if the hand's still there. I can flex my fingers now and they don't hurt."

Lin Hou Ying smiled. "Good. That's a sure sign it was only the unit that was damaged. If you had twisted it badly or damaged the nerve connections it might have been more difficult. As it is, I can fit you with a temporary unit until the old one is repaired."

"That thing there?"

Lin glanced across. "Yes. I'm sorry it's so ugly."

"No. Not at all. I think it's quite beautiful."

Meg laughed uncomfortably. "No. *Shih* Lin's right. It's ugly. Brutal."

"It's only a machine," Ben answered her, surprised by the vehemence, the bitterness in her voice. "It has no life other than that which we give it."

"It's horrible," she insisted. "Like the morph. Like all such things."

Ben shrugged and looked back at Lin Hou Ying. "Does it function like the other one?"

The small man had been studying the hand in the vise, probing it with one of the tiny scalpels. He looked up, smiling.

"In certain ways, yes; but in others it's a vast improvement on this model here. Things have changed greatly in the last five years. Prosthetics among them. The response time's much enhanced. It's stronger, too. And in that particular model"—he indicated the hand on the table with a delicate motion of his head—"there's a remote override."

Ben stared at it a moment, then looked back at Lin Hou Ying. "Why's that?"

Lin stood and went across to the carrying case that stood on the floor beside the table. Earlier he had taken the hand from it. "Look," he said, taking something from inside. "Here's the rest of the unit."

It was an arm. A silver arm. Ben laughed. "How much more of him have you?"

Lin laughed, then brought the arm across. In his other hand he held a control box. "Some of our customers have lost far more than you, *Shih* Shepherd. The arm is a simple mechanism. It is easy to construct one. But a hand. Well, a hand is a complex thing. Think of the diversity of movements it's possible to make with a hand. Rather than waste our efforts making a single unit of hand and arm together, we decided long ago to specialize—to concentrate on the hands. And this"—he handed Ben the control box—"controls the hand."

"Can I?"

Lin lowered his head slightly. "As you wish, *Shih* Shepherd."

For a while Ben experimented, making the fingers bend and stretch, the hand flex and clench. Then he turned it and made it scuttle, slowly, awkwardly, like a damaged crab, on the table's surface.

Ben set the box down. "Can I keep this?"

Lin bowed his head. "Of course. And the arm?"

Ben laughed, then looked across at Meg and saw how she was watching him. He looked down. "No. Take the arm."

Just then the door at the far end of the room opened and his mother came in, carrying a small tray. Behind her came the kitten, Zarathustra.

"Refreshments, *Shih* Lin?"

The small man bowed low. "You honor me, *nu shi.*"

Beth started to put the tray down on the table beside the silver hand, but as she did so, the kitten jumped up on the chair beside her and climbed up onto the table.

"Hey . . ."

Meg made to move forward, but Ben reached out, holding her arm with his right hand. "No. Leave him. He's only playing."

His mother turned, looking at him.

"There," he said, indicating a small table to one side of the room.

He watched her go across and put the tray down, then looked back at the kitten. It was sniffing at the fingers of the hand and lifting its head inquisitively.

"Don't . . ." Meg said quietly.

He half-turned, looking at her. "I won't hurt it."

"No," she said, brushing his hand aside and moving across to lift the kitten and cradle it. "He's real. Understand? Don't toy with him."

He watched her a moment, then looked down at the control box in his lap. *Real,* he thought. *But how real is real? For if all I am is a machine of blood and bone, of nerve and flesh, then to what end do I function? How real am I?*

Machines of flesh. The phrase echoed in his head. And then he laughed. A cold, distant laughter.

"What is it, Ben?"

He looked up, meeting his mother's eyes. "Nothing."

He was quiet a moment, then he turned, looking across at the Han. "Relax a while, *Shih* Lin. I must find my father. There's something I need to ask him."

———

HE FOUND HAL in the dining room, the curtains drawn, the door to the kitchen pulled to. In the left-hand corner of the room there was a low table on which were set the miniature apple trees the T'ang had given the Shepherds five years before.

The joined trees were a symbol of conjugal happiness, the apple an omen of peace but also of illness.

His father was kneeling there in the darkened room, his back to Ben, his forearms stretched out across the low table's surface, resting on either side of the tree, his head bent forward. He was very still, as if asleep or meditating; but Ben, who had come silently to the doorway, knew at once that his father had been crying.

"What is it?" he said softly.

Hal's shoulders tensed; slowly his head came up. He stood and turned, facing his son, wiping the tears away brusquely, his eyes fierce, proud.

"Shut the door. I don't want your mother to hear. Nor Meg."

Ben closed the door behind him, then turned back, noting how intently his father was watching him, as if to preserve it all. He smiled faintly. Yes, he thought, there's far more of me in you than I ever realized. Brothers, we are. I know it now for certain.

"Well?" he asked again, his voice strangely gentle. He had often questioned his own capacity for love, wondering whether what he felt was merely some further form of self-delusion; yet now, seeing his father there, his head bowed, defeated, beside the tiny tree, he knew beyond all doubt that he loved him.

Hal's chest rose and fell in a heavy, shuddering movement. "I'm dying, Ben. I've got cancer."

"Cancer?" Ben laughed in disbelief. "But that's impossible. They can cure cancers, can't they?"

Hal smiled grimly. "Usually, yes. But this is a new kind, an artificial carcinoma, tailored specifically for me, it seems. Designed to take my immune system apart piece by piece. It was *Shih* Berdichev's parting gift."

Ben swallowed. Dying. No. It wasn't possible. Slowly he shook his head.

"I'm sorry, Ben, but it's true. I've known it these last two months. They can delay its effects, but not for long. The T'ang's doctors give me two years. Maybe less. So you see, I've not much time to set things right. To do all the things I should have done before."

"What things?"

"Things like the shell."

For a moment Ben's mind missed its footing. Shells . . . He thought of Meg and the beach and saw the huge wave splinter along the toothlike rocks until it crashed against her, dragging her back, away beneath the foaming surface, then heard himself screaming—*Meg!!!*—while he stood there on the higher rocks, impotent to help.

He shivered and looked away, suddenly, violently displaced. Shells . . . Like the stone in the dream, the dark pearl that passed like a tiny, burning star of nothingness through his palm. For a moment he stared in disbelief at where his hand ought to have been; then he understood.

"What is it, Ben?"

He looked up. "I don't know. I've never . . ."

He stopped. It was like a wave of pure darkness hitting him. A sheer black cliff of nothingness erasing all thought, all being from him. He staggered and almost fell; then he was himself again, his father's hands holding his upper arms tightly, his heavily lined face thrust close to his own, the dark green eyes filled with concern and fear.

"Ben? Ben? What is it?"

"Darkness," he whispered. "It was like . . ."

Like what? He shuddered violently. And then the earlier thing came back to him. Shells . . . *Pai pi.* That was what his father meant. And that was why they had to make one. Because he was dying. Yes. It all made sense now.

"Like what?" his father asked, fleshing the thought.

"Nothing," he answered, calmer now. "The shell. I understand it now."

"Good. Then you'll help me sketch things out for the team?"

Ben frowned. "Team? What team?"

The pressure of Hal's hands on Ben's arms had eased, but he made no move to take them away. "I've arranged for a team of technicians to come here and work with us on the shell. I thought we could originate material for them."

Ben looked down. For a long time he was silent, thoughtful. Then he looked up again. "But why do that? Why can't we do the whole thing?"

Hal laughed. "Don't be daft, Ben."

"No. I'm serious. Why *can't* we do the whole thing?"

"Didn't you hear me earlier? It would take ages. And I haven't got ages. Besides, I thought you wanted to get away from here. To Oxford."

"I do. But this . . ." He breathed deeply, then smiled and reached up to touch his father's face with his one good hand. "I love you. So trust me. Three months. It's long enough, I promise you."

He saw the movement in his father's face; the movements of control, of pride and love and a fierce anger that it should need such a thing to bring them to this point of openness. Then he nodded, tears in his eyes. "You're mad, Ben, but yes. Why not? The T'ang can spare me."

"Mad . . ." Ben was still a moment, then he laughed and held his father to him tightly. "Yes. But where would I be without my madness?"

BEN TURNED from the open kitchen window. Behind him the moon blazed down from a clear black sky, speckled with stars. His eyes were dark and wide, like pools, reflecting the immensity he had turned from.

"What makes it all real?"

His mother paused, the ladle held above the casserole, the smell of the steaming rabbit stew filling the kitchen. She looked across at her son, then moved ladle to plate, spilling its contents beside the potatoes and string beans. She laughed and handed it to him. "Here."

She was a clever woman. Clever enough to recognize that she had given birth to something quite other than she had expected. A strange, almost alien creature. She studied her son as he took the plate from her, seeing how his eyes took in everything, as if to store it all away. His eyes devoured the world. She smiled and looked down. There was a real intensity in him—such an intellectual hunger as would power a dozen others.

Ben put his plate down, then sat, pulling his chair in closer to the table. "I'm not being rhetorical. It's a question. An honest-to-goodness question."

She laughed. "I don't know. It seems almost impertinent to ask."

"Why?"

She shrugged. It was scarcely the easiest of questions to raise at the dinner table. Who made the Universe? he might as well have asked. Or Why is Life? Who knew what the answer was?

Rabbit stew, maybe. She laughed.

Ben had gone very quiet, very watchful. A living microscope, quivering with expectancy.

"Two things come to mind," she said, letting the ladle rest in the pot. "And they seem to conflict with each other. The first is the sense that it'll all turn out exactly as we expect it. What would you call that?—a sense of continuity, perhaps. But not just that. There's also a sense we have that it *will* all continue, just as it ever did, and not just stop dead suddenly."

"And the second?" It was Meg. She was standing in the doorway, watching them.

Beth smiled and began ladling stew into a plate for her.

"The second's the complete opposite of the first. It's our ability to be shocked, surprised, or horrified by things we ought to have seen coming. Like death . . ." Her voice tailed off.

"A paradox," said Ben, looking down. He took a spoon from the table and began to ladle up the stock from his plate, as if it were a soup. Then he paused and nodded. "Yes. But how can I use that knowledge?"

There he had her. She in a lifetime had never fathomed that. She turned to Meg, offering her the plate. "Where's Father?"

"He'll be down. He said there was something he had to do."

She watched Meg take her place, then began to pour stew into another plate. It was unlike Hal to be late to table. But Hal had changed. Something had happened. Something he couldn't bring himself to tell her just yet.

"I'm sorry to keep you, Beth." Hal was standing in the doorway, something small hidden behind his back. He smiled, then came forward, offering something to her.

"What is it?" She wiped her hands on her apron, then took the tiny present from him.

He sat, then leaned back, his arms stretched wide in a gesture of expansiveness. The old fire still burned in his eyes, but she could see that he was unwell.

She shivered and looked down at the tiny parcel, then, with a brief smile at him, began unwrapping it.

It was a case. A tiny jewel case. She opened it, then looked up, surprised.

"Hal . . . It's beautiful!"

She held it up. It was a silver ring. And set into the ring was a tiny drop-shaped pearl. A pearl the color of the night.

Meg leaned forward excitedly, "It *is* beautiful! But I thought all pearls were white . . ."

"Most are. Normally they're selected for the purity of their color and luster—all discolored pearls being discarded. But in this instance the pearl was so discolored that it attained a kind of purity of its own."

Beth studied the pearl a moment, delighted, then looked up again. Only then did she notice Ben, sitting there, his spoon set down, his mouth fallen open.

"Ben?"

She saw him shiver, then reach out to cover the cold, silvered form of his left hand with the fleshed warmth of his right. It was a strangely disturbing gesture.

"I had a dream," he said, his eyes never leaving the ring. "The pearl was in it."

Meg laughed. "Don't listen to him. He's teasing you."

"No." He had turned the silvered hand and was rubbing at its palm, as if at some irritation there. "It was in the dream. A pearl as dark as nothingness itself. I picked it up and it burned its way through my palm. That's when I woke. That's when I knew I'd damaged the hand."

Hal was looking at his son, concerned. "How odd. I mean, it wasn't until this morning, just as I was leaving, that Tolonen brought it to me. He knew I was looking for something special. Something unusual. So your dream preceded it." He laughed strangely. "Perhaps you willed it here."

Ben hesitated, then shook his head. "No. It's serendipity, that's all. Coincidence. The odds are high, but . . ."

"But real," Meg said. "Coincidence. It's how things are, isn't it? Part of the real."

Beth saw how Ben's eyes lit at that. He had been trying to fit it into things. But now Meg had placed it for him. Had *allowed* it. But it was strange. Very strange. A hint that there was more to life than what they experienced through their senses. Another level, hidden from them, revealed only in dreams.

She slipped the ring on, then went across to Hal and knelt beside him to kiss him. "Thank you, my love. It's beautiful."

"Like you," he said, his eyes lighting momentarily.

She laughed and stood. "Well. Let's have some supper, eh? Before it all goes cold."

Hal nodded and drew his chair in to the table. "Fine. Oh, by the way, Ben, I've some news."

Ben looked across and picked up his spoon again. "About the team?"

"No. About the other thing. I've arranged it."

"Ah . . ." Ben glanced at Meg, then bent his head slightly, spooning stew into his mouth.

"What other thing?" Meg asked, looking at Ben, a sudden hardness in her face.

Ben stared down at his plate. "You know. Oxford. Father's said I can go."

There was a moment's silence; then, abruptly, Meg pushed her plate away and stood. "Then you *are* going?"

He turned and looked at her, a strange defiance in his eyes. "Yes."

She stood there a moment longer, then turned away, storming out down the steps. They could hear her feet pounding on the stairs. A moment later a door slammed. Then there was silence.

Ben looked across and met his mother's eyes. "She's bound to take it hard."

Beth looked at her son, then away to the open window. "Well . . ." She sighed. "I suppose you can't stay here forever." She looked down, beginning to fill her own plate. "When do you plan to go?"

"Three months," Hal answered for him. "Ben's going to work on something with me before then. Something new."

She turned, looking at Hal, surprised. "So you'll be here?"

But before Hal could answer, Ben pushed back his chair and stood. "I'd best go to her. See she's all right."

"There's no need . . ." she began. But Ben had already gone. Down the steps and away through the dining room, leaving her alone with Hal.

"You're ill," she said, letting her concern for him show at last.

"Yes," he said. "I'm ill."

T H E D O O R W A S partly open, the room beyond in shadow. Through the window on the far side of the room the moon shone, cold and white and distant. Meg sat on her bed, her head and shoulder turned from him, the moonlight glistening in her long dark hair.

He shivered, struck by the beauty of her, then stepped inside.

"Meg . . ." he whispered. "Meg, I've got to talk to you."

She didn't move; didn't answer him. He moved past her, looking out across the bay, conscious of how the meadows, the water, the trees of the far bank—all were silvered by the clear, unnatural light. Barren, reflected light; no strength or life in it. Nothing grew in that light. Nothing but the darkness.

He looked down. There, on the bedside table, beside the dull silver of his hand, lay a book. He lifted it and looked. It was Nietzsche's *Zarathustra*, the Hans Old etching on the cover. From the ancient paper cover Nietzsche stared out at the world, fierce-eyed and bushy browed, uncompromising in the ferocity of his gaze. So he himself would be. So he would stare back at the world, with an honest contempt for the falseness of its values. He opened the book where the leather bookmark was and read the words Meg had underlined. *To be sure, I am a forest and a night of dark trees. . . .* Beside it, in the margin, she had written "Ben." He felt a small shiver pass down his spine, then set the book down, turning to look at her again.

"Are you angry with me?"

She made a small noise of disgust. He hesitated, then reached out and lifted her chin gently with his good hand, turning her face into the light. Her cheeks were wet, her eyes liquid with tears, but her eyes were angry.

"You want it all, don't you?"

"Why not? If it's there to be had?"

"And never mind who you hurt?"

"You can't breathe fresh air without hurting someone. People bind each other with obligation. Tie each other down. Make one another suffocate in old, used-up air. I thought you understood that, Meg. I thought we'd agreed?"

"Oh yes," she said bitterly. "We agreed all right. You told me how it would be and what my choices were. Take it or leave it. I had no say."

"And you wanted a say?"

She hesitated, then drew her face back, looking down, away from him. "I don't know . . . I just feel . . . hurt by it all. It feels like you're rejecting me. Pushing me away."

He reached out again, this time with his other hand, not thinking. She pushed it from her, shuddering. And when she looked up, he could see the aversion in her eyes.

"There's a part of you that's like that, Ben. Cold. Brutal. Mechanical. It's not all of you. Not yet. But what you're doing, what you plan . . . I've said it before, but it's true. I fear for you. Fear that that—" she pointed to the hand—"will take you over, cell by cell, like some awful, insidious disease, changing you to its own kind of thing. It won't show on the surface, of course, but I'll know. I'll see it in your eyes, and know it from the coldness of your touch. That's what I fear. That's what hurts. Not you going, but your reasons for going."

He was silent for a moment, then he sat down next to her. "I see."

She was watching him, the bitterness purged now from her eyes. She had said it now, had brought to the surface what was eating at her. She reached out and took his hand—his human hand—and held it loosely.

"What do you want, Ben? What, more than anything, do you want?"

He said it without hesitation; almost, it seemed, without thought. "Perfection. Some pure and perfect form."

She shivered and looked away. Perfection. Like the hand. Or like the moonlight. Something dead. "Do you love me?"

She heard him sigh; sensed the impatience in him. "You know I do."

She turned slightly, looking at him, her smile sad, resigned now. Letting his hand fall from hers, she stood and lifted her dress up over her head, then lay down on the bed beside him, naked, pulling him down toward her.

"Then make love to me."

As he slipped from his clothes she watched him, knowing that for all his words, this much was genuine—this need of his for her.

You asked what's real, she thought. *This—this alone is real. This thing between us. This unworded darkness in which we meet and merge. This and this only. Until we die.*

"I love you," he said softly, looking down at her. "You know that."

"Yes," she said, closing her eyes, shuddering as he pressed down into her. "I know . . ."

And yet it wasn't enough. For him it would never be enough.

PART 3 | AUTUMN 2206

An Inch of Ashes

The East wind sighs, the fine rains come:
Beyond the pool of water-lilies, the noise of faint thunder.
A gold toad gnaws the lock. Open it, burn the incense.
A tiger of jade pulls the rope. Draw from the well and escape.
Chia's daughter peeped through the screen when Han the clerk
    was young,
The goddess of the river left her pillow for the great Prince of
    Wei.
Never let your heart open with the spring flowers:
One inch of love is an inch of ashes.

—LI SHANG-YIN, *Untitled Poem*, *ninth century A.D.*

CHAPTER SEVEN

The Pool in the Ruins

ERVANTS CAME running to take their horses, leading them back to the stables. Fei Yen seemed flushed, excited by the ride, her eyes wide with enjoyment. Li Yuan laughed, looking at her, and touched her arm.

"It suits you, my love. You should ride more often."

Tsu Ma came up and stood between them, an arm about each of their shoulders. "That was good, my friends. And this"—he gestured with his head, his strong neck turning to encompass the huge estate, the palace, the lake, the orchards, the view of the distant mountains—"it's beautiful. Why, the ancient emperors would envy you."

Tsu Ma's eyes sparkled and his pure white teeth—strong, square, well-formed teeth—flashed a smile.

"You are welcome here any time, Tsu Ma," Li Yuan answered him. "You must treat our stables as your own."

"Thank you, Li Yuan." Tsu Ma gave a slight bow, then turned, looking down at Fei Yen. "You ride well, Lady Fei. Where did you learn?"

She looked away, a slight color in her cheeks. "I've ridden since I was a child. My father had two horses." She turned back, the way she held her head displaying an intense pride. In a world where animals were rare, to own two horses was a matter of some prestige. Only the Seven took such things for granted.

Tsu Ma studied her a moment, then nodded. "Good. But let us go in. Your father will be expecting us."

Li Shai Tung was sitting in the Summer House, a small comset on his lap. Tiny three-dimensional holograms formed and faded in the air above the set, each figure giving its brief report before it vanished. Tsu Ma sat close by the old man, keeping silent, while Li Yuan went to get drinks. Fei Yen stood by the window looking down the steep slope toward the terrace and the ornamental lake. From time to time she would glance back into the room, her eyes coming to rest on the casually seated figure of Tsu Ma.

He was a broad-shouldered, handsome man. Riding, she had noticed how straight he held himself in the saddle, how unruffled he had been when leading his horse across a fast-flowing stream, how easily he brought his mount to jump a wall, as though he were part of the animal he rode. And yet he was immaculate, his hair groomed and beaded with rubies, his tunic an achingly sweet shade of pink that was almost white, edged with black, his trousers of a blue that reminded her of the summer skies of her youth. She had seen how tightly his thighs had gripped the flanks of the roan horse; how commanding he had seemed.

Li Shai Tung finished his business and put the comset down, smiling at Tsu Ma, then at his daughter-in-law, greeting them wordlessly. Li Yuan turned from the cabinet, carrying a tray of drinks. He was host here in this room.

Fei Yen took her drink and seated herself beside her husband, facing the other men. She was conscious of how Tsu Ma looked at her. So open. And yet not impolitely.

"You're looking well," Li Shai Tung said, looking across at Fei Yen. "You should ride more often."

Li Yuan leaned forward. "She was magnificent, Father. A born horsewoman! You should have seen how she leaped the meadow gate!" His eyes flashed wide as he said it, and when he looked at his wife it was with unfeigned admiration. Tsu Ma saw this and pushed his head back slightly, as if his collar were too tight. He reached into the inner pocket of his tunic and took out a slender silver case.

"May I smoke?" He held out the case and Li Yuan nodded, looking to his father for approval. The old man said nothing, merely smiled.

Tsu Ma removed one of the pencil-thin cheroots and lit it, then inhaled slowly, seeming to relax in his chair as he did so. The silver case lay on the arm of the chair.

He watched the smoke curl up, a thin, fragile thread of heated ash. "I must thank you, Li Yuan. Today has been perfect." His eyes settled on the young man's face, finding nothing but open friendship there, perhaps even a degree of admiration. He was used to it; accepted it as his due. But the look on Fei Yen's face— that was different. That, too, he recognized, but kept the knowledge to himself. He raised his glass, toasting his host and hostess silently, his smile serene, sincere.

Li Shai Tung watched all, nodding to himself. He seemed well pleased with things. For the first time in months he was smiling. Tsu Ma saw this and asked him why.

"I'll tell you. When we are alone."

The T'ang had not looked at Fei Yen, and his comment seemed quite innocuous, but she knew how traditional her father-in-law was. He was not like her own father; he would not discuss business in front of women. She set her drink down untouched and stood up, patting Li Yuan's hand, then turned to bow low to the two T'ang.

"Excuse me, *Chieh Hsia*, but I must go and change. The ride has made me tired."

It was untrue. She had never felt more alive. Her eyes shone with a barely contained excitement. But she lowered her head and went quietly from the room, turning only at the door to look back, finding, as she'd hoped, that Tsu Ma's eyes were on her.

"Well?" said Tsu Ma when she had gone. His manner seemed no different, and yet the word seemed somehow colder, more masculine than before.

"Good news. Both Wu Shih and Wei Feng have agreed to our little scheme."

Tsu Ma looked down. The development was unexpected. "Is that wise?"

"I thought so," Li Shai Tung continued, noting his hesitation. "In the present circumstances I felt it . . . safer . . . to have the balance of the Council know of my plans. It would not do to alienate my oldest friends."

Tsu Ma drew on the cheroot again, then looked up, meeting

his eyes. "No. But that's not exactly what I meant. This whole business of covert action. Surely it goes against the spirit of the Council? If we can't be open with each other—"

"And can we?" Li Yuan's words were bitter, angry, but at a look from his father he lowered his head, holding his tongue.

"I understand your feelings, Li Yuan," Tsu Ma answered him, smiling at the old T'ang to show he was not offended by his son's interruption. "But Wang Sau-leyan must surely not be allowed to triumph. This way, it seems we play into his hands."

Li Shai Tung was watching him closely. "Then you will not give your consent?"

Tsu Ma's smile broadened. "That is not what I said. I was merely pointing out the underlying logic of this course. Whatever you decide I will consent to, my father's oldest friend. And not only because of my respect for my father. I know you would not follow this course if there were any other way."

Li Shai Tung smiled then looked down into his lap. "If it helps reassure you, Tsu Ma, I will say to you what I have already said both to Wu Shih and Wei Feng. I do not wish to circumvent the Council in this matter. This is merely a question of research. A fact-finding exercise before I present my case to Council. The brief of the Project will be to study only the feasibility of wiring up Chung Kuo's population. It will fall far short of actual experimentation. After all, it would not do for me, a T'ang, to breach the Edict, would it?"

Tsu Ma laughed. "No, indeed. But tell me . . . who did you have in mind to look after the Project? It's a sensitive scheme. The security on it must be watertight."

"I agree. Which is why I'm placing Marshal Tolonen in charge."

"Tolonen?" Tsu Ma considered it a moment, then smiled. "Why, yes, I can see that that would work very well."

He met the old T'ang's eyes, a look of understanding passing between them that escaped the young Prince's notice. For Tolonen would be opposed to the scheme. He, if anyone, would be guaranteed to keep it in check.

"But see, I've talked enough already, and you still know so little about the scheme itself. Let Li Yuan speak for me now. Let him be my voice in this matter."

Tsu Ma looked across at the young man, interested. This was why he had come: to hear Li Yuan's proposal in detail. "Speak," he said, his left hand outstretched, palm open. A broad hand with long fingers clustered with heavy rings. Smoke curled up from beneath the hand.

Li Yuan hesitated; then, composing himself, he began itemizing the discoveries they had made at various SimFic establishments, discoveries that had broken the Edict—things meant to harm the Seven, now harnessed for their use.

Tsu Ma listened, drawing on the cheroot from time to time, his smile growing broader by the moment. Until, finally, he laughed and clapped his hand against his thigh.

"Excellent! My word, it *is* excellent." He rose and went to the window, looking down the slope. "You have my agreement, Li Shai Tung. I like this plan. I like it very much."

Tsu Ma turned, looking back at the young man. Li Yuan was smiling broadly, pleased with himself, proud of his scheme, and delighted that he had Tsu Ma's approval. Tsu Ma smiled back at him and nodded, then turned to the window again.

At the bottom of the slope, on the terrace above the ornamental lake, a woman was walking, looking back toward the house. She wore riding clothes and her long dark hair hung loose where she had just unfastened it. She was small, delicate, like a goddess made of the finest porcelain. Tsu Ma smiled and looked away; he turned to face the two men in the room with him.

"Yes," he said, the smile remaining on his lips. "It's perfect, Yuan. Quite perfect."

"Who is he?"

DeVore turned to Lehmann and smiled. "His name is Hung Mien-lo and he was Chancellor to Wang Ta-hung before his recent death."

Lehmann studied the screen a moment longer, then turned his back on it, staring at DeVore. "So what is he doing there?"

The film had been shot secretly by DeVore's man among the *Ping Tiao*. It showed a meeting Jan Mach had had that morning. A meeting he had been very anxious to keep a secret from the other *Ping Tiao* leaders.

"I don't know. But I'm sure of one thing. He wouldn't be there unless Wang Sau-leyan wanted him there. So the real question is—what does Wang Sau-leyan want of the *Ping Tiao*?"

"So Hung is the new T'ang's man now?"

"It seems so. Fischer, my man in Alexandria, thinks Sau-leyan wasn't responsible for his brother's death, but there's good reason to believe that Hung Mien-lo has been his man for some time now."

"And Mach? Why didn't he consult the others?"

"That's Mach's way. He didn't like it when I went to Gesell direct. If he'd had his way he would have checked me out beforehand, but I circumvented him. He doesn't like that. It rankles him. He likes to be in control of things."

"But you think he'll deal with Hung Mien-lo?"

DeVore nodded. "It makes sense. If I were he I'd do the same. He'll get what he can out of the T'ang. And he'll use that to keep us at a distance. To make the *Ping Tiao* less dependent on us. And, conversely, he'll use the alliance with us to keep the T'ang at a distance. It'll mean the *Ping Tiao* won't have to accept what either of us tell them to do. It'll give them the option to say no now and again. Mach will try to keep the deal with us secret from the T'ang, and vice versa. He'll try to make it seem as if the change—the strengthening of their position—comes from within the *Ping Tiao*."

Lehmann was silent awhile, thoughtful. "Then why not kill Hung Mien-lo and prevent Mach from making this deal? There has to be a reason."

DeVore smiled, pleased with his young lieutenant. He always enjoyed talking out his thoughts with him.

"There is. You see, Mach's scheme works only if we're unaware of the T'ang's role in things, if we're fooled by his tales of a great *Ping Tiao* renaissance. Oh, their fortunes will be on the up after Helmstadt, there's no doubt, but a deal with the T'ang could give them something they lack. Something they didn't get from Helmstadt. Funds."

"And you *want* that? You want them to be independently funded?"

"No. Not if that were all there was to it. But I don't intend to let them bargain with me. At the first sign of it I'll threaten to pull out altogether. That would leave them in a worse position than they began, because all the T'ang can offer them is money. They'd lose our contacts, our specialist knowledge, our expertise in battle. And the rest of the Bremen map . . ."

"I see. And then there's the question of what Wang Sau-leyan wants from this?"

"Exactly. He wouldn't risk contacting the *Ping Tiao* unless he had some scheme in mind. T'ang or not, if the other members of the Council of Seven heard of his involvement he would be dead."

Lehmann glanced at the screen. "It's a thought . . ."

"Yes. There's always that option. If things get really bad and we need something to divert the Seven."

"Then what do you intend to do?"

DeVore leaned forward and pressed the pad to clear the screen. At once the lights came up again.

"At present nothing. Mach is meeting Hung Mien-Lo again. In Alexandria in two weeks time. My man will be there to record it for me. It might be interesting, don't you think? And—who knows?—Mach might even give the T'ang his father's ears back."

———————

THE NIGHT WAS clear and dark, the moon a sharp crescent to the northeast, high above the distant outline of the mountains. It was a warm night. Laughter drifted across the water as the long, high-sided boat made its way out across the lake, the lanterns swinging gently on either side.

Tsu Ma had insisted on taking the oars. He pulled the light craft through the water effortlessly, his handsome mouth formed into a smile, his back held straight, the muscles of his upper arms rippling beneath his silks like the flanks of a running horse. Li Yuan sat behind Tsu Ma in the stern, looking past him at Fei Yen and her cousin, Yin Wu Tsai.

The two girls had their heads together, giggling behind their fans. It had been Fei Yen's idea to have a midnight picnic, and Tsu Ma had been delighted when the two girls had come to them with blankets and a basket, interrupting their talk. The two men had smiled and laughed and let themselves be led out onto the lake.

Li Yuan grinned broadly, enjoying himself. In the varicolored light from the lanterns Fei Yen looked wonderful, like a fairy princess or some mythical creature conjured from the rich legends of his people's past. The flickering patterns of the light made her face seem insubstantial, like something you might glimpse in a dream but which, when you came closer or held a clear light up to see it better, would fade or change back to its true form. He smiled at the fancifulness of the thought, then caught his breath, seeing how her eyes flashed as she laughed at something her cousin had whispered in her ear. And then she looked across at him, her dark eyes smiling, and his blood seemed to catch fire in his veins.

He shuddered, filled by the sight of her. She was his. *His.*

Fei Yen turned, looking out behind her, then turned back, leaning toward Tsu Ma. "To the island, Tsu Ma. To the island . . ."

Tsu Ma bowed his head. "Whatever you say, my Lady."

The boat began to turn. Beyond the temple on the small hill the lake curved like a swallow's wing. Near the wing's tip was a tiny island, reached by a wooden bridge of three spans. Servants had prepared it earlier. As they rounded the point, they could see it clearly, the bridge and the tiny two-tiered pagoda lit by colored lanterns.

Li Yuan stared across the water, delighted, then looked back at Fei Yen.

"It's beautiful, you clever thing. When did you plan all this?"

Fei Yen laughed and looked down, clearly pleased by his praise. "This afternoon. After we'd been riding. I . . . I did it for our guest, husband."

Tsu Ma slowed his stroke momentarily and bowed his head to Fei Yen. "I am touched, my Lady. You do me great honor."

Li Yuan watched the exchange, his breast filled with pride for his wife. She was so clever to have thought of it. It was just the right touch. The perfect end to a perfect day. The kind of thing a man would remember for the rest of his days. Yes, he could imagine it now, forty years from now, he and Tsu Ma, standing on the terrace by the lake, looking back . . .

She had even been clever enough to provide an escort for the T'ang, a clever, pretty woman who was certain to delight Tsu Ma. Indeed, had Fei Yen not been in the boat, he would have allowed himself to concede that Wu Tsai was herself quite beautiful.

For a moment he studied the two women, comparing them. Wu Tsai was taller than Fei Yen, her face, like her body, longer and somehow grosser, her nose broader, her lips fuller, her cheekbones less refined, her neck stronger, her breasts more prominent beneath the silk of her jacket. Yet it was only by contrast with Fei Yen that these things were noticeable: as if in Fei Yen lay the very archetype of Han beauty; and all else, however fine in itself, was but a flawed copy of that perfection.

The island drew near. Li Yuan leaned forward, instructing Tsu Ma where to land. Then the boat was moored and Tsu Ma was handing the girls up onto the wooden jetty, the soft rustle of their silks as they disembarked seeming, for that brief moment, to merge with the silken darkness of the night and the sweetness of their perfume.

They settled on the terrace, Fei Yen busying herself laying out the table while Wu Tsai sat and made pleasant conversation with Tsu Ma. Li Yuan stood at the rail, looking out across the darkness of the lake, his sense of ease, of inner stillness, lulling him so that for a time he seemed aware only of the dull murmur of the voices behind him and the soft lapping of the water against the wooden posts of the jetty. Then there was the light touch of a hand on his shoulder and he turned to find Fei Yen there, smiling up at him.

"Please, husband. Come sit with us."

He put his arms about her and lowered his face to meet her lips, then came and sat with them. Fei Yen stood by a tiny table to one side, pouring wine into cups from a porcelain jug; offering first to the T'ang, then to her husband, finally to her cousin. Only then did she give a little bow and pouring herself some wine, settle, kneeling at her husband's side.

Tsu Ma studied them both a moment, then raised his cup. "You are a lucky man, Li Yuan, to have such a wife. May your marriage be blessed with many sons!"

Li Yuan bowed his head, inordinately pleased. But it was no more than the truth. He *was* lucky. He looked down at the woman kneeling by his side and felt his chest tighten with his love for her. *His.* It was three days now since the wedding and yet he could not look at her without thinking that. *His.* Of all the men in Chung Kuo, only he was allowed this richness, this lifelong measure of perfection. He shivered and raised his cup, looking back at Tsu Ma.

"To friendship!" he offered, meeting Tsu Ma's eyes. "To we four, here tonight, and to our eternal friendship!"

Tsu Ma leaned forward, his teeth flashing as he smiled. "Yes. To friendship!" He clinked his cup against Li Yuan's, then raised it in offering, first to Wu Tsai and finally to Fei Yen.

Fei Yen had been looking up from beneath her lashes, her pose the very image of demure, obedient womanhood. At Tsu Ma's toast, however, she looked down sharply, as if abashed. But it was not bashfulness that made her avert her eyes; it was a deeper, stronger feeling, one that she tried to hide not only from the watchful T'ang, but from herself. She turned her head, looking up at Li Yuan.

"Would my husband like more wine?"

Li Yuan smiled back at her, handsome in his own way, and loving, too—a good man for all his apparent coldness. Yet her blood didn't thrill at his touch, nor did her heart race in her chest the way it was racing now in the presence of Tsu Ma.

"In a while, my love," he answered her. "But see to our guest first. Tsu Ma's cup is almost empty."

She bowed her head and, setting down her cup, went to fetch the wine jug. Tsu Ma had turned slightly in his seat and now sat there, his booted legs spread, one hand clasping his knee, the other holding out his cup. Turning, seeing him like that, Fei Yen caught her breath. It was so like the way Han Ch'in had used to sit, his strong legs spread arrogantly, his broad hands resting on his knees. She bowed deeply, hiding her sudden confusion, holding out the jug before her.

"Well . . . ?" Li Yuan prompted, making her start and spill some of the wine.

Tsu Ma laughed, a soft, generous laughter that made her look up at him again and meet his eyes. Yes, there was no doubting it; he knew what she was thinking. Knew the effect he had had on her.

She poured the wine then backed away, her head bowed, her throat suddenly dry, her heart pounding. Setting the jug down, she settled at her husband's feet again, but now she was barely conscious of Li Yuan. The whole world had suddenly turned about. She knelt there, her head lowered, trying to still the sudden tremor of her hands, the violent beating of her heart, but the sight of his booted feet beneath the table held her eyes. She stared at them, mesmerized, the sound of his voice like a drug on her senses, numbing her.

Wu Tsai was flirting with Tsu Ma, leaning toward him, her words and gestures unmistakable in their message; but Fei Yen could sense how detached the T'ang was from her games. He leaned toward Wu Tsai, laughing, smiling, playing the ancient game with ease and charm, but his attention was focused in herself. She could sense how his body moved toward her subtly; how, with the utmost casualness, he strove at each moment to include her in all that was said. And Li Yuan? He was unaware of this. It was like the poor child was asleep, enmeshed in his dream of perfect love.

She looked away, pained suddenly by all she was thinking. Li Yuan was her husband, and one day he would be T'ang. He deserved her loyalty, in body and soul. And yet . . .

She rose quietly and went into the pagoda, returning a moment later with a p'i p'a, the ancient four-stringed lute shaped like a giant teardrop.

"What's this?" said Li Yuan, turning to look at her.

She stood there, her head bowed. "I thought it might be pleasant if we had some music."

Li Yuan turned and looked across at Tsu Ma, who smiled and gave a tiny nod of his head. But instead of handing the lute to her cousin, as Li Yuan had expected, Fei Yen sat, the lute held upright in her lap, and began to play.

Li Yuan sat there, entranced by the fluency of her playing, the swift certainty of her fingers across the strings, the passionate tiny movements of her head as she wrought the tune from nothingness. He recognized the song. It was the *Kan Hua Hui*, the "Flower Fair," a sweet, sprightly tune that took considerable expertise to play. When she finished he gave a short laugh and bowed his head. He was about to speak, to praise her, when she began again—a slower, more thoughtful piece this time.

It was the *Yueh Erh Kao*, "The Moon on High."

He shivered, looking out across the blackness of the lake, his heart suddenly in his throat. It was beautiful: as if the notes were tiny silver fishes floating in the darkness. As the playing grew faster, more complex, his gaze was drawn to her face again and saw how her eyes had almost closed, her whole being suddenly focused in the song, in the movement of her fingers against the strings. It reminded him of that moment years before when she had drawn and aimed the bow. How her whole body had seemed to become part of the bow, and how, when the arrow had been released, it was as if part of her had flown through the air toward the distant target.

He breathed slowly, his lips parted in wonder. And Han was dead, and she was his. And still the Great Wheel turned . . .

It ended. For a time no one spoke. Then Wu Tsai leaned forward and took her cup from the table, smiling, looking across at Tsu Ma.

"My cousin is very gifted," she said. "It is said in our family that the gods made a mistake the day Fei Yen was born. They meant Yin Tsu to have another son; but things were mixed up and while she received the soul of a man, she was given the body of a woman."

Fei Yen had looked up briefly, only to avert her eyes again, but it was clear from her smile that she had heard the story often and was not displeased by it. Tsu Ma, however, turned to face Wu Tsai, coming to Fei Yen's defense.

"From what I've seen, if the gods were mistaken it was in one small respect alone. That Fei Yen is not *quite* perfect . . ."

Fei Yen met his eyes momentarily, responding to his teasing tone. "Not quite, *Chieh Hsia?*"

"No . . ." He held out his empty cup. "For they should have made you twins. One to fill my cup while the other played."

There was laughter all round. But when Fei Yen began to get up and pour for him, Tsu Ma took the jug and went around himself, filling their cups.

"There!" he said, sitting back. "Now I can listen once again."

Taking his hint, Fei Yen straightened the *p'i p'a* in her lap and after a moment's concentration, began to play. This time it was a song none of them had heard before. A strange, melancholy tune. And as she played she sang in a high contralto.

> A pretty pair of white geese
> Double, double, far from dusty chaos;
> Wings embracing, they play in bright sunlight,
> Necks caressing roam the blue clouds.
> Trapped by nets or felled by corded arrow
> Hen and cock are parted one dawn.
> Sad echoes drift down river bends,
> Lonesome cries ring out from river banks.
> "It is not that I don't long for my former mate,
> But because of you I won't reach my flock."
> Drop by drop she sheds a tear.
> "A thousand leagues I'll wait for you!"
> How happy to fall in love,
> So sad a lifetime parting.
> Let us cling to our hundred-year span,
> Let us pursue every moment of time,
> Like grass on a lonely hill
> Knowing it must wither and die.

Li Yuan, watching her, found himself spellbound by the song, transfixed by the pain in her face as she sang, and astonished that he had never heard her sing before—that he had never guessed she had these talents. When she had finished and the lute had fallen silent, he looked across at Tsu Ma and saw how the T'ang sat there, his head bowed, his hands clasped together tightly as if in grief.

Tsu Ma looked up, tears filming his eyes, his voice soft. "That was beautiful, Lady Fei. Perhaps the most beautiful thing I have ever heard."

Fei Yen was looking down, the *p'i p'a* resting loosely against her breasts, her whole frame bent forward, as if she had emptied herself with the song. She made a tiny motion of her head, acknowledging the T'ang's words; then she stood and with bows to Tsu Ma and her husband, turned and went back into the pagoda.

"Well . . ." said Tsu Ma, looking directly at Li Yuan. "What can I say, my friend? You honor me, tonight. I mean that."

"I, too, Tsu Ma. This has been an evening to remember."

Tsu Ma sat back. "That's true." He shivered, then seemed to come to himself again and smiled. "But come, I am neglecting the Lady Wu." He turned to Wu Tsai, his smile widening. "Do *you* play anything, my Lady?"

Li Yuan smiled, recognizing that Tsu Ma was hinting he should go after his wife. With a bow to his guests he went. But Fei Yen was not inside the pagoda. He stood there in the empty room a moment, frowning, hearing only the laughter from the terrace outside. Then he heard her calling him softly from the far side of the pagoda.

THEY STROLLED back across the bridge, his arm about her neck, her tiny body pressed warm and tight against his side. The night was mild and dark and comforting about them, but the terrace was empty, the pagoda, too. Li Yuan looked about him, puzzled, then stiffened, hearing a splash in the water close by.

He crouched, facing the danger. "Get behind me, Fei Yen!" he said, quietly but urgently, drawing the dagger from his boot.

A peal of laughter rolled out from the darkness in front of them, rich and deep and full of warmth. Li Yuan relaxed. It was Tsu Ma.

"Gods! What are you doing?"

Tsu Ma came closer, into the light of the lanterns. The water was up to his chest and his hair was slicked back wetly from his forehead.

"Swimming," he answered. "It's lovely. The water's much warmer than I thought it would be."

"And the Lady Wu? Has she gone back?"

In answer there was a splashing to their left and a second whoop of laughter.

"You should come in, you two!" she yelled. "It's marvelous!"

Li Yuan looked about him, puzzled. Tsu Ma saw and laughed.

"If you're looking for our clothes, they're in the boat. It was the Lady Wu's idea. She told me there were fish in the lake and I wanted to see for myself."

"And were there?" It was Fei Yen. She had come alongside Li Yuan and was standing there, looking across at Tsu Ma. He stood straighter in the water, his broad chest glistening wetly in the multicolored light.

"Only an eel," Wu Tsai answered, coming nearer, her naked shoulders bobbing above the surface of the water. "A rather stiff little eel . . ."

"Wu Tsai!" Fei Yen protested, but even Li Yuan was laughing now.

"They say the god Kung-Kung who brought the Great Flood was an eel," Tsu Ma said, scooping water up over his chest and arms as if he were washing. "A giant eel. But look, you two, if you're not going to join us, then perhaps you should let us join you. Li Yuan . . . if you would avert your eyes while the Lady Wu gets out and finds her clothes?"

"Of course . . ." Li Yuan turned away, hearing the giggling that went on behind his back as Fei Yen went across to help her cousin.

"All right," Wu Tsai said, after a while. "You can turn around now, Prince Yuan."

He turned back. Wu Tsai was kneeling in the boat, fastening her silks. She looked up at him, grinning. "You really should have joined us."

He hesitated, conscious of Tsu Ma, naked in the water close by, and of Fei Yen, crouched there beside the boat, watching him.

"It wouldn't have been right . . ."

Wu Tsai shrugged, and climbed up onto the bank. "I thought we had made a toast." Her eyes flashed mischievously. "You know, eternal friends, and all that . . ."

Tsu Ma had pushed forward through the water until he was standing just below the deep lip of the bank. Now he spoke, placing his hands flat on the flagstones at the lake's edge. "Prince Yuan is right, Lady Wu. Forgive me, I wasn't thinking. It would be most . . . improper."

Wu Tsai brushed past Li Yuan provocatively, then glanced back at Fei Yen, smiling. "I just thought it would have been fun, that's all. Something a little different."

Li Yuan turned angrily, glaring at her; then, biting back the retort that had come to mind, he turned back, looking at Fei Yen.

She was standing now, her head bowed, her whole stance submissive.

He took a step toward her, one hand raised in appeal. "You must see how wrong it would have been?"

Her eyes lifted, met his, obedient. "Of course, my husband."

He let his breathing calm, then turned back, looking across at the T'ang. "And you, Tsu Ma? What do you wish? Should we retire to the pagoda while you dress?"

Tsu Ma laughed, his body dark and powerful in the water. "Gods, no, Yuan. This is much too nice. I think I'll swim back. Float on my back a bit and stare up at the stars."

Yuan bowed his head. "Of course. As you will. But what will you do when you get to the far shore?"

But Tsu Ma had turned already and was wading out into the deeper water. He shouted back his answer as he slipped into the blackness. "Why, I'll get out of the water, Yuan! What else should I do?"

━━━━━

AT ELEVEN the next morning, Tolonen was standing at the West Window in the Room of the Five Directions in the East Palace at Tongjiang, looking out across the gardens toward the lake. He had been summoned to this meeting at short notice. That in itself was not unusual; but for once he had been told nothing of the reason for the meeting. It was this—a sense of unpreparedness—that made him feel restless standing there, made him turn and pace the room impatiently.

He had paused before the great mirror at the far end of the room, straightening the collar of his uniform jacket, when the door behind him opened. He turned, expecting Li Shai Tung, but it was the Prince, Li Yuan, who entered.

"Prince Yuan," he said, bowing.

Li Yuan came forward, extending an arm to offer the Marshal a seat. "Thank you for coming, Knut. My father will join us later."

Tolonen bowed again, then sat, staring pointedly at the folder in Li Yuan's lap. "Well, Yuan, what is it?"

Li Yuan smiled. He enjoyed the old man's bluntness, a trait that had grown more pronounced with every year.

"My father has asked me to talk to you on a certain matter. When I've finished, he'll come and speak with you himself. But what I have to say has his full approval. You can direct any questions—or objections—to me, as if you were speaking to my father."

"Objections?" Tolonen raised his chin. "If Li Shai Tung has approved it, why should I have objections? He has a job for me, neh?"

"A task, let's say. Something that he feels you should oversee."

Tolonen nodded. "I see. And what is this task?"

Li Yuan hesitated. "Would you like refreshments while we talk?"

Tolonen smiled. "Thank you, Yuan, but no. Unless your father wishes to detain me, I must be in Nanking three hours from now to meet Major Karr."

"Of course. Then we'll press on. It would be best, perhaps, if you would let me finish before asking anything. Some of it is quite complex. And please, record this if you wish."

Tolonen bowed his head, then turned his right hand palm upward and quickly tapped out the command on the grid of tiny flesh-colored blisters at his wrist. That done, he settled back, letting the young Prince speak.

Li Yuan watched the Marshal while he talked, barely referring to the folder in his lap, unless it was to take some diagram from it and hand it to Tolonen. He watched attentively, noting every frown, every look of puzzlement, every last betraying blink or twitch in the old man's face, anxious to gauge the depth of his feelings.

Tolonen had not smiled throughout the lengthy exposition. He sat there, grim-faced, his left hand gripping the arm of his chair. But when Yuan finished, he looked down, giving a great heave of a sigh.

"Can I speak now, Yuan?" Tolonen said, his eyes pained, his whole face grave.

"Of course. As I said, you must speak to me as if I were my father. Openly. As you feel."

Prepared as he was, Li Yuan nonetheless felt a sudden tightening in his stomach. He respected Marshal Tolonen greatly, had grown up in the shadow of the old man. But in this, he knew, they were of a different mind.

Tolonen stared at him a moment, nodding, his lips pressed

tightly together, his earnest gray eyes looking out from a face carved like granite. Then, with a deep sniff that indicated he had considered things long enough, he began.

"You ask me to speak openly. Yet I feel I cannot do that without offending you, Li Yuan. This is, I take it, your idea?"

Li Yuan could sense the great weight of the Marshal's authority bearing down on him, but steeled himself, forcing himself to confront it.

"It is."

"I see. And yet you command me—speaking with your father's voice—to answer you. Openly. Bluntly." He sighed. "Very well then. I'll tell you what I feel. I find this scheme of yours repugnant."

Li Yuan shivered, but kept his face impassive. "And I, Marshal Tolonen. And I. This is not something I *want* to do."

"Then why?"

"Because there is no other way. None that would not result in greater violence, greater bloodshed than that which we are already witnessing."

Tolonen looked down. Again he sniffed deeply. Then he looked up again, shaking his head. "No. Even were the worst to come, this is no path for us. To put things in men's heads. To wire them up and treat them like machines. Achh . . ." He leaned forward, his expression suddenly, unexpectedly, passionate. "I know what I am, Li Yuan. I know what I have had to do in the service of my T'ang. And sometimes I have difficulty sleeping. But this . . . this is different in kind. This will rob men of their freedom."

"Or the illusion of freedom?"

Tolonen waved the words aside impatiently. "It's no illusion, Prince Yuan. The freedom to choose—bad or good—that's real. And the Mandate of Heaven—those moral criteria by which a T'ang is adjudged a good or bad ruler—that too is real. Take them away and we have nothing. Nothing worth keeping, anyway."

Li Yuan sat forward. "I don't agree. If a man is bad, surely it is no bad thing to have a wire in his head—to be able to limit the effects of his badness? And if a man is good—"

Tolonen interrupted him. "You, I, your father—we are good

men. We act because we must—for the good of all. Yet when we have left this earth, what then? How can we guarantee that those who rule Chung Kuo after us will be good? How can we guarantee *their* motives? So you see, I'd answer you thus, my Prince. It does not matter if the man with the wire in his head is good or bad. What matters is the moral standing of the man who holds the wires in his hands like ten thousand million strings. Will he make the puppets dance? Or will he leave them be?"

Li Yuan sat back slowly, shaking his head. "You talk of dictatorships, Marshal Tolonen. Yet we are Seven."

Tolonen turned his head aside, a strange bitterness in his eyes. "I talk of things to be—whether they come in ten years or ten thousand." He looked back at Li Yuan, his gray eyes filled with sadness. "Whatever you or I might wish, history tells us this— nothing is eternal. Things change."

"You once thought differently. I have heard you speaking so myself, Knut. Was it not you yourself who said we should build a great dam against the floodwaters of Change."

Tolonen nodded, suddenly wistful, his lips formed into a sad smile. "Yes . . . but *this*!"

He sat there afterward, when the Prince had gone, staring down at his hands. He would do it. Of course he would. Hadn't his T'ang asked him to take this on? Even so, he felt heavy of heart. Had the dream died, then? The great vision of a world at peace—a world where a man could find his level and raise his family without need or care. And was this the first sign of the nightmare to come? Of the great, engulfing darkness?

He kept thinking of Jelka, and of the grandchildren he would someday have. What kind of a world would it be for them? Could he bear to see them wired, made vulnerable to the least whim of their lords and masters? He gritted his teeth, pained by the thought. Had it changed so much that even he—the corner- stone—began to doubt their course?

"Knut?"

He raised his head, then got to his feet hurriedly. He had been so caught up in his thoughts he had not heard the T'ang enter.

"*Chieh Hsia!*" He bowed his head exaggeratedly.

Li Shai Tung sat where his son had been sitting only moments before, silent, studying his Marshal. Then, with a vague nod of his head as if satisfied with what he had seen, he leaned toward Tolonen.

"I heard all that passed between you and my son."

"Yes, *Chieh Hsia*."

"And I am grateful for your openness."

Tolonen met his eyes unflinchingly. "It was only my duty, Li Shai Tung."

"Yes. But there was a reason for letting Yuan talk to you first. You see, while my son is, in his way, quite wise, he is also young. Too young, perhaps, to understand the essence of things—the place of *Li* and *Ch'i* in this great world of ours, the fine balance that exists between the shaping force and the passive substance."

Tolonen frowned, lowering his head slightly. "I'm afraid I don't follow you, *Chieh Hsia*."

The T'ang smiled. "Well, Knut, I'll put it simply, and bind you to keep this secret from my son. I have authorized his scheme, but that is not to say it will ever come about. You understand me?"

"Not fully, my Lord. You mean you are only humoring Li Yuan?"

Li Shai Tung hesitated. "In a way, yes, I suppose you could say I am. But this idea is deep-rooted in Yuan. I have seen it grow from the seed, until now it dominates his thinking. He believes he can shape the world to his conception, that this scheme of his will answer all the questions."

"And you think he's wrong?"

"Yes."

"Then why encourage him? Why authorize this madness?"

"Because Yuan will be T'ang one day. If I oppose him now in this, he will only return to it after my death. And that would be disastrous. It would bring him into conflict not only with his fellow T'ang but with the great mass of the Above. Best then to let him purge it from his blood while he is Prince, neh? To discover for himself that he is wrong."

"Maybe . . ." Tolonen took a deep breath. "But if you'll forgive me, *Chieh Hsia*, it still seems something of a gamble. What if this 'cure' merely serves to encourage him further? Isn't that possible?"

"Yes. Which is why I summoned you, Knut. Why I wanted you to oversee the project. To act as brake to my son's ambitions and keep the thing within bounds . . . and to kill it if you must."

Tolonen was staring at his T'ang, realization coming slowly to his face. Then he laughed. "I see, *Chieh Hsia* . . . I understand!"

Li Shai Tung smiled back at him. "Good. Then when Tsu Ma returns from riding, I'll tell him you have taken the job, yes?"

Tolonen bowed his head, all heaviness suddenly lifted from his heart. "I would be honored, *Chieh Hsia*. Deeply honored."

━━━━━

FIFTEEN *LI* north of Tongjiang, at the edge of the T'ang's great estate, were the ruins of an ancient Buddhist monastery that dated from the great Sung Dynasty. They stood in the foothills of the Ta Pa Shan, three levels of cinnabar-red buildings climbing the hillside, the once-elegant sweep of their gray-tiled roofs smashed like broken mouths, their brickwork crumbling, their doorways cluttered with weed and fallen masonry. They had stood so for more than two hundred and forty years, victims of the great *Ko Ming* purges of the 1960s, their ruin becoming, with time, a natural thing—part of the bleak and melancholy landscape that surrounded them.

On the hillside below the buildings stood the ruin of an ancient moss-covered stupa, its squat, heavy base chipped and crumbling, the steps cut into the face cracked, broken in places. It was a great, pot-bellied thing, its slender spire like an afterthought tagged on untidily, the smooth curve of its central surface pocked where the plaster had fallen away in places, exposing the brickwork.

In its shadow, in a square of orange brickwork partly hidden by the long grass, stood a circular pool. It had once been a well serving the monastery, but when the Red Guards had come they had filled it with broken statuary, almost to its rim. Now the water—channeled from the hills above by way of an underground stream—rose to the lip of the well. With the spring thaw, or when the rains fell heavily in the Ta Pa Shan, the well would overflow, making a small marsh of the ground to the southwest of it. Just now, however, the land was dry, the pool a perfect mirror, moss on the statuary below giving it a rich green color, like a tarnished bronze.

The sky overhead was a cold, metallic blue, while to the north, above the mountains, storm clouds were gathering, black and dense, throwing the farthest peaks into deep shadow.

To the south the land fell away, slowly at first, then abruptly. A steep path led down into a narrow, deeply eroded valley through which a clear stream ran, swift yet shallow, to the plains below.

At the southern end of the valley where the sky was brighter, a horseman now appeared, his dark mount reined in, its head pulling to one side as it slowed then came to a halt. A moment later, a second rider came up over the lip of rock and drew up beside the first. They leaned close momentarily then began to come forward again, slowly, looking about them, the first of them pointing up at the ruined monastery.

"What is this place?" Fei Yen asked, looking up to where Tsu Ma was pointing. "It looks ancient."

"It is. Li Yuan was telling me about it yesterday. There used to be two hundred monks here."

"Monks?"

He laughed, turning in his saddle to look at her. "Yes, monks. But come. Let's go up. I'll explain it when we get there."

She looked down, smiling, then nudged her horse forward, following him, watching as he began to climb the steep path that cut into the overhang above, his horse straining to make the gradient.

It was difficult. If it had been wet it would have been impossible on horseback, but he managed it. Jumping down from his mount, he came back and stood there at the head of the path, looking down at her.

"Dismount and I'll give you a hand. Or you can leave your mount there, if you like. He'll not stray far."

In answer she spurred her horse forward, willing it up the path, making Tsu Ma step back sharply as she came on.

"There!" she said, turning the beast sharply, then reaching forward to smooth its neck. "It wasn't so hard . . ."

She saw how he was looking at her, his admiration clouded by concern, and looked away quickly. There had been this tension between them all morning; a sense of things unspoken, of gestures not yet made between them. It had lain there beneath the stiff formality of their talk, like fire under ice, surfacing from time to time in a look, a moment's hesitation, a tacit smile.

"You should be more careful," he said, coming up to her, his fingers reaching up to smooth the horse's flank only a hand's length from her knee. "You're a good rider, Lady Fei, but that's not a stunt I'd recommend you try a second time."

She looked down at him, her eyes defiant. "Because I'm a woman, you mean?"

He smiled back at her, a strange hardness behind his eyes, then shook his head. "No. Because you're not *that* good a rider. And because I'm responsible for you. What would your husband say if I brought you back in pieces?"

Fei Yen was silent. What *would* he say? She smiled. "All right. I'll behave myself in future."

She climbed down, aware suddenly of how close he was to her, closer than he had been all morning; and when she turned, it was to find him looking down at her, a strange expression in his eyes. For a moment she stood there, silent, waiting for him, not knowing what he would do. The moment seemed to stretch out endlessly, his gaze traveling across her face, her neck, her shoulder, returning to her eyes. Then, with a soft laugh, he turned away, letting her breathe again.

"Come!" he said briskly, moving up the slope, away from her. "Let's explore the place!"

She bent down momentarily, brushing the dust from her clothes, then straightened up, her eyes following him.

"You asked me what monks were," he said, turning, waiting for her to catch up with him. "But it's difficult to explain. We've nothing like them now. Not since Tsao Ch'un destroyed them all. There are some similarities to the New Confucian officials, of course—they dressed alike, in saffron robes, and had similar rituals and ceremonies. But in other ways they were completely different."

She caught up with him. "In what way different?"

He smiled and began to climb the slope again, slowly, looking about him all the while, his eyes taking in the ruins, the distant, cloud-wreathed mountains, the two horses grazing just below them. "Well, let's just say that they had some strange beliefs. And that they let those beliefs shape their lives—as if their lives were of no account."

They had reached the pool. Tsu Ma went across and stood there, one foot resting lightly on the tiled lip of the well as he looked back across the valley toward the south. Fei Yen hesitated, then came alongside, looking up at him.

"What kind of beliefs?"

"Oh . . ." He looked down, studying her reflection in the pool, conscious of the vague, moss-covered forms beneath the surface image. "That each one of us would return after death, in another form. As a butterfly, perhaps, or as a horse."

"Or as a man?"

"Yes . . ." He looked up at her, smiling. "Imagine it! Endless cycles of rebirth. Each new-born form reflecting your behavior in past lives. If you lived badly you would return as an insect."

"And if well, as a T'ang?"

He laughed. "Perhaps . . . but then again, perhaps not. They held such things as power and government as being of little importance. What they believed in was purity. All that was important to them was that the spirit be purged of all its earthly weaknesses. And because of that—because each new life was a fresh chance to live purely—they believed all life was sacred."

A path led up from where they stood, its flagstones worn and broken, its progress hidden here and there by moss and weed. They moved on, following it up to the first of the ruined buildings. To either side great chunks of masonry lay in the tall grasses, pieces of fallen statuary among them.

In the doorway she paused, looking up at him. "I think they sound rather nice. Why did Tsao Ch'un destroy them?"

He sighed, then pushed through, into the deep shadow within. "That's not an easy question to answer, my Lady. To understand, you would have to know how the world was before Tsao Ch'un. How divided it was. How many different forms of religion there were, and every one of them 'the truth.' "

She stood there, looking in at him. "I know my history. I've read about the century of rebellions."

"Yes . . ." He glanced back at her, then turned away, looking about him at the cluttered floor, the smoke-blackened walls, the broken ceiling of the room he was in. There was a dank, sour smell to everything, a smell of decay and great antiquity. It seemed much colder here than out in the open. He turned back, shaking his head. "On the surface of things the Buddhists seemed the best of all the religious groups. They were peaceful. They fought no great holy wars in the name of their god. Nor did they persecute anyone who disagreed with them. But ultimately they were every bit as bad as the others."

"Why? If they threatened no one . . ."

"Ah, but they did. Their very existence was a threat. This place . . . it was but one of many thousand such monasteries throughout Chung Kuo. And a small one at that. Some monasteries had ten, twenty thousand monks, many of them living long into their eighties and nineties. Imagine all those men, disdainful of states and princes, taking from the land—eating, drinking, building their temples and their statues, making their books and their prayer flags—*and giving nothing back*. That was what was so threatening about them. It all seemed so harmless, so peaceful, but it was really quite insidious—a debilitating disease that crippled the social body, choking its life from it like a cancer."

Tsu Ma looked about him, suddenly angry, his eyes taking in the waste of it all. Long centuries of waste. "They could have done so much—for the sick, the poor, the homeless, but such things were beneath their notice. To purge themselves of earthly desires was all they were worried about. Pain and suffering— what did suffering mean to them except as a path to purity?"

"Then you think Tsao Ch'un was right to destroy them?"

"Right?" He came across to her. "Yes, I think he was right. Not in everything he did. But in this . . . yes. It's better to feed and clothe and house the masses than to let them rot. Better to give them a good life here than to let them suffer in the vague hope of some better afterlife."

He placed his right hand against the rounded stone of the upright, leaning over her, staring down fiercely at her as he spoke, more passionate than she had ever seen him. She looked down, her pulse quickening.

"And that's what you believe?" she asked softly. "That we've only this one life. And nothing after."

"Don't we all believe that? At core?"

She shivered, then looked up, meeting his eyes. "One life?"

He hesitated, his eyes narrowing, then reached out and brushed his fingers against her cheek and neck.

"Tsu Ma . . ."

He drew his hand back sharply. "Forgive me, I . . ." He stared at her a moment, his eyes confused, pained. "I thought . . ." He looked down, shaking his head, then pushed past her.

Outside the sky was overcast. A wind had blown up, tearing at the grass, rippling the surface of the pool. Tsu Ma knelt at its edge, his chest heaving, his thoughts in turmoil. *One life . . .* What had she meant if not that? What did she want of him?

He turned, hearing her approach.

"I'm sorry . . ." she began, but he shook his head.

"It was a mistake, that's all. We are who we are, neh?"

She stared at him, pained by the sudden roughness of his words. She had not meant to hurt him.

"If I were free . . ."

He shook his head, his face suddenly ugly, his eyes bitter. "But you're not. And the Prince is my friend, neh?"

She turned her face from him, then moved away. The storm was almost upon them now. A dense, rolling mist lay upon the hills behind the ruins and the wind held the faintest suggestion of the downpour to come. The sky was darkening by the moment.

"We'd best get back," she said, turning to him. But he seemed unaware of the darkness at the back of everything. His eyes held nothing but herself. She shuddered. Was he in love with her? Was that it? And she had thought . . .

Slowly he stood, his strong, powerful body stretching, as if from sleep. Then, turning his head from her, he strode down the slope toward the horses.

━━━━━

ON THE FLIGHT down to Nanking, Tolonen played back the recording, the words sounding clearly in his head. Listening to his own voice again, he could hear the unease, the bitterness there and wondered what Li Yuan had made of it. Prince Yuan was a clever one, there was no doubting it; so perhaps he understood why the T'ang had appointed him to oversee the Project rather than someone more sympathetic. Maybe that was why he had left things unresolved, their talk at an impasse. But had he guessed the rest of it? Did he know just how deeply his father was opposed to things?

He sighed, then smiled, thinking of the reunion to come. He had not seen Karr in more than three years. Not since he'd seen him off from Nanking back in November '03. And now Karr was returning, triumphant, his success in tracking down and killing Berdichev a full vindication of their faith in him.

Tolonen leaned forward, looking down out of the porthole. The spaceport was off in the distance ahead of them, a giant depression in the midst of the great glacial plateau of ice—the City's edge forming a great wall about the outer perimeter. Even from this distance he could see the vast, pitted sprawl of landing pads, twenty *li* in diameter, its southernmost edge opening out onto Hsuan Wu Lake, the curve of the ancient Yangtze forming a natural barrier to the northeast, like a giant moat two *li* in width. At the very center of that great sunken circle, like a vast yet slender needle perched on its tip, was the control tower. Seeing it, Tolonen had mixed feelings. The last time he had come to greet someone from Mars it had been DeVore. Before he had known. Before the T'ang's son, Han Ch'in, had died and everything had changed.

But this time it was Karr. And Karr would be the hawk he'd fly against his prey. So maybe it was fitting that it should begin here, at Nanking, where DeVore had first slipped the net.

Ten minutes later he was down and seated across from a young duty captain as they traveled the fast-link that connected the City to the spaceport. Things were tight here, tighter than he remembered them. They had banned all transit flights across the port. Only incoming or outgoing spacecraft were allowed in its air space. Anything else was destroyed immediately, without warning. So this was the only way in—underneath the port.

Karr's ship was docking even as Tolonen rode the sealed car out to the landing bay. The noise was deafening. He could feel the vibrations in his bones, juddering the cradle he was strapped into, making him think for a moment that the tiny vehicle was going to shake itself to pieces. Then it eased and the sound dropped down the register. With a hiss, a door irised open up ahead of him and the car slipped through, coming out into a great sunken pit, in the center of which stood the squatly rounded shape of the interplanetary craft.

He could see the *Tientsin* clearly through the transparent walls of the car, its underbelly glowing, great wreaths of mist swirling up into the cold air overhead. The track curved sharply, taking his car halfway around the ship before it slowed and stopped. Guards met him, helped him out, standing back, their heads bowed, as he stretched his legs and looked about him.

He smiled, looking back at the craft. It had come all the way from Mars. Like a great black stone slapped down upon the great *wei chi* board of Chung Kuo. Karr. He could see the big man in his mind's eye even now, lifting Berdichev and breaking him. Ending it quickly, cleanly. Tolonen sniffed. Yes, in that he and Karr were alike. They understood how things worked at this level. It was no good dealing with one's enemies as one dealt with one's friends. Useless to play by rules that the other side constantly broke. In war one had to be utterly ruthless. To concede nothing—unless concession were a path to victory.

As he watched, an R-shaped gantry-elevator moved on its rails across to the craft and attached itself to a portal on its uppermost surface. He walked toward it, habit making him look about him, as if, even here, he could expect attack.

Karr was in the first elevator, packed in with twenty or thirty others. As the cage descended, Tolonen raised a hand in greeting, but stayed where he was, just back from the others waiting there—maintenance crew, customs men, and guards. Karr was carrying a small briefcase, the handle chained to his arm. At the barrier he was first in the line, his Triple-A pass held out for inspection. Even so, it was some three or four minutes before he passed through.

The two men greeted one another warmly, Tolonen hugging the big man to him.

"It's good to see you, Gregor. You did well out there. I'm proud of you!"

"Thank you, sir. But you're looking well yourself."

Tolonen nodded, then pointed at the briefcase. "But what's

this? Don't we pay you enough that you have to go into the courier business?"

Karr leaned closer, lowering his voice. "It's my gift for the T'ang. I didn't want to say anything about it until I got back. You know how it is."

Tolonen sighed. "I know only too well. But tell me, what is it?"

Karr smiled. "Berdichev's files. His personal records. Coded, of course, but I'm sure we can crack them. If they're what I think they are, we can polish off the Dispersionists for good."

"Unless someone's done it already?"

Karr narrowed his eyes. "The Executive Killings, you mean?"

"Yes. It's one of the theories we're working on. Which is why I wanted you to take over the investigation from young Ebert. You've the nose for it."

"Hmmm . . ." Karr looked down. "I've read the files."

"And?"

"They make no sense. There's no real pattern to it. Good men and bad. It seems almost random. Except for the timing of it all."

"Yes. But there has to be a connection."

"Maybe . . ." Karr's face was clouded a moment, then he brightened. "But how's that darling daughter of yours? She was a little tiger!"

Tolonen's face lit up. "Gods, you should see her now, Gregor. Like Mu-Lan, she is. A regular little warrior princess. Yes . . . you must come and train with us some time!"

Karr bowed low. "I would be greatly honored."

"Good, then let's . . ."

Tolonen stopped. A man was standing just to Karr's right. Karr turned, reacting to the movement in Tolonen's eyes, then relaxed, smiling.

"First Advocate Kung!" Karr gave a small bow and put out his left hand to shake the outstretched hand of the Advocate. "I hope all goes well for you."

"Thank you, Major. And your own ventures . . . I hope they prove successful."

The Advocate hesitated, looking to Tolonen. Karr saw what his hesitation implied and quickly made the introduction.

"Forgive me. First Advocate Kung, this is Marshal Tolonen, Head of the Council of Generals."

Tolonen accepted the Advocate's bow with a tight smile. He knew this game too well to be caught in the web of obligation.

"I am delighted to make your acquaintance, Marshal Tolonen," Kung said, bowing again. Then he turned and clicked his fingers. At once his valet approached, handing him a small case. "However, it was you, Major Karr, whom I wanted to see. I was most grateful for your hospitality on board ship, and wanted to offer you a small token of my appreciation."

Tolonen smiled inwardly. He would have to brief Karr afterward on how to escape from this situation, otherwise First Advocate Kung would be calling upon him for favors from here until doomsday, playing upon the Major's need not to lose face.

"Thank you, Advocate, but . . ."

Karr saw the case falling away, Kung raising the handgun, both hands clasping the handle; and he reacted at once, straight-arming Tolonen so that the old man went down. It was not a moment too soon. The explosion from the big old-fashioned gun was deafening. But Karr was already swinging the case at the Advocate's head. He felt it connect and followed through with a kick to the stomach. Kung fell and lay still.

There was shouting all about them. The valet had gone down on his knees, his head pressed to the floor, his whole body visibly shaking. It was clear he had had nothing to do with the assassination attempt. Karr turned, looking for further assassins, then, satisfied there were none, looked down at Tolonen. The Marshal was sitting up, gasping, one hand pressed to his ribs.

Karr went down on one knee. "Forgive me, Marshal, I—"

Tolonen waved aside his apology, the words coming from him wheezingly. "You . . . saved my . . . life."

"I wouldn't have believed it. He was Senior Advocate on Mars. A highly respected man."

"Major!" The call came from behind Karr. He turned. It was one of the spaceport's Security captains.

"What is it?" he answered, standing, looking across to where the Captain was kneeling over the fallen man.

"There's no pulse."

Karr went across and knelt beside Kung, examining the body

for himself. It was true. Advocate Kung was dead. Yet the
wounds to the head and stomach were minimal. If he had *meant*
to kill the man . . .

"Shit!" he said, turning to look at Tolonen, then frowned.
"What is it, sir?"

Tolonen's eyes were wide, staring at the corpse. As Karr
watched him, the old man shuddered. "Gods . . ." he said softly.
"It's one of them."

Karr stared back at him a moment, then his eyes widened,
understanding. "A copy . . ." He turned and looked across at the
valet. The man had been forced to his feet and was being held
between two Security men, his head bowed in shame, his hands
trembling with fear.

"*You!*" Karr barked at him, getting up and going across to
him. "Tell me, and tell me fast, did you notice anything different
about your master? Anything unusual?"

The man shook his head abjectly. "Nothing, honored sir.
Believe me. I knew nothing of his intentions."

Karr studied the man a moment longer, then waved the guards
away. "Take him away and interrogate him. Whatever it takes. I
want the truth from him." He turned back. Tolonen was getting
to his feet, one of the guards giving him a hand.

Tolonen turned, smiling his thanks, then put out his hand.
"Give me your knife, sergeant."

The guard did as he was told, then stood back, watching as
Tolonen limped slowly across to the corpse.

He met Karr's eyes. "If it's like the others . . ." Karr nodded.
They both remembered that day when Han Ch'in had been
assassinated. Recalled the team of copy humans who had come
in from Mars to kill him. And now here they were again. A
second wave, perhaps. Tolonen knelt by the body, putting the
knife down at his side.

"Here," Karr said, coming to the other side of Kung. "I'll do
it."

If it was like the others it would have a metal plate set into its
chest. The real Kung would have been killed months ago.

Tolonen handed Karr the knife, then sat back on his knees,
rubbing at his ribs again, a momentary flicker of pain in his face.
"Okay. Let's see what it is."

Karr slit the Advocate's tunic open, exposing the flesh; then, leaning right over the body, he dug deeply into the flesh, drawing the blade across the corpse's chest.

Blood welled, flowed freely down the corpse's sides. They had not expected that. But there was something. Not a plate, as they'd both expected, but something much smaller, softer. Karr prised the knife beneath it and lifted it out. It was a wallet. A tiny black wallet no bigger than a child's hand. He frowned, then handed it across.

Tolonen wiped it against his sleeve, then turned it over, studying it. It seemed like an ordinary pouch, the kind one kept tobacco in. For a moment he hesitated. What if it was a bomb? He ought to hand it over to the experts. But he was impatient to know, for the man—and he *was* a man, there was no doubting that now—had almost killed him. He had been that close.

Gently he pressed the two ends of the wallet's rim toward each other. The mouth of the pouch gaped open. He reached in with two fingers, hooking out the thing within.

He stared at it a moment, then handed it across to Karr. He had known. The moment before he had opened it he had known what would be inside. A stone. A single white *wei chi* stone. Like a calling card. To let the T'ang know who had killed him.

Tolonen met Karr's eyes and smiled bitterly.

"DeVore. This was DeVore's work."

Karr looked down. "Yes, and when he hears about it he'll be disappointed. Very disappointed."

Tolonen was quiet a moment, brooding, then he looked back at Karr. "Something's wrong, Gregor. My instincts tell me he's up to something while we're here, distracted by this business. I must get back. At once. Jelka . . ."

Karr touched his arm. "We'll go at once."

━━━━━

DEVORE TURNED in his chair and looked across at his lieutenant.

"What is it, Wiegand?"

"I thought you should know, sir. The Han has failed. Marshal Tolonen is still alive."

"Ah . . ." He turned, staring out of the long window again, effectively dismissing the man. For a while he sat there, perfectly still, studying the slow movement of cloud above the distant peaks, the thin wisps of cirrus like delicate feathers of snow against the rich blue of the sky. Then he turned back.

He smiled. Like Wiegand, they would all be thinking he had tried to kill Tolonen, but that wasn't what he'd wanted. Killing him would only make him a martyr. Would strengthen the Seven. No, what he wanted was to destroy Tolonen. Day by day. Little by little.

Yes. Tolonen would have found the stone. And he would know it was his doing.

There was a secret elevator in his room, behind one of the full-length wall charts. He used it now, descending to the heart of the warren. At the bottom a one-way mirror gave him a view of the corridor outside. He checked that it was clear, then stepped out. The room was to the left, fifty *ch'i* along the corridor, at the end of a cul-de-sac hewn out of the surrounding rock.

At the door he paused and took a small lamp from his pocket, then examined both the locks. They seemed untouched. Satisfied, he tapped in the combinations and placed his eye against the indented pad. The door hissed back.

The girl was asleep. She lay there, facedown on her cot, her long, ash-blond hair spilling out across her naked shoulders.

He had found her in one of the outlying villages. The physical resemblance had struck him at once. Not that she would have fooled anyone as she was, but eighteen months of good food and expert surgery had transformed her, making the thousand *yuan* he'd paid for her seem the merest trifle. As she was now she was worth a million, maybe ten.

He closed the door and crossed the room, pulling the sheet back slowly, careful not to wake her, exposing the fullness of her rump, the elegance of her back. He studied her a moment, then reached down, shaking her until she woke and turned, looking up at him.

She was so like her. So much so that even her "father" would have had difficulty telling her from the real thing.

DeVore smiled and reached out to brush her face tenderly with the back of his hand, watching as she pushed up against it gratefully. Yes. She was nearly ready now.

"Who are you?" he asked her gently. "Tell me what your name is."

She hesitated then raised her eyes to his again. "Jelka," she said. "My name is Jelka Tolonen."

━━━━━

JELKA WAS KICKING for Siang's throat when the far wall blew in, sending smoke and debris billowing across the practice arena.

The shock wave threw her backward, but she rolled and was up at once, facing the direction of the explosion, seeing at a glance that Siang was dead, huge splinters jutting from his back.

They came fast through the smoke—three men in black clingsuits, breathing masks hiding their features, their heads jerking from side to side, their guns searching.

Ping Tiao assassins. She knew it immediately. And acted . . .

A backflip, then a singlehanded grab for the exercise rope, her other hand seeking the wall bars.

The middle assassin fired even as she dropped. Wood splintered next to her. She had only to survive a minute and help would be here.

A minute. It was too long. She would have to attack.

She went low, slid on her belly; then she was up, jumping high, higher than she had ever leaped before, her body curled into a tight ball. All three were firing now, but the thick smoke was confusing them; they couldn't see properly through their masks.

She went low again, behind Siang, taking a short breath before turning and kicking upward.

One of the men went down, his leg broken. She heard his scream and felt her blood freeze. The other two turned, firing again. Siang's body jerked and seemed to dance where it lay. But Jelka had moved on, circling them, never stopping, changing direction constantly, dipping low to breathe.

In a moment they would realize what she was doing and keep their fire at floor level. Then she would be dead.

Unless she killed them first.

The fact that there were two hindered them. They couldn't fire continuously for fear of killing each other. As she turned, they had to try to follow her, but the rapidity of her movements, the unpredictability of her changes of direction, kept wrong-footing them. She saw one of them stumble and took her chance, moving in as he staggered up, catching him beneath the chin with stiffened fingers. She felt the bones give and moved away quickly, coughing now, the smoke getting to her at last.

Fifteen seconds. Just fifteen seconds.

Suddenly—from the far end of the arena where the wall had been—there was gunfire. As she collapsed she saw the last of the assassins crumple, his body lifted once, then once again, as the shells ripped into him.

And as she passed into unconsciousness she saw her father standing there, the portable cannon at his hip, its fat muzzle smoking.

CHAPTER EIGHT

Shadows

～～～～

TOLONEN SAT at his daughter's bedside, his eyes brimming with tears.

"It was all a terrible mistake, my love. They were after me."

Jelka shook her head, but a huge lump sat in her throat at the thought of what had happened.

She had spent the last ten days in bed, suffering from shock, the after-reaction fierce, frightening. It had felt like she was going mad. Her father had sat with her through the nights, holding her hands, comforting her, robbing himself of sleep to be with her and help her through the worst of it.

Now she felt better, but still it seemed that everything had changed. Suddenly, hideously, the world had become a mask— a paper-thin veil behind which lay another nightmare world. The walls were no longer quite so solid as they had seemed, and each white-suited attendant seemed to conceal an assassin dressed in black.

The world had flipped over in her mind. Was now a thing of menace, a jagged landscape of threat.

It made it no better for her that they had been after her father. No, that simply made things worse. Far worse. For she had had vivid dreams—dreams in which he was dead and she had gone to see him in the T'ang's Great Hall, laid out in state, clothed from head to foot in the white cloth of death.

She stared at him a moment, her eyes narrowed slightly, as if she saw through the flesh to the bone itself; and while he met her staring eyes unflinchingly, something in the depths of him squirmed and tried to break away.

They had been *Ping Tiao*. A specially trained cell. But not Security-trained, thank the gods.

He looked down at where his hands held those of his daughter. The audacity of the *Ping Tiao* in coming for him had shaken them. They knew now that the danger was far greater than they had estimated. The War had unleashed new currents of dissent; darker, more deadly currents that would be hard to channel.

His own investigations had drawn a blank. He did not know how they would have known his household routines. Siang? It was possible, but now that Siang was dead he would never know. And if not Siang, then who?

It made him feel uneasy—an unease he had communicated to Li Shai Tung when they were alone together. "You must watch yourself, *Chieh Hsia*," he had said. "You must watch those closest to you. For there is a new threat. What it is, I don't exactly know. Not yet. But it exists. It's real."

Bombs and guns. He was reaping the harvest he had sown. They all were. But what other choice had they had?

To lay down and die. The only other choice.

Tolonen looked at his daughter, sleeping now, and felt all the fierce warmth of his love for her rise up again. A vast tide of feeling. And with it came an equally fierce pride in her. How magnificent she had been! He had seen the replay from the Security cameras and witnessed the fast, flashing deadliness of her.

He relinquished her hand and stood, stretching the tiredness from his muscles.

They would come again. He knew it for a certainty. They would not rest now until they had snatched his breath from him. His instinct told him so. And though it was not his way to wait passively for things to come to him, in this he found himself helpless, unable to act. They were like shadows. One strove to fight them and they vanished. Or left a corpse, which was no better.

No, there was no center to them. Nothing substantial for him to act against. Only an idea. A nihilistic concept. Thinking this, he felt his anger rise again, fueled by a mounting sense of impotence.

He would have crushed them if he could. One by one. Like bugs beneath his heel. But how did one crush shadows?

━━━━━━

FEI YEN jumped down from her mount, letting the groom lead it away, then turned to face the messenger.

"Well? Is he at home?"

The servant bowed low, offering the sealed note. Fei Yen snatched it from him impatiently, moving past him as if he were not there, making her way toward the East Palace. As she walked, she tore at the seal, unfolding the single sheet. As she'd expected, it was from Li Yuan. She slowed, reading what he had written, then stopped, her teeth bared in a smile. He would be back by midday, after four days away on his father's business. She looked about her at the freshness of the morning, then laughed, and pulling her hair out of the tight bun she had secured it in to ride, shook her head. She would prepare herself for him. Would bathe and put on fresh clothes. Perhaps the new silks he had sent her last week.

She hurried on, exhilarated, the delights of her early morning ride and the joy of his return coursing like twin currents in her blood.

She was about to go into her rooms when she heard noises farther down the corridor, in the direction of Li Yuan's private offices. She frowned. That part of the East Palace was supposed to be off-bounds while Li Yuan was away. She took two steps down the corridor, then stopped, relieved. It was only Nan Ho. He was probably preparing the offices for his master's return. She was about to turn away, not wishing to disturb the Master of the Inner Chamber, when she realized what it was she had found strange. There had been voices . . .

She walked toward him, was halfway down the corridor when he turned.

"Lady Fei . . ."

She could see at once that he had not expected her. But it was more than that. His surprise in finding her there had not turned to relief as, in normal circumstances, it ought. No. It was almost as if he had something to hide.

"You know Prince Yuan will be here in two hours, Master Nan?"

He bowed his head deeply. "He sent word, my Lady. I was preparing things for him."

"My husband is fortunate to have such an excellent servant as you, Master Nan. Might I see your preparations?"

He did not lift his head, but she could sense the hesitation in him and knew she had been right.

"You wish to see, my Lady?"

"If you would, Master Nan. I promise not to disturb anything. I realize my husband has his set ways, and I'd not wish to cause you further work."

"They are but rooms, my Lady . . ."

"But rooms are like clothes. They express the man. Please, Master Nan, indulge my curiosity. I would like to see how Prince Yuan likes his room to be. It would help me as a wife to know such a thing."

Nan Ho lifted his head and met her eyes. "My Lady, I . . ."

She smiled. "Is there some secret, Master Nan? Something I should know?"

He bowed his head, then backed away, clearly upset by her insistence. "Please, my Lady. Follow me. But remember, I am but the Prince's hands."

She hesitated, her curiosity momentarily tinged with apprehension. What could have flustered the normally imperturbable Nan Ho? Was it some awful thing? Some aspect of Li Yuan he wanted to keep from her? Or was it, instead, a surprise present for her? Something that she would spoil by insisting on seeing it?

For a moment she wondered whether she should draw back. It was not too late. Li Yuan would hate it if she spoiled his surprise. But curiosity had the better of her. She followed Master Nan, waiting as he unlocked the great double doors again and pushed them open.

She walked through, then stopped dead, her mouth fallen open in surprise. "*You!*"

The two girls had risen from the couch at her entrance. Now

they stood there, their heads bowed, their hands folded before them.

She turned, her face dark with anger. "What is the meaning of this, Master Nan? What are these creatures doing here?"

Nan Ho had kept his head lowered, bracing himself against her reaction. Even so, the savagery of her words surprised him. He swallowed and keeping his head low, looked past her at the girls.

"My master said to bring them here this morning. I was to . . ."

Her shriek cut him off. "Do you expect me to believe that, Nan Ho? That on the morning of his return my husband would have two such—*low* sorts brought to him?" She shuddered and shook her head, her teeth bared. "No . . . I don't know what your plan is, Master Nan, but I know one thing, I can no longer trust you in your present position."

He jerked his head up, astonished, but before he could utter a word in his defense, Fei Yen had whirled about and stormed across to where the two girls stood.

"And you!" she began. "I know your sort! Turtles eating barley, that's what you are! Good-for-nothings! You hope to rise on your backs, *neh*?"

The last word was spat out venomously. But Fei Yen was far from finished.

"You! Pearl Heart . . . that's your name, isn't it?"

Overwhelmed by the viciousness of the attack, Pearl Heart could only manage a slight bob of her head. Her throat was dry and her hands trembled.

"I know why you're here. Don't think I'm blind to it. But the little game's over, my girl. For you and your *pimp* here." Fei Yen shuddered, pain and an intense anger emphasizing every word. "I know you've been sleeping with my husband."

Pearl Heart looked up, dismayed, then bowed her head quickly, frightened by the look in Fei Yen's eyes.

"Well? Admit it!"

"It is true, my Lady . . ." she began, meaning to explain, but Fei Yen's slap sent her sprawling back onto the couch. She sat, looking up at Fei Yen, her eyes wide with shock. Sweet Rose was sobbing now, her whole frame shaking.

Fei Yen's voice hissed at her menacingly. "Get out . . . All of you . . . *Get out!*"

Pearl Heart struggled up, then stumbled forward, taking her sister's arm as she went, almost dragging her from the room, her own tears flowing freely now, her sense of shame unbearable. Li Yuan . . . How her heart ached to see him now, to have him hold her and comfort her. But it was gone. Gone forever. And nothing but darkness lay ahead of them.

▬▬▬▬

BACK IN HER ROOMS, Fei Yen stood looking about her sightlessly, the blackness lodged in her head like a storm trapped between high mountains. For a while she raged, inarticulate in her grief, rushing about the room uncontrollably, smashing and breaking, the pent-up anger pouring out of her in grunting, shrieking torrents. Then she calmed and sat on the edge of the huge bed, her respiration normalizing, her pulse slowing. Again she looked about her, this time with eyes that moved, surprised, between the broken shapes that lay littered about the room.

She wanted to hurt him. Hurt him badly, just as he had hurt her. But a part of her knew that that was not the way. She must be magnanimous. She must swallow her hurt and pay him back with loving kindness. Her revenge would be to enslave him. To make him need her more than he needed anything in the whole of Chung Kuo. More than life itself.

She shuddered, then gritted her teeth, forcing down the pain she felt. She would be strong. As she'd been when Han had died. She would deny her feelings and will herself to happiness. For the sake of her sons.

She went to the mirror, studying herself. Her face was blotchy, her eyes puffed from crying. She turned and looked about her, suddenly angered by the mess she had made, by her momentary lapse of control. But it was nothing she could not set right. Quickly she went into the next room, returning a moment later with a small linen basket. Then, on her hands and knees, she worked her way methodically across the floor, picking up every last piece of broken pottery or glass she could find. It took her longer than she had thought, but it served another purpose. By the time she had finished she had it clearly in her mind what she must do.

She took the basket back into the dressing room and threw a cloth over it; then she began to undress, bundling her discarded clothes into the bottom of one of the huge built-in cupboards that lined the walls. Then, naked, she went through to the bathroom and began to fill the huge, sunken bath.

She had decided against the new silks. Had decided to keep it as simple as she could. A single vermilion robe. The robe she had worn that first morning, after they had wed.

While the water streamed from the taps, she busied herself at the long table beneath the bathroom mirror, lifting lids from the various jars and sniffing at them until she found the one she was searching for. Yes . . . She would wear nothing but this. His favorite. *Mei hua*, plum blossom.

She looked at her reflection in the wall-length mirror, lifting her chin. Her eyes were less red than they'd been, her skin less blotchy. She smiled, hesitantly at first, then more confidently. It had been foolishness to be so jealous. She was the match of a thousand serving girls.

She nodded to her image, determined, her hands smoothing her flanks, moving slowly upward until they cupped and held her breasts, her nipples rising until they stood out rigidly. She would bewitch him, until he had eyes for nothing but her. She remembered how he had looked at her—awed, his eyes round in his face; she laughed, imagining it. He would be hers. Totally, utterly hers.

Even so, she would have her vengeance on the girls. And on that pimp, Nan Ho. For the hurt they had caused her.

Her smile softened. And after she had made love to him, she would cook for him. A recipe her grandmother had left to her. Yes, while he slept she would prepare it for him. As a wife would.

———

LI YUAN YAWNED and stretched as the craft descended, then looked at his personal secretary, Chang Shih-sen, who was gathering his papers together, softly humming to himself.

"We've got through a lot of work in the last four days, Chang," he said, smiling. "I don't think I've ever worked so hard."

Chang smiled back at him, inclining his head slightly. "It is good to work hard, my Lord."

"Yes . . ." Li Yuan laughed, feeling the craft touch down beneath him. "But today we rest, neh? I won't expect to see you until tomorrow morning."

Chang bowed low, pleased by his master's generosity. "As the Prince wishes."

He turned back, looking out the portal at the activity in the hangar. A welcoming committee of four servants, led by Nan Ho, was waiting to one side, while the hangar crew busied themselves about the craft. Chang was right. He felt good despite his tiredness. He had spent more than eighty hours scanning files and interviewing, and now all but two of the places on the Project were filled. If his father agreed, they could go ahead with it within the week.

For one day, however, he would take a break from things, set all cares aside and devote himself to Fei Yen.

He looked down, grinning at the thought of her. Life was good. To have important business in one's life and such a woman to return to; that, surely, was all a man could ask for.

And sons . . . But that would come. As surely as the seasons.

He heard the hatch hiss open and looked back at Chang Shih-sen. "Go now, Chang. Put the papers in my study. We'll deal with them tomorrow."

Chang bowed his head, then turned away. Li Yuan sat there a moment longer, thinking over the satisfactions of the last few days, recollecting the great feeling of *ch'i*, of pure energy, he had experienced in dealing with these matters. Unlike anything he had ever felt before. It made him understand things better, made him realize why men drove themselves instead of staying at home in the loving arms of their wives. And yet it was good to come home, too. Good to have that to look forward to.

"A balance . . ." he said softly, then laughed and climbed up out of his seat, making his way down the short gangway, the three servants standing off to one side of him as he passed, their heads bowed low.

Nan Ho came forward as he reached the bottom of the steps, then knelt and touched his head to the ground.

"Welcome home, my Lord."

"Thank you, Master Nan. But tell me, where is Fei Yen?"

Nan Ho lifted his head fractionally. "She is in her chambers, Prince Yuan. She has given orders for no one to disturb her. Not even her *amah.*"

Li Yuan grinned. "Ah . . ."

"My Lord—"

But Li Yuan was already moving past him. "Not now, Master Nan. I must go and see her."

Nan Ho turned, his extreme agitation unnoticed by the Prince. "But my Lord—"

"Later, Nan Ho . . ." Li Yuan called back, not turning, breaking into a trot as he crossed the flagged pathway between the hangar and the northern palace.

He ran through the palace, past bowing servants, then threw open the doors to her apartments.

She was waiting for him, sitting on the huge bed, her legs folded under her, the vermilion robe she had worn on their wedding morning pulled about her. Her head was lowered in obedience, but there was a faint smile on her cherry lips. He stood there in the doorway, getting his breath, drinking in the sight of her.

"My Lord?" she said, looking up at him, her eyes dark like the night, her voice warm, welcoming.

"My love . . ." he said, the words barely a whisper, the scent of plum blossom in the room intoxicating. Then, closing the doors firmly behind him, turning the great key, he went across to her and sat beside her on the bed, drawing her close.

He drew back, looking at her again, seeing at once the reflection of his love, there in her eyes. "I've missed you . . ."

In answer she shrugged the thin silk robe from her shoulders, then drew his head down into the cushion of her breasts, curling her legs about him.

"Make love to me, my Lord, I beg you."

Afterward he lay there, next to her, staring at her in wonder.

"My love. My darling little swallow . . ."

She laughed, then drew his face close, kissing him gently, tenderly. "Now you know how much I missed you."

"And I you . . ."

She pushed him back and sat up. "But you're tired, husband.

Why don't you sleep awhile. And when you wake I'll have a meal ready for you."

"But my love, you needn't . . ."

She put a finger to his lips. "I want to. Besides, I am your wife."

He started to protest again, but she shook her head. With a brief laugh he lay back on the bed, closing his eyes. Within a minute he was asleep.

She studied him a moment, laying her hand softly on his chest, feeling the soft rise and fall of his breath, then gently covered the soft fold of his spent manhood. She shivered. He was still such a boy.

She went into the tiny pantry and busied herself, preparing the ingredients she had had brought from the kitchen only an hour before. It would be two hours before it was ready. Time enough to bathe and change again.

She lay there a long time in the bath, soaking, looking through the open door at his sleeping figure on the bed. He was no bother really. Such a sweet boy. And yet . . .

As she floated there, she found herself remembering the sight of Tsu Ma in the water, his chest bared, his hair slicked back, the presence of his boots planted so solidly on the earth beneath the table, the deep, warm vibration of his voice.

Tsu Ma . . .

She opened her eyes again. The boy was still sleeping. Her husband, the boy.

She shivered, then stirred herself in the water. It was time she dressed and saw to his meal.

———

WHEN HE WOKE it was to find her sitting beside him on the bed, watching him. He turned his head, glancing at his timer, then yawned. He had slept more than two hours.

He sat up, breathing in deeply. "What's that? It smells delicious."

She smiled and turned away, returning moments later with a bowl and chopsticks. He took it from her, sniffed at it, then began eating, holding the bowl close to his mouth, smacking his lips in appreciation.

"This is excellent. What is it?"

She was kneeling by the bed, watching him. "It's a recipe of my grandmother's. Wolfberry stewed with beef. A tonic for *yang* energy . . ." She laughed at his frown. "An aphrodisiac, my husband. It enhances strength and endurance."

He nodded enthusiastically. "It's *good*. Your grandmother was a clever woman, and you, my love, are an excellent cook."

She looked down, smiling. "My husband is too kind."

He was still a moment, watching her, astonished for the hundredth time by the fragile beauty of her; then he began to eat again, realizing with a laugh just how hungry he had been.

"Is there anything else, husband? Anything I could get for you?"

He lowered the bowl, smiling at her. "No. But that reminds me. There is something I must do. One small thing, then the rest of the day is free. We could go riding if you like."

She looked back at him, her eyes bright. "I'd like that."

"Good. Then I'll call Nan Ho—"

Uncharacteristically, she interrupted him. "Forgive me husband, but that is not possible."

"Not possible?" Li Yuan frowned, then gave a short laugh. "I don't understand you."

She lowered her head, making herself small, submissive. "I am afraid I had to dismiss Master Nan. He—"

"*Dismiss* him?" Li Yuan put the bowl aside and stood, looking down at her. "Do I hear you rightly, Fei Yen? You have dismissed my Master of the Inner Chamber?"

"I had to, my Lord."

He shook his head, then looked away, past her. "Tell me. Why did you dismiss him? What did he do?"

She glanced up at him, then bowed her head again. "My Lord will be angry with me."

He looked back at her. "Have I reason, then, to be angry with you?"

She looked up, meeting his eyes, her own dewed with tears. He hardened himself against the sight of her; even so, he felt himself moved. He had never seen her as beautiful as at that moment.

"I am your wife, my Prince. Did I not have good reason to be angry with the man?"

He laughed, utterly confused now. "Fei Yen . . . talk sense. I don't follow what you're saying."

She looked down, swallowing, a sudden bleakness in her face that tore at his heart. "The girls . . . Nan Ho had brought girls . . ." A shudder passed through her. "Girls for your bed . . ."

He took a long breath. So—she had misunderstood him. "Forgive me, my love, but you have no reason to be angry with Nan Ho. It was not his doing. I asked him to bring those girls here. That was the thing I had to do."

"And that makes it better?" Her voice was broken, anguished. "How could you, Yuan? Am I not a good wife to you? Do I deny you anything?" She looked up at him, the hurt in her eyes almost too much for him. When she spoke again, her voice was a mere whisper. "Or have you tired of me already?"

He was shaking his head. "No . . . never. But you mistake me—"

"Mistake you?" Sudden anger flared in her eyes. "You bring those girls here—girls who have shared your bed—and say I have mistaken you."

"Fei Yen—"

"Then deny it! Look me in the eyes, husband, and deny that you haven't *had* them?"

He shivered. "It wasn't like that. I . . ."

But his hesitation was enough for her. She tucked her head down bitterly, her hands pulling anxiously at the lap of her dress, then stood angrily.

"Fei Yen! You must believe me . . ."

She glared at him. "*Believe* you?"

He bristled, suddenly angered that she could think this of him, after all he had done to purify himself for her. Hadn't he cast the maids off? Hadn't he denied himself the pleasures of their company this last year? He shuddered. "You had no business dismissing Master Nan! Who comes or goes in these rooms is *my* business, not yours!"

She turned away, suddenly very still. Her voice changed; became smaller and yet harder than before. "Then let a thousand singsong girls come. Let *them* be wives to you. But not Fei Yen . . ."

He went to her, taking her shoulders gently, wanting, despite his anger, to make things right between them; but she shrugged him off, turning violently to confront him, the fury in her eyes making him take a step back from her.

"What kind of a woman do you think I am, Li Yuan? Do you think me like them? Do you think I have no pride?" She drew herself up straighter. "Am I not the wife of a great Prince?"

"You know what you are, Fei Yen!"

"No. I only know what you would have me be."

He began to answer her, but she shook her head dismissively, her eyes boring into him. "I tried hard, Li Yuan. Tried to dispel my doubts and tell myself it was Nan Ho. I tried to be loving to you. To be a good wife in every way. And how did you repay me? By cheating on me. By bringing in those *whores* behind my back."

He felt something snap in him. This was too much. To call his girls whores. Even so, he answered her quietly.

"Be careful what you say, Fei Yen. Those girls were my maids. They took good care of me in my childhood. I have a great affection for them."

She laughed scornfully. "Whores—"

His bark of anger made her jump. "Hold your tongue, woman!"

He stood there commandingly, suddenly very different: all childishness, all concession gone from him. He was shouting now. "It is not your place to criticize *me*. *I* have done nothing wrong. Understand me? Nothing! But you . . ." He shivered with indignation. "To have the audacity to dismiss Master Nan . . . Who in hell's name do you think you are?"

She did not answer. But her eyes glared back at him, their look wild and dangerous.

"Nan Ho stays, understand me? And I shall see the girls, as that's my wish."

He saw a shudder of pure rage ripple through her and felt himself go cold inside. Her face seemed suddenly quite ugly— her lips too thin, her nose too brittle, her perfect brow furrowed with lines of anger. It was as if she were suddenly bewitched, her words spitting back at him through a mask of hatred.

"If that's your wish, so be it. But do not expect me in your bed, Prince Yuan. Not tonight. Nor any other night."

His laughter was harsh; a bitter, broken sound; the antithesis of laughter.

"So be it."

He turned and stormed from the room, slamming the door behind him as he went, his departing footsteps echoing, unrelenting, on the marble tiles.

━━━━━

DEVORE WAS PRESSED up against the wall, Gesell's knife at his throat.

"Give me one good reason why I shouldn't kill you."

DeVore stared back at Gesell, a vague, almost lazy sense of distaste in his eyes.

"Because I don't know what you're talking about."

"You lying bastard. You killed those two men. You must have. You were the only one outside the Central Committee who knew what they were doing. Only you knew how crucial they were to our plans."

There was a movement behind Gesell.

"Not the only one . . ."

Gesell turned. Mach had come in silently. He stood there, watching them. Ascher crossed the room, confronting him, her anger, if anything, more pronounced than Gesell's.

"I say we kill him. He's betrayed us. Spat on us."

Mach shook his head. "He's done nothing. Let him go."

"*No!*" Gesell twisted DeVore's collar tighter. "Emily's right. We can't trust him after this."

Mach pushed past the woman. "For the gods' sakes, let him go, Bent. Don't you understand? *I* killed them."

Gesell laughed uncertainly. "*You?*"

Mach took the knife from Gesell's hand and sheathed it, then removed his hand from DeVore's collar. Only then did he turn and look at DeVore, inclining his head slightly.

"I apologize, *Shih* Turner. You must excuse my brother. He did not know."

"Of course." DeVore stretched his neck slightly, loosening the muscles there.

Gesell rounded on Mach. "Well? What the hell's been happening?"

"I'm sorry, Bent. I had no time to warn you. Besides, I wasn't sure. Not until I'd checked."

"Sure of what?"

"They were Security. Both of them. They must have been sleepers. Records show they left Security five years ago—a year before they joined us."

A slight tightening about DeVore's eyes was the only sign that he was interested, but none of the others in the room noticed it, nor the way he rubbed at his wrist, as if relieving an itch there; they were watching Mach, horrified by this new development.

"Security . . ." Gesell hissed through his teeth. "Gods . . ."

"There are others, too. Three more. In two separate cells."

"You made checks?"

Mach nodded. "I'm keeping tabs on them. They'll hear what happened. I want to see what they'll do, whether they'll sit tight or run. If they run I want them. Alive, if possible. I want to find out what they're up to."

Ascher was shaking her head. "It doesn't make sense. If they had their men inside our organization, why didn't they act in response to Helmstadt?"

Mach glanced at DeVore, conscious of how much he was giving away simply by talking in front of him; but he'd had no choice. If Gesell had killed Turner, they'd have been back to square one. Or worse; they might have found themselves in a tit-for-tat war with Turner's lieutenants. It was almost certain that the man had given orders to that effect before he came here at Gesell's summons.

Mach turned, facing Ascher. "I thought of that. But that's how it works sometimes. They're ordered to sit tight until the thing's big enough and ripe enough to be taken. They obviously thought that Helmstadt was worth sacrificing."

"Or that you wouldn't succeed . . ." DeVore said.

Mach looked back at him again. "Maybe . . ."

The three men had been an advance squad; trained technicians. Their job had been to locate the communications nerve-centers surrounding Bremen. It was a delicate, sensitive job, one upon which the success or failure of the whole attack depended. The idea was for them to place special devices at these *loci*—devices that the regular maintenance crews would think were innocuous parts of the complex of delicate wiring. The devices would sit there, unused, for months, until the day when the *Ping Tiao* launched their attack. Then they would be triggered and Bremen would suffer a massive communications blackout.

That had been the plan. But now things were in chaos.

Gesell looked down. "Do you think they've passed on what they knew?"

Mach shrugged, his expression bitter. Even killing them had not appeased his anger. "I don't know. I hoped to keep one of them alive for questioning, but they fought hard. It was as if they'd been ordered not to be taken alive."

"That's so." Again De Vore entered the conversation. He moved closer. "You should take one of them now, before they hear of it."

Ascher nodded. "I think he's right. What if they take poison or something?"

Mach shivered, then bowed his head. "Okay. We'll take them now. But if it's like it was with the others, it won't be easy."

De Vore narrowed his eyes, studying Mach. His respect for the man had grown enormously. Matton and Tucker had been two of his best men, not merely good at their task of infiltrating the *Ping Tiao*, but good fighters, too. He was sorry to lose them. Sorry, too, to have had his network of spies uncovered, his eye among the *Ping Tiao* blinded. Now he would have to depend upon cruder means—on bribery and blackmail. Unsatisfactory means.

"Concentrate on just one of them," he said, meeting Mach's eyes. "Take him yourself. Then bind him tightly, so there's no chance of him harming himself. After that you should do things slowly. Time, that's all it needs. Time will break the spirit of any man. Then you'll find out what you want to know."

Mach stared back at him steadily. "You've done this?"

De Vore nodded. "Many times."

"Then I'll do as you say."

De Vore smiled. "Good." But it would be too late. As soon as Mach had revealed what he had done, De Vore had pressed the tiny panel at his wrist, opening the channel that switched everything he was saying direct into the heads of his three surviving agents. Already his men would have heard his words and taken the appropriate action.

"And if we discover nothing?" Gesell asked, looking directly at DeVore.

"Then we continue. We must assume now that they know about our plan to attack Bremen, but not when or where we will strike. Nor *how* precisely. Meanwhile it would profit us to seem to change our plans. To look for other targets. And let them know . . ."

Mach looked up again, smiling for the first time since he had entered the room. "I like that. A diversion . . ."

DeVore nodded and smiled back at him. "What does Sun Tzu say? 'The crux of military operations lies in the pretense of accommodating oneself to the designs of the enemy.' Well, we shall seem to back off, as if discovered; but in reality we shall continue with our scheme. If they know nothing of our plans, then no harm has been done today. And even if they do know, they'll not expect us to pursue it after this, neh?"

Mach studied him thoughtfully a moment, then nodded. "Yes. But I must go. Before they hear . . ."

◆◆◆◆◆

HAAVIKKO CLOSED the door behind him then gave a small shudder, staring at the tiny slip of plastic in his hand. His senior officer had been only too glad to approve his new posting. From Major Erickson's viewpoint it must have seemed a blessing to be rid of him. He had been nothing but trouble for the Major. But now he was Karr's man, part of his special services unit. Still a lieutenant, but with a future now. And a friend.

He was meeting Kao Chen in two hours, but first there was one more thing to sort out. His sister, Vesa.

Vesa had been living in a small apartment in the Mids since their aunt had died a year earlier. Wrapped up in his own debauchery he had not known of her plight until recently. But now he could do something. The job with Karr brought with it a private living unit in Bremen: four rooms, including the luxury of his own private bathroom. "But you'll not be there that often," Karr had warned him, "Why not move your sister in?"

Vesa had jumped at the idea. She had held on to his neck and wept. Only then had he realized how lonely she had been, how great his neglect of her, and he had cried and held her tightly. "It's all right," he had whispered, kissing her neck. "Everything will be all right."

He tucked the transfer document into his tunic, then hurried along the corridors, taking a crowded elevator down to the living quarters in the heart of the great multistack fortress.

She was waiting for him in the apartment. As he came in, she got up from the couch, crossed the room, and embraced him, her eyes bright with excitement.

"This is wonderful, Axel! We'll be happy here. I know we will."

He smiled and held her to him, looking about the room. The apartment she had been in had been a single room—like his own, spartanly furnished—and she had had to share washing and night-soil facilities. He gritted his teeth against the shame that welled up at the thought of what he'd let happen to her, then met her eyes again, smiling.

"We'll get a few bits and pieces, eh? Brighten things up a bit. Make it more personal. More *us.*"

She smiled. "That would be nice."

He let her go, then stood there, watching her move about the room, disturbed by the thoughts, the memories that insisted on returning to him in her presence. He kept thinking of the girl in Mu Chua's House of the Ninth Ecstasy, the singsong girl, White Orchid, who had looked so much like Vesa. He looked down. But all that was behind him now.

"I thought I might cook you something . . ."

He went across to her. "Vesa, look . . . I'm sorry, but there's something I have to do tonight. Something urgent."

She turned and looked at him, her disappointment sharp. "But I thought . . ."

"I know. I'm sorry, I . . ."

"Is it your new job?"

He swallowed. "Yes . . ." He hated lying to her, even over something as innocent as this, but it was important that she didn't get involved. It would be dangerous pinning Ebert down and he didn't want to put her at risk. Not for a single moment.

She came across and held his arms. "Never mind. Tomorrow night, eh? We'll celebrate. I'll cook something special." She hesitated, watching his face a moment, then smiled, her voice softening. "You know, Axel. I'm proud of you. I always have been. You were always something more to me than just my big brother. You were like—"

"*Don't* . . ." he said softly, hurt by her words. Even so, he could not disillusion her, could not tell her the depths to which he had sunk. One day, perhaps, but not now. Maybe when he had nailed Ebert and the truth was out he would tell her everything. But not before.

Her eyes blazed with her fierce sisterly love of him. That look, like purity itself, seared him and he let his eyes fall before it.

"I must go." He kissed her brow, then turned away. He went to his room and picked up the bag he had packed earlier; then he went to the small desk in the corner and took a tiny notebook from the drawer.

"Your new job . . . is it dangerous?" she asked, watching him from the doorway.

He looked back at her. "It might be."

"Then you'd best have this."

She placed something in his left hand. It was a pendant on a chain. A circle of black and white jade, the two areas meeting in a swirling S shape. A *tai chi*, the symbol of the Absolute—of *yin* and *yang* in balance. He stared at it a moment, then looked up at her.

"It was Father's," she said to his unspoken question. "He left it to me. But now it's yours. It will protect you."

He put his bag down and slipped the pendant over his neck, holding the jade circle a moment between his fingers, feeling the cool smoothness of its slightly convex surface; then he tucked it away beneath his tunic.

He leaned forward and kissed her. "Thank you . . . I'll treasure it."

"And Axel?"

He had bent down to lift his bag again. "Yes?"

"Thank you . . . for all of this."

He smiled. Yes, he thought, but I should have done it years ago.

KLAUS EBERT poured two brandies from the big decanter, offering one to his son.

"Here . . ."

Hans raised his glass. "To you, Father."

Klaus smiled and lifted his glass in acknowledgment. He studied his son a moment, the smile never leaving his face; then he nodded.

"There's something I wanted to speak to you about, Hans. Something I didn't want to raise earlier, while Mother was here."

Hans raised his eyebrows, then took a deep swig of the brandy. "The Company's all right, isn't it?"

His father laughed. "Don't you read your reports, Hans? Things have never been healthier. We're twice the size we were five years ago. If this continues . . ."

Hans reached out and touched his father's arm. "I read the reports, Father. But that isn't what I meant. I've heard rumors about trouble in the mining colonies."

"Yes . . ." Klaus eyed his son with new respect. He had only had the reports himself last night. It was good to see that, with all his other duties, Hans kept himself astride such matters. He smiled. "That's all in hand. But that's not what I wanted to talk to you about. It's something more personal."

Hans laughed, showing his fine, strong teeth. "I thought we'd settled that. The Marshal's daughter seems a fine young woman. I'm proud of the way she handled those assassins. She'll make me a good wife, don't you think?"

Klaus nodded, suddenly awkward. "Yes . . . Which is why I felt I had to speak to you, Hans. You see, I've been approached by Minister Chuang."

Hans's look of puzzlement warmed him, reassured him. He had known at once that it was only vicious rumor. For his son to be involved in such an unsavory business was unthinkable.

"I saw the Minister this morning," he continued. "He insisted on coming to see me personally. He was . . . most distressed. His wife, you see . . ."

He hesitated, thinking that maybe he should drop the matter. It was clear from Hans's face that he knew nothing about the allegations.

Hans was shaking his head. "I don't follow you, Father. Is his wife ill?"

"Do you know the woman?"

"Of course. She's quite a popular figure in social circles. I've met her, what?, a dozen, maybe fifteen, times."

"And what do you make of her?"

Hans laughed. "Why?" Then he frowned, as if suddenly making the connection. He put his glass down, anger flaring in his eyes. "What is this? Is the Minister alleging something between me and his wife?"

Klaus gave the slightest nod, grateful to his son for articulating it, gratified by the anger he saw in his son's face.

"Well, damn the man!" Hans continued. "And damn his wife! Is this the way they repay my friendship—with slurs and allegations?"

Klaus reached out and held his son's shoulder. "I understand your anger, Hans. I, too, was angry. I told the Minister that I found his allegations incredible. I said that I would not believe a son of mine could behave as he was alleging you had behaved." He shuddered with indignation. "Furthermore, I told him to either provide substantive proof of his allegations or be prepared to be sued for defamation of character."

Hans was staring at his father wide-eyed. "And what did the Minister say to that?"

Klaus shivered again; then he gave a small laugh. "He was most put out. He said his wife had insisted it was true."

"Gods . . . I wonder why? Do you think . . . ?"

"Think what?"

Hans let out a long breath. "Perhaps I spurned the woman somehow. I mean, without knowing it . . . She's always been one to surround herself with young bucks. Perhaps it was simply because I've never fawned over her or flattered her. Maybe her pride was hurt by that. Did the Minister say how or why she broke this incredible news to him? It seems most extraordinary."

Klaus shook his head. "I never thought to ask. I was so outraged . . ."

"Of course. Perhaps the Minister had a row with his wife and to wound him she used my name. After all, you'd not expect the woman to use the name of one of her real lovers, would you?"

Klaus shrugged, out of his depth. "I guess not."

"Still . . . the *nerve* of it! To drag me into her sordid affairs. I've a mind to confront her and her husband and have it out with them."

Klaus's fingers tightened on his son's shoulder. "No, Hans. I'd prefer it if you didn't. I think it best if we keep the Minister and his wife at a distance."

"But Father—"

"No. I felt I had to mention it to you, but let this be the end of it. All right?"

Hans bowed his head. "As my father wishes."

"Good. Then let us talk of more pleasant matters. I hear young Jelka is being sent home tomorrow. Perhaps you should visit her, Hans. You could take her a small gift."

Klaus nodded to himself, then drained his glass. Yes, it was probably as Hans said: there had been a row and Chuang's wife had used Hans's name to spite her husband. It was not Minister Chuang's fault. He had reacted as any man would. No, the woman was clearly to blame for everything. In the circumstances it would be inadvisable to allow bad feeling to develop from such shadows. Worse still to make an enemy of the Minister. Tomorrow he would send a gift—one of the new range of creatures, perhaps—to smooth things over.

He looked at his son again and smiled, pleased by what he saw. He could not have made a finer creature in his own vats. Though he said so himself, Hans was a masterpiece of genetics—the end product of two centuries of breeding. Like a god, he was. A king among men.

His smile softened. It was as the Seven said, there were levels among men; and Hans, his son, was at the pinnacle. He watched him drain his glass and smile back at him.

"I must get back. You know how it is . . ." Hans hesitated, then came forward and kissed his father's cheek. "But thank you."

Klaus grinned. "For what? I am your father, Hans. Who, if not I, should defend you against such slanders? Besides, who knows you better than I, neh?"

Hans stepped back, then gave a small bow. "Even so . . ."

Klaus lifted his chin, dismissing him. "Go on, boy. Duty calls."

Hans grinned, then turned away. When he was gone Klaus Ebert went across to the decanter and poured himself a second brandy. In times like these he was fortunate to have such a son. The kind of son a man could be proud of. A king. He smiled and raised the glass, silently toasting his absent son, then downed the drink in a single, savage gulp. Yes, a king among men.

━━━━━

HAAVIKKO WAS SITTING in Wang Ti's kitchen, Kao Chen's two-year-old daughter, Ch'iang Hsin, snuggled in his lap. Across from him Chen busied himself at his wife's side, preparing the meal. At his feet their five-year-old, Wu, was waging a ferocious battle between two armies of miniature dragons, their tiny power packs making them seem almost alive.

Looking about him, it was hard to imagine anything quite so different from the world he had inhabited these past ten years, a world as divorced from this simple domesticity as death is from life. He shuddered, thinking of it. A world of swirling smoke and smiling wraiths.

Wang Ti turned to him, wiping her hands on a cloth. "And your sister, Axel? How is she?"

He smiled. "She's fine, Wang Ti. Never happier, I'd say."

She looked at him a moment, as if to read him, then smiled. "That's good. But you need a woman, Axel Haavikko. A wife."

Chen laughed and glanced round. "Leave the poor boy alone, Wang Ti. If he wants a wife he'll find one soon enough. After all, he's a handsome young man. And if an ugly fellow like me can find a wife . . ."

Wang Ti shook her head. "Ugly is as ugly does. Never forget that, husband. Besides, if I close my eyes you are the handsomest of men!"

Husband and wife laughed, real warmth—a strong, self-deprecating humor—in their laughter.

"Anyway," Chen added after a moment, "marriage isn't always such a good thing. I hear, for instance, that our friend Ebert is to be married to the Marshal's daughter."

Haavikko looked down, his mood changed utterly by the mention of Ebert.

"Then I pity the girl. The man's a bastard. He cares for

nothing except his own self-gratification. Ask anyone who's served with him. They'll all tell you the same."

Chen exchanged a brief look with Wang Ti as she set the bowls down on the table, then nodded. "Or would, if they weren't so afraid of crossing him."

Haavikko nodded. "That's the truth. I've been watching him these past few weeks—spying on him, you might say—and I've seen how he surrounds himself with cronies. A dozen or more of them at times. He settles all their Mess bills and buys them lavish presents. In return they suck up to him, hanging on to his every word, laughing on cue. You know the kind. It's sickening. They call him 'the Hero of Hammerfest,' but he's just a shit. A petty little shit."

Chen wiped his hands, then sat down across from Axel, his blunt face thoughtful. "I know. I've seen it myself. But I can understand it, can't you? After all, as the world sees it he's a powerful man—a *very* powerful man—and those sucking up to him are only little men—*hsiao jen*. Socially they're nothing without him. But they hope to grow bigger by associating with him. They hope to rise on his coattails."

Wang Ti had been watching them, surprised by their change of mood. Gently, careful not to wake the sleeping child, she took Ch'iang Hsin from Haavikko's lap, then turned, facing her husband, the child cradled against her. "Why so bitter, husband? What has the man ever done to you?"

"Nothing . . ." Chen said, meeting her eyes only briefly.

Haavikko looked between the two momentarily, noting the strange movement of avoidance in Chen's eyes, knowing it signified something; then he leaned toward him again.

"There's one particularly vile specimen who hangs about with him. A man by the name of Fest. He was a cadet with me, and afterward he served with Ebert and me under Tolonen. He's a Captain now, of course. But back then . . ." Axel shuddered, then continued. "Well, he was partly to blame for my downfall."

Chen looked past Axel momentarily, lifting his chin, indicating to Wang Ti that she should wait in the other room; then he looked back at Axel, his face creased with concern, his voice suddenly softer, more sympathetic.

"What happened?"

Haavikko hesitated, then gave a small, bitter laugh. "It was different then. I can see that now. The world, I mean. It was shaped differently. Not just in my head, but in its externals. You could trust the appearance of things much more. But even then there were some—Ebert among them—who were made . . . crooked, you might say. *Twisted.* And it's in their nature to shape others in their own distorted form."

He glanced up, giving a little shiver, the sheer rawness of the hurt in his eyes making Chen catch his breath.

"We'd gone down to the Net, the day it happened. Ebert, Fest and I. We were after the assassins of the T'ang's Minister, Lwo Kang, and had been told to wait for a contact from our Triad connections there. Well, I didn't know that Ebert had arranged for us to stay in a singsong house. It began there, I guess. He had me drugged and I . . . well, I woke up in bed with one of the girls. That was the start of it. It doesn't seem much, looking back, but it's . . . well, it's like I was clean before then; another person, unsullied, untouched by all those darker things that came to dominate me."

"And that's what happened?"

Haavikko gave a bitter laugh. "No. But that was where it began. I can see that now. The two things are inseparable. That and what followed. They were part of the same process. Part of the twistedness that emanates from that man."

"Ebert, you mean?"

Haavikko nodded. "Anyway . . . It was later that day. After we'd found the corpses of the assassins. After we'd gone to the Pit and seen Karr defeat and kill the adept, Hwa. Ebert made us go to the dressing rooms after the fight. He wanted to take Karr out to supper and share in his victory. It was something he didn't own, you see, and he wanted to buy it. But Karr was having none of it. And then Tolonen arrived and accepted Karr's services as guide. Oh, it's all linked. I see that clearly now. But back then . . . well, I thought things just happened. You know the saying *Mei fa tzu,* 'It's fate.' But there was a design to it. A shape."

Haavikko paused, taking a deep, shuddering breath, then continued.

"It was when we were coming away from the assassin's apartment. We were in the sedan: Ebert, Fest, and I. Ebert was sounding off, first about Karr and then about the General. He said things that he would never have dared say to the General's face. When I called him out for it, Fest came between us. He told me to forget what was said. But I couldn't . . ."

Haavikko was silent a moment, looking down at his hands. When he looked up again there was a strange sadness in his eyes.

"I don't regret what I did. Even now I don't think I would have acted any other way. It was just . . . well, let me tell you. When I was alone with the General I asked to be transferred. I felt unclean, you see. Of course, the old man asked me for my reasons. But when I tried to avoid giving them he ordered me to tell him what was up. So I did. I told him what was said in the sedan."

Chen let out his breath. "I see . . ."

"Yes. You can imagine. Tolonen was livid. He called Ebert and Fest back at once. It wasn't what I wanted; even then I didn't feel it was right to get Ebert thrown out of the force for something he'd said in a heated moment. But it was out of my hands at that stage. And then . . ."

"Fest backed him up?"

Haavikko nodded. "I couldn't believe it. They were both so convincing. So much so that for months afterward I kept asking myself whether I'd been wrong. Whether I'd imagined it all. Whether their version of things was really the truth. It was as if I'd had a bad dream. But it was one I couldn't wake from. And it all began back then. On that day ten years ago."

A voice came from the shadows of the doorway behind them. "I remember that day well."

The two men looked around, surprised. There was a figure in the doorway, a giant of a man, his head stooped to clear the lintel, his broad shoulders filling the frame of the door. Karr.

Chen was up out of his chair at once. He went across and embraced the big man, smiling fiercely. "Gregor! You should have said you were coming!"

Karr held his friend's arms a moment, smiling down into his face; then he looked back at Axel.

"Yes. I remember you well, Axel Haavikko. I remember you coming to watch me fight that day. But I never understood until today why you disappeared from things so suddenly. You have good cause to hate Major Ebert."

Haavikko looked down, abashed. "If I spoke out of turn, Major Karr . . ."

Karr laughed. He had put his arm about Chen's shoulders familiarly, like a father about his son's. "Here, in Kao Chen's, we have an agreement, and you must be a party to it, Axel. In these rooms there is no rank, no formality, understand? Here we are merely friends. Kao Chen insists on it, and I . . ." his smile broadened. "Well, as your senior officer, I insist upon it, too. Here Chen is Chen. And I am Gregor."

Karr put out a hand. Haavikko stood up slowly, looking at the offered hand, hesitant even now to commit himself so far. But then he looked at Chen and saw how his friend's eyes urged him to take Karr's hand.

He swallowed dryly. "I'm grateful. But there's one further thing you should know about me before you accept me here." He looked from one to the other. "You are good men, and I would have no secrets from you. You must know what I am. What I have done."

"Go on," Karr said, his hand still offered.

Haavikko stared back at Karr, meeting his gray eyes unflinchingly. "You heard me say how it felt as though I were in a bad dream, unable to wake. Well, for ten years I inhabited that nightmare, living it day and night. But then, a month or so ago, I woke from it. Again I found myself in bed in a singsong house, and once again a strange girl was lying there beside me. But this time the girl was dead, and I knew that I had killed her."

Karr's eyes narrowed. "You *knew*?"

Haavikko shuddered. "Yes. I remember it quite vividly."

Karr and Chen looked at each other, some sign of understanding passing between them; then Karr looked back at Haavikko. His hand had not wavered for a moment. It was still offered.

"We have all done things we are ashamed of, Axel Haavikko. Even this thing you say you did—even that does not make you a bad man. Chen here, for instance. Would you say he was a good man?"

Haavikko looked at Chen. "I would stake my life on it."

"Then it would surprise you, perhaps, to learn that Kao Chen was one of the two assassins you were after that day ten years ago."

Haavikko shook his head. "No. He can't be. They were dead, both of them. I saw the *kwai*'s body for myself."

Karr smiled. "No. That was another man. A man Chen paid to play himself. It's something he's not proud of. Something he'd rather hadn't happened. Even so, it doesn't make him a bad man."

Haavikko was staring at Chen now with astonishment. "Of course . . . the scar." He moved forward, tracing the scar beneath Chen's left ear with his forefinger. "I know you now. You were the one on film. With your friend, the small man. In the Main of Level Eleven."

Chen laughed, surprised. "You had that on film?"

"Yes . . ." Haavikko frowned. "But I still don't understand. If you were one of the killers . . ."

Karr answered for Chen. "Li Shai Tung pardoned Kao Chen. He saw what I saw at once. What you yourself also saw. That Chen is a good man. An honest man, when he's given the chance to be. So men are, unless necessity shapes them otherwise."

"Or birth . . ." Haavikko said, thinking again of Ebert.

"So?" Karr said, his hand still offered. "Will you join us, Axel? Or will you let what's past shape what you will be?"

Haavikko looked from one to the other; then, smiling fiercely at him, tears brimming at the corners of his eyes, he reached out and took Karr's hand.

"Good," said Wang Ti, appearing in the doorway. She moved past them, smiling at Axel, as if welcoming him for the first time. "And about time, too. Come, you three. Sit down and eat, before dinner spoils."

━━━━━

OVER THE MEAL Karr outlined what had been happening since his return from Mars. Their one real clue from the Executive Killings had led them to a small *Ping Tiao* cell in the Mids fifty *li* south of Bremen. His men were keeping a watch on the comings and goings of the terrorists. They had strict orders not to let the *Ping Tiao* know they were being observed, but it was not something they could do indefinitely.

"I'm taking a squad in tonight," Karr said, sitting back from table and wiping at his mouth with the back of his hand. "In the small hours. I want to capture as many of the cell members as possible, so we'll need to be on our toes."

Chen nodded, his mouth full. He chewed for a moment, then swallowed. "That'll be difficult. They organize tightly and post guards at all hours. And then, when you do confront them, they melt away like shadows. You'll have to corner them somehow. But even if you do, I've heard they'd rather die than be captured."

"Yes . . . but then, so will most men if they're given no other option. Sun Tzu is right: leave but one avenue for a man to escape by and his determination to fight to the death will be totally undermined. He will recognize how sweet life is and cling to it. So it will be tonight. I'll offer them a pathway back to life. If I can capture just one of them, perhaps we'll get to the bottom of this."

Haavikko smiled. The man looked, even ate, like a barbarian, but he thought like a general. Tolonen had not been wrong all those years ago when he had recognized this in Karr. Haavikko put his chopsticks down and pushed his bowl away, then reached into his pocket and took the notebook from it.

"What's that?" Karr said, lifting his chin.

Haavikko handed it across the table. "See for yourself."

He watched as the big man thumbed through the notebook. At first Karr simply frowned, not understanding; then, slowly, he began to nod, a faint smile forming on his lips. Finally he looked up, meeting Axel's eyes.

"You did this all yourself?"

"Yes."

Chen pushed his bowl aside and leaned forward, interested. "What is it?"

Karr met his eyes thoughtfully. "It's an analysis of the official investigation into Minister Lwo Kang's murder. And if I'm not mistaken, there are a number of things here that were never included in the findings of the T'ang's committee."

Karr handed the book across to Chen, then looked back at Haavikko. "May I ask why you did this, Axel?"

"I was ordered to."

Karr laughed. "Ordered to?"

"Yes, by General Tolonen, shortly before I was dismissed from his service. He asked me to compile a list of suspects, however improbable. Men who might have been behind the assassins. It was a direct order, one he never rescinded."

Karr stared back at Haavikko, astonished. "I see. But then surely Marshal Tolonen ought to have it?"

Haavikko hesitated, then looked down, shaking his head.

"I understand," Karr said after a moment. "And maybe you're right. After what happened there's no reason why he should trust you, is there? The Marshal would see it only as an attempt to get back at Ebert. He'd think you had invented this to discredit your enemies."

Haavikko nodded, then looked up again, his eyes burning fiercely now. "But you two know Ebert. You know what he is. So maybe that,"—he indicated the notebook in Chen's hands— "incomplete as it is, will help us nail the bastard."

Chen looked up. "He's right, Gregor. This makes interesting reading."

"Interesting, yes, but not conclusive."

Chen nodded thoughtfully, smiling back at Karr. "Exactly. Even so, it's a beginning."

"Something to work on."

"Yes . . ."

Haavikko saw how the two men smiled knowingly at each other and felt a sudden warmth—a sense of belonging—flood through him. He was alone no longer. Now there were three of them, and together they would break Ebert, expose him for the sham—the hollow shell—he was.

Karr looked back at him. "Is this the only copy?"

"No. There's a second copy, among some things I've willed to my sister, Vesa."

"Good," Karr turned to Chen. "In that case, you hang on to that copy, Chen. I'm giving you two-weeks paid leave. Starting tomorrow. I want you to follow up some of those leads. Especially those involving men known to be friends or business acquaintances of the Eberts."

"And if I find anything?"

There was a hammering at the outer door to the apartment. The three men turned, facing it, Kao Chen getting to his feet.

There was an exchange of voices; then a moment later, Wang Ti appeared in the doorway.

"It's a messenger for you, Major Karr," she said, the use of Karr's rank indicating that the man was within hearing in the next room.

"I'll come," said Karr, but he was gone only a few moments. When he came back, his face was livid with anger.

"I don't believe it. They're dead."

"Who?" said Chen, alarmed.

"The *Ping Tiao* cell. All eight of them." Karr's huge frame shuddered with indignation; then, his eyes looking inward, he nodded to himself. "Someone knew. Someone's beaten us to it."

〰〰〰

EBERT WAS STANDING with his Captain, Auden, laughing, his head thrown back, when Karr arrived. Signs of a heavy fire-fight were everywhere. Body bags lay to one side of the big intersection, while the corridors leading off were strewn with wreckage.

Karr looked about him at the carnage, then turned, facing Ebert. "Who was it?" he demanded.

"Who was what?" Ebert said tersely, almost belligerently.

"Was it DeVore?"

Ebert laughed coldly. "What are you talking about, Major Karr? They were *Ping Tiao*. But they're dead now. Eight less of the bastards to worry about."

Karr went still, suddenly realizing what had happened. "You killed them?"

Ebert looked at Auden again, a faint smile reappearing. "Every last one of them."

Karr clenched his fists, controlling himself. "Is there somewhere we can talk?" he said tightly. "Somewhere private?"

Auden indicated a room off to one side. "I'll post a guard."

"No need," said Karr. "We'll not be long."

When the door closed behind them, Karr rounded on Ebert.

"You stupid bastard! Why didn't you report what you were doing? Who gave you permission to go in without notifying me?"

Ebert's eyes flared. "I don't need *your* permission, Karr."

Karr leaned in on him angrily. "In this instance you did!

Marshal Tolonen put me in charge of this investigation; and while it's still going on, you report to me, understand me, Major Ebert? Your precipitate action has well and truly fucked things up. I had this cell staked out."

Ebert looked up at the big man defiantly, spitting the words back at him. "Well, I've simply saved you the trouble, haven't I?"

Karr shook his head. "You arrogant bastard. Don't you understand? I didn't want them dead. We were going in tonight. I wanted at least one of them alive. Now the whole bloody lot of them will have gone to ground and the gods know when we'll get another chance like this."

Ebert was glaring back at him, his hands shaking with anger. "You're not pinning this on me, Karr. It's you who've fouled up, not me. I was just doing my job. Following up on evidence received. If you can't keep your fellow officers informed . . ."

Karr raised his hand, the fingers tensed, as if to strike Ebert in the face; then he slowly let the tension ease from him. Violence would achieve nothing.

"Did any of our men get hurt?"

There was an ugly movement in Ebert's face. He looked aside, his voice subdued. "A few . . ."

"Meaning what?"

Ebert hesitated, then looked back at him again. "Four dead, six injured."

"Four dead! *Ai ya!* What the fuck were you up to?" Karr shook his head, then turned away, disgusted. "You're shit, Ebert, you know that? How could you possibly lose four men? You had only to wait. They'd have had to come at you."

Ebert glared pure hatred at the big man's back. "It wasn't as simple as that . . ."

Karr turned back. "You fucked up!"

Ebert looked away, then looked back, his whole manner suddenly more threatening. "I think you've said enough, Karr. Understand? I'm not a man to make an enemy of."

Karr laughed caustically. "You repeat yourself, Major Ebert. Or do you forget our first meeting." He leaned forward and spat between Ebert's feet. "There! That might jog your memory. You were a shit then and you're a shit now."

"I'm not afraid of you, Karr."

"No . . ." Karr nodded. "No, you're not a coward; I'll give you that. But you're still a disgrace to the T'ang's uniform, and if I can, I'll break you."

Ebert laughed scornfully. "You'll try."

"Yes, I'll try. Fucking hard, I'll try. But don't underestimate me, Hans Ebert. Just remember what I did to Master Hwa that time in the Pit. He underestimated me, and he's dead."

"Is that a threat?"

"Take it as you want. But between men, if you understand me. You go before the Marshal and I'll deny every last word. Like you yourself once did, ten years ago."

Ebert narrowed his eyes. "That officer with you—it's Haavikko, isn't it? I thought I recognized the little shit."

Karr studied Ebert a moment, knowing for certain now that Haavikko had told the truth about him; then he nodded. "Yes, Haavikko. But don't even think of trying anything against him. If he so much as bruises a finger without good reason, I'll come for you. And a thousand of your cronies won't stop me."

━━━━━

TSU MA STOOD in the courtyard of the stables at Tong-jiang, waiting while the groom brought the Arab from its stall. He looked about him, for once strangely ill at ease, disconcerted to learn that she had ridden off ahead of him.

He had tried to cast her from his mind, to drive from his heart the spell she had cast over him; but it was no use. He was in love with her.

In love. He laughed, surprised at himself. It had never happened to him before. Never, in all his thirty-seven years.

He had only to close his eyes and the image of her would come to him, taking his breath. And then he would remember how it was, there on the island in the lantern light; how he had watched her lose herself in the tune she had been playing; how her voice had seemed the voice of his spirit singing, freed like a bird into the darkness of the night. And later, when he had been in the water, he had seen how she stood behind her husband, watching him, her eyes curious, lingering on his naked chest.

One life? she had asked, standing in the doorway of the ruined temple. *One life?* as if it meant something special. As if it invited him to touch her. But then, when he had leaned forward to brush her cheek, her neck, she had moved back as if he had transgressed; and all his knowledge of her had been shattered by her refusal.

Had he been wrong those times? Had he misjudged her? It seemed so. And yet she had sent word to him. Secretly. A tiny, handwritten note, asking him to forgive her moodiness, to come and ride with her again. Was it merely to be sociable—for her husband's sake—or should he read something more into it?

He could still hear her words. *If I were free . . .*

Even to contemplate such an affair was madness. It could only make for bad blood between the Li clan and himself and shatter the age-old ties between their families. He knew that. And yet the merest thought of her drove out all consideration of what he *ought* to do. She had bewitched him, robbed him of his senses. That, too, he knew. And yet his knowledge was as nothing beside the compulsion that drove him to see her again. To risk everything simply to be with her.

He turned, hearing the groom return with the Arab.

"*Chieh Hsia.*" The boy bowed, offering the reins.

Tsu Ma smiled and took the reins. Then, putting one foot firmly in the stirrup, he swung up onto the Arab's back. She moved skittishly but he steadied her, using his feet. It was Li Yuan's horse; the horse he had ridden the last time he had come. He turned her slowly, getting used to her again, then dug in his heels, spurring her out of the courtyard and north, heading out into the hills.

He knew where he would find Fei Yen; there at the edge of the temple pool where they had last spoken. She stood there, her face turned from him, her whole stance strangely disconsolate. Her face was pale, far paler than he remembered, as if she had been ill. He frowned, disconcerted by something; then with a shock, he recognized the clothes she was wearing. Her riding tunic was a pink that was almost white, edged with black; her trousers were azure blue; and her hair . . . her hair was beaded with rubies.

He laughed softly, astonished. They were the same colors—the same jewels—he had worn the first time they had met. But what did it mean?

She looked up as he approached, her eyes pained, her lips pressed together, her mouth strangely hard. She had been crying.

"I didn't know if you would come."

He hesitated, then went across to stand at her side.

"You shouldn't be riding out so far alone."

"No?"

The anger in her voice took him aback. He reached into his tunic and took out a silk handkerchief. "Here . . . What's wrong?"

He watched her dab her cheeks, and wipe her eyes, his heart torn from him by the tiny shudder she gave. He wanted to reach out and wrap her in his arms, to hold her tight and comfort her; but he had been wrong before.

"I can't bear to see you crying."

She looked at him, anger flashing in her eyes again, then looked down, as if relenting. "No . . ." She sniffed, then crushed the silk between her hands. "No, it's not your fault, Tsu Ma."

He wet his lips, then spoke again. "Where is your husband?"

She laughed bitterly, staring down fixedly at her clenched hands. "Husbands! What is a husband but a tyrant!"

Once more the anger in her face surprised him.

She stared up at him, her eyes wide, her voice bitter. "He sleeps with his maids. I've seen him."

"Ah . . ." He looked down into the water, conscious of her image there in front of him. "Maybe it's because he's a man."

"A man!" She laughed caustically, her eyes meeting his in the mirror of the pool, challenging him. "And men are different, are they? Have they different appetites, different needs?" She looked back at the reality of him, forcing him to look at her and meet her eyes. "You sound like my brothers, Tsu Ma. They think the matter of their sex makes them my superior when any fool can see—"

She stopped, then laughed, glancing at him. "You see, even the language we use betrays me. I would have said, not half the man I am."

He nodded, for the first time understanding her. "Yet it is how things are ordered," he said gently. "Without it—"

"I know," she said impatiently, then repeated it more softly, smiling at him. "I know."

He studied her a moment, remembering what her cousin Yin

Wu Tsai had said—that she had been born with a woman's body and a man's soul. It was true. She looked so fragile, so easily broken; yet there was something robust, something hard and uncompromising, at the core of her. Maybe it was that—the precarious balance in her nature—that he loved. That sense he had of fire beneath the ice. Of earthiness beneath the superficial glaze.

"You're not like other women."

He said it softly, admiringly, and saw how it brought a movement in her eyes, a softening of her features.

"And you? Are you like other men?"

Am I? he asked himself. Or am I simply what they expect me to be? As he stared back at her he found he had no answer. If to be T'ang meant he could never have his heart's desire, then what use was it being T'ang? Better never to have lived.

"I think I am," he answered after a moment. "I have the same feelings and desires and thoughts."

She was watching him intently, as if to solve some riddle she had set herself. Then she looked down, away from him, the faintest smile playing on her lips. "Yes, but it's the balance of those things that makes a man what he is, wouldn't you say, Tsu Ma?"

He laughed. "And you think my balance . . . different?"

She looked up at him challengingly. "Don't you?" She lifted her chin proudly, her dark eyes wide. "I don't really know you, Tsu Ma, but I know this much—you would defy the world to get what you wanted."

He felt himself go still. Then she understood him, too. But still he held back, remembering the mistake he had made before. To be rebuffed a second time would be unthinkable, unbearable. He swallowed and looked down.

"I don't know. I—"

She stood abruptly, making him look up at her, surprised.

"All this talking," she said, looking across to where their horses were grazing. "It's unhealthy. Unnatural." She looked back at him. "Don't you think so?"

He stood slowly, fascinated by the twist and turn of her, her ever-changing moods. "What do you suggest?"

She smiled, suddenly the woman he had met that first time,

laughing and self-confident, all depths, all subtleties gone from her.

"I know what," she said. "Let's race. To the beacon. You know it?"

He narrowed his eyes. "We passed it ten *li* back, no?"

"That's it." Her smile broadened. "Well? Are you game?"

"Yes," he said, laughing. "Why not? And no quarter, eh? No holding back."

"Of course," she answered, her eyes meeting his knowingly. "No holding back."

———————

FEI YEN REINED IN her horse and turned to look back down the steep slope beneath the beacon. Tsu Ma was some fifty *ch'i* back, his mount straining, its front legs fighting for each *ch'i* of ground.

Her eyes shone and her chest rose and fell quickly. She felt exhilarated. It had been a race to remember.

Tsu Ma reined in beside her. His mount pulled its head back, overexcited by the chase, and he leaned down to smooth it, stroking the broad length of its face. Then he looked up at Fei Yen, his strong features formed into a smile of pleasure.

"That was good. I haven't enjoyed myself so much in years!"

He laughed, a deep, rich laugh that sent a shiver down her spine. Then he reached out and drew the hair back from where it had fallen across her face. His hand rested against her cheek.

It was the first time he had touched her.

He withdrew his hand and turned from her, standing in his saddle and looking out across the valley. They were at the highest point for twenty *li* around. To their backs and distant were the foothills of the Ta Pa Shan, but before them was only the plain.

Or what had once been the plain. In his grandfather's time the City had stretched only as far as Ch'ung Ch'ing. Now it covered all the lowlands of Sichuan. From where he looked it glistened whitely in the afternoon sunlight, a crystalline growth come to within a dozen *li* of where they were. He could not see its full extent from where he stood, but he knew that it filled the

Ch'ang Chiang Basin, eight hundred *li* south to the mountains, a thousand *li* east to west. A vast plateau of ice.

He lowered himself in the saddle, then turned, looking back at her. She was watching him, concerned. Such a look as a wife gives her man. Thinking this, he smiled and remembered why he'd come.

He climbed down from his mount and walked across to her. "Come!" he said, offering her his hand to help her down. But this time he did not relinquish her. This time he turned her to face him, enveloping her in his arms.

She looked up at him expectantly, her mouth open, the bottom lip raised, almost brutal in what it implied. Her eyes seared him, so fierce was their demand. And her body, where he gripped it, seemed to force itself into him.

It was as he'd thought.

He kissed her, his mouth crushing hers, answering her need with his own. For a moment they struggled with each other's clothing, tearing at the lacing, freeing themselves; and then he had lifted her onto him and was thrusting deep into her, her legs wrapped about his back, her pelvis pushing down urgently to meet his movements.

"My love," she said, her dark eyes wide, aroused, her fine, small hands caressing his neck. "Oh my love, my Lord . . ."

CHAPTER NINE

The Veiled Light

L I YUAN STOOD with his father at the center of the viewing circle, looking down at the great globe of Chung Kuo, 160,000 *li* below. Down there it was night. Lit from within, the great, continent-spanning mass of City Europe glowed a soft, almost pearled white, bordered on all sides by an intensity of blackness. To the south—beyond the darkness of the Chung Hai, the ancient Mediterranean—glowed City Africa, its broad, elongated shape curving out of view; while to the east—separated from City Europe by the dark barrier of the East European Plantations—City Asia began, a vast glacier, stretching away into the cold heart of the immense land mass.

The room in which they stood was dimly lit; the double doors at the top of the steps leading to the T'ang's private rooms were closed. It was warm in the room, yet, as ever, the illusion of coldness prevailed.

"What have you decided, Father?"

The T'ang turned to his son, studying him thoughtfully, then smiled.

"To wait to hear what the Marshal says. He saw the boy this morning."

"Ah . . ." Li Yuan glanced at the slender folder he was carrying beneath his arm. In it were copies of the records Karr had brought back with him from Mars: Berdichev's personal files, taken from the corpse of his private secretary three days before Karr had caught up with Berdichev himself.

It had taken them two weeks to break the complex code, but it had been worth it. Besides giving them access to a number of secret SimFic files—files that gave them the location of several special projects Berdichev had instigated—they had also contained several items of particular interest.

The first was a detailed breakdown of the events leading up to the assassination of the Edict Minister, Lwo Kang, ten years earlier. It was similar in many respects to the document Tolonen had brought to Li Shai Tung shortly after the event—the papers drawn up by Major DeVore. That document, and the web of inference and connection it had drawn, had been enough to condemn the Dispersionist Edmund Wyatt to death for treason. But now they knew it for what it was. Though Wyatt had been against the Seven, he had played no part in the murder of Minister Lwo. No, he had been set up by his fellow conspirators. But Wyatt's death, almost as surely as the destruction of the starship *The New Hope*, had brought about the War that followed.

Li Yuan looked back at his father, conscious of how much he had aged in the years between. The War had emptied him, stripped him of all illusions. Five years ago he would not have even contemplated the Wiring Project. But times had changed. New solutions were necessary. The second file was confirmation of that.

"About the Aristotle File, Father. Do we know yet if any copies were made?"

Li Shai Tung looked down past his feet at the blue-white circle of Chung Kuo.

"Nothing as yet, Yuan. So maybe we've been lucky. Maybe it wasn't disseminated."

"Perhaps . . ." But both knew that the Aristotle File was too important—too potentially damaging to the Seven—for Berdichev to have kept it to himself. For it was no less than the true history of Chung Kuo, the version of events the tyrant Tsao Ch'un had buried beneath his own.

Li Yuan shivered, remembering the day he had found out the truth about his world, recollecting suddenly the dream he had had, a vision of a vast mountain of bones filling the plain from horizon to horizon. The foundations of his world.

"You know, Yuan, I was standing here the night you were born. It was late and I was looking down at Chung Kuo, wondering what lay ahead. I had been dreaming . . ."

He looked up, meeting his son's eyes.

"Dreaming, Father?"

The T'ang hesitated, then gave a small shake of his head. "No matter. Just that it struck me as strange. The boy and all . . ."

He knew what his father meant.

The third file concerned a boy Berdichev had taken a personal interest in, a Clayborn child from the Recruitment Project for whom Berdichev had paid the extraordinary sum of ten million *yuan*.

Part of the file was a genotyping—a comparison of the child's genetic material to that of a man alleged to be his father. The result of the genotyping was conclusive. The man *was* the child's father. And the man's name? Edmund Wyatt—the person wrongly executed for orchestrating the assassination of the T'ang's minister, Lwo Kang.

That had been strange enough, but stranger yet was a footnote to the file; it revealed that instead of being the work of Soren Berdichev, as was claimed on the file itself, the Aristotle File had, in fact, been compiled and authored by the boy.

The fact that had struck them both, however, was the date the genotyping had given for the conception of the boy, a date that coincided with a visit Wyatt, Berdichev, and Lehmann had made to a singsong house in the Clay.

It was the day Li Yuan had been born. The day his mother, Lin Yua, had died giving birth to him, three months premature.

It was as if the gods were playing with them. Taking and giving, and never offering an explanation. But which was the Clayborn boy—gift or curse? On the evidence of the Aristotle File he seemed—potentially, at least—a curse; yet if the reports on him were to be believed, he might prove the greatest asset the Seven possessed. The question that confronted them—the question they had met today to answer—was simple: should they attempt to harness his talents or should they destroy him?

There was a banging on the great doors at the far end of the room.

"Come in!" the T'ang answered, turning to face the new-comer.

It was Tolonen. He strode in purposefully, then stopped three paces from the T'ang, clicking his heels together and bowing his head.

"*Chieh Hsia.*"

"Well, Knut? You've seen the boy. What do you think?"

Tolonen lifted his head, surprised by the abruptness with which the T'ang had raised the matter. It was unlike him. He turned briefly to Li Yuan, giving a small bow, then turned back to Li Shai Tung, a smile forming.

"I liked him, *Chieh Hsia.* I liked him very much. But that's not what you asked me, is it? You asked me whether I thought we could trust the boy. Whether we could risk using him in such a delicate area of research."

"And?"

Tolonen shrugged. "I'm still not certain, *Chieh Hsia.* My instinct tends to confirm what was in the file. He's loyal. The bond he formed with his tutor, T'ai Cho, for instance, was a strong one. I think that's inbred in his nature. But then, there's the fight with the boy Janko to consider and the whole personality reconstruction business subsequent to that. He's not the same person he was before all that. We have to ask ourselves how that has affected him. Has it made him more docile and thus easier to control, or has it destabilized him? I can't answer that, I'm afraid. I really can't."

The T'ang considered a moment, then nodded, smiling at his Marshal. "Thank you, Knut. Your fears are the mirror of my own. I have already signed the death warrant. I was merely waiting to hear what you would say."

"But, Father . . ." Li Yuan started forward, then stepped back, lowering his head. "Forgive me, I . . ."

Li Shai Tung stared at his son a moment, surprised by his interruption, then frowned. "Well, Yuan?"

"A thousand apologies, Father. I was forgetting myself."

"You wished to say something?"

Li Yuan bowed. "I . . . I merely wished to caution against being too hasty in this matter."

"Too hasty?" The old T'ang laughed and looked across at Tolonen. "I've been told I was many things in my life, but too hasty . . . What do you mean, Li Yuan? Speak out."

"The boy . . ." Li Yuan looked up, meeting his father's eyes. "If what is written about the boy is true, if he is but a fraction as talented as is said . . . Well, it would be a great waste to kill him."

Li Shai Tung studied his son carefully. "You forget why we fought the War, Yuan. To contain change, not to sponsor it. This boy, Kim. Look at the mischief he has done already with his 'talent.' Look at the file he made. What is to prevent him making further trouble?"

Li Yuan swallowed, sensing that everything depended on what he said in the next few moments, that his father had not quite made up his mind, even now.

"With respect, Father, things have changed. We all know that. Our enemies are different now, subtler, more devious than ever before. And the means they use have changed, too. While we continue to ignore the possibilities of technology, they are busy harnessing it—against us." Li Yuan looked down. "It's as if the gods have given us a gift to use against our enemies. We have only to monitor him closely."

"It was tried before. You forget just how clever the boy is."

Li Yuan nodded. "I realize that, Father. Even so, I think it can be done."

The T'ang considered a moment, then turned back, facing Tolonen. "Well, Knut? What do *you* think?"

Tolonen bowed. "I think it could be done, *Chieh Hsia*. And would it harm to delay a little before a final decision is made?"

The T'ang laughed. "Then I am outnumbered."

Tolonen smiled back at him. "Your one is bigger than our two, *Chieh Hsia*."

"So it is. But I'm not a stupid man. Nor inflexible." He turned, facing his son again. "All right, Yuan. For now I'll leave this in your hands. You'll arrange the matter of security with Marshal Tolonen here. But the boy will be your direct responsibility, understand me? He lives because you wish him to. You will keep my warrant with you and use it if you must."

Li Yuan smiled and bowed his head low. "As my father wishes."

"Oh, and one more thing, Yuan. It would be best if you saw the boy yourself." He smiled. "You have two places left to fill on the Wiring Project, I understand."

"I was . . . keeping them in case."

"I thought as much. Then go. See the boy at once. And if your view of him confirms the Marshal's, we'll do as you say. But be careful, Yuan. Knowledge is a two-edged sword."

When his son was gone, the T'ang turned back, facing his Marshal.

"Keep me closely informed, Knut. Yuan is not to know, but I want us to know where Kim is at all times. Maybe he is what Yuan claims. But what can be used by us can just as easily be used by our enemies, and I'm loath to see this one fall back into their hands. You understand me clearly, Knut?"

"I understand, *Chieh Hsia.*"

"Good. Then let us speak of other matters. Your daughter, Jelka. How is she?"

Tolonen's eyes brightened. "Much better, *Chieh Hsia.* She is back home now."

Li Shai Tung frowned. "Was that wise, Knut? I mean . . . to be back where the attack happened."

"The doctors thought it best. And I . . . well, for all that happened, I felt she would be safest there."

"I see. But she is still not quite as she was, I take it?"

Tolonen looked down, his eyes troubled. "Not quite, *Chieh Hsia.*"

"I thought as much. Well, listen to me, Knut. Knowing how busy you'll be these next few weeks, I've come up with an idea that might put your mind at ease and allow Jelka to come to terms with her experience."

"*Chieh Hsia?*"

"You remember the island your family owned? Off the coast of Finland?"

"Near Jakobstad?" Tolonen laughed. "How could I forget? I spent a month there with Jenny, shortly after we were married."

"Yes . . ." The two men were silent a moment, sharing the

sweet sadness of the memory. "Well," said Li Shai Tung, brightening, "why not take Jelka there for a few weeks?"

Tolonen beamed. "Yes! Of course!" Then he grew quiet. "But as you say, I am far too busy, *Chieh Hsia*. Who would look after her? And then there's the question of passes . . ."

The T'ang reached out and touched his Marshal's arm. It was like Tolonen not to abuse the Pass Laws, not to grant permissions for his family or friends. In all the years he had known him he had not heard of one instance of Tolonen using his position for his own advantage.

"Don't worry, Knut. I've arranged everything already. Passes, supplies, even a special squad to guard her." He smiled broadly, enjoying the look of surprise on Tolonen's face. "Your brother, Jon, and his wife have agreed to stay with her while she's there."

Tolonen laughed, astonished. "Jon?" Then he shook his head, overcome with emotion. "I'm deeply grateful, *Chieh Hsia*. It will be perfect. Just the thing she needs. She'll love it, I know she will."

"Good. Then you'll take her yourself, tomorrow. After you've sorted out this business with the boy. And Knut?"

"Yes, *Chieh Hsia*."

"Don't hurry back. Stay with her a night. See her settled in, neh?"

"Is that an order, *Chieh Hsia*?"

The T'ang smiled and nodded. "Yes, dear friend. It is an order."

◆◆◆◆◆

AFTER TOLONEN HAD gone, Li Shai Tung went to his private rooms. He bathed and dressed in his evening silks, then settled in the chair beside the carp pond, picking up the *Hung Lou Meng*, the *Dream of Red Mansions*, which he had discarded earlier. For a while he tried to read, tried to sink back down into the fortunes of young Pao-yu and his beloved cousin, Tai-yu, but it was no good; his mind kept returning to the question of the Aristotle File and what it might mean for Chung Kuo.

His son Li Yuan had seen it all five years before, in those first few days after he had been told the secret of their world—the Great Lie upon which everything was built. He remembered how Yuan had come to him that night, pale and frightened, awakened by a terrible dream.

Why do we keep the truth from them? Yuan had demanded. *What are we afraid of? That it might make them think other than we wish them to think? That they might make other choices than the ones we wish them to make?*

Back then he had argued with his son, had denied Yuan's insistence that they were the jailers of Tsao Ch'un's City, the inheritors of a system that shaped them for ill. *We are our own men,* he had said. But was it so? Were they really in control? Or did unseen forces shape them?

He had always claimed to be acting for the best; not selfishly, but for all men, as the great sage Confucius had said a ruler should act. So he had always believed. But now, as he entered his final years, he had begun to question what had been done in his name.

Was there truly any real difference between concealing the truth from a man and the placing of a wire in his head?

Once he might have answered differently, might have said that the two things were different in kind; but now he was not so certain. Five years of war had changed him, soured him.

He sighed and looked back down at the page before closing the book.

"You were right, Pao-yu. All streams are sullied. Nothing is *ch'ing* . . . nothing pure."

He stood, then cast the book down onto the chair angrily. Where had his certainty gone? Where the clarity of his youth?

He had foreseen it all, sixteen years ago, on that dreadful evening when his darling wife, Lin Yua, had died giving birth to his second son, Li Yuan. That night he, too, had awoken from an awful dream—a dream of the City sliding down into the maw of chaos, of dear friends and their children dead, and of the darkness to come.

Such dreams had meaning. Were voices from the dark yet knowing part of oneself, voices you ignored only at your peril. And yet they *had* ignored them, had built a System and a City to deny the power of dreams, filling it with illusions and distractions, as if to kill the inner voices and silence the darkness deep within.

But you could not destroy what was inside a man. So maybe Yuan was right. Maybe it *was* best to control it. Now, before it was too late to act. For wasn't it better to have peace—even at such a price—than chaos?

He turned, annoyed with himself, exasperated that no clear answer came.

He stared down into the depths of the carp pool, as if seeking the certainty of the past, then shook his head. "I don't know . . ." he sighed. "I just don't know any longer."

A single carp rose slowly, sluggishly to the surface, then sank down again. Li Shai Tung watched the ripples spread across the pool, then put his hand up to his plaited beard, stroking it thoughtfully.

And Yuan, his son? Was Yuan as certain as he seemed?

He had heard reports of trouble between Yuan and Fei Yen. Had been told that the Prince, his son, had not visited his new wife's bed for several days, and not through pressure of work. He had been there in the Palace at Tongjiang with her, and still he had not visited her bed. That was not right. For a couple to be arguing so early in their relationship did not bode well for the future. He had feared as much—had *known* the match was ill-conceived—but once more he had refused to listen to the voice within. He had let things take their course, like a rider letting go the reins. And if he fell—if his son's unhappiness resulted—who could he blame but himself?

Again the carp rose, swifter this time, as if to bite the air. There was a tiny splash as its mouth lifted above the surface, then it sank down again, merging with the darkness.

Li Shai Tung coiled his fingers through his beard, then nodded. He would let things be. Would watch closely and see how matters developed. But the cusp was fast approaching. He had told Tolonen otherwise, but the truth was that he was not so sure Li Yuan was wrong. Maybe it *was* time to put bit and bridle on the masses, to master events before the whole thing came crashing down on them.

It would not hurt, at least, to investigate the matter. And if the boy Kim could help them find a way . . .

The T'ang turned, then bent down and retrieved the book, finding himself strangely reassured by its familiarity. He brushed at the cover, sorry that he had treated it so roughly. It was a book he had read a dozen times in his life, each time with greater understanding and a growing satisfaction. Things changed, he knew that now, after a lifetime of denying it; but certain things—intrinsic things—remained constant, for all men at all times. And in the interplay of change and certainty each man lived out his life.

It was no different for those who ruled. Yet they had an added burden. To them was ordained the task of shaping the social matrix within which ordinary men had their being. To them was ordained the sacred task of finding balance. For without balance there was nothing.

Nothing but chaos.

━━━━

IT WAS LATE afternoon when Li Yuan finally arrived at Bremen. General Nocenzi had offered his office for the young Prince's use, and it was there, at the very top of the vast, three-hundred-level fortress, that he planned to meet the boy.

Kim was waiting down below. He had been there since his early morning session with Tolonen, unaware of how his fate had hung in the balance in the interim; but Li Yuan did not summon him at once. Instead he took the opportunity to read the files again and look at extracts from the visual record—films taken throughout the eight years of Kim's stay within the Recruitment Project.

They had given the boy the surname Ward, not because it was his name—few of the boys emerging from the Clay possessed even the concept of a family name—but because all those who graduated from the Project bore that name. Moreover, it was used in the *Hung Mao* manner—in that curiously inverted way of theirs, where the family name was last and not first.

Li Yuan smiled. Even that minor detail spoke volumes about the differences in cultures. For the Han had always put the family first. Before the individual.

He froze the final image, then shut down the comset and leaned forward to touch the desk's intercom. At once Nocenzi's private secretary appeared at the door.

"Prince Yuan?"

"Have them bring the boy. I understand there's a Project official with him, too. A man by the name of T'ai Cho. Have him come too."

"Of course, Excellency."

He got up from the desk, then went to the window wall and stood there. He was still standing there, his back to them, when they entered.

T'ai Cho cleared his throat. "Your Excellency . . . ?"

Li Yuan turned and looked at them. They stood close to the door, the boy a pace behind the official. T'ai Cho was a tall man, more than five *ch'i*, his height emphasized by the diminutive size of the Clayborn child. Li Yuan studied them a moment, trying to get the key to their relationship—something more than could be gained from the summaries in the file—then he returned to the desk and sat, leaving them standing.

There were no chairs on the other side of the desk. He saw how T'ai Cho looked about him, then stepped forward.

"Excellency . . ." he began, but Li Yuan raised a hand, silencing him. He had noticed how the boy's eyes kept going to the broad window behind him.

"Tell me, Kim. What do you see?"

The boy was so small; more like a child of eight than a boy of fifteen.

Kim shook his head, but still he stared, his large eyes wide, as if afraid.

"Well?" Li Yuan insisted. "What do you see?"

"Outside," the boy answered softly. "I see outside. Those towers. The top of the City. And there," he pointed out past the Prince, "the sun."

He stopped, then shook his head, as if unable to explain. Li Yuan turned to look where he was pointing as if something wonderful were there. But there were only the familiar guard towers, the blunted edge of the City's walls, the setting sun. Then he understood. Not afraid . . . *awed.*

Li Yuan turned back, frowning; then, trusting to instinct, he came directly to the point.

"I've called you here because you're young, Kim, and flexible of mind. My people tell me you're a genius. That's good. I can use that. But I've chosen you partly because you're not a part of this infernal scientific setup. Which means that you're likely to have a much clearer view of things than most, unsullied by ambition and administrative politics, by a reluctance to deal with me and give me what I want."

He laced his fingers together and sat back.

"I want you to join a scientific team, a team whose aim is to develop and test out a new kind of entertainment system."

Kim narrowed his eyes, interested but also wary.

"However, that's not all I want from you. I want you to do something else for me—something that must be kept secret from the rest of the members of the team, even from Marshal Tolonen."

The boy hesitated, then nodded.

"Good." He studied the boy a moment, aware all the time of how closely the tutor was watching him. "Then let me outline what I want from you. I have a file here of R & D projects undertaken by the late Head of SimFic, the traitor Berdichev. Some are quite advanced, others are barely more than hypothesis. What I want you to do is look at them and assess—in your considered opinion—whether they can be made to work or not. More than that, I want you to find out what they *could* be used for."

He saw the boy frown and explained. "I don't trust the labels Berdichev put on these projects. What he says they were intended for and what their actual use was to be, were, I suspect, quite different."

Again the boy nodded. Then he spoke.

"But why me? And why keep these things secret from the Marshal?"

Li Yuan smiled. It was as they'd said; the boy had a nimble mind.

"As far as Marshal Tolonen is concerned, these things do not exist. If he knew of them he would have them destroyed at once, and I don't want that to happen."

"But surely your father would back you in this?"

He hesitated; then looking at the official sternly, he said, "My father knows nothing of this. He thinks these files have already been destroyed."

T'ai Cho swallowed and bowed his head. "Forgive me, Highness, but . . ."

"Yes?" Li Yuan kept his voice cold, commanding.

"As I say, forgive me, but . . ." The man swallowed again, knowing how much he risked even in speaking out. "Well, I am concerned for the safety of my charge."

"No more than I, *Shih* T'ai. But the job must be done. And to answer Kim's other question—he is, in my estimation, the only one who can do it for me."

Again T'ai Cho's head went down. "But, Highness . . ."

Li Yuan stood angrily. "You forget yourself, T'ai Cho!" He took a breath, calming himself, then spoke again, softer this time. "As I said, I, too, am concerned for Kim's safety. Which is why, this very day, I interceded on the boy's behalf."

He picked up the warrant and handed it to T'ai Cho, seeing his puzzlement change to a bewildered horror. The blood drained from the man's face. T'ai Cho bowed his head low, one trembling hand offering the warrant back. "And you had this rescinded, Highness?"

"Not rescinded, no. Postponed. Kim lives because I wish him to live. My father has made him my responsibility. But I am a fair man. If Kim does as I wish—if he comes up with the answers I want—then I will tear up this document. You understand, T'ai Cho?"

T'ai Cho kept his head lowered. "I understand, Highness."

━━━━━━

FEI YEN was sleeping when he came in. He stood above her, in partial darkness, studying her features, then turned away, noting her discarded riding clothes there on the floor beside the bed. He undressed and slipped into the bed beside her, her body warm and naked beneath the silken sheets; he pressed up close, his hand resting on the slope of her thigh.

In the darkness he smiled, content to lie there next to her. He was too awake, too full of things, to sleep; even so he lay there quietly, mulling things over, comforted by her warmth, her presence there beside him.

He understood now. It was only natural for her to be jealous. It was even possible that some strange, feminine instinct of hers had "known" about his earlier relationship with the girls.

He closed his eyes, listening to her gentle breathing, enjoying the sweet scent of her, the silkiness of her skin beneath his fingers.

After a while he rolled from her and lay there, staring up through layers of darkness at the dim, coiled shape of dragons in the ceiling mosaic, thinking of the boy. Kim was promising—very promising—and he would make sure he got whatever he needed to complete his work. And if, at the end of the year, his results were good, he would reward him handsomely.

That was a lesson he had learned from his father. Such talent as Kim had should be harnessed, such men rewarded well, or destroyed, lest they destroy you. Control was the key. Directed interest.

He stretched and yawned. He had not felt so good in a long time. It was as if everything had suddenly come clear. He laughed softly. It made him feel wonderful—hugely benevolent.

A smile came to his lips as he thought of the thing he had bought Fei Yen that very evening, after he had come from the boy. A thoroughbred, an Arab stallion bred from a line of champions. Its pure white flanks, its fine, strong legs, its proud, aristocratic face—all these combined to form an animal so beautiful that he had known at once she would want it.

He had had it shipped directly to his stables here at Tong-jiang. He would take her first thing in the morning to see it.

He smiled, imagining the delight in her face. Beside him Fei Yen stirred and turned onto her back.

He sat up, then turned, looking down at her. Slowly, carefully, he drew back the sheet, letting it slip from her body, exposing her nakedness. For a while he simply looked, tracing the subtle curves of her body, his fingers not quite touching the surface of her flesh. So delicate she was. So beautiful. A perfect sculpture of the living flesh.

Wake up, he thought. *Wake up, my love.* But the wish was unrequited. Fei Yen slept on.

He lay there a while longer, unable to relax, then got up and put on his robe. His desire had passed the point where he could lie there and forget it. He went into the marbled bathroom and stood there in the shower, letting the cold, hard jets of water purge him.

He stood there a while longer, mindlessly enjoying the flow of water over his limbs. It was lukewarm now, but still refreshing, like a fall of rain, clearing his mind. He was standing there, his arms loose at his sides, when she appeared in the doorway.

"Yuan . . . ?"

He looked up slowly, half conscious of her, and smiled. "You're awake?"

She smiled, looking at him. "Of course. I was waiting for you."

She slipped off her robe and came to him, stepping into the shower beside him, then gave a small shriek.

"Why, Yuan! It's freezing!" She backed out, laughing.

He laughed, then reached up to cut the flow. Looking across he saw how her skin was beaded with tiny droplets.

"Like jewels," he said, stepping out.

She fetched a towel and knelt beside him, drying him, tending to him obediently, as a wife ought. He looked down, feeling a vague desire for her, but he had doused his earlier fierceness.

She stood to dry his shoulders and his hair, her body brushing against his, her breasts and thighs touching him lightly as she moved about him. Turning from him she went to the cupboards, returning a moment later with powders and unguents.

"A treat," she said, standing before him, the fingers of one hand caressing his chest. "But come, let's go into the bedroom."

She laughed, then pushed him through the door before her. It was a raw, strangely sexual laugh, one he had not heard from her before. It made him turn and look at her, as if to find her transformed, but it was only Fei Yen.

"I've missed you," she said as she began to rub oils into his shoulders, his neck, the top of his back. "Missed you a lot." And as her fingers worked their way down his spine he shivered, the words echoing in his head. "Like breath itself, my husband. Like breath itself . . ."

━━━━━

SIX HOURS LATER and half a world away, in the Mids of Danzig Canton, Marshal Tolonen was standing in the main office of the newly formed Wiring Project. He had seen for himself the progress that had been made in the three days since he had last visited the laboratories. Then there had been nothing—nothing but bare rooms—now there was the semblance of a working facility, even though most of the equipment remained in cases, waiting to be unpacked.

Tolonen turned as Administrator Spatz came hurriedly into the room, bowing low, clearly flustered by the Marshal's unannounced arrival.

"Marshal Tolonen, please forgive me. I was not expecting you."

Tolonen smiled inwardly. *No*, he thought, *you weren't. And I'll make it my practice in future to call here unannounced.* He drew himself upright. "I've come to advise you on the last two appointments to your team."

He saw how Spatz hesitated before nodding and wondered why that was; then, pushing the thought from his mind, he turned and snapped his fingers. At once his equerry handed him two files.

"Here," Tolonen said, passing them across. "Please, be seated while you study them."

Spatz bowed, then sat at his desk, opening the first of the files, running his finger over the apparently blank page, the warmth of his touch bringing the characters alive briefly on the specially treated paper. After only a minute he looked up, frowning.

"Forgive me, Marshal, but I thought the last two places were to be filled by working scientists."

"That was the intention."

Spatz looked aside, then looked back up at the Marshal, choosing his words carefully. "And yet . . . well, this man T'ai Cho—he has no scientific background whatsoever. He is a tutor. His qualifications . . ."

Tolonen nodded. "I understand your concern, *Shih* Spatz, but if you would look at the other file."

Spatz nodded, still uncertain; then he set the first file aside, opening the second. Again he ran his finger over the page. This time, however, he took his time, working through the file steadily, giving small nods of his head and occasional grunts of surprise or satisfaction. Finished, he looked up, smiling broadly. "Why, the man's record is extraordinary. I'm surprised I've not heard of him before. Is he from one of the other Cities?"

Tolonen was staring past Spatz, studying the charts on the wall behind him. "You could say that."

Spatz nodded to himself. "And when will he be joining us?"

Tolonen looked back at him. "Right now, if you like."

Spatz looked up. "Really?" He hesitated, then nodded again. "Good. Then there's just one small thing. A mistake, here on the first page." He ran his finger over the top of the page again, then looked up, a bland smile on his lips. "The date of birth . . ."

Tolonen looked away, snapping his fingers. A moment later his equerry returned. This time he was accompanied. "There's no mistake," Tolonen said, turning back.

There was a look of astonishment on Spatz's face. "You mean, *this* is Ward?"

Tolonen looked across at the boy, trying to see him as Spatz saw him; as he himself had first seen him, before he had seen the films that demonstrated the boy's abilities. Looking at him, it seemed almost impossible that this scrawny, dark-haired creature was the accomplished scientist described in the personnel file; yet it was so. Berdichev had not been alone in believing the boy was something special.

Spatz laughed. "Is this some kind of joke, Marshal?"

Tolonen felt himself go cold with anger. He glared back at Spatz and saw the man go white beneath the look.

Spatz stood quickly, bowing his head almost to the desktop. "Forgive me, Marshal, I did not mean . . ."

"Look after him, Spatz," Tolonen answered acidly. "Allocate a man to take care of him for the next few days until his tutor, T'ai Cho, joins him." He shivered, letting his anger drain from him. "And you'll ensure he comes to no harm."

He saw Spatz swallow dryly and nodded to himself, satisfied that he had cowed the man sufficiently. "Good. Then I'll leave him in your custody."

━━━━━

SPATZ WATCHED Tolonen go, then turned his attention to the boy. For a moment he was speechless, still too astonished to take in what it all meant; then he sat heavily and leaned forward, putting his hand down on the summons button. At once his assistant appeared in the doorway.

"Get Hammond in here," he said, noting the way his assistant's eyes went to the boy. "At once!"

He sat back, steepling his hands together, staring across at the boy. Then he laughed and shook his head. "No . . ."

Now that the first shock was wearing off, he was beginning to feel annoyed, angered by the position he had been put in. Now he would have to return the money he had been given to put names forward for the vacancies. Not only that, but in the place of real scientists he had been lumbered with a no-hoper and a child. What had he done to deserve such a thing? Who had he angered?

He looked down at his desk, sniffing deeply. "So you're a scientist, are you, Ward?"

When the boy didn't answer, he looked up, anger blazing in his eyes. "I'll tell you now. I don't know what game people higher up are playing, but I don't believe a word of that file, understand me? And I've no intention of letting you get near anything important. I may have to nurse-maid you, but I'll be damned if I'll let you bugger things up for me."

He stopped. There was someone in the doorway behind the boy.

"You called for me, *Shih* Spatz?"

"Come in, Hammond. I want you to meet our latest recruit, Kim Ward."

He saw how Hammond glanced at the boy, then looked about the room before finally coming back to him.

"You mean, *you're* Ward?" Hammond asked, unable to hide his surprise. "Well, the gods save us!" He laughed, then offered a hand. "I'm Joel Hammond, Senior Technician on the Project."

Seeing how the boy stared at Hammond's hand a moment before tentatively offering his own, how he studied the meeting of their hands, as if it were something wholly new to him, Spatz understood. The boy had never been out in society before. Had never learned such ways. It made Spatz think, made him reconsider what was in the file. Or, rather, what wasn't. But he still didn't believe it. Why, the boy looked nine at the very most. He could not have done so much in so brief a time.

"I want you to look after the boy, Hammond. Until his . . . guardian arrives."

"His guardian?" Hammond looked at Kim again, narrowing his eyes.

"T'ai Cho," Kim answered, before Spatz could explain. "He was my tutor at the Recruitment Project. He was like a father to me."

Gods, thought Spatz, more convinced than ever that someone up-level was fucking with him, willing him to fail in this. A boy and his "father," that was all they needed! He leaned forward again, his voice suddenly colder, more businesslike.

"Look, Hammond. Get him settled in. Show him where things are. Then get back here. Within the hour. I want to brief you more fully, right?"

Hammond glanced at the boy again, giving the briefest of smiles; then he looked back at Spatz, lowering his head. "Of course, Director. Whatever you say."

━━━━━

"Well, Yuan, can I take it off yet?"

He turned her to face him, then untied the silk from her eyes, letting it fall to the ground. She looked up at him, wide-eyed, uncertain, then gave a small, nervous laugh.

"There," he said, pointing beyond her, smiling broadly now.

She turned, looking about her at the stables. The grooms were standing about idly, their jobs momentarily forgotten, watching the young Prince and his bride, all of them grinning widely, knowing what Li Yuan had arranged.

She frowned, not knowing what she was looking for, then turned back, looking at him.

"Go on," he said, encouraging her. "Down there, in the end stall."

Still she hesitated, as if afraid, making him laugh.

"It's a gift, silly." He lowered his voice, slightly. "My way of saying that I'm sorry."

"Down there?"

"Yes. Come, I'll show you."

He took her arm, leading her to the stall.

"There!" he said softly, looking down at her.

She looked. There in the dimness of the stall, stood the horse he had bought her. As she took first one, then another, slow step toward it, the horse turned its long white head, looking back at her, its huge dark eyes assessing her. It made a small noise in its nostrils, then lowered its head slightly, as if bowing to her.

He saw the tiny shudder that went through her and felt himself go still as she went up to the horse and began to stroke its face, its flank. For a moment, that was all. Then she turned and looked back at him, her eyes wet with tears.

"He's beautiful, Yuan. Really beautiful." She shivered, looking back at the horse, her hand resting in its mane, then lowered her head slightly. "You shouldn't have, my love. I have a horse already."

Yuan swallowed, moved by her reaction. "I know, but I wanted to. As soon as I saw him I knew you'd love him." He moved closer, into the dimness of the stall itself, and stood there beside her, his hand resting gently on the horse's flank.

She looked up at him, her eyes smiling through the tears. "Has he a name?"

"He has. But if you want to you can rename him."

She looked back at the Arab. "No. Look at him, Yuan. He is himself, don't you think? A T'ang among horses."

He smiled. "That he is, my love. An Emperor. And his name is *Tai Huo*."

She studied the Arab a moment longer, then turned back, meeting Li Yuan's eyes again. "Great Fire . . . Yes, it suits him perfectly." Her eyes searched Yuan's face, awed, it seemed, by his gift. Then, unexpectedly, she knelt, bowing her head until it touched her knees. "My husband honors me beyond my worth . . ."

At once he pulled her up. "No, Fei Yen. Your husband loves you. I, Yuan, love you. The rest . . ." he shuddered, "well, I was mistaken. It was wrong of me."

"No." She shook her head, then lifted her eyes to his. "I spoke out of turn. I realize that now. It was not my place to order your household. Not without your permission."

"Then you have my permission."

His words brought her up short. "Your permission? To run your household?"

He smiled. "Of course. Many wives do, don't they? And why not mine? After all, I have a clever wife."

Her smile slowly broadened; then, without warning, she launched herself at him, knocking him onto his back, her kisses overwhelming him.

"Fei Yen!"

There was laughter from the nearby stalls, then a rustling of straw as the watching grooms moved back.

He sat up, looking at her, astonished by her behavior; then he laughed and pulled her close again, kissing her. From the stalls nearby came applause and low whistles of appreciation. He leaned forward, whispering in her ear. "Shall we finish this indoors?"

In answer she pulled him down on top of her. "You are a Prince, my love," she said softly, her breath hot in his ear, "you may do as you wish."

━━━━

JOEL HAMMOND stood in the doorway, watching the boy unpack his things. They had barely spoken yet, but he was already conscious that the boy was different from anyone he had ever met. It was not just the quickness of the child, but something indefinable, something that fool Spatz hadn't even been aware of. It was as if the boy were charged with some powerful yet masked vitality. Hammond smiled and nodded to himself. Yes, it was as if the boy were a compact little battery, filled with the energy of *knowing*; a veiled light, awaiting its moment to shine out and illuminate the world.

Kim turned, looking back at him, as if conscious suddenly of his watching eyes.

"What did you do before you came here, *Shih* Hammond?"

"Me?" Hammond moved from the doorway, picking up the map Kim had set down on the table. "I worked on various things, but the reason I'm here is that I spent five years with SimFic working on artificial intelligence."

Kim's eyes widened slightly. "I thought that was illegal? Against the Edict?"

Hammond laughed. "I believe it was. But I was fortunate. The T'ang is a forgiving man. At least, in my case he was. I was pardoned. And here I am."

He looked back down at the map again. "This is the Tun

Huang star chart, isn't it? I saw it once, years ago. Back in college. Are you interested in astronomy?"

The boy hesitated. "I was." Then he turned, facing Hammond, his dark eyes looking up at him challengingly. "Spatz says he's going to keep me off the Project. Can he do that?"

Hammond was taken aback. "I—"

The boy turned away, the fluidity of the sudden movement—so unlike anything he had ever seen before—surprising Hammond. A ripple of fear passed down his spine. It was as if the boy were somehow more and, at the same time, less human than anyone he had ever come across. For a moment he stood there, his mouth open, astonished; then, like a thunderbolt, it came to him. He shuddered, the words almost a whisper.

"You're Clayborn, aren't you?"

Kim took a number of books from the bottom of his bag and added them to the pile on the desk, then looked up again. "Yes. I lived there until I was six."

Hammond shuddered, seeing the boy in a totally new light. "I'm sorry. It must have been awful."

Kim shrugged. "I don't know. I can't remember. But I'm here now. This is my home."

Hammond looked about him at the bare white walls, then nodded. "Yes. Yes, I suppose it is." He put the chart down and picked up one of the books. It was Liu Hui's *Chiu Chang Suan Shu*, "Nine Chapters on the Mathematical Art," the famous third-century treatise from which all Han science began. He smiled and opened it, surprised to find it in the original Mandarin. Flicking through, he noticed the notations in the margin, the tiny, beautifully drawn pictograms in red and black and green.

"You speak *Kuo-yu*, Kim?"

Kim straightened the books, then turned, looking back at Hammond. He studied him a moment, intently, almost fiercely; then he pointed up at the overhead camera. "Does that thing work?"

Hammond looked up. "Not yet. It'll be two or three days before they've installed the system."

"And Spatz? Does he speak *Kuo-yu*—Mandarin?"

Hammond considered a moment, then shook his head. "I'm not sure. I don't think so, but I can check easily enough. Why?"

Kim was staring back at him, the openness of his face disarming Hammond. "I'm not naive, *Shih* Hammond. I understand your position here. You're here on sufferance. We're alike in that. We do what we're told or we're nothing. *Nothing.*"

Hammond shivered. He had never thought of it in quite those terms, but it was true. He put the book down. "Yes. But I still don't follow you. What is all this leading to?"

Kim picked the book up and opened it at random, then handed it back to Hammond.

"Read the first paragraph."

Hammond read it, pronouncing the Mandarin with a slight southern accent, then looked back at Kim. "Well?"

"I thought so. I saw how you looked at it. I knew at once that you'd recognized the title."

Hammond smiled. "So?"

Kim took the book back and set it beside the others on the shelf.

"How good is your memory?"

"Pretty good, I'd say."

"Good enough to hold a code?"

"A code?"

"When you go back, Spatz will order you not to speak to me about anything to do with the Project. He'll instruct you to keep me away from all but the most harmless piece of equipment."

"You know this?"

Kim looked round. "It's what he threatened shortly before you arrived. But I know his type. I've met them before. He'll do all he can to discredit me."

Hammond laughed and began to shake his head; then he stopped, seeing how Kim was looking at him. He looked down. "What if I don't play his game? What if I refuse to shut you out?"

"Then he'll discredit you. You're vulnerable. He knows you'll have to do what he says. Besides, he'll set a man to watch you. Someone you think of as a friend."

"Then what *can* I do?"

"You can keep a diary. On your personal comset. Something that will seem completely innocent when Spatz checks on it."

"I see. But how will you get access?"

"Leave that to me." Kim turned away, taking the last of the objects from the bag and putting it down on the bedside table.

"And the code?"

Kim laughed. "That's the part you'll enjoy. You're going to become a poet, *Shih* Hammond. A regular Wang Wei."

━━◆◆◆━━

D E V O R E S A T at his desk in the tiny room at the heart of the mountain. The door was locked, the room unlit but for the faint glow of a small screen on one side of the desk. It was late, almost two in the morning, yet he felt no trace of tiredness. He slept little—two or three hours a night at most—but just now there was too much to do to even think of sleep.

He had spent the afternoon teaching Sun Tzu to his senior officers: the final chapter on the employment of secret agents. It was the section of Sun Tzu's work that most soldiers found unpalatable. On the whole they were creatures of directness, like Tolonen. They viewed such methods as a necessary evil, unavoidable yet somehow beneath their dignity. But they were wrong. Sun Tzu had placed the subject at the end of his thirteen-chapter work with good reason. It was the key to all. As Sun Tzu himself had said, the reason an enlightened prince or a wise general triumphed over their enemies whenever they moved—the reason their achievements surpassed those of ordinary men—was foreknowledge. And as Chia Lin had commented many centuries later, "An army without secret agents is like a man without eyes or ears."

So it was. And the more one knew, the more control one could wield over circumstance.

He smiled. Today had been a good day. Months of hard work had paid off. Things had connected, falling into a new shape—a shape that bode well for the future.

The loss of his agents among the *Ping Tiao* had been a serious setback, and the men he had bought from among their ranks had proved unsatisfactory in almost every respect. He had had barely a glimpse of what the *Ping Tiao* hierarchy were up to for almost a week now. Until today, that was, when suddenly two very different pieces of information had come to hand.

The first was simply a code word one of his paid agents had stumbled upon: a single Mandarin character, the indentation of which had been left on a notepad Jan Mach had discarded. A character that looked like a house running on four legs. The character *yu*, the Han word for fish, the symbol of the *Ping Tiao*. It had meant nothing at first, but then he had thought to try it as an entry code to some of the secret *Ping Tiao* computer networks he had discovered weeks before but had failed to penetrate.

At the third attempt he found himself in. *Yu* was a new recruitment campaign; a rallying call; a word passed from lip to ear; a look, perhaps, between two sympathetic to the cause. DeVore had scrolled through quickly, astonished by what he read. If this were true . . .

But of course it was true. It made sense. Mach was unhappy with what was happening in the *Ping Tiao*. He felt unclean dealing with the likes of T'angs and renegade Majors. What better reason, then, to start up a new movement? A splinter movement that would, in time, prove greater and more effective than the *Ping Tiao*. A movement that made no deals, no compromises. That movement was *Yu*.

Yu. The very word was rich with ambivalence, for *yu* was phonetically identical with the Han word meaning "abundance." It was the very symbol of wealth, and yet tradition had it that when the fish swam up-river in great numbers it was a harbinger of social unrest. *Yu* was thus the symbol of civil disorder.

And if the file was to be trusted, *Yu* was already a force to be reckoned with. Not as powerful yet as the *Ping Tiao*, nor as rich in its resources, yet significant enough to make him change his plans. He would have to deal with Mach. And soon.

The second item had come from Fischer in Alexandria. The message had been brief—a mere minute and three-quarters of scrambled signal—yet it was potentially enough, in its decoded form, to shake the very foundations of the Seven.

He leaned forward and ran the film again.

The first thirty seconds were fairly inconclusive. They showed Wang Sau-leyan with his Chancellor, Hung Mien-lo. As Fischer entered, the T'ang turned slightly, disappearing from camera view as the Captain bowed.

"Are they here?" Wang asked, his face returning to view as Fischer came out of his bow.

"Four of them, *Chieh Hsia*. They've been searched and scanned, together with their gift."

"Good," the T'ang said, turning away, looking excitedly at his Chancellor. "Then bring them in."

"*Chieh Hsia* . . ."

DeVore touched the pad, pausing at that moment. Wang Sau-leyan was still in full view of Fischer's hidden camera, his well-fleshed face split by a grin that revealed unexpectedly fine teeth. He was a gross character, but interesting. For all his sybaritic tendencies, Wang Sau-leyan was sharp, sharper, perhaps, than any among the Seven, barring the young Prince, Li Shai Tung's son Yuan.

He sat back, studying the two men for a time, unhappy that he had not been privy to their conversations before and after this important meeting. It would have been invaluable to know what it was they really wanted from their association with the *Ping Tiao*. But Fischer's quick thinking had at least given him an insight into their apparent reasons.

He let the film run again, watching as it cut to a later moment when Fischer had interrupted the meeting to tell the T'ang about the fire.

The camera caught the six men squarely in its lens—Wang Sau-leyan to the left; Hung Mien-lo just behind him; Gesell, Mach and their two companions to the right. It was an important moment to capture—one that, if need be, could be used against the T'ang of Africa. But equally important was the moment just before Fischer had knocked and thrown the doors open wide, a moment when Wang's voice had boomed out clearly.

"Then you understand, *ch'un tzu*, that I cannot provide such backing without some sign of your good intentions. The smell of burning wheat, perhaps, or news of a whole crop ruined through the accidental pollution of a water source. I'm sure I don't have to spell it out for you."

DeVore smiled. No, there was no need for Wang Sau-leyan to say anything more. It was clear what he intended. In exchange for funds he would get the *Ping Tiao* to do his dirty work—to burn the East European Plantations and create havoc with City Europe's food supplies, thus destabilizing Li Shai Tung's City. But would the *Ping Tiao* take such a radical action? After all, it was their people who would suffer most from the subsequent food shortages. Would they dare risk alienating public opinion so soon after they had regained it?

He knew the answer. They would. Because Mach was quite prepared to see the *Ping Tiao* discredited. He would be happy to see the *Yu* step into the gap left by the demise of the *Ping Tiao*. He was tired of deferring to Gesell. Tired of seeing his advice passed over.

Well, thought DeVore, pausing the film again, perhaps we can use all these tensions—redirect them and control them. But not yet. Not quite yet.

They had broken up their meeting temporarily while the fire was dealt with; but when Fischer returned, the *Ping Tiao* had already gone. Even so, the final forty seconds of the film provided a fascinating little coda on all that had happened.

Wang Sau-leyan was sitting in the far corner of the room, turning the gift the *Ping Tiao* had given him, in his hands, studying it. It was the tiny jade sculpture of Kuan Yin that DeVore had given Gesell only the week before.

"It's astonishing," Wang was saying. "Where do you think they stole it?"

Hung Mien-lo, standing several paces away, looked up. "I'm sorry, *Chieh Hsia?*"

"This." He held the tiny statue up so that it was in clear view of the camera. "It's genuine, I'd say. T'ang Dynasty. Where in hell's name do you think they got their hands on it?"

Hung Mien-lo shrugged, then moved closer to his T'ang, lowering his voice marginally. "More to the point, *Chieh Hsia*, how do you know that they'll do as you ask?"

Wang Sau-leyan studied the piece a moment longer, then looked back at his Chancellor, smiling. "Because I ask them to do only what is in their own interest." He nodded, then looked across, directly into camera. "Well, Captain Fischer, is it out?"

The film ended there, as Fischer bowed, but it was enough. It gave DeVore plenty to consider. Plenty to use.

And that was not all. The day had been rich with surprises. A sealed package had arrived from Mars: a copy of the files Karr had taken from Berdichev's private secretary.

DeVore smiled. He had been telling his senior officers the story only that afternoon—the tale of T'sao and the Tanguts. The Tanguts were northern enemies of the Han; and T'sao, the Han Chief of Staff, had pardoned a condemned man on the understanding that he would swallow a ball of wax, dress up as a monk, and enter the kingdom of the Tanguts. The man did so and was eventually captured and imprisoned by the Tanguts. Under interrogation he told them about the ball of wax, and when he finally shat it out, they cut it open and found a letter. The letter was from T'sao to their own Chief Strategist. The Tangut King was enraged and ordered the execution both of the false monk and his own Chief Strategist. Thus did T'sao rid himself of the most able man in his enemies' camp for no greater price than the life of a condemned man.

So it was with the boy. He would be the means through which the Seven would be destroyed; not from without, as Berdichev had imagined, but from within. The Seven would be the agents of their own destruction. For the boy carried within him not a ball of wax but an idea. One single, all-transforming idea.

DeVore sat back. Yes, and Li Yuan would fight to preserve the boy, for he honestly believed that he could control him. But Li Yuan had not the slightest conception of what the boy represented. No, not even the boy himself understood that yet. But DeVore had seen it at once, when Berdichev had first shown him the Aristotle File. The file was a remarkable achievement, yet it was as nothing beside what the boy was capable of. His potential was astonishing. Li Yuan might as well try to harness Change itself as try to force the boy's talents to conform to the needs of State.

Li Shai Tung had been right to sign the boy's death warrant. The old man's gut instincts had always been good. It was fortunate that the War had undermined his certainty. The old Li Shai Tung would have acted without hesitation. But the old T'ang was effectively dead—murdered along with his son Han Ch'in, eight years earlier.

DeVore nodded to himself, then cleared his mind of it, coming to the final matter. The report was brief, no more than a single line of coded message; yet it was significant. It was what he had been waiting for.

He took the tiny piece of crumpled paper from his top pocket and unfolded it. It had been passed from hand to hand along a chain of trusted men until it came into his own, its message comprehensible only to his eyes. "The tiger is restless," it read. He smiled. The tiger was his code word for Hans Ebert, the handwriting on the paper that of his man Auden.

He had recruited Auden long ago—years before he had had the man appointed sergeant under Ebert—but Hammerfest had been a heaven-sent opportunity. Auden had saved Ebert's life that day, eight years ago, and Ebert had never forgotten it. Hans Ebert was a selfish young man but curiously loyal to those about him. At least, to those he felt deserved his loyalty, and Auden was one such. But it did not do to use all one's pieces at once. Life was like *wei chi* in that respect; the master chose to play a waiting game, to plan ahead. So he with Auden. But now he was capitalizing upon his long and patient preparation. It had been easy, for instance, for Auden to persuade Ebert to launch the premature attack on the *Ping Tiao* cell; an attack that had prevented Karr from discovering the links between the terrorists and himself. But that had been only the start: a test of the young man's potential. Now he would take things much further and see whether he could translate Ebert's restlessness into something more useful. Something more constructive.

Yes, but not through Auden. He would keep Auden dark, his true nature masked from Ebert. There were other ways of getting to Ebert; other men he trusted, if not as much. His uncle Lutz, for instance.

DeVore folded the paper and tucked it back into the pocket. No, Auden was part of a much longer game; part of a shape that, as yet, existed in his head alone.

He smiled, then stood, stretching, his sense of well-being brimming over, making him laugh softly. Then he checked himself. Have a care, Howard DeVore, he thought. And don't relax. It's only a shape you've glimpsed. It isn't real. Not yet. Not until you make it real.

"But I will," he said softly, allowing himself the smallest of smiles. "Just see if I don't."

THE PIMP WAS SLEEPING, a girl on either side of him. The room was in semidarkness, a wall-mounted flat-lamp beside the door casting a faint green shadow across the sleeping forms. It was after fourth bell and the last of the evening's guests had left an hour before. Now only the snores of the sleepers broke the silence of the house.

Chen slid the door back quietly and slipped into the room. At once he seemed to merge with the green-black forms of the room. He hesitated a moment, his eyes growing accustomed to the subtle change in lighting, then crossed the room, quickly, silently, and stood beside the bed.

The pimp was lying on his back, his head tipped to one side, his mouth open. A strong scent of wine and onions wafted up from him; a tart, sickly smell that mixed with the heavy mustiness of the room.

Yes, thought Chen. It's him, all right. I'd know that ugly face anywhere.

He took the strip of plaster from the pouch at his belt and peeled off two short lengths, taping them loosely to his upper arm. He threw the strip down, then drew his gun. Leaning across one of the girls, he placed it firmly against the pimp's right temple.

"Liu Chang . . ." he said softly, as the pimp stirred. "Liu Chang, listen to me very carefully. Do exactly as I say or I'll cover the mattress with your brains, understand me?"

Liu Chang had gone very still. His eyes flicked open, straining to see the gun, then focusing on the masked figure above him. He swallowed, then gave a tiny, fearful nod.

"What do you want?" he began, his voice a whisper, then fell silent, as Chen increased the pressure of the gun against the side of his head.

Chen scowled at him. "Shut up, Liu Chang," he said, quietly but firmly. "I'll tell you when to speak."

The pimp nodded again, his eyes wide now, his whole body tensed, cowering before the gunman.

"Good. This is what you'll do. You'll sit up very slowly. Very slowly, understand? Make a sudden move and you're dead." Chen smiled cruelly. "I'm not playing games, Liu Chang. I'd as soon see you dead as let you go. But my people want answers. Understand?"

Liu Chang's mouth opened as if to form a question, then clicked shut. He swallowed deeply, sweat running down his neck, and nodded.

"Good. Now up."

The pimp raised himself slowly on his elbows, Chen's gun pressed all the while against his right temple.

Chen nodded, satisfied, then thrust his right arm closer to the pimp. "Take one of the strips of plaster from my arm and put it over this girl's mouth. Then do the same with the other. And get no ideas about wrestling with me, Liu Chang. Your only chance of living is if you do what I say."

Again there was that slight movement in the pimp's face— the sign of a question unasked—before he nodded.

As he leaned forward, Chen pushed slightly with the gun, reminding the pimp of its presence, but it was only a precaution. If the file was correct, he should have little bother with the man. Liu Chang had been an actor in the Han opera before he became a pimp, more noted for his prowess in bed than his ability with a knife. Even so, it was wise to take care.

Liu Chang moved back from Chen, then leaned forward again, placing the strip across the sleeping girl's mouth. It woke her and for a moment she struggled, her hands coming up as if to tear it away. Then she saw Chen and the gun and grew still, her eyes wide with fear.

"Now the other."

He noted the slight hesitation in Liu Chang and pressed harder with the gun.

"*Do it!*"

The pimp took the strip and placed it over the other girl's mouth. She, too, woke and, after a moment's struggle, lay still.

Good, Chen thought. Now to business.

"You're wondering what I want, aren't you, Liu Chang?"

Liu Chang nodded, twice.

"Yes, well, it's simple. A girl of yours was killed here, a month or two ago. I'm sure you remember it. There was a young officer here when it happened. He thinks he did it. But you know better than that, don't you, Liu Chang? You know what really happened."

Liu Chang looked down, then away; anything but meet Chen's gaze. He began to shake his head in denial, but Chen jabbed the gun hard against his head, drawing blood.

"This is no fake I'm holding here, Liu Chang. You'll discover that if you try to lie to me. I *know* you set Lieutenant Haavikko up. I even know how. But I want to know the precise details. And I want to know who gave the orders."

Liu Chang looked down miserably. His heart was beating wildly now and the sweat was running from him. For a moment longer he hesitated, then he looked up again, meeting Chen's eyes.

"Okay, Liu Chang. Speak. Tell me what happened."

The pimp swallowed, then found his voice. "And if I tell you?"

"Then you live. But only if you tell me everything."

Liu Chang shuddered. "All right." But from the way he glanced at the girls, Chen knew what he was thinking. If he lived, the girls would have to die. Because they had heard. And because Liu Chang could not risk them saying anything to anyone. In case it got back.

But it doesn't matter, Chen thought, listening as the pimp began his tale; *because you're dead already, Liu Chang. For what you did. And for what you would do, if I let you live.*

▼▼▼▼▼

HERRICK'S WAS forty *li* east of Liu Chang's, a tiny, crowded place at the very bottom of the City, below the Net.

It was less than an hour since Chen had come from the singsong house; not time enough for anyone to have discovered Liu Chang's body or for the girls to have undone their bonds. Nevertheless he moved quickly down the corridors—shabby, ill-lit alleyways that, even at this early hour, were busy—knowing that every minute brought closer the chance of Herrick being warned.

It was two years since he had last been below the Net, but his early discomfort quickly passed, older habits taking over, changing the way he moved, the way he held himself. Down here he was *kwai* again, trusting to his instincts as *kwai*, and, as if sensing this, men moved back from him as he passed.

It was a maze, the regular patterning of the levels above broken up long ago. Makeshift barriers closed off corridors, marking out the territory of rival gangs, while elsewhere emergency doors had been removed and new corridors created through what had once been living quarters. To another it might have seemed utter confusion, but Chen had been born here. He knew it was a question of keeping a direction in your head, like a compass needle.

Even so, he felt appalled. The very smell of the place—the same wherever one went below the Net—brought back the nightmare of living here. He looked about him as he made his way through, horrified by the squalor and ugliness of everything he saw, and wondered how he had stood it.

At the next intersection he drew in against the left-hand wall, peering around the corner into the corridor to his left. It was as Liu Chang had said. There, a little way along, a dragon had been painted on the wall in green. But it was not just any dragon. This dragon had a man's face; the thin, sallow face of a *Hung Mao*, the eyes intensely blue, the mouth thin-lipped and almost sneering.

If Liu Chang was right, Herrick would be there now, working. Like many below the Net, he was a night bird, keeping hours that the great City overhead thought unsociable. Here there were no curfews, no periods of darkness. Here it was always twilight, the corridors lit or unlit according to whether or not the local gang bosses had made deals with those Above who controlled the basic facilities such as lighting, sanitation, and water.

Now that he was working for the Seven, such thoughts made him feel uneasy, for it was they, his masters, who permitted the existence of this place. They who, through the accident of his birth here, had made him what he was—*kwai*, a hired knife, a killer. They had the wealth, the power, to change this place and make it habitable for those who wished it so, and yet they did nothing. Why? He took a deep breath, knowing the answer. Because without this at the bottom, nothing else worked. There had to be this place—this lawless pit—beneath it all to keep those Above in check. To curb their excesses. Or so they argued.

He set the thoughts aside. This now was not for the Seven. This was for Axel. And for himself. Karr's hunch had been right. If Ebert had been paying for Axel's debauchery, the chances were that he was behind the death of the girl. There were ways, Karr had said, of making a man think he'd done something he hadn't; ways of implanting false memories in the mind.

And there were places where one could buy such technology. Places like Herrick's.

Chen smiled. He was almost certain now that Karr was right. Liu Chang had said as much, but he had to be sure. Had to have evidence to convince Axel that he was innocent of the girl's murder.

Quickly, silently, he moved around the corner and down the corridor, stopping outside the door beside the dragon. At once a camera above the door turned, focusing on him.

There was a faint buzzing, then a voice—tinny and distorted—came from a speaker beside the camera.

"What do you want?"

Chen looked up at the camera and made the hand sign Liu Chang had taught him. This, he knew, was the crucial moment. If Liu Chang had lied to him, or had given him a signal that would tip Herrick off . . .

There was a pause. Then, "Who sent you?"

"The pimp," he said. "Liu Chang."

Most of Herrick's business was with the Above. Illicit stuff. There were a thousand uses for Herrick's implants, but most would be used as they had on Haavikko—to make a man vulnerable by making him believe he had done something that he hadn't. In these days of response-testing and truth drugs it was the perfect way of setting a man up. The perfect tool for blackmail. Chen looked down, masking his inner anger, wondering how many innocent men had died or lost all they had because of Herrick's wizardry.

"What's your name?"

"Tong Chou," he said, using the pseudonym he had used at one time in the Plantation, knowing that if they checked the records they would find an entry there under that name and a face to match his face. Apparently they did, for after a long pause, the door hissed open.

A small man, a Han, stood in the hallway beyond the door. "Come in, *Shih* Tong. I'm sorry, but we have to be very careful who we deal with here. I am Ling Hen, *Shih* Herrick's assistant." He smiled and gave a tiny bow. "Forgive me, but I must ask you to leave any weapons here, in the outer office."

"Of course," Chen said, taking the big handgun from inside his jacket and handing it across. "Do you want to search me?"

Ling Hen hesitated a moment, then shook his head. "That will not be necessary. However, there is one other thing."

Chen understood. Again, Karr had prepared him for this. He took out the three ten-thousand *yuan* "chips" and offered them to the man.

Ling smiled, but shook his head. "No, *Shih* Tong. You hold on to those for the moment. I just wanted to be sure you understood our house rules. Liu Chang's briefed you fully, I see. We don't deal in credit. Payment's up front, but then delivery's fast. We guarantee a tailored implant—to your specifications—within three days."

"Three days?" Chen said. "I'd hoped . . ."

Ling lowered his head slightly. "Well . . . Come. Let's talk of such matters within. I'm sure we can come to some kind of accommodation, neh, *Shih* Tong?"

Chen returned the man's bow, then followed him down the hallway to another door. A guard moved back, letting them pass, the door hissing open at their approach.

It was all very sophisticated. Herrick had taken great pains to make sure he was protected. But that was to be expected down here. It was a cutthroat world. He would have had to make deals with numerous petty bosses to get where he was today, and still there was no guarantee against the greed of the Triads. It paid to be paranoid below the Net.

They stepped through, into the cool semidarkness of the inner sanctum. Here the only sound was the faint hum of the air filters overhead. After the stench of the corridors, the clean, cool air was welcome. Chen took a deep breath, then looked about him at the banks of monitors that filled every wall of the huge, hexagonal room, impressed despite himself. The screens glowed with soft colors, displaying a thousand different images. He stared at those closest to him, trying to make some sense of the complex chains of symbols, then shrugged; it was an alien language, but he had a sense that these shapes—the spirals and branching trees, the clusters and irregular pyramids—had something to do with the complex chemistry of the human body.

He looked across at the central desk. A tall, angular-looking man was hunched over one of the control panels, perfectly still, attentive, a bulky wraparound making his head seem grotesquely huge.

Ling turned to him, his voice hushed. "Wait but a moment, *Shih* Tong. My master is just finishing something. Please, take a chair, he'll be with you in a while."

Chen smiled but made no move to sit, watching as Ling Hen went across to the figure at the control desk. If Karr was right, Herrick would have kept copies of all his jobs as a precaution. But where? And where was the guard room? Or had Herrick himself let them in?

He looked down momentarily, considering things. There were too many variables for his liking, but he had committed himself now. He would have to be audacious.

He looked up again and saw that Herrick had removed the wraparound and was staring across at him. In the light of the screens his face seemed gaunter, far more skeletal than in the dragon portrait on the wall outside.

"*Shih* Tong . . ." Herrick said, coming across, his voice strong and rich, surprising Chen. He had expected something thin and high and spiderish. Likewise his handshake. Chen looked down at the hand that had grasped his own so firmly. It was a long, clever hand, like a larger version of Jyan's, Chen's dead companion. He looked up and met Herrick's eyes, smiling at the recollection.

"What is it?" Herrick asked, his hawklike eyes amused.

"Your hand," Chen said. "It reminded me of a friend's hand."

Herrick gave the slightest shrug. "I see." He turned away, looking around him at the great nest of screens and machinery. "Well . . . you have a job for me, I understand. You know what I charge?"

"Yes. A friend of mine came to you a few months ago. It was a rather simple thing, I understand. I want something similar."

Herrick looked back at him, then looked down. "A simple thing?" He laughed. "Nothing I do is simple, *Shih* Tong. That's why I charge so much. What I do is an art form. Few others can do it, you see. They haven't the talent or the technical ability. That's why people come here. People like you, *Shih* Tong." He looked up again, meeting Chen's eyes, his own hard and cold. "So don't insult me, my friend."

"Forgive me," Chen said hastily, bowing his head. "I didn't mean to imply . . . Well, it's just that I'd heard . . ."

"Heard what?" Herrick was staring away again, as if bored.

"That you were capable of marvels."

Herrick smiled. "That's so, *Shih* Tong. But even your 'simple things' are beyond most men." He sniffed, then nodded. "All right, then, tell me what it was this friend of yours had me do for him, and I'll tell you whether I can do 'something similar.' "

Chen smiled inwardly. Yes, he had Herrick's measure now. Knew his weak spot. Herrick was vain, overproud of his abilities. He could use that. Could play on it and make him talk.

"As I understand it, my friend was having trouble with a soldier. A young lieutenant. He had been causing my friend a great deal of trouble; so to shut him up, he had you make an implant of the man committing a murder. A young *Hung Mao* girl."

Herrick was nodding. "Yes, of course. I remember it. In a brothel, wasn't it? Yes, now I see the connection. Liu Chang. He made the introduction, didn't he?"

Chen felt himself go very still. So it wasn't Liu Chang who had come here in that instance. He had merely made the introduction. Then why hadn't he said so?

"So Captain Auden is a good friend of yours, *Shih* Tong?" Herrick said, looking at him again.

Auden . . . ? Chen hesitated, then nodded. "Ten years now."

Herrick's smile tightened into an expression of distaste. "How odd. I had the feeling he disliked Han. Still . . ."

"Do you think I could see the earlier implant? He told me about it, but . . . well, I wanted to see whether it really was the kind of thing I wanted."

Herrick screwed up his face. "It's very unusual, *Shih* Tong. I like to keep my customers' affairs discreet, you understand? It would be most upsetting if Captain Auden were to hear I had shown you the implant I designed for him."

"Of course." Chen saw at once what he wanted and took one of the chips from his pocket. "Would this be guarantee enough of my silence, *Shih* Herrick?"

Herrick took the chip and examined it beneath a nearby desk light, then turned back to Chen, smiling. "I think that should do, *Shih* Tong, I'll just find my copy of the implant."

Herrick returned to the central desk and was busy for a moment at the keyboard; he came back with a thin film of transparent card held delicately between the fingers of his left hand.

"Is that it?"

Herrick nodded. "This is just the analog copy. The visual element of it, anyway. The real thing is much more complex. An implant is far more than the simple visual component." He laughed coldly, then moved past Chen, slipping the card into a slot beneath one of the empty screens. "If it were simply that it would hardly be convincing, would it?"

Chen shrugged, then turned in time to see the screen light up.

"No," Herrick continued. "That's the art of it, you see. To create the whole experience. To give the victim the *feeling* of having committed the act, whatever it is. The smell and taste and touch of it—the fear and the hatred and the sheer delight of doing something illicit."

He laughed again, turning to glance at Chen, an unhealthy gleam in his eyes. "That's what fascinates me, really. What keeps me going. Not the money, but the challenge of tailoring the experience to the man. Take this Haavikko, for instance. From what I was given on him it was very easy to construct something from his guilt, his sense of self-degradation. It was easy to convince him of his worthlessness, to make him believe he was capable of such an act. That, too, is part of my art, you see—to make such abnormal behavior seem a coherent part of the victim's reality."

Chen shuddered. Herrick spoke as if he had no conception of what he was doing. To him it was merely a challenge, a focus for his twisted genius. He lacked all feeling for the men whose lives he destroyed. The misery and pain he caused were, for him, merely a measure of his success. It was evil. Truly evil. Chen wanted to reach out and take Herrick by the throat and choke him to death, but first he had to get hold of the copy and get out with it.

An image began to form on the screen. The frozen image of a naked girl, sprawled on a bed, backing away, her face distorted with fear.

"There's one thing I don't understand, *Shih* Herrick. My friend told me that Haavikko took a drink of some kind. A drug. But how was the implant put into his head? He's only a junior officer, so he isn't wired. How, then, was it done?"

Herrick laughed. "You think in such crude terms, *Shih* Tong. The implant isn't a physical thing, not in the sense that you mean. It's not like the card. That's only storage—a permanent record. No, the implant *was* the drug. A highly complex drug made up of a whole series of chemicals with different reaction times, designed to fire particular synapses in the brain itself—to create, if you like, a false landscape of experience. An animated landscape, complete with a predetermined sequence of events."

Chen shook his head. "I don't see how."

Herrick looked away past him, his eyes staring off into some imaginary distance. "That's because you don't understand the function of the brain. It's all chemicals and electronics, in essence. The whole of experience. It comes in at the nerve ends and is translated into chemical and electrical reactions. I merely bypass those nerve ends. What I create is a dream. But a dream more real, more vivid, than reality!"

Chen stared at him, momentarily frightened by the power of the man, then looked back at the screen. He didn't want to see the girl get killed. Instinctively, he reached across, ejecting the card, and slipped it into his pocket.

Herrick started forward. "What the fuck—?"

Chen grabbed Herrick by the neck, then drew the knife from his boot and held it against his throat.

"I've heard enough, *Shih* Herrick. More than enough, if you must know. But now I've got what I came for, so I'll be going."

Herrick swallowed uncomfortably. "You won't get out of here. I've a dozen guards—"

Chen pulled the knife toward him sharply, scoring the flesh beneath Herrick's chin. Herrick cried out and began to struggle, but Chen tightened his grip.

"You'd better do as I say, *Shih* Herrick, and get me out of here. Or you're dead. And not pretend dead. Really dead. One more shit comment from you and I'll implant this knife in the back of your throat."

Herrick's eyes searched the room, then looked back at Chen. "All right. But you'll have to let me give instructions to my men."

Chen laughed. "Just tell them to open the doors and get out of the way." He raised his voice, looking up at one of the security cameras. "You hear me, *Shih* Ling? If you want to see your boss again, do as I say. Any tricks and he's dead, and where will you be then? Runner to some gang boss, dead in a year."

He waited a moment, searching the walls for sign of some technological trickery. Then there was a hiss and a door on the far side of the room slid open.

He pressed harder with the knife. "Tell them I want to go out the way I came in, *Shih* Herrick. Tell them quickly, or you're dead."

Herrick swallowed, then made a tiny movement of his head. "Do as he says."

They moved out slowly into the corridor, Chen looking about him, prepared at any moment to thrust the knife deep into Herrick's throat.

"Who are you working for?"

Chen laughed. "Why should I be working for anyone?"

"Then I don't understand . . ."

No, thought Chen. *You wouldn't, would you?*

They came to the second door. It hissed open. Beyond it stood four guards, their knives drawn.

"No further," said Ling, coming from behind them.

Chen met Ling's eyes, tightening his grip on Herrick's throat. "Didn't you hear me, Ling? You want your master to die?"

Ling smiled. "You won't kill him, Tong. You can't. Because you can't get out without him."

Chen answered Ling's smile with his own, then pulled Herrick closer to him, his knife hand tensed.

"This is for my friend, Axel. And for all those others whose lives you have destroyed."

He heard the cry and looked back, seeing how the blood had drained from Ling's face, then let the body fall from him.

"Now," he said, crouching, holding the knife out before him. "Come, *Shih* Ling. Let's see what you can do against a *kwai.*"

CHAPTER TEN

Islands

J ELKA LEANED out over the side of the boat, straining against the safety harness as she watched the rise and fall of the waves through which they plowed, the old thirty-footer rolling and shuddering beneath her, the wind tugging at her hair, taking her breath, the salt spray bitingly cold against her face.

The water was a turmoil of glassy green threaded with white strands of spume. She let her hand trail in the chill water then put her fingers to her mouth, the flesh strangely cold and hard, her lips almost numb. She sucked at them, the salt taste strong in her mouth, invigorating. A savage, ancient taste.

She turned, looking back at the mainland. Tall fingers of ash-gray rock thrust up from the water, like the sunken bones of giants. Beyond them lay the City, its high, smooth, clifflike walls dazzling in the morning light—a ribbon of whiteness stretching from north to south. She turned back, conscious suddenly of the swaying of the boat, the creak and groan of the wood, the high-pitched howl of the wind contesting with the noise of the engine—a dull, repetitive churring that sounded in her bones— and the constant slap and spray of water against the boat's sides.

She looked up. The open sky was vast. Great fists of cloud sailed overhead, their whiteness laced with sunlight and shadow; while up ahead the sea stretched away, endless it seemed, its rutted surface shimmering with light.

Sea birds followed in their wake, wheeling and calling, like

333

souls in torment. She laughed, the first laughter she had enjoyed in weeks, and squinted forward, looking out across the sun-dazzled water, trying to make out the island.

At first she could see nothing. Ahead, the sea seemed relatively flat, unbroken. And then she saw it, tiny at first, a vague shape of green and gray melding and merging with the surrounding sea as if overrun. Then, slowly, it grew, rising out of the sea to meet her, growing more definite by the moment, its basalt cliffs looming up, waves swelling and washing against their base.

Jelka looked across at her father. He sat there stiffly, one hand clenched and covered by the other, his neck muscles tensed; yet there was a vague, almost dreamy expression in his eyes. He was facing the island, but his eyes looked inward. Jelka watched him a moment; then looked away, knowing he was thinking of her mother.

As the boat slowed, drifting in toward the jetty, she looked past the harbor at the land beyond. A scattering of old stone houses surrounded the quayside, low, gray-green buildings with slate roofs of a dull orange. To the far right of the jetty a white crescent of shingle ended in rocks. But her eyes were drawn upward, beyond the beach and the strange shapes of the houses, to the hillside beyond. Pines crowded the steep slope, broken here and there by huge iron-gray outcrops of rock. She shivered, looking up at it. It was all so raw, so primitive. Like nothing she had ever imagined.

She felt something wake deep within her and raised her head, sniffing the air. The strong scent of pine merged with the smell of brine and leather and engine oil, filling her senses, forming a single distinctive odor. The smell of the island.

Her father helped her up onto the stone jetty. She turned, looking back across the water at the mainland. It was hazed in a light mist, its walls of ice still visible yet somehow less impressive from this distance. It was all another world from this.

Sea birds called overhead, their cries an echoing, melancholy sound. She looked up, her eyes following their wheeling forms, then looked down again as a wave broke heavily against the beach, drawing the shingle with it as it ebbed.

"Well," her father said softly, "here we are. What do you think of it?"

She shivered. It was like coming home.

She looked across at the houses, her eyes moving from one to another, searching for signs of life.

"Which one?" she asked, looking back at him.

Her father laughed. "Oh, none of those." He turned, giving orders to the men in the boat, then looked back at her. "Come on, I'll show you."

Where the cobbles of the jetty ended they turned left onto an old dirt track. It led up through the trees, away from the houses and the waterfront.

The track led up onto a broad ledge of smooth, gray rock. There was a gap in the screen of trees and a view across the water.

"Careful," he said, his grip on her hand tightening as she moved closer to the edge. "It can be slippery." Then she saw it.

Below her was a tiny bay enclosed on three sides by the dense growth of pines. But at one point the tree cover was broken. Directly across from her a great spur of rock rose abruptly from the water, and on its summit—so like the rock in color and texture that at first she had not recognized it—was the house.

It was astonishing. Huge walls of solid stone rose sheer from the rock, ending in narrow turrets and castellated battlements. A steep roof, gray and lichen-stained, ran almost the length of the house. Only at its far end, where the sea surrounded it on three sides, was its steep pitch broken. There a tower rose, two stories higher than the rest of the house, capped with a spire that shone darkly in the sunlight.

She stared at it openmouthed, then looked back at her father.

"I thought it was a house."

He laughed. "It is. It was my great-grandfather's house. And his grandfather's before that. It has been in our family for nine generations."

She narrowed her eyes, not understanding. "You mean, it's ours?"

"It was. I guess it still is. But it is for Li Shai Tung to say whether or not we might use it."

"It seems so unfair."

He stared at her, surprised, then answered her. "No. It has to be like this. The peasants must work the land. They *must* be outside. And the Seven carry a heavy burden; they need their estates. But there is not land enough for all those who wish to live outside. There would be much resentment if we had this and others didn't, don't you see?"

"But, surely, if it's ours . . ."

He shook his head firmly. "No. The world has grown too small for such luxuries. It's a small price to pay for peace and stability."

They walked on, still climbing. Then he turned back, pointing downward. "We have to go down here. There are some steps, cut into the rock. They're tricky, so you'd better take my hand again."

She let him help her down. It was cooler, more shaded beneath the ridge, the ground rockier, the long, straight trunks of the pines more spaced.

"There," he said, pointing between the trees.

She looked. About fifty *ch'i* distant was a gray stone wall. It was hard to tell how high it was from where she stood, but it seemed massive—twice her father's height at least. To the left it turned back on itself, hugging the cliff's edge, to the right it vanished among the trees. Partway along was a huge gate, flanked by pillars, and beyond that—still, silent in the late morning sunlight—the tower.

She turned to find him looking past her at the house, a distant smile on his face. Then he looked down at her.

"Kalevala," he said softly. "We're home, Jelka. Home."

━━━━━

"Do you know the thing I miss most?"

T'ai Cho looked up at Kim and smiled. Kim stood in the doorway, looking past him. "What's that?"

"The pool. I used to do all my best thinking in the pool."

He laughed. "Well, can't we do something about that?"

Kim made a small movement of his head, indicating the overhead camera. "Only if *Shih* Spatz wills it."

T'ai Cho stared at Kim a moment longer, then returned to his unpacking.

"I'll put in a request," he said, taking the last few things from the bag, then stowed it beneath the pull-down bed. "He can only say no, after all." He looked up again, meeting Kim's eyes with a smile. "Anyway, how have things been? Is the work interesting?"

Kim looked away. "No," he answered quietly.

T'ai Cho straightened up, surprised. "Really? But I thought you said the research would be challenging?"

"It is. But Spatz is not letting me get anywhere near it."

T'ai Cho stiffened. "But he can't do that! I won't *let* him do that to you, Kim. I'll contact the Prince."

Kim shook his head. "No. I don't want to go running to Prince Yuan every time I've a problem."

T'ai Cho turned angrily. "But you must. The Prince will have Spatz removed. He'll—"

But Kim was still shaking his head. "You don't see it, do you, T'ai Cho? You think this is just a piece of pure science research, but it's not. I saw that at once. This is political. And very sensitive. Practically all of the men they've recruited for it are vulnerable. They were on the wrong side in the War and now they've no choice but to work on this. All except for Spatz, and he's no scientist. At least, not a good enough scientist to be on a project of this nature. No, he's here to keep a lid on things."

"But that's outrageous."

"No. Not at all. You see, someone wants this project to fail. That's why Spatz was made Administrator. Why Tolonen was appointed overall Head of the Project."

"And you'll allow that to happen?"

"It's not up to me, T'ai Cho. I've no choice in the matter. I do as I'm told. As I've always done. But that's all right. There are plenty of things we can do. All that's asked of us is that we don't rock the boat."

T'ai Cho was staring at him, his eyes narrowed. "That's not like you, Kim. To lay down and do nothing."

Kim looked down. "Maybe it wasn't, in the past. But where did it ever get me?" He looked up again, his dark eyes searing T'ai Cho. "Five years of Socialization. Of brutal reconditioning. That was my reward for standing up for myself. But next time they won't bother. They'll just write me off as an unfulfilled investment. A bad debt." He laughed bitterly. "I'm not even a citizen. I exist only because Li Yuan wills my existence. You heard him yourself, T'ai Cho. That's the fact of the matter. So don't lecture me about doing something. Things are easy here. Why make trouble for ourselves?"

T'ai Cho stared back at him, open-mouthed, hardly believing what he was hearing. "Well, you'd better go," he said abruptly. "I've things to do."

"I'm sorry, T'ai Cho. I . . ."

But T'ai Cho was busying himself, putting clothes into a drawer.

"I'll see you later, then?" Kim asked, but T'ai Cho made no sign that he had even heard.

Back in his room Kim went to the desk and sat, the first of the poems Hammond had written on the screen in front of him.

It had not been easy, making T'ai Cho believe he had given up. It had hurt to disillusion his old tutor, but it was necessary. If he was to function at all in this setup, he had to allay Spatz's suspicions, make Spatz believe he was behaving himself. And what better way of convincing Spatz than by manipulating the reactions of the man supposedly closest to him? T'ai Cho's indignation—his angry disappointment in Kim—would throw Spatz off the scent. Would give Kim that tiny bit of room he needed.

Even so, it hurt. And that surprised Kim, because he had begun to question whether he had any feelings left after what they had done to him in Socialization. He recalled all the times he had met T'ai Cho since then, knowing what the man had once been to him, yet feeling nothing. Nothing at all. He had lain awake at nights, worried about that absence in himself, fearing that the ability to love had been taken from him, perhaps for good. So this—this hurt he felt at hurting another—was a sign of hope. Of change in himself.

He looked down at the poem on the desk, then sighed. What made it worse was that there was an element of truth in what he had said to T'ai Cho. Remove Spatz and another Spatz would be appointed in his place. So it was in this life. Moreover, it was true what he had said about himself. Truer, perhaps, than he had intended.

All his life he had been owned. Possessed, not for himself but for the thing within him—his "talent." They used him, as they would a machine. And, like a machine, if he malfunctioned he was to be repaired, or junked.

He laughed softly, suddenly amused by this vision of himself. Yes, he asked, *but what makes me different from the machines? What qualities distinguish me from them? And are those qualities imperfections—weaknesses—or are they strengths? Should I be more like them or less?*

They had conditioned him, walled off his past, taught him to mistrust his darker self; yet it was the very part of him from which it all emanated—the wellspring of his being.

The thinking part—they overvalued it. It was only the processor. The insights came from a deeper well than that. The upper mind merely refined it.

He smiled, knowing they were watching him, listening to his words. Well, let them watch and listen. He was better at this game than they. Much better.

He leaned forward, studying the poem.

To the watching eyes it would mean nothing. To them it seemed a meaningless string of chemical formulae; the mathematical expression of a complex chain of molecules. But Kim could see through the surface of the page and glimpse the Mandarin characters each formula represented. He smiled to himself, wondering what Spatz would make of it. Beyond the simple one-for-one code Kim had devised to print out the information taken from Hammond's personal files was a second code he had agreed upon with Hammond. That, too, was quite simple—providing you had the key to how it worked and a fluent understanding of Mandarin.

The poem itself was clumsy, its images awkward, clichéd—but that was understandable. Hammond was a scientist, not a poet. And although the examination system insisted upon the study of ancient poetry, it was something that most men of a scientific bias put behind them as quickly as possible. What was important, however, was the information contained within the central images. Three white swans represented how Spatz had divided the research into three teams. Then, in each of the next three lines, Hammond detailed—by use of other images—the area of study each team was undertaking.

It was a crude beginning, no more than a foundation, yet it

showed it could be done. As Hammond gained confidence he would develop subtlety: a necessity in the days to come, for the information would be of a degree of complexity that would tax their inventiveness to the limit.

That said, the most difficult part was already resolved. Kim had devised a means by which he could respond to Hammond. His co-conspirator had only to touch a certain key on his computer keyboard and Kim's input would automatically load into his personal files. That same instruction would effectively shut down Hammond's keyboard, render it useless, its individual keys unconnected to its regular program. Whichever key Hammond subsequently pressed would bring up one character of Kim's reply, until his message was complete.

It was a trick he had learned in Socialization. A game he'd played, haunting the files of others with his cryptic messages. And no one had dreamed it was possible.

He typed his queries out quickly, keeping this first response simple, modeling his poem on one by the fourth-century poet T'ao Ch'ien. It printed up on the screen as further chains of molecules. Then, happy with what he had done, he punched the code to send it to Hammond's file.

He switched off the set and sat back, stretching, suddenly tired. Then, unexpectedly, the comset came alive again, the printer at the side of the desk beginning to chatter. He caught his breath, watching the printout slowly emerge. A moment later it fell silent. He leaned forward and tore the printout off, then sat back, reading it through.

It was from Spatz, informing him that he had been given permission to use the recreational facilities of the local Security forces.

He studied it a moment and then laughed. A pool! Spatz had given him a pool!

━━━━━━

HER UNCLE JON had set and lit a fire in the huge hearth. Its flickering light filled the big tall-ceilinged room, making it seem mysterious and half-formed, as if, at any moment, the walls would melt and run. Her father was sitting in a big upright armchair by the window, staring out at the sea. Standing in the doorway, she looked across at him, then back at the fire, entranced. It was something she had never seen before. Something she had never thought to see. Outside, beyond the latticed windows, evening was falling, dark clouds gathering over the sea; but here, inside, the firelight filled the room with warmth.

She knelt beside the fire, putting her hands out to it, shivering suddenly, not from the cold, but from a feeling of familiarity; from a strange sense of having made the gesture before, in another life than this.

"Careful," her father said, almost lazily. "It's hot. Much hotter than you'd think."

She knelt there in the half-shadow, mesmerized by the flickering pattern of the firelight, its fierce heat, its ever-changing dance of forms; then she looked back at her father. His face was changed by the fire's light, had become a mask of black and gold, his eyes living, liquid jewels. For some reason it moved her deeply, sending a shiver down her spine. At that moment her love for him was like something solid: she could touch it and smell it, could feel its very texture.

She looked about her. There were shelves on the walls, and books. Real books, leather bound, like those she had seen in the museum once. She turned, hearing the door creak open, and looked up, smiling, at her uncle. Behind him came her aunt, carrying a tray of drinks.

"What are all the books?"

She saw how her uncle looked to her father before he answered her, as if seeking his permission.

"They're old things. History books and myth."

"Myth?"

Her aunt Helga looked up, a strange expression in her eyes, then looked down again, busying herself with the drinks.

Again her uncle Jon looked to his brother uncertainly. "They're stories, Jelka. Old legends. Things from before the City."

He was about to say more, but her father interrupted him. "There are things that belong here only. You must not take them back with you, understand me, child? You must not even mention them. Not to anyone."

She looked down. "Why?"

"Content yourself that they are."

She looked across at him again. His voice had been harsh, almost angry, but his eyes seemed troubled. He looked away, then back at her, relenting. "While you're here you may look at them, if that's what you want. But remember, these things are forbidden back in the City. If anyone knew . . ."

She frowned, not understanding. Forbidden? Why forbidden? If they were only stories.

"Jelka?"

She looked up, then quickly took the glass her aunt Helga was holding out to her. "Thanks."

She was silent a moment, then looked across at her uncle. "Daddy said this place had a name. Kalevala. Why is it called that?"

Jon laughed, then took a glass from his wife and came across, sitting in the chair nearest Jelka.

"You want to know why this house is called Kalevala? Well," he looked across at her father then back at Jelka, "it's like this . . ."

She listened, entranced, as her uncle talked of a distant past and a land of heroes, and of a people—her people—who had lived in that land; of a time before the Han and their great City, when vast forests filled the land and the people were few. Her mind opened up to the freedom of such a past—to a world so much bigger than the world she knew. A vast, limitless world, bounded by mist and built upon nothingness. Kalevala, the land of heroes.

When he was finished, she sat there, astonished, her drink untouched.

"Well?" her father said over the crackle of the fire, his voice strangely heavy. "Do you understand now why we are forbidden this? Can't you see what restlessness there would be if this were known to all?"

She looked back at him, not recognizing him for a moment, the vision still filling her mind, consuming her. Then she lowered her eyes and nodded. "Yes. I think so. And yet . . ."

He smiled back sadly at her. "I know. I feel it too, my love. It calls us strongly. But this is now, not then. We cannot go back.

This is a new age and the heroes are dead. The land of Kalevala is gone. We cannot bring it back."

She shivered. *No*, she wanted to say; *it's still alive, inside us—in that part of us that dreams and seeks fulfillment.* And yet he was right. There was only this left. This faint, sad echo of a greater, more heroic age. This only. And when it, too, was gone?

She closed her eyes, overwhelmed by a sudden sense of loss. The loss of something she had never known. And yet not so, for it was still a part of her. She could feel it—there in the sinew and bone and blood of her.

"Jelka?"

She looked up. Her uncle was standing by the shelves, watching her, concerned, the pain in his eyes the reflection of her own.

"The Kalevala . . . Would you like to read it?"

He stretched out his hand, offering one of the thick, leather-bound volumes. Jelka stared back at him a moment, then went across to him, taking the book. For a moment she simply stared at it, astonished, tracing the embossed lettering of the cover with her finger; then she turned, looking at her father.

"Can I?"

"Of course. But remember what I said. It belongs here. No-where else."

Jelka nodded, then looked back at the book. She opened the cover and read the title page.

"I didn't think . . ." she began, then laughed.

"Didn't think what?" said her uncle, standing beside her.

"This," she said, looking up into his face. "I never dreamed there would be a book of it."

"It wasn't a book. Not at first. It was all songs, thousands of songs, sung by peasants in the homelands of Karelia. One man collected them and made them into a single tale. But now there's only this. This last copy. The rest of it has gone—singers and songs, the people and the land—as if it had never been."

She looked back at him, then stared at the book in her hands, awed. The last copy. It frightened her somehow.

"Then I'll take good care of it," she said. "As if it were a sister to me."

CHEN RAISED HIMSELF uneasily in the bed, then pulled the cover up, getting comfortable again. His chest was strapped, his arm in bandages, but he had been lucky. The knife had glanced against a rib, missing anything vital. He had lost a lot of blood, but he would heal. As for the arm wound, that was superficial—the kind of thing one got in a hard training session.

Karr was sitting across from him, scowling, his huge frame far too big for the hospital chair. He leaned forward angrily, giving vent to what he had had to hold in earlier while the nurse was in the room.

"You were stupid, Chen. You should have waited for me."

Chen gritted his teeth against a sudden wash of pain, then answered his friend.

"I'm sorry, Gregor. There wasn't time."

"You could have contacted me. From Liu Chang's. You could have let me know what you planned. As it was I didn't even know you'd gone to see the pimp until half an hour ago. I thought we were waiting for the Security report on Liu Chang."

"I got it back before I went in. It confirmed what we'd thought. He was an actor, in opera, before he became a pimp. And there was one unproven charge of murder against him. That was the reason he was demoted to the Net."

Karr huffed impatiently. "Even so, you should have waited. You could have been killed."

It was true. And he *should* have waited. But he hadn't. Why? Perhaps because he had wanted to do it himself. It was mixed up somehow with Pavel, the boy on the Plantation who had been killed by DeVore's henchman. He still felt guilty about that. So perhaps he had put himself at risk to punish himself. Or maybe it was more complex than that. Maybe it had to do with the risks involved; he had enjoyed it, after all, had liked the way the odds were stacked against him.

Five to one. And he had come out of it alive. Had fought them hand to hand and beaten them. *Kwai* he was. He knew it now, clearer than he had ever known it before. *Kwai*.

"I'm sorry," he said again. "It was wrong of me."

"Yes." Karr sat back a little, then laughed, meeting Chen's eyes, his anger dissipating. "Still, you're alive."

There was a knock, then a head poked round the door.

"Axel!" Chen tried to sit up, then eased back, groaning softly.

Haavikko came into the room. Giving a small nod of acknowledgment to Karr, he went across and took Chen's hand, concerned.

"What happened? Gregor told me you'd been hurt, but not how."

Chen took a painful breath, then grinned up at Haavikko, squeezing his hand. "It was only a scrape."

Karr laughed. "Only a scrape! You know what our friend here has been doing, Axel?"

Haavikko looked, shaking his head.

"Shall I tell him, Chen, or do you want to?"

"Go ahead," said Chen, the pain from his ribs momentarily robbing him of breath.

Karr pointed beyond Haavikko, indicating a chair in the corner. "Those are Chen's clothes. Look in the top pocket of the tunic. You'll find something there that will interest you."

Haavikko turned and looked. The tunic was ripped and bloodstained, but the pocket was intact. He reached inside and drew out a thin piece of transparent card.

"This?"

Karr nodded and watched as Haavikko studied it a moment, then looked back at him, his expression blank. "So? What is it?"

Karr went across, taking the card. "I'll show you exactly how it works later on. For now take my word on it. This is what they call an implant. Or, at least, the record of one. On this card is stored all the information you'd need to make a special chemical. One that could create a false memory in someone's head."

Haavikko looked up, puzzled. "So?"

"So the information on this particular card was designed for one specific person. You."

"Me?" Haavikko laughed. "What do you mean?"

"Just this. Chen here did some digging into your friend Liu Chang's past. And then he paid the man a visit. From that he got confirmation of something he and I had suspected from the start. That, and an address below the Net. At that address he found a man named Herrick who makes these things. And from

Herrick he got this card, which is a copy of a false memory that was implanted in your head. The memory of killing a young singsong girl."

Haavikko had blanched. "No . . . It's not possible. I remember . . ." His voice faltered and he looked down, wetting his lips with his tongue. "It can't have been false. It was too real. Too . . ."

Karr reached out, touching his shoulder. "And yet it's true, Axel Haavikko. You didn't kill her. Someone else did. Probably Liu Chang. Your only mistake was to take the drug that was mixed in with your wine. It was that which made you think you'd killed her."

"No."

"It's true," said Chen. "Wait until you see the copy. You never touched her. You couldn't have done, don't you see? You're not that kind of man."

They watched him. Watched his chest rise and fall. Then saw how he looked at them again, disbelief warring with a new hope in him.

"Then I *really* didn't do it? I didn't kill that poor girl?"

"No," said Karr fiercely, taking his arm. "No, my friend. But we know who did. We can't prove it yet but we will. And when we do we'll nail the bastard. For all the lives he's ruined."

———

JELKA CRIED OUT, then sat up in the darkness, the terror of the dream still gripping her. She could see the three men vividly—tall, thin men, standing at the lake's edge, staring across at her, their eyes like black stones in their unnaturally white faces, their long, almost skeletal hands dripping with blood. And herself, at the center of the lake, the great slab of stone sinking slowly beneath her feet, drawing her down into the icy depths.

She heard footsteps on the flags of the corridor outside, then the creaking of her door as it opened. Her heart leaped to her mouth, certain they had come for her again, but as the lamplight spilled into the room she saw it was only her father.

"What is it, my love?"

He came to her and, setting the lamp down on the bedside

table, sat beside her on the bed, holding her to him. She closed her eyes a moment, shuddering, letting him comfort her; then she moved back slightly, looking up into his face.

"It was the dream again. But worse. This time I was in Kalevala, in the land of heroes. All about me was a wilderness of tree and rock and shallow pools. And still they came for me, following me through the trees. As if they had traveled back across the years to find me . . ."

His face creased in sympathetic pain. He drew her close again, pressing her head into his chest, comforting her. "There, my love. It's all right. I'm here now. No one will harm you. No one. I promise you."

His arms encircled her, strong, powerful arms that were like great walls of stone, protecting her; but still she could see the three assassins, see how they smiled, toothless, their mouths black like coals as she sank into the ice-cold water.

He moved back, looking down at her. "Shall I ask Helga to come?"

She hesitated, then nodded.

He went to the door, then turned, looking back at her. "And don't worry. No one will harm you here. No one."

━━━━━

SHE WAS UP early the next morning, watching her father pack. Later she sat there at the harbor's edge, watching the boat slowly disappear from sight. For a while she just stared at the nothingness, aching for him to return; then, with a start, she realized that the nothingness was filled with living things, was a universe of form and color.

She walked back slowly to the house, looking about her, while Erkki, the young guard her father had insisted on, trailed some twenty *ch'i* behind. There was a whole world here to explore, different in kind from the soft and sun-baked islands of Sumatra she had known during her father's exile. No, even the light was different here, was somehow familiar. Already the island seemed not strange but merely something she had forgotten, as if she knew it from another time.

In the days that followed she explored the island. Day by day she added to her knowledge of its places and its ways, its dark pools and tiny waterfalls, its narrow inlets and silent places, its caves and meadows. And slowly, very slowly, she fell in love with it.

Above all there was one special place . . .

It was the afternoon of her fourth day and she was making her way down from the island's summit, Erkki following. Usually he stayed close, calling her back when he felt she was taking too great a risk; but the path down from the crest was familiar now, and he relaxed, letting her go ahead.

She made her way across the grassy hilltop to a place where the land fell away. There, at the cliff's edge, stood a ruined chapel, its roof open to the sky, the doorway empty, gaping. It was a tiny building, the floor inside cracked and overgrown with weeds, one of the side walls collapsed, the heavy stones spilled out across the grass. Yet you could still read the lettering carved into the stone lintel and see the symbols of fish, lamb, and cross cut into the stone within.

She had asked her uncle about the words, words that seemed familiar despite their strangeness, that shared the same letters as her own tongue, yet were alien in their form. But he had not known their meaning, only that they were Latin, the ancient language of the *Ta Ts'in*. As for the symbols, he knew but he would not say.

For a moment she stood there, staring out at the sea beyond the ruin, then went on, finding the path down.

It was an old path, worn by many feet, and near the bottom, where the way grew steep, steps had been cut into the rock. She picked her way nimbly between the rocks and out beneath the overhang. There, on the far side of the broad shelf of rock, was the cave.

This was her special place, the place of voices. Here the island spoke to her in a thousand ancient tongues.

She went halfway across the ledge then stopped, crouching, looking down through the crack in the great gray slab. There, below her, the incoming tide was channeled into a fissure in the rock. For a moment she watched the rush and foam of the water through the narrow channel, then looked across at the young guard, noting how he was watching her, smiling, amused by what she was doing.

"Can't you hear it, Erkki? It's talking to me."

He laughed. "It's just a noise."

She looked down at it again, then lifted her head, listening for the other voices—for the sound of the wind, the branches singing overhead, the cry of seabirds calling out to sea. "No," she said finally. "They're voices. But you have to listen carefully."

Again he laughed. "If you say so, *Nu shi* Tolonen. But it's just noise to me. I haven't the ear for it, I guess."

She looked at him a moment, then smiled and turned away. No, he hadn't the ear for it; but, then, few had these days. A constant diet of trivee shows and holodramas had immunized them against it, had dulled their senses and filled their heads with illusions. But she could hear it—the inner voice of things. She could feel it in her blood, the pulse of the great world—more real, more alive, than anything within the levels.

She stood, wiping her hands against her thighs, then went across and stood at the edge of the rock, looking out across the rutted surface of the sea. She could feel the wind like a hand against her face, roughly caressing her, could taste the salt tang on her lips. For a moment she stood there, her eyes closed, imagining herself at the helm of a great ship, crossing the vast ocean, on her way to discover new lands. Then, smiling, she turned and went across to the cave, ducking beneath the low shelf of rock into the darkness beyond.

For a moment she paused, letting her eyes grow accustomed to the darkness, sniffing at the air. Then she frowned. Maybe it was only her imagination, but today it seemed different, less dank and musty than usual. Maybe that had to do with the weather. Her uncle had said a storm was on its way. Had warned her to be indoors when it came.

She smiled and turned, looking about her. On the wall behind her were the ancient letters, a hand's length in height, scored into the rock and dyed a burned ochre against the pale cream of the rock. Their sticklike angular shapes brought to mind a game she had played as a child with her *amah*'s yarrow stalks. Further in, where the ceiling sloped down to meet the floor of the cave, she had found a pile of tiny bones and the charred remains of an ancient fire. She bent down, squinting into the deep shadows, then frowned. They had been disturbed.

A tiny ripple of fear went up her back. And then she heard it. A strange, rustling noise at the back of the cave.

"Erkki!" she called, in a low, urgent whisper.

He was there in a moment, crouched in the cave's entrance, his gun searching the dark interior.

"What is it?" he said quietly.

She held her breath. Maybe she had imagined it. But then it came again, closer now. She shivered, then caught her breath as a pair of eyes looked back at her from the darkness. Dark, feral eyes that held her own, unblinking.

"It's an animal," she said softly, fear giving way to astonishment in her. "A wild animal."

She heard the click as Erkki took the safety off his gun and put her hand out, signaling him to hold still.

She took a slow step backward, then another, until she was beside him. "It won't harm us. It's more afraid of us than we are of it. It must have been sleeping at the back of the cave and I disturbed it."

Beside her Erkki shivered. "I thought all the animals were dead."

Yes, she thought. So did I. But there's one—probably more than one—here on the island. She could make out more of it now, could see how dark its fur was, how small, yet powerful its limbs. She had seen its like in her school textbooks. It was a fox. A real live fox.

Erkki touched her arm gently, making her look at him. "Shall I bring a cage? There's one in the house. We could catch it and take it back with us."

She shook her head then looked back at it. "No. Let it go free. It belongs here, not there. Look at it—it wasn't meant to be caged."

Nor are we, she thought, wondering how long ago the trap had been set on her own kind, the bars secured on every side. But she could do this much: could leave this tiny fragment of wildness here where it belonged. To make a pet of it . . . She shuddered. It would die if they put it in a cage.

"Come," she said, "let's get back. The storm is coming."

At the summit she stopped again, looking about her. Gulls circled overhead, their cries shrill, bad-tempered. She pulled her jacket close about her. The wind was growing stronger, more blustery. To the northeast storm clouds were gathering, dark and threatening, massing above the City. A storm was coming, just as her uncle had said. She laughed. Let it come! Let the heavens open! She would greet it here, if need be. Then she turned and saw Erkki watching her.

"Okay. I'm coming. Just a little longer . . ."

He nodded and started down. For a moment longer she stood there, looking about her, imagining herself mistress of all she saw. Then, with a sigh, she followed Erkki down toward the lights of the house.

———

DIRECTOR SPATZ sat back in his chair, pointing directly at the screen.

"Well, Ellis? What in the gods' names is that?"

The man standing just behind him shrugged. "We're not sure as yet, Director, but we're working on it. At first we thought it might be some kind of star chart, considering the boy's interest in astronomy. But we've run it through the computer for a possible match and there's nothing."

For a moment both men were silent, staring at the screen. There were forty-six points in all, most of them linked by straight lines to three or four other lines. They formed a tight cat's cradle on the screen, elliptical in structure, like the upper half of a skull.

Spatz huffed loudly. "You're absolutely certain it has nothing to do with what we're working on?"

"Absolutely. Apart from the fact that we've barely begun work on the actual positioning of the wires, those points simply don't correspond to the areas of the brain we'd be looking to use. In my opinion it's only coincidence that it has that shape."

"Hmm." Spatz leaned forward and blanked the screen, then turned, looking up at his assistant. "I know what you think, Ellis, but you're wrong. He's up to something. I'm sure of it. So keep looking. I don't want your team to relax until you've found out what he's doing."

Ellis bowed. Once outside the room, he drew a long breath, then shook his head. The Director's obsession with the boy was bordering upon the insane. He was convinced that the boy had been introduced for one of two reasons—to spy upon him or to ensure that the Project failed. Either way he felt threatened. But the truth was far simpler.

He had been studying the boy for ten days now and was convinced that he was genuine. He had watched Kim working on several of his own projects and had seen how he applied himself to problems. There was no faking that, no way of counterfeiting that quickness of mind. But Spatz would not hear of it. Second-rate himself, he would not have it that a mere boy—and a Clayborn boy at that—could be his intellectual superior.

But Spatz wasn't to have it all his own way. Ellis had seen the directive that had come down only moments before he had gone in to see the Director. And there was nothing Spatz could do about it.

He laughed, then walked on. No, not even Project Director Spatz would have the nerve to countermand Prince Yuan's direct command.

▰▰▰

KIM WAS LYING on his back in the pool, his eyes closed. It was late and the pool was empty, but from the gym nearby came the harsh hiss and grunt of the men working out on the exercise machines.

For a time he simply floated, relaxing for the first time that day; then, rolling over, he kicked out for the side, glancing up at the cameras overhead.

Did they watch him even here? He smiled and ducked his face under, then lifted it, throwing the water out from him in a spray. Almost certainly. Even when he was pissing they'd have a camera on him. Spatz was like that. But he wasn't atypical. There were many like Spatz. The City bred them in the hundred thousands.

He pulled himself up and sat on the side, moving his legs lazily in the water. He had always been watched—it was almost the condition of his existence—but he had never come to like it. At best he used it, as he did now, as a goad, challenging himself to defeat its constrictions.

In that the reports on him were accurate. In this one respect the Clay *had* shaped him, for he was cunning. And not just cunning, but inventive in his cunning, as if the very directness of his mind—that aspect of him that could grasp the essence of a thing at once and use it—needed this other "twisted" part to permit its function. He smiled and looked down, wondering, as ever, what they made of his smiles, what they thought when they saw him smile so, or so.

He looked up, looked directly into the camera. What do you see, *Shih* Spatz? Does the image you have of me bear any relationship to the being that I truly am?

No, he answered, looking away. *No relationship at all.* But then Spatz had no idea what Chung Kuo would be like if the Project succeeded. All that concerned him was his own position on the great social ladder, and whether he rose or fell. All else was irrelevant.

Kim stretched his neck, then yawned. He had slept little these past few nights, trying to see through the mesh of details to the heart of the problem.

What *would* Chung Kuo be like if everyone were wired?

He had run various scenarios through his head. For instance, the Seven might limit the use of wiring to known criminals and political dissidents. Or, at the other extreme, they might wire everyone, even their wives and cousins. Not only that, but there was the nature of the wiring to consider. Was it to be a simple tracing mechanism, or would it be more complex? Would they be content to use it as a method of policing Chung Kuo's vast population, or would they seek to change behavior by its use?

This last caused him much concern, for the wire held a far greater potential for manipulation than Li Yuan probably envisaged. When one began to tinker with the human mind there was no limit to the subtle changes one might make. It was possible—even quite simple—to create attractions and aversions, to mold a thousand million personalities to a single mental template and make the species docile, timid, uncreative. But was that worse than what was happening anyway? It could be argued that Chung Kuo, the great utopian City of Tsao Ch'un, had been created for that very purpose, to *geld* Mankind and to keep the curious beast within his bars. In such a light this latest step—this plan to wire each individual—was merely a perfection of that scheme. Restraint alone had failed. The bars were not enough. Now they must put the bars—the walls—within, or see the whole vast edifice come crashing down. It was an unsettling thought.

Against this he set three things: his 'duty' to Li Yuan; his certainty that with him or without, this thing would be; and, last, the simple challenge of the thing.

He had tried to convince himself that he owed nothing to any man, but the truth was otherwise. His fate had always been in the hands of others. And wasn't that so for all men? Wasn't even the most basic thing—a man's existence—dependent upon a consensus among those he lived with, an agreement to let him *be*? Hadn't he learned that much in the Clay? No man was truly free. No man had any rights but those granted him by his fellows. In Li Yuan's favor, the Prince at least had recognized his worth and given him this chance. Surely that deserved repayment of some kind?

As to the second matter, he was certain now that only total catastrophe could prevent Li Yuan's scheme from becoming a reality. Indeed, catastrophe now seemed the sole alternative to the Wiring Project. The fuse had been lit long ago, in the Seven's refusal to confront the problem of massive population increases. Their reluctance to tackle that fundamental, a decision shaped by their veneration of the family and of the right of every man to have sons, had hampered any attempt to balance the slow increase in resources against the overwhelming increase in demand and make of Chung Kuo the utopia it was meant to be. But that was nothing new; it was an age-old problem, a problem that the emperors of Chung Kuo had been forced to face for more than two thousand years. Famine and plague and revolution were the price of such imbalance, and they would come again—unless the tide were turned, the great generative force harnessed. But that would not happen without an evolutionary change in the species. In the meantime, this—this artificial means—would have to do. The Seven had no option. They would have to wire or go under.

And the challenge? That, too, he saw in moral terms. As he conceived it now, the scheme presented mainly technical problems that required not the kind of inventiveness he was good at but the perfecting of existing systems. In many ways it was a matter of pure organizational complexity, of breaking down the Wiring Project into its constituent parts and then rebuilding it. The end, however, was not unachievable. Far from it. Most of the technology required already existed. He could have said as much to Prince Yuan at their first meeting, but the challenge—the real challenge—lay in directing the research, in determining not the *quality* of the eventual wire, but its *kind*.

And there, perhaps, he overstepped the brief Li Yuan had given him, for he had not been asked to consider what the wire should be capable of; he had been asked only to determine whether the scheme would work. Again he was to be simply the tool—the vehicle—for another's needs, the instrument by which their dreams might become realities. As ever, he was supposed to have no say in the matter. Yet he *would* have his say.

Kim stilled the movement of his legs in the water and looked up.

"Joel!"

Hammond stood there on the far side of the pool. "Kim. I thought I'd find you here."

Kim clambered up and went around the pool to greet him. "How long have you been there?"

"I've just got here. You looked deep in thought. Troubles?"

They were both conscious of the watching cameras. Kim shrugged and smiled, moving past the older man, taking his towel from the rail; then he turned, looking back at him. "What brings you here?"

Hammond held out a wafer-thin piece of printout paper. "This came."

Kim took it. A moment later he looked up, his dark eyes wide with surprise. "This is for real?"

"Absolutely. Director Spatz confirmed it with Prince Yuan's secretary. I'm to accompany you. To keep you out of trouble."

Kim laughed, then handed the paper back, pulling the towel up about his shoulders. "But that's amazing. An observatory. Does that mean we'll be going into space?"

Hammond shook his head. "No. Quite the opposite, in fact. The observatory at Heilbronn is situated at the bottom of a mineshaft, more than three *li* underground."

Kim looked away, then laughed. "Of course. It makes sense."
He looked back. "When do we go?"

"Tomorrow. First thing."

Kim smiled, then drew closer, whispering. "Was Spatz
angry?"

Hammond bent down, giving his answer to Kim's ear. "Angry? He was furious!"

━━━━━

JELKA WOKE. Outside the storm was raging, hurling gusts
of rain against the windowpane. Throwing on her nightgown
she went out into the passageway. The night growled and roared
beyond the thick stone walls of the house. She stood there a
moment, listening, then started as the window at the far end of
the passage lit up brilliantly. Seconds later a huge thunderclap
shook the house.

She shivered, then laughed, her fear replaced by a surge of
excitement. The storm! The storm was upon them!

She hurried down the great stairway, then stood there in the
darkness of the hallway, the tiles cold beneath her naked feet.
Again there was a flash, filling the huge, stained-glass window at
the far end of the hallway with brilliant color. And then darkness, intense and menacing, filled by the tremendous power of
the thunderclap that followed.

She went on, finding her way blindly to the door at the far end
of the passageway. Usually it was locked, but for once she found
it open. She stood there a moment, trembling. Here behind the
thick stone of the outer wall, it was still, almost silent, only the
muted rumble of distant thunder disturbing the darkness. When
the next flash came, she pulled the door open and went up into
the tower.

At once the sound of the storm grew louder. She went up the
narrow, twisting steps in darkness, her left arm extended, steadying herself against the wall, coming out into a room she had not
seen before. Blindly, she began to edge toward the center of the
room, away from the hole in the floor, then froze as a blaze of
light filled the room from the narrow window to her left. The
accompanying thunderclap exploded in the tiny space and, in

the momentary brilliance, she glimpsed the sparse contents of the room.

She saw herself briefly in the mirror opposite—a tiny figure in an almost empty room, her body framed in searing light, her face in intense shadow, one arm raised as if to fend off the thunder, the dark square of the stair hole just behind her.

She found the steps in the darkness, then went up, as a sudden flash filled the stairwell with light.

She went to the window. The glass was cold against her face, beaded with brilliant drops. The wooden boards were smooth and cool beneath her feet. Wind and rain rattled the glass. And then a vast hand seemed to shake the building. The tower seemed alive. As alive as she. She pressed her hands against the wood of the window's frame and stared out, waiting for each vivid stroke, each growl of elemental anger.

As the window lit up again she turned, looking behind her. On the far side of the room a metal ladder had been set into the wall. Above it, set square and solid in the ceiling, was a hatch. For a moment she stared at it, then pushed away from the window.

In the sudden dark she stumbled and fell, then clambered up again, her hands held out before her until they met the cold stone surface. For a moment she searched the wall blindly, cursing softly to herself, then found the metal rung and pulling herself across, began to climb.

She was pushing upward when the next flash filled the room. Above her the great hatch shuddered against her hands as the thunderclap shook the tower. She shivered, momentarily frightened by the power of the storm, then pushed her head and shoulder up against the hatch until it gave.

Suddenly she was outside, the rain pouring down onto her, the wind whipping cruelly at her hair, soaking the thin nightgown she was wearing.

She pulled herself up and, in the half-light, went to the parapet, steeling herself against the sudden cold, the insane fury of the wind, her hands gripping the metal rail tightly. As the sky lit up she looked down. Below her the sea seemed to writhe and boil, then throw a huge, clear fist of water against the rocks at the base of the tower. Spray splintered all about her and, as if on cue, the air about her filled with a ferocious, elemental roar that juddered the tower and shook her to the bone. And then darkness. An intense, brooding darkness, filled with the fury of the storm.

She was breathing deeply now, erratically. It felt as though the storm were part of her. Each time the lightning flashed and forked in the sky she felt a tremor go through her from head to toe, as sharp as splintered ice. And when the thunder growled it sounded in her bones, exploding with a suddenness that made her shudder with a fierce delight.

She shivered, her teeth clenched tight, her eyes wide, her limbs trembling with a strange, unexpected joy. Water ran freely down her face and neck, cleansing her, while below her the sea raged and churned, boiling against the rocks, its voice a scream of unarticulated pain, indistinguishable from the wind.

"Jelka!"

She heard the call from far below, the cry almost lost in the roar of the storm, and turned, looking across at the open hatch. For one brief moment she failed to recognize what it was, then she came to herself. Her uncle Jon . . .

The call came again, closer this time, as if just below.

"Jelka? Are you up there?"

She turned, yelling back at him, her voice barely audible over the grumble of the storm. "It's all right! I'm here!"

She looked out across the sea again, trembling, her whole body quivering, awaiting the next flash, the next sudden, thrilling detonation. And as it came she turned and saw him, his head poking up from the hatch, his eyes wide with fear.

"What in heaven's name are you doing, Jelka? Come down! It isn't safe!"

She laughed, exhilarated by the storm. "But it's wonderful!"

She saw how he shuddered, his eyes pleading with her. "Come down! Please, Jelka! It's dangerous!"

The wind howled, tearing at her breath, hurling great sheets of rain against the tower. And then with a mighty crash of thunder—louder than anything that had preceded it—the hillside to her right exploded in flame.

For a moment the after-image of the lightning bolt lingered

before her eyes; then she shuddered, awed by the sight that met her eyes.

Seven pines were on fire, great wings of flame gusting up into the darkness, hissing, steaming where they met and fought the downpour. She gritted her teeth, chilled by what she saw. And still the fire raged, as if the rain had no power to control it.

She turned, staring at her uncle; then, staggering, she ran across to him and let him help her down. For a moment he held her to him, trembling against her, his arms gripping her tightly. Then, bending down, he picked up the gown he'd brought and wrapped it about her shoulders.

"You're soaked," he said, his voice pained. "Gods, Jelka, what do you think you were doing? Didn't you know how dangerous it was?"

The sight of the burning trees had sobered her. "No," she said quietly, shivering now, realizing just how cold she was. "It was so . . ."

She fell quiet, letting him lead her down, his pained remonstrances washing over her.

He helped her down the last few steps then let her move past him out into the passageway. The passage light was on. At the far end, at the bottom of the great staircase, stood her aunt, her look of concern mirroring her husband's.

"It's all right," Jelka said. "I couldn't sleep. The storm. I wanted to see."

Jon nodded, a look passing between him and his wife. Then he placed his arm about Jelka's shoulders.

"I can see that, my love, but it really wasn't safe. What if you'd fallen?"

But Jelka could think only of the power of the storm, of the way it had seemed a part of her; each sudden, brilliant flash, each brutal detonation bringing her alive, vividly alive. She could see it yet, the sea foaming wildly below, the huge sky spread out like a bruise above, the air alive with voices.

"There are fresh clothes in the bathroom," her uncle said gently, squeezing her shoulder, bringing her back from her reverie. "Get changed then come through into the kitchen. I'll make some toast and *ch'a*. We can sit and talk."

He looked up, waving his wife away, then looked back at Jelka, smiling. "Go on now. I can see you won't sleep until this has blown over."

She did as she was told, then went into the kitchen and stood by the window, staring out through the glass at the storm-tossed waters of the harbor while he brewed the *ch'a*.

"Here," he said after a while, handing her an old earthenware mug filled with steaming *ch'a*. He stood beside her, staring outward, then gave a soft laugh.

"I've done this before, you know, when I was much younger than I am now. Your mother was like you, Jelka. Knut could never understand it. If there was a storm he would tuck his head beneath the blankets and try to sleep through it, as if it were all a damned nuisance sent to rob him of his sleep and no more than that. But she was like you. She wanted to see. Wanted to be out there in the thick of it. I think she would have thrown herself in the water if she'd not had the sense to know she'd drown."

He laughed again and looked down at her. Jelka was staring up at him, fascinated.

"What was she like? I mean, what was she really like?"

He nodded toward the broad pine table. They sat, he in the huge farmhouse chair, she on the bench beside him, a heavy dressing gown draped about her shoulders.

"That's better. It gets in my bones, you know. The damp. The changes in pressure." He smiled and sipped at his mug. "But that's not what you want to know, is it? You want to know about your mother . . ."

He shook his head slowly. "Where to start, eh? What to say first?" He looked at her, his eyes grown sad. "Oh, she was like you, Jelka. So very much like you." He let out a long breath, then leaned forward, folding his big broad hands together on the tabletop. "Let me start with the first moment I ever saw her, there on the rocks at the harbor's mouth . . ."

She sat there, listening, her mouth open, her breathing shallow. The *ch'a* in her mug grew cold and still she listened, as if gazing through a door into the past.

Through into another world. Into a time before her time. A place at once familiar and utterly alien. That pre-existent world a child can only imagine, never be part of. And yet how she ached to see the things he spoke of; how she longed to go back and see what he had seen.

She could *almost* see it. Her mother, turning slowly in the firelight, dancing to a song that was in her head alone, up on her toes, her arms extended, dreaming . . . Or, later, her mother, heavily pregnant with herself, standing in the doorway of the kitchen where she now sat, smiling . . .

She turned and looked but there was nothing; nothing but the empty doorway. She closed her eyes and listened, but again there was nothing; nothing but the storm outside. She could not see it—not as it really was. Even with her eyes closed she couldn't see it.

Ghosts. The past was filled with ghosts. Images from the dark side of vision.

Hours passed. The storm died. And then a faint dawn light showed at the sea's far edge, beyond the harbor and the hills. She watched it grow, feeling tired now, ready for sleep.

Her uncle stood, gently touching her shoulder. "Bed, my child," he said softly. "Your father will be here tomorrow."

▼▼▼▼▼

THE DEEP-LEVEL telescope at Heilbronn was more than a hundred and fifty years old. The big satellite observatories at the edge of the solar system had made it almost an irrelevancy, yet it was still popular with many astronomers, perhaps because the idea of going deep into the earth to see the stars held some curious, paradoxical appeal.

"It feels strange," Kim said, turning to face Hammond as they rode the elevator down into the earth. "Like going back."

Hammond nodded. "But not uncomfortable, I hope?"

"No." Kim looked away thoughtfully, then smiled. "Just odd, that's all. Like being lowered down a well."

The elevator slowed, then shuddered to a halt. The safety doors hissed open and they stepped out, two suited guards greeting them.

"In there," said one of the guards, pointing to their right. They went in. It was a decontamination room. Ten minutes later they emerged, their skin tingling, the special clothing clinging uncomfortably to them. An official greeted them and led them along a narrow, brightly lit corridor and into the complex of labs and viewing rooms.

There were four telescopes in Heilbronn's shaft, but only one of them could be used at any one time, a vast roundabout, set into the rock, holding the four huge lenses. One of the research scientists—a young man in his early twenties—acted as their guide, showing them around, talking excitedly of the most recent discoveries. Few of them were made at Heilbronn now— the edge observatories were the pioneers of new research—but Heilbronn did good work nonetheless, checking and amassing detail, verifying what the edge observatories hadn't time to process.

Hammond listened politely, amused by the young man's enthusiasm, but for Kim it was different: he shared that sense of excitement. For him the young man's words were alive, vivid with burgeoning life. Listening, Kim found he wanted to know much more than he already did. Wanted to grasp it whole.

Finally, their guide took them into one of the hemispherical viewing rooms, settled them into chairs, and demonstrated how they could use the inquiry facility.

His explanation over, he bowed, leaving them to it.

Kim looked to Hammond.

"No, Kim. You're the one Prince Yuan arranged this for."

Kim smiled and leaned forward, drawing the control panel into his lap, then dimmed the lights.

It was like being out in the open, floating high above the world, the night sky all about them. But that was only the beginning. Computer graphics transformed the viewing room into an armchair spaceship. From where they sat they could travel anywhere they liked among the stars: to distant galaxies far across the universe, or to nearer, better-charted stars, circling them, moving among their planetary systems. Here distance was of little consequence and the relativistic laws of physics held no sway. In an instant you had crossed the heavens. It was exhilarating to see the stars rush by at such incredible speeds, flickering in the corners of the eyes like agitated dust particles. For a while they rushed here and there, laughing, enjoying the giddy vistas of the room. Then they came back to earth, to a night sky that ought to have been familiar to them, but wasn't.

"There are losses, living as we do," Kim said wistfully.

Hammond grunted his assent. "You know, it makes me feel, well—insignificant. I mean, just look at it." He raised his hand. "It's so big. There's so much power there. So many worlds. And all so old. So unimaginably old." He laughed awkwardly, his hand falling back to the arm of the chair. "It makes me feel so small."

"Why? They're only stars."

"Only stars!" Hammond laughed, amused by the understatement. "How can you say that?"

Kim turned in his chair, his face, his tiny figure indistinct in the darkness, only the curved, wet surfaces of his eyes lit by reflected starlight. "It's only matter, reacting in predictable ways. Physical things, bound on all sides by things physical. But look at you, Joel Hammond. You're a man. *Homo sapiens*. A beast that thinks, that has feelings."

"Four pails of water and a bag of salts, that's all we are."

Kim shook his head. "No. We're more than mere chemicals. Even the meanest of us."

Hammond looked down. "I don't know, Kim. I don't really see it like that. I've never been able to see myself that way."

"But we have to. We're more than earth, Joel. More than mere clay to be molded."

There was a hint of bitterness in the last that made the man look up and meet the boy's eyes.

"What is it?" he asked softly.

"Nothing. Just the memory of something."

It was strange. They had not really spoken before now. Oh, there had been the poems—the transfer of matters scientific— but nothing personal. They were like two machines passing information one to the other. But nothing real. As people they had yet to meet.

Hammond hesitated, sensing the boy's reluctance, then spoke, watching to see how his words were taken. "Do you want to talk about it?"

Kim looked back at him. "This feels like home."

"Home?"

"Down deep. Under the earth."

"Ah . . . the Clay."

Kim smiled sadly. "You should have seen me, Joel. Eight years ago. Such a tiny, skulking thing, I was. And thin. So thin. Like something dead." He sighed, tilting his head back, remembering. "A bony little thing with wide, staring eyes. That's how T'ai Cho first saw me."

He laughed, a tighter, smaller sound than before. More like surprise than laughter. "I wonder what it was he saw in me. Why he didn't just gas me and dispose of me. I was just"—he shrugged, and his eyes came up to meet the older man's, dark eyes, filled with sudden, half-remembered pain—"just a growth. A clod of earth. A scrap of the darkness from beneath."

Hammond was breathing shallowly, intent on every word.

"Twice I was lucky. If it weren't for T'ai Cho I'd be dead. He saved me. When I reverted he made a bargain for me. Because of what he saw in me. Five years I spent in Socialization. Doing penance. Being retrained, restructured, *tamed.*"

Hammond looked up, suddenly understanding. So that was why Kim's life was forfeit. "What did you do?"

Kim looked away. The question went unanswered. After a while, he began to speak again. Slower this time. Hammond's question had been too close, perhaps; for what Kim said next seemed less personal, as if he were talking about a stranger, describing the days in Socialization, the humiliations and degradations, the death of friends who hadn't made it. And other, darker things. How had he survived all that? How emerged as he was?

Kim turned away, leaning across to activate the viewer. Slowly the hemisphere of stars revolved about them.

"We were talking about stars, Joel. About vastness and significance." He stood and walked to the edge, placing his hand against the upward curving wall. "They seem so isolated—tiny islands in the great ocean of space, separated by billions of *li* of nothingness. Bright points of heat in all that endless cold. But look at them again." He drew a line between two stars, and then another two. "See how they're all connected. Each one linked to a billion-billion others. A vast web of light, weaving the galaxy together."

He came across, standing close to Hammond, looking down at him. "That's what's significant, Joel. Not the vastness or the power of it all, but how it's connected." He smiled and reached down to take Hammond's hand, clasping it firmly. "Apart or *a part*. There are always two ways of seeing it."

"A web," said Hammond, frowning; he shook his head and laughed, squeezing the hand that held his own. "A bloody web. You're mad, you know that, Kim Ward? Mad!"

"Not mad, Joel. Touched, perhaps, but not mad."

━━━━━

IT WAS HER last day on the island. She had slept late and had woken hungry. Now she walked the wooded slopes beside the house, Erkki shadowing her. It was a cool, fresh day. The storm had washed the air clean, and the sky, glimpsed through the tall, black bars of pine, was a perfect, unblemished blue.

At the edge of the clearing she turned and looked back at the young guard. He was walking along distractedly, looking down at the ground, his gun hung loosely about his left shoulder.

"Did you hear it?"

He looked up, smiling. "Hear what?"

"The storm."

He shrugged. "I must have slept through it."

She studied him a moment, then turned back. In front of her the fire had burned a great circle in the stand of trees. Charred branches lay all about her. No more than a pace from where she stood, the ground was black. She looked up. The trees on all sides of the blackened circle had been seared by the heat of the blaze, their branches withered. She looked down, then stepped forward into the circle.

The dark layer of incinerated wood cracked and powdered beneath her tread. She took a second step, feeling the darkness give slightly beneath her weight, then stopped, looking about her. If she closed her eyes she could still see it, the flames leaping up into the darkness, their brightness searing the night sky, steaming, hissing where they met the violent downpour.

Now there was only ash. Ash and the fire-blackened stumps of seven trees, forming a staggered H in the center of the circle. She went across to the nearest and touched it with the toe of her boot. It crumbled and fell away, leaving nothing.

She turned full circle, looking about her, then shivered, awed by the stillness, the desolation of the place. She had seen the violent flash and roar of the gods' touch; now she stood in its imprint, reminded of her smallness by the destructive power of the storm. And yet for a moment she had seemed part of it, her thinking self lost, consumed by the elemental anger raging all about her.

She crouched and reached out, putting her fingers to the dark, soft-crumbling surface, then lifted them to her mouth, tasting the darkness. It seemed sour, unappetizing. Wiping her fingers against her knee, she stood and moved further in, until she stood at the very center of the great circle.

"Kuan Yin! What happened here?"

She turned and looked back at Erkki. He stood at the circle's edge, his eyes wide with wonder.

"The lightning did it," she said simply, but saw at once that he didn't understand. Of course, she thought; you slept through it, didn't you? In that you're like my father—like all of them—you carry the City within you, wherever you are.

She turned back, looking down. This evening, after supper, her father was coming to take her back. She sighed. It would be nice to see her father again, and yet the thought of returning to the City was suddenly anathema. She looked about her, desperate to see it all one last time, to hold it fast in memory, in case . . .

She shuddered, then finished the thought. In case she never came again.

The nightmares no longer haunted her, the three gaunt men no longer came to the edge of the lake, their mocking eyes staring across at her. Even so, the threat remained. She was the Marshal's daughter, and while he remained important to the T'ang, her life would be in danger.

She understood it now: saw it vividly, as if her mind had been washed as clear as the sky. They had not been after her father. No. They had been after her. For her death would have left her father drained, emotionally incapacitated, a dead man filling the uniform of the Marshal.

Yes, she saw it clearly now. Saw how her death would have brought about her father's fall. And if the keystone fell, how could the arch itself hold up?

She knew her father's weaknesses, knew that he had four of the five qualities Sun Tzu had considered dangerous in the character of a general: his courage too often bordered on reck-lessness; he was impulsive and quick-tempered and would, if provoked, charge in without considering the difficulties; his sense of honor was delicate and left him open to false accusa-tions; and, lastly, he was deeply compassionate. Against these she set his strengths, chief of which was the loyalty he engen-dered in those who served under him. As Sun Tzu had said in the tenth book of the *Art of War*, "Because such a general regards his men as infants they will march with him into the deepest valleys. He treats them as his own beloved sons and they will die with him."

She nodded to herself. Yes, and weaknesses sometimes were strengths and strengths weaknesses. Take Hans Ebert, for in-stance. A fine, brave soldier he might be, handsome, too, and well-mannered, yet her father's eyes saw a different man from the one she had seen that day in the Ebert mansion. To her father he was the son he had never had and was thus born to be his daughter's life companion. But that was to forget her own exis-tence, to leave out her own feelings on the matter.

She turned, chilled by the thought, then looked across at the young guard. "Come, Erkki. Let's get back. I ought to pack."

She looked about her as she walked, seeing it all as if it had already passed from her. Yet she would never wholly lose it now. She had found herself here, had discovered in this harsh and forbidding landscape the reflection of her inner self, her *true* self; once awakened to it she was sure she would never feel the same about her world. The scent of pine and earth, the salt tang of the sea—these things were part of her now, inseparable, like the voices of the island. Before she had been but a shadow of her self, entranced by the dream that was the City, unaware of her inner emptiness. But now she was awake. Herself—fully herself.

———

THE MESS ORDERLY set the glasses down on the table between the two men, then, with a smart bow, left the room.

"*Kan pei!*" said Tolonen, lifting his glass to his future son-in-law.

"*Kan pei!*" Ebert answered, raising his glass. Then, looking about him, he smiled. "This is nice, sir. Very nice."

"Yes." Tolonen laughed. "A Marshal's privileges. But one day you'll be Marshal, Hans, and this room will be yours."

"Maybe so," Ebert answered, setting his glass down. "But not for many years, I hope."

Tolonen smiled. He liked young Ebert hugely, and it was reassuring to know that Jelka would be in such good hands when she was married. Just now, however, there was work to be done; there were other matters to occupy them.

"I've come from the T'ang,"he said, sitting back. "I had to deliver the interim report on the Executive Killings." He paused and sniffed, his features re-forming themselves into a frown. "Li Shai Tung wasn't pleased, Hans. He felt we ought to have got somewhere by now, and perhaps he's right. But the very fact that we've drawn so many blanks convinces me that DeVore's behind this somehow."

"Do you think so, sir?" Ebert looked away, as if considering the matter, then looked back, meeting Tolonen's eyes. "But surely we'd have found *something* to connect him. It would be rather too clever of him, don't you think, not to have left some trace somewhere? So many people were involved, after all."

"Hmm . . ." Tolonen sipped at his drink—a fruit cordial— then set his glass down again. "Maybe. But there's another matter, Hans. Something I didn't know about until the T'ang told me of it today. It seems that more was taken in the raid on Helmstadt than the garrison expenses. Jewelry for the main part, but also several special items. They were in the safe the *Ping Tiao* took. Three items of T'ang pottery. Items worth the gods know how much on the collector's market."

Tolonen reached into his tunic pocket and pulled out three thick squares of black ice. They were "flats," hologramic stills.

"Here," he said, handing them across.

Ebert held them up, looking at them a moment, then placed one on the table beside his drink and pressed the indented strip that ran along one edge. At once a hologram formed in the air above the flat.

He studied each in turn, then handed them back to the Marshal. "They're beautiful. And as you say, they'd fetch astronomical prices, even on the black market." He hesitated, looking down. "I realize it's awkward but . . . well, might I ask what they were doing in the safe at Helmstadt?"

Tolonen tucked the flats away and picked up his glass again. "I have the T'ang's permission to discuss this with you, Hans. But remember, this is mouth-to-ear stuff."

Ebert nodded.

"Good. Well, it seems Li Shai Tung was planning an experiment. The statuettes were to be sold to finance that experiment."

"An experiment?"

"Yes. There have been talks—highly secretive talks, you understand—between the T'ang's private staff and several of the Net's biggest Triad bosses."

Ebert sat back, surprised. "I see. But what for?"

Tolonen sniffed. "It seems that Li Shai Tung wanted to try to reclaim parts of the Net. To bring them back into the fold, so to speak. He would guarantee basic services and limited travel in the lower levels, as well as huge cash injections to bring facilities up to standard. In return the Triad bosses would guarantee to keep the peace, within the framework of existing law."

Ebert looked down. "It seems . . ." he sighed, then looked up again. "Forgive me for being candid, sir, but I'd say it was highly optimistic, wouldn't you?"

Tolonen lowered his voice. "Just between us, Hans, I fully agree. But ours is not to question policy, ours is to carry that policy out. We are our master's hands, neh?"

There was a moment's silence between the men, then Tolonen continued. "Anyway, it seems that the loss of the three statues has thrown things into flux for the time being. The T'ang is reluctant to part with any more of his treasures until it can be found what happened to these three. If the Triads were involved—if they *are* trying to have their cake and eat it—Li Shai Tung wants to know that. It may answer other questions, too. We've had our suspicions for some while that the *Ping Tiao* were working with another group in their raid on Helmstadt. If they were acting in conjunction with one or other of the larger Triad bosses, it would explain a lot. Maybe it would even give us a handle on these murders."

"I see. And you want me to investigate?"

"That's right, Hans. You see, some of the jewelry has already shown up on the black market. I want you to find out who's been trading the stuff. Then I want you to trace it back and get some answers."

Ebert was silent a moment, considering, then he looked up again, meeting the Marshal's eyes. "Why not Karr?"

"Major Karr has quite enough on his hands already." Tolonen leaned forward and covered Ebert's hand with his own. "No, Hans, you look after this for me, eh? Get me some answers that'll please the T'ang. It'll do you no harm, I guarantee. The murders, they're one thing. But this . . . Well, it could prove far more important in the long run."

Ebert smiled. "Of course. When do you want me to report?"

"The T'ang has given me three days."

"Then three days it is. Whatever it takes. I'll find out who's behind all this."

"Good." Tolonen beamed. "I knew I could count on you, Hans."

━━━━━

IT WAS THIRTY minutes later and Ebert was in the corridor outside his apartment when the woman approached him, grabbing his arm and shrieking into his face.

"You bastard! You *bought* her, didn't you? To humiliate me!"

Ebert turned and shook her off. "I don't know what you mean, Madam Chuang. Bought whom?"

"You know fucking well *whom*!" Her face was pale, her eyes dark with sleeplessness, her clothes . . .

"Gods, woman, look at you! You're a mess! And such language! You forget yourself, Madam Chuang. A Minister's wife!"

He gave her a look of disgust and started to turn away, but she grabbed at him again. He turned back angrily, taking her hand from his arm and squeezing it painfully. "If you don't desist . . ." he said quietly, but threateningly.

She tore her hand away, then leaned toward him, spitting full in his face.

He swore, rubbing at his face, then, glaring at her, turned

away. But as he did so, she pulled a knife from inside her clothes and struck out, catching him glancingly on the arm.

"Shit!"

He was turning as she struck the second blow, lifting his wounded arm to try to fend her off. She grunted as she delivered the blow, her full weight behind it, her face distorted with a mad lust of hatred as she thrust at him. This time the knife caught him squarely on the back of the head, knocking him forward onto his hands and knees. But the knife had gone scattering away.

Madam Chuang looked in horror. Where the knife had caught him, the hair had ripped away, revealing a shining metal plate. He half turned his head, looking up at her, stunned by the force of the blow, yet still alive. She shrieked and made to leap on him, but strong hands pulled her back, then threw her down roughly. A moment later she felt something hard press down brutally against her temple and knew it was a gun. She closed her eyes.

"No! Leave her!" The voice was Ebert's. He got to his knees, trying to steady himself. "Leave her . . ."

Auden looked across at his Major, then with a small shudder, pulled the gun back from the woman's temple and returned it to the holster. "She would have killed you, Hans."

Ebert looked up, smiling through his pain. "I know. She's got spirit, that one! Real spirit. Wouldn't you like to fuck her?"

Auden looked away.

Ebert laughed. "No. Maybe not. But perhaps we should frighten her off, neh? After all, I can't always be watching my back, can I? There are times . . ." He laughed again, then reached up and touched the back of his head tenderly.

"What do you suggest?" Auden asked, looking back at him.

"Her breasts," Ebert said, wincing. "She was always proud of them. Cut her breasts."

Auden turned, pushed the woman down, and tore her silks open roughly, exposing her breasts. Then he knelt over her, pinning down her arms.

She looked up at him, horrified, her voice a mere breath. "You can't . . ."

He hit her savagely with the back of his hand, splitting her lip, then drew his knife from his belt. There was a moment's hesitation, then pinning her neck down with his left hand, he drew the knife across her breasts, once, twice, a third time, ignoring her screams of pain, the razor-sharp blade ripping open the skin.

He stood, sheathing his knife, looking down at the distraught woman, then turned back, seeing at once how Ebert had been watching, how his eyes were wide with excitement, how his chest rose and fell.

"Thanks," Ebert said quietly. "You'll see to her?"

Auden nodded, then bent down, recovering the package he had dropped in coming to Ebert's aid. "Here," he said, handing it to Ebert. "It came this morning."

Ebert glanced at it then looked across at the woman again. "Who would have believed it, eh? Who'd have thought the old girl had it in her?" He laughed, then got unsteadily to his feet, swaying, closing his eyes momentarily. Auden went to him and put his arm about him, supporting him.

"Are you sure you're all right? Should I get a medic?"

Ebert shook his head, slowly, smiling through the pain he clearly felt. "No. I'll rest awhile. It'll be all right."

Auden turned, looking across at the Minister's wife. She had turned onto her side now, huddled into herself, whimpering, her bloodied silks pulled about her torn and ruined breasts. "I'll see to her. Don't you worry about that. I'll say she was attacked in the corridors by a gang. Fest will back me up."

Ebert swallowed, then put his hand on Auden's arm. "Good. Then get moving. I'll go inside and lie down for a while. There's help there if I need it."

He watched Auden go over to the woman and crouch down, speaking into his wrist-set, summoning assistance, then turned away. It would be all right; Auden would sort things out. He touched his arm. It was only a superficial wound, but the blow to his head . . . Well, perhaps Auden was right. Perhaps he should have the medics in. She had caught him a cracking blow, after all. He could easily be concussed.

He turned to face the door. "Fancy that . . ." he said softly, placing his hand against the lock and lifting his face to look directly into the overhead camera. At once the door hissed open. "She could have killed me," he said, going inside. "The fucking woman could have killed me!"

━━━━━

THE GREAT HALL of the Jakobstad Terminal was uncharacteristically silent, the departure lounge emptied of its normal crowds, the doors barred and guarded by soldiers. As the tiny party came through, their footsteps echoed across the massive space. It was almost a *li* from landing pad to platform, but Tolonen had waved away the sedan and had led his party on by foot, marching quickly, his daughter just behind him, the twelve-man elite corps squad fanned out about them, prepared for anything.

The Marshal had taken extraordinary steps to bring his daughter home. Things were in flux again and if their enemies were to strike anywhere, they would strike here, at one of the terminals. Which was why he was taking no chances.

The "bolt" was waiting for them, its normal crew of eighty pared down to ten trusted men, its usual complement of fifteen hundred passengers reduced to fourteen for this one journey. It was a fast-track monorail, cutting directly through the City, south to Turku, then east to Helsinki Terminal. From there they would commission another transporter and fly across the Baltic direct to Danzig.

Tolonen looked about him, tense despite his strict arrangements. For once he had chosen to trust no one; only he knew what he had planned. Even so, it would not be difficult for his enemies to second-guess him. If they could get into his home, what could they not do?

As they boarded the bolt he hesitated, scanning the platform both ways, then went inside. Jelka was already seated, her long legs stretched out in front of her. He smiled, studying her a moment, noticing how she had color from being outside, how her hair seemed even blonder than usual. He sat, facing her, leaning forward, his hands clasped together between his knees.

"Well?"

It was the first time they had relaxed together. On the flight across from the island he had been busy taking reports and giving orders, but now he could take time to talk, to ask her how she had enjoyed her stay.

She looked back at him and smiled, her eyes sparkling. "It was beautiful, Daddy. Just beautiful."

"So you enjoyed it?" He laughed. "That's good . . ."

She looked away. For a moment there was a strange wistfulness in her eyes, a wistfulness he shared and understood.

For a moment he just looked at her, realizing how precious she was to him. She was so like her mother now. So like the woman he had loved.

"You look tired," she said, concerned for him.

"Do I?" He laughed again, then nodded. "Well, perhaps I am." He smiled and leaned forward again, reaching out to take her hands in his. "Listen, we've got one stop-off to make, but then I've got the evening free. How do you fancy coming to the opera? I've booked a box. It's the T'ang's own company. They're doing *The South Branch*."

She laughed, delighted, for a moment forgetting her heaviness of heart. She had always liked opera, and if *The South Branch* wasn't the lightest of subjects, it was still opera.

"Where are we going first?"

He sat back, relinquishing her hands. "It's just business. It won't take long. A half hour at most. Then we can get back and get changed, neh?"

They felt the bolt judder then begin to move, picking up speed very quickly. Jelka looked away, watching the dragon pattern on the wall beyond the window flicker and then blur until it was just seven lines of red and green and gold.

"Did Uncle Jon tell you about the storm?"

"No." He laughed. "There was a storm, was there?"

"Yes." She turned, looking back at him. "It was so powerful. So . . ."

He looked down, as if disturbed. "Yes," he said quietly. "I'd forgotten."

She stared at him a moment, surprised by his sudden change of mood. "What is it?"

He looked up at her again, forcing a smile. "Nothing. Just that it suddenly reminded me of your mother."

"Ah . . ." She nodded. Then it was as her uncle had said. Yes, she could see it now, how different her father and mother had been and yet how much in love.

She turned her head, seeing their reflections in the glass of the window, and smiled sadly. It must have been hard for him, harder even than his exile.

She pushed the thought away, trying to cheer herself with the prospect of the evening ahead; but raising her hand to touch her cheek, she caught the unexpected scent of burnt pine on her fingers and felt herself go still.

"What is it?" her father asked, his eyes never leaving her.

"Nothing," she answered, turning, smiling at him again. "Nothing at all."

<hr />

"Who's that?"

Tolonen came back to the one-way mirror and stood beside his daughter. "That? Why that's Ward. Kim Ward. He's a strange one. Quite brilliant. They say his mind is quicker than a machine."

She laughed, surprised. "You mean, he's one of the team?"

"Yes, and probably the best, by all accounts. It's astonishing, considering . . ."

Jelka looked up at him. "Considering what?"

Her father looked away, as if the matter were distasteful. "He's Clayborn. Can't you see it in him—that darkness behind the eyes? He's been conditioned; but even so, it's never quite the same, is it? There's always that little bit of savagery left in them." He looked back at her, smiling. "Still . . . let's get on, eh? I've done here now and Hans is waiting back home."

She nodded vaguely, looking back at the boy, pressing her face close up against the glass to stare at him. She could see what her father meant. When he turned to face the glass it was as though something else—something other than the boy— looked back at her. Some wild and uncaged thing that owed nothing to this world of levels. She shivered, not from fear but from a sense of recognition. She laughed softly, surprised to find him here when she had thought him left behind her on the island. Then, as if coming to herself, she pushed back slightly from the glass, afraid.

And yet it was true. She could see it, there, in his eyes. Clayborn, her father had said. But he was more than that.

"Come, Jelka. Let's get on."

For a moment longer she hesitated, watching the boy, then turned, following her father, only then realizing what he had said earlier.

"The gods preserve us," she said almost inaudibly. "Hans Ebert! That's all I need!"

———————

KIM TURNED, looking across the table at Hammond.

"Who was that?"

"Who?"

"The girl. The one with Marshal Tolonen."

Hammond laughed. "Oh, her. That was his daughter, didn't you know?"

"Ah . . ." For a while he had thought it might have been his wife. It was the habit of such men, after all, to take young girls for wives. Or so he had heard. But he was strangely pleased that he'd been mistaken.

"Did you hear the rumors?" one of the other men said, keeping his voice low. "They say the *Ping Tiao* tried to assassinate her."

Kim frowned. "It wasn't on the news."

"No," one of the others said conspiratorially. "It wouldn't be. Just now they want everyone to believe that things are quiet and that they're in control. But I've heard—well, they say a whole squad of them attacked the Marshal's apartment. She killed six of them before her father intervened."

Kim felt a strange ripple of excitement—or was it fear?—move down his spine. He looked at Hammond again.

"What's her name?"

Hammond frowned. "I'm not sure. Jukka, or something."

"Jelka," one of them corrected him. "Jelka Tolonen."

Jelka. He shivered, then looked down. Yes, the name fitted her perfectly. Like something out of myth.

"What's going on here?"

Kim looked up, meeting Spatz's eyes. "Nothing," he said. "Nothing at all."

"Good. Then you can go now, Ward. I've no further use for you."

He bowed slightly, keeping all expression from his face, but inwardly he felt elated. Spatz had had no choice other than to take him into the laboratories for the duration of the Marshal's visit and Kim had made the most of it, calling up files and asking questions until he was as fully briefed of developments as the best of them. Yet as he walked back down the corridor to his room he found himself thinking not of the Project but of the girl. Who was she? What was she like? What did she sound like when she spoke? How did her face change when she laughed?

He paused at his door, thinking of how she had stood there at her father's side, her deeply blue eyes taking in everything. And then, briefly, her eyes had met his own and she had frowned. As if . . .

He shivered, then shook his head, palming the lock and stepping inside as the door irised open. No, it wasn't possible. It was only his imagination. And yet—well, for the briefest moment it had seemed that she had *seen* him. Not just the outward form of him, but his deeper self.

He smiled, dismissing the thought, then sat down on his bed, looking about him. What would you make of this, Jelka Tolonen? he wondered. It would be too alien, I'm sure. Too dull. Too esoteric.

Yes, for she was not of his kind. She was First Level, powerful, sophisticated, rich. No doubt she was in love with fine clothes and dances, opera and gallant young officers. It was ridiculous even to think . . .

And yet he *was* thinking it.

For a moment he closed his eyes, seeing her again: so straight and tall and perfectly proportioned, her skin so pure and white, her hair like gold and silver blended, her eyes— He caught his breath, remembering her eyes. Yes. Like something out of myth.

CHAPTER ELEVEN

King of the World

T SU MA STOOD on the grassy slope, looking south, the ruined monastery above him, at his back. He could see her in the distance, a tiny figure beneath the huge, cloudless sky, spurring her horse on along the narrow track between the rocks. For a brief moment he lost sight of her behind the great tor at the valley's head; then she reappeared, closer now, her dark hair streaming behind her as she leaned forward in the saddle, climbing the long slope.

He looked down, sighing. They had met here several times these last few weeks, and every time they had ended by making love despite his resolve to cast her off and mend his ways. But this time it was different. This time he had to end it. To break off with her, before they were discovered.

He was still in love with her; there was no denying that. But love was not enough, he knew that now. For this love—a love that had begun in passion and bewilderment—had now become a torment, keeping him from sleep, distracting him at every moment, until he felt he had to halt it or go mad. He could not now meet with Li Yuan or his father without wanting to throw himself at their feet and beg forgiveness for the wrong he had done them both.

So now an end to it. While it was yet within his power to end it.

He watched her come on, now hearing her voice encouraging the horse, seeing how she sat up in the saddle looking for him, then raised a hand in greeting. He returned the gesture uncertainly, steeling himself against the thoughts that came. Last time they had climbed the hill together, hand in hand, then gone into the ruined temple, and lain on his cloak for three hours, naked, their eyes, their hands and lips, feasting upon each other's bodies. The sweetness of the memory ate at him now, like sugar on a tooth. He groaned and clenched his fists against it. Even so, his sex stirred and his heart began to hammer in his chest.

He had never known how dreadful love could be, had never imagined how the heart could grieve and yet exult at the same time. But so his did.

She drew nearer, her horse laboring under her, snorting, straining to make the steep gradient. Seeing her thus reminded him of that first time, when she had ridden past him, ignoring his offer of help. Back then he had been thrilled by her defiance, for all he'd said to her of taking care; but now that recklessness in her seemed less attractive. Was the very thing, perhaps, that forged his determination to bring things to a head.

"Tsu Ma!"

She jumped down and ran to him, throwing her arms about him, her lips seeking his; but he held still against her, as if made of stone. She drew back, astonished, her eyes wide, looking up into his face.

"What is it, my love? What's happened?"

He looked down at her, his hands trembling now, her beauty, the warmth of her hands where they touched him, almost robbing him of his senses. Her perfume was intoxicating, her eyes like oceans in which a man could drown.

"I love you," he began, the full depth of what he felt for her concentrated in those few words.

"I know," she interrupted him, pressing closer, relief flooding her face. "And I've news—"

"Hear me out!" he said harshly, then relented, his hand brushing against her face, his voice softening. "Please, my love, hear me out. This is difficult enough . . ."

Her face changed again. She tried to smile, then frowned. "Difficult?"

"Yes. I . . ." He swallowed. Never had anything been so

difficult as this. Not even the death of his father and the ritual killing of the "copy" had prepared him for the hardship of this moment. "I . . ."

He fell silent. Even now it was not said. Even now he could take her in his arms and carry her up into the temple rooms and lay her on his cloak. Even now he could have that sweetness one last time.

But no. If this once, then he would want her forever. And that could not be. Not while there were Seven. Chung Kuo itself would have to fall before he could have Fei Yen.

He looked down, the pain of what he felt almost overwhelming him.

"You want to end it? Is that it?"

Her voice was strangely soft, surprisingly sympathetic. He looked up and saw how she was looking at him, saw how his own hurt was reflected in her face. And even as he watched he saw the first tears begin to gather in the corner of her eyes and fall, slowly, ever so slowly, down the porcelain perfection of her cheek.

"Fei Yen . . ." he said, his voice a whisper. "You know I love you."

"And I you." She shuddered, then stepped back from him. "I had a dream. A dream that I was free to become your wife."

He shivered, horrified by the words. "It cannot be."

Her eyes were pleading with him now. "Why not? I was his brother's wife. You know our laws."

"And yet you married him. The Seven put their seals to the special edict. It was done. It cannot be undone."

"Why not? You willed the law changed once, now will it back."

He shook his head. It was as he said; it could not be undone. Though all the seven T'ang agreed the match was ill-chosen, they would not change this thing. Not now. For one day Li Yuan would be T'ang, and to do this would be to wound him deeply. Only catastrophe could come of that. Only the end of everything they were.

He spoke clearly now, articulating each word separately. "I would we both were free, Fei Yen. I would give up all I have for that. But only ill—great ill—would come of it. And this, this *play* between us—it too must end. We must not meet like this again. Not ever."

She winced at his finality. "*Not ever?*"

The sweetness of the words, their pain and pleading, seemed to tear his soul from him, and yet he stood firm against her, knowing that to soften now would undo everything. "Not ever. Understand me, Li Yuan's wife? From now we are but— acquaintances who meet at functions and the like. All other thoughts must now be put aside."

"Would you forget . . . ?" she began, then fell silent, dropping her head, for he was glaring at her.

"Enough, woman! Would you have me die before you've done with me?"

"Never . . ." she answered, the word a mere breath, a whisper.

"Then go. At once."

She bowed, obedient, for a moment so like a wife to him that he caught his breath, pained, beyond all curing pained by the sight of her, broken, defeated by his own determination not to have her.

And then she was gone and he was alone again. He sat down heavily, feeling suddenly empty, hollowed of everything but grief, and wept.

━━━━━

FEI YEN JUMPED DOWN and, without waiting for her groom to come and take the horse, made toward the palace. As she ran through the stable yards, grooms and servants bowed low, then straightened up, watching her back, astonished. No one dared say a word, but their exchanged glances spoke eloquently. They had seen her ruined face and understood, for they, at least, knew what had been happening between the Princess and the handsome young T'ang.

And now, it seemed, it was over.

In the corridor Nan Ho made to greet her, but she ran past him as if he were not there. He turned, frowning, deciding not to pursue her but to go out to the stables and investigate the matter. It was his duty, after all, to serve his Prince. And how better than to understand and gauge the volatile moods of the woman closest to him?

Fei Yen herself went into her rooms and slammed the doors behind her, locking them; then she threw herself down onto the bed, letting the enormity of what had happened wash over her at last, her tiny body shaken by great shuddering sobs.

For a while she slept, then woke an hour later, all of the anger and hurt washed from her. She stood and looked about her, studying the hangings, the rich furnishings of her room, frowning at their strangeness, finding no connection between herself and these things. It was as if she had died and come to life again, for she felt nothing. Only an overpowering numbness where feeling ought to be.

She turned, catching her own reflection in the glass on the far side of the room. She took a step toward it, then stopped, looking down sharply.

Her news . . . She had never had a chance to tell him her news.

She stood there a moment, trembling, a single tear running down her cheek; then she lifted her head defiantly, taking control of herself again, knowing what she must do.

She bathed, then summoned her maids and had them put her hair up and dress her in a simple *chi pao*, the silk a pale lavender trimmed with blue. Then, to perfect the look, she removed all of her bangles and her rings, except his, wearing nothing about her neck. That done she stood before the mirror, examining herself minutely.

Yes. That was the look she wanted. Not sumptuous and sophisticated but plain and almost earthy—like a peasant girl. She had kept even her makeup simple.

Smiling she turned from the mirror and went out into the corridor.

"Master Nan!" she called, glimpsing the Master of the Inner Chamber at the far end of the corridor.

Nan Ho turned, acknowledging her; then, giving a small bow to the man he had been talking to, he hastened to her, stopping four paces from Fei Yen and bowing low, his eyes averted.

"Master Nan, is my husband back yet?"

Nan Ho kept his head lowered. "He is, my Lady. Twenty minutes ago."

"Good," she turned, looking away from him. "Then go to

him, Master Nan, and tell him his wife would welcome a few
moments of his time."

Nan Ho looked up, surprised, then looked down quickly.
"Forgive me, my Lady, but the Prince asked not to be disturbed.
He has important work to finish."

"He is in his study, then?"

Nan Ho bowed his head slightly. "That is so, my Lady. With
his personal secretary, Chang Shih-sen."

"Then you need worry yourself no longer, Nan Ho. I'll go to
him myself."

"But, my Lady—"

"You are dismissed, Nan Ho."

He bowed very low. "As my Lady wishes."

She watched him go, then turned away, walking quickly
toward her husband's study.

In front of the door she hesitated, composing herself, then
knocked.

There was a moment's silence, then footsteps. A second later
the door opened slightly and Secretary Chang looked out at her.

"My Lady . . ." He bowed, then opened the door wider, stepping back, at the same time looking across at Li Yuan.

"It is your wife, my Lord, the Princess Fei."

Li Yuan stood up behind his desk as Fei Yen entered, his face
lighting at the sight of her.

"Fei Yen. I thought you were out riding."

"I—" She hesitated, then crossed the room until only the desk
was between them. "The truth is, husband, I could not settle
until I had seen you. Master Nan said you had returned . . ."

Li Yuan looked past her at his secretary. "Go now, Shih-sen.
We'll finish this later." Then, smiling, he came round the desk
and embraced her, lifting her face to kiss her lips. "Your eagerness to see me warms me, my love. I've missed you too."

She let her head rest against his chest a moment, then looked
up at him again. "I've missed you, yes, but that isn't why I've
interrupted you."

He laughed gently. "You need no reason to interrupt me. You
are reason enough in yourself."

She smiled and looked down. "Even so, it wasn't only my
eagerness to see you. I have some news."

"News?" He moved her slightly back from him, taking her upper arms gently in his hands, studying her. Then he smiled again. "Well, let us go outside into the garden. We'll sit on the bench seat, side by side, like doves on a perch, and you can tell me your news."

Returning his smile she let herself be led out into the sunlit warmth of the garden. From somewhere near at hand a songbird called, then called again. They sat, facing each other on the sun-warmed bench.

"You look beautiful, my love," he said, admiring her. "I don't know what you've done, but it suits you." He reached out, his fingers brushing against her cheek, caressing the bare, un-adorned flesh of her neck. "But come, my love, what news is this you have?"

For a second or two her eyes searched his, as if for prior knowledge of what she was about to say; but he, poor boy, suspected nothing.

"What would you say if I told you I had fallen?"

He laughed, then shook his head, puzzled. "Fallen?"

She smiled, then reached out, taking his hands in her own. "Yes, my wise and yet foolish husband. *Fallen.* The doctors confirmed it this very morning." She saw how his eyes widened with sudden comprehension and she laughed, nodding her head. "Yes, my love. That's right. We're going to have a child."

━━━━

IT WAS LATE afternoon and the Officers Club at Bremen was almost empty. A few men stood between the pillars on the far side of the vast, hexagonal lounge, talking idly; only one of the tables was occupied.

A Han servant, his shaved head bowed, made his way across the huge expanse of green-blue carpet to the table, a heavily laden tray carried effortlessly in one hand. And as he moved between the men, scrupulously avoiding touching or even brushing against them as he put down their drinks, he affected not to hear their mocking laughter or the substance of their talk.

One of them, a tall mustached man named Scott, leaned forward, laughing, then stubbed out his cigar in one of the empty glasses.

"It's the talk of the Above," he said, leaning back and looking about him at his fellow officers. Then, more dryly, "What's more, they're already placing bets on who'll succeed the old bugger as Minister."

Their laughter spilled out across the empty space, making the Han working behind the bar look up before they averted their eyes again.

They were talking of Minister Chuang's marriage earlier that day. The old man had cast off his first wife and taken a new one—a young girl of only fourteen. It was this last that Scott had been rather salaciously referring to.

"Well, good luck to the man, I say," an officer named Panshin said, raising his glass in a toast. Again there was laughter. Only when it had died down did Hans Ebert sit forward slightly and begin to talk. He had been quieter than usual, preferring for once to sit and listen rather than be the focus of their talk; but now all eyes looked to him.

"It's a sad story," he began, looking down. "And if I'd had an inkling of how it would turn out I would never have got involved."

There was a murmur of sympathy at that, an exchange of glances and a nodding of heads.

"Yes, well—there's a lesson to us all, neh?" he continued, looking about him, meeting their eyes candidly. "The woman was clearly deranged long before I came across her."

For once there was no attempt to derive a second meaning from his words. All of them realized the significance of what had happened. An affair was one thing, but this was different. Events had got out of hand and the woman had overstepped the mark when she had attacked Ebert.

"No," Ebert went on. "It saddens me to say so, but I do believe Madam Chuang would have ended in the sanatorium whether I'd crossed her path or not. As for her husband, I'm sure he's much better off with his *tian-fang*," he smiled, looking to Scott, "even if the girl kills him from sheer pleasure."

There were smiles at that but no laughter. Even so, their mood was suddenly lighter. The matter had been there, unstated, behind all their earlier talk, dampening their spirits. But now it was said and they all felt easier for it.

"No one blames you, Hans," Panshin said, leaning forward to touch his arm. "As you say, it would have happened anyway. It was just bad luck that you got involved."

"That's so," Ebert said, lifting his shot glass to his lips and downing its contents in one sharp, savage gulp. "And there are consolations. The *mui tsai* for one."

Fest leaned forward, leering, his speech slurred. "Does that mean you've cooled toward the other one, Hans?" He laughed suggestively. "You know. The young chink whore . . . Golden Heart."

Fest was not known for his discretion at the best of times, but this once his words had clearly offended Ebert. He sat there, glaring at Fest. "That's my business," he said coldly. "Don't you agree?"

Fest's smile faded. He sat back, shaking his head, suddenly more sober. "Forgive me, Hans, I didn't mean . . ." He fell silent, bowing his head.

Ebert stared at Fest a moment longer, then looked about him, smiling. "Excuse my friend, *ch'un tzu*. I think he's had enough." He looked back at Fest. "I think you'd best go home, Fest. Auden here will take you if you want."

Fest swallowed, then shook his head. "No. I'll be all right. It's not far." He sought Ebert's eyes again. "Really, Hans, I didn't mean anything by it."

Ebert smiled tightly. "It's all right. I understand. You drank too much, that's all."

"Yes." Fest put his glass down and got unsteadily to his feet. He moved out from his seat almost exaggeratedly, then turned, bowing to each of them in turn. "Friends . . ."

When he was gone, Ebert looked about him, lowering his voice slightly. "Forgive me for being so sharp with him, but sometimes he forgets his place. It's a question of breeding, I suppose. His father climbed the levels, and sometimes his manners—" he spread his arms, "Well, you know how it is."

"We understand," Panshin said, touching his arm again. "But duty calls me, too, I'm afraid, much as I'd like to sit here all afternoon. Perhaps you'd care to call on me some time, Hans? For dinner?"

Ebert smiled broadly. "I'd like that, Anton. Arrange something with my equerry. I'm busy this week, but next?"

Slowly it broke up, the other officers going their own ways,
until only Auden was there with him at the table.

"Well?" Auden asked, after a moment, noticing how deep in
thought Ebert was.

Ebert looked up, chewing on a fingernail.

"You're annoyed, aren't you?"

"Too fucking right I am. The bastard doesn't know when to
hold his tongue. It was bad enough the Minister committing his
wife to the asylum, but I don't want to be made a total
laughingstock."

Auden hesitated, then nodded. "So what do you want me to
do?"

Ebert sat back, staring away across the sea of empty tables
toward the bar, then looked back at him, shuddering with anger.

"I want him taught a lesson, that's what I want. I want
something that'll remind him to keep his fucking mouth shut
and drink a little less."

"A warning, you mean?"

Ebert nodded. "Yes. But nothing too drastic. A little roughing
up, perhaps."

"Okay. I'll go there now, if you like." He hesitated, then
added, "And the pictures?"

Ebert stared back at him a moment. Auden was referring to
the package he had left with him the day he had been attacked
by the madwoman. He took a breath, then laughed. "They were
interesting, Will. Very interesting. Where did you get them?"

Auden smiled. "From a friend, let's say. One of my contacts in
the Net."

Ebert nodded. It had been quite a coincidence. There he'd
been, only half an hour before, talking to Marshal Tolonen
about the missing sculptures, and there was Auden, handing
him the package containing holograms of the self-same items he
had been instructed to find.

"So what do you want to do?" Auden prompted.

"Nothing," Ebert answered, smiling enigmatically. "Unless
your friend has something else for me."

Auden met his eyes a moment, then looked away. So he

understood at last. But would he bite? "I've a letter for you," he said, taking the envelope from his tunic pocket. "From your uncle Lutz."

Ebert took it from him and laughed. "You know what's in this?"

Auden shook his head. "I'm only the messenger, Hans. It wouldn't do for me to know what's going on."

Ebert studied his friend awhile, then nodded slowly. "No, it wouldn't, would it?" He looked down at the envelope and smiled. "And this? Is this your friend's work, too?"

Auden frowned. "I don't know what you mean, Hans. As I said—"

Ebert raised a hand. "It doesn't matter." He leaned forward, taking Auden's hand, his face suddenly earnest. "I trust you, Will. Alone of all this crowd of shits and hangers-on, you're the only one I can count on absolutely. You know that, don't you?"

Auden nodded. "I know. That's why I'd never let you down."

"No." Ebert smiled back at him fiercely, then sat back, releasing his hand. "Then get going, Will. Before that loud-mouthed bastard falls asleep. Meanwhile, I'll find out what my uncle wants."

Auden rose, then bowed. "Take care, Hans."

"And you, Will. And you."

━━━━━

FEST LEANED against the wall pad, locking the door behind him, then threw his tunic down onto the floor. Ebert had been right. He *had* had too much to drink. But what the hell? Ebert was no saint when it came to drinking. Many was the night *he'd* fallen from his chair incapable. And that business about the girl, the chink whore, Golden Heart. Fest laughed.

"I touched a sore spot there, didn't I, Hans old pal? Too fucking sore for your liking, neh?"

He shivered, then laughed again. Ebert would be mad for a day or two, but that was all. If he kept his distance for a bit it would all blow over. Hans would forget, and then . . .

He belched, then put his arm out to steady himself against the wall. "Time to piss."

He stood over the sink, unbuttoning himself. It was illegal to urinate in the wash basins, but what the shit? Everyone did it. It was too much to expect a man to walk down the corridor to the urinals every time he wanted a piss.

He was partway through, thinking of the young singsong girl Golden Heart and what he'd like to do to her, when the door chime sounded. He half-turned, pissing on his boots and trouser leg, then looked down, cursing.

"Who the hell . . . ?"

He tucked himself in and not bothering to button up, staggered back out into the room.

"Who is it?" he called out, then realized he didn't have his hand on the intercom.

What the fuck? he thought, it's probably Scott, come to tell me what happened after I'd gone. He went across and banged his hand against the lock to open it, then turned away, bending down to pick his tunic up off the floor.

He was straightening up when a boot against his buttocks sent him sprawling headfirst. Then his arms were being pulled up sharply behind his back and his wrists fastened together with a restraining brace.

"What in hell's name?" he gasped, trying to turn his head and see who it was, but a blow against the side of the head stunned him and he lay there a moment, tasting blood, the weight of the man on his back preventing him from getting up.

He groaned, then felt a movement in his throat. "Oh, fuck. I'm going to be sick . . ."

The weight lifted from him, letting him bring his knees up slightly and hunch over, his forehead pressed against the floor as he heaved and heaved. When he was finished he rested there for a moment, his eyes closed, sweat beading his forehead, the stench of sickness filling the room.

"Gods, but you disgust me, Fest."

He looked sideways, finding it hard to focus, then swallowed awkwardly. "And who the fuck are you?"

The man laughed coldly. "Don't you recognize me, Fest? Was it so long ago that your feeble little mind has discarded the memory?"

Fest swallowed again. "Haavikko. You're Haavikko, aren't you?"

The man nodded. "And this is my friend, Kao Chen."

A second face, that of a Han, appeared beside Haavikko's, then moved away. It was a strangely familiar face, though Fest couldn't recall why. And that name . . .

Fest closed his eyes, the throbbing in his head momentarily painful, then slowly opened them again. The bastard had hit him hard. Very hard. He'd get him for that.

"What do you want?" he asked, his cut lip stinging now.

Haavikko crouched next to him, pulling his head back by the hair. "Justice, I'd have said, once upon a time, but that's no longer enough—not after what I've been through. No. I want to hurt you and humiliate you, Fest, as much as I've been hurt and humiliated."

Fest shook his head slowly, restrained by the other's grip on him. "I don't understand. I've done nothing to you, Haavikko. Nothing."

"Nothing?" Haavikko's laugh of disbelief was sour. He tugged Fest's head back sharply, making him cry out. "You call backing Ebert up and having me dishonored before the General nothing?" He snorted, then let go, pushing Fest's head away roughly. He stood. "You shit. You call that *nothing?*"

Fest grimaced. "I warned you. I told you to leave it, but you wouldn't. If only you'd kept your mouth shut—"

Haavikko's boot caught Fest on the shoulder. He fell onto his side, groaning, then lay there, the pain lancing through his shoulder. For a time he was still, silent, then he turned his head again, trying to look back at Haavikko.

"You think you'll get away with this?"

It was the Han who answered him, his face pressed close to Fest's, his breath sour on Fest's cheek. "See this?" He brought a knife into the range of Fest's vision—a big vicious-looking knife, longer and broader than the regulation issue, the edge honed razor-sharp.

"I see it," Fest said, fighting down the fear he suddenly felt.

"Good. Then you'll be polite, my friend, and not tell us what we can or cannot do."

There was something coldly fanatical about the Han. Something odd. As if all his hatred were detached from him. It made him much more dangerous than Haavikko, for all Haavikko's threats. Fest looked away, a cold thrill of fear rippling through him.

"What are you going to do?"

The Han laughed. Again it was cold, impersonal. "Not us, Fest. You. What are *you* going to do? Are you going to help us nail that bastard Ebert, or are you going to be difficult?"

Fest went very still. So that was it. Ebert. They wanted to get at Ebert. He turned back, meeting the Han's eyes again. "And if I don't help you?"

The Han smiled. A killer's smile. "If you don't, then you go down with him. Because we'll get him, be assured of that. And when we do, we'll nail you at the same time, Captain Fest. For all the shit *you've* done at his behest."

Fest swallowed. It was true. His hands were far from clean. But he also sensed the unstated threat in the Han's words. If he *didn't* help . . . He looked away, certain that the Han would kill him if he said no. And then, suddenly, something broke in him and he was sobbing, his face pressed against the floor, the smell of his own vomit foul in his nostrils.

"I hate him. Don't you understand that? *Hate* him."

Haavikko snorted his disgust. "I don't believe you, Fest. You're his creature. You do his bidding. You forget, old friend, I've seen you at your work."

But Fest was shaking his head. He looked up at Haavikko, his face pained, his voice broken now. "I *had* to. Don't you understand that, Haavikko? That time before Tolonen—I *had* to lie. Because if I hadn't . . ."

The Han looked at Haavikko, something passing between them, then he looked back at Fest. "Go on," he said, his voice harder than before. "Tell us. What *could* he have done? You only had to tell the truth."

Fest closed his eyes, shuddering. "Gods, how I wished I had. But I was scared."

"You're a disgrace—" Haavikko began, but Fest interrupted him.

"No. You still don't understand. I *couldn't*. I . . ." He looked down hopelessly, then shook his head again. "You see, I killed a girl—"

Haavikko started forward angrily. "You lying bastard!"

Fest stared back at him, wide-eyed, astonished by his reaction, not understanding what he meant by it. "But it's true! I killed a girl. It was an accident—in a singsong house—and Ebert found out about it—"

Haavikko turned, outraged. "He's lying, Chen! Mocking me!"

"No!" Chen put his hand on Haavikko's arm, restraining him. "Hear him out. And think, Axel. Think. Ebert's not that imaginative a man. What he did to you—where would he have got that idea if not from Fest here? And what better guarantee that it would work than having seen it done once before?"

Haavikko stared back at him open-mouthed, then nodded. He turned, looking back at Fest, sobered. "Go on," he said, almost gently this time. "Tell us, Fest. Tell us what happened."

Fest shivered, looking from man to man, then, lowering his eyes, he began.

━━━━━

THE DOORMAN BOWED low, then stepped back, his fingers nimbly tucking the folded note into his back pocket as he did so.

"If the gentleman would care to wait, I'll let *Shih* Ebert know he's here."

DeVore went inside and took a seat, looking about him. The lobby of the Abacus Club was a big high-ceilinged room, dimly lit and furnished with low heavy-looking armchairs. In the center of the room a tiny pool was set into a raised platform, a fountain playing musically in its midst, while here and there huge bronze urns stood like pot-bellied wrestlers, their arms transformed to ornately curved handles, their heads to bluntly flattened lids.

Across from him the wall space was taken up by a single huge tapestry. It depicted an ancient trading hall, the space beneath its rafters overflowing with human life, busy with frenetic activity, each trader's table piled high with coins and notes and scrolled documents. In the foreground a clearly prosperous merchant haggled with a customer while his harried clerk sat at the table behind him, his fingers nimbly working the beads of his abacus. The whole thing was no doubt meant to illustrate the principles of honest trade and sturdy self-reliance, but to the eye of an impartial observer the impression was merely one of greed.

DeVore smiled to himself, then looked up as Lutz Ebert appeared at the far end of the lobby. He stood and walked across, meeting Ebert halfway.

Lutz Ebert was very different from his brother, Klaus. Ten years his brother's junior, he had inherited little of his father's vast fortune and even less, it seemed, of his distinctive personal traits. Lutz was a tall, slim, dark-haired man, more sauve in his manner than his brother—the product of his father's second marriage to an opera star. Years before, DeVore had heard someone describe Lutz as honey-tongued, and it was true. Unlike his brother he had had to make his own way in the world and the experience had marked him. He was wont to look away when he talked to people or to press one's hand overzealously, as if to emphasize his friendship. The blunt, no-nonsense aloofness that was his brother's way was not allowed him, and he knew it. He was not his brother—neither in power nor personality—though he was not averse to using the connection, letting others make what they would of his relationship with, and his possible influence over, one of Chung Kuo's most powerful men. He had swung many deals that way, deals that the force of his own personality and limited circumstances might have put outside his grasp. Here, in the Abacus Club, however, he was in his element, among his own kind.

Lutz smiled warmly, greeting him, then gave a small, respectful bow.

"What an unexpected pleasure, *Shih* Loehr. You'll dine with me, I hope. My private rooms are at the back. We can talk there undisturbed."

"Of course."

The rooms were small but sumptuously furnished in the latest First Level fashion. DeVore unbuttoned his tunic, looking about him, noting the bedroom off to one side. No doubt much of Lutz Ebert's business was transacted thus, in shared debauchery with others of his kind. DeVore smiled to himself again, then raised a hand, politely refusing the drink Ebert had poured for him.

"I won't, thanks. I've had a tiring journey and I've a few other visits to make before the day's over. But if you've a fruit juice or something . . ."

"Of course." Ebert turned away and busied himself at the drinks cabinet again.

"This is very nice, my friend. Very nice indeed. Might I ask what kind of rental you pay on these rooms?"

Ebert laughed, then turned, offering DeVore the glass. "Nominally it's only twenty thousand a year, but in reality it works out to three or four times that."

DeVore nodded, raising his glass in a silent toast. He understood. There were two prices for everything in this world. One was the official, regulated price: the price you'd pay if things were fair and there were no officials to pay squeeze to, no queues to jump. The other was the actual price—the cost of oiling palms to get what a thousand others wanted.

Ebert sat down, opposite him. "However, I'm sure that's not why you came to see me."

"No. I came about your nephew."

Ebert smiled. "I thought as much."

"You've written to him?"

"In the terms you suggested, proposing that he call on me tomorrow evening for supper."

"And will he come?"

Ebert smiled, then took an envelope from his top pocket and handed it to DeVore. Inside was a brief handwritten note from Hans Ebert, saying he would be delighted to dine with his uncle. DeVore handed the letter back. "You know what to say?"

"Don't worry, Howard. I know how to draw out a man. You say you've gauged his mood already. Well, fair enough, but I know my nephew. He's a proud one. What if he doesn't want this meeting?"

DeVore sat back, smiling. "He'll want it, Lutz, I guarantee it. But you must make it clear that there's no pressure on him, no obligation. I'd like to meet him, that's all—to have the opportunity of talking with him."

He saw Ebert's hesitation and smiled inwardly. Ebert knew what risks he was taking simply in being here, but really he'd had no option. His last business venture had failed miserably, leaving him heavily indebted. To clear those debts Ebert had to work with him, whether he wished it or not. In any case, he was being paid very well for his services as go-between—a quarter of a million *yuan*—with the promise, if things worked out, of further payments.

There was a knock at the door. It was the steward, come to take their orders for dinner. Ebert dealt with him, then turned back to DeVore, smiling, more relaxed now the matter had been raised and handled.

"Are you sure there's nothing else I can do for you, Howard? Nothing I can arrange?"

DeVore sat back, then nodded. "Now you mention it, Lutz, there is one small thing you can do for me. There's something I want to find a buyer for. A statuette . . ."

━━━━━━

IN THE TRANSPORTER returning to the Wilds, DeVore lay back, his eyes closed, thinking over his day's work. He had started early, going down beneath the Net to meet with Gesell and Mach. It had been a hard session, but he had emerged triumphant. As he'd suspected, Wang Sau-leyan had convinced them—Gesell particularly—that they ought to attack Li Shai Tung's Plantations in Eastern Europe. Once implanted, this notion had been hard to dislodge, but eventually he had succeeded, persuading Mach that an attack on Bremen would strike a far more damaging blow against the T'ang while damaging his own people less. His agreement to hand over the remaining maps and to fund and train the special *Ping Tiao* squads had further clinched it. He could still see how they had looked at each other at the end of the meeting, as if they'd pulled a stroke on him, when it had been he who had called the tune.

From there he had gone on to dine with Ebert's uncle, and then to his final meeting of the day. He smiled. If life were a great game of *wei chi*, what he had done today could be summarized thus. In his negotiations with the *Ping Tiao* he had extended his line and turned a defensive shape into an offensive one. In making advances to Hans Ebert through his uncle he sought to surround and thus remove one of his opponent's potentially strongest groups. These two were perfections of plays he had begun long ago, but the last was a brand-new play—the first stone set down on a different part of the board, the first shadowing of a wholly new shape.

The scientist had been easy to deal with. It was as his informer had said: the man was discontented and corrupt. The first made it possible to deal with him, the second to buy him. And bought him he had, spelling out precisely what he wanted for his money.

"Do this for me," he'd said, "and I'll make you rich beyond your dreams." And in token of that promise he had given the man a chip for twenty thousand *yuan*. "Fail me, however, and you had better have eyes in your back and a friend to guard your sleep. Likewise if you breathe but a single word of what I've asked you to do today." He had leaned forward threateningly. "I'm a generous man, *Shih* Barycz, but I'm also deadly if I'm crossed."

He had seen the effect his words had had on the scientist and was satisfied it would be enough. But just to make sure he had bought a second man to watch the first. Because it never hurt to make sure.

And so he had laid his stone down where his opponents least expected it, at the heart of their own formation—the Wiring Project. For the boy Kim was to be his own, when he was ready for him. Meanwhile he would keep an eye on him and ensure he came to no harm. Barycz would be his eyes and ears and report back to him.

When the time came he would take the boy off-planet. To Mars. And there he would begin a new campaign against the Seven. A campaign of such imaginative scope as would make their defensive measures seem like the ignorant posturings of cavemen.

He laughed and sat up, glimpsing the mountains through the portal to his left as the craft banked, circling the base.

But first he would undermine them. First he would smash their confidence, break the *Ywe Lung*, the great wheel of dragons, and make them question every act they undertook. Would set them one against another, until . . .

Again he laughed. Until the final dragon ate its own tail. And then there would be nothing. Nothing but himself.

HANS EBERT smiled and placed his arm about Fest's shoulders. "Don't worry, Edgar. The matter's closed. Now, what will you drink? I've a bottle of the T'ang's own finest *Shen*, if you'd like. It would be good to renew our friendship over such a good wine, don't you think?"

Fest lowered his head slightly, still ill at ease despite Ebert's apparent friendliness. He had thought of running when he'd first received Ebert's note summoning him to his apartment, but where would he run? In any case, it was only a bout of paranoia brought on by the visit of Haavikko and the Han to his rooms. There was no real reason why he should fear Ebert. And as for the other matter—the business with Golden Heart—not only had Ebert forgiven him, he had astonished him by offering him use of the girl.

"I've tired of her," Ebert had said, standing there in the doorway next to him, looking in at the sleeping girl. "I've trained her far too well, I suspect. She's far too docile. No, my preference is for a woman with more spirit. Like the *mui tsai*."

Fest had looked about for her, but Ebert had quickly explained that he'd sent the *mui tsai* away. For a day or two.

Ebert had laughed again. "It doesn't do to jade the appetite. A few days abstinence sharpens the hunger, don't you find?"

Fest had nodded. It had been six days since he'd had a woman and his own hunger was sharp as a razor. From where he stood he could see the girl's naked breasts, the curve of her stomach where she had pushed down the sheet in her sleep. He swallowed. How often he'd imagined it. Ever since that first time in Mu Chua's.

Ebert had turned his face, meeting Fest's eyes. "Well, Edgar? Wouldn't you like to have her?"

Slowly, reluctantly, he had nodded; and Ebert, as if satisfied, had smiled and drawn him back, pulling the door to.

"Well, maybe you will, eh? Maybe I'll let you use her."

Now they stood in the lounge, toasting their friendship, and Fest, having feared the very worst, began to relax.

Ebert turned, looking about him, then sat, smiling across at him.

"That's a nasty bruise you've got on the side of your face, Edgar. How did that come about?"

The question seemed innocuous—a mere pleasantry—yet Fest felt himself stiffen defensively. But Ebert seemed unconcerned. He looked down, sipping his drink, as if the answer were of no importance.

"I fell," Fest began. "Truth was, I was pissing in the sink and slipped. Caught myself a real crack on the cheek and almost knocked myself out."

Ebert looked up at him. "And your friends . . . how are they?"

Fest frowned. "My friends? Scott you mean? Panshin?"

Ebert shook his head slowly. "No. Your other friends."

"I don't know what you mean. What other friends?"

"Your new friends. The friends you made yesterday."

Fest swallowed. So he knew. Or did he? And if he did, then why the earlier show of friendship? Why the offer of the girl? Unless it was all a game to draw him out and make him commit himself.

He decided to brazen it out. "I still don't follow you, Hans. I've got no new friends."

The speed with which Ebert came up out of his chair surprised him. Fest took a step backward, spilling his drink.

"You fucking liar. You loud-mouthed, cheating liar. And to think I trusted you."

Fest shivered. The change in Ebert was frightening. His smile had become a snarl. His eyes were wide with anger.

"It's all lies, Hans. Someone's been telling lies . . ."

Again Ebert shook his head, his contempt for Fest revealed at last in his eyes. He spat the words out venomously. "You want to fuck the girl, eh? Well, I'd sooner see you dead first. And as for liars, there's only one here, and that's you, you fucking creep! Here, look at this."

He took the picture Auden had taken from outside Fest's apartment and handed it across. It showed Fest standing in his doorway, saying good-bye to Haavikko and the Han. All three of them were smiling.

"Well? What have you got to say for yourself? Give me one good reason why I shouldn't kick your ass from here to Pei Ching?"

Fest stood there a moment longer, staring down at the photo, then let it fall from his fingers. He looked back at Ebert and smiled, for the first time in a long while feeling free, unbeholden to the man.

"Go fuck yourself, Hans Ebert."

It was what he had wanted to say for more than fifteen years but had never had the courage until now. He saw how Ebert's eyes flared at his words and laughed.

"You little shit."

He reacted slowly. Ebert's hand caught him a stinging blow to the ear, making him stagger back, knocking his glass from his hand. Then he was crouched, facing Ebert, knife in hand.

"Try that again, Ebert, and I'll cut you open."

Ebert faced him, circling slowly, sneering now. "You were always a windy little sod, Fest, but you were never any good with a knife. Why, if I'd not kept you for my amusement you'd have never made sergeant, let alone captain."

Fest lunged, but again he was too slow. Ebert had moved. Fest's knife cut nothing but air. But Ebert caught his arm and held it in a vise-like grip, bringing it down savagely onto his knee.

Fest screamed, but his scream was cut short as Ebert smashed his face down onto his knee. Then, drawing his own knife, he thrust it once, twice, a third time into Fest's stomach, grunting with the effort, heaving it up through the mass of soft tissues until it glanced against the bone.

He thrust Fest away from him, then threw his knife down. For a moment Fest's eyes stared up at him, horrified, then he spasmed and his eyes glazed over. He had been disemboweled.

Ebert stood there a moment longer, shuddering, looking down at what he had done; then he turned and walked across to the doorway, looking into the room where Golden Heart lay. She lay on her side now, her back to him, but he could see at once that she was sleeping. He shivered, then closed the door, locking it from his side.

He turned back. Blood was still welling from the corpse, bubbling like a tiny fountain from a severed artery, pooling on the floor beside the body. He stared at it a moment, fascinated, then walked across the room to the comset and tapped in Auden's code.

In a moment Auden's face appeared. "What is it, Hans?"

Ebert hesitated, then smiled. "I had a little bother with our friend, I'm afraid. It—got out of hand. If you could come?"

"Of course. I'll be there directly. And Hans?"

"What?"

"Don't forget. You've supper with your uncle tonight. Get washed and ready. I'll deal with the rest."

GOLDEN HEART lay there, hardly daring to breathe, still trembling from what she had witnessed through the narrow gap in the door. She had seen Ebert draw his knife and stab the other man, not once, to disable him, but three times . . .

She had heard him come to the doorway and look in, then had tensed as she heard the door lock click, not daring to look and see if he were inside the room with her or not—expecting her own turn to be next. But then she had heard his voice speaking on the comset outside, and had almost wept with relief.

Yet when she closed her eyes she could still see him, his face distorted with a mad fury, grunting as he pulled his knife up through the other man's flesh, tearing him open. *Murdering* him.

She shuddered and pulled the sheet tight about her. Yes, Ebert had murdered Fest; there was no other word for it. Fest had drawn his knife first, but Ebert had disarmed him before he'd drawn his own. And what followed had been nothing less than vicious, brutal murder.

And if he knew . . . If for a single moment he suspected she had seen . . .

She lay there a moment longer, listening to him moving about in the next room, getting ready for his supper date, then got up and went into the tiny washroom, closing the door quietly behind her before she knelt over the basin, sluicing the cold, clear water up into her face again and again, as if to wash the awful image from her eyes.

ON THE WESTERN TERRACE at Tongjiang it was early evening. Long shadows lay across the sunlit gardens below the balcony, while from the meadows by the lake a peacock cried, breaking the silence.

On the terrace itself tables had been laid with food and drink. At one end, against the wall of the palace, a golden canopy had been erected, its platform slightly raised. There, enthroned in the dragon chair, sat the T'ang, Li Shai Tung, Prince Yuan, and the Lady Fei standing to one side of him beneath the bright red awning.

The T'ang had summoned all of the household servants who could be spared out onto the terrace. They stood there, crowded into the space in front of the canopy, more than six hundred in all, silent, wine tumblers in hand, waiting for the T'ang to speak.

To one side of this gathering the Master of the Inner Chamber, Nan Ho, stood among the grooms. He had spent the whole day looking into what had disturbed the Lady Fei that morning, interviewing staff and rooting through the tangle of rumor and counter-rumor to sort fact from fancy. And now he knew.

He looked across at her, seeing how sweetly she smiled up at her husband, how warmly he returned her gaze; he shivered, his sense of foreboding strong. In the warm glow of the late afternoon sunlight she seemed particularly beautiful, the simplicity of her attire setting her off, as the shell sets off the oyster. Yet that beauty was badly flawed. In time the mask she wore would slip and all would see her as he saw her now, with knowing eyes. He saw the Prince reach out and take her hand and looked down, knowing where his duty lay.

One thing was paramount, one thing alone—his Master's happiness. And if the Prince's happiness depended on this weak and foolish woman, then so it had to be; for it was not his place to change his Master's heart, merely to guard it against the worst the world could do. For that reason he had given special instructions to all he had discussed the matter with, warning them that from henceforth the smallest mention of the subject—even the most idle speculation—would be punished with instant dismissal. Or worse. For he was determined that no word of the matter would ever reach the ears of Li Yuan or his father. No. He would let nothing come between the Prince and his happiness.

He sighed and looked back, even as the great T'ang stood and began to speak, his joy like winter sunlight in his wizened face. But for Nan Ho that joy was hollow. Like the thin light, it only seemed to cast its warmth. Beneath the flesh his bones were cold, his feelings in suspense. A son! All about him his fellow servants raised their voices, excited by the news; he raised his, too, but he could hear—could *feel*—the falseness in his voice.

Strangely, his thoughts turned to Pearl Heart. Yes, he thought, *Pearl Heart would have made a better, finer wife than this false creature. Truer to you. She would have made you strong when you were T'ang. Would have made of you a paragon among rulers.*

Yes, but Pearl Heart was only a serving maid—a beast to warm your bed and teach you bedroom manners. What lineage she had was the lineage of unknown parenthood. She could not match the breeding of this whore.

Nan Ho looked up again, seeing once more his Prince's joy. That, at least, was no counterfeit. And that was why he would hold his tongue and keep this fragile boat afloat. Not for her, for what was she now but a painted thing?—a mask to hide corruption—but for Li Yuan.

And then who knew what change a child might bring?

He lifted his head, listening. There was the faint growl of engines in the distance, coming nearer. He turned, looking into the setting sun, and saw them—two craft, coming in low from the west. For a moment he was afraid; but then, looking across at his T'ang, he saw how Li Shai Tung looked, then nodded to himself, as if he were expecting two such craft to come.

"Let us drink to the health of my son and his wife," Li Shai Tung said, smiling, raising his glass. "And to my grandson. *Kan Pei!*"

The blessing echoed across the terrace as the craft came on.

━━━━━

LI SHAI TUNG paused in the coolness of the anteroom and looked about him. He had not been certain they would come, but here they were in answer to his request. Surely that meant something in itself? Surely that meant they were willing to take the first step?

Damn them! he thought, suddenly angry. *Damn them that I should have to make such deals with their like!* Then he looked down, realizing where his thoughts had led him, for both men, after all, were T'ang, whatever their personal faults.

T'ang! He shivered, wondering what his grandfather would have made of Wang Sau-leyan. Then, clearing his head of such thoughts, he went into his study, taking a seat behind his desk, composing himself, waiting for his Chancellor, Chung Hu-yan, to bring them through.

After long thought, he had decided to pre-empt matters, to make peace before the division in Council grew into enmity. And if that meant swallowing his pride and meeting Wang Sau-leyan and Hou Tung-po halfway, then he would do that. For balance. And to buy time, so that the Seven might be strong again.

Hou Tung-po was not the problem. The young T'ang of South America had merely fallen under his friend's charismatic spell. No, his only fault was to be weak-minded and impressionable. The real cause of dissent was Wang Hsien's fourth son, Sau-leyan, the present T'ang of Africa.

He laughed despairingly. How cruelly the times mocked them to make such a man a T'ang—a man who was fit only to be sent below the Net! For two whole cycles they had been strong, their purpose clear, their unity unquestioned, and now . . .

He shook his head, then let his fingers brush against the two documents he had had prepared. If all went well they would be shreds within the hour, their only significance having lain in the gesture of their destruction.

But would that be enough? Would that satisfy the T'ang of Africa?

Outside, in the corridors, two bells sounded, one low, one high. A moment later Chung Hu-yan appeared in the great doorway, his head lowered.

"Your guests are here, *Chieh Hsia*."

"Good." He stood and came around the desk. "Show them in, Chung. Then bring us wines and sweetmeats. We may be here some while."

The Chancellor bowed and backed away, his face registering an understanding of how difficult the task was that lay before his master. A moment later he returned, still bowed, leading the two T'ang into the room.

"Good cousins," Li Shai Tung said, taking their hands briefly. "I thank you for sparing the time from busy schedules to come and see me at such short notice."

He saw how Hou Tung-po looked at once to his friend for his lead, how his welcoming smile faded as he noted the blank expression on Wang Sau-leyan's face.

"I would not have come had I not felt it was important to see you, Li Shai Tung," Wang answered, staring past him.

Li Shai Tung stiffened, angered not merely by the hostility he sensed emanating from the young T'ang but also by the inference that a T'ang might even consider not coming at his cousin's urgent wish. Even so, he curbed his anger. This time, young Wang would not draw him.

"And so it is," he answered, smiling pleasantly. "A matter of the utmost importance."

Wang Sau-leyan looked about him with the air of a man considering buying something, then looked back at Li Shai Tung. "Well? I'm listening."

It was so rude, so wholly unexpected, that Li Shai Tung found himself momentarily lost for words. Then he laughed. *Is that really the way you want it?* he thought, *or is that too a pose— designed to throw me from my purpose and win yourself advantage?*

He put his hand to his beard thoughtfully. "You're like your father, Sau-leyan. He too could be blunt when it was called for."

"My father was a foolish old man!"

Li Shai Tung stiffened, shocked by the young man's utterance. He looked across at Hou Tung-po and saw how he looked away, embarrassed, then shook his head. He took a breath and began again.

"The other day, in Council—"

"You seek to lecture me, Li Shai Tung?"

Li Shai Tung felt himself go cold. Would the young fool not even let him finish a sentence?

He bowed his head slightly, softening his voice. "You mistake me, good cousin. I seek nothing but an understanding between us. It seems we've started badly, you and I. I sought only to mend that. To find some way of redressing your grievances."

He saw how Wang Sau-leyan straightened slightly at that, as if sensing concession on his part. Again it angered him, for his instinct was not to accommodate but to crush the arrogance he saw displayed before him; but he kept all sign of anger from his face.

Wang Sau-leyan turned, meeting his eyes directly. "A deal, you mean?"

He stared back at the young T'ang a moment, then looked aside. "I realize that we want different things, Wang Sau-leyan, but is there not a way of satisfying us both?"

The young man turned, looking across at Hou Tung-po. "Is it not as I said, Hou?" He raised a hand dismissively, indicating Li Shai Tung. "The *lao jen* wants to buy my silence. To bridle me in Council."

Li Shai Tung looked down, coldly furious. *Lao jen*, "old man," was a term of respect, but not in the way Wang Sau-leyan had used it. The scornful intonation he had given the word had made it an insult, an insult that could not be ignored.

"An offered hand should not be spat upon."

Wang Sau-leyan looked back at him, his expression openly hostile. "What could you offer me that I might possibly want, *lao jen?*"

Li Shai Tung had clenched his hands. Now he relaxed them, letting his breath escape him in a sigh. "Why in the gods' names are you so inflexible, Wang Sau-leyan? What do you want of us?"

Wang Sau-leyan took a step closer. "Inflexible? Was I not 'flexible' when your son married his brother's wife? Or by flexible do you really mean unprincipled, willing to do as you and not others wish?"

Li Shai Tung turned sharply, facing him, openly angry now. "You go too far! Hell's teeth, boy!"

Wang Sau-leyan smiled sourly. "Boy . . . That's how you see me, isn't it? A boy, to be chastised or humored. Or locked away, perhaps."

"This is not right——" Li Shai Tung began, but again the young T'ang interrupted him, his voice soft yet threatening.

"This is a new age, old man. New things are happening in the world. The Seven must change with the times or go under. And if I must break your power in Council to bring about that change, then break it I shall. But do not think to buy or silence me, for I'll not be bought or silenced."

Li Shai Tung stood there, astonished, his lips parted. *Break it? Break his power?* But before he could speak there was a knocking at the door.

"Come in!" he said, only half aware of what he said, his eyes still resting on the figure of the young T'ang.

It was Chung Hu-yan. Behind him came four servants, carrying trays. "*Chieh Hsia*—?" he began, then stepped back hurriedly as Wang Sau-leyan stormed past him, pushing angrily through the servants, knocking their trays clattering to the tiled floor as they hastened to move back out of the T'ang's way.

Hou Tung-po hung back a moment, clearly dismayed by what had happened. Taking a step toward Li Shai Tung, he bowed, then turned away, hurrying to catch up with his friend.

Li Shai Tung stood there a moment longer; then waving his Chancellor away, he went to the desk and picked up one of the documents. He stared at it a moment, his hands trembling with anger; then, one by one, he began to pick off the unmarked seals with his fingernails, dropping them onto the floor beside his feet until only his own remained at the foot of the page.

He would have offered this today. Would have gladly torn this document to shreds to forge a peaceful understanding. But what had transpired just now convinced him that such a thing was impossible. Wang Sau-leyan would not permit it. Well, then, he would act alone in this.

He turned his hand, placing the dark, dull metal of the ring into the depression at the desk's edge, letting it grow warm; then he lifted his hand and pressed the seal into the wax.

There. It was done. He had sanctioned his son's scheme. Had given it life.

For a moment longer he stood there, staring down at the document, at the six blank spaces where the seals had been; then he turned away, his anger unassuaged, speaking softly to himself, his words an echo of what the young T'ang had said to him.

"This is a new age, old man. New things are happening in the world."

He laughed bitterly. "So it is, Wang Sau-leyan. So it is. But you'll not break me. Not while I have breath."

━━━━━

KARR STOOD on the mountainside, shielding his eyes, looking about him at the empty slopes. It was cold, much colder than he'd imagined. He pulled the collar of his jacket up around his ears and shivered, still searching the broken landscape for some sign, some clue as to where to look.

The trouble was, it was just too big a place, too vast. One could hide a hundred armies here and never find them.

He looked down, blowing on his hands to warm them. How easy, then, to hide a single army here?

It had begun two days ago, after he had been to see Tolonen. His report on the Executive Killings had taken almost an hour to deliver. Even so, they were still no closer to finding out who had been behind the spate of murders.

Officially, that was. For himself, however, he was certain who was behind them—and he knew both the T'ang and Tolonen agreed. DeVore. It had to be. The whole thing was too neat, too well orchestrated, to be the work of anyone else.

But if DeVore, then why was there no trace of him within the City? Why was there no sign of his face somewhere in the levels? After all, every Security camera, every single guard and official in the whole vast City, was on the look-out for that face.

That absence had nagged at him for weeks, until coming away from his meeting with Tolonen, he had realized its significance. If DeVore couldn't be found inside, then maybe he wasn't inside—maybe he was outside? Karr had gone back to his office and stood before the map of City Europe, staring at it, his eyes drawn time and again to the long, irregular space at the center of the City—the Wilds—until he knew for a certainty that that was where he'd find DeVore. *There*, somewhere in that tiny space.

But what had seemed small on the map was gigantic in reality. The mountains were overpowering, both in their size and number. They filled the sky from one horizon to the other; and when he turned, there they were again, marching away into the distance, until the whole world seemed but one long mountain range and the City nothing.

So, where to start? Where, in all this vastness of rock and ice, to start? How to search this godsforsaken place?

He was pondering that when he saw the second craft come up over the ridge and descend, landing beside his own, in the valley far below. A moment later a figure spilled from the craft and began to make its way toward him, climbing the slope. It was Chen.

"Gregor!" Chen greeted him. "I've been looking all over for you."

"What is it?" Karr answered, trudging down through the snow to meet him.

Chen stopped, then lifted his snow goggles, looking up at him. "I've brought new orders. From the T'ang."

Karr stared at him, then took the sealed package and tore it open.

"What does it say?"

"That we're to close the files on the murders. Not only that, but we're to stop our search for DeVore—temporarily, at least— and concentrate on penetrating the *Ping Tiao* organization. It seems they're planning something big."

Chen watched the big man nod to himself, as if taking in this new information, then look about him and laugh.

"What is it?" he asked, surprised by Karr's laughter.

"Just this," Karr answered, holding the T'ang's orders up. "And this," he added, indicating the mountains all about them. "I was thinking—two paths, but the goal's the same. *DeVore.*"

"DeVore?"

"Yes. The T'ang wants us to investigate the *Ping Tiao*, and so we shall; but when we lift that stone, you can lay odds on which insect will come scuttling out from under it."

"DeVore," said Chen, smiling.

"Yes, DeVore."

———

HANS EBERT stood on the wooden veranda of the lodge, staring up the steep, snow-covered slope, his breath pluming in the crisp air. As he watched, the dark spot high up the slope descended slowly, coming closer, growing, until it was discernibly a human figure. It was coming on apace, in a zig-zag path that would bring it to the lodge.

Ebert clapped his gloved hands together and turned to look back inside the lodge. There were three other men with him, his comrades in arms. Men he could trust.

"He's here!" he shouted in to them. "Quick now! You know your orders!"

They got up from the table at once, taking their weapons from the rack near the door before going to their posts.

When the skier drew up beneath the veranda, the lodge seemed empty except for the figure leaning out over the balcony. The skier thrust his sticks into the snow, then lifted his goggles and peeled off his gloves.

"I'm pleased to see you, Hans. I didn't know if you would come."

Ebert straightened up, then started down the steps. "My uncle is a persuasive man, *Shih* DeVore. I hadn't realized he was an old friend of yours."

DeVore laughed, stooping to unfasten his boots. He snapped the clips and stepped off the skis. "He isn't. Not officially. Nor will you be. Officially."

He met the younger man at the bottom of the steps and shook both his hands firmly, warmly, flesh to gloves.

"I understand it now."

"Understand what? Come, Hans, let's go inside. The air is too keen for such talk."

Hans let himself be led back up into the lodge. When they were sitting, drinks in hand, he continued. "What I meant is, I understand now how you've managed to avoid us all these years. More old friends, eh?"

"One or two," said DeVore cryptically, and laughed.

"Yes," Ebert said thoughtfully. "You're a regular member of the family, aren't you?" He had been studying DeVore, trying to gauge whether he was armed or not.

"You forget how useful I once was to your father."

"No . . ." Ebert chose the next few words more carefully. "I simply remember how harmful you were subsequently. How dangerous. Even to meet you like this, it's—"

"Fraught with danger?" DeVore laughed again, a hearty, sincere laughter that strangely irritated the younger man.

DeVore looked across the room. In one corner a *wei chi* board had been set up, seven black stones forming an H on the otherwise empty grid.

"I see you've thought of everything," he said, smiling again. "Do you want to play while we talk?"

Ebert hesitated, then gave a nod. DeVore seemed somehow too bright, too at ease, for his liking.

The two men stood and went to the table in the corner.

"Where shall I sit? Here?"

Ebert smiled. "If you like." It was exactly where he wanted DeVore. At that point he was covered by all three of the marksmen concealed overhead. If he tried *anything* . . .

DeVore sat, perfectly at ease, lifting the lid from the pot, then placed the first of his stones in *tsu*, the north. Ebert sat, facing him, studying him a moment, then lifted the lid from his pot and took one of the black stones between his fingers. He had prepared his men beforehand. If he played in one particular place—in the middle of the board, on the edge of *shang*, the south, on the intersection beside his own central stone—then they were to open fire, killing DeVore. Otherwise they were to fire only if Ebert's life was endangered.

Ebert reached across, playing at the top of *shang*, two places out from his own corner stone, two lines down from the edge.

"Well?" he said, looking at DeVore across the board. "You're not here to ask after my health. What do you want?"

DeVore was studying the board as if he could see the game to come—the patterns of black stones and white, their shape and interaction. "Me? I don't want anything. At least, nothing from you, Hans. That's not why I'm here." He set down a white stone, close by Ebert's last, then looked up, smiling again. "I'm here because there's something *you* might want."

Ebert stared at him, astonished, then laughed. "What could I possibly want from you?" He slapped a stone down almost carelessly, three spaces out from the first.

DeVore studied the move, then shook his head. He took a stone from his pot and set it down midway between the corner and the center, as if to divide some future formation of Ebert's stones.

"You have everything you need, then, Hans?"

Ebert narrowed his eyes and slapped down another stone irritably. It was two spaces out from the center, between DeVore's and his own, so that the five stones now formed a broken diagonal line from the corner to the center—two black, one white, then two more black.

DeVore smiled broadly. "That's an interesting shape, don't you think? But it's weak, like the Seven. Black might outnumber white, but white isn't surrounded."

Ebert sat back. "Meaning what?"

DeVore set down another stone, pushing out toward *ch'u*, the west. A triangle of three white stones now sat to the right of a triangle of black stones. Ebert stared at the position a moment, then looked up into DeVore's face again.

DeVore was watching him closely, his eyes suddenly sharp, alert, the smile gone from his lips.

"Meaning that you serve a master you despise. Accordingly, you play badly. Winning or losing has no meaning for you. No *interest.*"

Ebert touched his upper teeth with his tongue, then took another stone and placed it, eight down, six out in *shang*. It was a necessary move; a strengthening move. It prevented DeVore from breaking his line while expanding the territory he now surrounded. The game was going well for him.

"You read my mind then, *Shih* DeVore? You know how I think?"

"I know that you're a man of considerable talent, Hans. And I know that you're bored. I can see it in the things you do, the decisions you make. I can see how you hold the greater part of yourself back constantly. Am I wrong, then? Is what I see really the best you can do?"

DeVore set down another stone. Unexpectedly it cut across the shape Ebert had just made, pushing into the territory he had mapped out. It seemed an absurd move, a weak move, but Ebert knew that DeVore was a master at this game. He would not make such a move without good reason.

"It seems you want me to cut you. But if I do, it means you infiltrate this area here." He sketched it out.

"And if you don't?"

"Well, it's obvious. You cut me. You separate my groups."

DeVore smiled. "So. A dilemma. What to choose?"

Ebert looked up again, meeting his eyes. He knew that De-Vore was saying something to him through the game. But what?

Was DeVore asking him to make a choice? The Seven or himself? Was he asking him to come out in the open and declare himself?

He put down his stone, cutting DeVore, keeping his own lines open.

"You say the Seven are weak, but you—are you any stronger?"

"At present, no. Look at me, I'm like these five white stones here on the board. I'm cut and scattered and outnumbered. But I'm a good player and the odds are better than when I started. Then they were seven to one. Now"—he placed his sixth stone, six down, four out in *shang*, threatening the corner—"it's only two to one. And every move improves my chances. I'll win. Eventually."

Ebert placed another black stone in the diagonal line, preventing DeVore from linking with his other stones, but again it allowed DeVore space within his own territory and he sensed that DeVore would make a living group there.

"You know, I've always admired you, Howard. You would have been Marshal eventually. You would have run things for the Seven."

"That's so . . ." DeVore smiled openly, showing his small but perfect teeth. "But it was never enough for me to serve another. Nor you. We find it hard to bow to lesser men."

Ebert laughed, then realized how far DeVore had brought him. But it was true. Everything he said was true. He watched DeVore set another stone down, shadowing his own line, sketching out territory inside his own, robbing him of what he'd thought was safely his.

"I see," he said, meaning two things. For a time, then, they simply played. Forty moves later he could see that it was lost. DeVore had taken five of his stones from the board and had formed a living group of half of *shang*. Worse, he had pushed out toward *ch'u* and down into *p'ing*. Now a small group of four of his stones was threatened at the center and there was only one way to save it—to play in the space in *shang* beside the central stone, the signal for his men to open fire on DeVore. Ebert sat back, holding the black stone between his fingers, then laughed.

"It seems you've forced me to a decision."

DeVore smiled back at him. "I was wondering what you would do."

Ebert eyed him sharply. "Wondering?"

"Yes. I wasn't sure at first. But now I know. You won't play that space. You'll play here instead." He leaned across and touched the intersection with his fingertip. It was the move that gave only temporary respite. It did not save the group.

"Why should I do that?"

"Because you don't want to kill me. And because you're seriously interested in my proposition."

Ebert laughed, astonished. "You *knew*?"

"Oh, I know you've three of your best stormtroopers here, Hans. I've been conscious of the risks *I've* been taking. But how about you?"

"I think I know," Ebert said, even more cautiously. Then, with a small laugh of admiration he set the stone down where DeVore had indicated.

"Good." DeVore leaned across and set a white stone in the special space, on the edge of *shang*, beside Ebert's central stone, then leaned back again. "I'm certain you'll have assessed the potential rewards, too." He smiled, looking down at his hands. "King of the world, Hans. That's what you could be. T'ang of all Chung Kuo."

Ebert stared back at him, his mouth open but set.

"But not without me." DeVore looked up at him, his eyes piercing him through. "Not without me. You understand that?"

"I could have you killed. Right now. And be hailed as a hero."

DeVore nodded. "Of course. I knew what I was doing. But I assumed you knew why you were here. That you knew how much you had to gain."

It was Ebert's turn to laugh. "This is insane."

DeVore was watching him calmly, as if he knew now how things would turn out between them. "Insane? No. It's no more insane than the rule of the Seven. And how long can that last? In ten years, maybe less, the whole pack of cards is going to come tumbling down, whatever happens. The more astute of the Above realize that and want to do something about it. They want to control the process. But they need a figurehead. Someone they admire. Someone from among their number. Someone capable and in a position of power."

"I don't fit your description."

DeVore laughed. "Not now, perhaps. But you will. In a year from now you will."

Ebert looked down. He knew it was a moment for decisiveness, not prevarication. "And when I'm T'ang?"

DeVore smiled and looked down at the board. "Then the stars will be ours. A world for each of us."

A world for each of us. Ebert thought about it a moment. This then was what it was really all about. Expansion. Taking the lid off City Earth and getting away. But what would that leave him?

"However," DeVore went on, "you didn't mean that, did you?" He stood and went across to the drinks cabinet, pouring himself a second glass of brandy. Turning, he looked directly at the younger man. "What you meant was, what's in it for me?"

Ebert met his look unflinchingly. "Of course. What other motive could there be?"

DeVore smiled blandly. Ebert was a shallow, selfish young man, but he was useful. He would never be T'ang, of course—it would be a mistake to give such a man *real* power—but it served for now to let him think he would.

"Your brandy is excellent, Hans." DeVore walked to the window and looked out. The mountains looked beautiful. He could see the Matterhorn from where he stood, its peak like a broken blade. Winter was coming.

Ebert was silent, waiting for him.

"What's in it for you, you ask? This world. To do with as you wish. What more could you want?" He turned to face the younger man, noting at once the calculation in his face.

"You failed," Ebert said after a moment. "There were many of you. Now there's just you. Why should you succeed this time?"

DeVore tilted his head, then laughed. "Ah yes . . ."

Ebert frowned and set his glass down. "And they're strong."

DeVore interrupted him. "No. You're wrong, Hans. They're weak. Weaker than they've been since they began. *We almost won.*"

Ebert hesitated, then nodded. It was so. He recognized how thinly the Families were spread now, how much they depended on the good will of those in the Above who had remained faithful. Men like his father.

And when his father was dead?

He looked up sharply, his decision made.

"Well?" DeVore prompted. "Will you be T'ang?"

Ebert stood, offering his hand.

DeVore smiled and put his drink down. Then he stepped forward and, ignoring the hand, embraced the young man.

Artifice and Innocence

The more abstract the truth you want to teach the more you
  must seduce the senses to it.

—FRIEDRICH NIETZSCHE, *Beyond Good and Evil*

Reach me a gentian, give me a torch
let me guide myself with the blue, forked touch of this flower
down the dark and darker steps, where blue is darkened on
    blueness
even where Persephone goes, just now, from the frosted Sep-
    tember
to the sightless realm where darkness is awake upon the dark
and Persephone herself is but a voice
of a darkness invisible enfolded in the deeper dark
of the arms Plutonic, and pierced with the passion of dense
    gloom,
among the splendour of torches of darkness, shedding darkness
    on the lost bride and her groom.

—D. H. LAWRENCE, *Bavarian Gentians*

CHAPTER TWELVE

The Feast of the Dead

BANK OF EIGHT screens, four long, two deep, glowed dimly on the far side of the darkened room. In each lay the outline image of a hollowed skull. There were other shapes in the room, vague forms only partly lit by the glow. A squat and bulky mechanism studded with controls was wedged beneath the screens. Beside it was a metallic frame, like a tiny fourposter stretched with wires. In the left-hand corner rested a narrow trolley containing racks of tapes, their wafer-thin top edges glistening in the half light. Next to that was a vaguely human form slumped against a bed, its facial features missing. Finally, in the very center of the room was a graphics art board, the thin screen blank and dull, the light from the eight monitors focused in its concave surface.

It was late—after three in the morning—and Ben Shepherd was tired, but there was this last thing to be done before he slept. He squatted by the trolley and flicked through the tapes until he found what he wanted, then went to the art board and fed in the tape. The image of a bird formed instantly. He froze it, using the controls to turn it, studying it from every angle as if searching for some flaw in its conception; then, satisfied, he let it run, watching as the bird stretched its wings and launched into the air. Again he froze the image. The bird's wings were stretched back now, thrusting it forward powerfully.

It was a simple image in many ways. An idealized image of a bird, formed in a vacuum.

He sorted through the tapes again and pulled out three, then returned to the art board and rewound the first tape. That done he fed the new tapes into the slot and synchronized all four to a preset signal. Then he pressed PLAY.

This time the bird was resting on a perch inside a pagoda-like cage. As he watched, the cage door sprung open and the bird flew free, launching itself out through the narrow opening.

He froze the image, then rotated it. This time the bird seemed trapped, its beak and part of its sleek, proud head jutting from the cage, the rest contained within the bars. In the background could be seen the familiar environment of the Square. As the complex image turned, the tables of the Cafe Burgundy came into view. He could see himself at one of the nearer tables, the girl beside him. He was facing directly into the shot, his hand raised, pointing, as if to indicate the sudden springing of the bird; but her head was turned, facing him, her flame-red hair a sharp contrast to the rich, overhanging greenery.

He smiled uncertainly and let the tape run on a moment at one-fifth speed, watching her head come slowly round to face the escaping bird. In that moment, as she faced it fully, the bird's wing came up, eclipsing the watchers at the table. There it ended.

It was a brief segment, no more than nine seconds in all, but it had taken him weeks of hard work to get it right. Now, however, he was thinking of abandoning it completely.

This was his favorite piece in the whole composition—the key image with which it had begun—yet as the work had progressed, this tiny fragment had proved ever more problematic.

For the rest of the work the viewpoint was established in the viewer's head, behind the eyes, yet for this brief moment he had broken away entirely. In another art form this would have caused no problems—might, indeed, have been a strength—but here it created all kinds of unwanted difficulties. Experienced from within the Shell, it was as if, for the brief nine seconds that the segment lasted, one went outside one's skull. It was a strange, disorienting experience, and no tampering with the surrounding images could mute that effect or repair the damage it did to the work as a whole.

In all the Shells he had experienced before, such abrupt switches of viewpoint had been made to serve the purpose of the story: were used for their sudden shock value. But then, all forms of the Shell before his own had insisted only upon a cartoon version of the real, whereas what he wanted was reality itself. Or a close approximation. Such abrupt changes destroyed the balance he was seeking, shattered every attempt of his to create that illusion of the really real.

Only now was he beginning to understand the cost—in artistic terms—of such realism, the limiting factors and the disciplines involved. It was not enough to create the perfect illusion; it was also necessary to maintain a sequential integrity in the experiencing mind. The illusion depended on him staying within his own skull, behind his own eyes, the story developing in real time.

There was, of course, a simple answer: abandon all breaches of sequential integrity. But that limited the kind of story one could tell. It was a straitjacket of the worst kind, limiting fiction to the vignette, briefly told. He had recognized this at once and agonized over it, but weeks of wrestling with the problem had left him without an answer.

Perhaps this was why all previous practitioners of the form had kept to the quasi-realism of a cartoon, leaving the experiencing imagination to suspend disbelief and form a bridge between what was presented and the reality. Maybe some of them had even tried what he was attempting now, had experimented with "perfected," realistic images and had faced the same constricting factors. Maybe so, but he had to make a choice—pursue his ideal of a perfect art form or compromise that vision in favor of a patently synthetic form, a mere embellishment of the old. It was no real choice at all, yet still he procrastinated.

He wound the tapes back and replayed, this time at one-tenth speed—five frames a second—watching the bird thrust slowly outward from the cage in an explosion of sudden, golden, living fire; seeing beyond it the girl's face, its whiteness framed in flames of red as it turned to face the screen.

He closed his eyes and froze the image. It was the best thing he had done. Something real and beautiful—a tiny, perfect work of art. And yet . . . He shivered, then pressed ERASE. In an instant it was gone, the tapes blanked. He stood there for a long time afterward, leaning against the machine, perfectly still, his eyes closed. Then, with a tiny shudder, he turned away. There was that much anyway. It was there—it would *always* be there—in his head.

He went to the bed and sat, not knowing what he felt, staring intently, almost obsessively at the narrow ridge of flesh that circled his left wrist. Then he got up again and went out into the other room.

For a while he stood there in the center of the room, his mind still working at the problem; but just now he could not see past his tiredness. He was stretched thin by the demands he had placed on himself these last few weeks. All he could see were problems, not solutions.

He took a long, shuddering breath. "Small steps," he told himself, his voice soft, small in the darkness. "There is an answer," he added after a moment, as if to reassure himself. Yet he was far from certain.

He turned away, rubbing at his eyes, too tired to pursue the thought, for once wanting nothing but the purging oblivion of sleep. And in the morning?

In the morning he would begin anew.

━━━━━

THE SQUARE was a huge, airy space at the top of Oxford Canton, the uppermost level of a complex warren of Colleges that extended deep into the stack below. To the eternal delight of each new generation of students, however, the Square was not square at all, but hexagonal, a whole deck opened up for leisure. Long, open balconies overlooked the vastness of the Green, leaning back in five great tiered layers on every side, while overhead the great dome of the stars turned slowly in perfect imitation of the sky beyond the ice.

Here, some seventeen years earlier, so rumor had it, Berdichev, Lehmann, and Wyatt had met and formed the Dispersionist party, determined to bring change to this world of levels. Whether the rumor was true or not, the Square was a place to which the young intelligentsia of all seven cities were drawn. If the world of thought were a wheel, this was its hub, and the Green its focus.

A line of oaks bordered the Green, hybrid evergreens produced in the vats of SynFlor; while at its center was an aviary, a tall, pagoda-like cage of thirteen tiers, modeled upon the *Liu he t'a*, the Pagoda of the Six Harmonies at Hang Chou. As ever, young men and women strolled arm in arm on the vast lawn or gathered about the lowest tier, looking in at the brightly colored birds.

The Square was the pride of Oxford Canton and the haunt of its ten thousand students. The elite of the Above sent their children to Oxford, just as the elite of a small nation state had done centuries before. It was a place of culture and for the children of First Level families, a guarantee of continuity.

No big MedFac screens cluttered the Green itself, but in the cool walkways beneath the overhang, small Vidscreens showed the local cable channels to a clientele whose interests and tastes differed considerably from the rest of the Above.

The overhang was a place of coffee shops and restaurants, CulVid boutiques and SynParlors. It was a curious mixture of new and old, of timelessness and state-of-the-art, of purity and decadence; its schizophrenic face a reflection of its devotees.

At the Cafe Burgundy business was brisk. It was a favorite haunt of the Arts Faculty students, who, at this hour, crowded every available table, talking, drinking, gesturing wildly with all the passion and flamboyance of youth. The tables themselves—more than two hundred in all—spread out from beneath the overhang toward the edge of the Green. Overhead, a network of webbing, draped between strong poles, supported a luxuriant growth of flowering creepers. The plants were a lush, almost luminous green, decorated with blooms of vivid purples, yellows, reds, and oranges—huge gaping flowers with tongues of contrasting hues, like the silent heads of monsters. Beneath them the tables and chairs were all antiques, the wood stained and polished. They were a special feature of the cafe, a talking point, though in an earlier century they would have seemed quite unexceptional.

Han waiters made their way between the packed tables, carrying trays and taking orders. They were dressed in the plain, round-collared robes of the Tang Dynasty, the sleeves narrow, the long er-silks a dark vermilion with an orange band below the knee: the clothes of an earlier, simpler age.

At a table near the edge sat four students. Their table was empty but for three glasses and a bottle. They had eaten and were on their third bottle of the excellent Burgundy from which the cafe took its name. A vacant chair rested between the two males of the party, as if they were expecting another to join them. But it was not so. All spaces at the table had to be paid for, and they had paid to keep it vacant.

There was laughter at the table. A dark-haired, olive-skinned young man was holding sway, leaning well back in his chair, a wineglass canted in his hand. The singsong tones of his voice were rather pleasant, well-modulated. He was a handsome, aristocratic man with a pronounced aquiline profile, a finely formed mouth, and dark, almost gypsy eyes. Strong-limbed and broad-shouldered, he looked more a sportsman than an artist, though a fastidiousness about his clothes somewhat redressed that impression. As he talked, his free hand carved forms from the air, the movements deft, rehearsed. He was older than the others by some four or five years, a factor that made them defer to him in most things; and often—as now—he monopolized their talk, leading it where he would.

His name was Sergey Novacek and he was a Masters student and a sculptor. His father, Lubos, was a well-to-do merchant who, at his wife's behest, indulged his only son, buying him a place at Oxford. Not that Sergey was unintelligent. He could easily have won a scholarship. It was simply a matter of prestige. Of status. At the level on which Lubos Novacek had his interests, it was not done to accept state charity.

Just now Sergey was telling them of the ceremony he had attended the previous day, a ceremony at which six of his sculptures had been on display. He had not long been fulfilling such commissions, yet he spoke as if he had great experience in the matter. But that was his way, and his friends admired him for it, even if others found it somewhat arrogant.

"It all went very well, at first," he said, his handsome features serious a moment. "Everyone was most respectful. They fed me and watered me and tried their best to be polite and hide from themselves the fact that I was neither family nor Han." He laughed. "None too successfully, I'm afraid. But, anyway . . . The tomb was magnificent. It stood in its own walled gardens next to the house. A massive thing, two stories high, clad all over in white marble, and with a gate you could have driven a team of four horses through." Sergey sipped at his drink, then laughed. "In fact, the tomb was a damn sight bigger than the house!"

There was laughter.

"That's so typical of them," said the second young man, Wolf, lifting his glass to his lips. He was taller and more heavily built than his friend, his perfect North European features topped by a close-cropped growth of ash-blond hair. "They're so *into* death."

Sergey raised his glass. "And a good job too, neh?"

"For you," one of the girls, Lotte, said teasingly, her blue eyes flashing. It was true. Most of Sergey's commissions were funerary—tomb statues for the Minor Families.

Lotte was a pale-skinned, large-breasted girl, who wore her blond hair unfashionably long and plaited, in defiance of fashion. These things aside, she looked exactly like what she was— the twin of her brother, Wolf. Beside her, silent, sat the fourth of their small group, Catherine. She was smaller than her friends, more delicately built; a slender redhead with Slavic features and green eyes.

Sergey smiled. "Anyway. As I was saying. It was all going well and then the ceremony proper began. You know how it is: a lot of New Confucian priests chanting for the souls of the departed. And then the eldest son comes to the front and lights a candle for the ancestors. Well . . . it had just got to that stage when, would you believe it, eldest son trips over his *pau*, stumbles forward, and falls against the lines of paper charms."

"No!" All three sat forward, Wolf amused, the two girls horrified.

"Unfortunate, you might think, and embarrassing, but not disastrous. And so it might have been, except that in falling he dropped the lighted candle among the charms." Sergey laughed shortly and nodded to himself. "You should have seen it. There must have been two or three thousand charms hanging up on those lines, dry as bone, just waiting to go up in one great sheet of flame. And that's exactly what they did. Eldest son was all right, of course. The servants pulled him away at once. But before anyone could do a thing, the flames set off the overhead sprinklers. Worse than that, no one knew the combination sequence to the cutout and the key to the manual override was missing. It just poured and poured. We were all soaked. But the worst was to come. Because the garden was enclosed, the water couldn't drain away. Much of it sank into the thin soil layer, but soon that became waterlogged, and when that happened the water began to pour down the steps into the tomb. Within minutes the water was up to the top step. That's when it happened."

He leaned forward and filled his glass, then looked about him, enjoying himself, knowing he had their full attention. "Well? What do you think?"

Wolf shook his head. "I don't know. The eldest son fell in, perhaps?"

Sergey narrowed his eyes. "Ah yes, that would have been good, wouldn't it? But this was better. Much better. Imagine it. There we all are, still waiting for someone to switch the damn sprinklers off, our expensive clothes ruined, the ground a total bog beneath our feet, no one willing to show disrespect by leaving the gardens before the ceremony's over, when what should happen but the unthinkable. Out floats the coffin!"

"Kuan Yin, preserve us!" Wolf said, his eyes round as coins.

"Poor man," murmured Catherine, looking down.

Sergey laughed. "Poor man, my ass! He was dead. But you should have seen the faces on those Han. It was as if they'd had hot irons poked up their backsides! There was a muttering and a spluttering and then—damn me if they didn't try to shove the coffin back into the tomb against the current! You should have seen the eldest son, slipping about in the mud like a lunatic!"

"Gods preserve us!" Wolf said. "And did they manage it?"

"Third time they did. But by then the sprinklers were off and the servants were carrying the water away in anything they could find."

The two men laughed, sitting back in their chairs and baring their teeth. Across from Wolf, Lotte smiled broadly, enjoying her brother's laughter. Only Catherine seemed detached from their enjoyment, as if preoccupied. Sergey noticed this and leaned toward her slightly. "What is it?"

She looked up. "It's nothing . . ."

He raised an eyebrow, making her laugh.

"Okay," she said, relenting. "I was just thinking about the painting I'm working on."

"You're having trouble?"

She nodded.

Wolf leaned across to nudge Sergey. "I shouldn't worry. She's not a real artist."

Catherine glared at him, then looked away. Wolf was always mocking her for working on an oil board, when, as he said, any artist worth their rice bowl worked in watercolors. But she discounted his opinion. She had seen his work. It was technically perfect, yet somehow lifeless. He could copy but he couldn't create.

She looked back at Sergey. "I was thinking I might go to the lecture this afternoon."

He lifted his chin slightly. "Lecture?"

She smiled. "Oh . . . I forgot. You weren't here when the College officials came around, were you?" She searched in her bag for something, then set a small hexagonal pad down on the table. She placed her palm against it momentarily, warming the surface, then moved her hand away. At once a tiny, three-dimensional image formed in the air and began to speak.

"That's Fan Liang-wei, isn't it?" said Wolf, leaning across to refill his glass.

"Shhhsh," Sergey said, touching his arm. "Let's hear what the old bugger has to say."

Fan Liang-wei was one of the most respected *shanshui* artists in City Europe. His paintings hung in the homes of most of the Minor Families. The Great Man's long white hair and triple-braided beard were familiar sights to those who tuned in to the ArtVid channel; and even to those whose tastes were less refined, Fan Liang-wei was the personification of the *wen ren*, the scholar-artist.

It was standard practice for professors of the College to advertise their lectures in this way, since their fees were paid according to attendance figures. Indeed, it was the practice for some of the less charismatic of them to bribe students to attend—filling the first few rows of the hall with sleepers. For the Great Man, however, such advertising was not strictly necessary. His fee was guaranteed whatever the attendance. Nonetheless, it was a matter of ego, a question of proving his supreme status to his fellow academicians.

The tiny figure bowed to its unseen audience and began to talk of the lecture it was to give that afternoon, its internal timer updating its speech so that when it referred to the lecture it reminded the listeners that it was "less than two hours from now." The lecture was to be on the two *shanshui* artists Tung Ch'i-ch'ang and Cheng Ro, and was entitled "Spontaneity and Meticulousness." Sergey watched it a moment longer, then smiled and reached out to put his hand over the pad, killing the image.

"It could be amusing. I've heard the old man's worth hearing."

"And Heng Chian-ye?" Wolf asked. "You've not forgotten the card game?"

Sergey looked across and saw how Catherine had looked away angrily. He knew how strongly she disapproved of this side of him—the gambling and the late-night drinking sessions—but it only spurred him on to greater excesses, as if to test her love.

He smiled, then turned back to Wolf. "That's all right. I told him I'd see him at four, but it'll do the little yellow bastard good to wait a bit. It'll make him more eager."

Wolf laughed. "Do you still intend to challenge him? They say he's a good player."

Sergey lifted his chin and looked away thoughtfully. "Yes. But Heng's an arrogant young fool. He's inflexible. Worse, he's rash when put under pressure. Like all these Han, he's more concerned with saving face than saving a fortune. And that will be his undoing, I promise you. So, yes, I'll challenge him. It's about time someone raised the stakes on young Heng."

Sergey leaned forward, looking across at Lotte. "And you, Lotte? Are you coming along?"

Again his words, his action in leaning toward Lotte, were designed to upset Catherine. They all knew how much Lotte was besotted with the handsome young sculptor. It was a joke that even she, on occasion, shared. But that didn't lessen the pangs of jealousy that affected Catherine.

As ever, Lotte looked to her brother before she answered, a faint color at her cheeks. "Well, I ought, I know, but—"

"You *must*," Sergey said, reaching out to cover her hand with his own. "I insist. You'd never forgive yourself if you didn't see the Great Man."

Wolf answered for her. "We were going to do some shopping. But I'm sure . . ."

Wolf looked at Lotte, smiling encouragement, and she nodded. Wolf still had hopes that his sister might marry Novacek. Not that it affected his relationship with Catherine. Not significantly.

"Good," said Sergey, leaning back and looking about the circle of his friends. "And afterward I'll treat you all to a meal."

———

THE TIERS of the lecture hall were packed to overflowing. Stewards scurried up and down the gangways, trying to find seats for the crowds pressing into the hall, clearly put out by the size of the attendance. Normally the hall seemed vast and echoing, but today it was like a hive, buzzing with expectation.

At three precisely the lights dimmed and the hall fell silent. On a raised platform at the front of the hall a single spotlight picked out a lectern. For a while there was no movement on stage, then a figure stepped out of the darkness. A murmur of surprise rose from the watching tiers. It was Chu Ta Yun, the Minister of Education. He stood to one side of the lectern, his head slightly bowed, his hands folded at his waist.

"*Ch'un tzu*," he began, his tone humble, "I have been given the great pleasure and honor of introducing one of the outstanding figures of our time. A man whose distinctions are too numerous to be listed here and whose accomplishments place him in the very first rank of painters. A man who, when the history of our culture is set down by future generations, will be seen as the epitome—the touchstone—of our art. *Ch'un tzu*, I ask you to welcome to our College the Honorable Fan Liangwei, painter to the court of His Most Serene Highness, Li Shai Tung."

As the Minister withdrew, head bowed, into the darkness, Fan Liang-wei came into the spotlight, resting his hands lightly on the edge of the lectern, then bowing his head to his audience. There was a faint shuffling noise as, in unison, the packed tiers lowered their heads in respect to the Great Man.

"Ch'un tzu," he began, in the same vein as the Minister, then, smiling, added, "Friends . . ."

There was a small ripple of laughter from the tiers. The ice had been broken. But at once his face grew serious again, his chin lifting in an extravagant yet thoughtful gesture, his voice taking on an immediate tone of authority.

"I have come here today to talk of art, and, in particular, of the art of shanshui painting, something of which I have, or so I delude myself, some small knowledge."

Again there was the faintest ripple of amusement, but, as before, it was tinged with the deepest respect. There was not one there who did not consider Fan Liang-wei to be Chung Kuo's foremost expert on the ancient art of shanshui.

The Great Man looked about the tiers, as if noting friends there among the crowd; then he spoke again. "As you may know, I have called today's talk 'Spontaneity and Meticulousness,' and it is upon these two extremes of expression that I wish to dwell, taking as my examples the works of two great exponents of the art of shanshui, the Ming painter Tung Ch'i-ch'ang and the Song painter Cheng Ro. But before I come to them and to specific examples of their work, I would like to take this opportunity of reminding you of the critic Hsieh Ho's Six Principles, for it is to these that we shall, time and again, return during this lecture."

Fan Liang-wei paused, looking about him. He had just opened his mouth to speak when the door to his right swung open and a young man strode into the hall, ignoring the hushed remonstrances of a steward. The steward followed him two or three paces into the hall, then backed away, head bowed, glancing up at the platform apologetically before drawing the door closed behind him. The young man, meanwhile, moved unselfconsciously along the gangway in front of the platform and began to climb the stairs. He was halfway up when the Great Man cleared his throat.

"Forgive me, young Master, but am I interrupting something?"

The young man half turned, looking back at the speaker, then, without a word, climbed the rest of the steps and sat down at their top.

There was a murmur of astonishment from the surrounding tiers and even a few harshly whispered words of criticism, but the young man seemed oblivious of it. He sat there, staring down at the platform, a strange intensity in his manner making him seem brooding, almost malicious in intent.

"Are we comfortable?" the Great Man asked, a faint trace of annoyance in his voice.

The young man gave the barest nod.

"Good. Then perhaps we might continue. As I was saying . . . Hsieh Ho, in his classic fifth-century work the *Ku Hua-p'in-lu*, set down for all time the Six Principles by which the great artist might be recognized. In reiterating these, we might remember that while Hsieh Ho intended that all six should be present in a great work of art, they do, nonetheless, form a kind of hierarchy, the First Principle, that of spirit-consonance, of harmony of spirit to the motion of life—that sense we have of the painting coming alive through the harmonizing of the vital force, the *ch'i*, of the painter with the *ch'i* of his subject matter—forming the first rank, the First Level, if you like."

There was a mild ripple of laughter at the Great Man's play on words. He continued quickly, his anger at the rudeness of the young man's interruption set aside momentarily.

"Bearing this in mind, we see how the Second Principle, the bone structure of the brushwork—and its strength in conveying the *ch'i*, or vital energy—stems from the First and is, indeed, dependent upon it, as a Minister is dependent upon the favor of his T'ang. Likewise, the Third Principle, the fidelity, or faithfulness of the artistic representation to the subject, is dependent upon these first two. And so forth."

He hesitated, then looked directly at the young man seated at the head of the stairs. "You understand me, young Master?"

Again the young man nodded.

"Good. Then let me move on quickly. Fourth of the Six Great

Principles is likeness in color. Fifth is the proper placing of the various elements within the scheme of the painting. And Sixth, and last in our great hierarchy, is the preservation of the experience of the past through making pictorial reference to the great classical paintings."

Fan Liang-wei smiled, looking about him, then moved to one side of the platform, half turning as the screen behind him lit up, showing an ancient painting.

"There is, of course, one further quality that Hsieh Ho demanded from the great artist—a quality that, because it is intrinsic to art, is enshrined in each of those six great Principles—that of *ching*. Of precision or minuteness of detail."

He indicated the painting. "This, as you may recognize, is Tung Ch'i-ch'ang's *Shaded Dwelling among Streams and Mountains*, one of the great works of Ming art. This hanging scroll . . ."

The Great Man had turned, looking back at his audience; but now he stopped, his mouth open, for the young man had stood and was making his way slowly down the steps again.

"Forgive me," he said tartly, his patience snapping, "but have I to suffer more of your interruptions?"

The young man stopped, a faint smile playing on his lips. "No. I've heard enough."

"Heard enough . . ." For the briefest moment Fan's face was contorted with anger. Then, controlling himself, he came to the edge of the platform, confronting the young man. "What do you mean, heard enough?"

The young man stared back at Fan Liang-wei, unperturbed, it seemed, by the hardness in his voice, undaunted by his reputation.

"I mean what I said. I've heard enough. I don't have to wait to hear what you have to say—you've said it all already."

Fan laughed, astonished. "I see—"

The young man lifted his arm, pointing beyond Fan at the screen. "That, for instance. It's crap."

There was a gasp of astonishment from the tiers, followed by a low murmur of voices. Fan Liang-wei, however, was smiling now.

"Crap, eh? That's your considered opinion, is it, *Shih* . . . ?"

The young man ignored the request for his name, just as he

ignored the ripple of laughter that issued from the benches on all sides. "Yes," he answered, taking two slow steps closer to the platform. "It's dead. Anyone with a pair of eyes can see it. But you . . ." He shook his head. "Well, to call this lifeless piece of junk one of the great works of Ming art is an insult to the intelligence."

Fan straightened, bristling, then gave a short laugh. "You're a student of painting, then, young Master?"

The young man shook his head.

"Ah, I see. Then what are you precisely? You *are* a member of the College, I assume?"

There was more laughter from the tiers, a harder, crueler laughter as the students warmed to the exchange. The young man had stepped out of line. Now the Great Man would humiliate him.

"I'm a scientist."

"A scientist? Ah, *I see.*"

The laughter was like a great wave this time, rolling from end to end of the great lecture hall. Fan Liang-wei smiled, looking about him, sensing victory.

"Then you know about things like *painting*?"

The young man stood there, the laughter in the hall washing over him, waiting for it to subside. When it did he answered the Great Man.

"Enough to know that Tung Ch'i-ch'ang was the dead end of a process of slow emasculation of a once-vital art form."

The Great Man nodded. "I see. And Cheng Ro . . . I suppose he *was* a great painter . . . in your estimation?"

There was more laughter, but it was tenser now. The atmosphere had changed, become electric with anticipation. They sensed blood.

The young man looked down. Then, unexpectedly, he laughed. "You know your trouble, Fan Liang-wei?" He looked up at the older man challengingly. "You're a slave to convention. To an art that's not a real art at all, just an unimaginative and imitative craft."

There was a low murmur of disapproval from the tiers at that. As for Fan himself, he was still smiling; but it was a tight, tense mask of a smile, behind which he seethed.

"But to answer your question," the young man continued. "Yes, Cheng Ro was a great painter. He had *lueh*, that invaluable quality of being able to produce something casually, almost uncaringly. His ink drawing of dragons—"

"*Enough!*" Fan roared, shivering with indignation. "How *dare* you lecture me about art, you know-nothing! How *dare* you stand there and insult me with your garbled nonsense!"

The young man stared back defiantly at Fan. "I dare because I'm right. Because I know when I'm listening to a fool."

The hall had gone deathly silent. Fan, standing there at the edge of the platform, was very still. The smile had drained from his face.

"A fool?" he said finally, his voice chill. "And you think you can do better?"

For a moment the young man hesitated. Then, astonishingly, he nodded, and his eyes never leaving Fan Liang-wei's face, began to make his way down to the platform.

———————

THE CAFE BURGUNDY was alive with news of what had happened.

At a table near the edge of the Green, the four friends leaned in close, talking. Wolf had missed the lecture, but Sergey had been there with Lotte and had seen the young man mount the platform.

"You should have seen him," Sergey said, his eyes glinting. "As cool as anything, he got up and stood at the lectern, as if he'd been meaning to speak all along."

Wolf shook his head. "And what did Fan say?"

"What *could* he say? For a moment he was so dumbfounded that he stood there with his mouth hanging open, like a fish. Then he went a brilliant red and began to shout at Shepherd to sit down. Oh, it was marvelous. 'It's my lecture,' the old boy kept saying, over and over. And Shepherd, bold as brass, turns to him and says, 'Then you could do us all the courtesy of talking sense.' "

They all roared at that; all but Catherine, who looked down. "I've seen him, I think," she said, "in here."

Sergey nodded. "You can't really miss him. He's an ostentatious little sod. Do you know what he does?" He looked about the table, then leaned back, lifting his glass. "He comes in at the busiest time of day and has a table to himself. He actually pays for all five places. And then he sits there, drinking coffee, not touching a bite of food, a pocket comset on the table in front of him." Sergey lifted his nose in a gesture of disdain, then drained his glass.

Wolf leaned forward. "Yes, but what happened? What did Fan say?"

Sergey gave a sharp little laugh. "Well, it was strange. It was as if Shepherd had challenged him. I don't know. I suppose it had become a matter of face . . . Anyway, instead of just sending for the stewards and having him thrown out, Fan told him to go ahead."

"I bet that shut him up!"

"No. And that's the most amazing part of it. You see, Shepherd actually began to lecture us."

"No!" Wolf said, his eyes wide with astonishment. Beside him, Catherine stared down into her glass.

"Yes . . . he droned on for ages. A lot of nonsense about the artist and the object, and about there being two kinds of vision. Oh, a lot of high-sounding mumbo-jumbo."

"He didn't drone, Sergey. And he was good. Very good."

Sergey laughed and leaned across the table, smiling at the red-haired girl who had been his lover for almost two years. "Who told you that? Lotte here?" He laughed. "Well, whoever it was, they were wrong. It's a pity you missed it, Catherine. Shepherd was quite impressive, in a bullshitting sort of way, but . . ." He shrugged, lifting his free hand, the fingers wide open. "Well, that's all it was, really. Bullshit."

Catherine glanced up at him, as ever slightly intimidated by his manner. She picked up her glass and cradled it against her cheek, the chill red wine casting a roseate shadow across her face. "I didn't just *hear* about it. I was there. At the back of the hall. I got there late, that's all."

"Then you know it was crap."

She hesitated, embarrassed. She didn't like to contradict him, but in this he was wrong. "I . . . I don't agree . . ."

He laughed. "You don't agree?"

She wanted to leave it at that, but he insisted.

"What do you mean?"

She took a breath. "I mean that he was right. There is more to it than Fan Liang-wei claims. The Six Principles . . . they strangle art. Because it *isn't* simply a matter of selection and interpretation. As Shepherd said, it has to do with other factors, with things unseen."

Sergey snorted.

She shivered, irritated by his manner. "I knew you'd do that. You're just like Fan Liang-wei, sneering at anything you disagree with. And both of you . . . well, you see only the material aspect of the art, its structure and its plastic elements. You don't see—"

Sergey had been shaking his head, a patient, condescending smile fixed on his lips, but now he interrupted her.

"What else *is* there? There's only light and shadow, texture and color. That's all you can put on a canvas. It's a two-dimensional thing. And all this business about things unseen, it's . . ." He waved it away lightly with his hand.

She shook her head violently, for once really angry with him. "No! What you're talking about is great design, not great art. Shepherd was right. That painting, for instance—the Tung Ch'i ch'ang. It *was* crap."

Sergey snorted again. "So you say. But it has nothing to do with art, really, has it?" He smiled, sitting back in his chair. "You fancy the fellow, don't you?"

She set her glass down angrily. Wine splashed and spilled across the dark green cloth. "Now *you're* talking bullshit!"

He shook his head, talking over her protestations. "My friend Amandsun tells me that the man's not even a member of the Arts Faculty. He really *is* a scientist of some kind. A *technician.*"

He emphasized each syllable of the final word, giving it a distinctly unwholesome flavor.

Catherine glared at him a moment, then turned away, facing the aviary and its colorful occupants. On one of the higher perches a great golden bird fluffed out its wings as if to stretch into flight. The long, silken underfeathers were as black as night. It opened its beak, then settled again, making no sound.

Sergey watched the girl a moment, his eyes half lidded; then, sensing victory, he pushed home with his taunts.

"Yes, I bet our dear Catherine wouldn't mind *him* tinkering with her things unseen."

That did it. She turned and took her glass, then threw its contents into his face. He swore and started to get up, wiping at his eyes, but Wolf leaned across, holding his arm firmly. "Too far, Sergey. Just a bit too far . . ." he said, looking across at Catherine as he spoke.

Catherine stood there a moment longer, her head held back, fierce, proud, her face lit with anger; then she took five coins from her purse and threw them down onto the table. "For the meal," she said. Then she was gone, was walking out into the Mainway, ignoring the turned heads at other tables.

Sergey wiped the wine from his eyes with the edge of the tablecloth. "It stings! It fucking well stings!"

"It serves you right," said Lotte, watching her friend go, her eyes uncharacteristically thoughtful. "You always have to push it beyond the limits, don't you?"

Sergey glared at her, then relented. The front of his hair was slick with wine, his collar stained. After a moment he laughed. "But I was right, wasn't I? It hit home. Dead center!"

Beside him Wolf laughed, looking across at his sister and meeting her eyes. "Yes," he said, smiling, seeing his smile mirrored back. "I've never seen her so angry. But who is this Shepherd? I mean, what's his background?"

Sergey shrugged. "No one seems to know. He's not from one of the known families. And he doesn't make friends, that's for sure."

"An upstart, do you think?" Lotte leaned across, collecting the coins and stacking them up in a neat pile.

"I guess so." Sergey wiped at his hair with his fingers, then licked them. "Hmm. It might be interesting to find out, don't you think? To try to unearth something about him?"

Wolf laughed. "Unearth. I like that. Do you think . . . ?"

Sergey wrinkled his nose, then shook his head. "No. He's too big to have come from the Clay. You can spot those runts from ten *li* off. No, Mid-Levels, I'd say."

Lotte looked up, smiling. "Well, wherever he comes from, he has nerve, I'll say that for him."

Sergey considered, then grudgingly agreed. "Yes. He's impressive in a sort of gauche, unpolished way. No manners, though. I mean, poor old Fan was completely at a loss. You can be sure *he* won't rest until he's found a way of getting even with our friend."

Wolf nodded. "That's the trouble with the lower levels," he said, watching his sister's hands as they stacked and unstacked the coins, "they've no sense of what's right. No sense of *Li*. Of propriety."

"Or of art," Sergey added.

"No . . ." And their laughter carried across the tables.

BEN DREW BACK into the shadows, watching. The two old men had gone down onto their knees before the makeshift shrine, the paper offerings and the bowls of food laid out in front of them. As he watched they bowed in unison, mumbling a prayer to the spirits of the departed. Then, while one of them stood and stepped back, his head still bowed, the other took a small brush from his inside jacket pocket and lifting the bowls one at a time, swept the space in front of the tablets.

The two men were no more than ten or fifteen paces from Ben, yet it seemed as if a vast gulf separated them from him—an abyss of comprehension. He noted the paper money they had laid down for the dead, the sprigs of plastic "willow" each wore hanging from his hair knot, and frowned, not understanding.

When they were gone he went across and stood there, looking at the wall and at the offerings laid out before it. It was a simple square of wall, the end of one of the many cul-de-sacs that led from Main, yet it had been transformed. Where one expected blankness, one came upon a hundred tiny tablets, each inscribed with the names and dates of the deceased. He looked, reading several of them, then bent down, picking up one of the paper notes of money. It was beautifully made, like the other presents here, but none of it was real. These were things for the dead.

For the last hour he had simply walked in the lowest levels of Oxford stack, trying to understand the events in the lecture hall; had drifted through the corridors like a ghost, purposeless.

Or so he'd thought.

Their laughter had not touched him. It had been an empty, meaningless noise, a braying to fill the void within. No, but the emptiness itself—that unease he had seen behind every eye as he was speaking—*that* worried him. It had been like speaking to the dead. To the hordes of hungry ghosts who, so the Han believed, had no roots to tie them to this world, no living descendants to fulfill their all-too-human needs. They were lost and they looked lost. Even their guide, the Great Man. He more than any of them.

These thoughts had filled him, darkening his mood. And then, to come upon this . . .

Ben turned, hearing a noise behind him, but it was only an old man, two pots slung from the yoke that rested on his shoulders, the one balancing the other. As the old man came on he noticed Ben and stopped, his ancient face wrinkling, as if suspicious of Ben's motives.

Ben stood. "Forgive me. I didn't mean to startle you. I was just looking." He smiled. "Are you a *ch'a* seller?"

"*Ch'a?*" The old man stared back at Ben, puzzled, then looked down at one of the pots he was carrying and gave a cackle of laughter. "No, Master. You have it wrong. This . . ." he laughed again, showing his broken teeth, "this isn't *ch'a*, Master. This is ash."

"Ash?"

The old man grinned back at him fiercely. "Of course. I'm *Lu Nan Jen* for this stack."

The Oven Man! Of course! So the ash . . . Ben laughed, surprised. "And all this?" he asked, half turning to indicate the shrine, the paper offerings, the bowls of food.

The old man laughed uneasily. "You're a strange one, Master. Don't you know what day it is? It's *Sao Mu*, the Feast of the Dead."

Ben's eyes widened. Of course! The fifteenth day of the third month of the old calendar. *Ch'ing Ming*, it was, the festival of brightness and purity, when the graves were swept and offerings made to the deceased.

"Forgive me," he offered quickly, "I'm a student. My studies . . . they've kept me very busy recently."

"Ah, a *student*." The old man bowed respectfully, the yoke about his neck bobbing up and down with the movement. Then he looked up, his old eyes twinkling. "I'm afraid I can't offer you any of this ash, Master, but the *ch'a* kettle is on inside if you'd honor me with your presence."

Ben hesitated a moment, then returned the old man's bow. "I would be honored, *Lu Nan Jen.*"

The old man grinned back at him, delighted, his head bobbing, then made his way to a door on the far side of the corridor. Ben followed him in, looking about the tiny room while the old man set down his pots and freed himself from the yoke.

"I must apologize for the state of things, Master. I have few visitors. Few *live* visitors, if you understand me?"

Ben nodded. There was a second door at the other end of the room with a sign in Mandarin that forbade unauthorized entry. On the wall beside it was a narrow shelf, on which were a meager dozen or so tape-books—the kind that were touch-operated. Apart from that there was only a bed, a small stool, and a low table on which were a *ch'a* kettle and a single bowl. He watched while the old man poured the *ch'a* then turned to him, offering the bowl.

"You will share with me, I hope?" he said, meeting the old man's eyes.

"I . . ." The old man hesitated, then gave a small bow. It was clear he had not expected such a kindness.

Ben sipped at the *ch'a*, then offered the bowl to the old man. Again he hesitated; then, encouraged by Ben's warm smile, he took the bowl and drank noisily from it.

"It must be strange, this life of yours, *Lu Nan Jen.*"

The Oven Man laughed and looked about him, as if considering it for the first time. "No stranger than any man's."

"Maybe so. But what kind of life is it?"

The old man sat, then leaned forward on the stool, the *ch'a* bowl held loosely in one hand. "You want the job?" he asked, amused by Ben's query.

Ben laughed. "No. I have enough to do, *lao jen.* But your work—it fascinates me."

The old man narrowed his eyes slightly. "Do you mean my work, or what I work with?"

"You can separate the two things that easily?"

The Oven Man looked down, a strange smile on his lips, then

he looked up again, offering the *ch'a* bowl to Ben. "You seem to know a lot, young Master. What is it that you're a student of?"

"Of life," Ben answered. "At least, so my father says."

The old man held his eyes a moment, then nodded, impressed by the seriousness he saw in the younger man's face.

"This is a solitary life, young Master." He gave a small chuckle, then rubbed at his lightly bearded chin. "Oh, I see many people, but few who are either able or inclined to talk."

"You've always been alone?"

"Always?" The old man sniffed, his dark eyes suddenly intense. "Always is a long time, Master, as any of my clients would tell you if they could. But to answer you—no, there were women, one or two, in the early years." He looked up, suddenly more serious. "Oh, don't mistake me, Master, I am like other men in that. Age does not diminish need and a good fuck is a good fuck, neh?"

When Ben didn't answer, the old man shrugged.

"Anyway . . . there were one or two. But they didn't stay long. Not after they discovered what was in the back room."

Ben turned, looking at the door, his eyebrows lifted.

"You want to see?"

"May I?"

Ben set the *ch'a* down and followed the old man, not knowing what he would find. A private oven? A room piled high with skulls? Fresh corpses, partly dissected? Or something even more gruesome? He felt a small shiver of anticipation run through him, but the reality of what met his eyes was wholly unexpected.

He moved closer, then laughed, delighted. "But it's— beautiful!"

"Beautiful?" The old man came and stood beside him, trying to see it as Ben saw it, with new eyes.

"Yes," Ben said, reaching out to touch one of the tiny figures next to the tree. Then he drew his finger back and touched it to his tongue. The taste was strange and yet familiar. "What did you use?"

The old man pointed to one side. There, on a small table were his brushes and paints and beside the paint pots a bowl like the two he had been carrying when Ben had first met him. A bowl filled with ashes.

"I see," said Ben. "And you mix the ash with dyes?"

The old man nodded.

Ben looked back at the mural. It almost filled the end wall. Only a few white spaces here and there, at the edges and the top left of the painting, revealed where the composition was unfinished. Ben stared and stared, then remembered suddenly what the old man had said.

"How long did you say you've been working at this?"

The old man crouched down, inspecting something at the bottom of the painting.

"I didn't."

"But—" Ben turned slightly, looking at him, seeing things in his face that he had failed to notice earlier. "I mean, what you said about the women, when you were younger. Was this here then?"

"This?" The old man laughed. "No, not this. At least, not all of it. Just a small part. This here . . ." He sketched out a tiny portion of the composition, at the bottom center of the wall.

"Yes. Of course." Ben could see it now. The figures there were much cruder than the others. Now that his attention had been drawn to it, he could see how the composition had grown, from the center out. The Oven Man had learned his art slowly, patiently, year by year adding to it, extending the range of his expression. Until . . .

Ben stood back, taking in the whole of the composition for the first time.

It was the dance of death. To the far left, a giant figure—huge compared to the other, much smaller figures—led the dance. It was a tall, emaciated figure, its skin glass-pale, its body like that of an ill-fed fighter, the bare arms lithely muscled, the long legs stretched taut like a runner's. Its body was facing to the left—to the west and the darkness beyond—but its horselike, shaven head was turned unnaturally on its long neck, staring back dispassionately at the naked host that followed, hand in hand, down the path through the trees.

In its long, thin hands Death held a flute, the reed placed to its lipless mouth. From the tapered mouth of the flute spilled a flock of tiny birds, dark like ravens, yet cruel, their round eyes like tiny beads of milky white as they fell onto the host below, pecking at eye and limb.

The trees were to the right. Willow and ash and mulberry. Beneath them and to their left, in the center of the mural, a stream fell between rocks, heavy with the yellow earth of Northern China. These were the Yellow Springs, beneath which, it was said, the dead had their domain, *ti yu*, the "earth prison." He saw how several among that host—Han and *Hung Mao* alike—looked up at that golden spill of water as they passed, despairing, seeing nothing of its shining beauty.

It was a scene of torment, yet there was compassion there, too. Beneath one of the trees the two figures he had first noticed embraced one final time before they joined the dance. They were a mother and her child, the mother conquering her fear to comfort her tearful daughter. And, further on, beneath the biggest of the willows, two lovers pressed their faces close in one last, desperate kiss, knowing they must part forever.

He looked and looked, drinking it in, then nodded, recognizing the style. It was *shanshui*—mountains and water. But this was nothing like the lifeless perfection Tung Ch'i-ch'ang had painted. These mountains were alive, in motion, the flow of water was turbulent, disturbed by the fall of rock from above.

It was a vision of last things. Of the death not of a single man but of a world. Of Chung Kuo itself.

He stood back, shivering. It was some time since he had been moved so profoundly by anything. The Oven Man was not a great painter—at least, not technically—yet what he lacked in skill he more than made up for in vision. For this was real. This had Ch'i—vitality. Had it in excess.

"I can see why they left you, *Lu Nan Jen*. Was this a dream?"

The old man turned, looking at Ben, his whole manner changed. There was no mistaking him now for a simple *ch'a* seller.

"You understand, then?"

Ben met his eyes. "When did it come?"

"When I was ten. My life . . ." He shrugged, then looked away. "I guess there was nothing I could be after that but *Lu Nan Jen*. There was no other school for me."

"Yes." Ben turned, looking at it again, awed by its simple power. "All this—your work—it must keep you busy."

"Busy?" The old man laughed. "There is no busier person in the Seven Cities than the Oven Man, unless it is the Midwife. They say eight hundred million die each year. Eight hundred million, and more, each year. Always more. There is no room for such numbers in the earth. And so they come to my ovens." He laughed, a strangely thoughtful expression on his face. "Does that disturb you, young Master?"

"No," Ben answered honestly, yet it made him think of his father. How long would it be before Hal, too, was dead—alive in memory alone? Yet he, at least, would lie at rest in the earth. Ben frowned. "Your vision is marvelous, *Lu Nan Jen*. And yet, when you talk, you make it all sound so—so prosaic. So meaningless."

"From nothing they come. To nothing they return."

"Is that what you believe?"

The old man shrugged, his eyes going to the darkness at the far left of the mural, beyond the figure of Death. "To believe in nothing, is that a belief? If so, I believe."

Ben smiled. There was more sense, more wisdom in this old man than in a thousand Fan Liang-weis. And himself? What did he believe? Did he believe in nothing? Was the darkness simply darkness? Or was there something there, within it? Just as there seemed to be a force behind the light, was there not also a force behind the dark? Maybe even the same force?

The old man sighed. "Forgive me, young Master, but I must leave you now. I have my ovens to attend. But please, if you wish to stay here . . ."

Ben lowered his head. "I thank you, *Lu Nan Jen*. And I am honored that you showed me your work. It is not every day that I come across something so real."

The Oven Man bowed, then met Ben's eyes again. "I am glad you came, young Master. It is not every day that I meet someone who understands such things. The dream uses us, does it not?"

Ben nodded, moved by the old man's humility. To create *this* and yet to know how little *he* had had to do with its creating. That was true knowledge.

He bowed again and made to go, then stopped. "One last thing," he said, turning back. "Do you believe in ghosts?"

The Oven Man laughed and looked about him at the air. "Ghosts? Why, there's nothing here *but* ghosts!"

━━━━━

"Catherine? Are you in there?"

She closed her eyes and let her forehead rest against the smooth, cool surface of the door, willing him to go and leave her in peace, but his voice returned, stronger, more insistent.

"Catherine? You are there, aren't you? Let me in."

"Go away," she said, hearing the tiredness in her voice. "You've a date with young Heng, haven't you? Why don't you just go to that and leave me be."

"Let me in," he said, ignoring her comment. "Come on. We need to talk."

She sighed, then stepped back, reaching across to touch the lock. At once the door slid back.

Sergey had changed. He was wearing his gambling clothes— dark silks that lent him a hard, almost sinister air. She had never liked them, least of all now, when she was angry with him.

"Still sulking?" he asked, making his way past her into the room.

She had thrown a sheet over the oil board to conceal what she had been working on, but he went straight to it, throwing back the sheet.

"Is this what's been causing all the difficulties?"

She punched the touch pad irritably, closing the door, then turned to face him.

"What do you want?"

He laughed, then came across to her. "Is that how you greet me?"

He tried to embrace her, but she pushed him away.

"You forget," she said, moving past him and throwing the sheet back over the oil board.

"It was a joke—" he began, but she rounded on him angrily.

"You're a child! Do you know that?"

He shrugged. "I thought that's what you liked about me. Besides, it wasn't you who had wine thrown in your face. That hurt."

"Good."

She turned away, but he caught her arm and pulled her back.

"Let go of me," she said coldly, looking down at where he held her.

"Not until you apologize."

She laughed, astonished by him. "*Me* apologize? After what you said? You can go rot in hell before I apologize to you!"

He tightened his grip until she cried out, tearing her arm away from his grasp.

"You bastard. You've no right—"

"No *right?*" He came closer, his face leaning into hers threateningly. "After what we've been to each other these last two years, you have the nerve to say I've no right?" His voice was hard, harder than she had ever heard it before, and she found herself suddenly frightened by this aspect of him. Had it always been there, just below the surface of his charm? Yes. She'd always known it about him. Perhaps that was even what had first attracted her to him. But now she was tired of it. Tired of his thoughtless domination of her. Let him drink himself to death, or take his whores, or gamble away all his money—she would have no more of it.

"Just go, Sergey. Now, before you make even more of a fool of yourself."

She saw his eyes widen with anger and knew she had said the wrong thing. He reached out and grabbed her neck roughly, pulling her closer to him. "A fool?"

Through her fear she recognized the strange parallel of the words with those Fan Liang-wei had used to Shepherd. Then she was fighting to get away from him, hitting his arms and back as he pulled her chin around forcibly and pressed his mouth against her own. Only then did he release her, pushing her back away from him, as if he had finished with her.

"And *now* I'll go see Heng."

She shivered, one hand wiping at her mouth unconsciously. "You bastard," she said, her voice small. "You obnoxious bastard . . ." She was close to tears now, her anger displaced suddenly by the hurt she felt. How *dare* he do that to her? How *dare* he treat her like his thing?

But he only shook his head. "Grow up, Catherine. For the gods' sake grow up."

"Me?" But her indignation was wasted on him. He had turned away. Slamming his fist against the lock, he pushed out through the door, barely waiting for it to open. Then he was gone.

She stood there awhile, staring at the open doorway, fear and hurt and anger coursing through her. Then, as the automatic lock came on and the door hissed closed, she turned and went into the kitchen. She reached up, pulled down a bottle of peach brandy, and poured herself a large glass, her hands trembling. Then, using both hands to steady the glass, she took a long, deep swig of it, closing her eyes, the rich, dark liquid burning her throat.

She shuddered. The bastard! How *dare* he?

Back in the other room, she set the glass down on the floor, then threw the sheet back from the oil board, looking at the painting. It was meant to be a joint portrait. Of her and Sergey. Something she had meant to give him for their second anniversary, two weeks away. But now . . .

She looked at it, seeing it with new eyes. It was shit. Lifeless shit. As bad as the Tung Ch'i-ch'ang landscape. She pressed ERASE and stood back, watching as the faces faded and the colored, contoured screen became a simple, silk smooth rectangle of uncreated whiteness.

For a moment she felt nothing, then, kneeling, she picked up her glass, cradling it against her cheek momentarily before she put it to her lips and drank.

She looked up again, suddenly determined. Fuck him! If that was what he thought of her, if that was how he was prepared to treat her, she would have no more of it. Let it be an end between them.

She swallowed, the warmth in her throat deceptive, the tears threatening to come despite her determination not to cry. She sniffed, then raised her glass, offering a toast to the silent doorway.

"Go fuck yourself, Sergey Novacek! May you rot in hell!"

SERGEY STOOD at the top of the steps looking down into the huge, dimly lit gaming room of the Jade Peony. Lights above the tables picked out where games were in progress, while at the far end a bar ran from left to right, backlit and curved like a crescent moon. The floor below was busy. Crowds gathered about several of the tables, the excited murmur of their voices carrying to where he stood.

There was a sweet, almost peppery scent in the air, like cinnamon mixed with plum and jasmine, strangely feminine, yet much too strong to be pleasant. It was the smell of them—of the sons of the Minor Families and their friends. The distinguishing mark of this Han elite, like a pheromonal dye. Sergey smiled. In theory The Jade Peony was a mixed club, membership determined not by race but by recommendation and election, but in practice the only *Hung Mao* here were guests, like himself.

Yang kuei tzu, they called his kind. "Ocean devils." *Barbarians*.

Even the Han at the door had looked down on him. He had seen the contempt that lay behind that superficial mask of politeness. Had heard him turn, after he had gone, and mutter a word or two of his own tongue to the other doorman. Had heard them laugh and knew it was about him.

Well, he'd wipe a few smiles from their faces tonight. And Heng? His smile broadened momentarily. He would make sure Heng would not be smiling for a long time.

He went down the plushly carpeted stairway, past the great dragon-head sculpture that stood to one side, making his way to the bar.

As he passed they stared at him openly, their hostility unmasked.

Heng Chian-ye was where he said he would be, at a table on the far left, close to the bar, a big, hexagonal table covered in a bright-red silk. Representations of the *wu fu*, the five gods of good luck, formed a patterned border around its edge, the tiny silhouettes picked out in green.

He smiled and bowed. "Heng Chian-ye . . . You received my message, I hope."

Heng Chian-ye was seated on the far side of the table, a glass and a wine bottle in front of him. To either side of him sat his friends, four in all, young, fresh-faced Han in their early twenties, their long fingernails and elaborately embroidered silks the calling card of their kind. They stared back at Sergey coldly, as if at a stranger, while Heng leaned forward, a faint smile playing on his lips.

"Welcome, *Shih* Novacek. I got your message. Even so, I did wonder whether you would make an appearance tonight." His smile broadened momentarily, as if to emphasize the jest. "Anyway, you're here now, neh? So please take a seat. I'll ask the waiter to bring you a drink."

"Just wine," he said, answering the unspoken query, then sat, smiling a greeting at the others at the table, inwardly contemptuous of them.

Then, taking the silken pouch from inside his jacket pocket, he threw it across the table so that it landed just in front of Heng Chian-ye. It was deliberately done; not so much an insult as an act of gaucheness. In the circles in which Heng mixed it was not necessary to provide proof of means before you began to play. It was assumed that if you sat at a gaming table you could meet your debts. Thus it was among the *ch'un tzu*. Only *hsiao jen*—little men—acted as Sergey was acting now.

Sergey saw the looks that passed among Heng and his friends and smiled inwardly. Their arrogance, their ready assumption of superiority—these were weaknesses. And the more he could feed that arrogance, the weaker they would become. The weaker they, the stronger he.

"What's this?" Heng said, fingering the string of the pouch as if it were unclean.

"My stake," Sergey said, sitting forward slightly, as if discomfited. "Look and see. I think you'll find it's enough."

Heng laughed and shook his head. "Really, *Shih* Novacek. That's not how we do things here."

Sergey raised his eyebrows, as if puzzled. "You do not wish to play, then? But I thought . . ."

Heng was smiling tightly. His English was clipped, polite. "It isn't what I meant." He lifted the pouch with two fingers and threw it back across the table. "You would not be here if I . . . doubted your ability to pay."

Sergey smiled. "Forgive me," he said, looking about him as he picked up the pouch and returned it to his pocket, "I did not mean to offend."

"Of course," Heng answered, smiling; yet the way he glanced at his friends revealed what he was really thinking. "I understand, *Shih* Novacek. Our ways differ. But the game . . ."

Sergey lowered his head slightly, as if acknowledging the wisdom of what Heng Chian-ye had said. "The game is itself. The same for Han and *Hung Mao* alike."

Heng gave the barest nod. "So it is. Well, shall we play?"

"Just you and I, Heng Chian-ye? Or will the *ch'un tzu* join us?"

Heng looked to either side of him. "Chan Wen-fu? Tsang Yi? Will you play?"

Two of the Han nodded, the other two—as if on cue—stood, letting the others spread out around the table.

"You will be west, *Shih* Novacek, I east. My friends here will be north and south."

Sergey sat back, taking the wine from the waiter who had appeared at his side. "That's fine with me. You have new cards?"

Heng lifted his chin, as if in signal to the waiter. A moment later the man returned with a sealed pack, offering them to Sergey. He took them and hefted them a moment, then set them down on the table.

"Bring another."

Heng smiled tightly. "Is there something wrong with them, *Shih* Novacek?"

"Not at all, Heng Chian-ye. Please, bear with me. It is a foible of mine. A *superstition.*" He spoke the last word quietly, as if ashamed of such a weakness, and saw the movement in Heng's eyes, the way he looked to north and south, as if to reinforce the point to his two friends.

"You have many superstitions, *Shih* Novacek?"

"Not many. But this . . ." He shrugged, then turned, taking the new pack from the waiter and putting it down beside the other. Then, to Heng's surprise, he picked up the first and broke the seal.

"But I thought . . ."

Sergey looked down, ignoring Heng's query, fanning the huge cards out on the table in front of him. There were one hundred and sixty cards in a pack of *Chou*, or "State," arranged into nine levels, or groupings. At the head of all was the Emperor, enthroned in golden robes. Beneath him were his seven Ministers, these graybeards plainly dressed, as if in contrast. At the third level were the Family Heads—the twenty-nine cards richly decorated, each one quite different from the others. At the next level down the four Generals seemed at first glance quite uniform; yet the staunch *Hung Mao* faces of the old men differed considerably. Beneath them came the four Wives of the Emperor, ranked in their household order, and beneath them—at the sixth level—came the two Concubines, their scantily dressed figures making them the most attractive of the cards. Next were the eight Sons, their resemblance to their respective mothers suggested by their facial features and cleverly underlined by use of color and decoration. Then, at the eighth level of this complex hierarchy came the eighty-one Officials, ranked in nine levels of nine, their great *chi ling* patches displayed on the chests of their powder-blue gowns. And finally, at the ninth level—last in the great pecking order of State—were the twenty-four Company Heads, their corporate symbols—some long forgotten, some just as familiar now as when the game was first played one hundred and twenty years before—emblazoned on the copy of the Edict scroll that each held.

Sergey turned one of the cards a moment, studying the reverse carefully for special markings, then compared it with a second. The backs of the cards were a bright, silken red, broken in the center by a pattern of three concentric circles, three rings of dragons—twenty-nine black dragons in the outer circle, seven larger dragons in the second, and at the very center, a single golden dragon, larger than all the others, its great jaws closing on its tail.

Sergey smiled and looked up. "These are beautiful cards, Heng Chian-ye. The faces . . . they look almost as if they were drawn from life."

Heng laughed. "So they were, my friend. These are copies of the very first *Chou* pack, hand-drawn by Tung Men-tiao."

Sergey looked down at the cards with a new respect. Then these were tiny portraits of the actual people who had filled those roles. Men and women whom the great artist and satirist Tung

Men-tiao had known in life. He smiled. Somehow it gave the game an added bite.

"Shall we start?" Heng asked. "If you'll stack the cards, we'll cut to see who deals."

For the first few hours he had tried to keep things fairly even, attributing his victories to good fortune, his defeats to his own stupidity. And all the while he had studied their play, had seen how the other two played to Heng, even while making it seem that they had only their own interests at heart. It was clever but transparent, and he could see how it would have fooled someone else, but he was not just any player. At *Chou* he excelled. He had mastered it as a child, playing his father and uncles for his pocket money.

In the last game he had drawn the Emperor and despite a strong hand, had proceeded to ensure that he lost; rather than consolidating power, he played into the hands of Heng's three Minister cards. Heng's rebellion had succeeded and Sergey had ended by losing a thousand *yuan*. He had seen the gleam in Heng's eyes as he noted down his winnings on the tab and knew that the time was ripe. Heng had won the last two games. He must feel he was on a winning streak. What better time, then, to up the stakes?

Sergey looked down, pretending not to see how Heng looked to his left at Tsang Yi, knowing what was to come.

"Forgive me, *ch'un tzu*," the Han began, getting to his feet and bowing, first to his friends, and then—his head barely inclined—to Sergey, "but I must go. My father . . ."

"Of course," Heng said smoothly, before Sergey could object. "We understand, don't we, *Shih* Novacek?"

We do, he thought, smiling inwardly, then watching as another of Heng's circle took Tsang's place at the table.

"I'll buy Tsang out," the Han said, his eyes meeting Sergey's briefly, challengingly. Then, turning to Heng, he added, "But look, Chian-ye, why don't we make the game more—*exciting.*"

Heng laughed, acting as though he didn't understand his friend. "How so, Yi Shan-ch'i? Was that last game not exciting enough for you?"

Yi inclined his head slightly. "Forgive me, honorable cousin, but that is not what I meant. The game itself was good. As enjoyable to watch as I'm sure it was to play. But such a game needs an added bite, don't you think? If the stake were to be raised to ten thousand *yuan* a game . . ."

Heng laughed, then looked across at Sergey. "Maybe so. But let's ask our friend here. Well, *Shih* Novacek? What do you say? Would you like to raise the stakes, or are you happy as it is?"

It was delicately put. Almost too delicately, for it was phrased to let him back off without losing face. But things were not so simple. He was not one of them, even though he sat at their table. He was *Yang kuei tzu*. A foreign devil. A *barbarian*. He looked down, wrinkling up his face as if considering the matter, then looked up again.

"Ten thousand *yuan* . . ." He laughed nervously. "It's more than I've lost in a whole evening before now. Still, Yi Shan-ch'i is right. It *would* make the game more interesting."

Heng looked to his two friends, then back at Sergey. "I would not like to pressure you."

"No." Sergey shook his head firmly, as if he had made up his mind and was now determined. "Ten thousand *yuan* it is. For good or ill."

He sat back, watching Yi deal. As ever Heng picked up each card as it was dealt, his face an eloquent map of his fortunes. For his own part, Sergey waited until all seventeen cards were laid facedown before him, watching the other two sort their cards before he picked up his own.

As he sorted his hand he thought back to the last time he had played Heng. The object of *Chou* was straightforward and could be expressed quite simply: it was to hold the most points in one's hand at the end of the final play. To do so, however, one had not only to strengthen one's own hand but to weaken one's opponents. The game's complex system of discards and exchanges, blind draws and open challenges was designed to simulate this aspect of political life, the sticky web of intrigue that underpinned it all. Heng played, however, as if he barely understood this aspect of the game, as if only the relative levels of the cards—their positive attributes—mattered to him. He sought to cram his hand full of high-scoring cards and bonus combinations—Ministers and Family Heads and Generals—failing, like so many of his kind, to understand the other side of things, the powerfully destructive potential of Concubines and Sons.

In *Chou* the value of a card did not always express its significance in the scheme of things. So it was with Concubines. At the end of the game they were worth only eight points—fifty-six points less than a Family Head and one hundred twenty points less than a Minister. Unless . . .

Unless the Emperor were without a Wife. In which case, the Concubine took on its negative aspect, canceling out not only its own value but the two hundred fifty-six points that the Emperor would otherwise score.

Likewise with the Sons. While they scored only four a piece at the final count, in the company of their respective mothers they became a liability, canceling out not merely their own value but that of any Minister held.

The skillful player sought, therefore, to pair Wives with Sons, hold back Wives from those who held the Emperor, and, at the last throw, to off-load their pairings and Concubines in an exchange of hostages. To win by undermining their opponents.

Sergey smiled, noting that he had both Concubines in his hand. Well, good. This time he would keep them. Would make it seem he had drawn them late in the play, before he could off-load them on another.

A half hour later he had lost.

"Another game, *ch'un tzu?*" Heng asked, jotting down Yi's victory on the tab. Sergey glanced across. He was eleven thousand down, Chan nine, Heng eight. Yi, who had taken on Tsang's deficit of two thousand, was now twenty-eight thousand up.

Heng dealt this time. "Has anyone the Emperor?" he asked, having sorted out his own hand.

Sergey laid it down before him, then reached across to take another card from the pile. Having the Emperor made one strong. But it also made one vulnerable—to Concubines and the scheming Sons of Wives.

Again he smiled. He had a good hand—no, an excellent hand. Three Wives and three Ministers and there, at the far left of his hand, one of the Concubines. The tiny, doe-eyed one.

He looked down, momentarily abstracted from the game,

thinking back to earlier that evening and to the row with Catherine. He had shut it out before, but now it came back to him. It had been his fault. He could see that now. But why did she always have to provoke him so? Why couldn't she be more like the other women he knew? He felt a mild irritation at her behavior. Why did she always have to be so stubborn? Didn't she know what it did to him? And all that business with the "technician," Shepherd. Why had she done that, if not to spite him? She knew how jealous he was. Why couldn't she be a bit more compliant? Then again, he liked her spirit. So different from Lotte and her kind.

He laughed softly, conscious of the contradiction.

"You have a good hand, *Shih* Novacek?" Heng asked, smiling tightly at him, misunderstanding the cause of his laughter.

"I think so, Heng Chian-ye," he answered, leaning forward to place two of the Ministers facedown onto the discard pile. "I think so."

Two hours later he was sixty-one thousand down. He wasn't the only one down, of course. Chan had a deficit of nineteen thousand marked against his name. But Yi was eighteen thousand up, and Heng, who had won three of the last four games, was sixty-two thousand in credit.

It had gone perfectly. Exactly as he'd planned. He looked across. Heng Chian-ye was smiling broadly. In the last hour Heng had begun to drink quite heavily, as if to buoy up his nerves. He had drunk so much, in fact, that he had almost made a simple mistake, discarding the wrong card. An error that could have lost him everything. Only Yi's quick action had prevented it, an intercession Sergey had pretended not to see.

Now was the time. While Heng was at the height of his pride. But it must come from Heng. In such company as this it must seem that it was not he but Heng who raised the stakes a second time.

In the last hour a small crowd had gathered about the table, intrigued by the sight of a *Hung Mao* playing *Chou* in the Jade Peony. Sergey had noted how a ripple of satisfaction had gone through the watchers each time he had lost and had felt something harden deep inside him. Well, now he would show them.

He leaned back in his seat, pretending to stifle a yawn. "I'm tired," he said. "Too many late nights, I guess." He smiled across at Heng. "Maybe I should stop now, while I've any of my fortune left."

Heng glanced across at his friends, then looked back at him. "You mean to leave us soon, *Shih* Novacek?"

He straightened up and took a deep breath, as if trying to sober up. "Fairly soon."

"Your luck must change."

"Must it?" He laughed harshly, then seemed to relent. "Well, maybe . . ."

"In which case . . ." Heng looked about him, then leaned toward Sergey again. "Maybe you'd like the chance to win your money back, eh, my friend? One game. Just you and I. For sixty-one thousand."

Sergey looked down. Then, surprisingly, he shook his head. "I wouldn't hear of it. Even if I won, well, it would be as if we hadn't played." He looked up, meeting Heng's eyes. "No, my friend. There must be winners and losers in this world of ours, neh? If we are to play, let it be for—seventy-five thousand. That way I at least have a small chance of coming out ahead."

Heng smiled and his eyes traveled quickly to his friends again. There was an expectant hush now about the table.

"Make it a hundred."

He made a mime of considering the matter, then shrugged. "All right. So be it." He turned, summoning a waiter. "Bring me a coffee. Black, two sugars. I might need my wits about me this time."

It took him twenty minutes.

"It seems my luck has changed," he said, meeting Heng's eyes, seeing at once how angry the other man was with himself; for he had made it seem as though victory were the Han's, only to snatch it away at the last moment. "I was fortunate to draw that last card."

He saw what it cost Heng to keep back the words that almost came to his lips and knew he had him.

"Anyway," he added quickly, "I really should go now. I thank you for your hospitality, Heng Chian-ye. Settle with me when you will. You know where to find me." He pushed his chair back from the table and got to his feet.

"Wait!"

Heng was leaning forward, his hand extended toward Sergey.

"Surely you won't go now, *Shih* Novacek? As you yourself said, your luck has changed. Why, then, do you hurry from your fortune? Surely you aren't afraid, my friend?"

Sergey stared back at him. "Afraid?"

Heng leaned back, a faint smile coming to his lips. "Yes. Afraid." He hesitated. "I'll play you again, *Shih* Novacek. One final game. But this time we'll make the stakes worth playing for. Two-hundred thousand. No. *Two-hundred-and-fifty* thousand."

Sergey looked about him at the watching Han, seeing the tension in every face. This was no longer about the money; for Heng it was now a matter of pride—of *face*.

He sat, placing his hands firmly on the edge of the table, looking back at Heng, fixing him in his gaze, his manner suddenly different—harder, almost brutal in its challenge.

"All right. But not for two-fifty. Let's have no half measures between us, Heng Chian-ye. If I play you, I play you for a million. Understand me?"

There were low gasps from all around the table, then a furious murmur of voices. But Heng seemed unaware of the hubbub that surrounded him. He sat staring back fixedly at Sergey, his eyes wide as if in shock. His hands were trembling now, his brow was beaded with sweat.

"Well?"

Unable to find his voice, Heng nodded.

"Good." Sergey leaned forward and took the cards; then, surprising them all, he handed them to Yi. "You deal, Yi Shan-ch'i. I want no one to say that this was not a fair game."

He saw Heng's eyes widen at that. Saw realization dawn in Heng's frightened face.

So now you know.

He kept his face a mask, yet inwardly he was exulting. *I've got you now, you bastard. Got you precisely where I wanted you.* A million. Yes, it was more than Heng Chian-ye had. More than he could possibly borrow from his friends. He would have no alternative. If he lost he would have to go to his uncle.

HENG YU TURNED in his seat, dismissing the servant, then went outside into the anteroom. Heng Chian-ye knelt there, on the far side of the room, his head bowed low, his forehead touched almost to the tiled floor. He crossed the room, then stood over the young man, looking down at him.

"What is it, Cousin?"

Heng Chian-ye stayed as he was. "Forgive me, Uncle Yu, but I have the most grave request to make of you."

Heng Yu, Minister of Transportation for Li Shai Tung and Head of the Heng Family, pulled at his beard, astonished. Chian-ye was fourteen years his junior, the youngest son of his uncle, Heng Chi-po, the former Minister, who had passed away eleven years earlier. Several times over the past five years he had had to bail the boy out when he was in trouble, but all that had changed six months ago, when Chian-ye had come into his inheritance. Now that he had his own income, Chian-ye had been a much rarer visitor at his "uncle" Yu's house.

"A grave request? At this hour, Chian-ye? Do you *know* what time it is? Can it not wait until the morning?"

Heng Chian-ye made a small, miserable movement of his head. "I would not have come, Uncle, were it not a matter of the utmost urgency."

Heng Yu frowned, confused, his head still full of figures from the report he had been studying.

"What is it, Chian-ye? Is someone ill?"

But he knew, even as he said it, that it was not that. Fu Hen would have come with such news, not Chian-ye. Unless . . . He felt himself go cold.

"It isn't Fu Hen, is it?"

Heng Chian-ye raised his head the tiniest bit. "No, honored Uncle. No one is ill. I . . ."

Heng Yu sighed with relief, then leaned closer. "Have you been drinking, Chian-ye?"

"I—" Then, astonishingly, Chian-ye burst into tears. Chian-ye, who had never so much as expressed one word of remorse over his own wasteful lifestyle, in tears! Heng Yu looked down at where Chian-ye's hand gripped the hem of his *pau* and shook his head. His voice was suddenly forceful, the voice of a Minister commanding an underling.

"Heng Chian-ye! Remember who you are! Why, look at you! Crying like a four-year-old! Aren't you ashamed of yourself?"

"Forgive me, Uncle! I cannot help it! I have disgraced our noble family. I have lost a million *yuan!*"

Heng Yu fell silent. Then he gave a small laugh of disbelief. "Surely I heard you wrong, Chian-ye? A million *yuan?*"

But a tiny nod of Chian-ye's bowed head confirmed it. A million *yuan* had been lost. Probably at the gaming table.

Heng Yu looked about him at the cold formality of the anteroom, at its mock pillars and the tiny bronze statues of gods that rested in the alcoves on either side, the unreality of it all striking him forcibly. Then he shook his head. "It isn't possible, Chian-ye. Even *you* cannot have lost that much, surely?"

But he knew that it was. Nothing less would have brought Chian-ye here. Nothing less would have reduced him to such a state.

Heng Yu sighed, his irritation mixed with a sudden despair. Was he never to be free of his uncle's failings? First that business with Lwo Kang, and now this. As if the father were reborn in his wastrel son to blight the family's fortunes with his carelessness and selfishness.

For now he would have to borrow to carry out his schemes. Would have to take that high-interest loan *Shih* Saxton had offered him. A million *yuan!* He cursed silently, then drew away, irritably freeing his *pau* from his cousin's grasp.

"Come into the study, Chian-ye, and tell me what has happened."

He sat behind his great ministerial desk, his face stern, listening to Chian-ye's story. When his cousin finished, he sat there silently, considering. Finally he looked back at Chian-ye, shaking his head.

"You have been a foolish young man, Chian-ye. First you overstretched yourself. That was bad enough. But then . . . well, to promise something that was not yours to promise, that was . . . insufferable."

He saw how Chian-ye blushed and hung his head at that. *So there is some sense of rightness in you,* he thought. *Some sense of shame.*

"However," he continued, heartened by the clear sign of his

cousin's shame, "you are family, Chian-ye. You are *Heng.*" He pronounced the word with a pride that made his cousin look up and meet his eyes, surprised.

"Yes. Heng. And the word of a Heng must be honored, whether given mistakenly or otherwise."

"You mean—?"

Heng Yu's voice hardened. "I mean, Cousin, that you will be silent and *listen* to me!"

Heng Chian-ye lowered his head again, chastened; his whole manner subservient now.

"As I was saying. The word of a Heng must be honored. So, yes, Chian-ye, I shall meet *Shih* Novacek's conditions. He shall have the *Ko Ming* bronze in settlement for your debt. As for the information he wanted, you can do that for yourself, right now. The terminal is over there, in the corner. However, there are two things you will do for me."

Chian-ye raised his head slightly, suddenly attentive.

"First you will sign over half of your annual income, to be placed in a trust that will mature only when you are thirty."

Chian-ye hesitated, then gave a reluctant nod.

"Good. And second, you will resign your membership to the Jade Peony."

Heng Chian-ye looked up, astonished. "But, Uncle . . . ?" Then, seeing the angry determination in Heng Yu's face, he lowered his eyes. "As you say, Uncle Yu."

"Good," Heng Yu said, more kindly now that it was settled. "Then go to the terminal. You know how to operate it. The codes are marked to the right. But ask me if you must. I shall be here a few hours yet, finishing my reports."

He watched Chian-ye go to the terminal, then sat back, smoothing at his beard with his left hand, his right hand resting on the desk. A million *yuan!* That, truly, would have been disastrous. But this—this deal. He smiled. Yes, it was a gods-given opportunity to put a bit and brace on his reckless cousin, to school him to self-discipline. And the price? One ugly bronze worth, at most, two-hundred thousand, and a small snippet of information on a fellow student!

He nodded, strangely pleased with the way things had turned

out, then picked up the report again. He was about to push it into the slot behind his ear when Chian-ye turned, looking across at him.

"Uncle Yu?"

"Yes, Chian-ye?"

"There seems to be no file."

Heng Yu laughed, then stood, coming round his desk. "Of course there's a file, Chian-ye. There's a file on everyone in Chung Kuo. You must have keyed the code incorrectly."

He stared at the screen. INFORMATION NOT AVAILABLE, it read.

"Here," he said, taking the scrap of paper from his cousin's hand. "Let me see those details."

He stopped dead, staring at the name that was written on the paper, then laughed uncomfortably.

"Is something wrong, Uncle Yu?"

"No . . . nothing. I . . ." He smiled reassuringly, then repeated what Chian-ye had tried before, getting the same response. "Hmm," he said. "There must be something wrong with this terminal. I'll call one of my men to come and see to it."

Heng Chian-ye was watching him strangely. "Shall I wait, Uncle?"

For a moment he didn't answer, his head filled with questions. Then he shook his head absently. "No, Chian-ye." Then, remembering what day it was, he turned, facing him.

"You realize what day it is, Chian-ye?"

The young man shook his head.

"You mean you have been wasting your time gambling when your father's grave remains unswept?"

Chian-ye swallowed and looked down, abashed. "*Sao Mu*," he said quietly.

"Yes, *Sao Mu*. Or so it is for another three-quarters of an hour. Now go, Chian-ye, and do your duty. I'll have these details for you by the morning, I promise you."

When Chian-ye was gone he locked the door, then came back to the terminal.

Ben Shepherd. Now what would *Shih* Novacek be doing wanting to know about the Shepherd boy? One thing was certain—it wasn't a harmless inquiry. For no one, Han or *Hung Mao*, threw a million *yuan* away on such a small thing. Unless it wasn't small.

He turned, looking across at the tiny chip of the report where it lay on his desk, then turned back, his decision made. The report could wait. This was much more important. Whatever it was.

CHAPTER THIRTEEN

Catherine

W OULD YOU MIND if I sat with you?"

He looked up at her, smiling, seeming to see her, to *create* her, for the very first time. She felt unnerved by that gaze. Its intensity was unexpected, unnatural. And yet he was smiling.

"With me?"

She was suddenly uncertain. There was only one chair at his table. The waiters had removed the others, isolating him, so that no one would approach him.

She felt herself coloring. Her neck and her cheeks felt hot, and after that first, startling contact, her eyes avoided his.

"Well?" he said, leaning back, his fingers resting lightly on the casing of the comset on the table in front of him.

He seemed unreachable, and yet he was smiling.

"I . . . I wanted . . ." Her eyes reached out, making contact with his. So unfathomably deep they were. They held hers, drawing her out from herself. ". . . to sit with you."

But she was suddenly afraid, her body tensed against him.

"Sit where?" His hand lifted, the fingers opening in a gesture of emptiness. The smile grew broader. Then he relented. "All right. Get a chair."

She brought a chair and put it down across from him.

"No. Closer." He indicated the space beside him. "I can't talk across tables."

She nodded, setting the chair down where he indicated.

"Better."

He was still watching her. His eyes had not left her face from the moment she had first spoken to him.

Again she felt a flash of fear, pure fear, pass through her. He was like no one she had ever met. So— She shook her head, the merest suggestion of movement, and felt a shiver run along her spine. No, she had never felt like this before—so—helpless.

"What do you do?"

Not "Who are you?." Nothing so formal as an introduction. Instead, this. Direct and unabashed. *What do you do?* Peeling away all surfaces.

For the first time she smiled at him. "I . . . paint."

He nodded, his lips pinched together momentarily. Then he reached out and took her hands in his own, studying them, turning them over.

So firm and warm and fine, those hands. Her own lay caged in his, her fingers thinner, paler than those that held them.

"Good hands," he said, but did not relinquish them. "Now, tell me what you wanted to talk to me about."

About hands, perhaps. Or a million other things. But the warmth, the simple warmth of his hands curled about her own, had robbed her of her voice.

He looked down again, following her eyes. "What is it, Catherine?"

She looked up sharply, searching his face, wondering how he knew her name. He watched her a moment longer, then gave a soft laugh.

"There's little you don't pick up, sitting here. Voices carry."

"And you hear it all? Remember it?"

"Yes."

His eyes were less fierce now, less predatory in their gaze; yet it still seemed as if he were staring at her, as if his wide-eyed look were drug-induced. But it no longer frightened her, no longer picked her up and held her there, suspended, soul-naked and vulnerable before it.

Her fear of him subsided. The warmth of his hands . . .

"What do you paint?"

Until a moment ago it had seemed important. All important.

But now? She tilted her head, looking past him, aware of the shape of his head, the way he sat there, so easy, so comfortable in his body. Again, so unexpected.

He laughed. Fine, open laughter. Enjoying the moment. She had not thought him capable of such laughter.

"You're a regular chatterbox, aren't you? So *eloquent* . . ."

He lifted his head as he uttered the last word, giving it a clipped, sophisticated sound that was designed to make her laugh.

She laughed, enjoying his gentle mockery.

"You had a reason for approaching me, I'm sure. But now you merely sit there, mute, glorious—and quite beautiful."

His voice had softened. His eyes were half-lidded now, like dark, occluded suns.

He turned her hands within his own and held them, his fingers lying upon her wrists, tracing the blood's quickening pulse.

She looked up, surprised, then looked down at his left hand again, feeling the ridge there. A clear, defined line of skin, circling the wrist.

"Your hand . . . ?"

"Is a hand," he said, lifting it to her face so that she could see it better. "An accident. When I was a child."

"Oh." Her fingers traced the line of flesh, a shiver passing through her. It was a fine, strong hand. She closed her hand on his, her fingers laced into his fingers, and looked at him.

"Can I paint you?"

His eyes widened, seeming to search her own for meanings. Then he smiled at her, the smile like a flower unfolding slowly to the sun. "Yes," he said. "I'd like that."

━━━━━

IT WAS NOT THE BEST she had ever done, but it was good, the composition sound, the seated figure lifelike. She looked from the canvas to the reality, sitting there on her bed, and smiled.

"I've finished."

He looked up distractedly. "Finished?"

She laughed. "The portrait, Ben. I've finished it."

"Ah . . ." He stood up, stretching, then looked across at her again. "That was quick."

"Hardly quick. You've been sitting for me the best part of three hours."

"Three hours?" He laughed strangely. "I'm sorry. I was miles away."

"Miles?"

He smiled. "It's nothing. Just an old word, that's all."

She moved aside, letting him stand before the canvas, anxious to know what he thought of it. For a moment she looked at it anew, trying to see it for the first time, as he was seeing it. Then she looked back at him.

He was frowning.

"What is it?" she asked, feeling a pulse start in her throat.

He put one hand out vaguely, indicating the canvas. "Where am I?"

She gave a small laugh. "What do you mean?"

"This . . ." He lifted the picture from its mechanical easel and threw it down. "It's shit, Catherine. Lifeless shit!"

She stood there a moment, too shocked to say anything, unable to believe that he could act so badly, so—*boorishly*. She glared at him, furious at what he'd done, then bent down and picked up the painting. Where he had thrown it down the frame had snapped, damaging the bottom of the picture. It would be impossible to repair.

She clutched the painting to her, her deep sense of hurt fueling the anger she felt toward him.

"Get out!" she screamed at him. "Go on, get out of here, right now!"

He turned away, seemingly unaffected by her outburst; then he leaned over the bed, picking up the folder he had brought with him. She watched him, expecting him to leave, to go without a further word, but he turned back, facing her, offering the folder.

"Here," he said, meeting her eyes calmly. "This is what I mean. This is the kind of thing you should be doing, not that crap you mistake for art."

She gave a laugh of astonishment. He was unbelievable.

"You arrogant bastard."

She felt like slapping his face. Like smashing the canvas over his smug, self-complacent head.

"Take it," he said, suddenly more forceful, his voice assuming an air of command. Then, strangely, he relented, his voice softening. "Just look. That's all. And afterward, if you can't see what I mean, I'll go. It's just that I thought you were different from the rest. I thought . . ."

He shrugged, then looked down at the folder again. It was a simple art folder—the kind that carried holo flats—its jet-black cover unmarked.

She hesitated, her eyes searching his face, looking for some further insult, but, if anything, he seemed subdued, disappointed in her. She frowned, then put the painting down.

"Here," she said, taking the folder from him angrily. "You've got nerve, I'll give you that."

He said nothing. He was watching her now, expectantly, those dark eyes of his seeming to catch and hold every last atom of her being, their gaze disconcerting.

She sat down on the edge of the bed, the folder in her lap, looking up at him through half-lidded eyes.

"What is this?"

"Open it and see."

For a long time she was silent, her head down, her fingers tracing the shapes and forms that stared up at her from the sheaf of papers that had been inside the folder. Then she looked up at him, wide-eyed, all anger gone from her.

"Who painted these?"

He sat down beside her, taking the folder and flicking through to the first of the reproductions.

"This is by Caravaggio. His 'Supper at Emmaus,' painted more than six hundred years ago. And this . . . this is Vermeer, painted almost sixty years later; he called it 'The Artist's Studio.' And this is by Rembrandt, 'Aristotle Contemplating the Bust of Homer,' painted ten years earlier. And this is 'Laocoon' by El Greco—"

She put her hand on his, stopping him from turning the print over, staring at the stretched white forms that lay there on the page.

"I've—I've never seen anything like these. They're—"

She shivered, then looked up at him, suddenly afraid.

"Why have I never seen them? I mean, they're beautiful. They're *real* somehow."

She stopped, suddenly embarrassed, realizing now what he had meant. She had painted him in the traditional way—the only way she knew—but he had known something better.

"What does it mean?" she asked, her fingers tracing the pale, elongated forms. "Who are they?"

He gave a small laugh, then shook his head. "The old man lying down in the center, he's Laocoon. He was the priest who warned the Trojans not to allow the wooden horse into Troy."

She gave a little shake of her head, then laughed. "Troy? Where was Troy? And what do you mean by wooden horse?"

He laughed, once again that openness, that strange naturalness of his surfacing unexpectedly. "It was an ancient tale. About a war that happened three thousand years ago between two small nation states. A war that was fought over a woman."

"A woman?"

"Yes." He looked away, a faint smile on his lips.

"How strange. To fight a war over a woman." She turned the page. "And this?"

Ben was silent for a time, simply staring at the painting; then he looked up at her again. "What do you make of it?"

She gave a little shrug. "I don't know. It's different from the others. They're all so—so dark and intense and brooding. But this—there's such serenity there, such knowledge in those eyes."

"Yes." He laughed softly, surprised by her. "It's beautiful, isn't it? The painter was a man called Modigliani, and it was painted some three hundred years after those others. It's called 'Last Love.' The girl was his lover, a woman called Jeanne Hebuterne. When he died she threw herself from a fifth-floor window."

She looked up at him sharply, then looked back down at the painting. "Poor woman. I . . ." She hesitated, then turned, facing him. "But why, Ben? Why haven't I heard of any of these painters? Why don't they teach them in College?"

He looked back at her. "Because they don't exist. Not officially."

"What do you mean?"

He paused, then shook his head. "No. It's dangerous. I shouldn't have shown you. Even to know about these—"

He started to close the folder but she stopped him, flicking through the remaining paintings until she came to one near the end.

"This," she said. "Why have I never seen this before?"

Ben hesitated, staring at the print she was holding out to him. He had no need to look at it; it was imprinted firmly in his memory. But he looked anyway, trying to see it fresh—free of its context—as she was seeing it.

"That's da Vinci," he said softly. "Leonardo da Vinci. It's called 'The Virgin and Child with Saint Anne and John the Baptist' and it was painted exactly seven hundred and eight years ago."

She was silent a moment, studying the print, then she looked up at him again, her eyes pained now, demanding.

"Yes, Ben, but why? And what do you mean, they don't exist? These paintings exist, don't they? And the men who painted them—they existed, didn't they? Or is this all some kind of joke?"

He shook his head, suddenly weary of it all. Was he to blame that these things had gone from the world? Was it his fault that the truth was kept from them? No. And yet he felt a dreadful burden of guilt, just knowing this. Or was it guilt? Wasn't it something to do with the feeling he had had ever since he'd come here, into the City? That feeling that only *he* was real? That awful feeling of distance from everything and everyone—as if, when he reached out to touch it all, it would dissolve, leaving him there in the midst of nothingness, falling back toward the earth.

He heard the old man's voice echo in his head—*Ghosts? Why, there's nothing here but ghosts!*—and shivered.

Was that why he had shown her these? To make some kind of connection? To reassure himself that he wasn't the only living, breathing creature in this vast mirage—this house of cards?

Maybe. But now he realized what he had done. He had committed her. Seduced her with these glimpses of another world. So what now? Should he back off and tell her to forget all that she'd seen, or should he take her one step further?

He looked at her again, taking her hand, for that one brief moment balanced between the two courses that lay open to him. Then he smiled and squeezed her hand.

"Have you ever read *Wuthering Heights*?"

She hesitated, then nodded.

"Good. Then I want you to read it again. But this time in the original version. As it was first written, three hundred and sixty years ago."

"But that's—" She laughed then looked down, disturbed by all of this. "What are you doing, Ben? Why are you showing me these things?"

"To wake you up. To make you see all of this as I see it." He looked away from her, his eyes moving back to the broken painting on the easel.

"I met someone yesterday. A *Lu Nan Jen*. You know, what they call an Oven Man. He painted, too. Not like you. He didn't have your skill with a brush, your eye for classical composition. But he did have something you haven't—something the whole of Han art hasn't—and that's vision. He could see clear through the forms of things. Through to the bone. He understood what made it all tick and he set it down—clearly, powerfully. For himself. So that he could understand it all. When you came up to me in the Cafe Burgundy I had been sitting there thinking about him—thinking about what he'd done, how he'd spent his life trying to set down that vision, that *dream* of his. And I wondered suddenly what it would be like to wake that in someone. To make it blossom in the soul of someone who had the talent to set it down as it really ought to be set down. And then there you were, and I thought . . ."

She was watching him closely now, her head pushed forward, her lips parted in expectation.

"You thought what?"

He turned back, looking at her. "What are you doing this afternoon?"

She sat back, disappointed. "Nothing. Why?"

"Would you like to come with me somewhere? Somewhere you've never been before?"

She narrowed her eyes. "Where?"

"Somewhere no one ever goes. Beneath here. Into the Clay."

▼▼▼▼▼

BEN HAD HIRED a man to walk ten paces in front of them, his arc lamp held high, its fierce white light revealing the facades of old graystone buildings, their stark shapes edged in deepest shadow.

Ben held a second, smaller lamp, a lightweight affair on a long, slender handle. Its light was gentler, casting a small, pearled pool of brightness about the walking couple.

Catherine held his hand tightly, fascinated and afraid. She hadn't known. She thought it had all been destroyed. But here it was, preserved, deserted, left to the darkness; isolated from the savage wilderness surrounding it.

As they walked, Ben's voice filled the hollow darkness, speaking from memory, telling her the history of the place.

"Unlike all previous architects, the man who designed City Earth made no accommodation for the old. The new was everything to him. Even that most simple of concessions—the destruction of the old—was, as far as possible, bypassed. The tallest buildings were destroyed, of course, but the rest was simply built over, as if they really had no further use for the past." He turned, looking back at her. "What we have now is not so much a new form of architecture as a new geological age. With City Earth we entered the Technozoic. All else was left behind us, in the Clay."

He paused, pointing across at a rounded dome the guide's lamp had revealed. "Have you ever noticed how there are no domes in our City, even in the mansions of First Level? No. There are copies of Han architecture, of course, though even those are quite recent developments, things of the last fifty years or so. But of the old West there's nothing. All that elegance of line has been replaced by harder shapes—hexagons, octagons, an interlacing of complex crystalline structures, as if the world had frozen over."

"But that . . ." She pointed up at the curved roof of the dome. "That's beautiful."

"It is, isn't it?"

She shook her head, not understanding. "But why?"

"The desire for conformity, I guess. Things like that dome induce a sense of individuality in us. And they didn't want that."

She shrugged. "I don't follow you."

Ben looked about him. The circle of light extended only so far. Beyond, it was as if the great stone buildings faded into uncreated nothingness. As if they had no existence other than that which the light gave them in its passage through their realm. Ben smiled at the thought, realizing that this was a clue to what he himself was doing. For he—as artist—was the light, creating that tiny circle of mock-reality about him as he passed.

He turned back, looking at the girl, answering her.

"When it all fell apart, shortly before City Earth was built, there was an age of great excess—of individual expression unmatched in the history of our species. The architects of City Earth—Tsao Ch'un, his Ministers, and their servants—identified the symptom as the cause. They saw the excesses and the extravagance, the beauty and the expression as cultural viruses and sought to destroy them. But there was too much to destroy. They would have found it easier to destroy the species. It was too deeply ingrained. Instead, they tried to mask it—to bury it beneath new forms. City Earth was to be a place where no one wanted for anything. Where everything the physical self could need would be provided for. It was to be Utopia—the world beyond Peach Blossom River."

She frowned at him, not recognizing the term, but he seemed almost unaware of her now. Slowly he led her on through the labyrinth of streets, the doubled lights, like sun and moon, reflected in the ceiling high above.

"But the City was a cage. It catered only to the grounded, physical being. It did not cater to the higher soul—the winged soul that wants to fly."

She laughed, surprised by him. But of course one caged birds. Who had ever heard of a bird flying free?

The walls closed about them on either side. They were walking now through a narrow back alley, the guide only paces in front of them, his lamp filling the darkness with its strong white light. For a moment it almost seemed they were walking in the City.

Unless you looked up. Unless you stopped and listened to the silence; sensing the darkness all around.

Ben had been silent, looking away. Now he turned, looking back at her.

"It was to be a landscape devoid of all meaning. A landscape of unrelated form."

He had paused and she had been obliged to stop with him. But all she wanted now was to get out, for all the strange beauty of this place. She felt uncomfortable here. Afraid, and vulnerable.

"We are creatures of the earth, Catherine," he said, his eyes sharing something of the darkness beyond the lamp's fierce circle. "Creatures of the earth and yet . . ." he hesitated, as if in pain, "and yet we want to fly. Don't you find that strange?"

She looked past him, at the old brickwork, itself a geometric pattern. "I don't know," she said. "Perhaps we were always looking to create something like the City. Perhaps it's only the perfection of something we always had in us."

He looked at her fiercely, shaking his head in denial. "No! It's death, that's what it is! Death!"

He shuddered. She felt it through her hand. A shudder of revulsion. She hadn't understood before, but now she saw. Why he had isolated himself. Why he always seemed so hostile.

"You talk as if you're not from the City," she said. "As if . . ." But she left her question unasked. He would tell her if he wanted to.

"We keep the names," he said, "but they mean nothing anymore. They're cut off. Like most of us, they're cut off."

"But not you," she said after a moment.

He laughed but said nothing. It irritated her for once, that enigmatic side of him. She freed her hand from his and walked on. He followed, the light from his lamp throwing faint shadows off to one side.

She was angry. Hurt that he made no concessions to her. As if she meant nothing to him.

She stopped, then turned to face him.

He stood there, the lamp held high, the light throwing his face into strange lines, the shadows making it seem wrong—a face half in brightness, half in dark.

"Shall we go on?" he asked. But she could make out no expression on his face. His features were a rigid mask of shadow and light.

"I hate it here."

He turned, looking about him once again, the light wavering with the movement, throwing ghostly shards of brilliance against the windows of the buildings to either side. Dead, black eyes of glass, reflecting nothing.

She reached out and touched his arm. "Let's go back, Ben. Please. Back to Oxford."

He smiled bitterly, then nodded. Back to Oxford then. The name meant nothing to her, after all. But it was where they had been these last two hours. A place, unlike the bright unreality that had been built over it. A real place. For all its darkness.

━━━━

IN HER DREAM she saw herself, walking beside him, the lamp held up above their heads, the shadowed, ancient town surrounding them, the floor of the City lost in the darkness overhead.

She saw the labyrinth again, saw its dark and secret rivers, the Isis and the Cherwell, flow silently, like blood in the veins of the earth. His words. His image for them. In her dream she stood there with him on the old stone bridge, her flesh connected to his at the palm. And when he lifted his lamp the water shone.

She woke, feeling hot, feverish, and switched on the bedside lamp. It was four in the morning. She sat up, rubbing her palms together, looking at them in amazement and relief. It had been so real. She had felt where her flesh sank into his and shared a pulse, seen the wine-dark flow where it passed beneath the stone arch of the bridge . . .

So real that waking seemed a step down.

For a while she sat there, shivering, not from cold but from a surreal sense of her other self. Of her sleeping, dreaming self who, like the figure in the dream, walked on in darkness, understanding nothing.

She closed her eyes, trying to recapture it, but the image was fading fast, the feeling of it slipping from her. Then the pulse of it faltered, died.

She got up, and went across to the canvas, then sat on the stool in front of it, the seat cold against her naked buttocks, her toes curled about the rounded bar. Her body was curved, lithe, like a cat's, while her fine, flamelike hair fell straight, fanning halfway down her back, her flesh like ivory between its livid strands.

She stared at the painting, studying it minutely.

It was dark. Reds and greens dominated the visual textures, sharply contrasted, framed in shapes of black that bled from the edge of the painting. Harsh, angular shapes, the paint laid thick on the canvas, ridged and shadowed like a landscape.

His face stared out at her, flecks of red and green like broken glass forming his flesh, the green of his eyes so intense it seemed to flare and set all else in darkness.

She had shown him seated in her chair, his shoulders slightly forward, his arms tensed, as if he were in the act of rising. His long, spatulate fingers gripped the arms firmly, almost lovingly.

There was a hard-edged abstract quality to the composition that none of her friends would have recognized as hers, yet something softer showed through, a secondary presence that began to dominate once that first strong sense of angularity and darkness diminished.

The painting lived. She smiled, knowing that in this she had transcended herself. It was a breakthrough. A new kind of art. Not the mimicry she had long accepted as her art, but a new thing, different in kind from anything she had ever done before.

Behind the firmness of the forms there was an aura. A light behind the darkness. A tenderness behind those harsh, sharp-sculpted shapes. His dark, fragmented face grew softer the more she looked, the eyes less fierce, more gentle.

She reached out with one hand to touch the bottom surface, her fingers following the line of whiteness where the figure faded into darkness. Below that line what at first seemed merely dark took on new forms, new textures—subtle variations of gray and black.

Buildings. Strange, architectural forms. Ghost images she had seen as real. All crowded there; trapped, pressed down beneath the thinnest line of white. Like a scar on the dark flesh of the canvas.

She tilted her head, squinting at the figure. It was stiff, almost lifeless in the chair, and yet there was the suggestion of pure force, of an intense, almost frightening vitality. A doubleness, there in everything: something she had not been aware of until he had shown it to her.

She relaxed, satisfied, and straightened her back, letting her hands drop to her knees. Then she stretched, her arms going up and back, her small, firm breasts lifting with the movement. She clawed the air with her fingers, yawning, then laughed to herself, feeling good.

Leaning forward, she activated the graphics keyboard beneath the painting's lower edge, then pressed one of the pads, making the canvas rotate a full 360 degrees.

Slowly the figure turned, presenting its left shoulder to the viewing eye, its face moving into profile.

She pressed PAUSE and sat back, looking. He was handsome. No, more than handsome: he was beautiful. And she had captured something of that. Some quality she had struggled at first to comprehend. A wildness—a fierceness—that was barely contained in him.

She shifted the focus, drawing out a detail of the wrist, the muscles there. She leaned forward, looking, touching the hard-edged textures of the projection, seeing what the machine had extrapolated from her intention.

She studied it a moment longer, then got to work, bringing the pallet around into her lap and working at the projection with the light-scalpels, making the smallest of alterations, then shifting focus again, all the while staring at the canvas, her forehead creased in a frown of intense concentration, her body hunched, curled over the painting, her hands working the plastic surface to give it depth.

When she had finished it was almost eight and the artificial light of the wake hours showed between the slats of her blinds, but she had worked all the tiredness from her bones.

She felt like seeing him.

Her robe lay on the chair beside her bed. She put it on and went across to the comset, touching his code from memory. In a moment his face was there, on the flatscreen by her hand. She looked down at him and smiled.

"I need to see you."

His answering smile was tender. "Then I'll be over."

The screen went dark. She sat there a moment, then turned away. Beside the bed she bent down, picking up the book she had left there only hours before. For a moment she stared at its cover as if bewitched, then opened it, and picking a passage at random, began to read.

She shuddered. It was just as Ben had said. There was no comparison. It was such a strange and wonderful book. Unseemly almost, and yet beautiful. Undeniably beautiful.

The novel she remembered had been a dull little morality tale—the story of a boy from the Clay who had been taken in by a First Level family and had repaid their trust by trying to corrupt the upright daughter of the house. In that version filial piety had triumphed over passion. But this . . .

She shook her head, then put the book down. For all its excesses, it was so much more real, so much more *true* than the other. But what did it mean? What did all of these things mean? The paintings, the strange buildings beneath the City, and now this—this tale of wild moors and savage passions? What did it all add up to?

Where had Ben found these things? And why had she never heard of them before?

Why?

She sat, a small shiver—like an after-shock—rippling down her spine. Things that existed and yet had no existence. Things that, if Ben were right, were dangerous even to know about. Why should such things be? What did they mean?

She closed her eyes, focusing herself, bringing herself to stillness, calming the inner voices, then leaned back on her elbows.

He was coming to her. Right now he was on his way.

"Then I'll be over."

She could hear his voice; could see him clearly with her inner eye. She smiled, opening her eyes again. He had not even kissed her yet. Had not gone beyond that first small step. But surely that must come? Surely? Else why begin?

She stood, looking about her, then laughed, a small thrill passing through her. No, he hadn't even kissed her yet. But maybe this time. *Maybe . . .*

BEN STOOD in the doorway, relaxed, one hand loosely holding the edge of the sliding panel, the other combing through his hair.

"Really . . ." he was saying, "I'd much rather treat you to breakfast."

He seemed elated, strangely satisfied; but with himself, not with her. He had barely looked at her yet.

She felt herself cast down. A nothing.

"I'd like to cook you something—" she began again, knowing she had said it already. Again he shook his head. So definite a movement. Uncompromising. Leaving her nowhere. A bitter anguish clenched the muscles of her stomach, made her turn from him, lest he see. But she had seen how his eyes moved restlessly about the room, not really touching anything. Skating over surfaces, as if they saw nothing.

As if what he *really* saw was not in her room.

She turned and saw that he was looking at the covered canvas. But there was no curiosity in his eyes. For once he seemed abstracted from the world, not pressed right up against it. She had never seen him like this before, so excited and yet so cut off from things.

She looked at him a moment longer, then shrugged and picked up her slender clutch bag. "All right. I'm ready."

They found a quiet place on the far side of the Green from the Cafe Burgundy. At first they ate in silence, the curtain drawn about them in the narrow booth, giving the illusion of privacy. Even so, voices carried from either side. Bright, morning voices. The voices of those who had slept and come fresh to the day. They irritated her as much as his silence. More than that, she was annoyed with him. Annoyed about the way he had brought her here and then ignored her.

She looked across the table's surface to his hands, seeing how at ease they were, lying there either side of the shallow, emptied bowl. Through the transparent surface she saw their ghostly images, faint but definite, refracted by the double thickness of the ice. He was so self-contained. So isolated from the world. It seemed, at that moment, that it would be easier for her to reach through the surface and take those ghostly hands than to reach out and grasp the warm reality.

She felt a curious pressure on her; something as tangible in its effect as a pair of hands pressed to the sides of her head, keeping her from looking up to meet his eyes. Yet nothing real. It was a phantom of her own creating—a weakness in her structure.

She looked away, stared down at her untouched meal. She had said nothing of her new painting. Of why she had called him. Of all she had felt, staring at that violent image of his face. He had shut her out. Cut off all paths between them. As she sat there she wished for the strength to stand up and leave him there sitting before his empty bowl.

As if that were possible.

She felt her inner tension mount until it seemed unendurable. And then he spoke, reaching out to take her hands in his own; the warmth of them dissipating all that nervous energy, destroying the phantoms that had grown vast in his neglect.

"Have you ever tasted real food, Catherine?"

She looked up, puzzled, and met his eyes. "What do you mean, *real*?"

He laughed, indicating her bowl. "You know, I've never seen you eat. Not a morsel." His hands held hers firmly yet without real pressure. There was a mischievous light behind his eyes. She had not seen him like this before.

"I eat," she said, making him laugh again at the assertiveness of her simple statement. "But I still don't understand you."

"Ah," he said. "Then the answer is no."

She shook her head, annoyed with him again, but in a different way. He was teasing her. Being unfair.

He looked down. "It's strange what becomes important. For no apparent reason. Things take hold. Won't release you."

He looked up again, all humor gone from his eyes. That intensity was back. That driven quality.

"And that's your obsession, is it? Food?"

She saw at once that her joke had misfired. In this, it seemed, he was vulnerable. Wide open.

Perhaps that was what obsession was. A thing against which there was no defense. Not even humor.

So, she thought. *And this is yours. The real.*

For a time he said nothing. She watched the movement in his dark expressive eyes. Sea moods beneath the vivid green. Surface and undertow. And then he looked out again, *at* her, and spoke.

"Come with me. I want to show you something."

━━━━━

BEN'S APARTMENT was to the north of Oxford Canton, on the edge of the fashionable student district. Catherine stood in the main room, looking about her.

"I never imagined . . ." she said softly to herself, then turned to find him there in the doorway, a wine-filled glass in each hand.

"You're privileged," he said, handing her a glass. "I don't usually let anyone come here."

She felt both pleased and piqued by that. It was hard to read what he meant by it.

It was a long, spacious room, sparsely decorated. A low sofa was set down in the middle of the plushly carpeted floor, a small, simply molded coffee table next to it. Unlike the apartments of her friends, however, there were no paintings on the wall, no trinkets or small sculptures on the tabletops. It was neat, almost empty.

She looked about her, disappointed. She had expected something more than this. Something like Sergey's apartment.

He had been watching her. She met his eyes and saw how he was smiling, as if he could read her thoughts. "It's bleak, isn't it? Like a set from some dreadfully tasteful drama."

She laughed, embarrassed.

"Oh don't worry. This is"—he waved his hand in an exaggerated circle—"a kind of mask. A front. In case I had to invite someone back."

She sipped her wine, looking at him sharply, trying to gauge what he was saying to her. "Well?" she said, "what were you going to show me?"

He pointed across the room with his glass. There was a panel in the far wall. A sliding panel with the faint indentation of a thumb-lock.

"The mystery revealed," he said. "Come."

She followed, wondering why he played these games. In all else he was so direct. So much himself. Then why these tricks and evasions? What was he hiding? What afraid of?

His fingers tapped out a combination on the touch-pad. The thumb-lock glowed READY and he pressed his right thumb into the depression. The door hissed back, revealing a second room as big as the one they were in.

She stepped through, impressed by the contrast.

For all its size it was cluttered, the walls lined with shelves. In the spaces between hung prints and paintings. A small single bed rested against the far wall, its sheets wrinkled, a simple cover drawn back. Books were piled on a bedside table and in a stack on the floor beside the bed. Real books, not tapes. Like the one he had given her. Her mouth opened in a smile of surprise and delight. But what really grabbed her attention was the apparatus in the center of the room.

She crossed the room and stood beside it.

"Is this what you do?" she asked, feeling the machine tremble, its delicate limbs quivering beneath her touch.

The scaffolding of the machine was laced with fine wires, like a cradle. Inside lay a lifesize marionette, a mock human, no features on its face, its palms smooth and featureless. The morph was like the machine, almost alive, tremblingly responsive to her touch. Its white, almost translucent surfaces reflected the ceiling light in flashes and sparkles.

It was beautiful, a work of art in itself.

"Does it do anything?"

"By itself, no. But yes, in a sense it's what I do."

She looked quickly at him, then back to the machine, re-membering what Sergey had said about him being a technician, a scientist. But how did that equate with what he knew about art? All that intuitive, deeply won knowledge of his? She frowned, trying to understand, trying to fit it all together. She looked down at the base of the machine, seeing the thick width of tape coiled about the spools, like some crude relic from the technological past. She had never seen anything like it.

She circled the machine, trying to comprehend its function. Failing.

"What *is* this?" she said finally, looking back at him.

He stood on the other side of the machine, looking at her through the fragile scaffolding, the fine web of wiring.

"It's what I brought you here to see."

He was smiling, but behind the smile she could sense the intensity of his mood. This was important to him. For some reason very important.

"Will you trust me, Catherine? Will you do something for me?"

She stared back at him, trying to read him, but it was impossible. He was not like the others. It was hard to tell what he wanted, or why. For a moment she hesitated, then nodded, barely moving her head, seeing how much he had tensed, expecting another answer.

He turned away momentarily, then turned back. The excitement she had glimpsed earlier had returned to his eyes, this time encompassing her, drawing her into its spell.

"It's marvelous. The best thing I've done. You wait. You'll see just how marvelous. How *real.*"

There was a strange, almost childish quality in his voice—an innocence—that shocked her. He was so open at that moment. So completely vulnerable. She looked at him with eyes newly opened to the complexity of this strange young man, to the forces in contention in his nature.

Strangely, it made her want to hold him to her breast, as a mother would hold her infant child. And yet at the same time she wanted him, with a fierceness that made her shiver, afraid for herself.

━━━━━

BEN STOOD at the head of the frame, looking down at her. Catherine lay on her back, naked, her eyes closed, the lids flickering. Her breasts rose and fell gently, as if she slept, her red hair lay in fine red-gold strands across her cheeks, her neck.

Stirrups supported her body, but her neck was encased in a rigid cradle, circled with sensitive filaments of ice, making it seem as if her head were caged in shards of glass. A fine mesh of wires fanned out from the narrow band at the base of her skull, running down the length of her body, strips of tape securing the tiny touch-sensitive pads to her flesh at regular intervals. Eighty-one connections in all, more than half of those directly into the skull.

The morph lay on the bed, inert. Ben glanced at its familiar shape and smiled. It was almost time.

He looked down at the control desk. Eight small screens crowded the left-hand side of the display, each containing the outline image of a skull. Just now they flickered through a bright sequence of primaries, areas of each image growing then receding.

Beneath the frame a tape moved slowly between the reels. It was a standard work—an original *pai pi*—but spliced at its end was the thing he had been working on, the new thing he was so excited about. He watched the images flicker, the tape uncoil and coil again, then looked back at the girl.

There was a faint movement in her limbs, a twitching of the muscles where the pads were pressed against the nerve centers. It was vestigial, but it could be seen. Weeks of such ghost movement would cause damage, some of it irreparable. And addicts had once spent months in their shells.

The tracking signal appeared on each of the eight small screens. Fifteen seconds to the splice. He watched the dark mauve areas peak on six of the screens, then fade as the composition ended. For a moment there was no activity, then the splice came in with a suddenness that showed on all the screens.

According to the screens, Catherine had woken up. Her eyes were open and she was sitting up, looking about her. Yet in the frame the girl slept on, her lidded eyes unmoving, her breasts rising and falling in a gentle motion. The faint tremor in her limbs had ceased. She was still now, perfectly at rest.

The seconds passed slowly, a countdown on the top-right screen showing when the splice ended.

He smiled and watched her open her eyes, then try to shake her head and raise her hands. Wires were in her way, restraining her. She looked confused, for a brief moment troubled. Then she saw him and relaxed.

"How are you?" he asked.

Her eyes looked back questioningly at him. Green eyes, the

same deep shade of green as his own. She looked quite beautiful, lying there. It was strange how he had not noticed it before. That he had *seen* it and yet not noted it.

"I don't understand . . ." she began, "I woke up and you were sitting next to me at the Cafe Burgundy. I'd had too much to drink and I'd fallen asleep. I . . . I had been dreaming. We were talking . . . something about colors . . . and then I turned and looked across at the pagoda. You said something about all the birds escaping, and, yes, across the Green, I could see that it was so. There were birds flying everywhere. They'd broken out of their cage. Then, as I watched, one flew right at me, its wings brushing against my face even though I moved my head aside to avoid it. You were laughing. I turned and saw that you had caught the bird in your hands. I reached across and . . ."

She stopped, her brow wrinkling, her eyes looking inward, trying to fathom what had happened.

"And?"

She looked straight at him. "And then I woke up again. I was here." She tried to shake her head and was again surprised to find it encased, her movements restrained. She stared at the webbing trailing from her neck, as if it should dissolve, then turned, looking back at him.

"I shouldn't be here, should I? I mean, I woke up once, didn't I? So this . . ." confusion flickered in her face and her voice dropped to an uncertain whisper, "this must be a tape."

He smiled. "Good," he said softly. "That's just what I wanted to hear."

He moved around her and began to unfasten the connections, working quickly, methodically, his touch as sure and gentle as a surgeon's.

"I don't follow you, Ben. Which was which. I mean, this is real now, isn't it? But that part in the cafe . . ."

He looked down into her face, only a hand's width from his own.

"That was the tape. My tape. The thing I've been working on these last four months."

She laughed, still not understanding. "What do you mean, your tape?"

He unclipped the band and eased it back, freeing her neck.

"Just what I said." He began to massage her neck muscles, knowing from experience what she would be feeling with the restraint gone. "I made it. All that part about the cafe."

She looked up at him, her head turned so that she could see him properly, her nose wrinkled up. "But you can't have. People don't make tapes. At least, not like that. Not on their own. That thing before—that cartoonlike thing. That was a *pai pi*, wasn't it? I've heard of them. They used to have dozens of people working on them. Hundreds sometimes."

"So I've been told."

He moved behind her, operating the stirrup controls, lowering her slowly to the floor. Then he climbed into the frame above her, untaping the lines of wire and releasing the pads from her flesh one by one, massaging the released flesh gently to stimulate the circulation, every action carried out meticulously, as if long rehearsed.

"I don't like teams," he said, not looking at her. Then, squatting, he freed the twin pads from her nipples, gently rubbing them with his thumbs. They rose, aroused by his touch, but he had moved on, working down her body, freeing her from the harness.

"I set myself a problem. Years ago. I'd heard about *pai pi* and the restrictions of the form, but I guess I realized even then that it didn't have to be like that. Their potential was far beyond what anyone had ever thought it could be."

"I still don't follow you, Ben. You're not making sense."

She was leaning up on her elbows now, staring at him. His hand rested on the warmth of her inner thigh, passive, indifferent to her, it seemed. She was still confused. It had been so real. Waking, and then waking again. And now this—Ben, crouched above her, his hand resting on her inner thigh, talking all this nonsense about what everyone knew had been a technological dead end. She shook her head.

His eyes focused on her, suddenly aware. "What's the matter?"

"I still don't understand you, Ben. It *was* real. I *know* it was. The bird flying at me across the Green, the smell of coffee and cigars. That faint breeze you always get sitting there. You know, the way the air circulates from the tunnels at the back. And other things, too."

She had closed her eyes, remembering.

"The faint buzz of background conversation. Plates and glasses clinking. The faint hum of the factories far below in the stack. That constant vibration that's there in everything." She opened her eyes and looked at him pleadingly. "It *was* real, Ben. Tell me it was."

He looked back at her, shaking his head. "No. That was all on the tape. Every last bit of it."

"No!" She shook her head fiercely. "I mean, I saw you there. Sitting there across from me. It *was* you. I know it was. You said . . ." She strained to remember, then nodded to herself. "You said that I shouldn't be afraid of them. You said that it was their instinct to fly."

"I said that once, yes. But not to you. And not in the Cafe Burgundy."

She sat up, her hands grabbing at his arms, feeling the smooth texture of the cloth, then reaching up to touch his face, feeling the roughness of his cheeks where he had yet to shave. Again he laughed, but softly now.

"You can't tell, can you? Which is real. This or the other thing. And yet you're here, Catherine. Here, with me. Now."

She looked at him a moment longer, then tore her gaze away, frightened and confused.

"That before," he said, "that thing you thought happened. That was a fiction. My fiction. It never happened. *I made it.*"

He reached out, holding her chin with one hand, gently turning her face until she was looking at him again. "But this— this is real. This now." He moved his face down to hers, brushing her lips with his own.

Her eyes grew large, a vague understanding coming into her face. "Then . . ." But it was as if she had reached out to grasp at something, only to have it vanish before her eyes. The light faded from her face. She looked down, shaking her head.

He straightened up, stepping out from the frame. Taking his blue silk *pau* from the bed he turned back, offering it to her. "Here, put this on."

She took the robe, handling it strangely, staring at it as if uncertain whether it existed or not; as if, at any moment, she would wake again and find it all a dream.

He stood there, watching her, his eyes searching hers for answers, then turned away.

"Put it on, Catherine. Put it on and I'll make some coffee."

━━━━━━

SHE LAY THERE on his bed, his blue silk *pau* wrapped about her, a mound of pillows propped up behind her, sipping at her coffee.

Ben was pacing the room, pausing from time to time to look across at her, then moving on, gesturing as he talked, his movements extravagant, expansive. He seemed energized, his powerful, athletic form balanced between a natural grace and an unnatural watchfulness, like some strange, magnificent beast, intelligent beyond mere knowing. His eyes flashed as he spoke, while his hands turned in the air as if they fashioned it, molding it into new forms, new shapes.

She watched him, mesmerized. Before now she had had only a vague idea of what he was, but now she knew. As her mind cleared she had found herself awed by the immensity of his achievement. *It had been so real . . .*

He paused beside the empty frame, one hand resting lightly against the upright.

"When I said I had a problem, I didn't realize how wrong it was to think of it as such. You see, it wasn't something that could be circumvented with a bit of technical trickery; it was more a question of taking greater pains. A question of harnessing my energies more intensely. Of being more watchful."

She smiled at that. As if anyone could be more watchful than he.

"So I began with a kind of cartoon. Ten frames a second, rough-cast. That gave me the pace, the shape of the thing. Then I developed it a stage further. Put in the detail. Recorded it at twenty-five a second. Finally I polished and honed it, perfecting each separate strand, rerecording at fifty a second. Slowly making it more real."

His hands made a delicate little movement, as if drawing the finest of wires from within a tight wad of fibers.

"It occurred to me that there really was no other way of doing it. I simply had to make it as real as I possibly could."

"But how? I can't see how you did it. It's . . ." She shrugged, laughing, amazed by him. "No. It's simply not possible. You *couldn't* have!"

And yet he had.

"How?" He grew very still. A faint smile played on his lips, then was gone. For a moment she didn't understand what he was doing with his body, with the expression on his face. Then, suddenly, her mouth fell open, shocked by the accuracy of his imitation, his stance, the very look of him.

And then he spoke. "But how? I can't see how you did it. It's . . ." He shrugged and laughed, a soft, feminine laugh of surprise. "No. It's simply not possible. You *couldn't* have!"

It was perfect. Not *her* exactly, yet a perfect copy all the same of her gestures, her facial movements, her voice. Every nuance and intonation caught precisely. As if the mirror talked.

She sat forward, spilling her coffee. "That's . . ."

But she could not say. It was frightening. She felt her nerves tingle. For a moment everything slowed about her. She had the sensation of falling, then checked herself.

He was watching her, seeing how she looked: all the time watching her, like a camera eye, noting and storing every last nuance of her behavior.

"You have to look, Catherine. Really look at things. You have to try to see them from the other side. To get right inside of them and see how they feel. There's no other way."

He paused, looking at her differently now, as if gauging whether she was still following him. She nodded, her fingers wiping absently at the spilled coffee on his robe, but her eyes were half-lidded now, uncertain.

"An artist—any artist—is an actor. His function is mimetic, even at its most expressive. And, like an actor, he must learn to play his audience." He smiled, opening out his arms as if to encompass the world, his eyes shining darkly with the enormousness of his vision. "You've seen a tiny piece of it. You've glimpsed what it can be. But it's bigger than that, Catherine. Much, much bigger. What you experienced today was but the merest suggestion of its final form."

He laughed, a short, sharp explosion of laughter that was like a shout of joy.

"*The* art—that's what I'm talking about! The thing all true artists dream of!"

Slowly he brought down his arms. The smile faded on his lips and his eyes grew suddenly fierce. Clenching his fists, he curled them in toward his chest, hunching his body into itself like a dancer's. For a moment he held himself there, tensed, the whole of him gathered there at the center.

"Not art like you know it now. No . . ." He shook his head, as if in great pain. "No. This would be something almost unendurable. Something terrible and yet beautiful. Too beautiful for words."

He laughed coldly, his eyes burning now with an intensity that frightened her.

"It would be an art to fear, Catherine. An art so cold it would pierce the heart with its iciness yet so hot that it would blaze like a tiny sun, burning in the darkness of the skull.

"Can you imagine that? Can you imagine what such an art would be like?" His laughter rang out again, a pitiless, hideous sound. "That would be no art for the weak. No. Such an art would destroy the little men!"

She shuddered, unable to take her eyes from him. He was like a demon now, his eyes like dark, smoldering coals. His body seemed transfigured; horrible, almost alien.

She sat forward sharply, the cup falling from her hands.

Across from her Ben saw it fall and noted how it lay; saw how its contents spread across the carpet. Saw, and stored the memory.

He looked up at her, surprised, seeing how her breasts had slipped from within the robe and lay between the rich blue folds of cloth, exposed, strangely different.

And as he looked, desire beat up in him fiercely, like a raging fire.

He sat beside her, reaching within the robe to gently touch the soft warmth of her flesh, his hands moving slowly upward until they cupped her breasts. Then, lowering his face to hers, he let his lips brush softly against her lips.

She tensed, trembling in his arms; then, suddenly, she was pressing up against him, her mouth pushing urgently against his, her arms pulling him down. He shivered, amazed by the sudden change in her, the hunger in her eyes.

For a moment he held back, looking down into her face, surprised by the strength of what he suddenly felt. Then, gently, tenderly, he pushed her down, accepting what she offered, casting off the bright, fierce light that had had him in its grasp only moments before, letting himself slip down into the darkness of her, like a stone falling into the heart of a deep, dark well.

CHAPTER FOURTEEN

The Lost Bride

⌐⌐⌐⌐⌐⌐⌐⌐⌐

"WELL, MINISTER HENG, what was it you wished to see me about?"

Heng Yu had been kneeling, his head touched to the cold, stone floor. Now he rose, looking up at his T'ang for the first time.

Li Shai Tung was sitting in the throne of state, his tall, angular body clothed in imperial yellow. The Council of Ministers had ended an hour earlier, but Heng Yu had stayed on, requesting a private audience with his T'ang. Three broad steps led up to the presense dais. At the bottom of those steps stood the T'ang's Chancellor, Chung Hu-yan. In the past few months, as the old man had grown visibly weaker, more power had devolved onto the shoulders of the capable and honest Chung; and it was to Chung that Heng had gone, immediately the Council had finished. Now Chung gave the slightest smile as he looked at Heng.

"I am grateful for this chance to talk with you, *Chieh Hsia*," Heng began. "I would not have asked had it not been a matter of the greatest urgency."

The T'ang smiled. "Of course. But please, Heng Yu, be brief. I am already late for my next appointment."

Heng bowed again, conscious of the debt he owed the Chancellor for securing this audience.

"It is about young Shepherd, *Chieh Hsia*."

The T'ang raised an eyebrow. "Hal's boy? What of him?"

"He is at College, I understand, Chieh Hsia."

Li Shai Tung laughed. "You know it for a certainty, Heng Yu, else you would not have mentioned the matter. But what of it? Is the boy in trouble?"

Heng hesitated. "I am not sure, Chieh Hsia. It does not seem that he is in any *immediate* danger, yet certain facts have come to my notice that suggest he might be in the days ahead."

Li Shai Tung leaned forward, his left hand smoothing his plaited beard.

"I see. But why come to me, Heng Yu? This is a matter for General Nocenzi, surely?"

Heng gave a small bow. "Normally I would agree, Chieh Hsia, but in view of the father's illness and the boy's possible future relationship with Prince Yuan . . ."

He left the rest unsaid, but Li Shai Tung took his point. Heng was right. This was much more important than any normal Security matter. Whatever Ben said just now of his intentions, he had been bred to be Li Yuan's advisor; and genes, surely, would win out eventually? For anything to happen to him now, therefore, was unthinkable.

"What do you suggest, Heng Yu?"

In answer, Heng Yu bowed, then held out the scroll he had prepared in advance. Chung Hu-yan took it from him and handed it up to the T'ang who unfurled it and began to read. When he had finished he looked back at Heng.

"Good. You have my sanction for this, Heng Yu. I'll sign this and give the General a copy of the authority. But don't delay. I want this acted upon at once."

"Of course, Chieh Hsia."

"And Heng Yu . . ."

"Yes, Chieh Hsia?"

"I am in your debt in this matter. If there is any small favor I can offer in return, let Chung Hu-yan know and it shall be done."

Heng Yu bowed low. "I am overwhelmed by your generosity, Chieh Hsia, but, forgive me, it would not be right for me to seek advantage from what was, after all, my common duty to my Lord. As ever, Chieh Hsia, I ask for nothing but to serve you."

Straightening, he saw the smile of satisfaction on the old

man's lips and knew he had acted wisely. There were things he needed, things the T'ang could have made easier for him; but none, at present, that were outside his own broad grasp. To have the T'ang's good opinion, however, that was another thing entirely. He bowed a second time, then lowered his head to Chung Hu-yan, backing away. One day, he was certain, such temporary sacrifices would pay off, would reap a thousandfold the rewards he now so lightly gave away. In the meantime he would find out what this business with the Novacek boy was all about, would get to the bottom of it and then make sure that it was from him that the T'ang first heard of it.

As the great doors closed behind him, he looked about him at the great halls and corridors of the palace, smiling. Yes, the old T'ang's days were numbered now. And Prince Yuan, when his time came, would need a Chancellor. A younger man than Chung Hu-yan. A man he could rely on absolutely.

Heng Yu walked on, past bowing servants, a broad smile lighting his features.

So why not himself? Why not Heng Yu, whose record was unblemished, whose loyalty and ability were unquestioned?

As he approached them, the huge, leather-paneled outer doors of the palace began to ease back, spilling bright sunlight into the shadows of the broad high-ceilinged corridor. Outside, the shaven-headed guards of the T'ang's elite squad bowed low as he moved between them. Savoring the moment, Heng Yu, Minister to Li Shai Tung, T'ang of City Europe, gave a soft small laugh of pleasure. *Yes*, he thought, looking up at the great circle of the sun. *Why not?*

⸻

CATHERINE STOOD in the doorway, looking across at him. Ben was sitting on the edge of the bed, his head pushed forward, his shoulders hunched, staring at the frame without seeing it.

He had awakened full of life, had smiled and kissed her tenderly and told her to wait while he brought her breakfast, but he had been gone too long; she had found him in the kitchen, staring vacantly at his hands, the breakfast things untouched. "What is it?" she had asked. "What's happened?" But he had walked past her as if she wasn't there. Had gone into the other room and sat down on the bed. So still, so self-engrossed that it had frightened her.

"Ben?" she said now, setting the tray down beside him. "I've cooked breakfast. Won't you have some with me?"

He glanced up at her. "What?"

"Breakfast." She smiled, then knelt beside him, putting her hand on his knee.

"Ah . . ." His smile was wan; was merely the token of a smile.

"What is it, Ben? Please. I've not seen you like this before. It must be something."

For a moment he did nothing. Then he reached into the pocket of his gown and took something out, offering it to her.

It was a letter. She took it from him, handling it with care—with a feeling for its strangeness.

She sat on the floor beside his feet, handling the letter delicately, as if it were old and fragile like the book he had given her, taking the folded sheets and smoothing them out upon her lap.

For a moment she hesitated, a sudden sense of foreboding washing over her. What if it were another woman? Some past lover of his, writing to reclaim him—to take him back from her? Or was it something else? Something he had difficulty telling her?

She glanced at him, then looked back, beginning to read. After only a few moments she looked up. "Your sister?"

He nodded. "She wants to come and visit me. To see what I'm up to."

"Ah . . ." But strangely, she felt no relief. There was something about the tone of the letter that troubled her. "And you don't want that?"

Again he nodded, his lips pressed tightly together.

For a moment she looked past him at the books on the shelf beside his bed. Books she had never heard of before, with titles that were as strange as the leather binding of their covers; books like Polidori's *Ernestus Berchtold*, Helme's *The Farmer of Inglewood Forest*, Poe's *Eleanora*, Brown's *The Power of Sympathy* and Byron's *Manfred*. She stared at them a moment, as if to make sense of them, then looked back at him.

Folding the sheets, she slipped them back inside the envelope, then held it out to him.

"I've come here to get away from all that," he said, taking the letter. He looked at it fiercely for a moment, as if it were a living thing, then put it back in his pocket. "This—" he gestured at the frame, the books and prints on the walls, the personal things that were scattered all about the room, then shrugged. "Well, it's different, that's all."

She thought of Lotte and Wolf, beginning to understand. "It's too close at home. Is that what you mean? And you feel stifled by that?"

He looked down at his hand—at the left hand where the wrist was ridged—then looked back at her.

"Maybe."

She saw how he smiled faintly, looking inward, as if to piece it all together in his head.

"Your breakfast," she said, reminding him. "You should eat it. It's getting cold."

He looked back, suddenly focusing on her again. Then, as if he had made his mind up about something, he reached out and took her hand, drawing her up toward him.

"Forget breakfast. Come. Let's go to bed again."

━━━━━━

"Well? Have you the file?"

Heng Chian-ye turned, snapping his fingers. At once his servant drew nearer and, bowing, handed him a silk-bound folder.

"I think you'll find everything you need in there," Heng said, handing it across. "But tell me, Novacek, why did you want to know about that one? Has he crossed you in some way?"

Sergey Novacek glanced at Heng, then looked back at the file. "It's none of your business, but no, he hasn't crossed me. It's just that our friend Shepherd is a bit of a mystery, and I hate mysteries."

Heng Chian-ye stared at Novacek a moment, controlling the cold anger he felt merely at being in his presence. The *Hung Mao* had no idea what trouble he had got him into.

"You've made your own investigations, I take it?" he said, asking another of the questions his uncle had insisted he ask.

Novacek looked up, closing the file. "Is this all?"

Heng smiled. "You know how it is, the richer the man, the less there is on file. If they can, they buy their anonymity."

"And you think that's what happened here?"

"The boy's father is very rich. Rich enough to buy his way into Oxford without any qualifications whatsoever."

Novacek nodded, a hint of bitterness overspilling into his words. "I know. I've seen the College records."

"Ah . . ." Heng gave the briefest nod, noting what he had said.

"And the bronze?"

Heng Chian-ye turned slightly. Again the servant approached him, this time carrying a simple ice-cloth sack. Heng took the sack and turned, facing Novacek. His expression was suddenly much harder, his eyes coldly hostile.

"This cost me dear. If there had been any way I could have borrowed a million *yuan* I would have done so, rather than meet my uncle's terms. But before I hand it over, I want to know why you wanted it. Why you thought it worth a million *yuan*."

Novacek stared at him a moment, meeting the Han's hostility with his own. Then he looked down, smiling sourly. "You call us big-noses behind our backs, but you've quite a nose yourself, haven't you, Heng?"

Heng's eyes flared with anger, but he held back, remembering what Heng Yu had said. On no account was he to provoke Novacek.

"And if I say you can't have it?"

Novacek laughed. "That's fine. You can pay me the million. In installments, if you like. However, I'll charge you interest on it. A hundred-and-fifty thousand a year." He looked up again, meeting Heng's eyes. "But that's rather more than what you get, so I hear. You might find it . . . *difficult* to make ends meet. It takes a fair bit to live as richly as you do."

Heng swallowed; then, almost brutally, he thrust the sack into the other man's hands.

Sergey watched Heng a moment, noting how angry he was and wondering about it, then looked down at the plain white sack he held, feeling the shape of the bronze through the flesh-thin cloth, a clear, clean sense of satisfaction—of fulfillment—washing through him.

"Good," he said. "Then we're clear, Heng Chian-ye. I'd say your debt to me was settled, wouldn't you?"

Heng Chian-ye turned, taking three angry steps away from him before turning back, his face almost black with anger, his finger pointing accusingly at his tormentor.

"Take care, Novacek. Next time you might not be so lucky. Next time you could meet with someone who counts honor a lesser thing than I. And then you'll find out what the world really thinks of scum like you."

Sergey stared back at him, smiling insolently. "Go fuck yourself, Heng Chian-ye. You've no more honor than a Triad boss's cock. The only reason you paid up was your fear of losing face in front of your friends. But that's your problem. I've got what I want."

Heng opened his mouth, as if to answer him in kind, then changed his mind. He laughed then shook his head, his voice suddenly colder, more controlled.

"Have you, my friend? Have you now?"

━━━━━

THEY WENT to the Cafe Burgundy and took a table close to the Green, paying to keep the three chairs empty. Catherine sat to Ben's right, the tiered cage of the central pagoda behind her, forming a frame to her pale, flamelike beauty. "My bird," he called her now, and so it seemed fitting. He smiled, studying her profile, then turned and raised a hand to order wine.

He had been quiet all evening, pensive. A second letter had come. It lay inside his jacket pocket unopened. He could feel its gentle pressure against his chest; sense the hidden shape of it.

She, too, had been quiet, but for different reasons. Hers was a broody, jealous silence, the kind he had come to know only too well these last few days.

The waiter came and poured their wine, leaving the unfinished bottle in an ice bucket on the table between them. Ben leaned across and chinked his glass against hers.

She turned her head and looked at him. "What does she want?"

He almost smiled at that, knowing what she really thought. His unexplained absences. The letters. Even his moods. He knew she took these things as signs of his infidelity. But she wasn't certain. Not yet, anyway. And so the brooding silence.

He sipped at his wine then set the glass down. "Here." He took the letter from his pocket and handed it to her.

She narrowed her eyes, suspicious of him, then took the letter from his fingers. For a time she simply stared at it, not certain what he meant by giving it to her. Then she lifted it to her nose and sniffed.

"Open it," he said, amused by her hesitation. "Or give it back and I'll open it. It's from my sister, Meg."

She nodded, only half-convinced, but gave the letter back, watching as he slit it open with his thumbnail and drew out the four slender sheets of paper. Without even glancing at them, he handed them to her.

"Here."

She lowered her eyes, beginning to read, reluctantly at first, but then with a growing interest. Finally, she looked up again, her face changed, more open to him.

"But why didn't you say? That was cruel of you, Ben, leaving me in the dark like that. I thought . . ."

She blushed and looked away. He reached across and took the letter from her.

"Aren't you pleased, Ben? I think it's sweet of her to worry about you. She could stay with me, if you'd like. I've a spare pull-down in my room. She could use that."

He glanced at her, then returned to the letter. Finished, he folded it neatly and slipped it back into his pocket.

"Well?" she said, exasperated by him. "It would be lovely to meet your sister. Really it would."

He poured himself more wine, then drank deeply from his glass, emptying it. She watched him, puzzled.

"What's the matter? What aren't you telling me?"

He shook his head.

"Don't you like her? Is that it?"

He laughed. "What, Meg? No, she's . . ." He smiled strangely, looking down into his empty glass. "She's just perfect." He looked up at her, then reached across, and gently lifting her chin, leaned forward to brush his lips against hers.

She smiled. "That's nice. But what about her?"

"She'll stay with me," he said, dismissing the subject. "Now, what shall we eat?"

She stared at him a moment, then let it go. "I don't care. Surprise me."

He laughed, suddenly, inexplicably, his old self. "Oysters. Let's have oysters."

"Just oysters?"

"No. Not *just* oysters, but a whole platter of oysters. The very best oysters. More than we could possibly eat." He puffed out his cheeks and sat back in his chair, his hands tracing an exaggerated curve about his stomach, miming a grossly swollen gut. He laughed, then sat upright again and turned in his chair, snapping his fingers for a waiter.

The abruptness of the transformation both delighted and disturbed her. It hinted at a side of him she had not seen before, unless it was in that moment when he had mimicked her. She poked her tongue between her teeth, watching him. Laughter at a nearby table distracted her momentarily, making her turn her head. When she looked back he was watching her again, a faint smile on his lips.

"Sometimes you're just plain strange," she said, laughing. "Like this business about your family. What's wrong with talking about them? You never tell me anything."

He shrugged. "It isn't important. That's home. This is here. I like to keep them separate."

She looked down, wondering if he realized what he was saying. She felt hurt by his exclusion, somehow lessened by it.

"It's too close there," he went on. "Too—" he laughed, a short, almost painful laugh, "too intense. You'll find that difficult to understand, I know. I don't hate it, it's just that I need distance from all that. Need something other than what I get there."

He had set down his glass and was pushing at the skin of his left hand with the fingers of his right, looking down at it as he smoothed and stroked the ridged flesh.

"And where, then, do I fit in? Am I real to you, Ben, or am I just something to be got?"

"Maybe," he said, meeting her eyes candidly. "Maybe that's all there is. Different kinds of getting."

She was about to speak—about to say something she would have regretted later—when the laughter rang out again, louder this time. She felt herself go cold, realizing whose voice it was that led the cold, mocking laughter.

Sergey . . .

She turned, seeing him at once. He was no more than twenty feet away from where they were sitting.

He turned in his chair, smiling at her. "Catherine! How *lovely* to see you!"

She could see that he was drunk. He pushed himself up unsteadily from his chair and came across, pulling out the empty chair beside her. Ignoring Ben, he sat, leaning toward her unpleasantly, almost threateningly, as he spoke.

"How *are* you, Catherine, my dear? It's quite a while since we saw *you* here, isn't it?"

He belched, then turned, a sneering smile lighting his reddened face.

"And who's this?" He feigned startled surprise. "My word, if it isn't our friend, the genius!" He made a mocking bow of politeness, but when he straightened up his face had hardened and his eyes were cold with malice.

"I've been wanting to have a few words with you, *friend.*"

There was an ugliness in the emphatic way he said the last word. A hint of violence.

She watched, her irritation with Ben transformed into fear for him. She knew just how dangerous Sergey could be when he was in this kind of mood.

Ben smiled and turned to call the waiter over. *Yes,* she thought, *that's best. End it now, before it gets out of hand.* But instead of asking the waiter to remove Sergey, Ben ordered a fresh bottle of the house wine and an extra glass. He turned back, facing his antagonist.

"You'll have a drink with us, I hope?"

Sergey gave a snort of surprise and annoyance. "I really can't believe you, Shepherd. You're such a smooth shit, aren't you? You think you can buy the world."

"Sergey—" she began, but he banged his fist down hard, glaring at her.

"Shut up, Catherine! You might learn a few things about smiling boy here."

She turned away, shutting her eyes, wishing it would stop.

Sergey leaned forward, his whole manner openly hostile now. "You're not from here, are you, Shepherd?"

Ben was silent, musing.

"You're not, are you?"

Catherine opened her eyes and looked across. There was a faint smile on Ben's lips, a wistful little smile.

"I've been doing a little digging," Sergey said, leaning across the table toward Ben, his breath heavy with wine. "And guess what I found out?" He laughed coldly. "Our friend here bought his way into Oxford. Just like he buys up everything. They waived the rules to let him in."

Catherine shook her head. "I don't follow you. I—"

Sergey huffed, disgust written large on his face. "He's a charlatan, that's what he is. He shouldn't be here. He's like all the other parasites. The only difference is that he's not a Han." He laughed brutally, then turned and looked at her again, angry now. "Unlike the rest of us, Shepherd here has no qualifications. He's never passed an exam in his life. As for work—" The laugh was broken, the sneer in the voice pointed. At nearby tables people had broken off their own conversations to see what was going on. "He's never attended a single tutorial. Never handed in a single essay. And as for sitting the end of year exams, forget it. He goes home before all that. He's above it, you see. Or at least, his money is."

There was a flutter of laughter at that. But Sergey was not to be distracted by it. He was in full flow now, one hand pointing at his target as he spoke.

"Yes, he's a strange one, this one. He's rich and he's obviously connected. Right up to the top, so they say. But he's something of a mystery, too. He's not from the City. And that's why he despises us."

She stared at Sergey, not understanding. What did he mean? *Everyone* came from the City. There was nowhere else to come from. Unless . . . She thought of the handwritten letters—of the strangeness of so many things connected with Ben—and for a moment felt uncertainty wash over her. Then she remembered what he was doing: recollected what she herself had experienced in the frame.

"You're wrong, Sergey. You don't understand—"

Sergey pulled himself up, went around the table, and stood there, leaning over Shepherd. "No. I understand only too well. He's a fucking toad, that's what he is. A piece of slime."

She watched the two of them anxiously, terrified of what was going to happen. "He's drunk," she said pleadingly. "He doesn't mean it, Ben. It's the drink talking." But she was afraid for him. He didn't know Sergey, didn't know how vicious his temper was.

Ben was looking at her, ignoring the other man. He seemed calm, unaffected by the words, by the physical presence of the other man above him.

"Let him have his say, love. It's only words."

It was the first time he had called her love, but she scarcely noticed it. All she could see was that the very mildness of Ben's words acted to inflame Sergey's anger.

"You're wrong," he said icily. "It's more than words."

Ben turned and looked up at him, undaunted. "When a fool tells you you're wrong, you rejoice."

It was too much. Sergey lunged at him with both hands, trying to get a grip on his neck, but Ben pushed him away and stood, facing him. Sergey was breathing heavily, furious now. He made a second grab at Ben and got hold of his right arm, trying to twist it round behind his back and force him down onto his knees.

Catherine was on her feet, screaming. "*No!* Please, Sergey! Don't hurt him! Please don't hurt him!"

Waiters were running toward them, trying to force a way through the crowd and break it up, but the press around the table was too great.

Using brute strength Sergey forced Ben down, grunting with the effort. Then, suddenly, Ben seemed to yield and roll forward, throwing his opponent off balance. Sergey stumbled and fell against a chair. When he got up, there was blood running from beneath his eye.

"You bastard . . ."

With a bellow of rage he threw himself at Ben again, but Ben's reflexes were much quicker. As Sergey lunged past him, he moved aside and caught hold of Sergey's right hand, turning the wrist.

The snap of breaking bones was audible. Sergey shrieked and went down onto his knees, cradling the useless hand.

For a moment Ben stood over him, his legs planted firmly apart, his chest rising and falling erratically; then he shuddered.

"I didn't mean . . ."

But it was done. The sculptor's hand was crushed and broken. Useless, it began to swell. Sergey pushed at it tenderly with one finger of the other hand, then moaned and slumped forward, unconscious.

Ben stepped back, away, his eyes taking in everything. Then he turned and looked at Catherine. She was standing there, her hands up to her mouth, staring down at the injured man.

"Ben . . ." she said softly, her voice barely in control. "Oh, Ben. What have you done?"

———————

M E G L O O K E D around her as they walked down Main toward the transit. The air was still, like the air inside a sealed box. It was the first thing she had noticed. There was no movement in the air, no rustling of leaves, none of the small, soft sounds that moving water makes, no hum of insects. Instead, small boys walked between the flower boxes with spray cans, pollinating the flowers, or watered the huge oaks that rested in deep troughs set into the floor. From their branches hung cages—huge, ornately gilded cages filled with bright-colored birds. But nothing flew here. Nothing bent and danced in the open wind.

"They like it like this," Ben said, as if that explained it all. Then he frowned and turned to look at her. "But it doesn't satisfy. Nothing here satisfies. It's all surfaces. There's nothing deep here. Nothing rooted."

It was Meg's first full morning in the City, though morning here meant little more than a change in the intensity of the overhead lighting. Outside, beyond the City's walls, it was still dark. But here that fact of nature did not matter. Throughout City Europe, time was uniform, governed not by local variation but in accordance with the rising and setting of the sun over the City's eastern edge.

Morning. It was one more imperfect mimicry. Like the trees, the flowers, the birds, the word lost its sharp precision here without a sun to make it real.

They went up fifty levels to the College grounds. This was what they termed an "open deck" and there was a sense of space and airiness. Here there were no tight warrens of corridors, no ceiling almost within reach wherever one went; even so, Meg felt stifled. It was not like being in a house, where the door opened out onto the freshness of a garden. Here the eyes met walls with every movement.

She had forgotten how awful it was. Like being in a cage.

"How can you stand it here?"

He looked about him, then reached out, taking her hand. "I've missed you, you know. It's been . . . difficult here."

"Difficult?"

They had stopped in the central hexagonal space. On every side great tiers of balconies sloped back gently toward the ceiling, their surfaces transparent, reflecting and refracting light.

"You should come home, Ben. All this," she looked about her, shaking her head, "it's no good for you."

"Maybe," he said, looking away from her. "And yet I've got to try to understand it. It may be awful, but this is what *is*, Meg. This is all that remains of the world we made."

She began to shake her head, to remind him of home, but checked herself. It was not the time to tell him why she'd come. Besides, talking of home would only infuriate him. And perhaps he was right. Perhaps he did have to try to understand it. So that he could return, satisfied, knowing there was nothing else— nothing *missing* from his world.

"You seem depressed, Ben. Is it just the place? Or is it something else?"

He turned, half smiling. "No. You're right. It's not just the place." He made a small despairing gesture, then looked up at one of the great tiers of balconies. Through the glasslike walls one could see people—dozens, hundreds, thousands of people. People, everywhere you looked. One was never alone here. Even in his rooms he felt the press of them against the walls.

He looked back at her, his face suddenly naked, open to her. "I get lonely here, Meg. More lonely than I thought it possible to feel."

She stared at him, then lowered her eyes, disturbed by the sudden insight into what he had been feeling. She would never have guessed.

As they walked on he began to tell her about the fight. When he had finished she turned to face him, horrified.

"But they can't blame you for that, Ben. He provoked you. You were only defending yourself, surely?"

He smiled tightly. "Yes. And the authorities have accepted that. Several witnesses came forward to defend me against his accusation. But that only makes it worse, somehow."

"But why? If it happened as you say it did."

He looked away, staring across the open space. "I offered to pay full costs. For a new synthetic, if necessary. But he refused. It seems he plans to wear his broken hand like a badge."

He looked back at her, his eyes filled with pain and hurt and anger. And something else.

"You shouldn't blame yourself, Ben. It was *his* fault, not yours."

He hesitated, then shook his head. "So it seems. So I made it seem. But the truth is, I enjoyed it, Meg. I enjoyed pushing him. To the limit and then . . ." He made a small pushing movement with one hand. "I *enjoyed* it. Do you understand that, Meg?"

She watched her brother, not understanding. It was a side of him she had never seen, and for all his words she couldn't quite believe it.

"It's guilt, Ben. You're feeling guilty for something that wasn't your fault."

He laughed and looked away. "Guilt? No, it wasn't guilt. I snapped his hand like a rotten twig. Knowing I could do it. Don't you understand? I could see how drunk he was, how easily he could be handled."

He turned his head, bringing it closer to hers, his voice dropping to a whisper.

"I could have winded him. Could have held him off until the

waiters came to break things up. But I didn't. I *wanted* to hurt him. Wanted to see what it was like. I engineered it, Meg. Do you understand? I set it up."

She shuddered, then shook her head, staring at him intently now. "No." But his eyes were fierce, assertive. What if he *had*?

"So what did you learn? What *was* it like?"

He looked down at her hand where his own enclosed it.

"If I close my eyes I can see it all. Can feel what it was like. How easily I led him. His weight and speed. How much pressure it took, bone against bone, to break it. And that knowledge is . . ." He shrugged, then looked up at her again, his hand exerting the gentlest of pressure on hers. "I don't know. It's power, I guess."

"And you enjoyed that?"

She was watching him closely now, forcing her revulsion down, trying to help him, to understand him.

"Perhaps you're right," he said, ignoring her question. "Perhaps I ought to go home."

"And yet something keeps you."

He nodded, his eyes still focused on her hand. "That's right. I'm missing something. I know I am. Something I can't see."

"But there's nothing here, Ben. Just look about you. Nothing."

He looked away, shrugging, seeming to agree with her, but he was thinking of the *Lu Nan Jen*, the Oven Man, and about Catherine. He had been wrong about those things—surprised by them. So maybe there was more, much more than he'd imagined.

He turned, looking back at her. "Anyway, you'd better go. Your appointment's in an hour."

She looked back at him, her disappointment clear. "I thought you were coming with me."

He had told Catherine he would meet her at eleven, had promised he would show her more of the old paintings; but seeing the look on Meg's face, he knew he could not let her go alone.

"All right," he said, smiling, "I'll come to the clinic with you. But then I've things to do. Important things."

BEN LOOKED about him at the rich decor of the anteroom and frowned. Such luxury was unexpected at this low level. Added to the tightness of the security screening it made him think that there must be some darker reason than financial consideration for establishing the Melfi Clinic in such an unusual setting.

The walls and ceiling were an intense blue, while underfoot a matching carpet was decorated with a simple yellow border. To one side stood a plinth on which rested a bronze of a pregnant woman—*Hung Mao*, not Han—her naked form the very archetype of fecundity. Across from it hung the only painting in the room—a huge canvas, its lightness standing out against the blue-black of the walls. It was an oak, a giant oak, standing in the plush green of an ancient English field.

In itself, the painting was unsurprising, yet in context it was, again, unexpected. Why this? he asked himself. Why here? He moved closer, then narrowed his eyes, looking at the tiny acorn that lay in the left foreground of the composition, trying to make out the two tiny initials that were carved into it.

AS. As what? he thought, smiling, thinking of all those comparatives he had learned as a very young child. As strong as an ox. As wily as a fox. As proud as a peacock. As sturdy as an oak.

And as long-lived. He stared at it, trying to make out its significance in the scheme of things; then he turned, looking back at Meg. "You've come here before?"

She nodded. "Every six months."

"And Mother? Does she come here, too?"

Meg laughed. "Of course. The first time I came, I came with her."

He looked surprised. "I didn't know."

"Don't worry yourself, Ben. It's women's business, that's all. It's just easier for them to do it all here than for them to come into the Domain. Easier and less disruptive."

He nodded, looking away, but he wasn't satisfied. There was something wrong with all this. Something . . .

He turned as the panel slid back and a man came through, a tall, rather heavily built Han, his broad face strangely nondescript, his neat black hair swept back from a polished brow. His full-length russet gown was trimmed with a dark-green band of silk. As he came into the room he smiled and rubbed his hands together nervously, giving a small bow of his head to Meg before turning toward Ben.

"Forgive me, *Shih* Shepherd, but we were not expecting you. I am the Senior Consultant here, Tung T'an. If I had known that you planned to accompany your sister, I would have suggested . . ." He hesitated, then not sure he should continue, he smiled and bowed his head. "Anyway, now that you *are* here, you had better come through, neh?"

Ben stared back at the Consultant, making him avert his eyes. The man was clearly put out that he was there. But why should that be if this were a routine matter? Why should his presence disturb things, even if this were "women's business"?

"Meg," the Consultant said, turning to her. "It is good to see you again. We expected you next week, of course, but no matter. It will take us but a moment to prepare everything."

Ben frowned. But she had said . . . He looked at her, his eyes demanding to know why she hadn't told him that her appointment was not for another week, but her look told him to be patient.

They followed Tung T'an into a suite of rooms every bit as luxurious as the first. Big, spacious rooms, decorated as if this were First Level, not the Mids. Tung T'an tapped out a combination on a doorlock, then turned, facing Ben again, more composed now.

"If you would be kind enough to wait here, *Shih* Shepherd, we'll try not to keep you too long. The tests are quite routine, but they take a little time. In the meantime, is there anything one of my assistants can bring you?"

"You want me to wait out here?"

"Ben . . ." Meg's eyes pleaded with him not to make trouble.

He smiled. "All right. Perhaps you'd ask them to bring me a pot of coffee and a newsfax."

The Consultant smiled and turned to do as Ben asked, but Meg was looking at him strangely now. She knew her brother well. Well enough to know he never touched a newsfax.

"What are you up to?" she whispered, as soon as Tung T'an was out of the room.

He smiled, the kind of innocuous-seeming smile that was enough to make alarm bells start ringing in her head. "Nothing. I'm just looking after my kid sister, that's all. Making sure she gets to the Clinic *on time.*"

She looked down, the evasiveness of the gesture not lost on Ben.

"I'll explain it all, Ben. I promise I will. But not now." She glanced up at him, then shook her head. "Look, I *promise.* Later. But behave yourself while you're here. Please, Ben. I'll only be an hour or so."

He relented, smiling back at her. "Okay. I'll try to be good."

A young girl brought him coffee and a pile of newsfax, then took Meg through to get changed. Ben sat there for a time, pretending to look at the nonsense on the page before him, all the while surreptitiously looking around. As far as he could see he was not being observed. At the outer gates security was tight, but here there was nothing. Why was that? It was almost standard for companies to keep a tight watch on their premises.

He stood up, stretching, miming tiredness, then walked across the room, looking closer at the walls, the vents, making sure. No. There was nothing. It was almost certain that he wasn't being observed.

Good. Then he'd delve a little deeper, answer a few of the questions that were stacking up in his head.

He went out into the corridor and made his way back to the junction. Doors led off to either side. He stopped, listening. There was the faintest buzz of voices to his right, but to his left there was nothing. He tried the left-hand door, drawing the sliding door back in a single silent movement. If challenged he would say he was looking for a toilet.

The tiny room was empty. He slid the door closed behind him and looked around. Again there seemed to be no cameras. As if they had no need for them. And yet they must, surely, if they had a regular clientele?

He crossed the room with three quick paces and tried the door on the far side. It too was open. Beyond was a long narrow room, brightly lit, the left-hand wall filled with filing cabinets.

Eureka! he thought, allowing himself a tiny smile. And yet it seemed strange, very strange, that he should be able to gain access to their files so easily.

As if they weren't expecting anyone to try.

His brow wrinkled, trying to work it out; then he released the thought, moving down the line of cabinets quickly, looking for the number he had glimpsed on the card Meg had shown at the gates. He found it without difficulty and tried the drawer. It opened at a touch.

Meg's file was missing. Of course . . . they would have taken it with them. Like a lot of private clinics most of the work was of a delicate nature, and records were kept in this old-fashioned manner, the reports handwritten by the consultants, no computer copy kept. Because it would not do . . .

He stopped, astonished, noting the name on the file that lay beneath his fingertips. A file that had a tiny acorn on the label next to the familiar name.

Women's business . . .

And then he laughed, softly, quietly, knowing now why Tung T'an had been so flustered earlier. *They were here! They were all here!* He flicked through quickly and found it. *His* file, handwritten like all the rest, and containing his full medical record—including a copy of his genetic chart.

He shivered, a strange mixture of pain and elation coursing through his veins. It was as he'd thought—Augustus *had* been right. Amos's experiment was still going on.

He stared at the genetic chart, matching it to the one he held in memory—the one he had first seen in the back of his great-grandfather's journal that afternoon in the old house, the day he had lost his hand.

The two charts were identical.

He flicked through the files again until he came across his father's. For a time he was silent, scanning the pages, then he looked up, nodding to himself. Here it was—confirmation. A small note, dated February 18, 2185. The date his father had been sterilized. Sterilized without knowing it, on the pretext of a simple medical procedure.

A date roughly five years before Ben had been born.

He flicked through again, looking now for his mother's file, then pulled it out. He knew now where to look. Anticipated what it would say. Even so, he was surprised by what he read.

The implant had been made seven months before his birth, which meant that he had been nurtured elsewhere for eight weeks before he had been placed in his mother's womb. He touched his tongue to his teeth, finding the thought of it strangely discomfiting. It made sense of course—by eight weeks they could tell whether the embryo was healthy or otherwise. His embryo would have been—what?—an inch long by then. Limbs, fingers and toes, ears, nose, and mouth would have formed. Yes. By eight weeks they would have been sure.

It made sense. Of course it did. But the thought of himself, in a false uterus, placed in a machine, disturbed him. He had always thought . . .

He let his hands rest on the edge of the drawer, overcome suddenly by the reality of what he had found. He had *known*—some part of him had believed it ever since that day when he had looked at Augustus's journal—even so, he had not been prepared. Not at core. It had been head knowledge, detached from him. Until now.

He shuddered. So it was true. Hal was not his father, Hal was his brother. Like his so-called great-great-grandfather Robert, his great-grandfather Augustus, and his grandfather James. Brothers, all of them. Every last one of them seeds of the old man. Sons of Amos Shepherd and his wife, Alexandra.

He flicked through until he found her file, then laughed. Of course! He should have known. The name of the clinic—Melfi. It was his great-great-great-grandmother's maiden name. No. His *mother's* maiden name.

Which meant . . .

He tried another drawer. Again it opened to his touch, revealing the edges of files, none of them marked with that important acorn symbol. And inside? Inside the files were blank.

"It's all of a piece," he said quietly, nodding to himself. All part of the great illusion Amos built about him. Like the town in the Domain, filled with its android replicants. Like the City his son had designed to his order. All a great charade. A game to perpetuate *his* seed, *his* ideas.

And this, here, was the center of it. The place where Amos's great plan was carried out. That was why it was hidden in the Mids. That was why security was so tight outside and so lax within. No one else came here. No one but the Shepherd women. To be tested, and when the time was right and the scheme demanded it, to have Amos's children implanted into their wombs. No wonder Tung T'an had been disturbed to see him here.

He turned, hearing the door slide back behind him.

It was Tung T'an.

"What in hell's name . . . ?" the Consultant began, then fell silent, seeing the open file on the drawer in front of Ben. He swallowed. "You should not be in here, *Shih* Shepherd."

Ben laughed. "No, I shouldn't. But I am."

The man took a step toward him, then stopped, frowning, trying, without asking, to ascertain how much Ben knew. "If you would leave now . . ."

"Of course. I've seen all I needed to see."

The Han's face twitched. "You misunderstand . . ."

Ben shook his head. "Not at all, Tung T'an. You see, I knew. I've known for some time. But not how. Or where. All this . . ." he indicated the files. "It just confirms things for me."

"You *knew?*" Tung T'an laughed and shook his head. "Knew what, *Shih* Shepherd? There's nothing to know."

"As you wish, Tung T'an."

He saw the movement in the man's eyes, the assessment and reassessment. Then Tung T'an gave a reluctant nod. "You were never meant to see any of this. It is why—"

"Why you kept the Shepherd males away from here." Ben smiled. "Wise. To make it all seem unimportant. Women's business. But old Amos wasn't quite so thorough here, was he?"

"I'm sorry?"

Ben shook his head. No, Tung T'an knew nothing of just how thorough Amos could be when he wanted to. The old town was an example of that, complete down to every last detail. But this—in a sense this was a disappointment. It was almost as if . . .

He laughed, for the first time seriously considering the idea.

What if Amos had *wanted* one of them to discover all this? What if that, too, were part of the plan—a kind of test?

The more he thought of it, the more sense it made. The boarded-up old house, the hidden room, the enclosed garden, the lost journal. None of them were really necessary unless they were meant to act as clues—doors to be passed through until the last door was opened, the final revelation made. No. You did not preserve what you wished to conceal. You destroyed it. And yet . . .

And yet he had stumbled on this by accident. Coming here had not been his doing, it had been Meg's. Unless . . .

She had come a week early. Why? What reason could she have had for doing that. A week. Surely it would have made no difference?

Tung T'an was still staring at him. "You place me in an impossible situation, *Shih* Shepherd."

"Why so, *Shih* Tung? Think of it. You can't erase what I've seen, or what I know. Not without destroying me. And you can't do that." He laughed. "After all, it's what all of this here is dedicated to preserving, isn't it? You have no other function."

Tung T'an lowered his head. "Even so—"

Ben interrupted him. "You need say nothing, Tung T'an. Not even that I was here. For my own part I will act as if this place did not and does not exist. You understand me?" He moved closer to the Han, forcing him by the strength of his will to look up and meet his eyes. "I was never here, Tung T'an. And this conversation . . . it never happened."

Tung T'an swallowed, aware suddenly of the charismatic power of the young man standing before him, then nodded.

"Good. Then go and see to my sister. She's like me. She doesn't like to be kept waiting. Ah, but you know that, don't you, Tung T'an? You, of all people, should know how alike we Shepherds are."

────

MEG SAT across from Ben in the sedan, watching him. He had been quiet since they had come from the clinic. Too quiet. He had been up to something. She had seen how flustered Tung T'an had been when he'd returned to her and knew it had to do with something Ben had said or done. When she'd asked, Ben had denied that anything had passed between him and Tung T'an, but she could tell he was lying. The two had clashed over something. Something important enough for Ben to be worrying about it still.

She tried again. "Was it something to do with me?"

He looked up at her and laughed. "You don't give up, do you?"

She smiled. "Not when it concerns you."

He leaned forward, taking her hands. "It's nothing. Really, sis. If it were important, I'd tell you. Honest."

She laughed. "That doesn't make sense, Ben. If it's not important, then there's no reason for you not to tell me. And if it is, well, you say you'd tell me. So why not just tell me and keep me quiet."

He shrugged. "All right. I'll tell you what I was thinking about. I was thinking about a girl I'd met here. A girl called Catherine. I should have met her, two hours back, but she's probably given up on me now."

Meg looked down, suddenly very still. "A girl?"

He squeezed her hands gently. "A friend of mine. She's been helping me with my work."

Meg looked up at him. He was watching her, a faint, almost teasing smile on his lips. "You're jealous, aren't you?"

"No—" she began, looking down, a slight color coming to her cheeks, then she laughed. "Oh, you're impossible, Ben. You really are. I'm curious, that's all. I didn't think . . ."

"That I had any friends here?" He nodded. "No. I didn't think I had, either. Not until a week ago. That's when I met her. It was strange. You see, I'd used her as a model for something I was working on. Used her without her knowing it. She was always there, you see, in a cafe I used to frequent. And then, one day, she came to my table and introduced herself."

A smile returned to her lips. "So when are you going to introduce her to me?"

He looked down at her hands, then lifted them to his lips, kissing their backs. "How about tonight? That is, if she's still speaking to me after this morning."

▬▬▬▬▬

BEN WAS SITTING with Meg in the booth at the end of the bar when Catherine came in. He had deliberately chosen a place where neither of them had been before—neutral ground—and had told Meg as much, not wanting his sister to feel too out of place. Ben saw her first and leaned across to touch Meg's hand. Meg turned, seeing how Catherine came down the aisle toward them, awkward at first, then when she knew they had seen her, with more confidence. She had put up her flame-red hair so that the sharp lines of her face were prominent.

Looking at her in the half-light Meg thought her quite beautiful.

Ben stood, offering his hand, but Catherine gave him only the most fleeting of glances. "You must be Meg," she said, moving around the table and taking the seat beside her, looking into her face. "I've been looking forward to meeting you." She laughed softly, then reached out to gently touch Meg's nose, tracing its shape, the outline of her mouth.

"Yes," she said, after a moment. "You're like him, aren't you?" She turned, looking at Ben. "And how are *you?*"

"I'm well," he said, noncommittally, taking his seat, then turning to summon a waiter.

Meg studied her in profile. Ben had said nothing, but she understood. The girl was in love with him.

She looked, as Ben had taught her, seeing several things: the fine and clever hands, the sharpness of the eyes that missed little in the visual field. An artist's eyes. And she saw how the girl looked at Ben: casual on the surface, but beneath it all uncertain, vulnerable.

Ben ordered, then turned back, facing them. "This, by the way, is Catherine. She paints."

Meg nodded, pleased that she had read it so well. "What do you paint? Abstracts? Portraits?" She almost said landscapes, but it was hard to believe that anyone from here would pick such a subject.

The girl smiled and glanced quickly at Ben before answering. "I paint whatever takes my interest. I've even painted your brother."

Ben leaned across the table. "You should see it, Meg. Some of her work's quite good."

Meg smiled. If Ben said she was good you could take it that the girl was excellent. She looked at Catherine anew, seeing qualities she had missed the first time: the taut, animal-like quality of her musculature and the way she grew very still whenever she was watching. Like a cat. So very like a cat.

The waiter brought their drinks. When he had gone, Ben leaned forward, toasting them both.

"To the two most beautiful women in the City. *Kan Pei!*"

Meg looked sideways at the girl, noting the color that had come to her cheeks. Catherine wasn't sure what Ben was up to. She didn't know him well enough yet. But there was a slightly teasing tone in his voice that was unmistakable, and his eyes sparkled with mischief. His mood had changed. Or, rather, he had changed his mood.

"This painting . . ." Meg asked, "is it good?"

Catherine looked down, smiling. There was no affectation in the gesture, only a genuine humility. "I think it is." She looked up, careful not to look at Ben, her cheeks burning. "It's the best thing I've done. My first real painting."

Meg nodded slowly. "I'd like to see it, if you'd let me. I don't think anyone has painted Ben in years. If at all."

The girl bowed her head slightly. There was silence for a moment, then Ben cleared his throat, leaning toward Meg. "She's far too modest. I've heard they plan to put on an exhibition of her work, here in the College."

Meg saw how the girl looked up at that, her eyes flying open, and knew it was not something she had told Ben, but that he had discovered it for himself.

She looked back at Catherine. "When is it being held?"

"In the spring."

"The spring . . ." Meg thought of that a moment, then laughed.

"Why did you laugh?" Catherine was staring back at her, puzzled, while from across the table Ben looked on, his eyes almost distant in their intensity.

"Because it's odd, that's all. You say spring and you mean one thing, while for me . . ." She stared down at her drink, aware of how strangely the girl was looking at her. "It's just that spring is a season of the year, and here . . ." she looked up, meeting the girl's deeply green eyes, "here there are no seasons at all."

For a moment longer Catherine stared back at her, seeking but not finding what she wanted in her face. Then she looked away, giving a little shrug.

"You speak like him, too. In riddles."

"It's just that words mean different things to us," Ben said, leaning back, his head pressing against the wall of the partition. It was a comment that seemed to exclude Catherine, and Meg saw how she took one quick look at him, visibly hurt.

Hurt and something else. Meg looked away, a sudden coldness in the pit of her stomach. It was more than love. More than simple desire. The girl was obsessed with Ben. As she looked back at Ben, one word formed clear in her head. *Difficult.* It was what he had said earlier. Now she was beginning to understand.

"Words are only words," she said, turning back and smiling at the girl, reaching out to touch and hold her hand. "Let's not make too much of them."

◆◆◆◆

SIX HOURS LATER, Catherine finished wrapping the present, then stood the canvas by the door. That done, she showered, then dressed and made herself up. Tonight she would take him out. Alone, if possible; but with his sister, if necessary. For a moment she stood there, studying herself in the wall-length mirror. She was wearing a dark-green, loose-fitting wrap tied with a cord at the waist. She smiled, pleased by what she saw, knowing Ben would like it; then she looked down, touching her tongue to her top teeth, remembering.

A card had come that afternoon. From Sergey. A terse, bitter little note full of recriminations and the accusation of betrayal. It had hurt, bringing back all she had suffered these last few weeks. But it had also brought relief. Her relationship with Sergey could not have lasted. He had tried to own her, to close her off from herself.

She shivered. Well, it was done with now. His clash with Ben had been inevitable and, in a sense, necessary. It had forced her to a choice. Sergey was someone in her past. Her destiny now lay with Ben.

The bolt took her north, through the early evening bustle. It was after seven when she reached the terminal at the City's edge. From there she took a tram six stacks east, then two north. There she hesitated, wondering if she should call and tell him she was coming; instead, she pressed on. It would give him less opportunity to make excuses. She had her own key now—she would surprise him.

She took the elevator up to his level, the package under her arm. It was heavy and she was longing to put it down. Inside, she placed it against the wall in the cloakroom while she took off her cape. The smell of percolating coffee filled the apartment. Smiling, she went through to the kitchen, hoping to find him there.

The kitchen was empty. She stood there a moment, listening for noises in the apartment, then went through to the living room. No one was there. Two empty glasses rested on the table. For a moment she looked about her, frowning, thinking she had made a mistake and they were out. Then she remembered the coffee.

She crossed the room and stood there, one hand placed lightly against the door, listening. Nothing. Or almost nothing. If she strained she thought she could hear the faintest sound of breathing.

She tried the door. It was unlocked. She moved the panel, sliding it back slowly, her heart pounding now, her hands beginning to tremble.

It was pitch black within the room. As she eased the panel back, light from the living room spilled into the darkness, breaching it. She saw at once that the frame had been moved from the center of the room; pushed back to one side, leaving only an open space of carpet and the edge of the bed.

She stepped inside, hearing it clearly now—a regular pattern of breathing. At first it seemed single, but then she discerned its doubleness. Frowning, she moved closer, peering into the darkness.

Her voice was a whisper. "Ben? Ben? It's me. Catherine."

She knelt, reaching out to touch him, then pulled her hand back sharply. The hair . . .

The girl rolled over and looked up at her, her eyes dark, unfocused from sleep. Beside her Ben grunted softly and nuzzled closer, his right arm stretched out across her stomach, his hand cradling her breast.

Her breath caught in her throat. *Kuan Yin! His sister!*

Meg sighed, then turned her face toward the other girl. "Ben?" she asked drowsily, not properly awake, one hand scratching lazily at the dark bush of her sex.

Catherine stood, the strength suddenly gone from her legs, a tiny moan of pain escaping her lips. She could see now how their limbs were entwined, how their bodies glistened with the sweat of lovemaking.

"I . . ." she began, but the words were swallowed back. There was nothing more to say. Nothing now but to get out and try to live with what she'd seen. Slowly she began to back away.

Meg lifted her head slightly, trying to make out who it was. "Ben?"

Catherine's head jerked back, as if she had no control of it, and banged against the panel behind her. Then she turned and, fumbling with the door, stumbled out—out into the harsh light of the living room—and fell against the table. She went down, scattering the empty glasses, and lay there a moment, her forehead pressed against the table's leg.

She heard the panel slide back and turned quickly, getting up, wiping her hand across her face. It was Ben. He put his hand out to her, but she knocked it away, her teeth bared like a cornered animal.

"You bastard . . ." she whimpered. "You . . ."

But she could only shake her head, her face a mask of grief and bitter disappointment.

He lowered his hand and let his head fall. It was an awkward, painful little gesture, one which Meg, watching from the other room, saw and understood. He hadn't told her. Catherine hadn't known how things were between Ben and herself.

Meg looked beyond her brother. Catherine had backed against the door. She stood there a moment, trembling, her pale, beautiful face wet with tears, racked with grief and anger. Then she turned and was gone.

And Ben? She looked at him, saw how he stood there, his head fallen forward, all life, all of that glorious intensity of his, suddenly gone from him. She shivered. He was hurt. She could see how hurt he was. But he would be all right. Once he'd got used to things. And maybe it was best. Yes, maybe it was, in the circumstances.

She went across and put her arms about him, holding him tightly, her breasts pressed against his back, her cheek resting against his neck.

"It's all right," she said softly, kissing his naked shoulder. "It's all going to be all right. I promise you it will. It's Meg, Ben. I'm here. I won't leave you. I promise I won't."

But when she turned him to face her, his eyes seemed sightless and his cheeks were wet with tears.

"She's gone," he said brokenly. "Don't you see, Meg? I loved her. I didn't realize it until now, but I loved her. And now she's gone."

━━━━━━

IT WAS MUCH LATER when Meg found the package. She took it through to the living room; then, laying it on the floor, she unwrapped it and knelt there looking down at it. It was beautiful. There was no doubt about it. Meg had thought no one else capable of seeing it, but it was there, in the girl's painting— all of Ben's power, his harsh, uncompromising beauty. She too had seen how mixed, how gentle-fierce he was.

She was about to wrap it again, to hide it away somewhere until they were gone from here, when Ben came out of the bedroom.

"What's that?" he asked, looking across at her, the faintest light of curiosity in his eyes.

She hesitated, then picked it up and turned it toward him.

"The girl must have left it," she said, watching him, seeing how his eyes widened with surprise, how the painting seemed to bring him back to life.

"Catherine," he corrected her, his eyes never leaving the surface of the painting. "She had a name, Meg, like you and I. She was real. As real as this."

He came closer, then bent down on his haunches, studying the canvas carefully, reaching out with his fingertips to trace the line and texture of the painting. And all the while she watched him, seeing how his face changed, how pain and wonder and regret flickered one after another across the screen of his features, revealing everything.

She looked down, a tiny shudder rippling through her. Their lives had been so innocent, so free of all these complications. But now . . . She shook her head, then looked at him again. He was watching her.

"What is it?" he asked.

She shook her head, not wanting to say. They had both been hurt enough by this. Her words could only make things worse. Yet she had seen the change in him. Had seen that transient, flickering moment in his face when pain had been transmuted into something else—into the seed of some great artifice.

She shuddered, suddenly appalled. Was this all there was for him? This constant trading in of innocence for artifice? This devil's bargain? Could he not just *be*? Did everything he experienced, every living breath he took, have to be sacrificed on the bleak, unrelenting altar of his art?

She wished there were another answer—another path—for him, but knew it was not so. He could not *be* without first recording his being. Could not be free without first capturing himself. Nor did he have any choice in the matter. He was like Icarus, driven, god-defiant, obsessed by his desire to break free of the element which bound him.

She looked back at him, meeting his eyes.

"I must go after her, Meg. I must."

"You can't. Don't you understand? She *saw* us. She'll not forgive you that."

"But this . . ." He looked down at the painting again, the pain returned to his face. "She saw me, Meg. Saw me clear. As I really am."

She shivered. "I know. But you can't. It's too late, Ben. Don't you see that?"

"No," he said, standing. "Not if I go now and beg her to forgive me."

She let her head fall, suddenly very tired. "No, Ben. You *can't*. Not now."

"*Why?*" His voice was angry now, defiant. "Give me one good reason why I can't."

She sighed. It was what she had been unable to say to him earlier—the reason why she had come here a week early—but now it *had* to be said. She looked up at him again, her eyes moist now. "It's Father. He's ill."

"I know—" he began, but she cut him off.

"No, Ben. You *don't* know. The doctors came three days ago. The day I wrote to you." There was a faint quaver in her voice now. She had let the painting fall. Now she stood there, facing him, the first tears spilling down her cheeks.

"He's *dying.*" She raised her voice suddenly, anger spilling over into her words. "Goddamnit, Ben, they've given him a month! Six weeks at most!" She swallowed, then shook her head, her eyes pleading with him now. "Don't you see? That's why you can't go after her. You've got to come home. You *must!* Mother needs you. She needs you badly. And me. I need you too, Ben. Me more than anyone."

◆◆◆◆

MEMORANDUM: 4th day of May, A.D. 2207

To His Most Serene Excellency, Li Shai Tung, Grand Counsellor and T'ang of *Ch'eng Ou Chou* (City Europe)

Chieh Hsia,

Your humble servant begs to inform you that the matter of which we spoke has now resolved itself satisfactorily. The girl involved, Catherine Tissan (see attached report, MinDis PSec 435/55712), has apparently returned to her former lover, Sergey Novacek (see attached report, MinDis PSec 435/55711), who, after pressure from friends loyal to Your Most Serene Excellency, has dropped his civil action against the Shepherd boy (see copies of documents attached).

Ben Shepherd himself has, as you are doubtlessly aware, returned home to tend his ailing father, abandoning his studies at Oxford, thus removing himself from the threat of possible attack or abduction.

This acknowledged, in view of the continuing importance of the Shepherd family to State matters, your humble servant has felt it his duty to continue in his efforts to ascertain whether this was, as appears on the surface of events, a simple matter of rivalry in love, or whether it was part of some deeper, premedi-

tated scheme to undermine the State. Such investigations
have revealed some interesting if as yet inconclusive results
regarding the nature of the business dealings of the father,
Lubos Novacek. Results which, once clarified, will, if of substance to this matter, be notified to Your Most Serene
Excellency.

Your humble servant,

Heng Yu,
Minister of Distribution, *Ch'eng Ou Chou* (City Europe)

Heng Yu read the top copy through; then, satisfied, he
reached out and took his brush from the inkblock, signing his
name with a flourish on each of the three copies. One would go
to Li Shai Tung. The second he would keep for his own records.
The third—well, the third would go to Prince Yuan, via Nan
Ho, his contact in the palace at Tongjiang.

Heng Yu smiled. Things could not have gone better. The boy
was safe, the T'ang pleased, and he was much closer to his
ambition. What more could a man ask for? Of course, not
everything had been mentioned in the documents. The matter
of the bronze statue, for instance, had been left out of the report
on Sergey Novacek.

It had been an interesting little tale. One that, in spite of
all, reflected well on young Novacek. Investigations into the
past history of the bronze had shown that it had once belonged
to his father, Lubos, who, to bail out an old friend, had had to
sell it. Sergey Novacek had known of this, and hearing Heng
Chian-ye talking of it, had set things up so that he might win
it back. The matter of Shepherd, it seemed, had been a secondary matter, spawned of jealousy and tagged on as an afterthought. The statue had been the prime mover of the boy's
actions. From accounts he had returned it to his father on his
sixtieth birthday.

And the father? Heng Yu sat back, stroking his beard. Lubos
Novacek was, like many of the City's leading tradesmen, a respectable man. His trade, however, was anything but respectable, for Lubos Novacek acted as a middleman between certain
First Level concerns and the Net. Put crudely, he was the pimp

of certain Triad bosses, acting on their behalf in the Above, buying and selling at their behest and taking his cut.

A useful man to know. And know him he would.

As for the Great Man—that pompous halfwit, Fan Liang-wei—Heng had enjoyed summoning him to his Ministry and ordering him to desist from his efforts to get Ben thrown out of the College. He had shown Fan the instrument signed by the T'ang himself and threatened him with instant demotion—even to the Net itself—should any word come back to him that Fan was pursuing the matter in any shape or form.

Yes, it had been immensely satisfying. Fan's face had been a perfect picture as he attempted to swallow his massive pride and come to terms with the fact of the boy's influence. He had been almost apoplectic with unexpressed anger.

Heng Yu gave a little chuckle, then turned to face his young cousin.

"Something amuses you, Uncle?"

"Yes, Chian-ye. Some business I did earlier. But come now, I need you to take these documents for me." He picked up two of the copies and handed them across. "This first copy must be handed directly to Chung Hu-yan and no one else, and this to Nan Ho at Tongjiang. Both men will be expecting you."

"Is that all, Uncle Yu?"

Heng Yu smiled. It was a moment for magnanimity. "No, Chian-ye. I am pleased with the way you have served me this past week. In view of which I have decided to review the matter of your allowance. In respect of past and future duties as my personal assistant, you will receive an additional sum of twenty-five thousand *yuan* per year."

Heng Chian-ye bowed low, surprised yet also greatly pleased. "You are most generous, Uncle Yu. Be assured, I will strive hard to live up to the trust you have placed in me."

"Good. Then get going, Chian-ye. These papers must be in the hands of their respective agents within the next six hours."

Heng Yu watched his cousin leave, then stood, stretching and yawning. There was no doubting it, this matter—of little substance in itself—had served him marvelously. He laughed, then looked about him, wondering momentarily what his uncle, Chian-ye's father, would have made of it.

And the matter of the Melfi Clinic?

That, too, could be used. Was something to be saved until the time was ripe. For though his uncle Heng Chi-po had been a greedy, venal man, he had been right in one thing. Information was power. And those who had it wielded power.

Yes. And never more so than in the days to come. For Chung Kuo was changing fast. New things were rising from the depths of the City. Things he would do well to know about.

Heng Yu, Minister to the T'ang, nodded to himself, then reached across and killed the light above his desk.

Which was why, in the morning, he had arranged to meet the merchant Novacek. To offer him a new arrangement—a new commodity to trade in, one he would pay handsomely to possess.

Information.

Fallen Petals

The guests are gone from the pavilion high,
In the small garden flowers are whirling around.
Along the winding path the petals lie;
To greet the setting sun, they drift up from the ground.

Heartbroken, I cannot bear to sweep them away;
From my eager eyes, spring soon disappears.
I pine with passing, heart's desire lost for aye;
Nothing is left but a robe stained with tears.

—LI SHANG-YIN, *Falling Flowers,* ninth century A.D.

L I Y U A N reined in his horse and looked up. On the far side of the valley, beyond the tall, narrow spire of Three Swallows Mount, a transporter was banking, heading for the palace, two *li* distant. As it turned he saw the crest of the *Ywe Lung* emblazoned on its fuselage and frowned, wondering who it was. As far as he knew his father was expecting no one.

He turned in his saddle, looking about him. The grassy slope led down to a dirt track that followed the stream for a short way, then crossed a narrow wooden bridge and snaked south toward Tongjiang. He could follow that path back to the palace or he could finish the ride he had planned, up to the old monastery, then south to the beacon. For a moment longer he hesitated, caught in two minds. It was a beautiful morning, the sky a perfect, cloudless blue; the kind of morning when one felt like riding on and on forever, but he had been out three hours already, so maybe it was best if he got back. Besides, maybe his father needed him. Things had been quiet recently. Too quiet. Maybe something had come up.

He tugged at the reins gently, turning the Arab's head, then spurred her on with his heels, leading her carefully down the slope and along the path, breaking into a canter as he crossed the bridge. He was crossing the long meadow, the palace just ahead of him, when a second transporter passed overhead, the insignia of the Marshal clearly displayed on the undersides of its stubby wings. Yuan slowed, watching as it turned and landed on the far side of the palace, a cold certainty forming in his guts.

It had begun again.

At the stables he all but jumped from the saddle, leaving the groom to skitter about the horse, trying to catch hold of the reins, while he ran on, along the red-tiled path and into the eastern palace.

He stopped, breathless, at the door to his father's suite of rooms, taking the time to calm himself, to run his fingers quickly through his unruly hair; but even as he made to knock, Chung Hu-yan, his father's Chancellor, drew the door of the anteroom open and stepped out, as if expecting him.

"Forgive me, Prince Yuan," he began, without preamble, "but your father has asked me if you would excuse him for an hour or so. A small matter has arisen, inconsequential in itself, yet urgent."

Yuan hesitated, wondering how far he could push Hu-yan on this, but again Hu-yan pre-empted him.

"It is nothing you can help him with, Prince Yuan, I assure you of that. It is a . . . *personal* matter, let us say. No one has died, nor is the peace of Chung Kuo threatened, yet the matter is of some delicacy. In view of special circumstances your father thought it best that he consult his cousin Tsu Ma and the Marshal. You understand, I hope?"

Yuan stood there a moment longer, trying to read something in Chung Hu-yan's deeply creased face, but the old man's expression was like a wall, shutting him out. He laughed, then nodded.

"I am relieved, Hu-yan. I had thought . . ."

But he had no need to say. It had been on all their minds these past few months. Where would their enemies strike next? Who would they kill? In many respects this peace was worse than the War that had preceded it; a tenuous, uncertain peace that stretched the nerves almost to breaking point.

He smiled tightly, then turned away, hearing the door pulled closed behind him. But even as he walked back he was beginning to wonder what it was that might have brought Tsu Ma so urgently to his father's summons. *A personal matter* . . . He turned, looking back thoughtfully, then shrugged and turned back, making his way past bowing servants and kneeling maids, hurrying now.

Maybe Fei Yen knew something. She was always hearing snippets of rumor that his own ears hadn't caught, so maybe she knew what this was. And even if she didn't, she had ways of finding such things out. Women's ways.

He laughed and broke into a run. And then maybe he would take her out in the palanquin. One last time before she was too far advanced in her pregnancy. Up to the monastery, perhaps. Or to the beacon.

Yes, they could make a picnic of it. And maybe, afterward, he would make love to her, gently, carefully, there on the grassy hillside, beneath the big open sky of northern China. One last, memorable time before the child came.

He stopped before her door, hammering at it and calling her name, laughing, all of his earlier fears forgotten, his head filled with the thought of the afternoon ahead.

"What is it, Yuan?" she asked, opening the door to him almost timidly, her smile uncertain. "Are you drunk?"

In answer he drew her to him, more roughly than he had meant, and lifted her up, crushing her lips with his own. "Not drunk, my love. No. But happy. Very happy. . . ."

━━━━━

LI SHAI TUNG had taken his guests through to the Summer House. Servants had brought *ch'a* and sweetmeats and then departed, leaving the three men alone. Tolonen stood by the window, looking down the steep slope toward the ornamental lake, while Tsu Ma and Li Shai Tung sat, facing each other, on the far side of the room. So far they had said nothing of importance, but now Li Shai Tung looked up at Tsu Ma and cleared his throat.

"Do you remember the first time you came here? That day you went riding with Yuan and the Lady Fei?"

Tsu Ma met his gaze unflinchingly. "That was a good day. And the evening that followed, out on the lake."

Li Shai Tung looked down. "Ah yes, Yuan told me of that. . . ." He smiled; sourly, Tsu Ma thought, fearing the worst.

The old T'ang raised his head again, the smile fading altogether. "And you recall what we spoke of that day?"

Tsu Ma nodded, his mouth dry, wishing the old man would be more direct. If he knew, why didn't he say something? Why this torment of indirectness? "We spoke of Yuan's Project, if I remember accurately," he said, looking across at Tolonen momentarily, recalling that they had appointed the old man to oversee the whole business. But what had this to do with Fei Yen and him? For surely that was why he had been summoned here this morning at such short notice. He looked down, filled with shame for what he had done. "I am sorry, Shai Tung, I—"

But Li Shai Tung seemed not to have heard. He carried on, as if Tsu Ma had said nothing.

"We spoke afterward, too, didn't we? A week or so later, if I recall. At which time I made you a party to my thoughts."

Tsu Ma looked up, frowning. He had heard of indirection, but this . . . Then he understood. This had nothing to do with Fei Yen and him. Nothing at all. He laughed, relief washing through him.

Li Shai Tung stared at him, astonished. "I am afraid I find it no laughing matter, cousin." He half-turned, looking at the Marshal. "Show him the file, Knut."

Tsu Ma felt himself go cold again. He took the file and opened it, the faintest tremor in his hands. A moment later he looked up, his face a picture of incomprehension.

"What in Hell's name is all this?"

The old T'ang held his head stiffly, his anger barely controlled. "Inventions. Machines. Devices that would be the ruin of Chung Kuo. Every last one of them breaking the Edict in a dozen, maybe twenty, different ways."

Tsu Ma glanced through the file, amazed by what he saw, then shook his head. "But where did they come from? Who invented them? And why?"

Tolonen spoke up for the first time. "They're SimFic mainly. From the traitor Berdichev's papers. We saw them long ago— three, maybe even four, years ago—but in a different form. Li Shai Tung ordered them destroyed. But here they are again, the same things but better than before."

"Better?"

Li Shai Tung nodded. "You recall that we talked of a young boy. A clever one, by the name of Kim Ward. Well, this is his work. Somehow he got hold of these papers and worked on them. The improvements are his. In one sense it's quite amazing, in another quite horrifying. But the fault does not lie with the boy."

Tsu Ma shook his head, still not understanding how all of this connected, or why Li Shai Tung should consult him on the matter. "Then who?"

"That's exactly what I asked the Marshal to find out. He came upon these files by accident, you understand. Six months had passed and I wanted to know what was happening with Yuan's Project. So, secretly, without the Project Director's knowledge, the Marshal trawled the Project's files."

Tsu Ma leaned back in his chair. "I see. You didn't want Yuan to know that you were checking up on him?"

Li Shai Tung nodded. "It seemed best. It was not that I felt he would lie to me, just that he might act as a . . . as a filter, let's say. But this. This shocked me."

"Then Li Yuan is responsible for this file? It was he who gave the originals to the boy to work on?"

"Yes. . . ." Bitterness and anger were etched starkly in the old man's face.

"I see. . . ."

He understood. Li Shai Tung had asked for him because he alone could be trusted, for he alone among the Seven knew of the existence of the Project. Even Wu Shih was under the impression that Li Shai Tung was only considering matters. Yes, and he understood the necessity for that; for were it to become common knowledge it could only do them harm. Wang Sauleyan, certainly, could be counted on to use it to foment trouble in Council and try to break the power of the Li family.

But that was not really the issue at hand. No. The real problem was that Li Shai Tung felt himself affronted. His son had not acted as a son should act. He had lied and cheated, no matter the good intent that lay behind the act. Indeed, to the old man that was probably the worst of it. Not that these things existed, for they could be destroyed, as if they had never been, but that Li Yuan had sought to conceal them from him. It was this part of it on which he sought Tsu Ma's advice. For who was closer to his son than Tsu Ma? As close, almost, as a brother. . . .

Li Shai Tung leaned closer. "But what should I do, Tsu Ma? Should I confront him with these . . . *things?*"

"No. . . ." Tsu Ma took a breath. "I would say nothing."

"Nothing?"

He nodded, holding the old man's eyes. "What good would it do? Yuan acted from your best interests. Or so he believes. So I'm sure he believes. There was no desire to harm you, only an . . . an eagerness, let us call it, an impatience in him, that can be set down to his youthfulness. Look upon these as folly. Arrange an accident and have all record of these things destroyed. The Marshal could arrange something for you, I'm certain. But say nothing. Do not damage what is between you and your son, Shai Tung."

The old man shook his head, momentarily in pain. "But he has lied to me. Deceived me."

"No. . . . Your words are too strong."

"It is unfilial. . . ."

Tsu Ma swallowed, thinking of his own far greater deceit, then shook his head again. "He loves you, Shai Tung. He works hard for you. Unstintingly hard. There is nothing he would not do for you. In that he is anything but unfilial. So let things be. After all, no real harm is done."

His words came strong and heartfelt, as if it were himself he was pleading for, and when Li Shai Tung looked up at him again there were tears in the old man's eyes.

"Maybe you're right. Maybe I am being too harsh." He sighed. "You are a good friend to him, Tsu Ma. I hope, for his sake, you are ever so." He turned, looking at the Marshal. "And you, Knut? What do you say?"

Tolonen hesitated, then lowered his head. "Tsu Ma is right. I had come here ready to argue otherwise, but having heard him I am inclined to agree. Say nothing. The rest I will arrange."

"And the boy?"

Tolonen looked briefly to Tsu Ma, then met his master's eyes again. "I would leave the boy for now, *Chieh Hsia.* Li Yuan will discover for himself how dangerous the boy is. And who knows, that may prove the most important thing to come from all of this, neh? To learn that knowledge is a two-edged sword?"

Li Shai Tung laughed; but it was an unhealthy, humorless sound. "Then it will be as you say, good friends. It will be as you say."

FEI YEN had been quiet for some while, staring out across the circular pool toward the distant mountains. Now she turned, looking back at him.

"Why did you bring me here?"

Li Yuan met her eyes, smiling vaguely, unconscious, it seemed, of the slight edge to her voice.

"Because it's beautiful. And . . ." He hesitated. A strange, fleeting expression crossed his features, then he looked down. "I haven't said before, but Han and I used to come here as boys. We would spend whole afternoons here, playing among the ruins. Long ago, it seems now. Long, long ago." He looked up at her again, searching her eyes, as if for understanding. "When I rode out this morning, I knew I had to come here. It was as if something called me."

She turned, shivering, wondering still if he was playing with her. If, despite everything, he *knew.* Behind him the ancient Buddhist stupa stood out against the blue of the sky, its squat base and ungainly spire like something alien in that rugged landscape. To its left rested the pale yellow silk palanquin he had insisted she be carried in, its long poles hidden in the waist-length grass, the six runners squatting nearby, talking quietly among themselves, their eyes averted. Farther up the hillside she could see the entrance to the ruined monastery where she had come so often with Tsu Ma.

It had all come flooding back to her; all of the old feelings reawakened, as sharp as ever. *Why now?* she had asked herself, horrified. *Why, when I have finally found peace, does it return to torment me?* She had listened to Yuan abstractedly, knowing Tsu Ma was once more in the palace, and had found herself wanting to run to him and throw herself upon his mercy. But it could not

be. She was this man's wife. This *boy's* wife. So she had chosen.
And now it could not be undone. Unless that was why the old
man had summoned Tsu Ma.

For one brief, dreadful moment she imagined it undone. Imagined herself cast off, free to marry Tsu Ma, and saw the tiny
movement of denial he would make. As he had done that time,
here, beside the pool. She caught her breath, the pain of that
moment returned to her.

*I should have been your wife, Tsu Ma. Your strength. Your second
self.*

Aiya, but it was not to be. It was not her fault that she had
fallen for Tsu Ma. No. That had been her fate. But this too was
her fate. To be denied him. To be kept from him forever. To be
married to this child. She looked down, swallowing back the
bitterness.

"What is it, my love?"

She looked at him, for the moment seeing nothing but his
youth, his naïvete; those and that awful old-man certainty of
his. Then she relented. It was not his fault. He had not chosen
to fall in love with her. No, he had been nothing but kindness to
her. Even so, her heart bled that it was he and not Tsu Ma who
had brought her here today.

"It's nothing," she answered him. "Only the sickness."

He stared at her, concerned, real sympathy in his expression
as he struggled to understand her. But he would never understand.

"Should we go back?" he asked softly, but she shook her head.

"No. It's all right. It'll pass in a while."

She looked away again, staring out toward the south and the
distant beacon, imagining him there, waiting for her, even now.
But there were only ghosts now. Distant memories. Those and
the pain.

She sighed. Was it always so? Did fate never grant a full
measure? Was it the lot of everyone to have this lesser satisfaction—this pale shadow of passion?

And was she to cast that to the winds? To choose nothing
rather than this sometimes-bitter compromise? She shook her
head, anguished. Oh, she had often thought of telling Yuan;
had had the urge to let the words float free from her, like acids,

eating into the soft dream of love he had built about him. And what had kept her from that? Was it pity for him? A desire not to be cruel? Or was it simple self-interest on her part?

She turned, looking at him again. Did she love him? *Did* she? No. But neither did she hate him. It was as she'd said so often to herself. He was a good man. A good husband. But beyond that . . .

She closed her eyes, imagining herself in Tsu Ma's arms again, the sheer physical strength of him thrilling beyond words, the strange, mysterious power of him enfolding her until her mind went dark and her nerve ends sang with the sweetness of his touch.

And could Li Yuan do that for her? She shuddered. No. Never in ten thousand years.

"If you would wait here a brief moment, *Shih* Nan, I will let my master know you are here."

Nan Ho, Li Yuan's Master of the Inner Chamber, returned the first steward's bow, then, when the man had gone, turned, looking about him. It was not often that he found himself in one of the mansions of the Minor Families and he was not going to miss this opportunity of seeing how they lived. He had seen the balcony on his way in; now he crossed the room quickly and stood there just inside the window, looking out across the grounds. Down below the *chao tai hui*—the entertainment—was in full swing, more than a thousand guests filling the space between the old stone walls.

He took a step further, out onto the balcony itself, fascinated by the range of outlandish fashions on display, amused by the exaggerated gestures of some of the more garishly dressed males, then froze, hearing voices in the gallery behind him. He drew in closer to the upright, drawing the long silk curtain across a fraction to conceal himself. It would not do to be seen to be so curious, even if he were here on the Prince's business.

At first he was unaware of the import of what was being said, then a single phrase made him jerk his head about, suddenly attending.

He listened, horrified, the laughter that followed the words chilling him. And as their footsteps went away down the stairs, he came out and, tiptoeing quietly across the tiled floor, leaned over the stairway to catch a sight of the men who had been talking, drawing his head back sharply as they turned on the landing below.

Gods! he thought, all consideration of the business he had come for gone from his mind. He must do something, and immediately, for this matter would not wait. He must nip it in the bud at once.

He was still standing there, his hands gripping the marble of the balustrade, when Pei Ro-hen entered the gallery from the far end.

"Master Nan? Is that you?"

He turned, flustered, bowing twice, then hurried forward, kissing Pei's offered ring hand. He straightened up and after the briefest pause to collect his thoughts, came directly to the point.

"Forgive me, my Lord, but something has just happened that I must attend to at once. I was waiting, by the window there, when four men entered the gallery, talking among themselves. Not wishing to disturb them, I took a step outside, onto the balcony, yet what I overheard is of the gravest importance. Indeed, I would go so far as to say that it threatens the security of our masters."

Pei Ro-hen had gone very still. There was a small movement in his normally placid face, then he nodded. "I see. And what do you wish to do, Master Nan?"

In answer Nan Ho went to the balcony again, his head bowed, waiting for Pei to come across. When the old man stood beside him, he pointed out across the heads of the crowd to four men who were making their way to one of the refreshment tents on the far side of the walled garden.

"Those are the men. The two in red silks and the others in lilac and green. If you could detain them on some pretext for an hour or two, I will see if I can bring the Marshal here. He will know best how to deal with this matter."

"Are you sure that is wise, Master Nan? Should we not, perhaps, simply keep an eye on them and prevent them from leaving?"

Nan Ho shook his head vigorously. "Forgive me, but no, my

Lord. They must be isolated at the earliest opportunity, for what they know is dangerous. I cannot say more, but the safety of my masters is at stake here and I would be failing in my duty if I did not act."

Pei smiled, pleased immensely by this show of loyalty. "I understand, Nan Ho. Then go at once and bring Marshal Tolonen. I, meanwhile, will act my part in this."

━━━━━

K I M S A T there in the semidarkness, the room lights doused, the soft, pearled glow of the screen casting a faint, silvered radiance over his face and upper arms. He had worked through the night, then slept, waking only an hour past, entranced, fearful, filled with the dream he'd had.

Her eyes. He had dreamed of Jelka Tolonen's eyes. Of eyes so blue that he could see the blackness beyond them; could see the stars winking through, each fastened on its silver, silken thread to where he stood, looking through her at the universe. He had woken, shivering, the intensity of the vision scaring him. What did it mean? Why was she there, suddenly, between him and the stars? Why could he not see them clearly but through the startling blueness of her eyes?

He had lain there awhile, openmouthed with astonishment, then had come and sat here, toying with the comset's graphics, trying to re-create the vision he had had.

A spider. As so often he had been a spider in his dream; a tiny, silvered, dark-eyed creature, throwing out his web, letting the threads fly outward to the stars on tiny spinners that caught the distant sunlight and converted it to silk, flying onward, faster and ever faster to their various destinations. But this time it had been as if a great wind were blowing, gathering all of the threads into a single twisted trunk, drawing them up into the blueness of those eyes that floated like twin planets above where he crouched. Only on the far side of those eyes, where the blue shaded into black, did the trunk seem to blossom, like the branches of a tree, a million tiny threads spreading out like the fine capillaries of a root system, thrust deep into the earth of the universe.

Kim shivered, staring down at the thing he had made, first in his dreams and then here in the flatness of the screen. So it had always been for him: first he would see something, then he would act on what he'd seen. But this? How could he act on this? How could he pass his web through the young girl's eyes?

Or was that what it meant? Was he being too literal? Did this vision have another meaning than all those that had preceded it?

He shook his head, then cleared the screen, only then realizing how fast his heart was beating, how hard it seemed suddenly to breathe. Why was that? What did it mean?

He stood, angry with himself. It was only a dream, after all. It didn't *have* to mean anything, surely? No, he was better off concentrating on finishing off the work for Prince Yuan. Another two, maybe three, days should see that done. Then he could send it through. He would ask Barycz for the favor.

He leaned forward, about to bring up the lights, when the screen came alive again. A message was coming through. He leaned back, waiting, one hand touching the keyboard lightly, killing the hardprint facility.

The words appeared in the official Project typescript, headed by the symbol of a skull surrounded by a tiny nimbus of broken lines. It was an instruction for him to go to the medical center at once for his three-month checkup.

Kim sat back thoughtfully. It was too early. He wasn't due his next medical for another ten days. Still, that wasn't so unusual. Not everyone was as punctilious as he. Even so, he would make sure it wasn't one of Spatz's tricks.

He tapped out the locking combination, then put in the code, touching Cap A to scramble it. Cap L would unscramble when the time came to unlock, but until then Prince Yuan's files would be safe from prying eyes. Yes, they could take the comset apart, component by component, and never find it.

He looked up at the watching camera and smiled, then, going across to the corner, poured water from the jug into the bowl and began to wash.

TOLONEN STOOD and came around his desk, greeting Prince Yuan's Master of the Inner Chamber.

"Master Nan, how pleasant to see you here. What can I do for you?"

Nan Ho bowed low. "Forgive me, Marshal. I realize how busy you are, but this is a matter of the most extreme urgency."

"So my equerry leads me to believe. But tell me, what has happened, Master Nan? Is the T'ang's life in danger?"

Nan Ho shook his head. "It is not the T'ang but young Prince Yuan who is threatened by this matter. Nor is it a matter of life but of reputation that is at stake."

The old man frowned at that. "I don't understand. You mean Prince Yuan's reputation is threatened?"

"I do indeed, Marshal. I was at Pei Ro-hen's mansion on my master's business, when I overheard something. A rumor. A most vile rumor, which, if it were to become common knowledge, might do irreparable damage not only to my master but to the Seven. Such damage might well have political consequences."

Tolonen was watching him, his lips slightly parted. "Could you be more specific, Master Nan? I mean, what kind of rumor is this we're talking of?"

Nan Ho lowered his eyes. "Forgive me, Marshal, but I would rather not say. All I know is that there are no grounds whatsoever for such a rumor and that the perpetrators have but one purpose: to create a most vile nuisance for the Family that you and I deem it an honor to serve."

He glanced up, seeing that his words had done the trick. At the thought of the Li Clan being harmed in any way, Tolonen had bristled. There was a distinct color at his neck, and his gray eyes bulged with anger.

"Then what are we to do, Master Nan? What steps might we take to eradicate this vileness?"

Nan Ho smiled inwardly, knowing he had been right to come direct to Tolonen. "Pei Ro-hen has detained the men concerned before they could spread their wicked rumor. He is holding them until our return. If, through them, we can trace the source of this rumor, then we might yet stand a chance of crushing this abomination before it takes root."

Tolonen gave a terse nod, then went back to his desk, giving brief instructions into his desktop comset before he turned back.

"The way is cleared for us. We can be at Lord Pei's mansion in half an hour. One of my crack teams will meet us there. Let us hope we are not too late, neh, Master Nan?"

Yes, thought Nan Ho, the tightness at the pit of his stomach returning. *For all our sakes, let us hope we can stop this thing before it spreads.*

━━━━━

THE TWO MEN STOOD at the barrier, waiting while the Marshal's party passed through on the down transit. When it had gone they turned, their eyes meeting briefly, a strange look passing between them.

"Passes . . ." the guard seated beyond the barrier said, waving them on with one hand.

Mach flipped open the tiny warrant card he was carrying in his left hand and offered it to the guard. The guard took it without looking at him. "Face up to the camera," he said tonelessly.

Mach did as he was told, staring up into the artificial eye. Somewhere in Central Records it would be matching his retinal prints to his service record. A moment later a green light flashed on the board in front of the guard. He handed the card back, again without looking at Mach, then held out his hand again.

Lehmann came forward a pace and placed his card into the guard's hand. This time the guard's eyes came up lazily, then took a second look as he noted the pallor of the man.

"You sick or something?"

Mach laughed. "So would you be if you'd been posted to the Net for four years."

The guard eyed Lehmann with new respect. "That so, friend?"

Lehmann nodded, tilting his face up to stare at the camera.

"Four years?"

"Three years, eight months," Lehmann corrected him, knowing what was in the false record DeVore had prepared for him.

The guard nodded, reading from the screen in front of him. "Says here you were decorated, too? What was that for?"

"Some bastard Triad runner got too nosy," Lehmann said, staring back at him menacingly. "I broke his jaw."

The guard laughed uncomfortably and handed back the card. "Okay. You can go through. And thanks. . . ."

Out of earshot Mach leaned close. "Not so heavy, friend."

Lehmann simply looked at him.

Mach shrugged. "Okay. Let's get on with this. We'll start with the boxes at the top of the deck."

They took the deck elevator up, passing through a second checkpoint, then sought out the maintenance shaft that led to the first of the eighteen communications boxes that serviced this deck.

Crouched in the narrow tunnel above the floor-mounted box, Lehmann took a small cloth bag from the pocket of his tunic. Tilting his head forward, he tapped first one and then the other of the false lenses out into his hand, placing them into the bag.

Mach was already unscrewing the first of the four restraining bolts. He looked up at Lehmann, noting what he was doing. "Are you sure you ought to do that? There are cameras in these tunnels, too."

Lehmann tucked the bag away. "It'll be okay. Besides, I can't focus properly with those false retinas in place."

Mach laughed. "So Turner doesn't think of everything."

Lehmann shook his head. "Not at all. He's very thorough. Whose man do you think is manning the cameras?"

Mach slowed, then nodded thoughtfully. "Uhuh? And how do you think he does that? I mean, he's got a lot of friends, your man Turner. It seems odd, don't you think? I mean, how long is it since he quit Security? Eight years now? Ten?"

"It's called loyalty," Lehmann said coldly. "I thought you understood that. Besides, there are many who feel like you and I. Many who'd like to see things change."

Mach shook his head slowly, as if he still didn't understand, then got to work on the second of the bolts.

"You think that's strange, don't you?" Lehmann said after a moment. "You think that only you lower-level types should want to change how things are. But you're wrong. You don't have to be on the bottom of this shit-heap to see how fuck-awful things are. Take me. From birth I was set to inherit. Riches beyond your imagination. But it was never enough. I never wanted to be rich.

I wanted to be free. Free of all the restraints this world sets upon us. Chains, they are. It's a prison, this world of ours, boxing us in, and I hate that. I've always hated it."

Mach stared up at him, surprised and, to a small degree, amused. He had never suspected that the albino had so much feeling in him. He had always thought him cold, like a dead thing. This hatred was unexpected. It hinted at a side to him that even Turner knew nothing of.

The second bolt came free. He set to work on the third.

"I bet you hated your parents, too, didn't you?"

Lehmann knelt, watching Mach's hands as they turned the bolt. "I never knew them. My father never came to see me. My mother . . . well, I killed my mother."

"You—" Mach looked back at him, roaring with laughter, then fell silent. "You mean, you really did? You *killed* her?"

Lehmann nodded. "She was a rich Han's concubine. An arfidis addict, too. She disgusted me. She was like the rest of them, soft, corrupt. Like this world. I set fire to her, in her rooms. I'd like to do the same to all of them. To burn the whole thing to a shell and pull it down."

Mach took a deep breath through his nose, then set to work again. "I see. And Turner knows this, does he?"

"No. He thinks I'm someone else, some*thing* else."

"I see. But why tell me?"

"Because you're not what he thinks you are either." Lehmann reached across him, beginning to unscrew the final bolt. "Turner sees only enemies or pale shadows of himself. That's how he thinks. Black and white. As if this were all one great big game of *wei chi.*"

Mach laughed. "You surprise me. I'd have thought—" Then he laughed again. "I'm sorry. I'm doing what you said he does, aren't I? Assuming you're something that you're not."

The last bolt came loose. Between them they gently lifted the plate from the connecting pins and set it to one side. Beneath the plate was a panel, inset with tiny slip-in instruction cards. At the base of the panel was a keyboard. Lehmann tapped in the cut-out code he'd memorized, then leaned close, studying the panel. His pale, thin fingers searched the board, then plucked five of the translucent cards from different locations. He slipped them into the pouch at his waist, then reached into his jacket and took out the first of the eighteen tiny sealed packets. When a certain signal was routed through this board, these five would be triggered, forming a circuit that overrode the standard instruction codes. To the backup system it would seem as if the panel were functioning normally, but to all intents and purposes it would be dead. And with all eighteen boxes triggered in this way, communications to the deck would be effectively cut off.

He slotted the five wafer-thin cards into place, reset the cut-out code, then, with Mach's help, lowered the plate back onto the connecting pins.

"There," Mach said. "One down, seventeen to go. Pretty easy, huh?"

"Easy enough," Lehmann said, taking one of the restraining bolts and beginning to screw it down. "But only if you've the nerve, the vision, and the intelligence to plan it properly."

Mach laughed. "And a few old friends, turning a blind eye."

Lehmann turned his head slightly, meeting Mach's eyes. "Maybe. And a reason for doing it, neh?"

◆◆◆◆◆

KIM HAD HEARD the alarm from three decks down but made nothing of it, yet coming out of the transit he remembered and, his pulse quickening, began to run toward his room.

Even before he turned the corner into his corridor he saw signs of what had happened. A long snake of hose ran from the corner hydrant, flaccid now. On the far side of it, water had pooled. But that was not what had alerted him. It was the scent of burning plastics.

He leapt the hose, took three small, splashing steps, then stopped. The door to his room was open, the fire-hose curving inside. Even from where he stood he could see how charred the lintel was, could see the ashy residue of sludge littering the floor outside.

"What in the gods' names . . . ?"

T'ai Cho jerked his head around the door. "Kim!" he cried, coming out into the corridor, his face lit up. "Thank the gods you're safe. I thought—"

He let himself be embraced, then went inside, facing the

worst. It was gone. All of it. His comset was unrecognizable, fused into the worktop as if the whole were some strange, smooth sculpture of twisted black marble. The walls were black, as was the ceiling. The floor was awash with the same dark sludge that had oozed out into the corridor.

"What happened?" he asked, looking about him, the extent of his loss—his books, his clothes, the tiny things he'd called his own—slowly sinking in. "I thought this kind of thing couldn't happen. There are sprinklers, aren't there? And air seals."

T'ai Cho glanced at one of the maintenance men who were standing around, then looked back at Kim. "They failed, it seems. Faulty wiring, it looks like."

Kim laughed sourly, the irony not lost on him. "Faulty wiring? But I thought the boxes used instruction cards."

One of the men spoke up. "That's right. But two of the cards were wrongly encoded. It happens sometimes. It's something we can't check up on. A mistake at the factory . . . You know how it is."

Only too well, Kim thought. *But who did this? Who ordered it done? Spatz? Or someone higher than he? Not Prince Yuan, anyway, because he wanted what was destroyed here today.*

He sighed, then shook his head. It would take weeks, months perhaps, to put it all back together again. And if he did? Well, maybe it would be for nothing after all. Maybe they would strike again, just as he came to the end of his task, making sure nothing ever got to Li Yuan.

He turned, looking at his old friend. "You shouldn't have worried, T'ai Cho. But I'm glad you did. I was having my three-month medical. They say I'm fine. A slight vitamin C deficiency, but otherwise . . ." He laughed. "It was fortunate, neh? I could have been sleeping."

"Yes," T'ai Cho said, holding the boy to him again. "We should thank the gods, neh?"

Yes, thought Kim. *Or whoever decided I was not as disposable as my work.*

━━━━━━

N A N H O stood in the cool of the passageway outside the room, mopping his brow, the feeling of nausea passing slowly from him. Though ten minutes had passed, his hands still trembled and his clothes were soaked with his own sweat. In all his forty years he had seen nothing like it. The man's screams had been bad enough, but the look in his eyes, that expression of sheer terror and hopelessness, had been too much to bear.

If he closed his eyes he could still see it. Could see the echoing kitchen all about him, the prisoner tied naked to the table, his hands and feet bound tight with cords that bruised and cut the flesh. He bared his teeth, remembering the way the masked man had turned, the oiled muscles of his upper arms flexing effortlessly as he lifted the tongs from the red-hot brazier and turned them in the half-light. He could see the faint wisp of smoke that rose toward the ceiling, could hear the faint crackle as the coal was lifted into cooler air, even before he saw the glowing coal itself. But most of all he could see the panic in the young man's eyes, and he recalled what he had thought.

Forgive me, Fan Ming-yu, but I had to do this. For my master.

The man had begun to babble, to refute all he had been saying only a moment before, but the torturer's movements seemed inexorable. The coal came down, slowly, ever so slowly it seemed, and the man's words melted into shrieks of fearful protest. His body lifted, squirming, desperate, but all of its attempts to escape only brought it closer to the implement of its suffering.

The torturer held back a moment. One leather-gloved hand pushed the man's hip down, gently, almost tenderly, it seemed. Then, with the kind of care one might see from a craftsman tracing fine patterns onto silver, he brought the coal down delicately, pressing it tightly against the man's left testicle.

Nan Ho had shuddered and stepped back, swallowing bile. He had glanced, horrified, at Tolonen, seeing how the old man looked on impassively, then had looked back at the man, unable to believe what he had seen, appalled and yet fascinated by the damage the coal had done. Then, turning away, he had staggered out, his legs almost giving out under him, the screams of the man filling his head, the smell of charred flesh making him want to retch.

He stood there a moment longer, calming himself, trying to fit what he had just seen into the tightly ordered pattern of the world he knew, then shook his head. It was not his fault. He had had no choice in the matter. If his master had been any other man, or if the Lady Fei had chosen any other man but Tsu Ma to be her lover, but . . . well, as it was, this had to be. To let the truth be known, that was unthinkable.

Tolonen came outside. He stood there, staring at Nan Ho, then reached out and held his shoulder. "I am sorry, Master Nan. I didn't mean it to upset you. It's just that I felt you ought to be there, to hear the man's confession for yourself." He let his hand fall, then shrugged. "There are more efficient ways of inflicting pain, of course, but none as effective in loosening a tongue. The more barbaric the means of torture, we find, the quicker the man will talk."

Nan Ho swallowed, then found his voice again. "And what did you discover?"

"I have a list of all those he spoke to. Few, fortunately. And his source."

"His source?"

"It seems you acted not a moment too soon, Master Nan. Fan Ming-yu had just come from his lover. A young man named Yen Shih-fa."

Nan Ho's eyes widened. "I know the man. He is a groom at the stables."

"Yes." Tolonen smiled grimly. "I have contacted Tongjiang already and had the man arrested. With the very minimum of fuss, you understand. They are bringing him here even now."

Nan Ho nodded abstractedly. "And what will you do?"

The Marshal swallowed, a momentary bitterness clouding his features. "What *can* I do? It is as you said, Master Nan. This rumor cannot be allowed to spread. But how prevent that? Normally I would trust to the word of such *ch'un tzu*, but in a matter of this seriousness it would not be enough to trust to their silence. A man's word is one thing, but the security of the State is another. No; nor would it serve to demote them below the Net. These four are men of influence. Small influence, admittedly, but their absence would be noticed and commented upon. No, in the circumstances we must act boldly, I'm afraid."

Nan Ho shuddered. "You mean they must die."

Tolonen smiled. "Nothing quite so drastic, Master Nan. It is a matter of a small operation." He traced a tiny line across the side of his skull. "An incision here, another there . . ."

"And their families?"

"Their families will be told that they took an overdose of something. Pei Ro-hen's surgeons had to operate to save them, but unfortunately there was damage—serious damage—to those parts of the brain that control speech and memory. Most unfortunate, neh? But the T'ang, in his generosity, will offer compensation."

Nan Ho stared at the Marshal, surprised. "You know this?"

"I have already written the memorandum. It will be on Li Shai Tung's desk this evening."

"Ah, then the matter is concluded?"

"Yes. I think we can safely say that."

"And the groom? Yen Shih-fa?"

Tolonen looked down, clearly angry. "Yen Shih-fa will die. After we have made sure he has done no further mischief."

Nan Ho bowed his head. "I understand . . ." Yet he felt no satisfaction, only a sense of dread necessity; that and a slowly mounting anger at his young master's wife. This was her fault, the worthless bitch. This was the price of her selfishness, her wantonness.

Tolonen was watching him sympathetically. "You have served your master well, Nan Ho. You were right. If this rumor *had* taken root . . ."

Nan Ho gave the slightest nod. He had hoped to keep the details from Tolonen, but it had not proved possible. Even so, no harm had been done. Fan Ming-yu's insistence on the truth of what he had said—that Tsu Ma *had* slept with the Lady Fei—had shocked and outraged the old man. Nan Ho had seen for himself the fury in Tolonen's face as he leaned over the man, spittle flecking his lips as he called him a liar and a filthy scandal monger. And thank the gods for that. No. Not for one moment had the Marshal believed it could be true. Tsu Ma and the Lady Fei. No. It was unthinkable!

And so it must remain. For a lifetime, if necessary. But how long would it be before another whispered the secret to one they trusted? How long before the rumor trickled out again, flowing from ear to ear like the tributaries of a great river? And then?

"I am pleased that it has all worked out so well, Marshal," he said, meeting the old man's eyes briefly. "But now, if you need me no longer, I must see Pei Ro-hen. I have yet to complete the business I came here to transact."

"Of course," Tolonen said, smiling now. "You have done all that needs to be done here, Master Nan. I can deal with the rest."

"Good. Then you'll excuse me."

He bowed and was beginning to turn away when Tolonen called him back.

"Forgive me, Master Nan, but one small thing. This morning, as I understand it, was the first time Tsu Ma had visited Tong-jiang for three, almost four months. Now, without saying for a moment that I believe it to be true, such rumors have no credibility—even among such carrion as these—unless there are some few small circumstances to back them up. What crossed my mind, therefore, was that this was possibly some old tale, renewed, perhaps, by Tsu Ma's visit this morning? I wondered . . ." He hesitated, clearly embarrassed by what he was about to say. "Well, to be frank, I wondered if you had heard any whisper of this rumor before today, Master Nan. Whether . . ."

But Nan Ho was shaking his head. "Maybe you're right, Marshal Tolonen, but personally I think it more likely that the T'ang's visit put the idea into the young groom's head, neh? Dig a little and I'm sure you'll find a reason for his malice. It would not be the first time that such mischief has come from personal disappointment."

Tolonen considered that a moment, then nodded, satisfied. "Well, it was just a passing thought. Go now, Master Nan. And may the gods reward you for what you have done here today."

━━━━

IT HAD TAKEN the best part of six hours to work their way down through the deck, but now they had only this last box to deal with and they were done. Both men had been quiet for some time, as if the stream of talk between them had dried up, but now Mach looked across at his pale companion and laughed.

"What is it?" Lehmann asked tonelessly, concentrating on unscrewing the last of the restraining bolts.

"I was just thinking—"

Again he laughed. This time Lehmann raised his eyes, searching his face. "Thinking what?"

"Just about what you might have become. With your father's money, I mean. You could have been a right bastard, neh? Beating them at their own game. Making deals. Controlling the markets. Undercutting your competitors or stealing their patents. Did that never appeal to you?"

Lehmann looked down again. "I considered it. But then, I considered a lot of things. But to answer you, *Shih* Mach—no, it never appealed to me. But this . . ." He eased the bolt out and set it down. "This is what I've always wanted to do."

"Always?" Mach helped him remove the plate, then sat back on his haunches, watching.

"Since I can remember," Lehmann went on, tapping the cut-out code into the keyboard. "I've always fought against the system. Ever since I knew I could. In small ways at first. And later . . ."

Mach waited, but Lehmann seemed to have finished.

"Are you really as nihilistic as you seem, Stefan Lehmann? Is there nothing you believe in?"

Lehmann's pale, thin fingers hovered over the panel a moment, then quickly plucked the five tiny cards from their slots. Mach had watched Lehmann do this eighteen times now, noting how he took his time, double-checking, making absolutely sure he took the right ones. It was impressive in a way, this kind of obsessive care. And necessary in this case, because the configuration of each panel was different. But there was also something machinelike about the way Lehmann went about it.

He waited, knowing the albino would answer him when he was good and ready; watching him take out the tiny sealed packet and break it open, then slip the replacement cards into their respective slots.

"There," Lehmann said. "That's all of them. Do you want to test the circuit out?"

Mach was about to answer when there was a banging on the tunnel wall beneath them.

"Shit!" Mach hissed between his teeth. "What the fuck is that?"

Lehmann had turned at the noise; now he waited, perfectly still, like a lizard about to take its prey. *Wait,* he mouthed. *It may be nothing.*

There was silence. Mach counted. He had gotten to eight when the banging came again, louder than before and closer, almost beneath their feet. Moments later a head appeared at the hatchway farther along.

"Hey!" the guard said, turning to face them. "Are you authorized to be in there?"

Mach laughed. "Well, if we're not we're in trouble, aren't we?"

The guard was pulling himself up into the tunnel, hissing with the effort. Mach looked to Lehmann quickly, indicating that he should do nothing. With the barest nod Lehmann leaned back, resting his head against the tunnel wall, his eyes closed.

The guard scrambled up, then came closer, his body hunched up in the narrow space. He was a young, dark-haired officer with the kind of bearing that suggested he had come out of cadet training only months before. "What are you doing here?" he asked officiously, one hand resting lightly on his sidearm.

Mach smiled, shaking his head. "Don't you read your sheets?"

The young guard bristled, offended by Mach's off-hand manner. "That's precisely why I'm here. I've already checked. There's no mention of any maintenance work on the sheets."

Mach shrugged. "And that's our fault? You should contact Admin and find out what asshole fucked things up, but don't get on *our* backs. Here." He reached inside his tunic and pulled out the papers DeVore had had forged for them.

He watched the guard's face; saw how the sight of something official-looking mollified him.

"Well? Are you satisfied?" Mach asked, putting out his hand to take the papers back.

The guard drew back a step, his eyes taking in the open box, the exposed panel. "I still don't understand. What exactly are you doing there? It says here that you're supposed to be testing the ComNet, but you can do that without looking at the boxes, surely?"

Mach stared back at him, his lips parted, momentarily at a loss, but Lehmann came to the rescue. He leaned forward casually and plucked one of the tiny cards from the panel in front of him, handing it to the guard.

"Have you ever seen one of these?"

The guard studied the clear plastic of the card, then looked back at Lehmann. "Yes, I—"

"And you know how they function?"

"Vaguely, yes, I—"

Lehmann laughed. A cold, scathing laughter. "You don't know a fucking thing, do you, soldier boy? For instance, did you know that if even a single one of these instruction cards gets put in the wrong slot then the whole net can be fucked up. Urgent information can be misrouted, emergency calls never get to their destinations. That's why we take such pains. That's why we look at every box. Carefully. Meticulously. To make sure it doesn't happen. Understand me?" He looked up at the guard savagely. "Okay, you've been a good boy and done all your checking, now just piss off and let us get on with the job, neh? Before we register a complaint to your superior officer for harassment."

Mach saw the anger in the young guard's face, the swallowed retort. Then the papers were thrust back into his hand and the guard was backing away down the tunnel.

"That was good," Mach said quietly when he was gone. "He'll be no more trouble, that's for sure."

Lehmann looked at him, then shook his head. "Here," he said, handing him the plate. "You finish this. I'm going after our friend."

Mach narrowed his eyes. "Are you sure that's wise? I mean, he seemed satisfied with your explanation. And if you were to kill him . . ."

Lehmann turned, his face for that brief moment very close to Mach's, his pink eyes searching the *Ping Tiao* leader's own eyes.

"You asked if I believed in anything, Mach. Well, there's one thing I do believe in—I believe in making sure."

━━━━━

LI YUAN RODE ahead, finding the path down the hillside. Behind him came the palanquin, swaying gently, the six carriers finding their footholds on the gentle slope with a practiced certainty, their low grunts carrying on the still evening air.

Li Yuan turned in his saddle, looking back. The sun was setting in the west, beyond the Ta Pa Shan. In its dying light the pale yellow silks of the palanquin seemed dyed a bloody red. He laughed and turned back, spurring his horse on. It had been a wonderful day. A day he would remember for a long time. And Fei Yen? Despite her sickness, Fei had looked more beautiful than ever. And even if they had not made love, simply to be with her had somehow been enough.

He threw his head back, feeling the cool breeze on his neck and face. Yes, motherhood suited Fei Yen. They would have many sons. A dozen, fifteen, sons. Enough to fill Tongjiang. And daughters too. Daughters who would look like Fei Yen. And then, when he was old and silver-haired, he would have a hundred grandchildren; would gather his pretties about his throne and tell them of a summer day—*this* day—when he had gone up to the ruins with their grandmother, the Lady Fei, and wished them into being.

He laughed, enjoying the thought, then slowed, seeing lights floating, dancing in the darkness up ahead. Looking back he raised a hand, signaling for the carriers to stop, then eased his mount forward a pace or two. No, he was not mistaken, the lights were coming on toward them. Then he understood. They were lanterns. Someone—Nan Ho, most likely—had thought to send out lantern bearers to light their way home.

He turned, signaling the carriers to come on, then spurred the Arab forward again, going down to meet the party from the palace.

He met them halfway across the long meadow. There were twenty bearers, their ancient oil-filled lanterns mounted on ten-*ch'i* wooden poles. Coming up behind were a dozen guards and two of the young grooms from the stables. Ahead of them all, marching along stiffly, like a young boy playing at soldiers, was Nan Ho.

"Master Nan!" he hailed. "How good of you to think of coming to greet us."

Nan Ho bowed low. Behind him the tiny procession had stopped, their heads bowed. "It was but my duty, my Lord."

Li Yuan drew closer, leaning toward Nan Ho, his voice lowered. "And the business I sent you on?"

"It is all arranged," Nan Ho answered quietly. "The Lord Pei has taken on the matter as his personal responsibility. Your maids will have the very best of husbands."

"Good." Li Yuan straightened up in his saddle, then clapped his hands, delighted that Pearl Heart and Sweet Rose would finally have their reward. "Good. Then let us go and escort the Lady Fei, neh, Master Nan?"

Li Yuan galloped ahead, meeting the palanquin at the edge of the long meadow. "Stop!" he called. "Set the palanquin down. We shall wait for the bearers to come."

As the chair was lowered there was the soft rustle of silk from inside as Fei Yen stirred. "Yuan?" she called sleepily. "Yuan, what's happening?"

He signaled to one of the men to lift back the heavy silk at the front of the palanquin, then stepped forward, helping Fei Yen raise herself into a sitting position. Then he stepped back again, pointing out across the meadow.

"See what Master Nan has arranged for us, my love."

She laughed softly, delighted. The darkness of the great meadow seemed suddenly enchanted, the soft glow of the lanterns like giant fireflies floating at the end of their tall poles. Beyond them on the far side of the meadow, the walls of the great palace of Tongjiang were a burnished gold in the sun's last rays, the red, steeply tiled roofs like flames.

"It's beautiful," she said. "Like something from a fairy tale."

He laughed, seeing how the lamplight seemed to float in the liquid darkness of her eyes. "Yes. And you the fairy princess, my love. But come, let me sit with you. One should share such magic, neh?"

He climbed up next to his wife, then turned, easing himself into the great cushioned seat next to her.

"All right, Master Nan. We're ready."

Nan Ho bowed, then set about arranging things, lining the lantern bearers up on either side of the palanquin, then assigning six of the guards to double up as carriers. He looked about him. Without being told the two grooms had taken charge of the Arab and were petting her gently.

Good, thought Nan Ho, signaling for the remaining guards to form up behind the palanquin. But his satisfaction was tainted.

He looked at his master and at his wife and felt sick at heart. How beautiful it all looked in the light of the lanterns, how perfect, and yet . . .

He looked down, remembering what he had done, what he had seen that day, and felt a bitter anger. *Things should be as they seem*, he thought. *No*, he corrected himself; *things should seem as they truly are.*

He raised his hand. At the signal the carriers lifted the palanquin with a low grunt. Then, as he moved out ahead of them, the procession began, making its slow way across the great meadow, the darkness gathering all about them.

<hr>

"Well, how did it go?"

Lehmann threw the pouch down on the desk in front of DeVore. "There was a slight hitch, but all the circuits are in place. I had to kill a man. A Security guard. But your man there, Hanssen, is seeing to that."

DeVore studied Lehmann a moment. "And nobody else saw you?"

"Only the guards at the barriers."

"Good." DeVore looked down, fingering the pouch, knowing that it contained all the communication circuits they had replaced, then pushed it aside. "Then we're all set, neh? Five days from now we can strike. There was no problem with Mach, I assume?"

Lehmann shook his head. "No. He seems as keen as we are to get at them."

DeVore smiled. *As he ought to be.* "Okay. Get showered and changed. I'll see you at supper for debriefing."

When Lehmann was gone he got up and went across the room, looking at the detailed diagram of Security Central that he'd pinned up on the wall. Bremen was the very heart of City Europe's Security forces; their "invulnerable" fortress. But it was that very assumption of invulnerability that made them weak. In five days' time they would find that out. Would taste the bitter fruit of their arrogance.

He laughed and went back to his desk, then reached across, drawing the folder toward him. He had been studying it all afternoon, ever since the messenger had brought it. It was a complete file of all the boy's work; a copy of the file Marshal Tolonen had taken with him to Tongjiang that very morning; a copy made in Tolonen's own office by Tolonen's own equerry, a young man DeVore had recruited to his cause five years earlier, when the boy was still a cadet.

He smiled, remembering how he had initiated the boy, how he had made him swear the secret oath. It was so easy. They were all so keen; so young and fresh and ripe for some new ideology—for some new thing they could believe in. And he, DeVore, was that new thing. He was the man whose time would come. That was what he told them, and they believed him. He could see it in their eyes; that urgency to serve some new and better cause—something finer and more abstract than this tedious world of levels. He called them his brotherhood and they responded with a fierceness born of hunger. The hunger to be free of this world ruled by the Han. To be free men again, self-governing and self-sustaining. And he fed that hunger in them, giving them a reason for their existence—to see a better world. However long it took.

He opened the file, flicking through the papers, stopping here and there to admire the beauty of a design, the simple elegance of a formula. He had underestimated the boy. Had thought him simply clever. Super-clever, perhaps, but nothing more. This file, however, proved him wrong. The boy was unique. A genius of the first order. What he had accomplished with these simple prototypes was astonishing. Why, there was enough here to keep several Companies busy for years. He smiled. As it was he would send them off to Mars, to his contacts there, and see what they could make of them.

He leaned back in his chair, stretching out his arms. It would be time, soon, to take the boy and use him. For now, however, other schemes prevailed. Bremen and the Plantations, they were his immediate targets—the first shots in this new stage of the War. And afterward?

DeVore laughed, then leaned forward, closing the file. The wise man chose his plays carefully. As in *wei chi*, it did not do to plan too rigidly. The master player kept a dozen subtle plays in his head at once, prepared to use whichever best suited the circumstances. And he had more than enough schemes to keep the Seven busy.

But first Bremen. First he would hit them where it hurt the most. Where they least expected him to strike.

Only then would he consider his next move. Only then would he know where to place the next stone on the board.

T HE TRANSCRIPTION of standard Mandarin into European alphabetical form was first achieved in the seventeenth century by the Italian Matteo Ricci, who founded and ran the first Jesuit Mission in China from 1583 until his death in 1610. Since then, several dozen attempts have been made to reduce the original Chinese sounds, represented by some tens of thousands of separate pictograms, into readily understandable phonetics for Western use. For a long time, however, three systems dominated—those used by the three major Western powers vying for influence in the corrupt and crumbling Chinese Empire of the nineteenth century: Great Britain, France, and Germany. These systems were the Wade-Giles (Great Britain and America—sometimes known as the Wade System), the Ecole Française de l'Extreme Orient (France), and the Lessing (Germany).

Since 1958, however, the Chinese themselves have sought to create one single phonetic form, based on the German system, which they termed the *hanyu pinyin fang'an* ("Scheme for a Chinese Phonetic Alphabet"), known more commonly as *pinyin*; and in all foreign-language books published in China since January 1, 1979, *pinyin* has been used, as well as being taught now in schools along with the standard Chinese characters. For this work, however, I have chosen to use the older and, to my mind, far more elegant transcription system, the Wade-Giles (in modified form). For those now accustomed to the harder forms of

pinyin, the following may serve as a basic conversion guide, the
Wade-Giles first, the *pinyin* after:

p	for b	ch'	for q
ts'	for c	j	for r
ch'	for ch	t'	for t
t	for d	hs	for x
k	for g	ts	for z
ch	for j	ch	for zh

The effect is, I hope, to render the softer, more poetic side of
the original Mandarin, ill-served, I feel, by modern *pinyin*.

The translations of Meng Chiao's "Impromptu" and Li Shang-
Yin's "untitled poem" are by A. C. Graham from his excellent
Poems of the Late T'ang, published by Penguin Books, London,
1965.

The translation of Po Chu-I's "To Li Chien" is by Arthur
Waley, from *Chinese Poems*, published by George Allen & Unwin, London, 1946.

The translation of Wu Man-yuan's "Two White Geese" (Fei
Yen's song in Chapter Seven) is by Anne Birrell from *New Songs
from a Jade Terrace: An Anthology of Early Chinese Love Poetry*,
published by George Allen & Unwin, London, 1982.

The quotations from Sun Tzu's *The Art of War* are from the
Samuel B. Griffith translation, published by Oxford University
Press, 1963.

The quotation from Arthur Koestler's *The Act of Creation*
is from the Hutchinson & Co. edition, published in London, 1969, reprinted with their permission and that of the
agents acting for Mr. Koestler's estate, Messrs. Peters, Fraser &
Dunlop.

The translations from Nietzsche's works are by R. J. Hol-
lingdale and are taken from the following volumes: *Thus Spoke
Zarathustra* (A Book for Everyone and No One), published by
Penguin Books, London, 1961; *Beyond Good and Evil* (Prelude
to a Philosophy of the Future), published by Penguin Books,
London, 1973; *Ecce Homo* (How One Becomes What One Is),
published by Penguin Books, London, 1979.

D. H. Lawrence's "Bavarian Gentians" can be found in *Last
Poems* (1932), but the version here is taken from an earlier draft
of the poem.

A marvelous recipe for Yang Sen's "Spring Wine"—mentioned in Chapter One—can be found on page 163 of *Chinese Herbal Medicine* by Daniel P. Reid, published by Thorsons, London, 1987.

The game of *wei chi* mentioned throughout this volume is, incidentally, more commonly known by its Japanese name of Go, and is not merely the world's oldest game but its most elegant.

DAVID WINGROVE, *April 1990*

A Glossary of Mandarin Terms

MOST OF THE MANDARIN terms used in the text are explained in context. However, as a few are used more naturally, I've considered it best to provide a brief explanation.

ai ya!—common exclamation of surprise or dismay.

amah—a domestic maidservant.

ch'a—tea.

Chieh Hsia—term meaning "Your Majesty," derived from the expression "Below the Steps." It was the formal way of addressing the Emperor, through his Ministers, who stood "below the steps."

chi pao—a one-piece gown, usually sleeveless, worn by women.

Chou—"state"; here the name for a card game based on the politics of the state of Chung Kuo.

Chu—the west.

chung—a porcelain *ch'a* bowl, usually with a lid.

ch'un tzu—an ancient Chinese term from the Warring States period, describing a certain class of noblemen, controlled by a code of chivalry and morality known as the *li*, or rites. Here the term is roughly, and sometimes ironically, translated as "gentlemen." The *ch'un tzu* is as much an ideal state of behavior—as specified by Confucius in the *Analects*—as an actual class in Chung Kuo, though a degree of financial independence and a high standard of education are assumed a prerequisite.

fu jen—"Madam," used here as opposed to *t'ai t'ai*—"Mrs."

hei—literally "black"; the Chinese pictogram for this represents a man wearing warpaint and tattoos. Here it refers to the genetically manufactured (GenSyn) half-men used as riot police to quell uprisings in the lower levels.

ho yeh—*Nelumbo nucifera*, or lotus, the seeds of which are used in Chinese herbal medicine to cure insomnia.

hsiao chieh—"Miss" or "unmarried woman"; an alternative to *nu shi*.

hsiao jen—"little man/men." In the *Analects*, Book XIV, Confucius writes: "The gentleman gets through to what is up above; the small man gets through to what is down below." This distinction between "gentleman" (*ch'un tzu*) and "little men" (*hsiao jen*), false even in Confucius' time, is no less a matter of social perspective in Chung Kuo.

hsien—historically an administrative district of variable size. Here the term is used to denote a very specific administrative area: one of ten stacks—each stack composed of thirty decks. Each deck is a hexagonal living unit of ten levels, two *li*, or approximately one kilometer, in diameter. A stack can be imagined as one honeycomb in the great hive of the City.

hun—the "higher soul," or spirit soul, which, the Chinese believe, ascends to Heaven at death; joins Shang Ti, the Supreme Ancestor; and lives in his court forever more. The *hun* is believed to come into being at the moment of conception (see also *p'o*).

Hung Mao—literally "red heads," the name the Chinese gave to the Dutch (and later English) seafarers who attempted to trade with China in the seventeenth century. Because of the piratical nature of their endeavors (which often meant plundering Chinese shipping and ports) the name has connotations of piracy.

kang—the Chinese hearth, serving also as oven and, in the cold of winter, as sleeping platform.

Kan Pei!—"good health" or "cheers"; a drinking toast.

k'ang hsi—a Ch'ing, or Manchu, Emperor whose long reign (1662–1722) is considered a golden age for the art of porcelain-making. The lavender-glazed bowl in "The Sound of Jade" is, however, not *K'ang Hsi* but *Chun Chou* ware from the Sung period (960–1127) and considered among the most beautiful (and rare) wares in Chinese pottery.

kao liang—a strong Chinese liquor.

Ko Ming—"revolutionary." The *T'ien Ming* is the Mandate of Heaven, supposedly handed down from Shang Ti, the Supreme Ancestor, to his earthly counterpart, the Emperor, *Huang Ti*. This Mandate could be enjoyed only so long as the Emperor was worthy of it, and rebellion against a tyrant—who broke the Mandate through his lack of justice, benevolence, and sincerity—was deemed not criminal but a rightful expression of Heaven's anger. In this sense *Ko Ming* means a breaking of the Mandate.

Kuan Yin—the Goddess of Mercy; originally the Buddhist male bodhisattva, Avalokitsevara (translated into Han as "He who listens to the sounds of the world" or *Kuan Yin*). The Chinese mistook the well-developed breasts of the saint for a woman's and since the ninth century, have worshipped *Kuan Yin* as such. Effigies of *Kuan Yin* will show her usually as the Eastern Madonna, cradling a child in her arms. She is also sometimes seen as the wife of *Kuan Kung*, the Chinese God of War.

Kuo-yu—Mandarin, the language spoken in most of Mainland China. Also known as *Kuan hua* and *Pai hua*.

kwai—an abbreviation of *kwai tao*, a "sharp knife" or "fast knife." It can also mean to be sharp or fast (as a knife). An associated meaning is that of a "clod" or "lump of earth." Here it is used to denote a class of fighters below the Net whose ability and self-discipline separate them from the usual run of hired knives.

lao jen—"old man" (also *weng*); used normally as a term of respect.

li—a Chinese "mile," approximating to half a kilometer or one-third of a mile. Until 1949, when metric measures were adopted in China, the *li* could vary from place to place.

liu k'ou—the seventh stage of respect, according to the "Book of Ceremonies." Two stages above the more familiarly known *k'ou t'ou*, it involves kneeling and striking the forehead three times against the floor, rising onto one's feet again, then kneeling and repeating the prostration with three touches of the forehead to the ground. Only the *san kuei chiu k'ou*—involving three prostrations—was more elaborate and was reserved for Heaven and its son, the Emperor (see also *san k'ou*).

mui tsai—rendered in Cantonese as "mooi-jai." Colloquially it means either "little sister" or "slave girl," though generally, as here, the latter. Other Mandarin terms used for the same status are *pei-nu* and *ya-tou*. Technically, guardianship of the girl involved is legally signed over in return for money.

nu shi—an unmarried woman; a term equating to "Miss."

pai pi—"hundred pens"; term used for the artificial reality experiments renamed "shells" by Ben Shepherd.

pau—a simple long garment worn by men.

Ping—the east.

Ping Tiao—leveling. To bring down or make flat.

p'i p'a—a four-stringed lute used in traditional Chinese music.

p'o—the "animal soul," which, at death, remains in the tomb with the corpse and takes its nourishment from the grave offerings. The *p'o* decays with the corpse, sinking down into the underworld (beneath the Yellow Springs) where—as a shadow—it continues an existence of a kind. The *p'o* is believed to come into existence at the moment of birth. (see also *hun*)

san k'ou—the sixth stage of respect, according to the "Book of Ceremonies." It involves striking the forehead three times against the ground before rising from one's knees (in *k'ou t'ou* one strikes the forehead but once) (see also *liu k'ou*).

Shang—the south.

shanshui—literally "mountains and water," but the term is normally associated with a style of landscape painting that depicts rugged mountain scenery with river valleys in the foreground. It is a highly popular form, first established in the T'ang Dynasty, back in the seventh to ninth centuries A.D.

shih—"Master." Here used as a term of respect somewhat equivalent to our use of "Mister." The term was originally used for the lowest level of civil servants, to distinguish them socially from the run-of-the-mill "Misters" (*hsian sheng*) below them and the gentlemen (*ch'un tzu*) above.

Ta Ts'in—the Chinese name for the Roman Empire. They also knew Rome as *Li Chien* and as "the Land West of the Sea." The Romans themselves they termed the "Big *Ts'in*"—the *Ts'in* being the name the Chinese gave themselves during the Ts'in Dynasty (265–316 A.D.).

tian-fang—literally "to fill the place of the dead wife"; used to signify the upgrading of a concubine to the more respectable position of wife.

ting—a freestanding, open-sided pavilion found in formal Chinese gardens.

tou chi—Glycine Max or the black soybean, used in Chinese herbal medicine to cure insomnia.

Tsu—the north.

wei chi—"the surrounding game," known more commonly in the West by its Japanese name of "Go." It is said that the game was invented by the legendary Chinese Emperor Yao in the year 2350 B.C. to train the mind of his son, Tan Chu, and teach him to think like an Emperor.

yang—the "male principle" of Chinese cosmology, which with its complementary opposite, the female *yin*, forms the *tai-chi*, derived from the Primeval One.

yuan—the basic currency of Chung Kuo (and modern day China). Colloquially (though not here) it can also be termed *kwai*—"piece" or "lump." One hundred *fen* (or cents) make up one *yuan*.

Ywe Lung—literally, the "Moon Dragon," the wheel of seven dragons that is the symbol of the ruling Seven throughout *Chung Kuo*: "At its center the snouts of the regal beasts met, forming a roselike hub, huge rubies burning fiercely in each eye. Their lithe, powerful bodies curved outward like the spokes of a giant wheel while at the edge their tails were intertwined to form the rim." (from "*The Moon Dragon*," Chapter Four of *The Middle Kingdom*).

Acknowledgments

THANKS MUST GO, once again, to all those who have read and criticized parts of *The Broken Wheel* during its long gestation. To my editors—Nick Sayers, Brian DeFiore, John Pearce, and Alyssa Diamond—for their patience as well as their enthusiasm. To my "Writers Bloc" companions, Chris Evans, David Garnett, Rob Holdstock, Garry Kilworth, Bobbie Lamming, and Lisa Tuttle. To Andy Sawyer, for an "outsider's view" when it was much needed. And, as ever, to my stalwart helper and first-line critic, Brian Griffin, for keeping me on the rails.

Thanks are due also to Rob Carter, Ritchie Smith, Paul Bougie, Mike Cobley, Linda Shaughnessy, Susan and the girls (Jessica, Amy, and baby Georgia) and Is and the Lunatics (at Canterbury) for keeping my spirits up during the long, lonely business of writing this. And to "Nan and Granddad" Daisy and Percy Oudot, for helping out when things were tight . . . and for making the tea!

Finally, thanks to Magma, IQ and the Cardiacs for providing the aural soundtrack to this.

In Times to Come . . .

In *The White Mountain*, the third volume in the *Chung Kuo* saga, events take a dramatic turn as City Europe is thrust once more into turmoil. In the immediate aftermath of the attack on Bremen, the Seven are unified in their determination to strike back at their enemies and eliminate the terrorist *Ping Tiao*. But their unity is short-lived. Dissension among them—promoted by the young T'ang of Africa, Wang Sau-leyan—runs deep, and soon the cracks reappear, hardening into real divisions.

DeVore, meanwhile, thrives on this, using every weapon in his vast arsenal of cunning and deceit to destabilize the situation and bring about the fall of the Seven. Working with both the T'ang's own Security forces and the *Ping Tiao*, he flits between the levels like a ghost, striking at the very heart of Chung Kuo with the ruthless discrimination that is his trademark.

Against DeVore, Li Shai Tung lets fly his "hawk," Gregor Karr. Karr's single-minded pursuit of DeVore results in a final bloody confrontation. But before then Karr comes upon something wholly unexpected—love.

Karr's friend, Kao Chen, meanwhile, continues his covert hounding of Hans Ebert, joined in this task by Ebert's enemy, the young Lieutenant Haavikko. What they unearth in these investigations is to have a dramatic and tragic outcome—an outcome that strikes deep at the roots of the great tree of State.

For Li Yuan this is, at first, the very best of times. Happy in love and experiencing a deep satisfaction in his work for his father, he looks forward to the birth of his first son. But Prince Yuan's happiness is not to last. Circumstances conspire to cast him down and crush his fragile expectations, leaving him a wiser, more bitter man, tempered in the unsparing forge of experience.

Li Yuan's pet scheme—the "wiring up" of Chung Kuo's vast population—continues apace. It is, he convinces himself, the only answer to Chung Kuo's mounting problems; the only means of preventing total catastrophe. Despite setbacks he grows more and more determined to see the idea become a reality. At whatever cost . . .

For the young scientific genius Kim Ward these are frustrating times. Prevented from working on the Project, his thoughts turn inward. Yet when disaster strikes the Project, it is Kim who proves Prince Yuan's savior and the Prince rewards Kim handsomely. But Kim is given a new dilemma—in which direction should he channel his undoubted talents? Should he pursue his dream of the Web or should he set aside his dream temporarily and make his mark in Chung Kuo's cutthroat markets?

One ray of sunlight in Kim's darkness was his glimpse of the Marshal's daughter, Jelka Tolonen. For her too these are dark days as she continues to be the target of terrorist attentions while her forthcoming marriage to the loathed Hans Ebert fills her with a real foreboding. Moreover, the visit to her family home in the north of the ancient Finnmark has opened her up to the vast mystery of the world—a mystery seemingly denied by the great world of levels in which she lives. Once opened to this, she can no longer feel at home in the City.

But Jelka's restlessness is not hers alone. In the depths of the City a long-nurtured dissatisfaction with how things are has been transformed by events into anger and a widespread fervor for change. What began as a struggle among the elite for control of Chung Kuo has become, in the space of a few short years, a struggle to determine what kind of society will exist in the future. The time is coming when this generalized feeling of anger and frustration will find its channel and rip the great City asunder. Here we see the first small sign of this new destructive tide, as rioting in the lower levels spreads and gets out of hand.

For Chung Kuo these are dark times. On all sides the great storm clouds are gathering as the old order crumbles. What will replace it? Will DeVore succeed in his aim of leveling the levels, or will Li Yuan's scheme to "wire up" Chung Kuo's billions prevail? In *The White Mountain* we see the great world-encompassing empire of the Han in its final days of stability. Ahead lie only darkness and uncertainty and Li Yuan's disturbing vision of a great white mountain of bones filling the plain where the City once stood. . . .